The Mammoth Book of

NOSTRADAMUS AND OTHER PROPHETS

Also available

The Mammoth Book of
NOSTRADAMUS
AND
OTHER PROPHETS

Damon Wilson

Carroll & Graf Publishers, Inc.
NEW YORK

Carroll & Graf Publishers, Inc.
19 West 21st Street
New York
NY 10010–6805

This edition first published in the UK
by Robinson Publishing Ltd 1999

ISBN 0–7867–0628–7

Printed and bound in the UK

10 9 8 7 6 5 4 3 2 1

Contents

Introduction

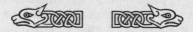

In the *Sunday Times* for 4 October 1998, journalist Stephen Farrar interviewed Julian Barbour, one of the most eminent cosmologists at Cambridge. The subject of the interview: Barbour's theory that time does not exist, that it is an illusion.

Thirty-five years ago, in October 1963, Barbour, then twenty-six years old, was on a train from Munich to the Bavarian Alps, where he intended climbing a mountain called the Watzmann. He happened to be reading a magazine article about Einstein's ideas of space and time, with which, of course, he was perfectly familiar. But reading about them in this popularized version made him suddenly aware that Einstein had never really grappled with the problem: what is time?

Now, as everyone knows, Einstein's theory of relativity declares that time is not some kind of constant, which flows at the same speed everywhere in the universe. The Argentinian writer Jorge Luis Borges underlined the point in a story called "The Secret Miracle", in which a Czech writer who has been condemned to death prays that he will have time to finish a play, and as the firing squad prepare to pull the triggers, time suddenly stands still. For a whole year the writer stands before the soldiers, and finishes his play in his head.

Einstein never suggested that time can stand still. But he argues that it goes more slowly for any object that moves at great speed – his best-known example being the story of the twins, one of whom stays on earth while his brother flies off in a space ship at half the speed of light. When the voyager returns, many years later, his brother is an old man; yet he himself is only slightly older than when he left.

As Julian Barbour lay awake in a mountain lodge on the slopes of the Watzmann, he tossed and turned, and brooded on the implication of Einstein's idea. If time can differ for each one of us, then time cannot "exist" in any objective sense. Of course, we all recognize that time is "subjective" – that if I am sitting in a dentist's waiting room with a toothache, it passes very slowly, whereas if I have a pretty girl on my knee, it flashes past. But Einstein is also talking about the kind of time measured by clocks.

Now the Greek philosopher Parmenides had argued that reality is timeless and unchangeable, and that therefore time itself is merely a figment of the imagination. But Sir Isaac Newton thought that time is a kind of river that flows throughout the universe, the same everywhere. And Einstein, of course, argued that time itself does not exist; what exists is a blend of space and time called space-time. They are like length and breadth, incapable of existing apart.

Barbour's starting point was quantum theory, which has some very odd paradoxes, such as that you cannot observe both the speed and the position of a subatomic particle at the same time. (This is Heisenberg's famous "Uncertainty Principle".) Niels Bohr went on to say that this uncertainty is not just a matter of our measuring instruments, but is inherent in quantum reality itself. Erwin Schroedinger protested, and invented his famous example of a cat locked in a box, in which some chance subatomic process can trigger the breaking of a cyanide capsule, killing the cat. And, said Schroedinger, Bohr was saying that the cat was neither dead nor alive until someone opened the box. That was absurd. But that was precisely what Bohr was saying. Until it is observed, he claimed, the cat is in a state of "probability", neither one thing nor the other.

In fact, Barbour turned to a pupil of Schroedinger, Bruno Bertotti, for co-operation on his new time theory. And the conclusion he has reached would no doubt have upset Schroedinger as much as Bohr's interpretation of the Uncertainty Principle.

Before we speak of this, let me add that there is another quantum paradox that is just as contrary to common sense as Schroedinger's cat. This is called Bell's Inequality (the word "theorem" is usually added, to make it sound less unfinished).

Suppose two electrons collide at the speed of light, and fly off in opposite directions. Einstein declared that, in that case, there would be nothing to stop you measuring the speed of one and the position of the other. And since they are exactly equal, you have disproved the Uncertainty Principle that both cannot be measured.

But apparently that is not true, either. Experiments based on Bell's theorem have shown that, no matter how far they fly apart, each particle seems to know what is happening to the other – as if they were mirror images. And anything you do to one affects the other. In quantum physics, distance seems to be an illusion. And if space and time are really linked, as Einstein said, then time must also be an illusion.

According to Barbour, every moment of time is like a snapshot. Einstein said the snapshots are threaded together, as if a string connected them like beads. Barbour points put that if this is true, then all the "beads" exist at the same time, and there is no such thing as past and future time. It is all now. Like Schroedinger's cat, we are all alive and dead at the same time.

Another baffling possibility of quantum physics (which is mentioned later in this book) is that there are billions of "parallel universes", a notion argued by the cosmologist Hugh Everett Jnr. The cat is dead in one universe and alive in another. And so, according to Everett – and Barbour – a woman who has just become pregnant might conceive a boy in one universe and a girl in another.

Now, at this point, the reader probably feels like saying: "Oh, come on, that's nonsense!" And, in fact, we can easily see that the apparent nonsense arises out of our notion of time as a kind of "fourth dimension" (as Wells put it, in *The Time Machine*.) If you could really travel along this fourth dimension, you could go back into yesterday and persuade an earlier "self" to climb back into the time machine and accompany you back to the present. In fact, you could go on collecting thousands of versions of yourself from different "times", until you had enough to fill a football stadium.

Yet, just as we feel we have won that argument, we have to confront some of the mysteries described in this book – for example, how thousands – no, millions – of people have foreseen the future, which ought to be impossible. In *An Experiment with Time*, J. W. Dunne described how he had repeatedly dreamed of the future – and claimed that this is true of all of us – except that most of us forget our dreams. (For more about Dunne, see the chapter in this book called "The Mystery of Time".) Moreover, saints and mystics have always said that time is unreal. So it would seem that Julian Barbour, instead of being the latest revolutionary in modern physics, is simply reviving a theory that is as old as philosophy.

In this book, my son Damon Wilson (who began collaborating on books with me about ten years ago, when he was twenty-three) tries to offer the widest overview of time ever attempted.

His project started as a book about Nostradamus, the sixteenth-century prophet whose *Centuries* seem to contain an amazing number of accurate glimpses of the future. It is true that many of Nostradamus's prophecies are so obscure that interpretation is virtually impossible; but, as this book shows, some of them – like the quatrain about the death of Henry II in a tournament, or the arrest of King Louis XVI and Marie Antoinette at Varennes – seem so accurate that it is hard to dismiss them as a product of chance. And then, the mention of Marie Antoinette reminds us of that strange experience of the two English ladies, Miss Moberly and Miss Jourdain, who were apparently transported back into the eighteenth century while visiting Versailles.

And so, like Harriet Beecher Stowe's Topsy, this book just growed, and went on growing – strange premonitions about the *Titanic*, the predictive powers of the *I Ching* and the Tarot, the Delphic Oracle, the Brahan Seer, Old Mother Shipton, astrology, even palmistry (I was amazed and impressed by the observations of Gale Jones about the ability of palmistry to predict crime from hand-prints). Every page offers some example of Julian Barbour's contention that time is not "continuous", but is like a massive snapshot album whose photographs exist simultaneously.

Another chapter of this book points out that the retired Cambridge archaeologist T. C. Lethbridge became convinced, through the use of his pendulum, that many "worlds" exist on different "vibratory rates", and that one of these is a timeless realm, rather like a museum, in which time stands still. Again, it looks as if Barbour has been anticipated.

If, as seems almost certain, time is not what it seems, then the next major question is: what is the reality that lies behind it? Nostradamus used to sit in his study, when the rest of the house was asleep, and stare into a candle flame or bowl of water; it was then he saw his visions of the future. It seems that his mind had access to some timeless realm, like a balcony from which he could look down on the crowd passing in the street below. And if Damon is correct, then perhaps we all possess this ability, to a greater or lesser degree, and fail to grasp it because we are so accustomed to being swept along by the crowd.

In which case, I would suggest, the best way of escaping the illusion of time is to begin to question its reality. This book is an excellent first step in that direction.

Colin Wilson

1 Impossible Dreams

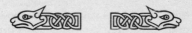

"These rabbits," [the chief rabbit] said, "who claim to have second sight – I've known one or two in my time. But it's not usually advisable to take much notice of them. For one thing, many are plain mischievous. A weak rabbit who can't hope to get far by fighting sometimes tries to make himself important by other means and prophecy is a favourite. The curious thing is that, when he turns out wrong, his friends seldom seem to notice, as long as he puts on a good act and keeps talking. But then again, you may get a rabbit who really has this odd power, for it does exist."

(Richard Adams, *Watership Down*)

Morgan Robertson was a haunted man. A highly productive author – of two novels and more than 200 short stories – his own life reads like a Victorian melodrama.

Born in Oswego, New York, in 1861, Morgan Andrew Robertson was the son of a pilot on Lake Erie, and in due course he went to sea as a cabin boy; until 1886, he was in the merchant service. He became a jeweller, but his eyes suffered from the close work, and he took up writing sea stories. They were better than average but, although they were published in English and American magazines, he was poorly paid, and never achieved the success of fellow sea veterans like Herman Melville and Joseph Conrad. He was dogged by bad luck; a periscope he invented could not be patented because a description of a similar device had appeared in a French fantasy story. His wife was an

invalid, and poverty and discouragement led him to drink ex-
cessively. But another reason for his alcoholism was a strange
obsession that inhibited him from taking up a more profitable
trade.

Robertson believed that he was possessed. According to II. W.
Francis – a journalist acquaintance – he "implicitly believed that
some discarnate soul, some spirit entity with literary ability,
denied physical expression, had commandeered his body and
brain." He was, in effect, "a mere amanuensis, the tool of the
'real writer'." Robertson himself spoke of his "astral writing-
partner".

He may have been correct – such things are not unknown. In
January 1907, a goldsmith named Frederic Thompson called on
Professor James Hyslop, president of the American Society for
Psychical Research, to explain that he believed he was possessed
by the spirit of a landscape painter named Robert Swain Gifford.
Thompson had actually met him once or twice and, after Gifford
died on 15 January 1905, Thompson began to hear the artist's
voice, urging him to paint. Although he had no artistic training,
he began producing work of considerable merit in the style of
Gifford. Hyslop heard from a number of mediums who claimed
to be receiving messages from a spirit that identified itself as
Gifford, and which mentioned that it was trying to influence
Thompson. When Hyslop saw some of Gifford's final sketches,
made just before his death (and never seen by Thompson), he
was amazed to discover their similarity to some of Thompson's
sketches – sketches of New England swamps and coastal islands
that Gifford knew well and Thompson had never visited. That
finally convinced Hyslop that Thompson was genuinely being
inspired by the spirit of Gifford. Thompson went on to become a
fairly successful painter in New York, and later in Florida; his
remarkable story is told by D. Scott Rogo in *The Infinite
Boundary*.

So Morgan Robertson's claims may well have had some basis
in fact. However, he seems to have been less fortunate than
Frederic Thompson, whose possessing spirit made sure he never
ran short of inspiration. "For months at a time," wrote Robertson's friend Francis, "although mentally alert, he would be
incapable of writing a single sentence." The "entity" would
totally abandon him at these times and he, believing he had
no imaginative skill of his own, was left to starve.

Before he could write a word, Robertson would have to lie for some time in a semi-sleeping, hypnogogic state. In this condition the "entity" (when it deigned to be available) could dictate stories to him, using dream-like images. These he later formed into a solid block of narrative. The periods of "communication" often lasted many hours, according to another friend, J. O'Neill. Afterwards, Robertson would "sit at the typewriter and pound out his story in a steady stream of words until he had finished what had been communicated in his somnolent state." Then he would be obliged to pause for the next section, which sometimes kept him waiting for days or weeks.

O'Neill explained that "his ideas would marshal themselves into a consecutive, coherent narrative up to a certain point, and then they would stop, whether he liked it or not, and that stopping, sometimes in the middle of an exciting situation, was the plague of his literary existence."

It must have been tempting for his acquaintances to dismiss Morgan Robertson's odd working practices as the delusions of an alcoholic who lacked real talent. Certainly his volume of short stories entitled *Futility*, published in 1898, struck many of his readers as the product of whisky-sodden pessimism. At a time when Jules Verne-style optimism about technology and the future was solidly in fashion, Robertson (or his erratic muse) chose to write depressing tales of shipwreck and marine disaster: little wonder it was another flop.

The subject of one story, "The Wreck of the *Titan*", came to Robertson, as usual, in one of his semi-trances. He saw, in his mind's eye, an ocean liner ploughing through a foggy Atlantic night. Initially he was both amazed and delighted by the vision. The ship was truly vast – at least 1,000 feet long – and his sailor's eye was entranced by its beautiful yet sturdy design. He was also amazed to see that the vessel was driven forward by three huge propellers, bigger than any he had ever encountered. But here he noted ominously that the ship must be making at least 23 knots, which was too fast for mid-Atlantic with poor visibility.

In his mind's eye, he saw many people moving about on deck, and suddenly knew that the ship carried over 2,000 passengers and crew. Here again, the sheer scale of the vessel stunned him – no other passenger ship had ever carried that many people, including the *Great Eastern*, the 692-foot leviathan built by Isambard Kingdom Brunel. (The *Great Eastern*'s run of non-stop bad luck, which some described as a "curse", ended in the Liverpool wreckers' yard in 1889; in its double hull the wreckers found the skeletons of the riveter and his boy apprentice, who had vanished while it was being built in 1856.)

With a growing sense of foreboding, Robertson turned his attention to the lifeboats. There were only twenty-four – an absurdly small number, that would not accommodate a quarter of the passengers. As he realized the unsettling implications of this fact, he seemed to hear a ringing voice uttering the word, "Unsinkable!" Then he saw a mountain of ice loom before the ship and knew they were going to strike. As the vision faded, he saw the ship's name. It was the *Titan*.

Robertson hurried to his typewriter. The first line he hammered out was: "She was the largest craft afloat and the greatest of the works of man . . ."

In "The Wreck of the *Titan*", Robertson described a ship that was a kind of floating palace. The luxury cabins were as big as city apartments, the decks as wide as promenades, and the passengers felt as safe from drowning as on dry land. Nineteen watertight compartments in the bows "would close automatically in the presence of water . . . [Even] with some compartments flooded, the ship would still float." The self-satisfied designers stressed that "no known accident of the sea could possibly fill so many". So the *Titan* was described by its builders as effectively unsinkable.

But on her third voyage – in the month of April – travelling from New York to England, the 75,000-ton liner strikes an iceberg in a fog bank. A long gash is torn below the waterline, and too many of the nineteen bow compartments are flooded for the vessel to stay afloat. As the ship sinks, the cold night air echoes with "nearly three thousand voices, raised in agonized screams".

Fourteen years later, on the evening of 14 April 1912, the White Star liner *Titanic* – which, together with her sister ship the *Olympia*, was one of the largest ships ever built – was steaming at 22 knots (roughly 22 miles an hour) on the final leg of her maiden voyage from Southampton to New York. The sea was calm, and there seemed no reason to anticipate danger. It was true that the recent winter had been the mildest in years, and many icebergs had broken off the polar caps and floated down the Labrador current into the Atlantic; but the *Titanic* had charted a southerly course, and the nearest iceberg was reported 250 miles away. There was no moonlight, but the stars were so bright that visibility was good.

At 9.40 p.m., the *Titanic* received a message from the *Mesaba*, which was sailing in front of her; it reported that there were many icebergs about. But the wireless officer, John Phillips, was not particularly concerned; he had received several messages about icebergs that day. And he was overwhelmed with messages that wealthy passengers wanted him to send to New York.

At about 11.30 p.m., the seaman in the crow's nest saw an iceberg straight ahead, about a quarter of a mile away. He phoned the bridge and first officer Murdock yelled at the helmsman, "Hard to starboard!"

It looked as if they could miss it easily. They had about two and a half minutes to change course.

The order was immediately given to reverse the propellers and turn to starboard – which, later commentators remark, may well have been a mistake, for reversing the engines would prevent the turn from being so effective; it would have been better to simply order the turn. The total result of the manoeuvre was the iceberg brushed past them.

As far as those on deck were concerned, collision had been avoided. What no one guessed was that, under the surface, there was an enormous spur of ice, which sliced along the side like a tin opener, causing a tremor so slight that few passengers noticed it. The 330-foot gash cut into three holds and two boiler rooms.

As soon as someone told Thomas Andrews, one of the ship's two designers, that there had been a noise like tearing calico, he rushed below to inspect the damage. He was relieved to find that the doors of the damaged holds had closed automatically. Unfortunately, this was because they were full of water . . . and they were huge. Inevitably, the vessel began to list forward and starboard, and Andrews belatedly grasped the fatal flaw in her layout. For, unlike the *Titan*'s completely sealed compartments, as described by Robertson, the *Titanic*'s bow compartments had a gap between the top of the wall and the ceiling. As water in a flooding compartment topped the rim, it would gush into its previously dry neighbour. At first, Captain Edward J. Smith and J. Bruce Ismay (the other designer) believed that the ship could survive even this appalling damage, but Andrews knew better. He saw that the flooding process could not be arrested; the *Titanic* was going down in a sea as calm as a village duckpond.

Although the news spread quickly, there was none of the mass panic described by Robertson in "The Wreck of the *Titan*". As people crowded onto the decks, asking why the ship had stopped, the stewards told them cheerfully that it was only a minor problem, and the ship would be on its way in a couple of hours. Yet the captain and its designers recognized that no amount of organization or level-headedness could save 2,220 passengers when there were only twenty lifeboats; at the most, they could save twelve hundred people.

SOS signals were radioed and emergency rockets fired. Unfortunately, Stanley T. Lord, the captain of the *California*, the only ship close enough to have saved them – which had stopped for the night at the edge of the ice field – thought the exploding flares were signs of a party on board, and went to sleep.

The battered old Cunard liner, the *Carpathia*, picked up the SOS signals and turned about, making full speed, but she was an hour away, and the *Titanic* was sinking fast. Below decks, 325 men continued working in the holds and boiler rooms. The ship's band played jazz, including the popular number "Poor Butterfly." The fifty officers helped the passengers into boats – women and children first. Ismay, the designer – and White Star director – panicked as he saw the last boat lowered, and jumped in, pushing ahead of women. He was branded for the rest of his life as a coward, just as Captain Lord of the *California* would forever be known as the man who went to sleep and let the *Titanic* passengers drown.

If the *Carpathia* had arrived earlier, nearly all passengers and crew could have been saved – as it was, the ship saved 711 people – but before it arrived, the *Titanic*'s boilers had exploded and hurtled like rockets along the ship. The *Titanic* up-ended and went down like a stone. 1,513 people died with her, including Captain Smith, who had been due to retire at the end of the voyage.

Morgan Robertson's *Futility*, which had hardly been a best seller in 1898, now achieved belated fame as the incredible similarities between the real and the fictional tragedies were noted, and was serialized in newspapers across the United States. Unfortunately, even this was unable to save Morgan Robertson's career. After publishing fourteen volumes with titles like *Ship-mates* and *Down to the Sea*, his "astral writing-partner" finally deserted him. In 1914, the humorist and actor Irving J. Cobb found him living penniless with his wife in a Harlem tenement, and raised enough money to set him again on his feet. He even bought Robertson a fur coat and gold-headed cane, which Robertson confessed he had always wanted. Yet Robertson was still unable to write. And in March 1915, he was found dead – of heart failure – in a hotel in Atlantic City, wearing his fur coat, and with his gold-headed cane across his knees, staring out at the sea.

Whether Morgan Robertson had seen the future through his own innate psychic faculty, or had somehow received the information from his "astral writing-partner", there can be no doubt that he had accurately described an event that had not yet taken place.

Inevitably, many disagree with this assessment – even among those who accept the possibility of precognition. Writing in 1960, Dr Ian Stevenson, Professor of Psychiatry at the University of Virginia, published a paper called: "A Review and Analysis of Paranormal Experiences connected with the Sinking of the *Titanic*". Although he could hardly be described as a sceptic – having been the President of the American Parapsychological Association – he nevertheless took a negative view:

> "A writer of the 1890s, familiar with man's repeated hubris, might reasonably infer that he would overreach himself in the construction of ocean liners which then . . . were man's greatest engineering marvels . . . A large ship would probably have great power and speed; the name *Titan* has connoted power and security for several thousand years; recklessness would race the ship through the areas of the Atlantic icebergs; these drift south in the spring, making April a likely month for a collision . . . Having reached the general conclusion of the probability of such a disaster, inferences, such as those I have suggested, might fill in details to provide correspondences which would have an appearance of precognition, but which we should, I believe, consider only successful inferences."

Stevenson might have instanced a poem called *The Tryst*, by the American poetess Celia Thaxter, and published in 1874, which is cited in a book called *Titanic, Triumph and Tragedy*, by John P. Eaton and Charles A. Haas, as an instance of a work of literature that seemed to presage the *Titanic* disaster. *The Tryst* describes an iceberg drifting "from out the desolation of the North" to the "warm airs of the sweet South", where a ship full of "brave men, sweet women, little children bright" sails before a fair wind. The inevitable "tryst" occurs, and "dully through wind and sea, one awful crash/Sounded, with none to mark." Certainly, *The Tryst* captures that disturbing sense of inevitability that seems to mark the tragedy of the *Titanic*; but can a poem about a sailing ship really be regarded as a kind of premonition about a massive engine-driven liner?

On the other hand, it is possible to make an altogether stronger case for the striking predictions of the campaigning newspaper editor W. T. Stead, who in March 1886 wrote an article entitled "How the Mail Steamer Went Down in Mid-Atlantic, by a Survivor", published in the *Pall Mall Gazette*. It describes how a fictional steamer sinks after colliding with another vessel, and how hundreds of passengers are lost because there are not enough lifeboats. Stead concluded the article: "This is exactly what might take place and what will take place if liners are sent to sea short of boats – Ed."

Now it is known that W. T. Stead, as well as being fascinated by nautical matters, was a convinced spiritualist and an active medium. Through a "spirit guide" called Julia, he obtained many "messages from the other side" in automatic writing (a practice in which the medium's hand appears to be controlled by an unknown entity). We do not know whether Stead received the same sort of "supernatural" inspiration as Robertson, but there can be no doubt that he remained obsessed by the threat of an ocean liner disaster to – literally – the end of his life. And in 1893, seven years after his first tale of maritime disaster, he wrote for the Christmas issue of *The Review of Reviews* (which he edited) a fictional account of a collision between an Atlantic iceberg and a passenger liner.

What makes *From the Old World to the New* so remarkable is the fact that the captain of the White Star liner *Majestic* – a real ship, which Stead described rescuing the survivors of the doomed vessel – was, at the time of publication, Edward J. Smith, the man who captained the *Titanic* on its last voyage.

In the story, the survivors are rescued because a clairvoyant passenger has a precognitive vision of the disaster. In 1903, Stead was involved in a seance that provides fairly convincing evidence that "spirits" have the power of precognition.

On 20 March a Bradford medium named Mrs Burchell was dining with Stead and a group of fellow spiritualists in Gatti's restaurant, and Stead asked her to hold an envelope he had obtained from the Serbian ambassador. Mrs Burchell had no idea of its contents, but it was, in fact, the signature of King Alexander of Serbia. Mrs Burchell said immediately: "Royalty! He is a king." Then she gave an accurate description of the king and, with increasing agitation, described how he would be murdered in his palace, together with his queen. While this was happening, another medium in the room fell into a trance and added the detail that the assassins were wearing what looked to her like Russian uniforms. Stead wrote an account of this seance, and it was in due course sent to the unpopular King Alexander – and his even less popular wife, Queen Draga. Alexander, a rationalist, ignored it. Four months later, on 16 June 1903, the king and queen were murdered in the palace in Belgrade by a group of army officers.

It should be noted at this point that psychical investigators have frequently stated that the "world of spirits" has no time in our earthly sense – or rather, all time seems to co-exist – and that this is why accurate prophecies of the future have been received so often via mediums. Which leads inevitably to the speculation: was Robertson's "astral writing-partner" trying to give a warning that the *Titanic* would sink?

In 1909, Stead had again showed a flash of something that in retrospect looked like clairvoyance. Speaking before the members of the Cosmos Club, he criticized what he felt to be the excessive rigour demanded by the Society for Psychical Research regarding what it considered sound evidence and, by way of illustration, conjured up a picture of himself drowning in the sea after a shipwreck. Suppose, he said, that rescuers, instead of throwing him a rope, asked, "What is your name?" and, when he replied, "W. T. Stead", shouted back: "How do we know you are Stead? Where were you born? Tell us the name of your grandmother."

"It is quite astonishing," remarks Leslie A. Shephard, in the *Encyclopedia of Occultism and Parapsychology*, "how often the picture of a sinking ocean liner with its attendant horrors recurred in Stead's writings."

On 21 April 1912, Stead was due in New York to appear at Carnegie Hall, where he had been invited by President Taft to speak on the subject of world peace.[1] He booked a passage for the *Titanic*'s maiden voyage. In a letter to his secretary, written just before his departure, he wrote: "I feel as if something was going to happen, somewhere or somehow." Whether this was a foreboding of his fate may be questioned in view of his next comment: "And that it will be for good." Stead was one of those who died on the *Titanic*.

Archdeacon Thomas Colley, who would later write a pamphlet on *The Foreordained Wreck of the Titanic* actually sent Stead a warning of the disaster before he sailed; Stead replied that he sincerely hoped that it would not happen, and that he would be in touch with Colley when he returned.

Two days after the sinking of the *Titanic*, before the news of its loss had been made public, a Detroit medium named Etta Wriedt (who had intended to return to England with Stead) went into a trance. She stated that Stead had been killed and also mentioned the names of several other prominent people who had been drowned. The following evening, an entity purporting to be Stead himself spoke through her, describing his end on the *Titanic*.

Stead's reservations about sea travel had been thoroughly reinforced by other spiritualists in the months before his death. For example, Cheiro, the most famous palmist of his time, sent Stead a warning almost a year before the *Titanic* set sail. Stead had gone to consult Cheiro because he was worried in case his crusading zeal (he had once gone to prison for a series of articles exposing child prostitution) might lead to an attempt on his life. Cheiro studied Stead's horoscope as well as his palm, and noted:

". . . any danger of violent death to you must be by water and nothing else. Very critical and dangerous for you should be April, 1912, especially about the middle of the month. So don't travel by water then if you can help it. If you do, you will be liable to meet with such danger to your life that the very worst may happen. I know I am not wrong about this 'water' danger; I only hope I am, or at least that you won't be travelling somewhere about that period."

1 By then, statesmen were well aware of the danger of a potentially catastrophic war in Europe.

Stead received Cheiro's warning in June, 1911. The following winter, he consulted the clairvoyant W. de Kerlor, whose speciality was crystal-ball gazing. The psychic claimed to see Stead travelling to America "on a huge black ship, but I can only see half of the ship – when one will be able to see it in its whole length, it is perhaps then that you will go on your journey." The *Titanic* was, in fact, completed in the Harland and Wollf shipyard in Belfast by then. But it may also be noted that the *Titanic* broke in half as she sank.

There are many stories of psychic premonitions of the disaster. Mrs Esther Hart, wife of Benjamin Hart, whose ticket cost them £26 and 5 shillings (a reasonably large sum, for those days) was horrified when she heard that the ship was described as unsinkable. She felt sure this was tempting fate. The family, including seven-year-old daughter Eva, was emigrating to Canada. She begged her husband to choose another ship; even as they were climbing the gangplank, she pressed him to change his mind. He told her that if she was so worried, she should return home with Eva, and come over when he had arrived safely. Understandably, she refused but, after dinner in the ship's dining room, she would change out of her dinner-dress into warm woollen clothes, and sit up all night, knitting or sewing.

On the night of the fourteenth, she was sitting in her cabin when the *Titanic* was holed by the iceberg; the bump was so slight that it did not even cause her glass of orange juice to slop over on the table top. Yet she knew immediately that this was what she had been expecting. She woke her husband and sent him up to the boat deck. When he returned, he said: "You'd better put my thick coat on. I'll wear another."

Years later, her daughter – who, like her mother, had been rescued – asked her why she had not asked her father what had happened. She said: "There was nothing to ask him." She already knew that the impending disaster had happened. Benjamin Hart was drowned.

An engineer called Colin MacDonald turned down an offer to become second engineer on the *Titanic* because he had a hunch that it would sink.

Many others cancelled their reservations, including the steel magnate Henry Clay Frick, the multi-millionaire George W. Vanderbilt (whose mother-in-law felt that maiden voyages were unlucky) and the banker J. Pierpont Morgan, whose mercantile combine owned the White Star line.

Ten days before the *Titanic* was due to sail, a London businessman named J. Connon Middleton, who had booked a week earlier, had a dream of the *Titanic* floating keel upward, her passengers swimming in the sea. The next night, he had the same dream. Yet, although worried, he was too practical-minded to cancel his passage. Fortunately, a week before sailing, he received a telegram from business associates saying the conference had been postponed for a week, asking him to delay his trip for a few days. Middleton mentioned his premonition to many people before the ship sailed, so was able to call on them for corroboration later.

As the ship passed the Isle of Wight on its way out of Southampton, the family of a man named Jack Marshall stood on their roof and waved their handkerchiefs. Suddenly, Mrs Marshall – the mother of novelist Joan Grant – grabbed her husband by the arm and screamed: "It's going to sink, it's going to sink before it reaches America." She was so certain that she refused to be soothed, shouting: "Do something, you fools – I see hundreds of people struggling in the icy water." In her autobiography, *Far Memory*, Joan Grant tells how the whole family was in such a state of tension for the following five days that it was almost a relief to hear that the *Titanic* had sunk.

At Queenstown in Ireland, a young fireman had a premonition of disaster, and deserted the ship.

On the *Titanic*'s last evening, the Rev. E. C. Carter held a service in the second-class dining room – and included among the hymns the rather odd choice "For those in peril on the sea". In Winnipeg, Canada, the Rev. Charles Morgan of the Rosedale Methodist Church had already chosen the hymns for that evening's service when he drifted into a doze on the sofa, and heard the words, "For those in peril on the sea". He did not know the hymn, but nevertheless went and looked out the music, and took it to church. At the same time as the Rev. Carter's congregation were singing the hymn on the *Titanic*, the Rev. Morgan's congregation were singing it in their church.

In his paper for the American Society for Psychical Research, already mentioned, Dr Ian Stevenson (best known for his studies of reincarnation) lists no less than nineteen cases of premonitions of the sinking of the *Titanic*, from England, America and Brazil.

On the day the *Titanic* sailed, a psychic named V. N. Turvey had a sudden intuition that the ship would be lost, and wrote a letter to this effect to Madame I. de Steiger. The letter actually arrived on 15 April by which time the *Titanic* had sunk; Turvey's letter was published in *Light* on 29 June 1912.

There is an interesting postscript to this tale of disaster. Precisely twenty-three years later, in April 1935, a young seaman named William Reeves was standing watch on the deck of a tramp steamer called the *Titanium*, carrying coal from the Tyne to Canada. Reeves knew all about the *Titanic* – the story of the great liner fascinated him. His watch was due to end at midnight – the time the *Titanic* struck the iceberg – and he knew that they were in roughly the same spot where this had happened. A sudden intuition of danger filled him with alarm, but he could see nothing ahead. Then, as he recalled that the *Titanic* had sunk on the day he was born, the intuition turned to certainty. He shouted a danger warning. The *Titanium*'s engines reversed, and it came to a halt just before it struck an iceberg.

The story of the *Titanic* disaster not only suggests that precognition of the future can occur, but that it may occur more often than we might assume. Of course, this outrages common sense, which takes the view that what has not yet happened cannot possibly be known – unless it happens to be predictable, like the movements of heavenly bodies.

But suppose our view of space and time is badly wrong, and the future can be known? This is not as absurd as it sounds. Although this world that surrounds us looks solid and real and unproblematic, we only have to ask ourselves when time began, or when it will end, to see that things are less simple than they seem. Cosmologists assure us that in the beginning was the big bang, and that the "background hiss" of interstellar space is evidence for it – having said which, they sit back, as if to say, "Next question, please." And we cannot help feeling much like the ancient Hindus when they were told that the world is supported on the back of an elephant, which is supported on the back of a camel, and so on . . . It is quite obvious that what we call science cannot embrace certain problems because they cannot be reduced to a kind of symbolic logic. The problem of time is one of these.

So, for example, the problem of the future has been tackled in hypnotic regression. In an issue of *Science* in 1954, Robert

Rubinstein and Richard Newman describe how, working with a group of hypnotic subjects, they told a medical student that it was now October 1963 (ten years ahead) and asked him what he was doing. He went on to describe his day in detail – an operation on an emergency case, complete with symptoms and diagnosis. When asked if he felt pleased, he mentioned that he had dealt with a similar case in 1958 – five years ahead of the date of the hypnotic session.

Another of the subjects described her anguish in 1963 at the death of her three-month-old son.

The authors go on: "We believe that each of our subjects, to please the hypnotist, fantasized of future . . ." It seems a pity that they did not try asking their subjects about some time closer to the present, and then checking on whether their reports were accurate.

However, the same experiment was carried out in the early 1970s by an American academic, Charles H. Hapgood, who began experimenting in hypnotism with his students at Keene State University in New Hampshire. One student was a youth named Jay and, on a Sunday evening, he was told that it was the following Wednesday, and was asked what he was doing. He said he had been to Keene airport, and had met a pilot who was able to give him details of an accident at Montpellier in which he was deeply interested.

On the following Wednesday evening, Hapgood asked Jay what he had been doing all day, and Jay replied that he had been to Keene airport, and had met a pilot who was able to tell him about the cause of the Montpellier crash.

A comparison of the details of the whole day showed that they corresponded exactly to what Jay had said three days earlier.

Another student named Henry was told under hypnosis that it was the following Thursday, and asked what he intended doing that day. He said he meant to borrow a friend's car, and to drive to Brattleboro to "have a good time". Progressed a few hours by the hypnotist, he explained that he was in a bar drinking beer with two women, who were saying critical things about their husbands and making improper suggestions, which Henry declined to repeat. Taken forward a few hours, he described getting back to Keene slightly the worse for wear, and waking up the dogs when he went home.

The following Friday, Hapgood saw Henry, and said: "Henry, I know where you were last night."

"I bet you don't."

"You went to Brattleboro in –'s car, and went to a diner and had a lot of beer."

When Hapgood came to the women, Henry looked worried and said: "But you don't know what they said, do you?"

Hapgood replied: "No, Henry, you refused to tell us."

Hapgood goes on: "Now where does all this leave us? There appears to be good evidence that the human psyche is not bound by the limitations of time and space. Our bodies exist in this physical world, where the laws of time, space, mass and energy operate in a finite way; but they are only the peaks of icebergs that jut above the sea, leaving nine-tenths of their mass out of sight below sea level. All the phenomena I have mentioned here can be easily duplicated. All that is necessary to demonstrate them is a good hypnotist and a few good subjects."

All this may seem to suggest a negative view of the human capacity for freedom – that we are living lives that have been scripted in advance. Indeed, there is a certain amount of evidence that this is so. Dr Michael Shallis, an Oxford science don, describes in his book *On Time* how he often had a sudden feeling of *déjà vu* in which he knew what would be happening in the immediate future. As a child of twelve, he asked his mother what they were to have for dinner and knew suddenly that she was going to answer: salad. He also describes how, giving a tutorial on radioactivity, he had the same *déjà vu* feeling, and knew that the next thing that had to happen was that he would suggest that he needed a certain book from his office, and would go and get it. He decided to resist this impulse, just to break the pattern – then heard his voice saying, "I will pop down to my office to get a book . . ."

But it would surely be a mistake to assume we have no free will. What about the young fireman who decided to get off the *Titanic* at Queenstown harbour, because of his premonition of the sinking? Was that pre-ordained, too, like the sinking? And if the answer to that might seem to be "yes", then how about a case described by J. B. Priestley in *Man and Time*, borrowed from the paranormal researcher Louisa Rhine? A mother described a dream in which she was camping with some friends on the shores of a creek. She went down to the creek with her baby to wash some clothes, then realized she had forgotten the soap. She put down her baby while she went back to the tent and, when she returned, found the baby face-down in the creek, obviously drowned.

Months later, she went camping with some friends on the bank of a creek. She took the baby with her to wash some clothes, realized she had forgotten the soap, and started back for it. The baby began throwing stones in the water, when she suddenly remembered her dream. So she picked up the baby and took him back to the tent with her.

This seems to suggest that the future is not predetermined – at least, not rigidly so. Since most self-observant persons are aware how far their lives are mechanical (we have only to note that we cannot recall if we have remembered to take a pill), then we might conclude that we exercise free will only in rare moments of "non-mechanicalness".

It might seem to follow that, where large masses of people are concerned, there is less chance of an individual exercise of free will making any difference. History itself obeys mechanical laws – a point of view Tolstoy argues in *War and Peace*. If so, then we may well feel that the sinking of the *Titanic* was somehow pre-ordained. This argument – between free will and determinism, or free will and compulsion – will obviously recur throughout this book.

This is, perhaps, the place to raise another important point: whether the phrase "written in the stars" can mean anything to any rational person. In their book *Astrology, the Divine Science*, Marcia Moore and Mark Douglas point out that the transit of the planet Neptune (called after the sea god) through "watery Cancer" was marked by the sinking of the *Titanic*. In *Prophecy and Prediction in the Twentieth Century*, Charles Neilson Gattey quoted the astrologer Dennis Elwell, who pointed out that, in April 1912, two major planets, Neptune and Jupiter, became stationary in the sky (that is, of course, looked as if they had become stationary from earth). The planets were in what astrologers call "biquintile", an angle of 144 degrees. (A quintile is an angle of seventy-two degrees, signifying strain, so a double quintile would indicate a double strain.) Jupiter, as the planet of the ruler of the gods, signifies mastery, while Neptune, the planet of the sea, is associated with ships. Elwell sees this as a strain between man's craving for mastery over nature – as in the declaration that the *Titanic* was unsinkable – and the immense forces he is challenging. Moreover, says Elwell, the sinking took place between two eclipses, one of the moon (1 April) and one of the sun (17 April), and eclipses tend to magnify such effects.

This may sound like the kind of nonsense with which newspaper astrologers mystify the public, but Elwell goes on to offer supporting evidence.

Early in 1987, he noticed that the same two planets, Jupiter and Neptune, would soon be coming into an aspect that astrologers call a square, which is when there is an angle of ninety degrees between two planets and the centre of the zodiac. A square indicates conflict. Furthermore, there was an eclipse of the sun on the Jupiter arm of the square, increasing the possibility of conflict.

Recalling the *Titanic*, Elwell wrote letters to the P&O and Cunard lines – not so much to warn them of some unspecified disaster, as to place his prediction on record. But Elwell also offered to try and pinpoint the danger. He stressed in his letters that it was the first time in forty years as an astrologer that he had felt the need to give such warnings. Both companies replied that their safety procedures were adequate.

In fact, the *Queen Elizabeth II* was making her way to New York when Elwell wrote these letters in February, and one was passed on to the commodore of the fleet, who was on board. The voyage was beset with disaster – failed air-conditioning, flooded cabins that caused the ship to list fifteen degrees so the passengers had to eat their meals at an angle, and various other problems. Perhaps as a precaution, the ship made a 250-mile detour to avoid the place where the *Titanic* sank.

Cunard may well have felt they had suffered their disaster, but P&O, the owners of the ferry company Townsend Thoreson, still had theirs to come. And if Elwell had known that P&O owned Townsend Thoreson, he might have had more success in pinpointing their disaster. For one of their ferries was called the *Herald of Free Enterprise*. The sign Aries is associated with pioneers and precursors – hence with heralds. And Jupiter has been traditionally associated with the idea of freedom. So a time when Jupiter was in Aries was obviously one when a disaster waiting to happen might finally make up its mind.

The *Herald of Free Enterprise* disaster *had* been waiting to happen for, as the enquiry later revealed, the car ferry often sailed with her bow doors still open, which was strictly against the rules. And in Zeebrugge, on 6 March 1987, with Jupiter in Aries on the horizon, the *Herald of Free Enterprise* left harbour with her bow car-loading doors wide open. Water gushed onto the car deck and the ferry began to list. Fortunately, she did not sink, but the excess water made her wallow and eventually capsize. 188 people were killed before rescuers could evacuate the hulk.

Gattey notes that a number of marine disasters occurred during that period of Jupiter in Aries in 1987: on 24 April, a ship called the *Hengist* collided with a French trawler, which capsized; on 1 May, two ferries collided in the fog, and two days later, there was another collision between a Townsend Thoreson ferry and another vessel in Calais harbour.

Elwell also pointed out that the *Olympic*, the *Titanic*'s sister ship, had not escaped that heavenly warning of disaster; seven weeks after the *Titanic* went down, an extraordinary steering error brought her close to running aground off Land's End. The incident was hushed up, to avoid alarming the public, but was finally revealed a few weeks after the *Herald of Free Enterprise* disaster.

Let me admit that, while I find Elwell's comments on marine accidents deeply interesting, there is in me a stubborn disinclination to accept that the movements of the planets can foretell such events. Yet I must also admit to a personal conclusion that will inevitably colour the following chapters: that human beings often make predictive statements that later prove to be true, but cannot be explained in terms of either intellectual foresight or inspired guesswork. How and why this happens, I shall have to leave readers to decide for themselves, my business being merely to provide the evidence.

2 Gut Knowledge

One of the oldest forms of divination[1] has become quite incomprehensible to the modern mind. Ancient methods such as astrology, dream interpretation and the *I Ching* have, as we will see later, survived the millennia and continued to flourish, but "extispicy" – the reading of the future in the ritually spilled viscera of a dead animal – has largely fallen out of fashion.

Nevertheless, "reading the entrails" was the most popular method of prediction in the cultures around the Mediterranean for thousands of years. Translations of cuneiform texts have shown that ritual evisceration was central to the religion and daily life of the Babylonian civilization (existing from around 1800 BC to 600 BC), and was probably inherited from their cultural forebears, the Sumerians (the first known civilization, dating from around 2800 BC to 1800 BC). We also know that extispicy (Latin: from *exta*, entrails, and *specere*, to inspect) was the chief form of augury in the Roman Empire up to and into the Christian era. In the period separating these cultures – about three thousand years – this practice was zealously followed by virtually all the civilizations of Western Asia and those around the Mediterranean Sea. Indeed, through modern anthropological research, it can be argued that just about every ancient culture world-wide has indulged in some form of extispicy at one time or another (and modern spirit-religions like Santeria and Vodun still do).

---

1 A magical or religious ritual aimed at divining the future.

It may be difficult for a modern mind to accept, but there are numerous recorded incidents of entrail-reading successfully predicting future events; indeed, why else would our forebears have continued such an unpleasant custom for so long, if they did not see some evidence of it actually working?

The most famous incident of accurate extispicy known today was the prediction that Julius Caesar would die on 15 March, 44 BC. It is notable that many modern sources, when describing Caesar's assassination, gloss over just how the soothsayer, Vestricius Spurinnia, came to give the warning: "Caesar! Beware the Ides of March."[2] Perhaps our historians' reluctance to mention this detail is understandable, as many of their readers might find it ridiculous that a goat's liver was the source of one of the best-known prophecies in history.

In Shakespeare's *Julius Caesar*, the doomed dictator contemptuously dismisses the soothsayer as a "dreamer" but, in fact, Spurinnia was both a patrician and a high priest – a man of great respect in Rome. As a Haruspex (Latin: *haruga*, a victim; *specere*, to inspect), Spurinnia would have been considered a very holy man by most Romans; only certain members of Rome's intellectual elite would have dismissed him as a superstitious fool or a bloody-handed fraud.[3]

On the morning of 14 March, 44 BC, Spurinnia was performing the daily ritual sacrifice: a goat had its throat cut as suitable prayers were chanted.[4] When the animal was quite dead it was laid, belly-up, on the altar stone. Temple servants pulled on its legs to keep it steady and the Haruspex opened it from ribs to genitals with a sacred knife. He then reached into the steaming cavity, severed the internal organs from their respective anchorages and carefully arranged the whole stinking mass on the altar stone. While the servants took the empty corpse away,

2 The "Ides" were monthly dates on the Roman calendar, which in March fell on the fifteenth day.
3 Just over a century before, Cato the Elder had wryly commented: "I wonder how one Haruspex can keep from laughing when he sees another." Julius Caesar – unfortunately, as we shall see – seems to have shared this deprecatory opinion.
4 Other animals, such as pigs, geese and sheep were also "read" by Haruspex, but Apollo, god of light and prophecy, particularly favoured goats, so these were usually the sacrifice when important matters were being divined.

Spurinnia carefully studied the state of the viscera, paying special attention to the liver and intestines – the organs thought most likely to predict the future.

To the priest's horror, according to the contemporary statesman Cicero, "there was no head to the liver of the sacrifice. These portents were sent by the immortal gods to Caesar that he might foresee his death . . ." By this we can guess that Spurinnia was either commissioned to make an augury on Caesar's behalf, or that he was himself curious to know the future of Rome's most powerful politician. Either way, he communicated the bad news immediately to the dictator.[5]

Caesar refused to consider the warning. He had good reason to believe that on the next day, 15 March, he would be proclaimed *Rex* in the Senate House – the first king of Rome in four hundred and sixty-six years. Even if he had been a true believer in extispicy, it would have been political suicide to show cowardice on that of all days. Also, as a shrewd political animal, Caesar must have suspected that those who wished to block the coronation might have bribed Spurinnia.

The following day, Caesar met Vestricius Spurinnia as he made his way to the Senate House. Despite the fact that his own wife had dreamed the night before that he would be murdered, Caesar was in buoyant spirits.

"Well, Spurinnia," he called, "the Ides of March are come!"

"Aye, Caesar," was the gloomy reply, "come, but not yet gone."

Less than an hour later, Caesar was dead: stabbed to death by men he had considered friends and colleagues.

The "head," missing from the liver of the goat sacrificed by Spurinnia, was what anatomists now call the *processus pyramidalis*. This is a pointed protuberance found on one side of the organ and contains approximately ten to fifteen per cent of the liver's overall volume. It therefore may seem surprising that so much of a vital organ could be missing and yet the goat still seem healthy enough to be a fit sacrifice. Yet veterinary research has shown that an animal living in reasonably unstressful conditions can still appear healthy with over eighty per cent of its liver dysfunctional. The fact that the *processus pyramidalis* was

5 Then a term simply meaning the military Commander-in-Chief, with little of the modern connotation of a tyrant.

actually absent is also less surprising than it may first seem. The liver is not a compact, muscular organ like the heart; various diseases can cause parts of it literally to dissolve away.

If, on the other hand, the liver had been undiseased, complete and a healthy shade of red, the soothsayer would have proclaimed it a good omen. A complex set of rules and references existed to guide a Haruspex. Each section of the liver had traditional, partially descriptive names such as the "Gate" and the "Table"; a particular mark on one these would indicate a specific portent. This would be then cross-referenced with other signs found on the liver and on the other organs. Furthermore, certain areas of the liver were connected with specific portions of the sky – thus creating a link with the sister trade of astrology. All in all, a soothsayer could produce a highly complex prediction from the entrails of a single sacrificial beast, and often many animals were "read" at one time to further honour the god and provide a thorough divination.

The liver and intestines were considered particularly indicative of the gods' influence on the future, largely due to their physical appearance. The intestine of an animal, for example, seems a confused mass of tubing when inside the creature's body. Yet, when it is removed and stretched out, it can be seen that it forms a neat double spiral; from the top of the stomach, the intestine curves in a clockwise direction, then doubles back within the first set of coils in an anti-clockwise route to the anus. This finding of order within apparent chaos must have been attractive to men attempting to divine the future. The intestine was linked with the planet Mercury, whose orbit also seems to double back on itself when viewed from the Earth. Whether the traditional role of the god Mercury – that of messenger and magician – was influenced by the practice of extispicy or, indeed, vice versa is now a moot point.

The ancients considered the liver the seat of the emotions and home of the immortal soul. Even as late as Shakespeare's day, Elizabethans tended to describe the liver instead of the heart as the originator of non-intellectual reactions. In *Love's Labours Lost*, for example, Biron says in an aside, "This is the liver-vein, which makes flesh deity." The reason that the heart later came exclusively to represent the emotions was simply because an excited person could feel it beating faster. The liver, on the other hand, won its reputation during a period when people tended to do their own butchery and regularly saw an aspect of the organ that is today largely forgotten. When freshly removed, the liver has a glossy, mirrored appearance: a Haruspex could literally see his face in it.

Numerous ancient texts refer to the liver as a "mirror of the soul", not least Plato's *Timaeus*:

> "God . . . placed the liver in the house of lower nature [the belly] contriving that it should be solid and smooth, and bright and sweet . . . in order that the power of thought, which proceeds from the mind, might be reflected as in a mirror . . . and so might strike terror into the desires."

Plato believed, in other words, that pure, intellectual thoughts originated in the head and were "reflected" in the liver, thus having a controlling influence on the animalistic desires of our "lower nature". "Such is the nature of the liver," Plato went on, "which is placed as we have described in order that it may give prophetic intimations." The liver, he thought, literally reflected the future.

This mirroring aspect of the liver may have been considered as religiously important in the sacrificial cultures outside those of the ancient Mediterranean. Robert Temple, in *Conversations with Eternity*, points out that the Toltec civilization of Mexico sacrificed men to a god called Tezcatlipoca, meaning "Smoking Mirror". The method of killing was disembowelment with an obsidian dagger. Temple suggests that the name of the slaughter god came from the mirror-like aspect of the fresh liver, combined with the "smoke" or steam that would rise from the organ on all but the hottest days. Unfortunately, we do not know enough about the Toltecs (who ruled in Mesoamerica from around 700 to the twelfth century AD) to determine whether they too believed the liver was in any way predictive.

The priests of the Celtic Druid cult of Britain and northern Europe often ritually sacrificed human beings and, occasionally, "read" their entrails. The Romans, when they first conquered France and south-east Britain under Julius Caesar, were horrified to discover the Druids practising extispicy on people instead of animals. Although usually tolerant of different religions, the Roman Empire afterwards made several attempts to smash Druidism as a matter of basic human decency. However, the cult survived all violent attempts to destroy it, only withering away when confronted by the peaceful invasion of Christian missionaries into Celtic lands.

Generals of the ancient world often used extispicy as a form of supernatural scouting. For example, when Hannibal and his Carthaginian army ravaged northern Italy in 216 BC, the people of Rome marshalled their troops to counter-attack. At times of national emergency, the city was commanded by two elected consuls. In this case the consuls were called Marcellus and Crispinus, and these opted to lead an army against the Carthaginians before they reached the gates of Rome.

When the opposing forces met, the Romans could not understand why Hannibal – who had arrived in the area first – had not taken the most strategically advantageous position, apparently leaving it for them. Plutarch gives the following account of what followed:

> "Now Marcellus determined to ride forward to reconnoitre [the intervening ground], so he sent for a soothsayer and offered sacrifice. When the first victim was slain, the soothsayer showed him that the liver had no head [i.e. the *processus pyrmidalis* was missing]. On sacrificing for the second time, the head appeared of unusual size, while all the other organs were excellent, and this seemed to set at rest the fear caused by the former. Yet the soothsayers said that they were even more disturbed and alarmed at this; for when, after very bad and menacing victims, unusually excellent ones appear, the sudden change is itself suspicious."

Any modern soldier will wince at the obvious trap the consuls now fell into, but it should be remembered that this was still the era of grand sweeps of massed troops and set-piece battles. Guerrilla war was considered dishonourable – the strategy of a cattle-raider, not a general. Moreover, the vital importance of keeping the army's leaders out of the mêlée was then rarely considered. Just over a hundred years before, Alexander the Great had always taken the point position of the first cavalry charge, and in two battles had come within striking distance of the enemy king himself. Following this example, Roman generals believed that the highest glory was to defeat the leader of the opposing army personally in hand-to-hand combat.

Plutarch goes on:

"Marcellus rode forth with his colleague Crispinus and his son, who was a military tribune, in all two hundred and twenty horsemen . . . On the overhanging crest of the woody hill, a man, unseen by the Romans, was watching their army. He signalled the men in ambush what was going on, so that they permitted Marcellus to ride close to them, and then suddenly burst out upon him, surrounding his little force on all sides . . . Marcellus was pierced through the side with a lance . . . Crispinus [escaped, but] after a few days, died of his wounds. Such a misfortune as this, losing both consuls in one engagement, never before befell the Romans."

In the subsequent Battle of Cannae, the Roman army of 50,000 men was shattered and forced to retreat in disorder. Hannibal lost only 6,700 men in the engagement, but the niggardliness of his countrymen, who refused to send him reinforcements, meant that he could ill afford such a loss. Despite their enemy's temporary helplessness, the Carthaginian army was forced to retreat from Italy before it could sack Rome. When the Romans eventually counter-attacked, it was Carthage that fell. Thus the Haruspex's prediction apparently came true – a great loss, followed by a great victory.

Through modern archaeological discoveries, it is now possible to trace the traditional development of extispicy. From the Romans the trail leads to the mysterious Etruscans of western-central Italy. This people, whose few surviving writings have yet to be deciphered, were completely obsessed with augury and specifically extispicy. At the time of the decadent collapse of their empire, it seems that individual Etruscans were unable to make even minor decisions without examining some unlucky creature's innards. The Roman statesman Cicero once commented that, "the whole Etruscan nation [was] stark mad on the subject of entrails . . ."

The origins of the Etruscan people, who apparently colonized Italy some time before 700 BC, remains a mystery. However, their main cultural influence seems to have been that of the Greeks, and it may have been from this link that their passion for reading livers came.

The Greeks practised extispicy as a matter of religious habit. So, when one reads of the building of the Athenian Acropolis, the preparations before the battle of Salamis or the assembly of ships for the siege of Troy, you can be certain that a priest with knife and a goat was there to divine the gods' will before any strategic decisions were made.

Of course, this sometimes caused dangerous delays, especially if the auspices were consistently unpropitious. In 415 BC, for example, Nicias, the general in charge of the Athenian attack on the island of Syracuse, wasted so much time on the beach waiting for Apollo's sign of favour that the Syracusians were able to outflank and annihilate his entire army.

Fourteen years later, on the coast of Asia Minor, the Athenian general Xenophon found himself in a similar predicament. His force of 10,000 Greek mercenaries had fought on the wrong side in a Persian civil war and was now being hunted by the victorious enemy army. Bereft of ships and provisions, it was vital that they find food, then march north and cross the Straits of Hellespont to Greece before the Persians were strong enough to crush them.

Before they set out, Xenophon ordered a sacrifice to read the omens. The entrails were unfavourable, so they stayed put for twenty-four hours. The next day the priest sacrificed again, but the sheep's entrails still indicated that they should not move. Xenophon was a young and untried general – elected to the post when his superiors had been captured and tortured to death. He probably would have faced a revolt among his starving troops when he ordered another day's delay, had it not been for the fact that his men believed in extispicy as keenly as he did.

On the third day, all the food was gone. Xenophon later wrote (modestly in the third person), "the soldiers came to Xenophon's tent, and told him they had absolutely no provisions left. He replied that he would not lead them out while the victims were adverse . . . 'The victims,' he said, 'as you have seen, fellow soldiers, are not yet favourable for our departure.'"

Neon, another officer, could not bear to watch his men starving for want of food that could easily be taken from neighbouring villages. So, despite the risk of incurring the displeasure of the gods, he led out a raiding party. However, as soon as they had dispersed to find food the Persian cavalry attacked and scattered them. On hearing this, Xenophon ordered another sacrifice – this time for the favour of the gods, rather than for the auspices – and immediately led out a relief force of veterans. The five hundred scavengers were rescued with only a few losses, but no food was secured.

This practical evidence that the Persians were almost ready to attack further demoralized the hungry troops. The priests had by now run out of sheep to sacrifice, and were forced to kill precious baggage oxen. Although the meat of these animals could be eaten following the sacrifice, their deaths only served to make moving all the more difficult. The three-day delay seemed to have doomed them to the same fate as the Athenians on Syracuse.

Finally, on the fourth day, the entrails of the sacrificial ox gave a favourable augury. Within hours, a Greek ship laden with food arrived – completely unexpectedly – and the army got its first full meal since the beginning of the crisis. Xenophon then gave orders to prepare for battle, saying: "It is better for us to fight now, when we have dined, than tomorrow, when we may be without dinner. The sacrifices, soldiers, are favourable, the omens encouraging, the victims most auspicious. Let us march against the foe."

The Persians were caught on the hop by this sudden advance; they presumably had thought that the Greeks had given up completely and were passively waiting for the death-blow. A Persian tactical withdrawal soon dissolved into a panicked rout and the Greeks found their road home clear (for the time being).

Xenophon did get his army back to Greece, and his account of their long trek through hostile territory, entitled *Xenophon's Anabasis* (Xenophon's Campaign), is still required reading in many military schools today. At every major decision point on the 1,500-mile march, he made sacrifice and had the priests read the entrails: never once, later on, did he feel the omens found therein were false – they were simply confusing now and again.

One general who read Xenophon's account with considerable interest was Alexander the Great. A few decades after the Greek army's retreat from Asia Minor, Alexander led a Macedonian-Greek allied force back across the Hellespont and, often using *Xenophon's Anabasis* as a guide to the territory, annexed the entire Persian Empire. His army conquered as far as north-west India and, by the age of thirty-three, he had conquered the largest empire yet known (only later surpassed by the Mongols under Genghis Khan and the British in Victorian times). Fortunately, Alexander's dream of combining Greek and Persian cultures into one state was greatly aided by the fact that both peoples shared many of the same beliefs, including extispicy.

On their exhausted return from India, Alexander's army headed for Babylon – one of the most ancient cities in the world and, as we have already seen, among the earliest known locations for the practice of extispicy. On the road, a message arrived from the Chaldaean[6] astrologers of the city, warning that a black fate would hang over Alexander's head if he entered Babylon.

The king had been away from his western empire for eight years at this point and now found corruption rife. So he ignored the warning, doubtless thinking that the Chaldaeans – who were city administrators, as well as priests – hoped to delay him while they tried to clean up the evidence of their wrong-doings. However, as Alexander approached the famous cyclopean walls of Babylon, a rumour came to him that his own Macedonian governor of the city had made sacrifice and received a hideous omen in the entrails. Setting up camp outside the gate, the king sent for and questioned the priest who had performed the rite. As the historian Plutarch tells: "The soothsayer answered that the victim's liver had lacked one lobe. 'Really!' exclaimed Alexander. 'That is a terrible omen!' He did the soothsayer no harm, but regretted that he had not listened to the warning [of the Chaldaeans]."

As a devoutly religious man, Alexander was fully schooled in extispicy, and often performed and read sacrifices in person. To try to reduce the threat of the omen, he spent as much time as possible outside the walls of Babylon, but soon caught a fever (or was poisoned) and died in the city.

Extispicy seems a perfect example of how a ridiculous practice can become a fervently held act of religious faith over the course of generations. A sceptic will say that the above cases of apparent prophecy were actually simple matters of coincidence, magnified by superstition and ignorant beliefs: those times when an

6 The Chaldaeans were such accurate prophets that the term was synonymous with astrology up to modern times. Many theologians believe that the "Three Wise Men" of the Christian nativity were Chaldaeans.

entrail-reading proved self-evidently false were not recorded, and so comparative study is impossible. Indeed, this argument is often levelled against all forms of religious, magical or scientific faith (excepting, perhaps, those adopted by the critic himself). However, it is important to consider the point of view of the pre-Scientific Age peoples when trying to understand their need and use of augury.

Our modern world is enthused with the intellectual confidence of scientific assurance. We are educated to believe that where a mystery exists, we have, or will find, the mental tools to unravel it. Possibly the boundary to this self-confidence may have been set by the quantum physicist who pointed out that "the sub-atomic universe is not only weirder than we imagine, it is weirder than we *can* imagine". Nevertheless, even if we accept this intellectual limitation, we are still far beyond our forebears, for whom almost everything was beyond their understanding.

The origins of rain and wind, the inner mechanics of repro-duction and disease, the regular movement of the stars and the unpredictability of the sea – all were total mysteries to ancient man and just had to be lived with as best as possible. This was not because they were less intelligent than we are today, but because their civilizations simply failed to record and communicate ideas as consistently as ours has done over recent centuries.

For example, the discovery of the value of pi[7] is generally attributed to the Greek philosopher Pythagoras in the sixth century BC. However, a nineteenth century study of the Great Pyramid at Giza showed that its builders encoded the exact value of pi into the structure's dimensions. Since this is highly unlikely to be a coincidence, it seems that the Ancient Egyptians knew the value of pi in 2,500 BC. Unfortunately, because they did not pass it on (perhaps because it was a religious secret or maybe because the papyrus scrolls they wrote upon were just too fragile to survive down the millennia), the information was lost until it was rediscovered by Pythagoras. Even then, it might have been lost again, had it not been for the followers of Pythagoras recording and then actively disseminating his ideas throughout the Mediterranean world.

Some ideas, of course, are universal to all developing civiliza-tions and thus do not need to be communicated – one of the most

7 The ratio of the circumference of a circle to its diameter.

common being the belief in omnipresent gods and/or super-natural beings.[8] In the face of great calamity, natural wonder or just plain incomprehension, mankind's typical reaction has been to suspect that somebody, somewhere is pulling switches to make it happen. Since, as we will see in this book, acts of precognition and clairvoyance also appear to be regular, if inexplicable, features of human life, it was only natural that gods would be credited for their occurrence. Here it is important to consider a fundamental aspect of the ancient forms of prophecy: propitiation.

Propitiation was exemplified by practices like extispicy. Mighty gods ran the universe, so offering sacrifice to them was a man's way to bribe them to be on his side: much like making "protection" payments to the Mafia. A natural extension of this idea was the belief that the "insides" of the sacrifice might indicate whether the gods were pleased with the gift or not. If the animal's innards were diseased, it would be easy to guess that the gods would not be favoured by the gift. Unfortunately, until it was killed, such hidden things could not be inspected – and afterwards, it was too late. Over time, a sceptical anthropologist might argue, cause and effect became confused and it came to be believed that portents on the entrails of the animal specifically indicated future events. The guts of the animal were not bad, thus making the god angry: the god was already angry, and said so by making the guts bad.

Yet, to study extispicy as a practice on its own, separate from the other beliefs of the time, is to misrepresent the people involved. For our ancient ancestors, omens were to be found everywhere. Moreover, they saw apparent evidence of these omens coming true on a daily basis. For them, accurate prophecy was a self-evident, if largely inexplicable truth – much as magnetism is for you or me. Their argument against modern scepticism would be the existential evidence of their own lives.

The Roman politician Cicero once wrote: "There are two types of divination: one comes from art, and the other from nature." By "art", he meant that the future could be read through intellectual skills such as geomancy,[9] astrology and palm-reading. This

8 This is why priesthood is sometimes said to be the second oldest profession, after prostitution.
9 Reading the future in the position of landforms.

presupposed that educated observation of the mundane world would lead to clues and insights from the metaphysical sphere. By "nature", he meant dreams, visions and direct contact with supernatural beings that knew the course of future events. Indeed, extispicy may have combined both these aspects. As we will see later, prophets like John Dee seem to have induced vision-trances by gazing fixedly into a reflective surface like a bowl of water, a crystal ball or, perhaps, the glossy surface of a freshly removed liver. Admittedly, there is little evidence that extispicy relied on visionary skills in the Haruspex, but, it should be remembered, the craft was sacred to those contemporaries who wrote about it; the inner mysteries may have been a taboo subject for public discussion. Certainly the detailed mechanics of an entrail-reading (what each mark meant and how they were cross-referenced) have not found their way into the historical record.

Before we ridicule the apparently childish beliefs of our ancestors, it is worth remembering that, until the discoveries of Sir Isaac Newton were made, the idea that one could deduce some of the inner workings of the universe by mathematics was at best laughed at, and at worst punishable as heresy. Even in the twentieth century, physicists like Einstein and Niels Bohr found themselves attacked by the more conservative in the scientific community. It should also be remembered that in many ways we are still as ignorant as to the nature of time as Cicero was in the first century BC.

A fault of modern, scientifically confident mankind is that we all too often decide that, if we do not understand a phenomenon, it can't have happened. However we may rationalize the development of extispicy, we cannot actually prove that it did not, in some strange way, predict future events as its practitioners fervently believed. At the very least, we should keep an open mind towards any available evidence of accurate prediction, even if, as with extispicy, we may find the actual method deeply repugnant.

3 The Voice of the Oracle

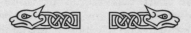

The modern view of prophets tends to be mildly satirical: they are people who utter dire warnings, like the soothsayer based on Cassandra in the 1970s television comedy *Up Pompeii*, who always burst on the scene with shouts of "Woe! Woe!" However, in ancient times, prophets were taken seriously because they played a specific role in society – something between a priest and a political advisor. As we have seen in the last chapter, the practice of augury was deliberately institutionalized in most pre-Christian civilizations; for many of our ancestors, the voice of the Oracle (the socially established prophet) was the voice of the gods.

Two of the oldest known oracles in the western world were at Dodona at Epirus – in Greece – and the Siwah oasis in the Libyan Desert. The Greeks believed that two sacred black doves were once dedicated to Isis and released from Egyptian Thebes: one flew to Dodona, the other to Siwah, indicating that the gods especially favoured these places. The Egyptians, at the same time, told of two elderly priestesses who, in the service of Isis, travelled and preached as far as their strength would carry them. The place where each finally stopped was dedicated as sacred ground. In an interesting link between the two fables, the word for "dove" in the ancient language of Epirus also meant "old woman".

The temple built at Siwah was dedicated to the goat-headed Theban god of wisdom, Amun, while the ancient grove of oaks at Dodona was dedicated to Zeus – the chief of the Greek gods. A link between the two was always maintained, since the Greeks considered Amun an aspect of Zeus and, when they went to ask his advice at Siwah, addressed him as "Zeus-Ammon".

Alexander the Great, having freed Egypt from the Persians in 331 BC, made a celebratory 200-mile pilgrimage to the Oracle of Siwah. This was no luxurious royal progress: Alexander set off into the trackless desert with only a handful of men and scanty supplies. The sheer harshness of the desert conditions took them by surprise and, after only a few days, their water ran out. Fortunately, the god indicated his favour by sending a sudden rainstorm that provided just enough water to enable them to reach their destination.

The ritual of the oracle at Siwah was rather odd. "When an oracle is wanted," Alexander was told, "the priests carry forth the bejewelled symbol of the god in a gilded boat, from whose sides dangle cups of silver; virgins and ladies follow the boat, singing the traditional hymn in honour of the deity." The supplicant would then make his question known, and the god would push the boat in a certain direction: forward meant "yes", backwards "no". (It sounds reminiscent of a modern ouija board.) Furious shaking meant the god thought the questioner was a fool.

Alexander, as liberator of Egypt and a crowned pharaoh, also had the right to speak directly to the deity in a private chamber. Not surprisingly, he decided to forgo the bizarre boat ceremony in favour of the latter option, but as such we do not know what he actually asked Zeus-Ammon. Alexander would only say afterwards that he had been given the answer he was seeking. Most historians now believe that he was either asking whether his planned conquest of the vast Persian Empire would succeed or, on a more personal note, if his mother's claim that he was actually the son of a god was true.

As a pharaoh, Alexander was ritually greeted by the head priest as "Son of Amun", and this may well have settled the latter question. His later unshakeable confidence, often in the face of overwhelming Persian forces, suggests that his private audience with the god may have convinced him of the certainty of his eventual victory. Whatever the truth, Alexander later ordered that coins stamped with his head should feature a band or circlet sporting two small goat horns – a possible show of respect or kinship with goat-headed Amun.

Modern excavation has revealed that Alexander may have been duped; it has revealed a ten- by twenty-foot chamber off the main courtyard with a secret passage running along the wall. Small holes link the passage with the inner chamber, suggesting that the voice of the god was actually the voice of a priest.

The oracle at Dodona was less elaborate. It was sited in southern Macedon in the Epirote hills, which were, until the time of Alexander's father Philip, barbaric to the point of savagery. Those who were allowed access by the neighbouring tribes were led up a stream to a grove of oak trees. The oak was sacred to Zeus, and the trees in this grove were said to be especially ancient, even for that long-lived species. Tending the grove were oracle-priestesses, usually elderly women trained to read the voice of the god in the whispering sound made by the wind in the trees.

Homer, writing between 750 and 650 BC, describes in the Iliad the hero Achilles invoking the chief of the gods as: "King Zeus, Dodonaen, Pelasgian, thou that dwellest afar ruling over wintry Dodona – and around dwell the Selloi, thy prophets, with unwashed feet and crouching on the ground . . ."

The priestesses had to go barefoot, even in the bitter Epirote winters, and were, understandably, filthy and unkempt. Only women were permitted to serve the oracle of Zeus; the reason may be that the Pelasgians, the original inhabitants who were conquered by the Greeks, were a matriarchal people who worshipped an earth-mother goddess. When the Greeks took over the grove, they replaced the goddess with masculine Zeus, but kept the other traditions of the sanctuary.

The stream that ran through the grove was said to be magical – running dry at noon each day and restarting twelve hours later. Since no normal stream behaves in this way, it sounds as if some blocking device was used to divert the stream while the priestesses listened to the sacred trees. In time, this noise-abatement policy was allowed to become one of the mysteries of the sacred grove.

Questions were written on small tablets and given to the priestess. She would then sit in the grove listening to the sound of the trees and to seven copper bowls hung like wind-chimes in the branches of the "voiceful oak" – the tree said to foretell the future. Having memorized every rustle and clink, the priestess would then consult the scrolls of ritual, which con-

tained meanings attached to numerous combinations of arbor-
eal sounds.

Modern excavations at Dodona have unearthed hundreds of
question tablets. Most are mundane to the point of tedium. A
local man called Agis asked "whether he has lost his blankets and
pillows himself, or has someone stolen them." Another man
asked if the child his wife Nyla was carrying was indeed his
own, and a farmer and his wife asked, "by what prayer or form of
worship they may enjoy greatest good fortune."

Others – envoys of powerful men or city-states – came to ask
more momentous questions, and were often baffled by the
answers. One story tells how emissaries from Boeotia consulted
the oracle on some question of grave national importance. Having
listened to the grove and consulted the scrolls, the priestess
Myrtile advised them that "it would be best for you to do the
most impious thing possible". The envoys went into a solemn
huddle, then leapt on Myrtile and threw her into a nearby
cauldron of simmering water – this being the most impious thing
they could think of on the spur of the moment.

Presumably these Boeotian supplicants had already tried the
oracle in their native country – or perhaps they had simply
decided that a long and dangerous trip to Dodona was preferable
to the ordeal of the oracle of Trophonius. Sited in a deep cave on
the Boeotian Hercynus River, this was, quite literally, a "holy
terror". The priests of the shrine of Trophonius – dedicated to
Apollo, the god of light – answered questions by granting "divine
visions" to the supplicants themselves: no intermediary oracle
was necessary.

The preparation was extremely harrowing. The questioner
was first locked in the nearby Temple of Fortuna for three days
and nights and made to fast for the whole period. On the fourth
night, he was led to the Shrine of Trophonius and given two cups
of water. The first was from the spring called *Lethe*, and was said
to blot out all previous memories for the duration of the oracle.
The second was from the stream called *Mnemosyne* (from which
we derive the words memory and mnemonic) and was said to help
the supplicant to remember the visions that were about to appear.

Visitors were then directed to the cavern beneath the shrine,
which involved clambering down a ladder in total darkness; at the
bottom of this there was a long narrow tunnel. Having struggled
down this grim stretch of cold rock (feet-first), the supplicant was

placed on a low trolley and handed two sacred honey-cakes. The
trolley then hurtled away into the darkness at break-neck speed.
Quite apart from the risk of falling off, the questioner had to hang
on to the cakes, no matter what happened, as the penalty for
arriving at the other end without them was death.

Timarchus, a disciple of the recently executed Socrates, told
how he went to the shrine of Trophonius to ask "What he should
think of the daimon [a spiritual guide] by which Socrates believed himself inspired." After the terrifying descent into the
depths of the cavern, he was left alone for a long time in darkness
and silence.

Suddenly, he saw a vision of a lake of fire, dotted with beautiful
coloured islands and a voice called: "Timarchus! The radiant
isles that float on the lake of fire are the sacred regions, inhabited
by pure souls . . . Those who keep their original purity amid the
ordeals of their first experience are clothed in divine radiance by
crossing the lake of fire, source of eternal life . . . The soul of
Socrates was one of these; always superior to his mortal body, his
soul had become worthy of entering communion with the invisible worlds and his familiar spirit, a deputy from them, taught
him a wisdom that men did not appreciate and therefore killed.
You cannot yet understand this mystery; in three months it will
be revealed to you."

The historian Plutarch wrote that Timarchus never recovered
from the ordeal. He died three months later "babbling about
luminous islands, lakes of fire and holding out his hands to the
picture of Socrates who, he said, was coming closer to him."

A modern psychologist may feel that the unnerving ceremonies
of the oracle at Trophonius represent a classic brainwashing
technique. Social isolation (in the Temple of Fortuna), starvation, dehydration, prolonged terror and finally sensory deprivation in the depths of the cave: all these (possibly combined with
drugs in the cups of water) would be likely to induce powerful
hallucinations. We may also see in these rituals typical "rites of
passage": physical and mental rigours designed to enhance consciousness and facilitate contact with higher planes of reality.

This argument does not dismiss the "ordeals" of Trophonius
as some kind of deception. It could well be that one of the
faculties acquired in such states of heightened awareness is that
of precognition.

The oracle in Boeotia was named after the architect who

designed the shrine above the sacred cave. The same Trophonius, and his brother Agamedes, also designed the temple for the most famous of all soothsayers: the oracle of Delphi, which was at Phocis in central Greece.

For over a thousand years, kings and commoners from Greece, Asia Minor, the Roman Empire, Egypt and north Africa relied on the Delphic *Pythia* (the oracle-priestess) for accurate predictions of the future. Wars were waged, colonies founded, peace treaties signed and the fates of individuals decided on the "word of the god", pronounced through the medium of the Pythia, who was usually a low-born and uneducated woman. Because of the veneration the oracle was held in all over the civilized world, Delphi became a nexus of religious and spiritual influence, not unlike the Vatican in the Middle Ages. Greece was transformed from a cultural backwater to the "cradle of western civilization" largely through the multicultural influence of visiting foreign supplicants to Delphi.

Yet the oracle's reputation, and all the riches in offerings that came with it, existed only because its priests knew something nobody else knew: how to choose, train and maintain seers and visionaries.

At the height of its power in the sixth century BC, Delphi – situated on the River Pleistus, beneath the awesome ramparts of Mount Parnassus – was a glittering temple of white marble, surrounded by a town of the kind that always springs up around tourist attractions. But, before the sixth century, it was almost as rustic as the oak grove of Dodona, and had been for about five hundred years.

The Delphic Oracle probably dated back to the period of the Mycenaean Empire, around 1500 to 1100 BC. In this earlier period of Greek power, often called the Age of Heroes, the nature goddess Gaea (or Gaia) was worshipped as the fount of Delphic prophecies. Later, following the post-Trojan War Dark Age, the religion of Apollo, the masculine god of light, replaced the waning cult of the goddess.

The legend tells how Gaea gave birth on Mount Parnassus to a titanic serpent called Python (after which the species of snake was named). Apollo slew this monster, which lived in a crack in the ground, and won the right to be worshipped at Delphi; the oracle became known as the "Pythia", meaning *pythoness*.

The original dedication to Gaia came about because the

oracle's power came out of the ground – in fact, from the crevasse in which the serpent had lived. The Greek historian Diodorus Siculus, writing in the first century BC, gave the following account of the discovery of the prophetic influence at Delphi:

"It was the goats of ancient times that first discovered the divine presence at Delphi – this is why, in our day, the people there still prefer such an animal when they offer sacrifice before consulting the god. The discovery is supposed to have occurred in this fashion. At the spot where the adytum [inner sanctum] of the present temple is, there was once a chasm in the ground where the goats used to graze. Whenever one of them approached this opening and looked down, it would begin skipping about in a startling fashion and bleating in a quite different voice to its normal one. Then, when the goatherds went to investigate this bizarre phenomenon, they too were similarly affected but, in their temporary possession by the god, would prophesy the future. As news of what was happening at the chasm spread across the countryside, many peasants flocked to test its strange power. As each approached the cleft, and breathed the vapour that emerged from the recesses, they would also fall into a sacred trance, through which Apollo would voice the coming of things yet to pass."

Thus, according to Diodorus Siculus, the Delphi fissure itself came to be called miraculous. At first, those who came to commune with the god would proclaim oracles to one another. However, many in the "divine rapture" hurled themselves down the bottomless chasm, so the local inhabitants decided that a single woman should take the burden of the god's possession and speak all the oracles.

The choice of a woman as the priestess might have been – as at Dodona – a survival from the prehistoric cult of the Earth Goddess. A more likely explanation is that in patriarchal ancient Greek society, women were considered more expendable than men, so it mattered less if a woman threw herself down the hole.

The choosing of a candidate to be the new Pythia was apparently a virtually random affair. Any local woman of the right age, who was willing to take the vow of chastity, was eligible. The testing of an applicant was itself absurdly straightforward. The priests would throw buckets of icy mountain-stream water on to the woman's bare skin – and could tell from how much she shuddered whether she was both robust and sensitive enough to be the "voice of Apollo". That was all that was involved, according to contemporary accounts.

This suggests that it was the vapour itself that created the trance in which the woman became the mouthpiece of Apollo. Unfortunately, we cannot scientifically test this theory because the chasm of Apollo no longer exists. (That it survived so long in a highly active earthquake region is in itself miraculous.) Modern geologists who have thoroughly examined the area state that there is nothing unusual about the earth or the bedrock at Delphi.

Becoming the new Delphic Oracle was a doubtful privilege. The lives of the Pythia were stressful, pleasureless and usually brief. Although the risk of falling down the fissure was minimized by seating the oracle on a large bronze tripod, the fumes themselves (presumably with a large admixture of sulphur dioxide) were unhealthy, and shortened their lives. Following an early scandal involving a handsome, virile supplicant and a lonely young Pythia, only chaste middle-aged women were chosen for the task.

Questioners approaching the oracle were first ritually purified, then told to sacrifice a goat to Apollo. They were then led into the sanctuary, but were kept far enough away from the rock cleft to avoid breathing the fumes or disturbing the reverie of the Pythia. The philosopher Apollonius of Tyana (born in the first century AD) described the air in the adytum as "a wonderfully sweet perfume", but admits that incense was burned all around, so we cannot be sure that the sacred vapours smelled as pleasant.

He goes on to describe the effect of the prophetic trance on the Pythia. Her chest heaved, her face flushed then went pale and her limbs shook convulsively. Soon she was foaming at the mouth and her hair was standing on end. Then she gabbled something that Apollonius could not make out, grabbed the sacred woollen fillet from her head and threw it on the ground. At this, the attending male priests, who had carefully transcribed the Pythia's words, hurried Apollonius outside.

Apollonius had asked if his name would live after his death. A priest later handed him a piece of paper carrying a "translation" of the Pythia's holy ranting: *You shall be spoken of in centuries to come, but only for insults to be levelled against your name.*

Not surprisingly, Apollonius tore the prediction to shreds and marched away: a reaction he later ruefully noted as being common to those who did not like or understand the Pythia's replies.

We are in a position to note the accuracy of the prediction. After his death, Apollonius and his Pythagorean beliefs were selected for ridicule by the early Fathers of the Christian Church. Since it is doubtful that the oracle knew anything about Apollonius's teachings, it seems unlikely she could have guessed this without some knowledge of the future.

Not all the Pythia's accurate predictions were induced by the vapour. When Alexander the Great visited Delphi, he is said to have arrived "off-season", during a period when the oracle was not giving predictions. Furious at the priests' flat refusal to prepare the Pythia, Alexander strode into her private chamber and started to haul her out to the sanctuary. Having no idea who he was, but realizing he was too strong to fight against, the Pythia is said to have shouted despairingly: "This young man is unstoppable!"

Realizing that he had his answer, Alexander released her, thanked her politely and left to invade Asia. He never lost a battle in his life.

Such clarity of speech – accidental as it may seem, in the above case – was a rarity in Delphic oracles. More often than not, the answer babbled by a Pythia and transcribed by the priests of Apollo was infuriatingly obscure. (The wilful obfuscation of the meaning of predictions is something we shall often encounter in this study of seers and prophecy.)

In the case of the Delphic Oracle, an element of despair at the inevitability of certain events in the future may be partly to blame. For example, when Polycrates, ruler of the island of Delos – the birthplace of Apollo – asked whether a festival he was planning should be named Delian, after the island, or Pythian, in honour of the oracle, the Pythia answered tersely: "It will not matter what you choose to call it."

This apparent self-effacement later turned out to be a strict, if misleading, statement of the truth. Before the festival could be initiated, a Persian satrap captured Polycrates and tortured and crucified him. The event did not need a name because it was destined never to take place.

On another occasion, the people of the island of Siphnos petitioned the oracle to tell them whether their recent good fortune would continue. The Pythia replied: "Whenever in Siphnos the town hall becomes white-browed, then wise men ought to beware of an ambush of wood and a herald in red."

Siphnos, a fairly small island, had recently become wealthy through the mining of gold and silver. To show off their new wealth, the Siphnians had recently gilded the outside of their town hall, making it appear – in bright sunlight – to be "white-browed". Therefore the warning of immediate danger was plain in the oracle, as was its probable origin: the reference to "an ambush of wood" apparently pointed to the wooden galleys of pirates. In fact, a few days after news of the oracle arrived on Siphnos, the Samian pirates – in ships with red-painted prows – raided the island and kidnapped many important personages. A ransom of a hundred talents of gold was eventually paid for them.

The islanders probably breathed sighs of relief that the prophesied danger had passed, leaving them still comparatively rich; but then the sea broke into the over-extended mine workings and reduced them all to poverty again.

The reason the oracle gave so little information was, in hindsight, readily apparent – the Siphnians might have protected themselves against pirate raids, but no advice could have stopped them from mining, so there was no way of saving their wealth.

A similarly worded oracle once saved all of Greece from conquest. In 480 BC, the Persian king Xerxes led a massive invasion of the Greek mainland, crushing all resistance before him. When it became plain that the Persian army would soon arrive, the Athenians asked the advice of the Pythia. The grim answer was: "Hence from my temple! Prepare for doom."

The Athenians pressed for more information. This time she pronounced that the "fortress of Cecrops" – the rock hill at the heart of Athens – must fall, but that "walls of wood unshaken" would save their dear ones. Still baffled, the envoys petitioned a third time and were told: "Stay not to meet the advancing horse and foot that swarms over the land, but turn and flee to fight another day." She added: "Oh, blessed Salamis! How many children of women will thou slaughter!"

The envoy now guessed that wooden walls meant ships, and the Athenians trusted the oracle enough to abandon their city to the enemy and fight the Persians at sea in galleys. Greatly outnumbered, the Athenians lured the Persians into the Bay of Salamis, restricting their manoeuvrability and allowing the

Greeks to close in for hand-to-hand fighting. The Persian army specialized in cavalry and chariot combat – now useless – while the Greek marine hoplites were probably the best infantry in the ancient world. The Persians lost two hundred ships to the Athenians' forty.

So many men died in the battle that the playwright Aeschylus later described the sea as invisible for broken ships and hacked corpses. With no fleet to back his invasion, Xerxes was unable to consolidate his conquest and was forced to withdraw to Asia Minor.

Again, in 431 BC, when the Spartans asked if they should invade northward into Athenian territory, the Pythia answered: "If you press the war with energy, then victory will be on your side." She added that Apollo – as the god of healing (and disease) – would aid the Spartans. Within days of the launch of the invasion, a plague struck Athens and her Theban allies. Sparta, inexplicably, was not affected.

Sparta eventually won the Pelopponesian war, but to the cost of the whole of Greece, for it eventually led to subsequent conquest first by the Macedonians under Alexander, and then Rome.

The oracle also played a major part in the peaceful spread of Greek civilization, for her word was automatically sought whenever a new Greek settlement was planned. It was on the Pythia's advice that the Cretans colonized Sicily, Archias founded Syracuse, the Boeotians built Heraclea in Pontus, the Spartans created another Heraclea in Thessaly and the city of Byzantium (now Istanbul) was constructed on the Hellespont. These colonizing projects owed much of their success to the belief of the colonizers that Apollo protected them.

It is ironic, but not surprising, that both the later conquerors of Greece – Macedonia and Rome – either aspired to be Greek or believed themselves the spiritual heirs of Greece – the highest aspect of which was the Delphic Oracle. It is impossible to imagine what our western culture would have been like, if the Pythia at Delphi had never existed.

The most famous single story about the oracle's prophetic powers dates from 548-547 BC, and is told by Herodotus. The richest country in the eastern Mediterranean at that time was Lydia (situated in present-day northern Turkey) and its king, Croesus, was (and still is) a by-word for magnificent wealth.

Croesus had ruled Lydia for eleven years of peace and prosperity, but now faced a major crisis. The Persians, an upstart nation of barbarian horsemen from the hills, had recently conquered his neighbours, the Medes, and Croesus suspected that he would be the next target. It seemed common sense to pre-empt them, and some of Croesus' councillors wanted to attack at once. Others argued for caution. Croesus decided to consult an oracle, but could not decide which of them would be the best. So he decided to test them.

He sent ambassadors to Dodona, Trophonius, Siwah, Delphi and other sanctuaries. All the supplicants were instructed to ask the same question at midday, one hundred days after they set out: "What is King Croesus doing at this moment?"

The Pythia at Delphi answered: "*I know the number of the sands and all measures of the sea. I understand the dumb and hear the voice that speaks not. A smell comes to my nostrils: strong-shelled tortoise boiled with lamb's flesh in bronze, covered above and below.*"

Croesus – having decided to do something that nobody could possibly guess – had boiled up some tortoise and lamb meat in a closed bronze pot. Although one of the other oracles is said to have come close to describing the uncommon act of a king cooking his own lunch, it was the Pythia who described it exactly.

The next envoys sent to Delphi took gifts for Apollo and his priests, which included a fortune in gold ingots, gold and silver dishes, jars and vases, a four-and-a-half-foot high solid gold statue of a woman (known as "Croesus's pastry cook") and two wine bowls, one of gold and the other of silver. Herodotus noted that the gold wine bowl weighed half a ton and could hold over 5,000 gallons. Croesus clearly hoped that he could buy the favour of Apollo; unfortunately, he does not seem to have heard about the Greek notion of *hubris* – the legendary "pride before a fall".

The Pythia was asked three separate questions. The first concerned the issue at hand: "Should Lydia attack the Persians?" The reply was: "After crossing the Halys [the river on the Lydian-Persian border], Croesus will destroy an empire."

The second question concerned the future: "Will Croesus' reign be a long one?" The Pythia replied: "When a mule becomes king of the Medes, then flee, soft-soled Lydian, by the pebbly Hermus [another Lydian river]. Stay not, nor feel shame for showing cowardice."

The final question was personal: "Will Croesus's son (dumb from childhood) ever speak?" To which the reply was: "Croesus, you prince of fools, hope to be not at home when your son finds his voice. Be far away on that day, for it will not be propitious for you."

Since the first prediction was exactly what he was hoping to hear, Croesus was inclined to find a favourable interpretation for the second two answers. He assumed they meant that he would rule a long time (for how could an animal rule over the Medes?) and that his son would one day regain his voice.

Whether Croesus saw the obvious risk – that the empire he would crush might be his own – is hard to say. Given the growing threat posed by Persian expansionism, he may have already decided that attack was his only defence. If he had known that King Cyrus was born of Persian and Mede parents – and was thus a "mule", of mixed race – he may not have risked the venture.

Croesus and the Lydian army crossed the Halys River in the autumn of 547 BC, and were met by a much larger Persian force led by Cyrus. After a day of fighting both armies were badly mauled, and neither could claim decisive victory. At dusk, Cyrus made a tactical withdrawal and Croesus returned to Lydia to gather a stronger army.

If Cyrus had been a less enterprising leader, Croesus might have ultimately won the war – having much greater resources and a number of allies to strengthen him. In the event, Cyrus made a surprise attack into Lydia while Croesus' army was partially disbanded for the winter: the traditional non-campaigning season. The Lydians fought hard, but it was only a matter of time before their capital, Sadis, fell.

As Persian soldiers marched into the Lydian throne room to capture Croesus (who had refused to flee), his son is said to have overcome his speech impediment to shout: "Swine! How dare you lay hands on King Croesus?"

What happened next depends on who we believe. Herodotus says that Croesus was recognized to be a worthy man by Cyrus the Great, and later became a trusted advisor in the Persian court. However, a recently discovered Babylonian message cylinder of that period states: "Cyrus, king of Persia, has marched into Lydia, killed its king, taken its wealth and left a garrison there."

The oracle's advice did not always lead to disaster. When an undistinguished visitor called Battus sought the counsel of the oracle, she assured him that he would successfully build an empire in Libya. Battus went on to organize an expedition and successfully founded the trading port of Cyrene in 631 BC – the colony went on to flourish for nearly 1,300 years. Battus himself was doubtless rather bemused by the oracle, since he had only gone to Delphi to ask if his stutter could be cured.

On another occasion, the Spartan monarch Lycurgus visited Delphi to ask the god's advice. For some years he had been exiled from his own kingdom, but had now been invited back. Lycurgus asked what he should do and the Pythia replied: "Beloved of God; the commonwealth that observes your laws will be the most famous in the world." Thus encouraged, Lycurgus returned to Sparta and drew up a fundamentally reforming set of laws that won the city universal respect for centuries to come.

In later years, the oracle was less trusted and consulted. Many people believed that the priests of Apollo were prone to twist their interpretations to please wealthy or powerful patrons. In other cases, where even they seemed unable to comprehend the words of the Pythia, the priests were said to give nebulous and meandering translations that could be understood to mean anything.

The Greek biographer Plutarch, writing in the last century BC, became a Delphic priest himself in the hope of reforming the sanctuary. When he found the task impossible, he retired and recorded his regret in *The Decline of the Oracles*.

Our modern attitude is understandably sceptical; it is tempting to believe that the oracle pronounced obscure nonsense that would take in the ignorant and credulous. The objection to this theory is the consistent reliability of Delphic predictions for over a millennium. As we have seen, many of the oracle's obscure predictions accurately revealed future events, and no amount of educated guesswork could account for this.

The fifth-century BC historian Thucydides – the archetype of the objective chronicler – ruefully admitted that Delphic predictions had repeatedly changed the course of Greek history. This, he could confirm from events in his own lifetime, was because the prophetic answers given by the Pythia were reliable enough to allow the complete redirection of state policies. If a city like Athens or Sparta had followed Delphic advice, later to find it totally inaccurate, historians like the sceptical Thucydides would have been delighted to record the fact, but they never got the opportunity.

The priests of Apollo kept detailed records of all the transactions of the oracle. This Delphic treasure-trove eventually found its way to Constantinople, and remained there for centuries. Sadly, the records vanished, following the capture of the city by the Ottoman Turks in 1453.

Like so many prophets, the Delphic Oracle foresaw her own end: "Aye, if you will hear it, if you endure to know that Delphi's self with all things gone must go. And thus, even thus, on some long destined day shall Delphi's beauty shrivel and burn away. Shall Delphi's fame from earth expire at that bright bidding of celestial fire?"

In its time, that prediction carried much the same shock value for the ancient Greeks that medieval Christians would have felt if someone had prophesied the downfall of the Church.

It was towards the beginning of the second century AD that Delphi faced the growth of this new and hostile religion of the crucified man-god. The early Christian Fathers attacked all previous Greek forms of belief. Interestingly, the Christians did not question the accuracy of Delphic oracles – they simply ascribed to them demonic powers.

However, it was not Christianity, but its own success that brought about the end of the Delphic Oracle. A young Roman nobleman called Hadrian visited Delphi around the turn of the first century AD and learned that he would one day be the emperor of Rome. On winning the laurel crown in 117, Hadrian ordered the oracle closed down and the sacred spring blocked. He had no intention of letting any would-be usurper receive the same encouragement . . .

In 362, the Emperor Julian – known as the Apostate, because he preferred paganism to Christianity – sent his personal physician to try to revive the oracle at Delphi. But it was too late; the age of oracles had passed. As the Oxford Classical Dictionary sadly notes, after the third century AD, "international attention was now confined to tourism and the Pythian games".

4 The Book of Changes

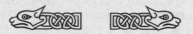

In 1949, admirers of the world's most eminent living psychologist, Carl Gustav Jung, must have suspected that he had lost his mind. At the age of seventy-four, this venerated founding member of psychoanalysis had written the foreword to the German translation by his friend Richard Wilhelm of a work called the *I Ching*, or *Book of Changes*: a collection of oracles used in fortune-telling. In his foreword, Jung actually confessed to consulting the oracle – the "ancient book that purports to be animated" – about his intention of presenting it to the western world.

The method of consulting it, apparently, consisted of throwing down three coins. Each throw produces a line; either a straight line, or a line with a break in the middle, depending on whether there is a preponderance of heads or tails. The procedure is repeated six times, and the lines are written down from the bottom upwards, six of them forming a "hexagram". What Jung obtained was a hexagram labelled *Ting*, "The Cauldron":

The "judgement" said: "Supreme good fortune. Success."

Jung interpreted "The Cauldron" as meaning that the *I Ching* was describing itself as a cauldron, a cooking-pot full of nourishment.

In the *I Ching*, each major "judgement" is followed by six

minor ones, known as "the lines", because each one applies to the separate lines – but only if these lines were obtained by throwing three heads or three tails. Three heads has a numerical value nine, three tails a numerical value six. Jung had a nine in the second place, which read:

> "My comrades are envious,
> But they cannot harm me.
> Good fortune."

Jung assumed this meant that the *I Ching* aroused envy, but he might well have taken it to mean that his fellow psychologists, many of whom regarded him with envy, might take this as an opportunity to attack him, but that their attacks would not succeed.

If so, he was right. The publication of the *I Ching* did indeed meet with a steadily snowballing success, until millions of copies were sold. In spite of colleagues who thought that his brain had softened, Jung not only weathered the storm, but emerged as one of the major gurus of the 1950s and, when he died in 1961, was more widely venerated than his old friend – and later enemy – Freud had ever been.

The sceptics – like Martin Gardner of the *Scientific American* – were not only scathing, but also bitter. It seemed to them appalling that a psychologist as widely respected as Jung should lend his name to puerile superstition.

It is only fair at this point to add that some sinologists[1] of distinction have also been sceptics. James Legge, the first scholar to translate the *I Ching* into English, in the mid-nineteenth century, displayed irritability when he talked about the tendency of Chinese scholars to declare that the hexagrams of the *I Ching* contain truths about electricity and other discoveries of contemporary western science. When he asked why, in that case, their ancestors had not discovered electricity, his Chinese colleagues replied that *they* had indeed to learn of such matters from western books, but that they then looked into the *I Ching* and found that they were already known to Confucius . . . Legge remarks that "the vain assumption thus manifested is childish, and until the Chinese drop their hallucination about the

1 Those who study Chinese language, history and culture.

I Ching . . . it will prove a stumbling-block to them, and keep them from entering upon the true path of science."

In volume two of his vast *Science and Civilization in China*, Joseph Needham comments that the *I Ching* "resembled . . . the astrological pseudo-explanations of medieval Europe, but the abstractness of the symbolism gave it a deceptive profundity." He goes on to say that Chinese scholars "would have been wiser to tie a millstone about the neck of the *I Ching* and cast it into the sea."

But then, Needham belonged to a pre-Jungian generation of scholars and, since he is writing a history of science in China, his attitude is hardly surprising. He would certainly have been equally outraged by the view of modern scientists like Percy Seymour, Hans Eysenck and Michel Gauquelin, that there is a great deal to be said for astrology.

In fact, sceptics like Legge and Needham are simply displaying ignorance of the Chinese religious attitude. The Chinese regard the earth as a living being and mountains as living organisms that diffuse vital breath throughout nature. For Taoists in particular, mountains are the means by which humans communicated with immortals and primeval earth forces. While Confucianism lays emphasis upon moral duties and social conduct, Taoism stresses individual freedom, self-transformation and mystical experience.

Chinese Buddhism has four sacred mountains in the north, south, east and west. For the Chinese, they are full of "telluric force", a sacred force inherent in the earth itself. These sacred "dragon paths", *lung mei*, carry this force as our arteries carry our blood. In the west, such lines have become known as "ley lines". These seem to differ from the winding Chinese dragon lines in being usually "old straight tracks", but (as the scholar John Michell has pointed out, in *The View Over Atlantis*) the difference is only superficial.

Out of this belief in telluric force springs the science the Chinese call *feng shui* (pronounced *fang shway*), the science of wind and water, known in the west as geomancy. Experts in *feng shui* (also known as the "dragon force") were traditionally consulted on the siting of buildings and tombs. Indeed, in modern Hong Kong or Peking, *feng shui* experts are still called in every day to explain persistent illness – or bad luck – and to rearrange the furniture. (The same thing occasionally happens in England, where a dowser might point out that someone's bed is pointing the wrong way, or that their favourite armchair is directly above an underground spring, and should be moved; but this is a rarity. In China it is as widely accepted as calling in the plumber.)

1998 saw the publication in Britain of a monthly magazine called *Feng Shui for Modern Living*, and, in an article on Hong Kong, *feng shui* expert Raymond Lo writes:

> "*Feng shui*, which means 'wind and water', originates from an ancient Chinese book called the 'Book of Burial' written by Kuan P'o in around 265 AD. This book describes the features of landscapes which will generate good *feng shui*. It says: 'The energy of the dragon will be dissipated by wind and will stop at the boundary of water.'
>
> The sentence tells us two important criteria in finding a good *feng shui* place. Firstly, the site must be sheltered from strong wind, secondly it must be near the boundary of a watercourse. In *feng shui*, we believe that there are energies called *aki* which are to be found in mountain ranges, which we call 'dragons'. To preserve such prosperous energy, the place must have shelter or natural protection against strong wind. Also, the 'dragon' is thought to move forward until it reaches water. At the boundary of water and land, the 'dragon' halts. Where the dragon stops, the energy accumulates. So a good *feng shui* place must meet these two requirements. It must be sheltered on all four sides, front, back, left and right, and it must be near water with an open space to accumulate ch'i."[2]

As can be plainly seen – and as Jung and Richard Wilhelm have pointed out – understanding Chinese religious thought demands a complete change in our western attitudes. This change has been brought about very largely by Wilhelm's *I Ching*, with its introduction by Jung.

In fact, Jung had prepared for the sceptical onslaught by developing a new "scientific" concept, which he called synchronicity, an "acausal" (or non-causal) "connecting principle". "Synchronicity" went on to become as much a part of the language as his earlier coinages *introvert* and *extrovert*.

2 This is elsewhere defined as "the magnetic field that occurs naturally around living things".

A synchronicity is the kind of coincidence that seems too preposterous to be explainable by mere chance. Jung illustrates it with the story of a mother who took a photograph of her small son in the Black Forest. She took it to be developed in Strasbourg but, with the outbreak of the 1914 war, gave it up for lost. In 1916, she bought a film in Frankfurt and took a picture of her daughter. When the film was developed, it proved to be a double exposure that included the picture she had taken of her son in 1914 – the film had somehow got back into circulation as a new roll.

Now it is, admittedly, hard to think of this as "mere coincidence". We are inclined to feel that there must have been some underlying "reason", some "connecting principle", that explained how the film, against a chance of millions to one, came back into the hands of its owner, but what could such a connecting principle be?

Jung's original theory of the *I Ching* as an "ancient book that purports to be animated", seems to suggest spirits. One might, for example, imagine that the spirit of the woman's dead mother followed the progress of the roll of film, and provided the mental impulse that made her daughter go to the shop, and the mental impulse that made the assistant take down that particular roll of film. But although Jung came, during the course of his lifetime, to believe in the existence of "spirits", he would have found such a theory too complicated to explain all synchronicities.

What precisely does an "acausal connecting principle" mean? Presumably Jung meant a way in which two events might be connected without an obvious material cause, but that seems equally difficult to conceive.

A better possible explanation might be found in a phrase of that remarkable Egyptologist, Schwaller de Lubicz, who wrote in *Sacred Science*: "The higher animals, as well as the human animal, are totally bathed in a psychic atmosphere which establishes the bond between the individuals, a bond as explicit as the air which is breathed by all living beings . . . Every living being is in contact with all the rhythms and harmonies of all the energies in his universe."

This seems to go to the heart of the matter. A commuter on his way to the office certainly does not feel in touch with all the rhythms and harmonies of the surrounding world. On the contrary, he feels as most of us feel most of the time – trapped inside a fairly narrow present, and cut off from the wider universe around him. As Eliot put it, in *The Waste Land*: "We each think of the key, each in his prison."

Yet, if the commuter was sitting on a train carrying him to a holiday in the south of France, he might well see the world quite differently. Somehow, everything would seem more interesting and exciting. If, later, he happened to be sitting outside a café on Marseilles harbourfront at half past five in the evening, drinking a glass of wine and looking at the people wandering past, he might well feel that the whole world is full of interesting vibrations and memories. For example, looking at the Chateau D'If out in the harbour, he might recall reading *The Count of Monte Cristo* at the age of twelve, and remember the hero's famous escape, and this in turn might lead him to think about *The Three Musketeers* and the siege of La Rochelle . . . So he comes to recognize that, in a state of relaxation, one thought or feeling leads to another, bringing a sense that everything in the universe is somehow connected.

Anyone who has experienced this feeling, whether or not he formulates it intellectually, has encountered the insight that produced the *Book of Changes*.

The *I Ching* probably began as two lines, the unbroken and the broken one, (called *yang* and *yin*, meaning light and darkness) signifying "yes" and "no". The person who consulted it probably tossed a coin or token and noted whether it came down heads or tails.

Now all ancient philosophers attached tremendous importance to the number three, regarding it as the source of creation. It can be found in ancient Egypt, ancient Greece, even in the Bible, where the word *logos* ("In the beginning was the Word": *logos* being Hebrew for "word") means a three-term proportion.

Their argument went like this. Creation sprang out of unity – in other words, by the division of unity. Schwaller de Lubicz says that we can see this process throughout nature – for example, when a branch of a tree divides to form two more branches. But when we look at the divided branch from below, what we see is a "trinity" – three branches joined, as in a schoolboy's catapult or a dowsing rod. Three, then, springs naturally out of two.

At all events, for whatever reason, the ancients saw three as a sacred number. So it was natural for the inventor of the original *I Ching* to see the two basic lines arranged in a kind of club sandwich:

In his little book *Changes: Eight Lectures on the I Ching*, Helmut Wilhelm, the son of Richard Wilhelm, explains its further development.

Originally, the three negative lines were associated with moisture and the sea, while the three positive lines were associated with dryness and the earth. Much later, the positive lines became associated with heaven, and the three negative lines took the place of earth. In other words, heaven became the masculine principle and earth the feminine principle.

Now anyone who looks at these two "sandwiches" can see that there are six possible combinations of the lines. All you have to do is to replace each line in turn with its opposite, and you get half a dozen arrangements.

The first of these arrangements is as follows:

Why the first? Because, in Chinese philosophy, the female trigram is regarded as the Abyss, the emptiness out of which everything arose, or, alternatively, as the sea that gave birth to the land. Since, in the *I Ching*, change always moves upward, from the bottom to the top, we start by changing the bottom line from negative to positive.

In this trigram, the female has been aroused and impregnated by the male, and bears a son, her first. And since the Chinese sages associated arousal with thunder, it is called *Chen*, Thunder – or the Arousing.

Readers who are already beginning to find this confusing are asked to persist just a little longer – at least, if they wish to understand what the *I Ching* is all about.

In fact, it would probably help if we move the bottom line up to the middle:

and stare at it, asking what it suggests.

The Chinese answer is that the female lines at the top and

bottom suggest a deep gorge or abyss, and the male line between them a fast-flowing river in the bottom of the gorge. Why a river, when water is feminine? Because these are the sons, and they start life as closer to the mother than the father. This set of lines is called *K'an*: and signifies Water and Danger.

This image of a gorge with a swift river suggests the idea of danger. Since a gorge is also a place in which one can hide, it also suggests the idea of effeminacy, withdrawal, sick melancholy. To the modern mind, the trigram suggests the romantic artists and poets of the nineteenth century, who found life such a burden.

Move the positive line up to the top:

$$\overline{}\\ == \\ ==$$

and the image suggests a slab resting on two supports, or a mountain. A mountain suggests keeping still, so the "third son" is known as *Ken*: Keeping Still. The third son is strong and unmoving.

We can now begin to see the way that Chinese thought works. The changes move upward. The first son is a burst of thunder, like the thunderclap of creation. The second son is also full of energy, but it is the subjective energy of the artist. And the third son is strong and silent, like a mountain, his energy under control.

The next three trigrams represent the three daughters, and we shall not go into these except to say that the eldest is *Sun*, the Gentle, whose image is the wind, the second eldest *Li*, the Clinging, whose image is fire, and the youngest *Tui*, the Joyous, whose image is a still lake.

And so we have eight *trigrams*, the mother, the father and their six sons and daughters.

The next stage in the development of the *I Ching* was to combine the trigrams into *hexagrams*, figures of six lines. The reasoning behind this is probably that each trigram represents one attribute – the Creative, the Arousing, the Joyous, etc – and the whole Chinese mode of thought springs from the notion of two elements, *yin* and *yang*, in combination, symbolized by a circle divided into light and dark by a wavy line, and known as *t'ai chi t'u*, the "great pole".

So the trigrams are combined into hexagrams – sixty-four of

them (eight times eight.) Then, once again, the sage contemplates the meaning of the hexagrams – what their combined elements signify – and draws his conclusions.

Towards the end of his life, Confucius is supposed to have remarked that if he had another fifty years to live, he would devote it to the study of the *I Ching*. At first that sounds absurd – how could anyone devote fifty years to studying sixty-four hexagrams? But the Chinese sages felt that these hexagrams contain the permutations and combinations of all life on earth, every situation that can possibly arise.

So, for example, if the upper trigram consists of three strong lines, and the lower one of three weak lines, as in Hexagram 11, this symbolizes peace. The Creative moves upward, and the Receptive moves downward, and the two perfectly balance one another. If, on the other hand, the weak lines are below and the strong above (as in Hexagram 12) then the two forces are moving in opposite directions, signifying stagnation and decline.

So studying the hexagrams was regarded by Confucius as studying life itself. All the lines in the *I Ching* change continually, but consistently, so that someone who studies them gradually comes to know them as a musician knows every phrase in a symphony, and recognizes how it develops from earlier phrases.

Moreover, a man who knew them intimately might be extremely valuable as a statesman, or as an adviser of the ruler, for he could see a situation in the real world that would instantly strike him as, let us say, Hexagram 38, *Opposition*, or as Hexagram 39, *Obstruction*. He would also know that a creative intervention – a strong line entering at the bottom – would push all the other lines upward (the top one would, of course, be lost), transforming opposition into Hexagram 5, *Waiting* or *Nourishment*, or transforming obstruction into Hexagram 21, *Biting Through*, which suggests the teeth closing to bite through an obstruction. On the other hand, he might recognize clearly that what is required is non-intervention, waiting until the darkness gradually gives way to light.

We can see, then, why the Chinese regarded the *I Ching* as a book of wisdom, and why they believed that it can foretell the future.

The sceptic, of course, will feel that this whole argument consists of fallacy piled on fallacy. Why should we regard these notions about alternating lines as anything more than a kind of pseudo-logic dreamed up by primitive thinkers, in the days when the principles of science were imperfectly understood?

To this we can only reply that the principles of western science also regard prophecy and precognition as nonsense, and this book has already attempted to show that there are circumstances in which human beings seem to have had undeniable glimpses of the future. This is a fact, and science progresses by attempting to absorb new facts, even if they seem to contradict its basic presuppositions.

In 1768, the French Academy of Sciences asked the great chemist Lavoisier to go and investigate a report of a huge stone that had hurtled down from the sky. Lavoisier, convinced that stones do not fall from the sky, reported that all the witnesses were mistaken or lying. It took many more decades before science admitted that stones do fall from the sky – and that, although most meteors are burnt up before they reach the earth, there are thousands every day. They are the rule, not the exception.

Now in fact, most people who have devoted some time to studying the *I Ching* soon become convinced that it can be surprisingly accurate. This could, of course, be chance or self-deception, but we must also admit that the scepticism most of us feel about such matters is based upon the notion that it hardly makes sense. How can throwing three coins (or dividing up a bundle of yarrow stalks – the more traditional method of divination) produce anything but a chance result?

Of course, Jung addressed this question in formulating the concept of synchronicity (although the biologist Paul Kammerer had already anticipated him). However, the concept of synchronicity still fails to explain it. It merely points to something that most of us have experienced. (I have yet to meet a person who has not experienced at least one remarkable synchronicity.) So why do synchronicities happen, and how can they explain the workings of the *I Ching*?

I would suggest that a good starting point might be that quotation from Schwaller de Lubicz: "Every living being is in contact with all the rhythms and harmonies of all the energies in his universe."

In other words, we could be wrong to assume that each of us is alone, "each in his prison". We think of ourselves as small, separate globules of life, each one alone, like a single-celled organism floating in a pond – an organism that may end up in the stomach of some living creature. But is it not possible that we are part of something larger, like all the cells in a mass of frogspawn – or indeed, in the human body? The body is a whole; its cells and parts are aware of one another. What Schwaller seems to be implying is that we may be connected to other parts of our "universe" by nerves and tissues that carry electrical impulses.

A better image is suggested by the hologram – which, as everybody knows, is a solid-looking object in space which turns out to a three-dimensional picture made of light beams. This is made by the interaction of two laser beams – beams of light in which all the waves "march in step" – on a photographic plate. One of the beams has just been reflected off some object, like a book. And when a laser beam is passed through the photographic plate, the book appears suspended in the air, looking quite real and solid.

Yet that book is actually a pattern of ripples on the plate. This is the reality of the hologram. Some modern physicists, like David Bohm, have even suggested the breathtaking idea that perhaps this world around us is not as real and solid as it looks. Perhaps it is also a "projection" of some *underlying* pattern which may not look remotely like the so-called "real world".

As soon as we enter this universe of modern physics, we are in a world in which Jung's synchronicity no longer sounds like some odd superstition. Perhaps we are wrong to think of the Frankfurt woman who recovered her son's photograph as a chance in a million. Perhaps in the "real" world that underlies our physical world, there was a connection. We feel that Frankfurt and Strasbourg are so far apart that the "chance" is infinitely unlikely. But suppose the woman's mind itself was the "thread" that connected them, and that led to her recovery of the roll of film?

Seen from that point of view, the idea of receiving sensible answers by throwing down three coins may not be as silly as it sounds – particularly if we bear in mind that we must formulate the question as clearly and simply as possible. Formulating the question may be like writing a message on a computer screen. Throwing the coins may be the means by which this message is sent to the e-mail address on the other side of the world. In fact, as we can see, the existence of computers and of the Internet provides an analogy that makes the operation of the *I Ching* seem altogether more acceptable.

To recapitulate this argument: the *I Ching* depends upon the notion that we are surrounded by vibrations and harmonies, of which we are largely unconscious, and which nevertheless respond to our own living vibrations and harmonies. So the mind is able to produce effects which are not measurable by purely our materialistic science. What happens when a question is clearly formulated, and coins are thrown, is an example of these effects.

Let us now look a little more closely into the history and the mechanics of the *I Ching*.

As we have seen, *I Ching* means *Book of Changes* (the "I" meaning "change"). It embodies sixty-four "hexagrams" (or *kua*) – each consisting of a sequence of six yin or yang lines, and each hexagram having a name such as *Sung*, Conflict, *Ku*, Decay, or *P'i*, Stagnation. The meaning of the hexagram is illustrated in a short verse, and this in turn is explained further in the *Image*, which enables us to understand the meaning the sages attached to the two trigrams that make up the hexagram.

For example, Hexagram 20, *Kuan*, meaning Contemplation, consists of the trigram meaning "the gentle, wind", above the trigram meaning "the receptive, earth". And the *Image* explains:

The wind blows over the earth
The image of Contemplation.
Thus the kings of old visited the regions of the world
Contemplated the people
And gave them instruction.

After this, in the Wilhelm version, comes a commentary on individual lines. These commentaries are supposed to be the philosophical musings of the Chou Dynasty's King Wen (circa 1150 BC), his son, the Duke of Chou, and finally the philosopher Confucius (circa 551-479 BC). Joseph Needham dismisses this, suggesting that it is more plausible to believe that the earliest part of the *I Ching* dates back to the eighth century BC. On the other hand, he quotes the view of the scholar Kuo Mo-Jo, who believed that the work may be as late as the third or fourth century BC. Needham himself provisionally accepts that the "peasant omens" that formed the basic *I Ching* date from around the eighth century BC, but reached their present form as late as the end of the Chou dynasty around 256 BC. He is sceptical of the view that King Wen, the Duke of Chou and Confucius had anything to do with the work.

According to the traditional view, the invention of the *I Ching* is attributed to the legendary god-king Fu Hsi, who is said to have ruled China around 30,000 years ago, although his actual historical date is probably about 2,400 BC. Fu Hsi is said to have lived in a time when men were primitive hunter-gatherers – he is credited with civilizing his contemporaries by inventing the art of cookery. (In fact, by 2,400 BC, the Chinese had been cultivating rice for over 3,000 years.)

One of the earliest methods of divination in China was heating scapula bones or tortoise-shells with red-hot metal, and interpreting the cracks that formed.

According to legend, the inspiration for the *I Ching* came to Fu Hsi from markings on the back of a sacred tortoise. Presumably this refers to the *yin* and *yang* symbol, the circle divided into light and dark by a wavy line. Around this circle were then arranged the eight trigrams, already mentioned, and around these, the sixty-four hexagrams.

This, according to traditional scholars, seems to have been the form in which the *I Ching* was transmitted to succeeding generations for more than a millennium. The only development during that period was the replacement of heat-cracked bones and tortoise-shells with fifty stalks of the "magical" yarrow plant (*Achilles Millefolium*). The ritual of the yarrow stalks is a complex ceremony involving picking up small handfuls of the dried stems and deriving *yin* and *yang* lines from the random numbers created. Both time-consuming and difficult, the yarrow stalk method remains favoured by those who see a deep religious significance in the oracle, but has elsewhere, as we have seen, been supplanted by the "coin method".

Around 1150 BC, the *I Ching* oracles were recorded in text form for the first time. About that period Wen-wang, or King Wen, the ruler of Chou – a semi-barbaric state on the western frontier of China – threatened the Shang dynasty, but was captured and imprisoned by the powerful eastern emperor Chou Hsin. One legend states that Wen somehow became a member of the Shang court, but soon found the corruption and cruelty impossible to bear. Unable to escape and powerless to improve matters, Wen – like Hamlet – pretended to be mad.

The tyrant had him imprisoned and, to pass the time, Wen consulted and meditated upon the *I Ching*. He decided that, in its basic form, the oracle lacked precision. So, with what he believed to be divine guidance, he wrote sixty-four short verses – the *Judgements* – to illustrate each hexagram's meaning and content. For example, in Hexagram 11, *T'ai*, Peace, in which the trigram for earth stands above the trigram for heaven:

> Peace.
> The small departs,
> great approaches.
> Good fortune.
> Success.

His reasoning was that Earth, the Receptive, moved naturally downward, while Heaven, the Creative, moves upward; so the two meet and counterbalance one another in harmony and peace.

On the other hand, when Heaven is above, and Earth beneath, as in Hexagram 12, Standstill, they are moving in opposite directions, and the result is lack of contact and stagnation.

Some of the prose expansions of the less favourable hexagrams Wen is believed to have illustrated with descriptions of his own bleak situation. Yet his attitude throughout remains that of a Taoist – a belief in the cyclical nature of all things and that intelligent inaction often achieves more than impulsive action. A persistent theme in the *Judgements* of the *I Ching* is that one must quietly persevere through bad times in the certainty of better times to come.

It should be noted that, although the official founder of Taoism was Lao Tze, born about 604 BC, the doctrine of the *Tao* (the Way) is regarded as one of the primary religions of China, possibly founded by the Yellow Emperor Huang Ti around 2600 BC.

After three years, Wen was ransomed (tradition states for a fine horse, four chariots and a beautiful girl), and returned to Chou, where he spent the rest of his life criticizing corruption and cruelty, and thereby becoming a hero of Confucian historians. His son, the Duke of Chou, overthrew the Shang dynasty, and initiated the Chou dynasty, which ruled for over 800 years.

The Duke of Chou added to the complexity of meaning of the *I Ching* by adding "line-by-line" commentaries. These were based on the visual image of a hexagram as well as questioner's progression through the situation predicted.

For example, in Hexagram 36, *Ming I*, The Darkening of the Light, the trigram for the Receptive, Earth, stands above that of the Clinging, Fire (the sun).

The sun has sunk under the earth, and is therefore darkened.

The Duke of Chou added a meaning to each of the six lines based firstly on their aspect as *yin* or *yang*, and secondly on their position within the hexagram.

The (unbroken) *yang* line at the bottom would be the first to be obtained when throwing coins or calculating yarrow stalks. It is therefore indicative of the beginning of a period of darkness. His advice attached to this line is that despite having energetic (*yang*) intentions, one should not take action as the difficult situation is just at its beginning. Each line thereafter offers advice based on their *yin* or *yang* form, added to the concept of a darkness (or difficult time) gradually lifting. Hence the *yin* (broken) line at the top suggests that "dawn" is at hand and that those who had profited by the dark (*yin*) aspect of the time will now fall

In the sixth century BC, as we have seen, Confucius followed the example of King Wen and the Duke of Chou and added his own *Judgements* on each hexagram, which Wilhelm labels the *Images*. Since Confucius was mainly concerned with "right conduct", his contributions to the *I Ching* are more concerned with advice on day-to-day living than with divination.

Helmut Wilhelm has an interesting chapter on the later history of the *I Ching*, and upon such scholars as Wang Pi, born in 226 AD, whose commentaries treat the *I Ching* as a book of wisdom rather than of divination, Chou Tun-i of the Sung period (960-1127 AD), who restored the Confucian emphasis on the *I Ching* as a guide to conduct, and Shao Yung, another Sung Confucian, whom Wilhelm describes as a speculative genius, who worked out a different order for the trigrams and hexagrams.

More than six hundred years later, the philosopher Leibniz saw Shao's diagram, and recognized in it something he himself had struck upon – the binary system of mathematics (now the basis of all computer calculations). Writing the numbers from 0 to 64 in the binary system, he recognized that they corresponded exactly to Shao's arrangement (with *yin* as 0, *yang* as 1), with only one difference: it inverts Shao's arrangement. Perhaps one day a mathematician will write a treatise on Shao's arrangement of the hexagrams, and explain by what curious chance or synchronicity they came to correspond inversely to the binary code.

Since Confucius, Chinese scholars have always regarded the philosophical outlook of the *I Ching* as its most important aspect. It is not, as an oracle, regarded as the voice of immutable fate, but rather an advisor on developing situations in the questioner's life. Good or bad, the prediction offered is open to change or even total reversal by the future actions of the questioner. Richard Wilhelm has commented on the additions by King Wen and the Duke of Chou:

> ". . . they endowed the hitherto mute hexagrams and lines, from which the future had to be defined as an individual matter in each case, with definite counsels for correct conduct. Thus the individual came to share in shaping fate. For his actions intervened as determining factors in world events, the more decisively so, the earlier he was able with the aid of the *Book of Changes* to recognize situations in their germinal phases."

Here we become aware of the basic difference between the *I Ching* and most other oracles, seers and prophets considered in this volume. The future is not, in Taoist philosophy, a fixed, pre-ordained road, but a meandering river that can be navigated to desired ends by suitably enlightened persons. The *I Ching* offers a view of possible futures and advice on present dilemmas, but never loses sight of man's freedom to choose.

Undoubtedly, the best introduction to *I Ching* is to consult it for oneself. There are now many translations, but Richard Wilhelm's 1951 translation has retained its lead. For readers who do not possess their own copy, the following truncated version is offered.

It consists of the sixty-four main hexagrams, each with their King Wen *Judgement*. I have expanded and illustrated these slightly, basing elucidations on King Wen's own prose descriptions.

For those interested in experimenting with it as an oracle, the "coin method" follows.

The Coin Method

Questions put to the *I Ching* should not be too specific. "What time will such-and-such happen?" and "How many people might be involved?" are not the kind of questions with which the oracle is intended to deal. A better line of enquiry would be: "What will be the result if I continue my present course of action?" or "How will such-and-such turn out?"

Take three lightweight coins (British two-penny bits and US one-cent pieces are ideal) and a pen and paper. Shake the coins vigorously in cupped hands – as if shaking dice – while clearly framing the question in your mind.

Let them fall, bearing in mind the following:

Three heads, or two heads and a tail = *yang*.

Three tails, or two tails and a head = *yin*.

For *yin*, draw a broken line:

— —

For *yang*, an unbroken line:

————

Repeat the above process six times, and, starting from the bottom, build up the hexagram.

The hexagram is made of two trigrams of three lines each. Using the table below, work out the number of the hexagram you have obtained. (For example, if all six lines were made up of heads, then the number will be 1, *Ch'ien*, the Creative; if of tails, then the trigram will be 2, *K'un*, the Receptive.)

Remember that the *I Ching* is geared to advise as much as prophesy. To derive anything but the most superficial value from a consultation, one must carefully consider the reply in the context of the question. Often a series of linked queries – one leading to another – can provide a very full and detailed answer. On the other hand, excessive questioning can only lead to increasing confusion. Hexagram 4 (Inexperience) gives a tongue-in-cheek warning against asking questions without trying to understand previous answers. If the *I Ching* does not give you food for thought – either as philosophy or prediction – you are not consulting it properly.

Glossary of Terms

Appropriate Perseverance = Firm, continuous action that the questioner knows (or hopes) to be correct in the given circumstances.

Supreme/Sublime Success = Great advancement in the situation in question. The extent and effect of the good fortune is, of course, defined by the bounds of the original question.

Ultimate Success = A fortunate outcome, but one that may lie at some distance in the future and may still have to be worked for.

Superior/Enlightened Person = One in touch with events and aware of their own strengths and shortcomings. The phrase often indicates that a moral or benevolent attitude is appropriate, but this will, of course, depend on the question asked.

The Basic 64 Hexagrams of the I Ching

1 – *Ch'ien*, The Creative
Active use of your creative power brings sublime success.
Further advantage will come through appropriate perseverance.

2 – *K'un*, The Receptive
Allow your natural receptivity to bring about sublime success.
One should persevere, but with the gentleness of a mare (the *I Ching*'s symbol of the feminine).
If you try to lead, you will become lost.
If, on the other hand, you follow the guidance of others, the way ahead will become clear.
Advantage will come through responsive reaction rather than dogmatic insistence.
Quiet perseverance will bring good fortune.

3 – *Chun*, Difficulty at the Beginning
You will encounter difficulty at the beginning of a new project but, accepted philosophically, this will lead to supreme success.
One must persevere, but far-reaching aims should not be undertaken. Helpers should be enlisted.

UPPER	Sky	Thunder	Moon	Mountain	Earth	Air	Sun	Water
LOWER								
Sky	1	34	5	26	11	9	14	43
Thunder	25	51	3	27	24	42	21	17
Moon	6	40	29	4	7	59	64	47
Mountain	33	62	39	52	15	53	56	31
Earth	12	16	8	23	2	20	35	45
Air	44	32	48	18	46	57	50	28
Sun	13	55	63	22	36	37	30	49
Water	10	54	60	41	19	61	38	58

4 – *Meng*, Youthful Folly

Inexperience, if coupled with a willingness to learn, will bring success.
I do not seek out the inexperienced;
It is the inexperienced who seek me.
At first I inform him.
If he continues to pester me, it is an importunity.
I do not inform the importunate.
Appropriate perseverance will be advantageous if you are either a teacher or a student.

5 – *Hsu*, Waiting

A period of waiting, while maintaining a confident attitude, will later bring you success.
Patient perseverance will bring good fortune.
Important projects may then be launched.

6 – *Sung*, Conflict

You will face conflict over the situation in question.
Although you are sincere, you will meet with obstructions.
A considered yielding in this situation will bring you good fortune.
Regardless pressing ahead for your own ends will bring you misfortune.
It will be advantageous to meet with an authority in this matter.
Important projects should not be launched in these circumstances.

7 – *Shih*, The Army – Unified Strength

The situation demands unified strength.
Like an army, individuals – or your personal energies – need to be ordered and directed to a single purpose.
This will demand perseverance and strong leadership.
When this is achieved, there will be good fortune and freedom from recriminations.

8 – *Pi*, Holding Together

Building unity – in your personal motivations or with people around you – will bring good fortune.
Further consultation with the oracle will determine the correctness, endurance and strength of your aims.

If you consider these now, you will avoid recriminations later. Those who are uncertain must be allowed to join in their own time, but those who decide to join too late will meet with misfortune.

9 – Hsiao Ch'u, The Taming Power of the Small (Restraint)
The situation demands restraint if you are ultimately to achieve success.
Forces gather in your favour, like rain clouds that may end a drought, but you must patiently wait for them to manifest their influence.

10 – Lu, Treading Carefully (Cautious Risk)
A cautious man may tread on a tiger's tail and yet avoid being attacked.
Take risks when you need to, but remember that suitable caution must be employed if you are to enjoy success.

11 – T'ai, Peace
A time of peace and prosperity is imminent.
Negative influences will wane.
Positive influences will grow.
There will be good fortune and success.

12 – P'i, Standstill (Stagnation)
A period of standstill and stagnation must be endured.
Even the efforts of the good and unselfish will count for nothing.
Negativity is growing.
Positive influences wane.

13 – T'ung Jen, Fellowship with Men (Affinity)
Pursue fellowship with those who openly share your interests.
Good fortune results.
Friends will help you to launch major projects at this time.
Persevere in an enlightened fashion and you will further your aims.

14 – Ta Yu, Possession in Great Measure
Being open and responsive while in a position of authority will bring you wealth and supreme success.

15 – *Ch'ien*, Modesty
Acting with moderation and personal modesty will win you success.
Persist in your efforts until you are sure that all matters are
properly concluded.

16 – *Yu*, Enthusiasm.
Encourage enthusiasm in those around you by harmonizing
interests and leading as the first among equals.
It is a good time to find helpers and get matters moving in the
right direction.

17 – *Sui*, Adaptation
Ready adaptation to changing circumstances will bring you
supreme success.
Appropriate perseverance will further matters.
An adaptive person will avoid recrimination.

18 – *Ku*, Work on What Has Been Spoiled (Repairing the
Situation)
Repairing matters that have started to go awry will bring about
ultimate success.
Important projects can then be launched.
Consider carefully what has already happened in this matter, and
what you think may come in the future.

19 – *Lin*, Approach (Spring)
The situation is undergoing a burst of new growth – like the
coming of spring – and there will be great success.
Appropriate perseverance will further your goals.
Remember, however, that after summer comes cold autumn.
Always be prepared for future misfortunes.

20 – *Kuan*, Contemplation
Carefully contemplate the situation:
Preparations have been made, but matters have yet to be concluded. Your deep understanding of matters will inspire confidence in others.

21 – *Shih Ho*, Decisive Resolve (Biting Through Obstacles)
You must decisively act to change the situation.
Allowing justice to be administered is favourable.

22 – *Pi*, Graceful Behaviour
Graceful behaviour will bring you success.
However, as grace is of little consequence in important matters,
only rely on it in minor undertakings.

23 – *Po*, Splitting Apart (Collapse)
Your interests in this situation are threatened with disastrous
collapse.
Anything you now try to do will only damage matters further.
Simply wait for the time being and watch for improvement.

24 – *Fu*, Return (The Turning Point)
A period of recuperation after bad times brings success.
Do not fret at the comings and goings of life.
Friends leave and return again, but it is not a mistake.
To and fro goes the way, but all things move in cycles.
Just as after seven days we return to the beginning of the week, so
the present situation must renew itself again.
Gently rebuild your powers and have a goal to aim for.

25 – *Wu Wang*, Innocent Response
An attitude of spontaneous and thus naturally innocent response
toward the matter of enquiry brings ultimate success.
Appropriate perseverance will further your aims.
Inappropriate or overly premeditated actions will bring misfortune.
This sort of questionable behaviour would halt progress to your
goal.

26 – *Ta Ch'u*, The Taming Power of the Great (Potential Energy)
You have much potential energy stored away, so there is advantage in appropriate perseverance.
Getting out and mixing with new people and elements will bring
you good fortune.
With such reserves of potential energy, it is a good time to launch
a major project.

27 – *I*, Correct Nourishment
Correct nourishment, applied with appropriate perseverance,
will bring good fortune.
Consider what around you needs to be nourished and how you
can best go about feeding it.

In this way you will come to a deeper understanding of your situation, your fellows and yourself.

28 – Ta Kuo, Breaking Point
The situation has come to a breaking point.
For good or bad, matters have reached critical mass and a major change will result.
Concentrate on your goals.
These will give you direction in a possibly chaotic period.

29 – K'an, Danger
If treated correctly, the threat of danger refines the spirit.
A concentrated mind will create the skill and confidence you need in this dangerous situation.
With skill and confidence, you can succeed under any circumstances.

30 – Li, The Clinging (Fire)
Two elements can join and create something greater than their combined whole.
Proceed with appropriate perseverance to achieve success.
As with a caring farmer and a docile cow, both parties can enjoy good fortune greater than any effort they must exert.

31 – Hsien, Influence (Natural Attraction)
Here natural attraction will bring success.
Appropriate perseverance will further your aims.
Choosing to join with that which you desire will bring good fortune.

32 – Heng, Continuation
The continuation of your situation, with as few disturbances as possible, will bring success and freedom from recrimination.
There is advantage in appropriate perseverance.
Nevertheless, don't just go with the flow.
Keeping your goal in mind will help you to advance toward it.

33 – Tun, Organized Withdrawal
Successful retreat from a superior opponent is a form of victory and, in this case, is your way to progress.
It is worth pressing for advantage only in small matters.

34 – *Ta Chuang*, Great Responsibility
In a position of great power, you are loaded with an equal measure of responsibility.
It is to your best advantage to act with fairness and correctness.

35 – *Chin*, Rapid Progress
Your aims will enjoy rapid progress in the situation in question. You will be like the prince who, in recognition of his enlightened leadership, was rewarded with many horses and allowed to meet with the Emperor three times in a single day.

36 – *Ming I*, Darkness
Your situation resembles that of a man trying to make progress in darkness.
Conditions are trying, but persevere and you will eventually come to better times.

37 – *Chia Jen*, The Family
Allow things and people in your present situation to find their natural roles – just as a family divides tasks to the members best suited to them.
Advantageous progress will come from the quiet and moderating influence that a mother might exert.

38 – *K'uei*, Contradictions
The situation in question is fraught with contradictions caused by you, other people or just circumstances.
In minor matters, however, you can still achieve good fortune.

39 – *Chien*, Obstruction.
An immovable object blocks your progress in the matter in question. Trying to force it out of your way will do no good.
The answer lies in finding a way around the obstruction.
Discuss the matter with knowledgeable people to gain insight.
Appropriate perseverance will bring good fortune.

40 – *Hsieh*, Relief
Relief from difficulty comes.
The time calls on you to be responsive to conditions.
If you can see no advantage in pressing ahead, a return to normal conditions will bring good fortune.

If you see something you might achieve, act quickly to take advantage of the propitious time and you will enjoy good fortune.

41 – *Sun*, Decrease
Energy is being sapped from the situation in question and it is going into a period of retraction and decline.
Nevertheless, a confident attitude will lead you to ultimate success and freedom from blame.
Keep your goals in mind.
How can you achieve the right state of mind?
You must learn to live in reduced circumstances until they take a turn for the better.

42 – *I*, Increase
Energy is being channelled into the situation in question and it will enjoy a period of growth and increase.
Keep your goals in mind.
Take advantage of the propitious time by launching important projects.

43 – *Kuai*, Resolution
The time has come to resolutely confront any problems in the situation in question.
Raise the issue in the place of judgement and be aware that there may be some danger as a result.
Warn friends if your action will affect them and refrain from the unjust use of force.
At all times remember your ultimate goal.

44 – *Kou*, Temptation
You are influenced by an apparently minor, but nevertheless dangerous temptation.
The risk is more hazardous than it seems.
Do not indulge your desires in this matter.

45 – *Ts'ui*, Consolidation
It is time to consolidate matters or perhaps form a group of like-minded people.
This will bring success.
The time is as propitious as when the King himself acted as a priest in the temple.

An authority should be consulted to create greater success.
Perseverance will further your aims.
Personal sacrifice will incur good fortune.
It would be good to undertake something at this time.

46 – *Sheng*, Self-Promotion

Pushing yourself to the forefront of events will bring you great success.
Meet with the authority in this matter and do not fall prey to fear or excessive modesty.
Hard work will bring you good fortune.

47 – *K'un*, Adversity

You face a period of adversity in the situation in question.
Nevertheless, perseverance may still bring forth success.
A person of sterling character can even enjoy good fortune at this trying time.
Do your best and nobody will have cause to blame you.
If you try to remedy the situation with words alone, however, you will receive no support.

48 – *Ching*, The Source of Inner Strength

Just as a town may change its boundaries over the years, but its well will remain in the same place, so your life may change drastically but the source of your inner strength will always remain the same.
Your inner strength neither increases nor decreases.
The only control on its beneficial power is how effectively you manage to draw upon it.
Like a well with too short a rope or a broken jug, a person who does not know how to employ his inner strength is bound to suffer misfortune.

49 – *Ko*, Revolution

Revolutionary change is called for – or is coming of its own accord.
You may be reluctant to join in because a revolution is never trusted until its ends have been visibly fulfilled.
In this case, however, place yourself at the forefront of the change because it will bring great success.
Your aims will be furthered by your perseverance and all regret will disappear.

50 – *Ting*, The Cauldron
Your present course in this matter is aligned with the Tao – the natural and spiritual flow of the universe.
You can expect supreme good fortune and success.
The situation is like winning a great cauldron filled with all that your heart desires.

51 – *Chen*, The Shock of the New (The Arousing)
A shock will come, but will bring you success if you can maintain your composure.
Sudden change, like thunder, makes everyone start.
Then, seeing that it is harmless, they laugh with relief.
Thunder might frighten everyone for a hundred miles, but the wise man remains calm and does not interrupt his activities.

52 – *Ken*, Meditation
You must meditate on the matter in question.
This is more than simple thought – you must compose your body and mind and raise your consciousness above the chattering of the ego.
In this way you will gain a vantage point above that of the worm's-eye view and learn deeper insights.
As a result, you may feel somewhat out of touch with everyday life, but there is no blame in this.

53 – *Chien*, Development
The situation calls for easy and sensible development – like the careful preparations for an important wedding.
Aiming to fulfil your desires in an unhurried fashion will bring good fortune.
Patient perseverance is the key to your advancement.

54 – *Kung Mei* , Subordinate Reserve.
You are thoroughly subordinate to the demands of the situation.
Any undertakings attempted from such an untenable position will only bring you misfortune.
Nothing, for the time being, should be set into motion.

55 – *Feng*, The Height of Success
You will reach a pinnacle of possible success and abundance.
Like a wise king, you should not be saddened that the only way on from this point is downwards.

Revel in the immediate moment and shine like the sun at its zenith.

56 – *Lu*, Strange Territory
You are passing through a situation that is new and strange to you. The actions you take in this unknown territory must be restricted in scope, but on this restrained level will enjoy success.
The cautious perseverance of a stranger in a strange land will win you good fortune.

57 – *Sun*, Gradual Influence (The Gentle)
Only take small and gentle actions to affect the issue in question. Breezes may seem weak and ineffectual but, given time, the wind can erode a mountain down to sand.
Keep your goal in mind, discuss matters with those more knowledgeable than yourself and your aims will be furthered.

58 – *Tui*, Joyous Exchange
It is a time for happiness and social exchange.
You will find success in a relaxed, but not over-indulgent atmosphere. Even under such pleasant circumstances, remember to remain persevering to further your aims.

59 – *Huan*, Dispersion
Reforming separated elements or factions back into a new whole will bring success in the situation in question.
The time for new leadership and unified direction approaches. Important projects may then be launched.
Appropriate perseverance will further your aims.

60 – *Chieh*, Limitation
Limitations refine the character and channel energies into new success.
Excessive limitation, however, stunts growth and restricts new possibilities.

61 – *Chung Fu*, Insight
Cultivated insights may enlighten even pigs and fishes.
A person moved by insight will enjoy good fortune.
Such knowledge allows the launch of important projects.
Appropriate perseverance will further your aims.

62 – *Hsiao Kou*, Sensible Ambitions
The trick of a happy life lies in sensible ambitions – this way, you are certain of success.
Appropriate perseverance will further your aims.
Small things may be undertaken, but great things must not.
When a bird flies too high, its song is lost.
It is best not to strive upward, but to remain below.
Such precaution will reap great good fortune.

63 – *Chi Chi*, After Completion
The present situation has been, or is being, concluded.
If there are still some small matters to deal with, success in these is indicated.
For the time being there will be good fortune but, as you enter into a wholly new situation, your uncertainty and confusion will mount.

64 – *Wei Chi*, Before Completion
You will enjoy success as the conclusion of a matter draws near.
When a fox swims a river, however, it must not relax prematurely or it will get its tail wet.
You too must remain vigilant to the end or you may lose all the advantage you have worked for.

In conclusion, it should be emphasized that using the *Book of Changes* purely as an oracle is to miss its true value. The person who wishes to understand the *I Ching* should begin by studying the eight trigrams and their meaning, then set out to learn how the philosophers who created the *I Ching* combined these trigrams to produce the images. It should not be regarded as a book of fortune-telling, but as a logical work whose whole meaning sprang from the basic two lines. The individual Lines, particularly those derived from a six or a nine, also deserve careful study, which suggests that it is worth acquiring your own copy of the complete book. Whether or not Confucius really said that he would like to spend fifty more years studying it, there can be no doubt that the *I Ching* is a work that repays a close and intimate acquaintance.

5 Old Mother Shipton

Sixteenth-century Yorkshire was not a safe place to look or behave like a witch. The religious hysteria that swept Europe in the late Middle Ages led to thousands of people being burned or hanged; England, although somewhat less affected than Central Europe, was no exception.

In spite of this, "Mother" Ursula Shipton, one of Yorkshire's most famous daughters, is said to have openly paraded her supernatural powers, and defied the most powerful clergyman in the land. Possibly the fact that she was so surpassingly ugly – she possessed a face like a Halloween mask – explains why she survived into her eighties and died in her bed – no one who has studied the witchcraft trials can doubt that there was a sexual element in the persecutions. If a suspect was reasonably attractive, she was more likely to be stripped and searched for "Devil's marks" than a withered old harridan.

Nevertheless, given the evidence, it is tempting to believe that Mother Shipton had the Devil's own luck.

The Yorkshire prophetess was born in Knaresborough around 1488, although accounts differ because several Yorkshire municipalities have claimed her as their own. Ursula's mother was called Agatha Sontheil, and had been orphaned at the age of fifteen with no other living relatives. She inherited her parents' small house, but owned very little else and was often forced to live off the charity of the parish. It was therefore some surprise to her neighbours that, at about the age of sixteen, she began to spend money that nobody had seen her earn or borrow.

It was a sign of the times that, shortly afterwards, when her belly began to swell, local gossip favoured the belief that Satan was the responsible party. Agatha cheerfully confirmed this rumour, describing a meeting with a very handsome gentleman on the riverbank, and how, after listening to her problems, he offered to banish them all if she would be "ruled by him". Thereafter he visited her cottage regularly, but in secret, and after each dalliance Agatha would find coins scattered about her house. Needless to say, when Agatha became pregnant, the fiend was seen no more.

Whether the father was Beelzebub or just an out-of-town rake, he seems to have had good connections with the Church. Following Ursula's birth, the Abbot of Beverley Minster travelled sixty miles to baptize the babe – a privilege usually reserved for the children of noblemen.

The abbot is also said to have maintained a friendly eye on the child in later years, even seeing to it that she received an education (a rarity for peasant girls, at that time). The local gossips therefore added his name to the list of suspected fathers.

In his 1997 book *The World's Greatest Unsolved Mysteries*, Lionel Fanthorpe suggests that the choice of the name Ursula might offer a clue to the babe's real procreator. *Ursus* is Latin for bear, and Fanthorpe points out that the Bear Clan is a secret bloodline that is supposed to include King Arthur and various other nobles in British history and mythology. Perhaps, Fanthorpe continues, the illegitimate baby was named Ursula to indicate that she was the daughter of a member of the Bear Clan. So perhaps her later freedom from persecution was due to the influence of her father's family.

Ursula Sontheil was born late at night during a storm – complete with thunder and lightning. Her physical deformity was immediately apparent, as described in this 1686 pamphlet *The Strange & Wonderful History of Mother Shipton*:

> "*Nor could the Tempest affright the Women more than the prodigious Physiognomy of the Child; the Body was long, but very big-bon'd, great Gogling eyes, very sharp and fiery, a Nose of unproportionable length, having in it many crooks and turnings, adorned with great Pimples, which like vapours of brimstone gave such a lustre in the night, that her Nurse needed no other candle to dress her by.*"

Although the author has clearly allowed his imagination free rein, all accounts of Mother Shipton agree that her deformity was striking. She was born with a hunchback and, as she grew older and her face developed, her nose and chin both became remarkably long and pointed. Woodcuts of the seeress became common in England, following the first publication of a pamphlet about her in 1641. Some scholars have even suggested that these portraits might have been one of the original inspirations for the nineteenth century *Mr Punch* glove puppet and the archetypal witch portrayed in children's books and Disney cartoons.

During her infancy, she was apparently the centre of a whirlpool of paranormal activity. Her harassed mother was "daily Visited by Spirits in divers shapes and forms", according to the 1684 *Life and Death of Mother Shipton* by Benjamin Harris. She attracted dozens of stray cats and dogs, and neighbours had no doubt that these were demons in disguise. Apart from such earthly pests, Ursula's mother was plagued by non-corporeal manifestations:

> "*The poor woman's work for the major part, was only to rectifie what these Spirits disordered about her house: the Chairs and Stools would frequently march upstairs and down, and they usually plaid below at Bowles with the Trenchers and dishes: Going to dinner, the meat was removed before she could touch a bit of it.*"

A modern paranormal investigator would categorize the above phenomena as typical poltergeist activity. One widely accepted view holds that such "hauntings" are actually the result of the unconscious telekinetic powers of a disturbed child or teenager. If so, then the young mother herself would seem the most likely "focus". However, since the haunting continued after Agatha left the house for good, we must consider Ursula herself as the most likely catalyst.

Ursula lost her mother when she was still just a toddler. Accounts differ as to whether Agatha simply died or, under the patronage of the Abbot of Beverley Minster, sought peace and redemption in the local convent. Either way, the child was left in the hands of a long-suffering nurse and the haunting continued unabated. Finally, when Ursula was inexplicably found sitting on an iron support bar high up inside the chimney

– quite unharmed and laughing happily – the poor woman's nerve broke and the child was sent to a church-run boarding school.

Ursula proved to be an amazingly gifted student. Although classroom jealousy, coupled with her deformity, made her the butt of some cruel teasing, she apparently "gave as good as she got". It is said that invisible hands would pinch her enemies until they screamed in terror, while others were struck dumb as they were about to recite aloud in class. Modern parapsychologists would regard this as evidence of a powerful psychic ability in the child, but Ursula's contemporaries were, however, in no doubt that she was under the protection of demons.

The Strange and Wonderful History of Mother Shipton tells the following story: a meeting of the important people of the parish was held at the local hostelry, and the teenage Ursula happened to pass through the room on an errand:

". . . *some of them abused her by calling her the Devils Bastard and Hagface, and the like, whereupon she went away grumbling, but so ordered affairs, that when they was set down to dinner, one of the principal Yeomen, that thought himself spruce and fine, had in an instant his Ruff* [a fluffed collar, shaped like a dinner-plate] *pull'd off, and the seat of the House of Office* [a euphemistic name for the toilet] *clapt in its place* . . . [the man sitting opposite him] *had his Hat invisibly convey'd away, and the Pan of a Close-stool* [a sort of potty on legs] *put instead thereof."* [A] *"modest young Gentlewoman"* [sitting at the table tried to suppress her laughter,] *"but could not, and withal continued breaking of wind backward for above a quarter of an hour together, like so many broadsides in a Sea-fight."*

A priest's attempts to exorcise the "demon powers" in Ursula had no effect.

By the time she was old enough to leave school, Ursula Sontheil already had a considerable reputation for "second sight", and from her mother's little cottage was able to make a reasonable living foretelling the future. Her major customers were hopeful young maidens who wanted to learn about future husbands.

Despite her obvious skill in this area, everyone was surprised when Ursula quickly landed herself a good husband. Toby Shipton was a carpenter by trade, and was also a good-natured soul who was devoted to his ugly but strangely gifted wife. Accounts vary as to whether the couple had any children, but Ursula soon earned the honorific title "Mother Shipton" out of the respect that her neighbours held for her as a "wise woman".

Even in the late Middle Ages, there was always a place in any village for a wise woman. In the Dark Ages, the Church Fathers had shown a grudging acceptance of such people because – despite being of the female sex and therefore tainted with the sin of Eve – their opinions carried great weight in the community. The local priest often found their influence as strong as his own. Later, as the Church became institutionalized in every town and village, the priests began to undermine and usurp the position and respect previously held by local shamen and wise women.

These village wise women were usually healers and fortune-tellers who had probably learned their skills from their mothers or grandmothers; such skills usually involved charms, and the use of toads and wax figures. These activities were taken for granted, and not regarded as particularly sinister. Things began to change after 1490, when a village healer named Jehane de Brigue was charged with being a witch, and sentenced to death by the Parlement in Paris; Jehane and a fellow "witch" were burned in August 1491.

The previously sporadic witchcraft persecution had turned into a flood after the publication of a book called *Malleus Maleficarum* (meaning *The Hammer of Witches*) by two Dominican monks, Jacob Sprenger and Heinrich Kramer, in 1484. Its emphasis on sexual matters ("the foulest venereal acts are performed by such devils . . .") caused it to be widely read by celibate monks, and the recent invention of the printing press made it the first bestseller. The European witchcraft craze lasted from around 1500 until the early eighteenth century and thousands of people (mostly women) were tortured, then hanged or burned at the stake.

So, by the time of Mother Shipton, the ancient societal power of the local wise woman was only a dim memory. Nevertheless, women who were expert midwives, and who could also cure fevers or foretell the size of the harvest, were indispensable in most communities. It was only during the Enlightenment, with the rise of the natural philosophers (later called scientists) that the wise woman became superfluous to requirement and went back to the kitchen sink.

At the time of Mother Shipton – born at the beginning of the witchcraft craze, but before it had fully spread to England – the wise woman still commanded both respect and superstitious fear in her local community. Nevertheless, by the time she became a famous witch, she was also undoubtedly protected by her reputation for integrity . . .

When a young man came to her, asking when his sick father would die and pass on his inheritance, Mother Shipton flatly refused to help him. A few days later, the father himself arrived and told her that his greedy son had become very ill. When he begged her to foretell whether his heir would live, Mother Shipton replied:

> For other Deaths who do gape out,
> Their own, unlook't for, comes about:
> Earth he did seek, ere long shall have,
> Of Earth his fill, within his Grave.[1]

As predicted, the young man was soon in the grave.

Mother Shipton also foretold public events in the nearby city of York:

> When there is a Mayor living in Minster Yard,
> Let him beware of a stab . . .

The Lord Mayor of York who moved his official residence to Minster Yard was stabbed to death by thieves, one night.

> Before Owse Bridge and Trinity Church meet they shall build in the day and it shall fall in the night, 'til they get the highest stone of Trinity Church to the lowest stone of Owse Bridge.

The steeple of the Trinity church was blown down in a storm and, at the same time, a flood broke the nearby bridge over the River Owse. Efforts to repair the damage went badly, with work by day collapsing again at night. When the bridge was finally repaired, it was noted that some stones from the Trinity spire had

1 Note the medieval rhyming of "have" with "grave".

accidentally been added to the bridge; indeed, the top of the spire
was now part of the base of one of the bridge supports.

If she had confined herself to such local predictions, Mother
Shipton would have been forgotten long ago. Her reputation was
based on her prophecies about the future of the whole of England, such as:

> Triumphant Death rides London through
> And men on tops of houses go.

We know that this prediction was commonplace outside
Yorkshire in 1666 because the diarist Samuel Pepys noted
it in his entry for 20 October of that year. He was writing
about the arrival, from the Thames, of Sir Jeremy Smith
during the great fire: "[Sir Jeremy] says he was on board
the *Prince* when news came of the burning of London; and all
the [crew of the] *Prince* said that now Shipton's prophecy was
out."

The reference to "Death riding triumphant" would have made
anyone in the sixteenth century think of the plague, since everyone was familiar with woodcuts of a skeletal Death riding over
plague victims. London was ravaged by the plague in 1665 – the
Great Fire came the following year.

The reference to men climbing to the tops of houses seems an
odd anticipation of a city-wide fire – surely a rooftop is the last
place one would want to be during a conflagration – until we read
of fire-watchers posted to note the direction and spread of the
blaze. In that light, the certainty of people at the time that
Mother Shipton had foretold the twin disasters becomes more
understandable.

The sailors on the *Prince* may have also been thinking of
another of Mother Shipton's prophecies:

> *A time shall happen, when a ship shall sail up the Thames, till
> it come against London, and the master of the ship shall weep,
> and the mariners of the ship shall ask him why he weeps, since
> he has made so good a voyage? And he shall say: "Ah! What a
> goodly city this was, none in the world to compare with it, and
> now there is scarce left an house that can let us have a drink for
> our money."*

The only other similar catastrophe to befall London was the Blitz of the Second World War.[2]

Mother Shipton became nationally famous for a prediction that came true in her own lifetime. It concerned Cardinal Wolsey, Henry VIII's Lord Chancellor and arguably the most powerful man in the country. Wolsey had also been appointed to the deanery of York but, due to his London schedule, rarely left the capital to visit his diocese.

In the autumn of 1529, Wolsey made preparations to travel to York and sent word ahead to prepare for his coming. Upon hearing this, Mother Shipton publicly proclaimed that the Cardinal would never visit the city again. She was by then famous enough to attract the attention of several aristocratic members of the Cardinal's faction. These, led by a local gentleman called Beasley, paid the seeress a visit. They were amazed that before they could knock on her door she called out: "Come in, Master Beasley. You lead, as their lordships do not know the way."

Once they were inside, she greeted each by name and called for refreshments. The Duke of Suffolk replied that she would not be so welcoming if she knew that they were visiting on behalf of the Cardinal. He would doubtless burn her as a witch when he arrived in York. Mother Shipton airily replied that if her handkerchief burned, then so would she, and threw it straight onto the roaring fire. A quarter of an hour later, she picked it out with a poker and handed it round the assembly: all agreed that it was not even singed.

Doubtless rather unnerved, they then asked why she had said that Cardinal Wolsey would never see York again. Mother Shipton replied that, on the contrary, the Cardinal would *see* York, but he would never reach the city. She then went on to prophesy the fate of each of the visiting lords. Being the reign of the turbulent and execution prone Henry VIII, it is not overly surprising that most were told that they would suffer early deaths – but it is the accurate detail she is said to have given that impressed later chroniclers. For example, she told Lord Percy that, "Your body will be buried in York pavement and your head will lie in France."

At the time, Percy made light of this prediction, commenting

---

2 A less grim interpretation of this prediction might suggest an imposition of alcohol prohibition laws some time in our future (a prospect horrible to a sailor, but probably quite acceptable to the morally Christian Mother Shipton).

that his neck would have to stretch a long way. In fact, he was later executed and buried in York but, as was the custom with condemned traitors, his severed head was stuck on a public spike as a warning to others. This was then stolen and taken to his relatives who had fled to France.

Cardinal Wolsey spent the last night of his journey at Cawood Castle, within sight of York. He is said to have ascended a tower to look at the city in the evening light, and was there told of Mother Shipton's prophecy. He angrily declared that he would have her arrested and burned, but that same night Wolsey was recalled to London to stand trial for high treason. The fifty-five-year-old priest died of "the flux" on the way back.

Today, Mother Shipton is most famous for her prediction of the developments of the industrial age. The very popular *Life, Prophecies and Death of the Famous Mother Shipton*, written by Charles Hindley and published in 1862, gives the following version of these prophecies:

> *Carriages without horses will go*
> *And accidents fill the world with woe . . .*
> *Around the world thoughts shall fly,*
> *In the twinkling of an eye . . .*
> *Through hills men shall ride,*
> *And no horse or ass be by his side,*
> *Underwater men shall walk,*
> *Shall ride, shall sleep, shall be seen,*
> *In white, in black, in green . . .*
> *Iron in water shall float,*
> *As easy as a wooden boat . . .*
> *All England's sons that plough the land,*
> *Shall be seen book in hand.*
> *Learning shall so ebb and flow,*
> *The poor shall most wisdom know . . .*
> *The world to an end will come*
> *In eighteen hundred and eighty-one.*

Apart from the embarrassingly inaccurate prediction of Armageddon, the rest seems strikingly prescient: trains (or cars), the proliferation of accidents, global communications, the replacement of the horse, submarines and undersea dwellings, metal-hulled ships and even universal education.

Unfortunately, all these "prophecies" were the fictional invention of the aforementioned Charles Hindley – he later confessed as much, admitting he did it to boost the sales of his book. Yet, even today, books quote this doggerel as genuine prophecies by Mother Shipton.

How many of the other predictions attributed to Mother Shipton were later inventions is now impossible to say. It is only with prophets like Nostradamus or Edgar Cayce, where we are certain that we are reading their own words, that we can be free of doubt.

Most of the prophecies attributed to Mother Shipton seem to concern events during her own lifetime and the hundred or so years following her death. For example, she is credited with predicting that Henry VIII would marry Anne Boleyn, and would then break with Rome:

> *When the Cow doth ride the Bull*
> *Then the Priest beware thy skull.*

A cow was part of Henry VIII's personal heraldry, while there was a black bull on the standard of Anne Boleyn's father. The conversion of the state religion from Catholic to Protestant (and the destruction of the power of the monasteries) started during the period of this marriage.

She is also said to have predicted the four-decade reign of Elizabeth I and the defeat of the Spanish Armada:

> *A Maiden Queen full many a year*
> *Shall England's War-like sceptre bear.*
> *The Western Monarch's Wooden Horses*
> *Shall be destroyed by the Drake's Forces.*

The English Civil War and execution of Charles I were foretold in the following verse:

> *Forth from the North shall mischief blow,*
> *And English Hob* [the Devil] *shall add thereto;*
> *Mars shall rage as he were wood,*
> *And Earth shall drunken be with blood.*
> *But tell us what's next, Oh cruel fate!*
> *A King Martyr'd at his gate.*

Nevertheless, not all her prophecies had such obvious explanations for the seventeenth-century pamphlet-buying public.

> *In time to hereafter,*
> *Our land will be ruled by two women.*
> *A child of ours will be contested*
> *By a child of Spain . . .*
> *In this time, blood will be shed*
> *Yet shall the child stay.*

This prediction, quoted in Lionel Fanthorpe's *World's Greatest Unsolved Mysteries,* is believed by some to refer to the 1982 Falklands War between Britain and Argentina. At the time Britain was governed by Prime Minister Margaret Thatcher and ruled by Queen Elizabeth II. Argentina was a colony of Spain, while Britain developed settlements on the Falkland Islands: both places were therefore "children" of European nations.

A rather odd prophecy seemed to predict a prosperous period, followed by a scarcity of men:

> *Then may a man take House or Bower, Land or Tower for one and twenty years; but afterwards shall be a white Harvest of Corn gotten by Women. Then shall it be, that one woman shall say to another: "Mother! I have seen a man today!"*

One commentator suggests that this is a prediction of British prosperity at the turn of the nineteenth century. This was followed, during the First World War, by the women labouring in fields and factories while their men were slaughtered in great numbers in France.

There are other prophecies of Mother Shipton that continue to defy explanation. Some are too short on comparative detail . . .

> *The North shall Rue it wondrous sore,*
> *But the South shall Rue it for evermore.*
> *The Time shall come, when Seas of Blood,*
> *Shall mingle with a greater flood.*

Others hardly seem to fit any known historical event up to the time of this writing . . .

You shall have a year of Pining Hunger, & shall not know of the War over-night, yet shall you have it in the Morning, and when it happens, it shall last three years, then will come a woman with one Eye, and she shall tread in many men's blood up to the knee.

The Fiery Year as soon as 'ore,
Peace shall then be as before.
Plenty everywhere is found,
And Men with Swords shall plow the ground.

Great noise there shall be heard, Great Shouts and Cries.
And Seas shall Thunder, louder than the Skies,
Then shall three Lions fight with three and bring
Joy to a people, Honour to their King.

Mother Shipton, like many seers, is said to have accurately predicted the time of her own death. A hospitable countrywoman to the last, she invited her friends and relatives to come and see her off, lay down on her bed and promptly passed away. The date is not known, but she is said to have lived well into her eighties, which would make it some time after 1570.

Benjamin Harris' *Life and Death of Mother Shipton* (1684) says of her: ". . . she was generally believed to be a witch, yet all persons whatever, that either saw or heard her, had her in great esteem: her memory to this day is much honoured by those of her own Country."

A stone was erected near Clifton, about a mile from the city of York, from which the following is taken:

Here Lies she who never ly'd,
Whose skill often has been try'd,
Her Prophecies shall still survive,
And ever keep her name alive.

6 Nostradamus

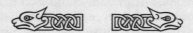

Michel de Nostredame – known universally as Nostradamus – has had more impact on the world than any other prophet since the golden age of the Delphic Oracle. His predictions have remained consistently in print since he first published them in 1555. His life and work have inspired novels, plays, Hollywood movies and any number of academic studies and treatises. As a figure of French national pride he ranks only behind Charles de Gaulle and Joan of Arc. Political leaders since the sixteenth century have seen in his prophecies optimistic portents for their own futures (although few seem to have been prepared to consider any potential warnings of doom from the seer). Indeed, in the public eye, the name Nostradamus has become synonymous with foretelling the future.

Yet we know very little about this man. Much of his life, his training, his method of prediction and his reasons for publishing remain largely unknown to us. Everything concerning Nostradamus seems touched with mystery and, as we shall see, this was probably due to the seer's own deliberate policy.

Nostradamus was born in the French city of Saint-Remy de Provence on 14 December 1503. The Nostredame family originally belonged to the Jewish faith, but had been Catholic converts for at least two generations. (The name Nostredame means "our lady", while the pen-name *Nostradamus* was a Latinization of his surname.) They made a fortune through trade but, according to Nostradamus' son Caesar, they were also respected as a line of scholars and doctors. Unfortunately, at that time, this combination of money, esoteric training and Jewish roots placed them in a rather dangerous position.

In the fifteenth and sixteenth centuries, many European countries – including France – expelled or executed all Jews who refused to convert to Christianity. The Inquisition – virtually an independent power since the rift with the Protestants – was responsible for widespread persecution of Jewish "enemies of Christ", often blaming them for crop failures and outbreaks of plague. Even those Jews who, like the Nostredame family, were willing to renounce Judaism, lived under continual suspicion. An accusation by a jealous neighbour could lead to a trial for witchcraft and forfeiture of family assets. Nostradamus' favourite pupil, Jean Aimes de Chavigny, later vehemently denied that his master was a Jew, although he certainly knew better.

Michel de Nostredame showed signs of remarkable intelligence from an early age, so his scholarly maternal grandfather, Jean de Saint-Remy, offered to educate the boy personally. By his early teens, Michel had mastered Latin, Greek and basic medical knowledge . . .

Tradition also holds that his grandfather taught him Hebrew and astrology – both regarded by the Inquisition as bordering on witchcraft.

Many Nostradamus commentators believe that his writings reveal evidence of a detailed knowledge of the Jewish esoteric tradition called the *Kabbala* (which we will discuss in the chapter on the Tarot). It is quite possible that he also learned this from his grandfather. If so, this was the most dangerous of his studies, even more so than astrology, for any reference to kabbalism in public could have led to both of them being accused of anti-Christian magic. Fortunately, even when young, Nostradamus knew when to keep his mouth shut.

In his early teens, he was sent to study in Avignon, and soon outstripped his classmates in most subjects. As a result, in 1522, he was sent to study medicine at Montpellier – at that time, one of the greatest medical universities in Europe. It took Michel only three years to be granted permission to practise as a doctor. His apprenticeship was probably shortened by an outbreak of plague in Montpellier, when every available doctor battled day and night to halt a form of plague called *le charbon*, which covered the victim's skin with black pustules. By the end of the epidemic, Nostradamus had earned a reputation as a gifted physician.

His pupil, Jean de Chavigny, would claim that even at this early stage in his medical career, Nostradamus employed anti-plague techniques of his own invention. It has even been implausibly suggested that Nostradamus may have used his power of precognition to anticipate treatments of later centuries, a theory that can be categorically denied, since we have some of Nostradamus' remedies – which he himself noted down – and they were not miracle cures by any definition. They include burning a powder of dried rose petals, cloves, lignum aloes, iris and sweet flag roots to "cleanse the air" (it was believed that plague was caused by "ill humours" in the atmosphere), and concocting pills of the same harmless mixture. The best that can be said is that the vitamin C in the rose petals may have helped.

For more general problems associated with male ageing, Nostradamus prescribed an ointment containing powdered coral, lapis lazuli and flecks of gold leaf.

> "If a man's beard is turning grey, [the ointment] retards that ageing process. It prevents headaches and constipation, and multiplies his sperm to such an extent that a man may enjoy marital pleasures as frequently as he desires without impairing his health. It keeps the four humours in such health that were a man to take it from birth, he could live forever."

This is enough to convince us that, whatever his powers of prophecy, Nostradamus the physician was a typical child of his time.

Even so, there were some respects in which his medical practices seemed an anticipation of the future. He insisted that patients be kept in sunlit, well-ventilated rooms, and be given daily baths – at a time when many people, even the aristocracy, were content with one bath per year. (Nostradamus himself bathed daily.) It is hard for us to appreciate how revolutionary this was; yet it was not until the twentieth century that doctors came to appreciate that patients in sunlit beds tend to recover quicker than those in dark ones. Before that, it was widely accepted that sickness travels in the form of vapour on the air, so it seemed logical to close the windows and doors of the sick chamber.

Even more extraordinary was his refusal to bleed the sick, at a time when bleeding was perhaps the most common remedy for anything from migraine to pneumonia. It was believed that the sick produced excess blood and, since blood was supposed to be the fluid in the body's central heating system, that draining off the blood could cure fever. No one but Nostradamus seemed to notice that bleeding did no good and often killed the patient. He must have been regarded as eccentric as a modern doctor who refuses to believe in transplant surgery.

Reports of Nostradamus' cures, as well as of his courage in facing the plague (many doctors fled at the first sign of it) led to invitations from other stricken towns. So, for a period, he practised as an itinerant physician in Toulouse, Narbonne and Bordeaux.

What does this tell us about Nostradamus? Simply that he was a brave man? Surely there is more to it than that. A modern reader finds it quite impossible to imagine what it was like to live in a plague-stricken city (although anyone who wants to find out should read the shattering account in Manzoni's great novel *The Betrothed*). The air was full of the stench of rotting corpses and, since most people believed that this smell carried the plague (and kept scented handkerchiefs pressed to their noses), it required more than courage to remain. It may be simply that, having studied astrology from his eighteenth to his twenty-sixth year, Nostradamus was convinced that he had a long time to live. But even astrology must seem a doubtful comfort amid the stench of death, and it is surely more likely that Nostradamus simply had a deep and powerful intuition of his own destiny, and that fate had something more interesting in store for him than the "black death".

We know that when the plague outbreak receded, some time before 1533, he returned to Montpellier to complete his studies and receive his doctor's degree. He was then invited to teach on the faculty, but his unorthodox ideas seem to have aroused the hostility of his senior colleagues and, after two years, he decided to resume his travels.

The wandering scholar and doctor returned to his native Provence and to the life of an itinerant doctor. It was at this time that he made a translation of the *Book of Orus Apollo, Son of Osiris, King of Egypt*, which he dedicated to the Princess of Navarre. He must have at least made Her Royal Highness' acquaintance to do this, so we can assume he was mixing in the highest circles.

After a year of wandering, Nostradamus decided to settle in Agen, in Aquitaine. De Chavigny believes he chose this town because it was the home of Julius Caesar Scaliger – one of the greatest scholars of the sixteenth century and a man with a strong interest in esoteric lore. It is certainly almost impossible that scholars like Nostradamus and Scaliger can have lived in the same small town without getting to know one another. Some writers have suggested that Scaliger initiated Nostradamus into a secret occult society and showed him forbidden books and methods of prediction, but the truth is that we simply do not know their relationship.

There may be another reason why Nostradamus chose Agen. That pleasant town had belonged to the English crown since 1152, when Eleanor of Aquitaine married Henry II of England, and continued to be English, on and off, for the next three centuries, until the English withdrew at the end of the Hundred Years' War (1453). It had a more international atmosphere than most French cities. In an article on Nostradamus, James Randi makes the penetrating comment that many of the quatrains of Nostradamus were "actually political commentaries and justifiable critiques of the activities of the Catholic Church, which was then busily tossing heretics on to bonfires wherever the Holy Inquisition could reach." England became Protestant in 1529, four years before Nostradamus received his degree at Montpellier. The intellectual atmosphere in Agen was probably freer than in the oppressively Catholic Montpellier. Randi goes on to state that Nostradamus was a secret Protestant, basing his theory on revealing letters discovered in the *Bibliothèque Nationale*. Since his own family had been forced to convert to Catholicism, Nostradamus had no reason to love the Catholic Church. It is perhaps ironic that Catherine of Navarre, the person most responsible for the St Bartholomew Massacre of Protestants, should later have become Nostradamus' admirer and patron.

Nostradamus married a girl of "high estate" soon after he arrived in Agen – and fathered two children. Sadly, in 1538, plague broke out in the town, and the great physician was unable to save the lives of his wife and two children. His wife's family promptly went to law to regain her dowry. It was a grim year for Nostradamus, because he was not only bereaved, but was also caught up in a petty row with his late wife's family concerning the return of her dowry.

Worse still, he was accused of heresy. The details are not clear; one version has him watching a workman casting a statue of the Virgin and making some tactless remark about making brazen images, while another has him saying that it was a statue of the devil. Nostradamus is said to have claimed that he meant it was as ugly as the devil. But, rather than defend himself before an ecclesiastical court, he set out once more on his travels.

Over the next eight or nine years, he wandered through France, Italy and Sicily. Little is known about this period of his life, but some writers have suggested that he became an initiate of the secret Priory of Sion while he was in Lorraine. The Priory was a heretical Rosicrucian order which, according to modern commentators, taught that Jesus survived the crucifixion, married Mary Magdalene, and moved to France. As we shall see in a later chapter, it is indeed possible that Nostradamus was an occult "initiate", but whether he was connected with the Priory is unknown . . .

His pupil Jean de Chavigny states that it was during this last period as a wanderer that Nostradamus' gifts as a prophet began to manifest themselves. There is a famous story of how he was riding along a dusty road near the Italian city of Ancona when he passed a line of mendicant friars, and dismounted and knelt before a young novice. Asked why he abased himself before the youth, he replied: "Because I must kneel before His Holiness." The friar, Felice Peretti, later became Pope Sextus V.

Another story tells how, when Nostradamus was staying in the Château de Fains, in Lorraine, his host, the Seigneur de Florinville, decided to test his gift of foreseeing the future. Pointing to two piglets, he asked what their fate would be. Nostradamus replied that the black one would be eaten for dinner, but that a wolf would eat the white piglet. Florinville then took his cook aside, and told him to kill and roast the white piglet for dinner. After the meal, the cook was summoned and asked to tell Nostradamus the colour of pig he had just eaten. The man looked embarrassed, then admitted that although he had killed the white piglet, as instructed, a pet wolf had stolen it from the kitchen, and he had been forced to kill and roast the black one.

In 1544, there was an outbreak of plague in Marseilles and, forcing his way through a tide of escaping refugees, Nostradamus hurried to the city to help. Two years later, he was in Aix-en-Provence doing the same – this time so successfully that he was granted a permanent pension by the city fathers. In Lyon, he fought an outbreak of whooping cough so effectively that he was rewarded with a sack of gold, which he immediately gave to the poor.

In 1547, he decided to settle again, this time in Salon-en-Craux (now known as Salon-de-Provence; the French still refer to Nostradamus as the Seer of Salon). Here he married a rich and well-connected widow and started a new family. His wife's wealth and his pension from nearby Aix-en-Provence allowed him to devote most of his time to his esoteric studies, the cultivation of his precognitive skill and a new passion: writing.

He had moved with his new wife into a house in a narrow, dark street, whose spiral staircase led to Nostradamus' study on the top floor, from which he could look over the pointed roofs of the town, and at the old castle of the archbishop on a steep rock. Here, surrounded by books and manuscripts, this short, vigorous man who looked more like a farmer than a sage, meditated upon the future, practised divination and scratched out sheet after sheet with his quill pen. The house can still be seen in Salon.

From 1550, Nostradamus published yearly almanacs – month by month diaries of the coming year's events, together with astrological tables of celestial conjunctions. These soon spread his celebrity far and wide. In 1552, he published a description of his "wonder drugs" and his eccentric medicinal theories – such as boiling water thoroughly before drinking. This book also listed a number of feminine cosmetics of his own concoction, as well as jam recipes that he particularly favoured. The *Trâite des Fardemens et Confitures* ("Treatise on Cosmetics and Jams") also achieved wide popularity.

At that time, printed volumes were still a novelty, but the spirit of the Renaissance had swept through French society, and new books were bought as quickly as they came off the presses. (These included the works of Nostradamus' contemporary and fellow medical graduate of Montpellier, Francois Rabelais.) Nostradamus became widely known for his almanacs and his treatise on cosmetics (which had been made popular by Catherine de Medici), so when, on 1 May 1555, he brought out his volume of prophetic quatrains, it quickly became something of a bestseller.

The courtier and poet Jean Dorat praised Nostradamus so highly to his students that one of them, Jean Aimes de Chavigny, travelled from Burgundy to Salon to meet the seer. De Chavigny was a distinguished man in his own right, having been mayor of Beaune. He soon became a lodger in the house of Nostradamus, and became the prophet's devoted helper and pupil; he also wrote a biography of Nostradamus to which this present account, like all the others, is indebted.

Nostradamus was in his early fifties when he met de Chavigny – an old man by the standards of sixteenth-century Europe. Chavigny described his master as being a "little less than middle height, robust, cheerful and vigorous. His brow was high and open, the nose straight, the grey eyes gentle, though in wrath they would flame . . . a severe but laughing face, so one saw allied with the severity a great humanity. His cheeks were ruddy even into extreme age, his beard thick, his health good."

Nostradamus' *Centuries* was so-called because each book (there were eventually twelve) contained one hundred predictions, each consisting of a four-line rhymed verse. In his preface, dedicated to his son Caesar, he makes it clear that he was not aiming at a wide audience. His knowledge, he says, derives from "astronomical effects" – that is, study of the heavens – but if he were to tell all he knows of the future, it would cause such offence among "those of the present Reign, Sect, Religion and Faith" that he would be angrily condemned. In spite of which he had decided, for the common good, to speak his mind about the future in "dark, abstruse sentences", and to ignore the advice of St Matthew not to cast his pearls before swine.

Nostradamus succeeded all too well in disguising his meanings – so well that the first reaction of the unprepared reader is to dismiss them as some kind of a joke. The two preliminary verses describe how he sits in his study, looking into a "thin flame" (presumably a candle) in a brass bowl of water and, using a divining rod, experiences "divine splendour", which "sits nearby". Then he plunges straight into obscurity:

> *Quands le littière du tourbillon versée,*
> *Et seront faces de leurs manteaux couvers,*
> *La Republique par gens nouveau vexée,*
> *Lors, blancs et rouges jugeront a l'envers.*

Translation:

> When the litter is overturned by the whirlwind,
> And faces will be covered by their cloaks,
> The Republic by new men is vexed,
> Then the whites and reds will judge conversely.

The first two lines are an excellent description of litter caught up by the wind, and men covering their faces with their cloaks, but *what* Republic is vexed by new men (upstarts?), and who are the whites and the reds who will pass perverse (or wrong) judgements? Henry C. Roberts, who translated the *Centuries* in 1937, concludes that Nostradamus is forecasting the Russian Revolution of 1917, with its Reds and Whites. But the Reds overthrew the Russian monarchy, not a republic. Besides, the Russians of 1917 did not wear cloaks. And if we add that "litter" can also mean a kind of chair in which wealthy people are carried by their lackeys, we have to admit that it sounds like a prophecy that applies to Nostradamus' own country rather than to Russia.

In fact, Nostradamus seems to foresee the future of France more than of any other country, so it is unlikely that the quatrain refers to the Russian Revolution – which leaves the French Revolution. The republicans and the royalists were also known as reds and whites. "Tourbillon" can mean a whirlpool or a whirlwind but, since men are holding their cloaks over their faces, a whirlwind seems the more likely. We have to remember that the Republic had been established by the time the "new men" – Robespierre, Danton and Marat – gained their power. If the "whites and reds" are royalists and republicans, then the last line means that the reds and whites hold opposite opinions about one another. This is certainly a far more reasonable interpretation than Henry C. Roberts' Russian Revolution.

There are a thousand of these verses (plus another thirteen from the two "lost books", 11 and 12), all virtually as incomprehensible as this. Just occasionally, a verse seems to score a direct hit on some historical event – as we shall see in the following pages – but, for the most part, they are as obscure as the utterances of the Delphic oracle.

A few months after the publication of the first seven *Centuries*, Nostradamus' life changed dramatically. He was summoned to the court of Henry II and arrived there on 15 August 1555.

It was almost certainly the queen, Catherine de Medici, who was responsible for summoning him; her husband was more interested in hunting than in the occult sciences. Catherine was fascinated by astrology and fortune-telling. One of the most calculating and ruthless women of the sixteenth century, she used astrological prediction rather as a modern politician uses polling organizations to help formulate policy. As the wife of the monarch, she could indulge her passion for the occult without fear of the Inquisition, and could offer similar protection to her favourites. Therefore, for Nostradamus, an invitation to the court was the most precious gift his increasing reputation could have brought.

In her excellent novelized biography of Nostradamus, *The Dreamer and the Vine,* astrologer Liz Greene speculates that the real reason Nostradamus was summoned to Paris was that someone had given the queen a copy of the *Centuries,* and she had seen the one that seemed to foretell her husband's death. *Century I,* quatrain 35 reads:

> *Le Lion jeune le vieux surmontera,*
> *En champ bellique par singulier duelle:*
> *Dans cage d'or l'oeil il lui crevera,*
> *Deux plays une puis mourrir mort cruelle.*

Translation:

> The young Lion shall overcome the old one,
> In a field by a single duel:
> In a golden cage he shall put out his eyes,
> Two blows from one then he shall die a cruel death.

In fact, the queen was anxious to get a second opinion from Nostradamus concerning a prediction made by another famous seer, Luc Gaurico. This Neapolitan astrologer had warned that the king's stars suggested death or blindness if he fought a duel in an enclosed space in his forty-first year. Catherine was not much emotionally attached to her husband – who had numerous mistresses, including his aged childhood nurse – but she was anxious that he should survive at least until 1562, when their eldest son Francis would be old enough to legally rule without a regent. Unfortunately, the threat to Henri's life was due to fall between 1559 and 1560.

What Nostradamus told his new royal patrons was not recorded. Tradition states that he gave a copy of the *Centuries* to Henri, with an offer to explain the meaning of each quatrain, but the king, being no intellectual, refused a privilege that future monarchs would have given fiefdoms for. The same tradition states that the Seer of Salon privately showed Queen Catherine a magic mirror, in which she saw three of her seven children attaining the crown of France.

Fantasy or truth, their majesties' known reaction to Nostradamus was in line with these stories: Henri politely ignored him, but Catherine thereafter ardently sought his prophetic advice. A Spaniard at the French court, Francisco de Alova, later remarked that Queen Catherine always quoted Nostradamus' words with a confidence "as if citing St John or St Luke". All threat of questioning by the Inquisition receded in the light of such high patronage. Queen Catherine even had Nostradamus lodged in the town house of the Archbishop of Sens. There, a steady stream of nobility visited the seer, who is said to have made a small fortune from medical and astrological consultations. However, Nostradamus had no intention of becoming a court magician, and soon requested, and was given, leave to return to Salon.

It seems unlikely that Nostradamus was altogether candid, at least with the king. The first volume of the *Centuries* contained specific predictions that Henri would die in agony and that his children would be the last of the ruling house of Valois. "Ill news is an ill guest" as the saying goes, so if the seer did elucidate these quatrains, we must assume that he was not taken seriously by the queen, or that what he had to tell her did not disturb her unduly.

The event foretold by Gaurico and Nostradamus, the death of King Henri, occurred in his forty-first year, just as Luc Gaurico had predicted. The "*duelle*" in question was a jousting competition that took place on 10 July 1559. King Henri had already won two jousts that morning. Queen Catherine sent a messenger to ask him to "toil no more" as it was "late, and the weather exceeding hot", but the king replied that, as champion of the field, it was his duty to accept three challenges. Gabriel de Lorges – the Comte de Montgomery – was already in the saddle at the far end of the jousting ring and, without another word, King Henri spurred towards him.

They struck and passed each other twice in succession but, as neither was unhorsed, they turned and charged for a third time.

To everyone's horror, de Lorges' blunted wooden lance shattered when it struck the king's breastplate and the sharp broken end slammed upward and pierced the visor of Henri's gold-embossed helmet. (These were, of course, "two blows in one" pass.) The splintered lance struck and entered just behind Henri's right eye socket, drove through that side of the brain case and exited near the right ear. Amazingly, he did not die instantly, but suffered ten days of blind agony before a gangrene infection finally put him out of his misery.

The Comte de Montgomery was seven years younger than the king and was commander of his Scottish Guard. Henri II used a lion as his unofficial badge and the emblem of Scotland was, and is, a lion rampant.

Detail for detail, Nostradamus' prediction was exactly correct and many people, especially Queen Catherine, saw it as such. If she was angry that the seer had not given a specific warning to King Henri – which might have saved his life – she showed no sign of it. When somebody suggested that Nostradamus was plainly a sorcerer and should be handed to the Inquisition, she angrily refused, restating that he was under her protection.

The attitude was generous – particularly if she suspected the meaning of the tenth quatrain of *Century I*:

> *Sergens transmis dans la cage de fer,*
> *Où les enfans septaines du Roy sont Pris:*
> *Les vieux et peres sortiront bas de l'enfer,*
> *Ains mourir voir de fruict mort et cris.*

Translation:

> Sergeants sent into an iron vault,
> Which holds the seven children of the King:
> The ancestors and forefathers will emerge from Hell,
> Lamenting to see death of the fruit of their line.

Catherine de Medici and Henri II had seven children and therefore, in 1555, had some reason to hope that their offspring would continue the line of kings. Unfortunately, this was not to happen. With the death of Queen Margot of Navarre in 1615 – the last of the seven children – the Valois line of kings came to an end.

Quatrain 11 of the sixth volume of the *Centuries* seems to be an even more specific prediction of the end of the Valois dynasty.

> *Des sept rameaux à trois seront reduicts,*
> *Les plus aisnez seront surprins par mort,*
> *Fraticider les deux seront seduicts,*
> *Les conjurez en dormans seront morts.*

Translation:

> The seven branches will be reduced to three,
> The older ones will be surprised by death,
> The two will be seduced towards fratricide,
> The conspirators will die while asleep.

Three of Catherine's five sons lived to ascend the throne of France (under French law, her two daughters were ineligible to rule). Of the seven, only Queen Margot lived to relative old age, the rest being prematurely "surprised by death" in their teens, twenties and thirties. Two of the brothers, Henri III and François, Duc d'Alenon, became mortal enemies and certainly would have indulged in fratricide, had the opportunity arisen.

Guessing the identity of the conspirators predicted to die in their sleep in the last line of the quatrain is now virtually impossible; sixteenth-century France was full of likely candidates. Some researchers have suggested it might have been the Guise brothers – co-conspirators with François, later assassinated by Henri III – but, although killed early in the morning, neither was asleep at the time.

Over the next decade, Nostradamus and his second wife lived peacefully in Salon. He never returned to Paris, even after it was generally recognized that he had correctly predicted the circumstances of the death of Henri II. Although he could doubtless have made a fortune at the court of the new king, François II, Nostradamus still declined offers to become the royal astrologer. This choice of a quiet life may have been to do with his age and health – by his late fifties, he already suffered from severe gout – but it is also possible that he had foreknowledge of the difficult times the French crown would soon undergo.

François II, son and heir of Henri II, was only sixteen when he came to the throne and was easily dominated by the powerful

Duc de Guise (just what Queen Catherine had feared might happen if her husband died before 1562). In 1560, after only a year as king, François died and was replaced by his fourteen-year-old brother, who was crowned Charles IX. This time, however, it was Queen-Mother Catherine who dominated her royal son – her intrigues and plots throughout his fourteen-year reign were to split France and sour the sectarian dispute between Protestant and Catholic to the point of massacre and civil war.

Nostradamus was apparently well aware of the tragic events shortly to befall France, because his *Centuries* foretold them in specific, if deliberately obscure, detail. He was visited personally by Catherine and King Charles in 1564, when the royal party went out of its way to pass through Salon. If he warned them of the coming massacre of Saint Bartholomew's Day, it failed to influence their later actions.

Two years following this royal visit, on 2 July 1566, Nostradamus died of a massive heart attack, in part brought on by his crippling gout. Following his death, his pupil de Chavigny republished the ten *Centuries* together with two partial volumes and two other posthumous works, *Sixains* (containing sixty-eight quatrains) and *Presages* (containing a further 141 predictions). In this later book, the last quatrain reads:

> *De retour d'Ambassade, don de Roy mis au lieu*
> *Plus n'en fera: sera allé à Dieu*
> *Parans plus proches, amis, frères du sang,*
> *Trouvé tout mort près du lict et du banc.*

Translation:

> On returning from an embassy, the King's gift safely stored
> No more will I labour for I will have gone to God
> By my close relatives, friends and blood brothers,
> I shall be found dead, near my bed and the bench.

Nostradamus had, just before his death, returned from an embassy to Arles, where he had been an official representative for Salon. The "King's gift", also mentioned in the first line, might have been the princely one hundred gold ecus Queen-Mother Catherine had given him, in the name of King Charles, two years before; we know that the seer left his family plenty of money when he died. On the night before his death, Nostradamus called for a priest to give the last rites – although he seemed healthy enough for de Chavigny to be surprised when the seer told him: "You will not see me alive at sunrise."

This was Nostradamus' last prophecy. The next morning, de Chavigny and the seer's family found him dead, lying between his bed and a bench he used to use to help get his gouty foot in and out of bed.

In his biography of his master, de Chavigny tells us that Nostradamus had asked "not to hear feet passing over him when he slept for the last time". Therefore, Nostradamus was entombed upright in a niche in the wall of the chapel of the Convent of Les Cordeliers. The plaque on the tomb reads:

Here lie the bones of the most illustrious Michel Nostradamus, the only one, in judgement of all mortals, worthy to write with a pen almost divine, under the influence of the stars, of events to come in the whole world.
He lived sixty-two years, six months and seventeen days.
He died at Salon in the year 1566.
Posterity disturb not his repose.
Anne Ponsart Gemelle, his wife, wishes her spouse true felicity.

The penultimate line was, not surprisingly, read by many to be a warning against disturbing the seer's bones. Indeed, quatrain 7, *Century IX*, was said to be a direct warning against this from the seer himself:

> *Qui ouvrira le monument trouvé*
> *Et ne viendra le serrer promptement,*
> *Mal lui viendra et ne pourra prouvé,*
> *Si mieux doit estre roi Breton ou Normand.*

Translation:

He that shall open the discovered monument [tomb],
And shall not close it again promptly,
Evil will befall him and no one will be able to prove it,
Better he were a Breton or Norman king.

There are two tales, possibly apocryphal, concerning the disturbance of Nostradamus' tomb. The first states that, in the year 1600, the citizens of Salon decided that their famous seer should be moved to a more prominent section of the chapel wall. On opening the tomb they found Nostradamus' body had been buried with a lead disc on a chain around its neck. The disc was quite unadorned, except for the printed numbers "1600".

Presumably the tomb was quickly resealed, or the bones were moved "*promptement*" enough for the curse of quatrain 7 *Century IX*, not to take effect, because no "evil" effects were reported following this incident.

The same cannot be said of the second tradition concerning Nostradamus' bones.

During the French Revolution, some soldiers are said to have broken into the seer's tomb in the hope of finding the magic mirror they had heard he used to see the future. When they found only his skeleton, they decided to get drunk and one soldier broke open Nostradamus' skull and swigged wine from it. As they were leaving the chapel, a hail of gunfire – fired by whom, the legend does not make plain – killed the sacrilegious trooper stone dead.

One fact we know for certain, following the Revolutionaries' ransacking of the convent of Les Cordeliers, the people of Salon decided that his bones should be moved to the church of Saint-Laurent, where his tomb can still be seen today. Strangely enough, when Nostradamus' original will and testament of 1566 was subsequently discovered, a section of text was noted to have been scored out, but still remained legible. It read: "In the sepulchre in the collegial church of Saint Laurens of the said Salon, and in the Chapel of Our Lady, in the wall of which it is desired to be made a monument."

A coincidence, perhaps, but the fact that Nostradamus asked for a monument to be placed in the very spot where his bones would eventually rest seems in keeping with his reputation for foreseeing the future.

In the remainder of this chapter, we shall consider some of the quatrains that seem to have been fulfilled in the lifetime of Nostradamus or soon after. Later chapters will deal the centuries that follow and, finally, with those that may reveal our future.

The main sources I have used are Erica Cheetham's *The Prophecies of Nostradamus*, Henry C. Roberts' *The Complete Prophecies of Nostradamus*, Jean-Charles de Fontbrune's *Nostradamus: Countdown to Apocalypse* and David Ovason's *The Secrets of Nostradamus*. I cite the theories appropriate to each and, where there is a significant difference of opinion, I summarize the various arguments.

The historical titles are my own. Nostradamus, of course, gave no such clues. The Roman numeral beneath gives the *Centuries* volume, and is followed by the quatrain number.

Due to the seer's unparalleled skill at poetic riddles, no one researcher can claim absolute certainty over the true meaning of *any* of Nostradamus' prophecies, and the reader is always left to think and decide for themselves where any truth may lie. Of course, this indeed may have been Nostradamus' purpose in publishing the *Centuries* in the first place.

Francis II and Mary Queen of Scots, 1558–60
X.55

> *Les malheureuses noces celebreront,*
> *En grand joye mais la fin malheureuse:*
> *Mary et mere Nore desdaigneront.*
> *La Phybe mort et Nore plus piteuse.*

Translation:

> The unhappy marriage will be celebrated,
> With great joy, but the end will be unhappy:
> Mary will be detested by the mother.
> The *Phybe* dead and the daughter-in-law most piteous.

In 1558, shortly before the accidental death of Henri II, the heir apparent to the French throne, Prince Francis, was married to Mary Stuart – later known as Mary Queen of Scots. Naturally the match was celebrated throughout both France and Scotland, but the marriage was destined to be tragically short.

The mothers of Mary (Marie de Guise) and of Francis (Catherine de Medici) loathed each other: the former referring to Catherine as "the merchant's daughter".[1] Mary's return to

---

1 A sneering allusion to the unaristocratic roots of the Medici family, whose name means "doctors".

Scotland, following the death of King Francis in 1560, dashed any hope of a closer alliance between the two kingdoms.

The reference to "Mary" in line three seems to suggest a prediction of the above events – note that Nostradamus did not use the French spelling, "Marie". Mary is a name rarely found in French history.

But what of "Phybe", a name that simply does not exist? This in itself tells us to look for one of Nostradamus' anagrams or words in code. The first syllable, "*phy*" suggests the Greek *phi*, the letter F, the initial letter of Francis, her husband. "*Be*" suggests *beta*, the second letter of the Greek alphabet, so "Phybe" becomes F2, Francis the Second.

The Conspiracy of Amboise, March 1560
IV.62

> Un coronel machine ambition,
> Se saisira de la grande armée,
> Contrée son prince faite invention,
> Es descouvert sera souz sa ramée.

Translation:

> A colonel intrigues a plot by his ambition,
> He shall seize upon the best part of the army,
> Against the prince he shall have a feigned invention.
> And shall be discovered under the branches.

Here we have a classic case of different interpretations by different Nostradamus scholars.

De Fontbrune believes this quatrain refers to the 1560 attempt to kidnap Francis II from Castle Amboise. The plotters, many from the army, thus hoped to remove the sixteen-year-old king from the manipulative influence of the Duc de Guise. They were, however, discovered in the neighbouring forest and slaughtered.

Roberts, on the other hand, believes this to be a prediction of the rise to power of Oliver Cromwell, but does not offer any supporting detail.

Erica Cheetham offers a third interpretation: the rise to power of Colonel Qaddafi in 1971 and his overthrow of King Idris of Libya.

Mary Queen of Scots and the "Casket Letters", 1567
VIII.23

> *Lettres trouves de la roine les coffres,*
> *Point de subscrit sans aucun nom d'hauteur*
> *Par la police seront caché les offres,*
> *Qu'on ne scaura qui sera l'amateur.*

Translation:

> Letters are found in the queen's coffers,
> No signature and no name of the author
> The ruse will conceal the offers,
> So they do not know who the lover is.

Following the death of the teenage Francis II, his widow, Mary Queen of Scots, married the Scottish noble, Lord Darnley. Although the match was at first happy enough to produce a son (later James VI of Scotland, then James I of England), Mary soon came to hate her syphilitic, conniving husband.

In 1567, Lord Darnley died under suspicious circumstances (the house in which he was sleeping exploded). The chief suspect in the murder was Mary's close friend, the Earl of Bothwell. This seemed to be confirmed when a silver casket of love letters and sonnets – apparently from Mary to Bothwell – came to light soon afterwards. After a mock trial, however, Bothwell was acquitted and, a few weeks later, divorced his wife and married Mary.

Although they could fix a trial, Queen Mary and her new consort could not control public opinion. The scandalous marital behaviour of the monarch led to a short but decisive civil war in Scotland, at the end of which Mary was forced to abdicate and flee to England. There she was placed under house arrest by her cousin, Queen Elizabeth I. Following an attempt to escape and take the English throne, Mary was beheaded in 1587.

The casket of letters, that implicated Bothwell and, indirectly,

Mary in Darnley's murder, is now thought by some historians to have been a set of forgeries produced by Mary's enemies. Whether this is true or not, however, it was not the casket but the Queen's own shameless remarriage that brought her downfall.

Perhaps it should be noted that Nostradamus almost certainly knew Mary Queen of Scots personally, as both visited the court of Henri II in 1556.

The Turkish Sack of Cyprus, 1570–1
XII.36

> *Assault farouche en Cypre se prepare,*
> *Larme a l'oeil, de ta ruine proche;*
> *Byzance class, Morisque, si grand tare,*
> *Deux differente, le grand vast par la roche.*

Translation:

> A savage attack prepared on Cyprus,
> Tears in my eye, thy ruin approaches,
> Byzantine fleet, Muslims, do great damage,
> Two different ones, the great waste by the rock.

Most sources agree that this quatrain refers to the savage invasion of Cyprus by the Ottoman Army.

Byzantium (now Istanbul) has been in Turkish hands since 1453, thus any fleet from there would be (as line three states) Muslim. In 1570, Sultan Selim II ordered the invasion of the island of Cyprus, which was at that time under Venetian rule. The Turkish fleet blockaded towns and landed 60,000 men. When Nicosia fell after forty-five days, 20,000 inhabitants were butchered and the rest were enslaved. Famagusta held out for almost a year before it was forced to surrender; the Venetian governor was tortured, then flayed alive, while the Ottoman troops ravaged the town and slaughtered its inhabitants. Repressive Turkish rule on Cyprus continued until 1878.

The Battle of Lepanto, 7 October 1571
III.64

> Le chef de Perse remplira grands Olchades,
> Classe tririme contre gent Mahometique:
> De Parthe et Mede, et pilliers les Cyclades,
> Repos long temps au grand port Ionique.

Translation:

> The lord of Persia shall prepare great Ships,
> A fleet of triremes against the Muslims:
> From Parthia and Media they shall come to plunder
>   the Cyclades,
> A long rest shall come to the great Ionic port.

The idea of a Persian leader sending a fleet against Muslims in the Cyclades (the Greek islands) seems rather odd. If, however, one reads the second line to indicate an opposing fleet attacking the first, a certain famous historical encounter seems to be suggested: the Battle of Lepanto.

Following its successful capture of Cyprus in 1571, the Ottoman Empire launched a fleet to invade the rest of the Aegean islands. This was met by an allied Christian fleet and destroyed in the Gulf of Lepanto (now called the Gulf of Corinth). Although this defeat did little harm to the military strength of the Ottoman Empire, it was of great psychological importance to the Christian states and marked the beginning of a long period of decline for the Turks. Ionian ports (those of the west coast of Asia Minor and the Greek islands) thereafter enjoyed a long period of comparative peace.

The battle of Lepanto is also notable in history as the last in which both sides utilised oared galleys (called triremes, in ancient times).

The 1572 Supernova
II.41

> La grand éstoile par sept jours bruslera,
> Nuée fera deux soleils apparior:

Le gros mastin toute nuict hurlera,
Quand grand pontife changera de terroir.

Translation:

> The great star shall burn for seven days,
> A cloud will make two suns appear:
> The huge mastiff will howl all night,
> When the great pope changes territory.

David Ovason believes that this quatrain specifically indicates the formation of a new star in the summer skies of 1572. This supernova appeared near Cassiopeia and burned visibly, night and day, for sixteen months. Thus, says Ovason, two "suns" were visible. He adds that the nova had a distinctly perceptible cloud of stellar gases around it at night.

This astronomical event caused consternation across Europe. Since the Dark Ages, it had been a fixture of Church belief that the "heavenly realm" of the sky was perfect and unchanging. The arrival of a new star was a painful blow to the Church's doctrinal authority just when men like Columbus and Copernicus were already undermining it with their strange theories and discoveries.

The supernova of 1572 highlighted the corrosion of the absolute authority of the Church through the growth of scientific reasoning in European society. It also heralded a new era of invention, reform and bloody conflict.

In Denmark, an alchemist called Tycho Brahe was so amazed by the new star that he dropped all his other work and dedicated his life to the study of the heavens – he was later to be called the "Father of Astronomy".

In Rome, Pope Pius V died during the time of the supernova and was replaced by Gregory XIII – designer of the Gregorian calendar now in almost universal use.

Finally, in Paris, Queen-Mother Catherine de Medici instigated a slaughter that was to lead to the most savage religious wars in Europe's history . . .

The St Bartholomew's Day Massacre, 24 August 1572
IV.47

> *Le noir farouche quand aura essayé*
> *Sa main sanguine par fué, fer, arcs tendus:*
> *Trestout le peuple sera tant effrayé,*
> *Voir les plus grans par col et pieds pendus.*

Translation:

> The savage black one, when his bloody hand
> Shall have done its worst with fire, sword and bows:
> Then will his people be terror-stricken
> At the sight of great ones hanged by the neck and feet.

Erica Cheetham suggests that "*noir*" in the first line is a partial anagram for *roi* (French: "king"). She goes on to speculate that this quatrain refers to the bloody St Bartholomew's Day Massacre that was to escalate the Protestant-Catholic troubles into a savage religious war.

In 1572, Catherine de Medici – mother of the then King of France, Charles IX – instigated a plot to assassinate Admiral Coligny, the leader of the Huguenot (French Protestant) faction. The plot failed – Coligny was only wounded – and, while gathered in Paris for the wedding of the king's sister Margot to Henry of Navarre, leading Huguenots demanded an investigation.

King Charles was at first ready to comply, but he soon changed his mind when his mother informed him to whom the trail would lead. With breathtaking cold-heartedness, the king and his mother decided to close the city gates and kill every Protestant their troops could find. Estimates vary, but at least 2,000 – possibly even as many as 100,000 – men, women and children were butchered on St Bartholomew's Day 1572. The slaughter soon spread to the French provinces and acted as fuel to the religious troubles that were to culminate in the disastrous Thirty Years' War, half a century later.

Cheetham suggests that the last line of Nostradamus' quatrain might be a reference to the fate of Admiral Coligny, whose attempted assassination set off the whole gruesome chain of events. As soon as the killings began, the violently pro-Catholic Duke de Guise sent men to Coligny's house. The admiral, who had won several campaigns for King Charles, was stabbed to death, then hung from a gibbet by one foot. Other Huguenot nobles were hanged by the neck.

On the other hand, Henry Roberts suggests that this quatrain might be a reference to the Italian Fascist (black clad) dictator Mussolini. After helping to instigate World War II and uncounted deaths, Mussolini was himself executed and hung from a lamp-post by his feet in 1945.

French Religious Unrest, 1574–6
III.98

> Deux Royals Frères si fort guerroyeront,
> Qu'entre'eux sera la guerre si mortelle:
> Qu'un chacun places fortes occuperont,
> De regne et vie sera leur grand querelle.

Translation:

Two royal brothers shall battle so much one against the other,
That the war between then shall be mortal:
Each shall occupy a strong place
Their quarrel will concern their kingdom and lives.

Both de Fontbrune and Erica Cheetham agree that this quatrain seems to concern the so-called Fifth French War of Religion.

The Duke d'Alençon, younger brother of King Henri III, was a liberal Catholic who championed the rights of the Huguenot Protestants. This placed him in direct opposition to (then) anti-Protestant Henri. In 1576, following two years of sectarian unrest and bloodshed, Alençon's faction led 30,000 men to the gates of Paris and forced the king to sign a conciliatory edict. Afterwards an uneasy, well-armed peace was maintained between the two brothers. With some difficulty, each maintained a rein on his detestation for the other for the greater good of France.

Had sixteenth-century religious differences always been settled in this relatively reasonable fashion, later European history might have been a good deal less bloody. Unfortunately, as Nostradamus seemed to have known, the war between Catholic and Protestant was destined to be "mortal".

The Murder of the Duc de Guise, 23 December 1588
III.51, III.55

> *Paris conjure un grand meurtre commettre*
> *Blois le fera sortir en plain effect;*
> *Ceux d'Orléons voudront leur chef remmettre,*
> *Angiers, Troye, Langres leur foront grand forfait.*

Translation:

> Paris conspires to commit great murder,
> Blois shall make it come to pass,
> The people of Orléans will replace their leader,
> Angiers, Troyes and Langres will harm them.

This quatrain seems to deal with an important political assassination that took place in the reign of Henri III.

One of the most influential families of late sixteenth-century France were the Dukes of Guise – a clan that led the Roman Catholic backlash against the growth of Protestantism. François, the second duke to carry the title, had already tried puppet-mastering the reign of the weakling Francis II (see "the Conspiracy of Amboise", above) following the death of Henri II. Eighteen years later, his son, Henri de Lorraine, was a close friend and supporter of Henri III. Unfortunately the pair argued over the king's growing favouritism towards the Protestant faction, so Guise formed a "Holy League" of pro-Catholics to counter the king's liberal turn of policy.

King Henri, with the typical ruthlessness of his family, decided to have his friend murdered. The Duc was invited to the palace at Blois, where several people tried to warn him that his life was in danger, including a beautiful marchioness who spent the night with him for that purpose. They failed because de Guise was too certain that the king would never dare harm him. The king did dare, however. Guise was asked into a room next to the bedchamber and was killed by the king's guards as Henri watched from behind the bed curtains; it was two days before Christmas, 1588.

At the same time the citizens of Orléans overthrew their governor and replaced him with a relation of the late Duc de Guise. The last line of Nostradamus' quatrain names the other towns that sided with the Holy League and the de Guise faction.

Nostradamus seems to have a second prophecy about the murder of Guise:

> En l'an qu'un oeil en France regnera,
> La Cour sera en un bien fascheux trouble,
> Le Grand de Blois son ami tuera,
> La regne mis en mal et doubte double.

Translation:

> In the year when an eye reigns in France,
> The court will be greatly troubled and embarrassed,
> The great one will kill his friend at Blois
> The reign thrown into evil and double doubt.

Why the king is described as "an eye" is difficult to fathom – although Fontbrune thinks it means a king who has been forced to share power, as Henry III was virtually sharing it with the Duc de Guise. ("Keeping an eye on" and "under someone's eye" also identify the eye with power.) The court was certainly deeply troubled and divided when Henri III had Guise assassinated, and his reign was plunged into even deeper trouble when the Pope excommunicated him.

The king and the Protestant Henry of Navarre became allies, but another assassination was soon to end that alliance.

The Assassination of Henri III, 2 August 1589
I.97

> Ce que fer, flamme, n'a sceu paracheuer,
> La douce langue au conseil viendra faire
> Par repos, songe, le roy fere resuer,
> Plus l'ennemy en feu, sang militaire.

Translation:

> What neither fire nor iron could achieve,
> A sweet tongue in council shall manage:
> In a sleeping dream the king will see,
> An enemy, not in war or military blood.

Erica Cheetham sees this quatrain as clear prediction of the murder of Henri III. If so, it was typical of Nostradamus' habit of concealing the meaning until after the event. No details in the quatrain could have warned Henri, even if he had read it the night before his assassination.

On 30 July 1589, King Henri told friends that the night before his sleep had been troubled by a strange dream. He had seen the royal ceremonial regalia – the crown, sceptre, sword, spurs and blue cloak – being trodden into the mud by a rabble of common people and monks. Although he was uncertain what this meant, he feared it was a premonition of death.

Three days later, at St Cloud, a young monk called Jacques Clement – who was, in fact, a fanatical anti-Protestant – approached the king. He told Henri that he had news concerning a secret letter and, as the king leaned down for the monk to whisper in his ear, Clement stabbed him in the stomach. Henri struck the monk with his own dagger, and Clement was quickly killed by the guards. But after a day of agony, Henri died of peritonitis.

Cheetham points out that the phrase "*douce langue au conseil*" seems to be one of the clever double-meanings of which Nostradamus was so fond. The king, despite his many war-like enemies, was killed in council by a man who pretended to be a friend. She also notes another typical Nostradamian twist: "douce" means sweet, as does "Clement".

The Victory of Henri de Navarre, 1589
X.18

> *Le ranc Lorrain fera place à Vendosme,*
> *Le hault mis bas et le bas mis en haut,*
> *Le filz d'Hamon sera esleu dans Rome,*
> *Et les deux grands seront mis en deffault.*

Translation:

> The House of Lorraine shall give place to Vendosme,
> The high shall fall, the low shall be exalted,
> The son of Hamon shall be chosen by Rome,
> And the two great ones will be defeated.

Henry III was the last king of the direct Valois line. Although, as Nostradamus predicted, three of Catherine de Medici's sons inherited the throne, all died without leaving an heir. Catherine herself – the Lady Macbeth of sixteenth-century France – died seven months before Henri's assassination and the fall of the dynasty.

The French throne was thus open to any noble who could claim direct descent from the Emperor Charlemagne. The man with the strongest claim to this bloodline was Henri, ruler of the little kingdom of Navarre, but he had virtually no chance, in most people's opinion. This was because, on one side, he had to compete for the crown with the powerful house of de Guise, and on the other, as already noted, Henri was a Protestant.

Indeed, Henri of Navarre might have been killed in the St Bartholomew's Day Massacre, if it had not been for two factors. The first was his immediate conversion to Catholicism when he realized what was happening. The second was his marriage that day to Princess Margot, the king's sister. (This marriage of a Catholic princess to a Protestant prince was, in fact, the very reason so many Huguenots were in Paris at the time of the slaughter.) Henri remained a virtual captive of King Charles until 1576, when he returned to Navarre and reconverted to Protestantism.

Henri immediately claimed the throne on the death of Henri III, but was blocked by a combination of the Guise family and their Holy League, the Pope – who obviously did not want a Protestant king of France – and the opposition of the generally Catholic French people. Despite his brilliant generalship and a string of victories against this coalition, Henri eventually won the crown by converting to Catholicism and thus undermining his opponents' popular support.[2] Thus, in 1593, Henri III of Navarre became Henri IV of France – the first of the Bourbon kings.

---

2 Henri cynically summed up his decision to change religion with the phrase: "Paris is worth a Mass".

The above quatrain predicts the defeat of the "House of Lorraine" – another name of the Guise clan – by "Vendosme" – Henri of Navarre was also Duke of Vendome. Thus, in the second line, the fall of the "high" de Guises and rise of the "lowly" King of Navarre. The "son of Hamon" being chosen by Rome in the third line is a correct prediction that Henri IV's accession would be eventually accepted by the papacy (Hamon was a heretic, and Henri inherited his Protestant "heresy" from his mother's teachings). The "two great ones" defeated in the last line were probably meant to indicate the two other main contenders for the throne, the Duc de Guise and the Duc de Mayenne.

Like the prediction of the death of Henri II in a joust, this quatrain was seen – immediately after the event – to be an exactly accurate prediction of an improbable happening. It further cemented Nostradamus' posthumous reputation across Europe as a major prophet.

In fact, if tradition is to be believed, Nostradamus took pains to confirm his premonition that Henri of Navarre would one day be king of France.

When, in 1563, Catherine de Medici had visited the aging Nostradamus, the ten-year-old Henri was taken along in the royal party. During the visit, the seer asked Henri's tutor if he could see the boy naked. Unsurprisingly, the boy flatly refused and his tutor decided not to force the issue. Nevertheless, Nostradamus is said to have gained access to young Henri's bedroom and peeked under his blankets. There he saw the birthmark he had foreseen on the first king of the Bourbon line and was satisfied that his vision had been true.

The Spread of Protestantism in the Late Sixteenth Century
III.67

> *Une nouvelle secte de Philosophes,*
> *Mesprisant mort, or, honneurs et richesses*
> *Des monts Germains ne seront limitrophes,*
> *A les ensuivre auront appuy et presses.*

Translation:

> A new sect of Philosophers,
> Despising death, gold, honours and riches:
> They will not be limited by the mountains of Germany,
> They shall have crowds of followers and much support.

The chief question of Nostradamus' day was the Protestant-Catholic split, later called the Reformation. Racially a Jew, Nostradamus took care to appear a faithful son of the Catholic Church but, as we have seen, his sympathies were possibly with the Protestants. Certainly he was under no illusion – as many of his fellow Catholics and several popes were – that the "Protestant heresy" might one day be stamped out.

Catholic fanatics like the Ducs de Guise and the Holy League aimed either to reconvert all Protestants or – as at the St Bartholomew's Day Massacre – kill them to a man, in the name of Christ. This ambition depended, however, on the containment of the Protestant teachings to the Teutonic nations that spawned them. Many Nostradamus scholars believe the above quatrain was Nostradamus' flat prediction that Protestantism would continue to spread and prosper.

The "new sect of philosophers" named by Nostradamus in the first line of the quatrain might well be the Protestants. Quite apart from the seer's habit of disguising identities in his quatrains, he may have used this oblique phrase to avoid trouble with the Inquisition.

Again, the description of the "new sect" as despising gold, honour and riches in the second line may seem odd today, but it should be remembered that Martin Luther's original disgust with the Catholic Church sprang from the hierarchy's obsession with such things. As to despising death, we have already seen how many Protestants killed and died in the name of their faith.

The last two lines apparently contain the prophecy of the future spread and popularity of Protestantism. Just how prophetic this was in Nostradamus' day is a moot question. By the time he published the *Centuries*, Protestantism had successfully spread to England, Holland, Scandinavia and large areas of France. One might, therefore, read this quatrain as a statement of political fact as much as a prediction of the future.

7 The Queen's Astrologer, the Rogue Necromancer and the Angel of Light

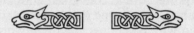

John Dee (1527–1608) is one of the most misunderstood-men in the history of magic and occultism. A scholar of undeniable genius, born at a time when the difference between superstition and science was virtually indistinguishable, he was a pioneer of the new movement to structure research and preserve knowledge. He should be remembered along with such thinkers as Roger Bacon and Isaac Newton. He would be shocked to realize that, four centuries after his death, he is remembered mainly as a student of necromancy – or what we might today call the paranormal – instead of as one of the founding fathers of modern science.

Dee wrote ground-breaking works on optics that, among other things, predicted the theory and practical value of telescopes (although some decades were to pass before Lippershey and Galileo succeeded in constructing the device that Dee had envisaged). When he saw that vital knowledge was being lost almost as fast as it was being accumulated, Dee proposed the setting-up of a cartographic arm of the English Navy, to centralize and store navigational maps, and a national manuscript library to do the same for general knowledge. Sadly, these institutions came into existence only after his death.

Again, during his lifetime, he was as highly regarded an astronomer as Tycho Brahe and Johannes Kepler. His lectures on Euclidean geometry at the University of Paris were always packed, and created a sensation among European mathematicians. Scholars stood in awe of Dee the mathematician and Dee the writer on natural philosophy (as science was then called), not Dee the necromancer.

Modern students of Dee agree that his scientific work compares favourably with that of Sir Isaac Newton a hundred years later. Indeed, it seems likely that, as a student, Newton studied Dee's speculations on light and mathematics; certainly Newton's *Principia* contains some suppositions that were first aired by Dee.

Like Kepler, Dee was an astrologer and, like Newton, he was an alchemist. Unfortunately he was also a crystal-gazer, a necromancer (i.e. someone who tries to raise the dead) and a man who had no doubt that he had conversed with angels and spirits. Add the fact that he also believed that he could foretell the future and it can be seen why he is now classified with Simon Magus, Cornelius Agrippa and Faust rather than with the scientific pioneers among whom he belongs. Shakespeare probably did him as much harm as anyone; it is generally accepted that he based Prospero in *The Tempest* on Dee.

So let us try to put the record straight.

John Dee was born in London on 13 July 1527. His father was a personal servant to Henry VIII – to be precise, the man who carved his meat – which explains why Dee always felt perfectly comfortable with life at court.

Dee was a gifted child, with a remarkable memory, and was able to work out complicated mathematical problems in his head. Although the son of a servant, he obviously deserved to be educated, and was accordingly sent to the Chantry School, in Essex, when he was ten, to learn Latin and the three Rs. At the age of fifteen he went on to St John's College, Cambridge, where he learned Greek and Hebrew. Despite his youth, he apparently proved a dedicated student. In his own words:

> "[I was] so vehemently bent to studie, that for those years I did inviolably keep to this order: only to sleep four hours every night; to allow to meat and drink (and some refreshing after) two hours every day, and of the other eighteen houres all (except the tyme of going to and being at divine service) was spent in my studies and learning."

In addition to Greek and Hebrew, he also studied mathematics, astronomy (then considered an impractical, star-gazing branch of the serious subject of astrology) and the properties of light. Today he would have taken a physics degree, but in the sixteenth century the concept of "science", separate from philosophy, was quite unknown.

At the age of nineteen, Dee graduated as a Bachelor of the Arts in Natural Philosophy. His academic career soon prospered; Trinity College had just been founded, and Dee was invited to become a Fellow. He was also offered the post of Under-Reader in Greek.

Now he had achieved the sixteenth century's equivalent of tenure, Dee permitted himself to relax with some amateur dramatics. The result was the first scandal associated with his name.

He was directing a student production of Aristophanes' satirical comedy *The Peace*, written at a time when the Athenians and the Spartans were about to declare a truce in the Pelopponesian War (which, alas, never happened), and naturally chose the leading role for himself. In the first scene, the peace campaigner Trygaeus (played by Dee) seats himself on a giant dung beetle (overfed until it is the size of a horse) and flies to visit Zeus on Mount Olympus. The audience probably expected a winch to raise the hero and his steed but, to their amazement and terror, Dee mounted the prop beetle and seemed to actually fly up to the roof of the theatre unassisted. We still do not know how he did it; probably he used his knowledge of projected light and a few mirrors. However, at the time, the rumour went around Cambridge that the young man was a sorcerer. Dee himself later noted – with a certain air of smugness – that there "was great wondering, and many vain reports spread abroad of the means how [the flight] was effected."

Two years later, with a growing realization that books alone would not feed his appetite to grasp the inner nature of the world, Dee took a sabbatical in Europe – doubtless to the relief of his still scandalized fellow academics. He never returned to his post at Trinity.

He travelled through the Low Countries, meeting eminent scholars such as Gerard Mercator, the celebrated mapmaker, and eventually settled at the University of Louvain in Belgium – one of the oldest universities in Europe. To support himself, he advertised as a tutor. His first students probably came out of curiosity – he was, after all, little older than they were, yet was offering to teach advanced logic, rhetoric, arithmetic and astrology. In fact, Dee proved to be a sensation – one suspects because he was a natural actor.

He returned to Cambridge long enough to take his MA degree (but would never obtain his doctorate – hence the title 'Dr Dee' is incorrect), then (in 1548) hastened back to Louvain. What attracted him may have been the fact that the legendary Cornelius Agrippa spent some time at Louvain towards the end of his restless life, a mere twelve years before Dee arrived there. Agrippa, who had died in Grenoble in 1535, at the age of forty-nine, had been the first and most influential of the "occult philosophers", and his *Occult Philosophy*, published three years before his death, had been widely read. Agrippa had a reputation for practising black magic – almost certainly undeserved – and the tall stories about him influenced the popular legends about Dr Faustus.

However, what was significant about Agrippa was a belief in the power of the mind, and the reality of telepathy. "Resolute imagination is the beginning of all magical operations," he says, and declares that people can cause damage to others by "ardent will alone". He points out that lovers sometimes feel one another's illnesses. If the will goes to sleep, he says, people can die of gloom and a sense of defeat.

So, no matter how much we incline to agree with Lynn Thorndike's judgement that Agrippa is something of a charlatan, it cannot be denied that his belief in the hidden power of the mind over nature was a new and exciting insight. Certainly, it exercised a great influence on Dee at a time when he was young and highly impressionable.

The real importance of Agrippa, as far as Dee was concerned, was that he had rescued magic from the medieval notion that it was a tool of the Devil. England, being a nation of pragmatists, took no interest in magic but, insofar as anyone cared about it, it was associated with witches and broomsticks. Agrippa, and his remarkable contemporary Paracelsus, taught the French and Germans to think of magic as part of the mystical quest for God. It was a serious study aimed at gaining control of unknown forces. Dee found the whole intellectual ferment of the continent as exciting as young British students found existentialism, immediately after the Second World War. Certainly it must have been exhilarating for Dee to find that his own brilliance was soon recognized, so that he felt himself a contributor to the intellectual ferment.

During the two years he spent in Louvain, Dee's reputation spread fast. The court of the Emperor Charles V was in Brussels at the time, and nobles from the court came to visit Dee. One of these, Sir William Pickering – who would become English ambassador to France – spoke of the 22-year-old Dee as: "this tall, slighte youthe, lookynge wise beyond his years, with fair skin, good lookes and a brighte colour."

Of course, Louvain was not the Mecca of the intellectuals; Paris had occupied that position ever since Abelard had founded its University in the twelfth century. At the earliest opportunity – which happened to be July 1550 – Dee travelled to the French capital, where his reputation had preceded him, and lost no time in delivering public lectures on "mathematics, physics and the teachings of Pythagoras".

The inclusion of the name of Pythagoras makes it clear that Dee was not confining himself to ordinary mathematics. Pythagoras was the Greek mystic who believed that mathematics (and music) held the secrets of the universe. Agrippa had been convinced that Pythagoras was a great religious magus. There are, Agrippa says, three worlds: the physical world, the mathematical (or celestial) world, and the Pythagorean, or supercelestial world, which is the world of religion. So when Dee chose as his subject the second world, and expounded its mysteries through Euclid, his listeners must have found it brilliant, exciting and faintly scandalous. (Agrippa had spent his whole life fighting charges of heresy – even the University of Louvain had condemned him.) His lectures were packed, and students climbed the outside walls to listen through the windows. As usual, Dee received several offers of appointments, but turned them down, since he felt that his place was in England.

Yet England must have been something of a disappointment after Louvain and Paris. It was still the intellectual backwater it had always been, and the young man's European reputation failed to impress his own pragmatic countrymen, who had never heard of Cornelius Agrippa and had no desire to.

Since Dee had left, Henry VIII had died, and his nine-year-old son Edward had come to the throne. Henry VIII had turned England into a Protestant country – out of a desire to defy the

Pope (who refused to grant him a divorce from his first wife, Catherine of Aragon, in order that he could marry Anne Boleyn). Prince Edward, like his father, was a Protestant (although it should be noted that Henry never called himself a Protestant – he remained what might be called a Henry-ite Catholic). Unfortunately, Edward was too young to bear the burden of sovereignty, and the strain killed him within seven years.

Meanwhile, Dee found that his post at Trinity College had been filled. Fortunately, one of his old Cambridge colleagues, John Cheke (who would soon become Sir John), offered to help him. Cheke had been appointed tutor to the fourteen-year-old boy-king and his sister Elizabeth, and felt that it ought to be possible to find his friend some similar position. As it turned out, nothing could be found for Dee at the palace. Luckily, King Edward remembered him as the son of his father's body-servant and had him awarded a pension of a hundred pounds a year. Thus provided for, but at an intellectual loose end, Dee was desperate for something to engage his restlessly energetic mind. He set about writing a treatise on the relation of the esoteric art of alchemy to the re-emerging science of mathematics.

In 1552, Sir John Cheke had another houseguest: the esteemed Italian doctor, Geronimo Cardano. What came to be called the Renaissance – a French word, meaning "rebirth" – had been fermenting in Italy since the fourteenth century (when the rediscovery of the Ancient Greek texts made learning and research fashionable again after hundreds of years of near extinction). As a result, Italian physicians were considered the most advanced, and were the most sought after, in Europe. England, in 1552, on the other hand, was only just beginning to join the new educational enlightenment, so it was only natural that a man like Cardano would be sent for when King Edward began to show signs of the health problems that would eventually kill him.

Cardano, who in many ways was well ahead of his time in his medical methods, backed his medical skills with a profound knowledge of astrology and occult law. Having ministered to the king, he drew up a horoscope which, he said, predicted that Edward would live to the age of fifty-five. He was deeply embarrassed therefore when, in 1553, Edward VI died at the age of sixteen.

The Italian was jeered at court, but John Dee remained fascinated by Cardano, and quizzed him thoroughly before he returned to Italy. Already an expert in the theory of astrology,

and an admirer of Cornelius Agrippa (as Cardano was not), Dee
plunged even deeper into the study of occultism, and eventually
accumulated a personal library of more than four thousand
books, which was probably more than there were in the royal
library. He also began to practise astrology, and his horoscopes
proved so accurate that he soon found that he had achieved the
ambition earlier denied him: a place at court.

In 1543, Edward VI died of the strain, and his elder sister Mary
took the throne, snatching it from under the nose of Lady Jane
Grey, Henry VIII's niece. (Lady Jane was executed, a year later.)

"Bloody Mary", as she is known to history, was by no means as
black as she is painted. The daughter of Henry VIII's first wife,
Catherine of Aragon – and the only survivor of six children – she
had had a miserable life, snubbed and humiliated because she was
an ardent Catholic. She had been declared a bastard (because
Henry had got rid of her mother by declaring the marriage illegal)
and given a minor place in the household of her younger half-
sister Elizabeth. She had also seen her old tutor and her mother's
chaplain burnt at the stake. So, perhaps understandably, she felt
no love of Protestants.

Yet, when she first came to the throne in 1553, she behaved in a
highly reasonable manner, so that one historian calls her "the
most human, the most merciful, the most sincerely religious, the
least worldly and the most moral of all the Tudors". But it was
her lack of worldliness that was her downfall. She was quite
determined to undo her father's reformation, and turn England
again into a Catholic country, so she restored England's allegiance to the Pope, and married a Catholic, Philip II of Spain.

Ordinary Englishmen were outraged; they were rather proud of
Henry VIII for defying the Pope, and they had no love of a church
that never stopped picking their pockets. They were even more
outraged when Mary gave the church the power to burn heretics,
which Henry VIII had taken away. So although she was gentle and
good-tempered by disposition, Mary was largely responsible for
the burning of Protestants (300 or so) that followed. Thereafter,
things never went right for her, and she realized her life had been a
failure. If she had had any sense, she would have been fair-minded
and moderate; as it was, she made it quite certain that England
would never again be a Catholic country.

Nevertheless, during the first year of her reign, it looked as if
she would be as reasonable as her dead brother. She even asked

Dee to cast her horoscope, and that of Philip II of Spain. She certainly indicated that she was ready to encourage Dee's researches.[1]

The problem was that Dee had no desire to be court astrologer under Mary. He disliked what was happening, particularly the notion of England becoming virtually Spanish. At that time, Spain and France had no love for one another, and Dee was naturally on the side of France. His whole temperament was naturally Protestant, so he placed all his hopes on his ex-pupil, Elizabeth, succeeding Mary on the throne. As an expert astrologer, he looked closely at Mary's horoscope and concluded that her reign was going to be short.

When Elizabeth was exiled to Woodstock, Dee began secretly corresponding with her. He made it his business to encourage her and prevent her from becoming demoralized. His cousin Blanch Parry had been Elizabeth's nurse, and was now a maid of honour. Through her, Dee visited the princess in exile and cast her horoscope, which predicted that she would become queen. He even showed her the grim horoscope he had cast for Queen Mary. It was this indiscretion that almost cost Dee his life. A spy called George Ferrys reported that Dee was attempting to "enchant" the queen – which really meant kill her by sorcery. Dee was arrested and his papers searched; he was imprisoned at Hampton Court.

In August 1555, he was brought before the Star Chamber.[2] But even under Mary – possibly because her excesses were already causing such revulsion – there was justice in England, and since there was no confirmatory evidence of treasonable intent, the judges found for acquittal. Dee, nevertheless, decided a period out of the public eye would be the safest course. He certainly could not show his face at court again – at least, not until his prediction for Princess Elizabeth came to fruition.

Even so, Dee wrote to the queen, not long after his release, to propose the formation of a national library. The dissolution of the monasteries, he pointed out, had caused many priceless

1 This was rather a surprise from the devout Mary. It should be remembered that the Catholic Church frowned on astrology when it claimed to predict the future. Many churchmen considered it a borderline heresy because knowledge of the future could only come from God or, more likely, Satan.
2 A judicial court primarily concerned with matters of interest to the Crown.

collections of books to be dispersed and lost. He offered, if she would provide the money, to dedicate the rest of his life to locating copies of unique books in private collections, then making copies for the library. Thus London might one day be a place of pilgrimage for scholars, much as Alexandria had been before the Moslems burned the Great Library.

He probably did not expect her to agree; perhaps he only raised the matter to give her an opportunity of discharging some of her resentment by turning him down. So he can hardly have been very surprised when Mary refused to give any support for the project. The National Library was to remain an academic's fantasy until the reign of Queen Victoria.

Deprived of the lucrative horoscope market at court, Dee spent the next three years pursuing rare texts at his own expense. To everyone's relief, Mary I died in 1558 at the age of forty-two, detested and generally deserted, and Princess Elizabeth replaced her on the throne. The new monarch remembered that Dee had accurately predicted this surprising turn of events and sent for him at once. She asked Dee to predict a favourable day for her coronation and he, after casting the appropriate horoscope, suggested 14 January 1559. The weather in London at that time of year is usually abominable, but the day of the coronation proved to be as pleasant as springtime and Dee got the credit. Much pleased, Queen Elizabeth promised to find him a profitable sinecure, so long as he promised to continue to act as her personal fortune-teller. Thereafter, court nobles referred to Dee as "Hyr Astrologer".

There then followed one of the most mysterious periods of John Dee's life. With everything at home at last in his favour, he suddenly decided to return to Europe. He had recently finished a treatise on natural magic and alchemy called *Monas Hieroglyphica* – a work that had taken him seven years. Strange to say, instead of dedicating the work to his new royal patron, he travelled halfway across the continent to present the work to the new Holy Roman Emperor, Maximilian II.

This seemed not only a political gaffe, but a religious blunder as well. One of Elizabeth's first acts as queen had been to reinstate Protestantism as the State Religion of England. For her personal astrologer to go to such trouble to dedicate a book to one of the most important Catholic leaders in Europe was tantamount to a direct insult to the new monarch. Yet when Dee returned in 1564, having taken an extensive trip around the capitals of Europe, Queen

Elizabeth went out of her way to welcome him home. It leads one to suspect that there is more here than meets the eye.

Dee's *Monas Hieroglyphica* had received the usual ungracious reception among academics in England. It was a complex study of the relationships between alchemy, magical practice and mathematics, and many scholars accused Dee of being impossibly abstruse. If they were hoping to curry favour with the practical-minded queen, they were disappointed. Dee later noted that "Her Majestie graciously defended my credit in my absence beyond the seas." On his return to London, Elizabeth made a point of inviting him to discuss the work with her personally and afterwards "did comfort and encourage me in my studies philosophicall and mathematicall." For a monarch with a notoriously short temper when it came to public slights, Elizabeth seemed to be acting quite out of character.

Lord Burghley, the queen's Chief Minister, also joined the unexpected chorus of praise by remarking that the book was "of the utmost value for the securities of the Realme". Some historians have suggested that he had his tongue in his cheek, but Dee's biographer, Richard Deacon, suggests the phrase is the key to Dee's mysterious European tour.

Sir Francis Walsingham, a close associate of Burghley, was then engaged in creating one of the most efficient foreign and domestic espionage operations ever known. Deacon suggests that the complex system of magical symbols described in Dee's *Monas Hieroglyphica* were used by Walsingham's agents to encode messages – perhaps on Dee's own suggestion. It also seems quite possible that Dee was himself an agent for the English Secret Service. It would explain his travels around Europe and the trip he later made to the Duchy of Lorraine, on the queen's authority with apparently secret orders.

We may also note that Elizabeth began her letters to him: "My noble Intelligencer" or "My Ubiquitous Eyes". As a visual pun on this last epithet, Dee always signed his letters to the queen with two zeros (representing his eyes) and the number seven (in numerology, the number of mystery).[3]

3 In 1952, the author Ian Fleming was looking for a code-name for his new fictional secret agent, James Bond, and settled on Dee's "007" as a historian's in-joke. The ironic result has been that Dee's secret code-number is now more famous than he ever was.

In December 1564, Elizabeth kept her promise to find Dee a lucrative position; he was offered the deanery of Gloucester. This would have provided for his material needs, while not occupying too much of his time. Unfortunately, by this time, Dee's interest in the occult (and his Cambridge reputation as a sorcerer) had earned him enemies in the Church. Although this was not as dangerous as it would have been in a Catholic country, it still meant that important ecclesiastic posts could be barred to him. Much to Elizabeth's annoyance, the deanship was given to another candidate without her consent.

Two years later, the queen managed to find her astrologer a couple of minor lay-rectorships, but these did little to provide him with a living income. Dee had already exchanged his small pension from Edward VI for a similarly unlucrative posting, and for the rest of his life was desperately short of cash.

Dee was understandably angry about the absurd accusations that blocked his advancement outside court circles. In his preface to Sir Henry Billingsley's translation of Euclid's *Elements*, he bitterly complained of the difficulties faced by researchers like himself:

"Is any honest student, or a modest Christian philosopher, to be, for such [inventive] feats, mathematically and mechanically wrought, counted and called a conjuror? . . . Shall that man be condemned as a companion of Hellhounds and a caller and conjuror of wicked damned spirits?

"Should I have fished so large and costly a nett, and been so long drawing, even with the helpe of Lady Philosophie, and Queen Theologie, and at length have catched but a frog, nay a Devill? . . . How great is the blindness and boldness of the multitude in things above their capacitie!"

Dee undoubtedly considered himself a devout Christian as well as an "honest student", and his studies, although limited by his penury, were certainly aimed at aiding his fellow man.

For example, as the queen's astrologer, he was called upon to cast horoscopes for the expeditions of naval explorers like Drake, Frobisher and Hawkins. As a result of his friendship with such men he published, in 1576, *General and Rare Memorials Pertayning to the Perfect Arte of Navigation*. The paper pointed out that many ships were yearly being lost on coasts and shoals, simply for the want of good maps. Dee suggested the creation of a "Petty Navy Royal" to chart the coasts and protect merchant shipping – in fact, what we now call the coastguard.

In passing, it should also be noted that in Dee's *Memorials*, he describes navigational benefits going to supporting "the British Empire". This is the first time the phrase has been found in print. It may indicate Dee's undoubted breadth of vision – the growth of the "Empire" was not to be generally recognized for at least another hundred years – or that, maybe, he had foreseen such glory in the nation's horoscope.

While continuing his many scientific and occult studies, Dee was also called upon regularly to act as the Royal astrologer and magical trouble-shooter. In 1577, a comet appeared in the northern sky and caused much consternation, since comets were the traditional signal of the death of kings (and possibly queens). Dee was called to Windsor post haste, and ordered to divine the portent's meaning. After three days' frenzied astrological calculation, Dee announced that the comet was not a sign sent to England, but portended doom for mainland Europe some time in the future.[4]

Shortly thereafter, a wax effigy – apparently representing Queen Elizabeth – was found at Lincoln's Inn Fields (now a borough of London, but then a village some distance from the capital). A pin had been thrust through the heart of the doll, and the queen feared an attempt at magical assassination. Dee was again sent for and ordered to investigate.

Nobody had dared move the effigy, so Dee was forced to go and inspect it *in situ*. Dee's area of expertise was not low witchcraft, but complex magical law – Elizabeth might just as well have sent the Royal Cook to investigate. Nevertheless, Dee was politically minded enough to see that the naturally paranoid monarch needed to be soothed quickly, before she instigated a witch-hunt. It was with apparent relief, therefore, that he was able to report that the wax doll was a very poor likeness of the

---

4 It is interesting to note that Johannes Kepler, the father of modern astronomy, also dabbled in astrology. Some decades after the 1577 comet's appearance, Kepler announced that it had actually foretold the rise of a northern prince who would ravage Germany, then die in 1632. Gustavus Adolphus, champion of the Protestants in the Thirty Years' War, died in 1632, killed in battle two years after Kepler's own death.

queen – if it was at all – and consequently it could not do her any harm. He was effusively thanked but, as usual, received no payment for his trouble.

In 1578, at the age of 51, Dee married Jane Fromond – a lady in waiting to Queen Elizabeth, very attractive and half the scholar's age. Dee seems to have fallen in love with her at court, and persuaded the queen to give her consent. Due to an on-going shortage of money, they were forced to settle in Dee's mother's house in Mortlake-on-Thames. They would produce eight children.

Unfortunately, Dee's reputation as a sorcerer made their neighbours wary of the household, but this did not stop them consulting him when they needed predictions made. For example, when a local servant lost a bundle of silverware, Dee was able, through an astrological reading, to tell him that the parcel had been taken by accident. If he returned to the ferry crossing (where the parcel was originally lost) on a certain day at a certain time, the silver plates would be honestly returned – as indeed they were.

On another occasion his neighbour, Goodwife Faldo, lost a basket of washing. In a dream, Dee saw the place where she had thoughtlessly dropped the clothes and directed her straight to them.

This second anecdote seems to indicate that Dee had some psychic powers beyond the art of astrology. It is certainly true that he tried to develop such abilities all his life but, by his own confession, he was never very successful. Indeed, John Dee would only warrant a passing note in this volume if it had not been for a particular line of research which he did not begin until he was almost sixty (an old man by contemporary standards).

In 1581, Dee obtained a "Chrystallo": a "great crystalline globe" – or what we would nowadays call a "crystal ball". Crystal-gazing, or *scrying*, involves staring into a translucent or reflective surface and seeing past, present and future events. Objects used in this way are not believed to form images of their own accord (like a television set) but instead induce visions in the mind of the viewer. As such, the scrying stone or mirror was only a prop for those who already possessed a psychic gift.

Although not particularly gifted himself, Dee stared intently into the globe, and became aware that a picture was forming. This was enough to whet his appetite, but he quickly realized that he would need a research assistant with better psychic talents, if his researches were to advance. He hoped that such a person would act as his "medium"[5] – by which he doubtless meant a tool, just as a microscope is a "medium" to a biologist. The reality, as we shall see, turned out quite differently.

In 1581, Dee met a young preacher called Barnabas Saul, who claimed to be a scryer. Saul came to stay at the Mortlake house and, on 22 December, they had their first session with the *Chrystallo*. Gazing deep into the crystal, Saul saw the Angel Anael – the being empowered, according to the Talmud, to reveal God's secrets. Dee, in his diary, said that he could also see the being, but that only Saul could hear its voice.

Anael told Dee, through Saul, that he would learn many truths through the magic stone, but Saul would not continue to be his interpreter. Only through "him that is assigned to the stone", the Angel said, could further secret matters be revealed. Whether this message was a true prophecy or Saul invented it to escape the unearthly situation, it proved correct.

Two months later, according to court records, Barnabas Saul was brought to trial in Westminster Hall. No record survives of the charge, but "witchcraft" seems a likely possibility. He seems to have succeeded in getting himself acquitted through a legal technicality, but it was clearly a close shave that he did not wish to repeat. When afterwards Dee asked him to continue their studies, Saul claimed to have lost the power of psychic sight.

"He confessed he never herd or saw any spiritual creature any more," Dee wrote disconsolately in his diary. Luckily, a few weeks after, in March 1582, another "medium" arrived at his front door – the old scholar's life would never be the same again.

The man introduced himself as Edward Talbot, although he soon admitted his real surname was Kelly. An erudite twenty-seven-year-old apothecary's apprentice from Worcester, Kelly claimed that a "spirituall creature" had recently appeared to him and told him of Dee's need of an assistant with second sight. Against the advice of Jane Dee, the astrologer gave his visitor the benefit of the doubt and took him in.

John Dee seems to have been a trusting soul, writing that in the first days of their acquaintance that "Talbot" had not "shewed

5 Dee may well have coined this word to describe a living, human link to the "higher realms".

himself dishonest in any thinge". This, as it turned out, was
something of a misjudgement: Kelly was, at the very least, one of
the most colourful scoundrels of the sixteenth century. Rumoured to have dabbled in black magic and necromancy,[6] he
had already been found guilty of forgery at Lancaster and had his
ears cut off. If John Dee wondered why his new assistant never
took off his skullcap (with the ear-encompassing sideflaps), he
was obviously too polite to ask.

Nevertheless, to write off Kelly as a confidence trickster, and
Dee as his foolish dupe, would be to underestimate both of them.
Dee later acknowledged that he learned his alchemy from Kelly.
He was certainly shrewd enough to recognize the younger man's
emotional and unreliable nature – complaining in his diary of
Kelly's "abominable lyes" and fits of childish melancholy – but,
as a medium through whom he could communicate with the
spirit world, Dee considered Kelly indispensable. He came to
this conclusion, he stated, through seeing the evidence with his
own eyes.

On 10 March 1582, Dee put Kelly to the test and recorded the
events as follows:

> "[Kelly] settled himself to the Action, and on his knees at
> my desk, setting the stone before him, fell to prayer and
> entreaty. In the mean space, I in my Oratory did pray and
> make motion to God and his good creatures for the further-
> ing of this Action. And within a quarter of an hour (or less)
> he had sight of one in the stone."

This spirit told Kelly that it was Uriel, Angel of Light. Kelly's
description of the angelic being was close enough to what Dee

---

6 A term that today has become the sole property of sword-and-sorcery
writers, but in the sixteenth century was seen as a real – if universally
vilified – profession. Necromancers were magicians with the power to talk
to the dead – seeking knowledge of hidden treasures or of future events.
There is an eighteenth-century print in the British Library showing Dee
and Kelly standing in a protective magic circle in a graveyard, speaking to
a disinterred corpse dressed in a shroud. The inscription explains that they
are "questioning the dead or an evil spirit speaking through his organs
respecting the future of a young gentleman, then a minor." In fact, there is
no evidence whatever that the religiously devout Dee ever joined Kelly in
conjuring the dead.

had himself seen in the *Chrystallo* to convince him that the younger man was telling the truth. The ex-forger was taken on as Dee's magical research-assistant at £20 a year.

Over the next year, the pair conducted many successful scrying sessions. An academic to the bone, Dee took careful notes of what happened each time, and later presented them in a work called *The Book of Mysteries*. This reads rather like a book of sermons, but this in itself is indicative. Thanks to his scholarly training, Dee recorded every word and detail with scientific exactitude but, at the same time, he believed that he was engaged on a project of the most profound religious significance: direct intercourse with God's angels.

As with Barnabas Saul, Dee often saw Kelly's angels himself and even managed to converse personally with them. These creatures not only appeared within the *Chrystallo*, but were also seen to walk about Dee's study, apparently made of solid flesh and blood. Nevertheless, Dee was certain that they were non-corporeal. At one point in his careful account of these experiments, Dee told an angel:

> "I do not think you have no organs or Instruments apt for voyce, but are meere spiritual and nothing corporeall, but have the power and property from God to initiate your message or meaning to ear or eye so that man's imagination shall be that they hear and see you sensibly."

Their reality was apparently affirmed by a childlike angel that appeared as the rays of the setting sun struck the *Chrystallo* on 21 November 1582. It presented Dee with a new crystal "as big as an egg: most bryght, clere, and glorious". This Dee referred to as his "*Angelicall Stone*", and now used instead of the *Chrystallo* for his scrying experiments. Unsurprisingly, he prized it greatly and carried it wherever he went for the rest of his life. (Charles Nicholl states in *The Chemical Theatre* (1980) that this "small globe of smoky polished quartz, the colour of moleskin . . . is now at the British Museum, along with his 'magic mirror', a disc of polished obsidian, apparently of Aztec origin.")

What exactly was happening? Two explanations suggest themselves. First is that Dee was engaging in pure self-deception, but that sounds doubtful, since another person was present. The second will strike anyone who is familiar with the history of nineteenth-century spiritualism, which begins around 1850 (after the strange manifestations at the home of the Fox sisters in New York State). Although there can be no doubt that a great deal of fakery went on, it also became clear from the careful investigations of the Society for Psychical Research (founded 1881) that many of the manifestations must have been genuine. In which case, there can be little doubt that Dee's "scryers" were what nineteenth-century researchers called "mediums" – people who could act as intermediaries between our world and the "spirit world".

Certainly, mediums were known long before the nineteenth century. All "primitive" peoples have their shamans who establish contact with the dead, and even the early Christian church took this for granted. Early church services involved mediums, and in a book called *The Teachings of the Twelve Apostles* (*circa* 140 AD) there is advice to mediums and others with psychic gifts who took part in church services. Another book from the same period, *The Shepherd of Hermas*, was regarded by the theologian Origen as divinely inspired, and by Bishop Irenaus as being equal to the scriptures; it explains at some length how to distinguish the true medium from the false. The Roman theologian Tertullian (150-230 AD) describes in *De Anima* ("Of the Soul") church services that sound like modern spiritualist meetings – with divine spirits controlling the mediums.

It may be added that anyone who has studied the history of witchcraft soon comes to suspect that it was not entirely a matter of the delusions of a few half-crazy old women and their equally unbalanced accusers. The Rev. Montague Summers is not being as reactionary as he sounds when he declares in his *History of Witchcraft* that nineteenth-century spiritualism was really a revival of medieval witchcraft. The accounts of communication with demons or spirits given in evidence at witch trials echo accounts of hundreds of seances in the files of the Society for Psychical Research – and of Dee's account of Kelly's angels:

"They that now come in are jolly fellows, all trymmed after the manner of Nobilitie now-a-dayes with gylt tapiers and curled haire, and the bragged up and downe. Bobagel [a frequent angelic visitor] standeth in a black velvet coat, and his hose, close round hose of upper-socks, over layd with gold lace. He hath a velvet hat cap with a black feather in it,

with a cape on one of his shoulders; his purse hanging at his
neck, and so put under his girdell . . . Seven others are
apparelled like Bobogel, sagely and gravely."

On another occasion, another "child angel" appeared: ". . . a
Spirituall creature, like a pretty girl of seven or nine years of
age . . . with her hair rolled before, and hanging down very long
behind, attired in a gown of Sey, changeable green and red, with
a Train . . . She seemed to play up and down . . . to go in and out
behind my books, lying in heaps . . ."

When questioned, the child said her name was Madimi, and
chirruped: "I am the last but one of my mother's children, I have
little Baby-children of my own at home . . ."

Madimi, like Uriel and Bobogel, became a regular visitor and,
over the years, Dee noted that she visibly grew into a young
woman. If this was all delusion, it was singularly persistent.

The angels taught Dee and Kelly many other "secrets",
including a strange language, *Enochian*, which they said had
been spoken by the Old Testament prophet, Enoch. The angels
taught Dee and Kelly various incantations in this language to
facilitate better contact while scrying. For example, the phrase
"Madariatza das perifa Lil cabisa micaolazoda saanire caosago of
fifa balzodizodarasa iada" meant "Oh, you heavenly denizens of
the first air, you are mighty in the parts of the earth, and execute
judgement of the highest." (If this language is indeed from the
ancient Middle East, examples of it have yet to be uncovered by
archaeologists.)

That Dee was not hallucinating these encounters – perhaps
hypnotized by Kelly – is suggested by the fact that the spirits
proved remarkably accurate in predicting future events. At one
point in Dee's original manuscript of the *Book of Mysteries*, the
author drew an axe in the margin. This was probably meant to serve
as a bookmark, since the entry on that page describes Kelly's vision
of a woman kneeling at an execution block. Uriel, their most regular
angelic visitor, explained that the woman was Mary Queen of Scots,
and that she was fated to be executed by Queen Elizabeth.

Mary was indeed in Elizabeth's keeping at that time, having so
infuriated her own people that, in 1568, she had been forced to
seek asylum in England. By 1583, although Mary had been kept a
prisoner for fifteen years, the idea that Elizabeth would actually
have her own cousin killed must have sounded unlikely. Regi-

cide, even by another monarch, was considered a crime against
God. Nevertheless, four years later, on 1 February 1587, Mary
was executed for plotting with Catholic rebels to assassinate
Elizabeth and seize the English throne.

On another occasion, the crystal showed an image of a "sea full
of ships". Uriel explained that an "enemy nation" would soon
begin to build a huge fleet to attack "the welfare of England".
Dee guessed that the enemy was Spain and hurried to inform the
queen. Some authors have suggested that John Dee's espionage
contacts were more likely to have been the source of this information than the Angel of Light – however, a little historical
research undermines this theory. It is a matter of record that Dee
informed Queen Elizabeth of the Armada prediction in 1583; but
it was not until 1585 that Philip II of Spain decided to muster an
invasion fleet.

Kelly and Dee's experiments with scrying aroused feverish
interest among gossips at court, and this led to a meeting between
Dee and the visiting Prince Albert Laski of Bohemia. This was
rather less impressive than it sounded, since Laski, although in
line for the throne of Poland, was virtually penniless and had
come to England to seek his fortune. Naturally, the parsimonious
Queen Elizabeth did little to help, but she did introduce Laski to
Dee and even offered to pay for a small banquet at the house in
Mortlake, to cement their friendship.

Prince Laski got on well with Dee and Kelly and was invited to
attend a scrying session. He believed that he too saw the angels in
Dee's study, and became a regular spectator thereafter. The little
girl, Madimi, seems to have developed a schoolgirl crush on the
prince. She told him that he would one day be the King of Poland
and that his family would eventually stop the Turkish encroach-
ment into Europe. Understandably, Laski was inclined to believe
in the angels.

As we shall see, they proved inaccurate on both these matters.
On others, their record was better. One day, while an angel called
Jubanladee was advising the prince to "look to the steps of his
youth, measure the length of his body, live better and see himself
inwardly", an attendant called Tanfield barged into the room
without knocking. Jubanladee turned coldly to the astonished
man and told him that within five months he would be "devoured
by fishes". This presumably happened as, less than half a year
later, Tanfield was lost at sea.

Laski's real goal was the *Philosopher's Stone*: a magical substance that alchemists declared to be the key to turning base
metals into gold, to living forever and transmuting the sinful soul
into a being cleansed of evil. Dee, who had made a lifelong study
of alchemy, regretfully told the prince that the angels had not yet
given him the secret. At this point, Kelly let it fall that he might
be able to help.

During a journey in Wales, Kelly said, an innkeeper had given
him an ancient parchment and two small ivory bottles of powder.
The publican told him that a grave robber had taken them from
the tomb of St Dunstan during the looting of Glastonbury
Abbey. The thief had paid for his lodgings with the objects
but, on thinking it over, the innkeeper decided he wanted nothing
to do with such a sacrilege.

Kelly claimed that the parchment was a treatise on alchemy
and contained a strange formula which, unfortunately, he had yet
to decode.

This was enough for Prince Laski. He insisted that Dee and
Kelly return with him to Poland and help fulfil Madimi's
prophecy. Uriel, Angel of Light, was consulted and gave his
approval. So Dee uprooted his family (along with Kelly and
Kelly's newly acquired wife) and set off to adventure in Europe
with what he believed to be God's blessing. He did not return
home for six years.

Now it should be stated at this point that the kind of alchemy
practised by Dee and Kelly was not the kind practised by
medieval alchemists like Arnold de Villanova and Nicholas
Flamel – for whom alchemy was a practical quest, like any other
form of research. Paracelsus and Cornelius Agrippa believed in a
new kind of magic, which emphasized the importance of the
mind and spirit – they could be considered the original exponents
of "mind over matter". It followed that the spirit would play an
equally important role in alchemy.

The new tradition is neatly summed up by Charles Nicholl in
The Chemical Theatre:

"There is the ancient esoteric tradition of alchemy, typified
by the medieval adept with his darkly elaborate chemical
procedures for probing, changing and perfecting matter.
And there were two currents of sixteenth-century alchemy,
promoting a dual image of the alchemist – the Hermetic

mystic-magician, intent on revealing the transforming Mercury, philosophical gold or perfect Stone within man's nature; and the Paracelsian chemist-physician, labouring to extract the healing virtues and arcana hidden in 'the bosom of Nature'."

Nicholl goes on to talk about what he calls "the occult efficacy of spirit".

That was the real difference between Dee and the older tradition. Dee believed that the alchemical transformation of lead into gold was a kind of magic, not just a chemical reaction, and that a hidden mystic will – exerted by the magician – was the transforming agent.

This is the secret that Prince Laski hoped would bring them all riches, and make him king of Poland.

They left in September 1583. European travel was then painfully slow (and slowly painful), so it was not until 3 February the next year that the party arrived at Prince Laski's castle outside Cracow. By this time, Laski's debts had made discovering the Philosopher's Stone an urgent necessity; he had an enormous loan to pay back by the end of April.

Dee and Kelly hurriedly set up an alchemical laboratory and hurled themselves into experiments; but it was on the angels that everyone placed their hopes. Laski's servants had hauled along all Dee's scrying apparatus – including a six-foot high "table", which the Archangel Michael had demanded for the "Angelicall Stone" to rest upon during scrying sessions. On every propitious night Dee, Kelly and the prince gazed into the crystal but, although the angels continued to appear, they were unable to offer any hint about turning lead into gold. Dee's biographer Richard Deacon believes that in his anxiety to uncover treasure, Kelly began to deviate from the path of white magic, and to invoke spirits usually associated with the path of darkness.

Even so, Madimi was able to tell Dee on one occasion: "I would not come into your study. The queen has caused it to be sealed," – a comment that proved to be quite accurate, although Dee was not able to confirm it until his return to England. He learned then that, soon after his departure for Europe, those jealous of his favour with the queen began to spread rumours about him. The old charge of sorcery was resurrected, but this in itself did him little damage, since he still had powerful friends and was self-evidently a devout Christian. It was his friendship with Kelly that turned out to be Dee's Achilles' heel. Legal charges from Wales were discovered, accusing Kelly of digging up newly buried corpses to question them magically about future events. Dee was regarded as guilty by association, and outraged neighbours at Mortlake ransacked his home. Furniture was damaged, as was a marvellous mechanical bird (given to him by a Dutch master-engineer), and part of his priceless library was burned. The queen, who refused to countenance the rumours, had her royal seal placed on the door to Dee's study, thus making it a matter of treason if anyone broke in again.

The April deadline for Prince Laski's debts came and went without any sign of an alchemical breakthrough, so he was forced to mortgage a large portion of his family's land. He does not seem to have held this against Dee and Kelly – he had, after all, given them only nine months to uncover a secret that had eluded the greatest alchemists for centuries. In August 1584, Laski took the pair to Prague to meet Emperor Rudolf. Dee – used to having a sympathetic ear from royalty – told the monarch of his long search for knowledge through study, and how the truth had been revealed to him through angels in his crystal. Rudolf had a reputation for being curious about such matters, and even attended a scrying session, but the angels proved uncooperative, and he lost interest.

In April 1585, Laski managed to arrange an audience for Dee with King Stephen of Poland. Running short of cash to support the luxury of in-house alchemists, Laski had decided to offer their services to Stephen in exchange for their upkeep. Once again Dee spoke at length about crystals, angels and the Philosopher's Stone, and once again the spirits declined to back up his claims, so Stephen's initial interest evaporated. Madimi's prediction, that Laski would become the King of Poland and defeat the Turkish hordes was also to prove sadly inaccurate.

The Dees and the Kellys stayed with Prince Laski at his townhouse in Prague until the spring of 1586. John Dee's fame – trumpeted by Prince Laski for all it was worth – then drew the unfavourable attention of the new pope, Sextus V. He proclaimed a specific bull[7] against Dee and Kelly, ordering them

---

7 A papal edict. The word "bull" comes from the Latin *bulla*, meaning "rounded" – a reference to the round, lead seals affixed to papal orders.

out of Prague in no more than six days. Prince Laski could no longer afford to keep the alchemists at his mortgaged castle, so they and their wives were forced to flee with nowhere to go.

Although this turn of events was upsetting, it did no harm to Dee's reputation – for, as we would put it nowadays, it was "good publicity". Almost immediately a new patron, Count Rosenberg of Tribau, offered to harbour them, provided they continue to search for the Philosopher's Stone. Moving to Rosenberg's castle at Tribau, Dee was offered a "goodly chapel" adjoining his living quarters to conduct scrying activities at night and to make alchemical experiments during the day. Kelly continued working with Dee as a scryer, but preferred to work alone on the St Dunstan's parchment, obviously hoping to be the first to discover the Great Secret. In their approaches to alchemy, the two men could hardly have been more different; Kelly was a sorcerer by nature and Dee was a scientist. While Kelly intoned incantations in one room, Dee experimented with chemical combinations in another. Their relationship by this time was less that of employer and servant than of senior and junior researcher.

The ripples from the papal edict carried as far as Russia – where it was rumoured that Dee had already discovered the secret of alchemy. The young Tsar, Fyodor I, sent an offer of £2,000 a year if the astrologer would agree to come to Moscow. As an added incentive – in case a man who could *make* gold would laugh at £2,000 a year – Fyodor added that the Dees would be escorted there by five hundred Cossacks, would live in the royal palace and eat the best food from his own kitchen. Dee turned the offer down, partly as a matter of basic honesty, but also because the son of Ivan the Terrible was probably someone it was better to disappoint from a safe distance.

Soon after Dee rejected the Tsar's offer, Kelly discovered the method of turning base metal into gold. Dee wrote that his assistant had "made projection with his powder [which had come in the little bottles with the innkeeper's parchment] in the proportion of one minim (upon an ounce and a quarter of mercury) and produced nearly an ounce of best gold."

Naturally – Kelly told everyone – the actual process was much more complicated than this and, furthermore, was to remain his secret. Dee was delighted for his friend's sake, declaring that he himself was quite satisfied to have played a lesser role in such a great discovery. Kelly was a less generous soul, and treated his former employer with an arrogant superiority only just short of contempt. Dee seems to have accepted all this with his usual quiet good nature.

Understandably, most biographers doubt that Kelly actually turned mercury into gold, even though it is theoretically possible (provided one has a fifty-mile-long particle accelerator). What seems more likely is that, following the Tsar's impressive offer, Kelly must have realized that, whether or not they found the Philosopher's Stone, they stood to make a fortune. If it had been left to him, they would have hastened to Moscow and risked the consequences. Under the circumstances, it seems probable that he worked out a way to fake the transmutation of mercury into gold, and tried out the deception on Dee and the Count.

Kelly's criminal leanings appear to have been a result of his flawed personality, rather than the need to survive in a hard world. Even as a young man, he could have made a perfectly good living as an apothecary, but apparently preferred to sell forged land deeds. Like many criminals, Kelly seems to have been unable to resist the temptation of short-term profit.

But now he seems to have embarked on his most audacious plan so far – the seduction of Jane Dee. At least, this seems to most reasonable interpretation of what happened next . . .

Dee was, as we have seen, about fifty-one when he fell in love with Jane Fromond, and she seems to have been about half that age. So, by 1587, he was sixty and his wife was in her mid-thirties. Kelly had married a nineteen-year-old girl named Joan Cooper, from Chipping Norton, in 1582, apparently on the advice of the angels. But Kelly is on record as having made a few slighting references to his wife's physical attractions, and compared her unfavourably to Jane Dee.

Now Kelly told Dee he wished to give up scrying, and advised Dee to use his son Arthur, then about eight. Unfortunately, Arthur was unable to see anything in the "shew stone" and, after a while, Kelly volunteered to try again. But he seemed unwilling to tell Dee what he had seen and heard. Dee insisted, and finally Kelly agreed to tell him.

He had seen Madimi doing a strip-tease until she was completely naked. Then she had told him that, just as she had revealed herself to him, so Dee and Kelly should put aside all barriers between them. In short, they were to share their wives in common.

Dee was shocked. Did Madimi mean on a physical, as well as a spiritual, level? Yes, indeed that was what she meant, said Kelly, and professed himself as shocked by the idea as Dee. But apparently this "cross-matching" would also cure Joan Kelly of her barrenness, as well as bring the alchemists within sight of their goal.

Dee and Kelly sat up most of the night arguing about it. Reluctantly, Dee began to come around to the idea of cross-matching. When he finally went to bed, he found Jane still awake, and told her what had happened. She was even more outraged than he had been, until he told her: "Jane, I can see there is no other remedy, but as hath been said, of our cross-matching."

After bursting into tears, Jane said that she wanted further consultation with the spirits. It seems they simply confirmed what they had already said. So on 3 May 1587, the four of them signed a document agreeing that "all things between us" should be common.

History draws a veil over what happened subsequently; Dee either decided not to write the sequel, or destroyed the account. We only know that he once again protested his unwillingness to go through with it. Dee's final comment is cryptic. On 19 July he wrote: "A certaine kinde of recommendation between our wives. Next day saw relenting of E. K., also by my Lord's entreaty." So we shall never know whether Kelly achieved his goal of seducing Jane Dee.

There is, one should add, another possible interpretation of this whole strange business. Dee makes it clear on other occasions that he often saw the spirits. If we are correct to conclude that Dee's intercourse with spirits was indeed genuine, then it is possible that the spirits were to blame. As all mediums know, spirits can be untruthful and deceptive. If Madimi and the other "angels" were, in fact, bored denizens of the "spirit world", glad to amuse themselves at the expense of human beings, perhaps they decided that the relationship would be enlivened by a little wife-swapping.

The only thing we can say with certainty is that, if Dee and Kelly exchanged wives, it would have been only for a brief period. Jane Dee was virtuous by nature, and Joan Kelly has been described as "a rare example of youthful holiness, chastity and all the virtues". Whether or not they were obeying the command of angels, it is unlikely that either woman would have wanted to commit adultery more than once.

As far as the trust between Dee and Kelly was concerned, this curious episode was the last straw. Kelly had always had an ungovernable temper, and their relationship had been strained by many harsh words. Now they probably felt that they had both said things that could not be taken back. We learn that Kelly, vindictive by nature, used his new-found influence to poison Count Rosenberg's mind against Dee. Now the Kellys were moved to a more luxurious suite of rooms, and the Dees ceased to be visited by Rosenberg at all.

As if this were not galling enough for the old man, Kelly now took to sending for him as if he were a servant. Keen as he doubtless was to be rid of his former master, Kelly was clever enough to realize that John Dee's encyclopaedic knowledge was indispensable. And since both had signed an agreement to "share everything", dictated (so Kelly said) word for word by the Archangel Raphael, Dee was obliged to provide his former employee with whatever information he might demand.

So, for over a year and a half (May 1587 to January 1589), Kelly used the "angelic agreement" to milk Dee for "magical" information, while maintaining a cold and superior manner towards him. At the same time, Dee's real work was marking time, for the Count never consulted him, Kelly would not act as his medium for scrying and, now that the secret of the Philosopher's Stone had been found by another, there seemed little point in alchemical experimentation.

This intolerable situation came to an end in mid-1588, with a letter from Queen Elizabeth, telling him that the Spanish invasion, that Dee had predicted in 1583 was imminent. Some of her naval advisers insisted that the only way to defeat the Armada was to destroy its ships before they left port. Sir Francis Drake had already shown how devastating "fireships"[8] could be, during an attack on Cadiz the year before, but Elizabeth wavered without the advice of "Hyr Astrologer".

Dee fell back on astrology, for which he did not need Kelly, and told her that the stars pointed to success off the English coast, not in the Spanish harbours. Dee had always held that the smaller and more manoeuvrable English fleet would have the advantage over Philip of Spain's massive galleons in a hand-to-

8 Unmanned vessels that were filled with gunpowder, set alight and floated into a busy harbour to act as incendiary bombs.

hand encounter. He also had the insight to realize that one of the chief dangers to the British fleet lay in the weather, and accordingly advised the queen to keep the British fleet in port until the last minute. Following his advice, Elizabeth held her navy back until the Armada had passed Plymouth. What defeated the Armada in July 1588 was not simply the skill and determination of the queen's commanders, but the unpredictable weather. More Spanish galleons were wrecked by storms than suffered from English gunfire.

Although Elizabeth was brutally ungrateful to her sailors, keeping them penned aboard their ships to avoid paying them until dozens had died of scurvy, she was fulsome in her expressions of gratitude to Dee, who might be regarded as the man most responsible for saving England from a Spanish invasion. In fact we now know that Dee's advice was doubly correct because, following Drake's assault on Cadiz, the Spanish had thoroughly prepared their ports for similar attacks.

Now in his sixties, John Dee was sick of adventures in Europe, and this was obviously a good time to return home. This, however, might take some time, as he was virtually penniless and could count on little or no help from Count Rosenberg or Edward Kelly. Fortunately, showing uncharacteristic generosity, Elizabeth arranged for a coach and a guard of honour to bring the Dees all the way back to Mortlake.

On 4 January 1589, Dee gave Kelly all his alchemical equipment and what books he could spare, then headed for home. The pair were never to meet again.

Unjust as it may seem, Edward Kelly would go on to become the most celebrated alchemist in Europe. Ben Jonson's alchemist (in the play of that name) is described as "a man the Emperour has courted above Kelley", while the novelist Thomas Nashe said that Kelly was better than Paracelsus or Raymond Lull, another famous contemporary alchemist. John Donne said that the city of Plymouth was so poor that even "77 Kelleys could [not] distill £10 out of all the towne". Kelly continued to produce quantities of gold, which he claimed he had transmuted from mercury, and became so famous that Emperor Rudolf – who had previously been unimpressed by Kelly's scrying – invited him to Prague.

There, under the scrutiny of the various scholars attached to the Emperor's Court, he continued to "make" large amounts of gold. At the house of Thadeus de Huzek, the Imperial Physician, Kelly was seen to change a pound of mercury into purest gold by simply adding a drop of a red oil of his own secret concoction. If we believe that he was faking these transformations, we must take it for granted that he was a brilliant conjuror[9] who must have secretly spent a fortune just to obtain the necessary gold, which leaves us with the puzzling question of how Kelly acquired the money.

At the height of his fame, Kelly did not forget his homeland. He sent Queen Elizabeth a warming-pan with an ingot of gold which fitted perfectly into the rectangular hole in the pan, into which the hot coals would normally be placed. He said that he had poured cool mercury into the hole, then transformed it, so that Her Majesty could see how easily transmutation could be achieved. Lord Burghley was so impressed that he immediately set his agents in Prague to try to woo Kelly back to England.

It may have been these overtures that cost Kelly his liberty and life. We do not know why Kelly – who had by now been knighted by the Emperor – fell from grace only two years after Dee returned to England. Emperor Rudolf, who was only eccentric when he met first Dee and Kelly in 1584, was now quite mad. In 1591 he quarrelled with Kelly and had him imprisoned at the castle of Pürglitz – possibly to stop him running away to England. He was tortured, released, imprisoned again, and is believed to have died as a result of a fall from a window while trying to escape in 1595 – although one commentator cites evidence that he was still alive two years later at the castle of Most.

When they first met in 1582, Kelly had told Dee that, during a scrying session two years earlier, a "spirit" had warned him that he would die a violent death.[10]

9 The infamous twentieth-century magician, Aleister Crowley, often claimed to be the reincarnation of Edward Kelly. However, it should be noted that Crowley seems to have respected Kelly for his skill as a con man as much as for his professed magical powers.

10 An interesting alternative view of Kelly can be found in Charles Nicholl's book *The Chemical Theatre* (1980). Nicholl is obviously inclined to take the evidence of contemporary observers seriously. Sir Edward Dyer had no doubt that Kelly was able to transmute base metals into gold. A. E. Waite, in his introduction to *The Alchemical Writings of Edward Kelly* (1893) also seems to take Kelly's claims seriously.

Dee outlived Kelly by thirteen years, but his last years were rarely happy. He returned to the house at Mortlake to find, as angel Madimi had predicted, that his priceless library had been ransacked. He was also virtually bankrupt. His lay-rectorships had paid him nothing while he was abroad, and his few savings were all but gone. In his sixty-fifth year, he was too worn out to begin again from scratch.

In 1595, after four years of near-penury, the queen eventually fulfilled her promise to find him an appointment, and allowed Archbishop Whitgift to offer him the post of Warden of Christ's College, Manchester, then a small but flourishing cotton town. But the institution was run by puritans, and his duties were so heavy that he had little time to study. The place became uncomfortable when rumours of his "sorcery" reached Manchester, and within months Dee was begging the queen to allow him to return to London. She promised to find him a better appointment, but did nothing. Dee succeeded in spending 1598 in London, but then had to return. He was often forced to sell books, and borrowed money by pledging cups and bowls.

The death of the queen in 1603 was the greatest blow so far. Dee knew this was the end of his hopes. The new king, James I, was strongly opposed to witchcraft, and had no use for a "sorcerer"; he began his reign by asking Parliament to enact a statute against the "evils of enchanters".

James should not be dismissed as a bigot; the case of the North Berwick witches, which had taken place in Scotland in 1590, left little doubt that a group of "witches" had really plotted the king's death. James himself had been as sceptical as anyone when a maidservant named Gilly Duncan confessed under torture, and implicated about seventy other people, including an elderly gentlewoman named Agnes Sampson. Agnes Sampson confessed under torture, as did a schoolmaster called John Fian, who had been secretary to the king's cousin, the Earl of Bothwell – the latter had a reputation for dabbling in black magic, and, as the heir to the throne, had good reason for wanting to kill the king.

Agnes Sampson confessed to raising the storm that had almost wrecked the king's ship when he was on his way back from Denmark with his new bride. But what finally convinced the king that she was telling the truth was when she whispered in his ear certain words he had spoken to his bride on her wedding night –

no one but the king and queen knew what they were. Naturally, the king ceased to be a sceptic.

All of which explains why the king became the author of a famous book called *Daemonologie*, and why his accession to the throne was bad news for Dee, who had already suffered from the prejudice of his colleagues at Manchester.

Racked with anxiety, Dee decided to try and clear the air with a petition to the new king to absolve him of the charge of being "a conjuror or caller or invocator of divils". However, Dee may have been overreacting; the king ignored his petition, but is believed to have given orders that Dee was to be left alone.

In March 1605 came an even greater blow than the death of the queen: the death of his wife Jane from the plague. His daughter Katherine took over the running of the household. Dee finally returned to Mortlake, where he continued his scrying experiments with his first scryer, Bartholomew Hickman, now also an old man. The angels continued to appear, promising him better times to come if he returned to Europe. But although Dee toyed with the idea, it was really out of the question – he was too weak to travel far. Still believing that he was close to finding the answer he had sought all his life, he died in 1608, at the age of eighty-one.

When Dee's son Arthur had been born in 1579, Dee had drawn up a horoscope, and had told Jane Dee that he would "have good fortune from a prince". Following his father's death, Arthur Dee became a physician and, when the Tsar of Russia asked to be sent an English doctor, James I personally recommended him. Thanks to the patronage of both the English king and the Tsar, Arthur Dee was more successful than his father had ever been, and became wealthy in Moscow, "supporting twelve children [and his wife] in luxury". When he fell out of favour thirteen years later, he returned to England and became the physician to Charles I. His friend Sir Thomas Browne wrote that Arthur Dee swore he had witnessed the transmutation of gold in Bohemia.

John Dee's biographer John Hort remarks that Dee cannot claim to rank among the world's successes. In the sense of worldly success, this is undoubtedly true. Yet this man who so often predicted the future with remarkable accuracy may undoubtedly be cited as a proof that the power of prophecy actually exists, and in that sense was more successful than any astrologer since Nostradamus.

8 Astrology

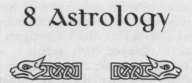

We noted in the last chapter that, although John Dee acknowledged that his own magic powers were virtually non-existent, he could nevertheless be an extremely accurate astrologer. How could this be? The answer, astrologers would reply, is that astrology is a science, and can be applied even by someone who does not believe in it. (Admittedly, it requires a natural talent and intuition, but so does any science.)

Astrology is a Greek word meaning science (or knowledge) of the stars. The odd thing is that stars actually seem to have little or nothing to do with it; they are too far away to have any influence on the earth or its inhabitants. What do have influence, according to astrologers, are the planets. The whole solar system is a kind of spider-web of gravitational forces, stretching through space like a giant cat's cradle. These forces, claim the modern astrologer, are what influence human beings. That may sound absurd, but, as we will see, there is far more scientific backing for astrology than, for example, the *I Ching*, the Tarot, palmistry, or any other form of divination explored in this book.

This is, for example, the view of Dr Percy Seymour, principal lecturer in astronomy at the South West Polytechnic, and director of the Plymouth Planetarium. Seymour himself began as a total sceptic, and in *Astrology: The Evidence of Science*, he points out that even in ages when everyone believed in astrology, many intelligent men regarded it as a preposterous delusion. For example, Chaucer, in "The Franklin's Tale", dismisses astrology (which in his day was the same as astronomy) as a method of predicting the tides, and calls it an abominable superstition. Even Galileo dismissed the notion that the moon might influence the oceans as "occult nonsense". Yet we now know that they were wrong: the movement of the tides is indeed due to the gravitational pull of the moon, and can be predicted precisely.

We also know that the moon really does influence "lunatics". Many psychiatrists agree that certain patients are influenced by the full moon. Human blood is influenced by sunspot activity, as Dr Maki Takata discovered when the flocculation index (the rate at which the blood albumin curdles) of patients began to rise all over the globe at a time of high sunspot activity. Giorgio Piccardi, head of the Institute for Physical Chemistry at Florence University, has discovered that chemical reactions vary according to sunspot reactions and moon cycles, and concludes that this is possible through the mediating effect of water. Professor Yves Rocard has established that human beings have an extremely delicate sensitivity to the earth's magnetic field, and that this explains the phenomenon of dowsing. We also know now that the homing instinct of birds is due to their sensitivity to earth magnetism.

Once it is established that man is surrounded by these magnetic forces, to which he responds like a magnetometer, we can see that it would be extremely unlikely that he would not be influenced by the field of the planets which, in turn, acts upon the field of the earth.

Astrology has always been a target for sceptics because phrases like "it is written in the stars" sound like an obvious piece of superstition. In nineteenth-century France, interest in astrology was so undermined by "the Age of Reason" that it was virtually forgotten (whereas in England, a certain interest remained alive).

In the 1890s, a French artillery officer named Paul Choisnard became sufficiently interested in it to wonder if it might not be possible to "prove" astrology by statistics. For example, there was a persistent tradition that members of the same family – particularly parents and children – might have the same features in their horoscopes. He studied various families, and concluded that this was the case. His *Proofs and Bases of Scientific Astrology* appeared in 1908.

German interest in astrology also began to revive around this time. Elsbeth Ebertin, born in 1880, was a graphologist (i.e. a handwriting expert) who became interested in astrology in 1910 when another graphologist asked not only for a sample of her handwriting, but for her date and time of birth. The resulting character assessment was so accurate that Frau Ebertin was stunned. She pressed the woman about her methods, and the woman finally admitted that she was not a graphologist at all, but an astrologer, who pretended to be a handwriting expert to avoid being harassed by the police.[1] Her results were a result of reading horoscopes.

Frau Ebertin was astonished. After all, graphology is a science, while astrology was supposed to be a kind of confidence-trickery. She began to study astrology, soon discovered that she had that natural intuitive ability that all good astrologers have, and began issuing yearbooks called *A Glimpse into the Future (Blick in die Zukunft)* in 1917. It was the first of a regular series, which were all best-sellers because of her natural writing ability.

In 1923, she was asked by a female admirer of the young political firebrand Adolf Hitler to cast his horoscope. The result was that, in the yearbook published in July 1923, she described him (although without mentioning his name) as "a man of action" who was "destined to play a Führer ['leader'] role", and went on to say that he would "sacrifice himself for the whole German nation". She added that an incautious action could trigger off an uncontrollable crisis.

On 8 November 1923, Hitler's followers staged their Munich "putsch", an attempt to take power that was quickly defeated and led to Hitler's arrest. Frau Ebertin achieved sudden notoriety with her remarkable prophecy. She explained in the following year's almanac that when she cast Hitler's horoscope, she had recognized immediately that this was a man who would not be favoured by good fortune if involved in major actions – a prophecy to be (partially) borne out by the Second World War.

Hitler was born 20 April 1889, and was therefore an Aries – but only just. The sign Aries is traditionally associated with enterprise and originality. But Frau Ebertin also noted the opposition between Hitler's sun and the planet Saturn – the latter usually a planet of adversity, and correctly foresaw problems.

In the 1920s, a young Swiss-German named Karl Ernst Krafft

1 Several nineteenth-century European countries had laws against people who told fortunes for payment.

studied Choisnard, and became convinced that "certain factors would repeat themselves in the charts of the members of the same family" (to quote Ellic Howe's book on Krafft, *Urania's Children*). He studied the birth data of 2,800 musicians, and decided that their birth charts revealed musical talent. To distinguish his own scientific astrology from the superstitious variety, Krafft called it *Cosmobiology*.

After a decade or more of frustrating work on cosmobiology and attempts to make a living, Krafft finally published his *Treatise on Astro-Biology* in French in 1939, but it failed to bring him the fame he had hoped for.

Then chance favoured him. Krafft was known as an authority on Nostradamus, and someone recommended him to Goebbels, who wanted to use the prophecies for propaganda purposes. (Quatrain number 57 of *Century III* seemed to foretell a "change of dynasty" in Britain in 1939, and the invasion of Poland.) Krafft had also been issuing a periodic Economic Bulletin that was partly political, partly economic and partly astrological and when, in 1939, he went to Germany, he was paid a small monthly sum to write reports for Himmler's Intelligence Service – Himmler had always been interested in occultism.

On 2 November 1939, Krafft's report included a prediction that Hitler's life would be in danger, due to use of explosive material, between November 7 and 10. Due to a ban on all predictions concerning Hitler, this was not shown to anyone in the Nazi high command.

In fact, on 8 November Hitler went to the annual reunion in the Burgerbrau beer hall in Munich, to commemorate the 1923 putsch, and a bomb exploded behind the speaker's rostrum just after Hitler had left, killing seven and wounding sixty-three. A man named Georg Elser was arrested a few days later, and was later confined in a concentration camp.

Krafft, with his craving for recognition, lost no time in sending a telegram to Deputy Führer Rudolf Hess – another senior Nazi with mystic leanings – pointing out that he had foretold the assassination attempt. Krafft and his wife were summoned to Berlin in January 1940, and Krafft began studying Nostradamus for Dr Goebbels. Whether he was a good interpreter is anybody's guess. For example, Howe cites one of his elucidations – of quatrain 94 of *Century V*:

Translatera en a Grande Germanie,
Brabant et Flanders, Gand, Bruges et Boulogne,
La traifue fainte, le grand duc d'Armenie,
Assaillira Vienne et la Cologne.

Translation:

He shall translate into Greater Germany,
Brabant and Flanders, Ghent, Bruges and Boulogne,
The treaty feigned, the grand duke of Armenia,
Will attack Vienna and Cologne.

The first two lines certainly look like Hitler's 1939–40 campaign, which added Brabant and Flanders, Bruges, Ghent and Boulogne to Greater Germany. But who is the Grand Duke of Armenia, and why should he attack Vienna and Cologne? Krafft discussed this with another Nostradamus enthusiast, Professor H. H. Kritzinger, whose opinion was that perhaps the "grand duke" was Stalin, born in Georgia, which is close to Armenia. Krafft preferred an altogether less likely interpretation: that Armenia was actually the great German hero Arminius, who had lured three Roman legions into a forest in 9AD and wiped them out. Krafft argued that, by Arminius, Nostradamus meant another great German hero, Adolf Hitler, who annexed both cities during his rise to power. It can be seen that Krafft was willing to stretch a point to please Goebbels.

Regrettably for Krafft, Rudolf Hess had decided to fly to England, convinced that the British were only too anxious to make peace. On 10 May 1941, he landed in Scotland and was promptly placed under arrest – he would remain in detention until his suicide in 1987. Hitler needed a story to explain what had happened to the German people. The story he and his advisers decided upon was that Hess's brain had become addled by crackpot astrologers, who had convinced him that his intervention would end the war. Mass arrests of astrologers and occultists followed quickly. Krafft was arrested on 12 June 1941. He was released a year later to work once more for the propaganda ministry. However, he soon developed a strong persecution mania and began writing accusatory letters to various officials, including an ominous forecast that bombs would fall on the Propaganda Ministry. He was arrested again in February

1942, and spent the rest of the war in jail, dying on his way to Buchenwald concentration camp on 8 January 1945.

In 1950, the French statistician Michel Gauquelin would feed Krafft's statistics – on which he based his *Treatise on Astro-Biology* – into a computer, and conclude that Krafft had been deluding himself.

Yet did that mean that Krafft's astrology was also self-deception? It seems not. Ellic Howe quotes many examples of his accuracy – quite apart from the Hitler assassination prophecy. Krafft was handed two specimens of handwriting and the birth data of two men, and asked about their individual destinies. A week later, Krafft produced his "forecast". He reported that one man (who, it turned out, was Corneliu Codreanu, the Rumanian Fascist leader) suffered from a schizoid personality, was probably of partly Jewish descent, and would not survive November 1938. Codreanu was indeed of partly Jewish descent – his mother was Jewish – and he was accused of high treason and shot while attempting to escape on 30 November 1938.

The second man was King Carol of Rumania, and of him (or rather, his birth data) Krafft said that while he at present enjoyed a position of considerable authority, he would experience a disastrous reverse about September 1940. King Carol was obliged to abdicate in favour of his son in September 1940, and the Germans marched into Rumania a month later.

Again, when Krafft was working on the charts of various enemy generals, he looked at the chart of General Montgomery, and remarked that it was certainly stronger than Rommel's. Montgomery, of course, defeated Rommel in the North Africa campaign.

The son of Frau Ebertin, the woman who foresaw Hitler's rise (and fall), tells how his mother, living in Freiburg in 1944, foresaw that she would die in an air raid, since the horoscopes of people in neighbouring houses revealed that they would all die at the same time. Frau Ebertin did not dare to move, afraid of causing panic among the neighbours, and she – and they – died in November 1944.

Howe also tells the interesting story of the Jewish-Hungarian astrologer Louis de Wohl, who fled from Hitler in the 1930s and worked in London. He was used by British Intelligence to try to counter Gobbels' "occult" propaganda. At a conference in Ohio, de Wohl compared the birth charts of Hitler and Napoleon, pointing out that both had Saturn in the same position, suggesting a sudden change of fortune at the height of success. Wohl also stated (on the basis of his chart) that Hitler had a mistress who would die violently. Hitler's Russian campaign, said de Wohl, would end as disastrously as Napoleon's.

In *The Last Days of Hitler*, Hugh Trevor Roper reveals that, after Himmler's arrest, two horoscopes were found on him, one for Hitler, and one for the Weimar Republic (which came into being in 1919 and was toppled by the Nazis in 1933). Both foretold the outbreak of war in 1939, remarkable victories until 1941, then a series of defeats culminating in disaster in 1945. They were, however, inaccurate in one essential: they showed a great victory in the second half of April 1945, then a stalemate until August, after which there would be peace. In April 1945, trapped in his bunker, Hitler eagerly awaited this great victory, which failed to materialize.

Does this not prove that astrology is unreliable? Not according to Charles Neilson Gattey, the author of *They Saw Tomorrow* (1988). Gattey points out that, in Hitler's horoscope, Neptune was at the cusp (i.e. on the edge of one sign and another) at the beginning of the opening degree of the twelfth field of his chart in April, while Neptune was his "death significance". The likeliest date for this – assuming that it was Hitler's death, and not that of some enemy – would be 1 May when Saturn was at an angle of 180 degrees to Hitler's moon.

When Roosevelt died on 13 April 1945, Goebbels rang Hitler triumphantly and announced that this was the turning point foretold. But Himmler's own astrologer Wilhelm Wulff told Himmler that it was Hitler's death that was foretold. Hitler committed suicide on 30 April.

Wulff had encountered a similar ambiguity when he was asked by General Arthur Nebe, head of the Kriminalpolizei, to cast the horoscope of someone called Franz Schwartz, and he produced a long horoscope. Nebe's friend Ernst Teichmann, a lawyer, was asked to read "Schwarz's" horoscope, and quickly saw that Schwarz was Nebe himself, and congratulated the unknown astrologer on his accurate description of Nebe's character. Nebe went pale and told him to read on. The horoscope went on to foretell disaster and death – a horrible death. Teichmann tried to reassure Nebe by replying that the death could be that of Nebe's worst enemy.

On 4 March 1945, Nebe was executed for his part in the Hitler bomb plot – strangled slowly with piano wire.

Wulff had also show how accurate astrology could be when Nebe asked him, in July 1943, if he could use his astrology to discover what had happened to Mussolini, who had fled from the Allied invasion of Italy. Using an Indian method, Wulff was able to tell Nebe that Mussolini was at present hidden about seventy-five miles south-east of Rome. It was later confirmed that Mussolini was then imprisoned on the island of Ponza, in just that location.

After the war, a statistician named Michel Gauquelin, studying psychology and statistics at the Sorbonne, came upon the work of Choisnard and Krafft, and fed Krafft's statistics into a computer. He concluded that Krafft's idea of statistics was extremely crude, and that Krafft's book was totally unconvincing. Yet Gauquelin was by no means a total sceptic – on the contrary, he had been fascinated by astrology since he was a schoolboy (for reasons he still finds it impossible to grasp). So when he realized that Krafft and Choisnard could not be taken seriously, he decided to try testing some of the basic assertions of astrology with the use of his newly acquired statistical methods and his computer.

One of the assertions he decided to test was that the signs of Aries and Scorpio should be prominent in the horoscopes of military men and sports champions, since they should, presumably, be governed by the planet of physical energy: Mars. This also turned out to be untrue.

Yet Aries and Scorpio are *star* signs. Gauquelin decided that he ought to look at the planets themselves. He chose to consider the planets just after dawn and, later, when they are directly overhead in the sky. This time his statistics showed that there appeared to be a correlation between certain professions and planets in these sectors. For example, doctors tended to have Mars or Saturn in these key sectors at birth. For actors and soldiers, it was Jupiter. For writers and politicians, it tended to be the moon. Sports champions had Mars on the horizon or overhead. That was impressive, as the odds were five million to one against these results occurring randomly.

A Belgian sceptic named Comte Para looked carefully at this latter effect, and decided it had to be accepted. Another sceptic, Professor Hans Eysenck, checked Gauquelin's results, expecting to find them erroneous; he was startled to find they stood up to thorough examination. Eysenck had the courage to say so, and he went on to conduct some of his own tests, with the help of the astrologer Jeff Mayo. They wanted to test whether people born under the odd signs of the zodiac (Aries, Gemini, Leo, etc) are extroverts, while those born under the even signs (Taurus, Cancer, Virgo etc) are introverts. They also wanted to know if people born under the three water signs (Cancer, Scorpio and Sagittarius) are more emotional than others. The study of two thousand people produced results that were well above the laws of chance.

It was Gauquelin who went on to argue (in *The Cosmic Clocks*) that lunatics are influenced by the full moon, that blood is influenced by sunspots, and that chemical reactions vary according to both sunspot activity and moon cycles.

These claims for astrology enraged many scientists, who felt that science was about to be engulfed by what Freud called "the black tide of occultism". A group calling itself the Committee for the Scientific Investigation of Claims of the Paranormal (CSI-COP) attacked aggressively. Unfortunately, the one thing this group failed to do was actually to investigate claims of the paranormal; they contented themselves by asserting loudly that the paranormal had to be nonsense, according to their own notion of what science ought to be.

The committee soon lost face embarrassingly when it was caught trying to suppress evidence in a manner reminiscent of the Watergate scandal. One of its founders, the physicist Dennis Rawlins, read a violent attack on Gauquelin, organized by the committee, in the sceptical magazine *The Humanist*. A total sceptic himself, Rawlins nevertheless tried to persuade his fellow committee members that they were opening themselves to ridicule by lending support to this kind of unreasoned attack. His fellow committee members became increasingly angry at Rawlins' insistence that Gauquelin should be fought with honest arguments. Rawlins then denounced their attempts to suppress him in a pamphlet called "Starbaby", which states that the committee were "would-be debunkers who bungled their major investigation, falsified the results, covered up their errors, and gave the boot to a colleague who threatened to tell the truth".

The "new intolerance" was most completely typified in a comment made by the physicist John Wheeler, at a meeting of the American Association for the Advancement of Science in 1979, when he demanded that the "pseudos" (meaning paranormal investigators) should be driven out of the "workshop of science".

Wheeler meant not only people like Gauquelin, but also people like Professor J. B. Rhine, who had been investigating parapsychology in his laboratory at Duke University in North Carolina since 1935.

In spite of the roar of approval that greeted Wheeler's words, scientific mavericks continued to challenge the rigid materialism of Wheeler and CSICOP. However, this chapter on astrology is no place to describe that controversy, which involved such works as Rupert Sheldrake's *New Science of Life*, David Bohm's *Wholeness and the Implicate Order*, Fritjof Capra's *The Tao of Physics* and Gary Zukav's *The Dancing Wu Li Masters* – all seeking to show that quantum physics and the Uncertainty Principle have made the old materialism untenable.

Yet one orthodox astronomer who was drawn into the controversy was to make an important contribution to the case for astrology. His name was Percy Seymour, and his speciality was magnetic fields – he had done some important work on the magnetic field of the Milky Way. As a member of a committee whose purpose was to try to introduce more astronomy into the British school curriculum, Seymour met the Professor of Astronomy at Glasgow University, Archie Roy – who happened to be a member of the Society for Psychical Research. Roy had no doubt whatever of the existence of spirits and the reality of life after death. The two became close friends, and Seymour came to recognize that to accept evidence for the paranormal is not necessarily a sign of feeble-mindedness.

So when Seymour came to meet Michel Gauquelin in 1987, he was prepared to listen with an open mind. Archie Roy was not in the least interested in astrology and was basically sceptical. On the other hand, Seymour read the books of Gauquelin, then Eysenck's book *Astrology: Science or Superstition* (with David Nias), and had to admit that their case seemed very strong indeed.

Because his speciality was magnetism, he was able to accept their findings because they fitted in with his own. The earth is a giant magnet – but so are the moon, the sun and the planets. They affect the magnetic field of the earth. We now know that birds and animals use this magnetic field for "homing" – even bacteria are affected by it. So it is certain that we are all sensitive to the earth's field, and to the fluctuations in it caused by the other planets. It is, as Seymour says, "as if the whole Solar System – the sun, moon and planets – is playing a complex symphony on the lines of force of the Earth's field".

We are all, says Seymour, genetically tuned to receiving vibrations from the solar system, and when we are born, we suddenly "hear" this music loud and clear, and have it imprinted on us. Our "fate" is not necessarily written in the stars or planets, but our character is. So Krafft, by looking at the birth charts of Rommel and Montgomery, was able to see that Montgomery was more of a "winner".

This, of course, fails to explain how Krafft was able to predict Elser's bomb attempt but, in another book – perhaps his most important – called *The Paranormal*, Seymour comes very close to an explanation. He suggests that large areas of the universe consist of what he calls "plasma space". Plasma is a gas that is so hot that its outer electrons have been stripped off by impacts, leaving charged particles called ions. They will thread themselves along magnetic lines of force like beads. These lines are the "strings" that vibrate between planets, and which explain why astrology works.

Seymour also accepts the existence of what he (and Einstein) call "world lines or geodesics". For example, you could make a graph that describes the flight of a plane from London to New York, with the time along one axis and the distance along the other. Similarly, you could make a graph of your life, with your birth at one end of the chronological bar and your death at the other, and your overall distance travelled on the other axis. The result would be your "world line". (A globe-trotter might have a long, shallow world line, while a man who spent all his life in the same village would have a nearly vertical world line.)

We are inclined to feel that this world line is merely an abstraction. Yet Einstein believed that space and time are not separate entities, but unite in what he called space-time. So Seymour also believes that world lines are real, and that they can influence one another. He explains what he means in a chapter called "The Evidence from Twins", and speaks, for example, of the Lewis twins, Sheila and Jacqueline, separated when they were born in Bristol in 1950. They met by chance in hospital, when they were put in the same treatment room, and found that both had double-jointed little fingers, birthmarks on their necks, moles on the left knee, and that both had suffered from kidney trouble.

Now this sounds reasonable enough, since they were mono-zygotic twins (both from the same ovum). But how do we explain the "Jim twins" of Ohio, who met for the first time when they were thirty-nine? Both had been called Jim by the families who adopted them, both had dogs called Troy, both had worked as attendants at filling stations, then in the same hamburger chain, they had the same hobbies, and had been married twice, first to women called Linda then to women called Betty. Both drove Chevrolets and took their holidays at the same time of the year at the same stretch of beach in Florida.

Clearly that, and dozens of similar cases (a whole book has been devoted to them) cannot be dismissed as examples of coincidence. Yet we have no rational way of explaining such similarities (although Jung tried, in his work on synchronicity). Seymour is suggesting that the twins have almost identical world lines, and that these involve the same things happening to them. This, we can see, offers a kind of explanation for what is otherwise inexplicable, how their "fates" could be so similar. It would obviously also explain why the horoscopes of Frau Ebertin's neighbours indicated that they would share the same fate – an Allied bomb.

Since we have mentioned the word synchronicity, discussed in the chapter on the *I Ching*, we can also see that we might need a very similar theory to that of "world lines" to explain astrology and synchronicity.

At this point, let us look a little more closely at what astrology is, and what it claims to be able to do.

Although the stars are too far away to play any active part in this "cat's cradle" of gravitational forces in our solar system, they nevertheless play a passive part – like the numbers around the edge of a clock. Like a clock, the "zodiac" (or signs of the heavens) has twelve major figures, called constellations. Each one comes up over the horizon at dawn, and then moves across the sky, along the semicircle overhead called the ecliptic. (Of course, we know it is the earth that moves, but that makes no practical difference to our chronological measurements of the apparent movement of the stars.) Because the earth moves round the sun, as well as rotating on its axis, a different constellation comes up over the horizon each month. These twelve constellations are called Aries (the Ram), Taurus (the Bull), Gemini (the twins), Cancer (the crab), Leo (the lion), Virgo (the virgin), Libra (the scales), Scorpio (the scorpion), Sagittarius (the centaur), Capricorn (the goat), Aquarius (the water carrier), and Pisces (the fishes); but they are no more than the figures around the clock face, which enable us to tell the time. If, by any chance, the earth's axis tilted at ninety degrees (like that of Uranus) another twelve would do just as well.

Nevertheless, we can tell the time even when a clock has no figures round the edge; what is important on a clock are the hands. In astrology, the hands are the planets. There are eight of these: Mercury, Venus, Mars, Jupiter, Saturn, Uranus, Neptune and Pluto. In addition there are the sun and moon, which are regarded as planets in astrology. This makes ten in all.

So the clock face has ten hands, and the face itself is divided into twelve segments, like slices of pie – called the Houses, or twelve signs of the zodiac – beginning with Aries. This sign is situated on the clock face where the figures eight and nine would be situated on a clock. And the next house, Taurus, is situated between seven and eight. (In other words, in astrology, our "clock" goes anticlockwise.) The line drawn from the figure nine to the centre of the clock is known as the ecliptic, and represents dawn, the eastern horizon, where the sun comes up.

You can see that, when the sun comes over the horizon at dawn, one of the signs of the zodiac also rises behind it – Aries in March-April, Taurus in April-May, and so on. If your birthday occurs during that month, then this is your "sun sign", and you are an Aries, Cancer, Pisces or whatever.

Various character traits are also associated with the sun signs. Aries characters are supposed to be pioneers and leaders, Taurus characters to be stubborn and practical, Gemini to be mercurial and articulate, Cancer to be home lovers, Leo to be extrovert and assertive, Virgo critical and analytical, Libra charming and helpful, Scorpio strong-willed and passionate, Sagittarius ambitious and optimistic, Capricorn patient and persevering, Aquarius idealistic and progressive, and Pisces sensitive and romantic.

Each of these signs also has negative characteristics. Aries characters can be assertive and selfish, Taurus pig-headed and materialistic, Gemini changeable and inconsistent, Cancer moody and inclined to stick in the mud, Leo a bully and show-off, Virgo pernickety and obsessive, Libra lazy and indecisive, Scorpio jealous and given to harbouring grudges, Sagittarius restless and boastful, Capricorn nagging and over-conventional, Aquarius unconventional and idiosyncratic, and Pisces temperamental and impractical.

It is also worth noting (as we observed above) that alternate signs are introvert or extrovert. Aries is extrovert, Taurus introvert, Gemini extrovert, Cancer introvert, and so on.

When an astrologer is asked to cast your horoscope, the first thing he wants to know is exactly what time you were born, and also where – the latitude and longitude. He will then take a book called an ephemeris, which tells him exactly where each planet is or was at various times during any given year. These positions refer to Greenwich, through which the line of 0° longitude passes, so if you were born in Moscow or Buenos Aires, then you must make adjustments accordingly.

He will then take a blank astrological chart, which looks like a clock face with twelve divisions, and mark on it where the various planets were at the moment you were born. If, like me, you were born in early August, then your sun will be in Leo. The rest of your planets will be distributed around the various houses. Exactly which house each planet is in has great significance for an astrologer. For example, if your Mercury happened to be in the third house (Gemini), this would indicate that you are an excellent communicator, since both Mercury and Gemini are associated with communication.

The astrologer would then begin looking at the "aspects" – that is, the angles between various planets. Of course, only certain angles are regarded as significant, such as conjunctions (two planets in the same place), oppositions (two planets 180° apart, on opposite sides of the chart), squares (two planets at right angles to one another), trines (where the angle is 120°) and others less important called sextiles, semi-sextiles, quincunx and so on.

The twelve houses are associated with our outlook and self. They have much in common with the twelve signs of the zodiac, so the fourth house refers to home, just as Cancer does, the fifth to self-expression, just as Leo does . . .

The first house is our personality, the second money, the third environment and communication, the fourth our home, the fifth self-expression, the sixth servants and service, the seventh partnership, the eighth legacies, the ninth understanding (including philosophy and religion), the tenth our profession and place in life, the eleventh friends and hopes, and the twelfth, hidden support and limitations.

When the astrologer looks at a birth chart, he notes instantly which planets are in various houses. Mercury in the house of personality means a communicator, quick-witted and adaptable, while a Venus in the fourth house (Cancer) reinforces the love of home with love of family and children.

The planets each have their own characteristics. The Sun represents strength and durability, the Moon changeability and receptiveness, Mercury intelligence and communication, Venus attraction and love, Mars aggression and conquest, Jupiter wisdom and growth, Saturn limitation and adversity, Uranus science and explosions (presumably Krafft found Uranus in Hitler's horoscope at the time of the beer-hall explosion), Neptune idealism and peace, and Pluto volcanic force, the great surge of energy. Astrologers quickly come to feel the planets as personalities, and to see immediately what is implied when a planet is in a certain sun sign, or in a certain house.

This, then, is astrology, and anyone can learn about the sun signs, planets and houses in a couple of days, with the help of a simple textbook. Then he will move on to more complex matters, such as what it means when a planet is in a certain sign, and when it is in a certain house. After learning what sun signs mean – if you are a Taurus, Pisces, etc. – you will want to go on to learn what it means to have a certain planet "in the ascendant" (or, more simply, "rising") – that is to say, the planet that is coming up over the horizon at the moment of birth. As one can see, astrology is a complex business when removed beyond the pedestrian scope of the newspaper horoscope page . . .

But let us return for a moment to astronomy. Apart from the movement of the earth around the sun, there is another movement that is far more tiny and subtle. The earth's axis, the imaginary line round which it spins, does not stay perfectly still. If you imagine the axis as a long pencil stuck through the earth, the ends of this pencil also describe a small circle, like a child's top that wobbles from side to side as it spins.

It takes a very long time for the axis to complete one of these tiny circles – just under 26,000 years. And yet, incredibly, there seems to be no doubt that our remote ancestors knew about this slight movement, which is known as the precession of the equinoxes. Professor Giorgio de Santillana has written a book, *Hamlet's Mill* (with Hertha von Dachend), that studies myths from all over the world, and establishes that this precession of the equinoxes seems to have been known to our ancestors for thousands of years. But why? Why was primitive man studying the sky so closely that he was able to notice a tiny movement that takes 26,000 years to complete?

We can imagine why Greeks and Babylonians were interested in the heavens; they were speculative thinkers who took a special interest in such philosophic matters. But why should Native Americans, Eskimos, Norsemen, Chinese, Finns, Hawaiians, Japanese, Hindus, Ancient Egyptians and the rest? Astronomy is only supposed to be between 2,000 and 3,000 years old, so how did these "primitive" people come to know about a slight difference in the rising of the constellations, which means that after 2,200 years of Pisces rising at dawn on the spring equinox, Aquarius takes its place? (Which, incidentally, is why, at this point in history, we are about to enter "the Age of Aquarius", after two thousand years or so in the Age of Pisces.)

Now the "precession" is supposed to have been discovered by the Greek Hipparchus around 160 BC. How is it possible that it could have become known to civilizations that predate it by thousands of years? We have to recognize that there is a great deal about civilization, and about our ancestors, that we do not even begin to know or understand. To the modern city-dweller, the stars are unimportant, except when we read our horoscope in the papers. Yet it would seem that for our ancestors – perhaps even to Palaeolithic cavemen – they were of vital importance. Why? If we understood that, we might begin to understand some of the great mysteries of astrology.

All the great astronomers of the past – Kepler, Tycho Brahe, Galileo, Newton – believed in astrology as a matter of course. Yet, after Newton, scientists became more sceptical, until by the end of the eighteenth century, astrology was widely regarded as mere superstition – in certain countries, like France, it was virtually forgotten. During most of the twentieth century, it has been associated with newspaper horoscopes (which obtusely attempt to find some common "destiny" for all Cancers, Leos, Capricorns on the same day) and dismissed as an absurd fallacy.

(In fact, even newspaper astrology can, in theory, be accurate within limits, since all persons of the same sun sign are supposedly subjected to the same planetary influences.) The change of view represented by Gauquelin, Eysenck and Seymour is virtually a revolution, and astrology has come into its own for the first time since the time of the ancients.

All this can at least suggest an answer to the question: why was ancient man so interested in the heavens? It seems more than he just made up mythical stories about the sun, moon and so on. Perhaps it was because he was consciously aware of living in a web of forces created by the heavens. He did not distinguish planets from the background of stars by merely noticing that they moved ("planet" means a wanderer). Maybe he felt the influence of the planets, just as "lunatics" presumably feel the influence of the full moon. Why did our ancestors regard Jupiter – the largest of the planets – as the king of the gods, although to the naked eye it is no bigger than other planets? Perhaps it was because they could sense its more ponderous influence – and the part it played in the cat's cradle of forces that make up the solar system. In ceasing to feel himself part of that great system, maybe modern man has lost a fundamental connection with the universe.

Let us move on to a practical illustration of the use of astrology. Nicholas Campion is President of the British Astrological Association, and became interested in the curious case of James Maybrick, the Liverpool cotton merchant who died in 1889, apparently poisoned with arsenic by his young wife Florence.

She was tried for the murder, and sentenced to death; this was later commuted to life imprisonment, of which she served twenty years.

In 1993, a book called *The Diary of Jack the Ripper*, by Shirley Harrison, caused a sensation. The "diary", signed "Jack the Ripper", had appeared in Liverpool, apparently given to a scrap metal dealer named Mike Barrett by his drinking companion Tony Devereux, who died soon after. The opening pages were missing, but the diary appeared to show that James Maybrick was in a state of frantic jealousy about his wife Florence, who was more than twenty years his junior, and who had banished him from her bed when she discovered that he had a mistress. His reaction to his violent emotional turmoil was to go to Whitechapel, in London, to "rip whores". According to Shirley Harrison, who studied both the Maybrick case and the Ripper case, the writer of the diary revealed both a close knowledge of Maybrick's life, and of certain unpublished details about the case.

Was Maybrick Jack the Ripper? Or was the diary a forgery, as many believe?

Nicholas Campion offered his own contribution to the debate when he agreed to cast the horoscope of James Maybrick for Shirley Harrison. (Maybrick's astrological chart is included at the end of this chapter.) Campion begins by pointing out that Maybrick was born (on 24 October 1838) with his Sun in Scorpio: an intense and secretive sign. (As noted above, those born under it are often prone to violent jealousy.) His Moon, equally important, is in Capricorn, a conservative sign (described earlier as patient and persevering).

Regrettably, the time of birth is not known, so we do not know Maybrick's rising sign. If, for example, he had been born at dawn, and his rising sign had therefore been Scorpio, the chances of his being Jack the Ripper would certainly be increased.

Venus, the planet of love, and Mercury, the planet of communication are together in Libra, the most likeable and appealing of the signs, and suggest that he could exercise great charm (which may have been the secret of his business success) and conceal deeper feelings behind an acceptable public face.

His Mars is in square (ninety degrees) with Saturn, the two indicating the threat of violence. Venus is in opposition to Pluto, which Campion describes as "one of the key astrological symbols of sexual violence". Venus is the symbol of the maiden, Pluto (who abducted Persephone) of the rapist. Campion quotes Liz Greene, who speaks of Pluto as the "destroyer rapist". Campion goes on to say that such a person is an individual who cannot tolerate imperfection, and who, if the object of desire is found to be flawed, would wish to destroy it. Since destroying Florence was out of the question, he may have turned to destroying prostitutes, who again affronted his idealism, his feeling that women ought to be goddesses.

Campion goes on to point out that, on the night of the first murder (of Mary Ann Nichols), Maybrick's Mars-Saturn alignment was powerfully aspected, and that his Mars-Venus alignment was strongly connected with Uranus, a planet of instability, and of uncontrollable events. There was also a square alignment of the Moon in Gemini with Venus in Virgo, indicating emotions bordering on hysteria.

Campion concludes that "whether Maybrick was Jack the Ripper or not, his horoscope repeatedly describes psychological complexes appropriate to the Ripper".

What Campion found even more surprising was the astonishing similarity between the horoscopes of James Maybrick and of Peter Sutcliffe, the "Yorkshire Ripper", who killed and disembowelled thirteen women between 1975 and 1981. In fact, during Sutcliffe's first murder, on 30 October 1975, Venus and Mars were repeating the positions they were occupying in Maybrick's horoscope during the Nichols murder.

Campion also notes that there is an interesting similarity between the birth chart of Maybrick and that of Hitler. Maybrick's Sun at birth was in exactly the same degree as Hitler's. Maybrick's Moon (which governs emotions) is also in the same degree as Hitler's. Hitler's temperament was, as we saw earlier in this chapter, notoriously explosive. It is interesting to think of Maybrick as a kind of Hitler who, unable to express his frustrations with violent explosions of rage and paranoia, as Hitler did, found his relief in disembowelling prostitutes.

The remarkable insight revealed by Campion's remarks on Maybrick and Jack the Ripper led my father, Colin Wilson, to ask him (in the autumn of 1998) for further comments about the nature of astrology, and the Maybrick case specifically. This is his reply:

"I have studied astrology for around twenty-five years and am known as an expert in its history and philosophy. I am also one of a number of astrologers who are attempting to redefine modern astrology, partly by reference to ancient concepts and partly in relation to the limitations of contemporary science. I am aware that there is no one theory that can explain astrology. All we have are models, each of which has to cope with the fact that astrology is practised in a variety of ways, ranging from the scientific to the magical, from the overtly materialist to the devoutly religious. There is little to connect a Wall Street trader running his planetary data through his computer to the Hindu priest prescribing rituals to designed to placate a planetary deity, yet both are 'astrologers'.

"The problem that astrologers face is that, although the naturalistic explanations of astrology proposed by scientists such as Percy Seymour may ultimately be found to explain such phenomena as the relationship between time of birth, temperament and professional success, many uses of astrology cannot be explained according to such models. There is no way in which every application of astrology can be justified by the familiar formula, first proposed by the Greek astrologer Claudius Ptolemy two thousand years ago, that if the Moon pulls the tides we must assume that its effects (and those of the other planets) on our bodies must influence our characters and destinies. For example, in 'horary' astrology, the astrologer notes the times at which specific questions are asked and casts a horoscope which is then interpreted according to strict rules.

"In my opinion, such uses of astrology should be seen as precisely the sort of one-off exercises which are dismissed by contemporary science as anomalies and hence disregarded. Karl Popper, the twentieth century's greatest philosopher of science, recognized as much when he defined astrology as a pseudoscience, by which he meant that it could ultimately be neither proved nor disproved. He saw clearly that as the precise coincidence of earthly events with celestial patterns on which astrology depends never recur, it is almost impossible to test its claims under controlled conditions.

"There are various philosophical approaches which can explain non-scientific models of astrology. For example, the Greek philosopher Plato, who lived in Athens from around 428–348 BC, took a fundamentally religious view. He believed that God placed the stars in the sky as 'moving images of eternity', and argued that, by studying their movements, we can find out more about both God's plan and the ever-changing qualities of time. He also believed that, because everything is in a constant state of change, the same conditions never recur and we can never establish any final knowledge about anything. From a Platonic point of view, a verified scientific astrology is therefore impossible.

"I myself have been particularly influenced by the Babylonian model of astrology, in which astrology is essentially seen as a language. The Babylonians, who developed the foundations of our modern western astrology between 2,000 and 500 BC, believed that the gods and goddesses moved the stars and planets, and that the perceptive astrologer could therefore deduce their divine intentions by studying celestial phenomena and offer the king appropriate advice. If we dispense with the gods and goddesses, then we are still left with an astrology in which the onus is put on the astrologer as interpreter of possibilities, rather than as the scientific analyst of objective realities.

"Carl Jung, the father of modern depth psychology, provided an additional perspective. In his theory of synchronicity, events are connected not necessarily because one causes the other, but because they happen at the same time. For example, if the bomb attack on Hitler coincided with a violent Mars transit then it's not that Mars 'caused' the attack which is significant, but that the two events coincided. Further, Jung argued that such coincidences are only valid if they are 'meaningful', and to be meaningful there needs to be an astrologer to attribute such meaning.

"The rather alarming conclusion is that there is no astrology without the presence of the astrologer! This point of view is actually not a million miles away from the opinion of Paul Kurtz (the founder of the sceptical organization, CSICOP)[2] that astrology is all 'in the eye of the beholder'. To all intents and purposes, the astrologer is therefore the centre of the exercise!

"We can, however, find ancient and modern justifications for this proposition as well. From the ancient world comes the idea that we are in a constant state of communication with the stars, and that if they 'influence' us then we can also 'influence' them, and that in our own small way we are 'co-creators' in the universe. In other words, astrology requires the presence of the astrologer, and is not something 'out there', independent of us. Some astrologers seek support for this position from the startling fact that the outcome of certain experiments in quantum physics appears to be influenced by the presence of the scientist conducting the experiment.

"From modern cosmology comes the 'strong Anthropic Principle' which states that 'the universe is the way it is because we are the way we are'. It is as if, just as we have made God in our own image, so astrology has been invented to serve very human purposes. I see astrology as a language of symbols which serves as a framework for thought, rather than a science which gives us

2 The Committee for Scientific Investigation of Claims of the Paranormal.

absolutely verifiable knowledge about the universe. It's a way of making connections which more conventional forms of analysis might miss, and an aid to lateral thinking. This in no way invalidates Michel Gauquelin's statistics or Percy Seymour's theories, which may be defined, in Krafft's term, as Cosmobiology or, in Gauquelin's own phrase, 'Neo-astrology'.

"So, what underpinned my comparison between Maybrick, Jack the Ripper and Peter Sutcliffe? Well, if astrology is a language, then it can tell us about the labels we apply to cultural phenomena. If it deals with symbols then it can also tell us about the myths, both ancient and modern, in which symbols play such an important part. Thus the mythology of Jack the Ripper is far larger then the precise fact that over a hundred years ago a sex murderer stalked the streets of London: such murders are not especially unusual but the haunting, terrifying image of the Ripper overshadows almost all other such crimes. Thus it is natural to mythically connect Jack the Ripper to the Yorkshire Ripper: both are manifestations of the mythical figure we call the Ripper, the terrible destroyer of women. The notion that we can make such verbal connections was suggested by Ludwig Wittgenstein, the founder of linguistic philosophy. He suggested, for example, that we can connect games, whether they are emotional games, for example, or ball games. One Ripper is therefore linked to the other by the use of a common label.

"In addition, the astrological measures which connected Maybrick's birth chart to those for both the Rippers' murders were based on 'secondary progressions'. These are planetary movements based on the same number of days after birth as the subject is old. Thus, to investigate events in Maybrick's fiftieth year, we would look at the planetary positions fifty days after his birth. In other words, we are not looking only at the actual planets when the murders were committed, but at their position many years earlier. The rationale for such a system is the idea that the Sun's apparent motion around the Earth in one day is 'equivalent' to its motion around the Earth in one year. It is does not take a genius to work out that the only justification for such a view lies in ancient solar religion, far away from the routine logic of twentieth century science.

"The last piece of the puzzle is the significance of the planet Pluto which, as Liz Greene pointed out, was the mythical archetype of the 'destroyer rapist'. It will be remembered that, in the Greek legends, Pluto was the underworld god who kidnapped and raped the young goddess Kore. His abduction of her represented both the onset of winter in the natural world, and the soul's journey through the underworld from a metaphysical point of view. Her subsequent release symbolized the onset of spring and the soul's resurrection. The planet's presence in the investigation into the Maybrick saga suggests that, as larger than life figures, both Jack the Ripper and the Yorkshire Ripper have somehow inherited the mythical power of the ancient god Pluto. Jung would have said that astrology is a matter of psychic projection, and that we have projected the myth on to both the Rippers, perhaps in an attempt to understand or cope with the awfulness of their crimes. Moreover, the language and interpretations of modern astrology are also still based on classical mythology, if only because the names of the planets are still those used by the Greeks and Romans.

"That is to say, I have used astrology as a mythical system to provide a framework for understanding the Ripper mythology.

"My conclusion, as far as Maybrick was concerned, is not that he could neither be definitively identified as the Ripper, nor ruled out of consideration, but that his horoscope draws him into the Ripper mythology. Perhaps this is evident in the fact that he has himself now been accused of being the Ripper. Perhaps it is evident in other aspects of his lifestyle, his visits to prostitutes and so on."

Campion ends: "My conclusion about astrology, though, is that, as a language of symbols rather than as a precise science, it can only be understood if we understand the nature of consciousness and, in spite of a hundred years of investigation into psychology, that is still a very long way off."

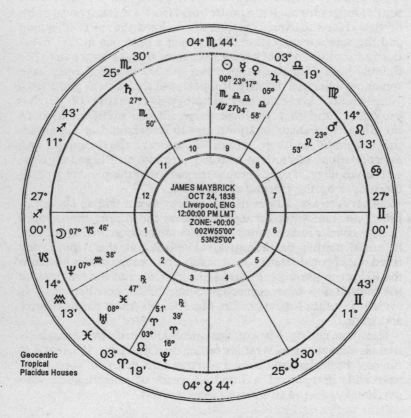

04° ♏ 44'

03° ♎ 19'

25° ♏ 30'

43' ♐ 11'

27° ♐ 00'

14° ♒ 13'

03° ♈ 19'

04° ♉ 44'

25° ♉ 30'

43' ♊ 11'

27° ♊ 00'

14° ♌ 13'

⊙ ☿ ♀
00° 23° 17'
♏ ♎ ♎
40' 27° 04'

♃ 05°
♎ 58'

♂ 23°
♌ 53'

☽ 07° ♑ 46'

♆ 07° ♒ 38'

♇ 47' ♓ Rx

♅ 08° ♓

♄ 27° ♏ 50'

51' ♈ 03°

Rx 39'

16° ♈ ☋

JAMES MAYBRICK
OCT 24, 1838
Liverpool, ENG
12:00:00 PM LMT
ZONE: +00:00
002W55'00"
53N25'00"

10 9
11   8
12   7
1   6
2   5
3 4

Geocentric
Tropical
Placidus Houses

Birth Chart of James Maybrick

9 Nostradamus and Astrology

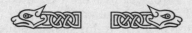

Most portraits of Nostradamus show him holding astronomical instruments, such as an astrolabe or mathematical dividers. The implication – that he obtained his predictions through astrology – seems reasonable, not least because Nostradamus is known to have supplemented his income by casting horoscopes for rich patrons. Yet even a cursory knowledge of the *Centuries* and the seer's life will show that this cannot be the whole explanation.

For example, while Nostradamus was visiting the court of Henri II in 1555, he was lodged in the Parisian townhouse of the Archbishop of Sens. Following his enthusiastic reception by Queen Catherine, it became fashionable for nobles to visit the "Prophet from Provence" to commission astrological birth charts. Yet one visitor was neither rich or of noble birth: he was a pageboy, in a state of desperation because his master's favourite hunting dog had run away and could not be found. The seer agreed to see him and, before the boy could tell him his problem, announced: "You are worrying about a lost dog. Go and search on the Orléans Road. You will find him there on a leash."

Sure enough, as soon as the page reached the road leading to Orléans, he met another servant leading the run-away dog on a lead.

Another, rather more whimsical story tells of the seer taking a walk outside the town walls of Salon. A young woman passed him and said, "*Bonjour, Monsieur Nostradame,*" to which he replied, "*Bonjour, pucelle,*" ("Good day, maiden"). Later that day, they passed each other again. The girl again said demurely, "*Bonjour, Monsieur Nostradame,*" but this time he replied – with a wry smile – "*Bonjour, petite femme,*" ("Good day, little grown-up woman.") The story goes on to state that the girl had secretly spent the morning with a young man . . .

Both stories may, of course, be apocryphal, but the fact that both seem to have been in circulation during Nostradamus' lifetime suggests that they were based on fact. They seem to show what seems obvious: that Nostradamus possessed a degree of clairvoyance or second sight.

Even a famous astrologer like Luca Gaurico could only warn Henri II to avoid fighting in an enclosed space (in armour, as it turned out) because of a risk to his sight and life. Nostradamus, on the other hand, apparently foresaw minute details of the accidental death of the king. In four short lines (*Century I,* quatrain 35) he gives clues to the colour of the king's armour, the heraldic badge of both men, the position of the fatal wound and the fact that Henri would die an excruciating death. This kind of accuracy points more to an actual vision of the future, than the kind of knowledge gained by astronomy, which tends to be less exact. (i. e. astrology: "You will be in mortal danger from wood and iron on such and such a date;" clairvoyance: "Don't walk down the High Street at noon on such and such, or a grand piano being winched into a high window will fall and kill you.")

Nostradamus himself gave confusing signals concerning his use of astrology. In the first sentence of his introduction to the first *Century,* he apparently admits that he used astrology to obtain his predictions:

"Your late birth, Caesar Nostradamus, my son [to whom he was dedicating the book] has caused me to spend much time in continual and nocturnal watchings, so that I might leave a memorial of myself after my death, to the common benefit of mankind, concerning the things the Divine Essence has revealed to me by *astronomical revolutions.*" (My italics.)

It should be noted that, in Nostradamus' day, astrology was popularly known as "practical astronomy" – astrology's daily usefulness being seen as the only real difference between the related practices. Certainly his contemporary readers would have transposed the two disciplines when reading this sentence – interpreting it as a direct endorsement of astrology – and there seems little obvious reason for modern readers to do otherwise. Yet, despite his apparently specific backing for astrology as the voice of "the Divine Essence", Nostradamus gives the following warning at the end of *Century VI*:

> *LEGIS CAUTIO CONTRA INEPTOS CRITICOS.*
> *Qui legent hos versus, mature censunto;*
> *Prophanum vulgus & inscium ne attrectato.*
> *Omnesque Astrologi, Blenni, Barbari procul sunto,*
> *Qui aliter faxit, is rite sacer esto.*

Translation:

> INVOCATION OF THE LAW
> AGAINST INEPT CRITICS.
> Those who read these verses,
> let them consider with mature mind.
> Let not the profane, vulgar and ignorant
> be attracted to their study.
> All *Astrologers*, Fools, Barbarians draw not near,
> He who acts otherwise, is cursed according to rite.
> (My italics.)

Interpretations of this apparently hypocritical statement vary. The simplest is that he actually meant "foolish astrologers" as opposed to "astrologers and fools"; in other words, he was attacking the many charlatans in his profession. This seems unlikely, however: Nostradamus was well versed in Latin and it is hard to believe he could make such an elementary grammatical error.

Another theory is that he was trying to avoid criticism by the Holy Inquisition. However, it was not astrology, but fortune-telling the Church disliked – and Nostradamus was, by any definition, a fortune-teller.

In *Nostradamus – Prophecies of Present Times?* (published in 1985), David Pitt Francis offers a statistical study of the astrological references found in the first ten *Centuries*. Of 942 quatrains, he found only eighty-five which, in his opinion, contained specifically astrological images or references – in other words, less than ten per cent of the prophecies. Surely, he argues, if Nostradamus was actually an astrologer, more astrological references would have found their way into the quatrains. Francis concludes that Nostradamus probably only dabbled in astrology, utilizing it solely for its poetic imagery – and for making money from courtiers by casting horoscopes, in which he was undoubtedly skilled.

David Francis' theory is partially supported by David Ovason in *The Secrets of Nostradamus* (1997): both agree that Nostradamus' use of astrological imagery in the *Centuries* is not primarily predictive. But where Francis dismisses the material as basically poetic, Ovason sees an occult dating system that reveals the seer's actual power to foresee the future.

"Nostradamus," says Ovason, "used astrology in a form which is so arcane as to be beyond the understanding of most modern astrologers. There is no evidence that, in the quatrains, at least, Nostradamus used astrology in a conventional way at all, either as a tool for prediction, or as a standard system of symbols for elucidation. In this sense, his quatrains are not astrological predictions. On the other hand, there is a vast body of evidence to show that Nostradamus made use of astrological references to designate specific time-periods in his quatrains."

What Ovason suggests is that Nostradamus did indeed foresee future events, then constructed the quatrains in such a way as to enlighten only those readers with the esoteric knowledge to understand the references he used.[1] As we have already seen, the seer was very fond of word puzzles. Medieval heraldry, ancient Latin and Greek mythology, sixteenth-century political in-jokes and astrological references were all utilized to construct these wordplays. But he used astrology, Ovason says, for a second purpose: through his remarkable knowledge of planetary

1 Ovason complains that most modern commentators have been prone to judge Nostradamus' astrological references in terms of their own knowledge of the subject: that is, from the viewpoint of the post-nineteenth century astrology revival. This movement had a tendency to "dumb down" the practice to make it accessible to a newspaper-reading public. The result, Ovason says, is that we fail to understand Nostradamus' use of astrology because he was utilizing it on a much higher level than most of us can even conceive: we dabble with kindergarten horoscopes while Nostradamus was an initiate of doctorate level.

conjunctions, he could give his knowledgeable readers very exact clues as to when the predicted events would take place.

For example, *Century III*, quatrain 3, reads:

> *Mars et Mercure et l'argent joint ensemble*
> *Vers le midy extréme siccité,*
> *Au fond d'Asie on dira terre tremble,*
> *Corinthe, Ephese lors en perplexité.*

Translation:

> Mars and Mercury and the silver [the moon] joined together,
> Towards the south extreme drought,
> From the depths of Asia comes report of an earthquake,
> Corinth and Ephesus then in perplexity.

A typically obscure Nostradamus prediction, one might think. But, Ovason argues, with a little astronomical knowledge and historical hindsight, we can see a precise prophecy emerge.[2]

The first line is obviously astrological in meaning. The planets Mars and Mercury are mentioned, and the moon is implied by the phrase "l'argent". (Any sixteenth-century peasant would have recognized "the silver" to describe the Moon: the two had been connected in popular myth and poetry for time out of mind.)

Mars, Mercury and the moon align every few years, so the first line does not give a precise date or even a reasonably short list of likely possibilities. Nevertheless, Ovason suggests, the rest of the quatrain allows us to narrow the prediction down to a specific event.

Ovason believes that a fourth astrological reference is hidden in the quatrain. The first word of line two is "Vers". Directly beneath it, at the start of line three, is the word "Au". The French word "Versau" is their name for the zodiac sign of

---

2 Perhaps the most convincing aspect of Nostradamus' predictions is that they seem to have been written with the aid of a modern-day history book. If he could not foresee future events, his defenders argue, how could he have constructed such clever historical puzzles, most of which were totally undecipherable to his contemporaries, only being recognizable after the events described?

Aquarius. Line two as a whole may also confirm this Aquarian hidden message. In the complex astrology practised by Nostradamus and his contemporaries, Aquarius was considered a symbol of "heat" (thus dryness or drought) as well as being a "midy" (southern) sign. Therefore, this might be a typically erudite joke by Nostradamus: an ironic comment that a water sign, also being the representative of southern heat, could be the symbol of "drought". If we accept these riddling references as genuine clues, Ovason suggests that we should look for a time when Mars, Mercury and the Moon align in the House of Aquarius.

The mention of Corinth and Ephesus in the fourth line would have had an ominous meaning for readers in Nostradamus' time: that of the encroaching Turkish Empire. Ephesus was on the Turkish coast, and the Turks had conquered Corinth (with the rest of Greece) almost a hundred years before. At the time of the publication of the *Centuries*, the Islamic hordes of the Ottoman Empire were the chief cause of unease in Christian Europe. The nightmare of a mass Turkish invasion hung over the nations of the Mediterranean, just as the fear of a pre-emptive nuclear strike did during the Cold War. Any mention of these Turkish-held towns would have caught the readers' attention like a magnet.

The mention of a major earthquake in Asia in line three, Ovason suggests, was a poetic hint that the Turkish Empire would be shaken to its foundations by events in a year of a Mercury-Moon-Mars-Aquarius conjunction. The next such year, following the publication of *Century III*, was 1571. In that year, a navy of allied Christian states destroyed that of the Turks at the Battle of Lepanto (also predicted by Nostradamus in *Century III*, quatrain 64 – see chapter 6). This unexpected defeat shook the Ottoman Empire to its roots. As a direct result, the Turkish armies became less aggressively expansionist and their empire began a long process of collapse.

In passing, it should also be noted that the Battle of Lepanto took place in the Bay of Corinth. Afterwards, commerce in the Turkish ports of Corinth and Ephesus suffered, as Christian pirates became bolder in the eastern Mediterranean; a "perplexity" possibly reflected in the fourth line of the quatrain.

Apart from Nostradamus' preference for riddles, there may have been a second reason for his use of astrology to suggest dates: it is possible that he knew that the calendar familiar to his readers would soon become redundant.

In 1582, sixteen years after Nostradamus' death, Pope Gregory XIII reformed the Christian calendar. The previous system, the Julian calendar (instituted by Julius Caesar), was eleven minutes and fourteen seconds longer than the solar year. This apparently negligible miscalculation had accumulated, year on year, since 45 BC. By the mid-sixteenth century, all dates were ten days later than they should have been. The calendar twenty first of June, for example, was not the longest day of the year – that had taken place ten days earlier. The Church was embarrassed that religious festivals were beginning to fall in the wrong season, and so decided on reform.

Pope Gregory realized that the Julian method of calculating leap years – by simply nominating one year in four – was the root of the problem.[3] The new Gregorian system decreed that if the first year of a century was evenly divisible by 400, it was a leap year. Thus, 1600 AD was a leap year, but 1700, 1800 and 1900 AD were not. This effectively removed several days every four hundred years and balanced the Julian discrepancy.

To begin the new calendar, the ten-day discrepancy had to be removed. This was achieved by the simple expedient of "jumping back" ten days in 1582, then continuing as normal. Nostradamus seems to have known that this would happen because in *Century I*, quatrain 42, he wrote:

> Le dix Kalende d'Avril de faict Gothique,
> Resuscité encor par gens malins:
> Le feu estainct assemblé diabolique,
> Cherchant les os du d'Amant et Pselin.

Translation:

> The tenth of the Calends of April calculated Gothic,
> Resuscitated by the wicked people:
> The fire put out, a diabolical assembly,
> Seek for bones of the demon of *Psellus*.

---

3 The solar year (the time it takes the earth to travel around the sun) is actually 365 days, 5 hours, 48 minutes and 45.5 seconds long. To rectify the discrepancy, a "leap year" (with an extra day in February) needed to be added at correct intervals.

We will look at the magical significance of this strange quatrain in a later chapter, but for now we are only interested in the first line. The "Calends" was the first day of the month in Ancient Rome. During the date conversion in 1582, the tenth of April and the first of April became the same day, but only in Catholic countries. Protestant nations obstinately stuck to the Julian calendar, in some cases for centuries (the Orthodox Church is still using it today). In Nostradamus' day, the most notably Protestant nations were the Germanic states of central Europe: the so-called "Gothic" states. Therefore, we might paraphrase the first line to read: "The Julian tenth of April, as the Protestants of Germany will calculate it . . ."

Sceptics will point out that the problem of the calendar was widely debated in Nostradamus' day, so this line hardly proves him a prophet; still, his recognition that the normally progressive Gothic nations would be slow to follow suit is altogether harder to dismiss.

Whether through precognition or through a common-sense certainty that the calendar must soon lose ten days, Nostradamus must have known that any date he gave in the quatrains would have been incorrect, either for his own day or for post-Julian readers. So the use of astrological conjunctions as a dating system would certainly have solved the problem.

Before leaving the subject of Nostradamus' use of astrology, I would like to add a personal experience that may support David Ovason's theory.

While I was conducting research for this volume, I came across *Century II*, quatrain 5, which reads:

> *Qu'en dans poissan, fer et lettres enfermée,*
> *Hors sortira qui puis fera la guerre:*
> *Aura par mer sa classe bien ramée,*
> *Apparoissant pres de Latine terre.*

Translation:

> In a fish, iron and letters are enclosed,
> He goes out and will then make war.
> His fleet will have travelled far across the sea,
> Appearing near the *Latine* Shore.

The word "fish" in the first line has often been translated as a submarine. For example, Henry Roberts (in *The Complete Prophecies of Nostradamus*) suggests that the quatrain predicts the secret preparations by General Mark Clark, prior to the invasion of North Africa in World War II. Other commentators, who translate "iron and letters" as "weapons and documents", suggest the quatrain is darkly reminiscent of atomic submarines: these carry codebooks to translate orders to launch their nuclear missiles.

Erica Cheetham, on the other hand, suggests that "iron" may indicate the planet Mars (also the god of weapons) and "letters" may indicate the planet Mercury (god of messengers). The "fish" might therefore be the zodiac sign of Pisces. She suggests that the quatrain may indicate the beginning of World War III – on a date when Mars and Mercury are both in the House of Pisces.

In *The Prophecies of Nostradamus* (1974), Cheetham notes that the next such conjunction was due on 26 March 1996. I read this explanation during mid-March 1996, when one of the main topics in the news was the up-coming Taiwanese General Election, due to be held on the twenty-sixth of that month.

Taiwan is a large island, south-west of Japan and only a few miles off the coast of China. For centuries the island's sovereignty has been a bone of contention between Japan, China, the European Imperial powers and Taiwanese nationalists. In 1949, the anti-communist Chinese leader Chaing Kai-shek was driven out of mainland China, so set up a new independent government on Taiwan. The Red Chinese would certainly have gone on to invade the island, but the United States quickly signed a treaty with Taiwan, effectively guaranteeing war if Communist China attacked their escaped enemy. Since that time, China has loudly maintained its right to reabsorb its old province but, to avoid starting a third world war, has limited its actions to bellicose posturing and military exercises in the Strait of Taiwan.

The Taiwanese general election in 1996 was considered highly significant across the world, because the Chinese government had virtually promised to invade the island if an anti-Chinese-leaning government were voted in. Since this seemed highly likely, considering Taiwanese public opinion, the Chinese sent a huge war fleet to "conduct war games" within sight of the Taiwanese coast. America, reacting to protect a major trading partner and to honour their treaty commitments, sent most of the US Pacific fleet, also to "conduct war games" near Taiwan.

Since Taiwan was, at that time, one of the most productive economies in the world, it seemed to me that the word "*Latine*" in the fourth line of *Century II*, quatrain 5, might have been a reference to the island. In Nostradamus' day, the most prolific traders were unquestionably the Latin cities of Genoa, Venice and Florence. It therefore seemed possible that Nostradamus might have used the term "Latine" not to indicate Italy, but a major trading nation for which he could think of no other representative reference. Of course, the above interpretation is open to doubt; yet the fact that a major trading nation was brought to the brink of war when Mars and Mercury were conjunct in Pisces is an interesting coincidence.

Fortunately the international incident did not escalate. Although an anti-Communist government was returned on the island, China decided that diplomatic loss of face was preferable to a major war. The only "*guerre*" to be seen in the incident were the fleet war games and the diplomatic posturing on both sides.

10 Nostradamus and the Seventeenth Century

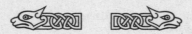

The following are some of the quatrains that Nostradamus scholars have attributed to the events of the seventeenth century. The reader should keep in mind the fact that Nostradamus deliberately obfuscated the meaning in his quatrains. Even the most erudite translator can only guess at the poems' possible meanings and implications.

Sceptics have claimed that Nostradamus did this to hide the fact that he could not actually foresee the future. The quatrains, they argue, are a poetic version of Rorschach inkblots. These are symmetrical ink stains that psychiatric patients are asked to contemplate and describe as if they were pictures with some specific meaning. The viewer's imagination "translates" the image and a trained psychiatrist can deduce aspects of a patient's psyche from listening to the process. For example, a healthy person might see a butterfly or a tree; a sex-maniac might see genitalia or a bloodstain.

The vagueness of most of Nostradamus' quatrains certainly demands imaginative "filling" by the translator, and the scholar's own interests can colour the result. For example, Henry C. Roberts (in *The Complete Nostradamus*) attributes many of the quatrains to events in the twentieth century. Erica Cheetham (in *The Prophecies of Nostradamus*) disagrees with Roberts on the translation of a number of these quatrains, finding pre-twentieth century historical events to match with their nebulous descriptions. Neither can claim to have positive proof to back any of these translations.

Yet most people who have studied the *Centuries* closely believe that there is more to Nostradamus' predictions than the desire of the reader to see their own historical interests reflected in the riddles of a sixteenth-century doctor. As we will see in this chapter, some quatrains contain partially hidden historical details that later appeared to be stunningly accurate predictions of real events after the seer's death. Of course, it is still possible to put these down as mere coincidences, but in some cases this explanation strains credibility to its limit.

The Catholic Church's Persecution of Astronomers in the Early Seventeenth Century
VIII.71 & IV.18

> Croistra le nombre si grand des Astronomes,
> Chassez, bannis et livres censurez,
> L'an mil six cens et sept par sacre glomes,
> Que nul aux sacres ne seront asseurez.

Translation:

> The number of Astronomers shall grow great,
> Driven away, banished and books censured,
> The year one thousand six hundred and seven years
>   by *glomes*,
> None shall be safe from the sacred.

By the early seventeenth century, the Catholic authorities were growing increasingly uneasy. Attacked by Protestants on one hand and undermined by free-thinking "natural philosophers" on the other, Church leaders began to show increasing signs of paranoia. The most obvious signs of this malady were the growing power of the Inquisition and the active participation of the Church in the European witch-hunting craze.

Students of the fledgling science of astronomy were under particular suspicion during this period. The date Nostradamus gives – 1607 – is not particularly significant, as far as we can now discover. In 1600, the Inquisition burned the philosopher and astronomer Giordano Bruno (see below). In 1633, the astronomer and mathematician Galileo was sentenced to life imprisonment by the same authority. Between these dates, we know that the Inquisition acted against many thinkers who the ecclesiastical authorities felt were overstepping the mark in their research. Perhaps the date 1607 may refer to one of these, but the key to understanding may be, of course, contained in the mysterious and unknown word "*glomes*" in the third line.

> *Des plus lettrez dessus les faits celestes,*
> *Seront par princes ignorans reprouvez,*
> *Punis d'edit, chassez comme celestes,*
> *Et mis a mort la ou seront trouvez.*

Translation:

> The most learned in the celestial sciences,
> Will be found at fault by ignorant princes,
> Punished by edicts, chased like criminals,
> And put to death where they shall be found.

This prediction fits several periods of history since Nostradamus' day. In the twentieth century alone, it may refer to both the Nazi and Stalinist mass execution of "subversive" intellectuals, Mao Tse-tung's "Cultural Revolution", Pol Pot's Cambodian "Killing Fields" or even the "Atom Spy" trials in Britain and America at the beginning of the Cold War. However, the use of the word "princes" suggests that Nostradamus may have meant the "Princes of the Church", and had in mind the Church's persecutions of astronomers and astrologers in the seventeenth century.

There is an unmistakable hint of personal bitterness in both the above quatrains. It is worth remembering that Nostradamus' family had lived in fear because of their Jewish roots and that the seer himself had undergone investigation by the Inquisition in 1538. Given that Nostradamus was a practising astrologer and, almost certainly, an initiate of "occult sciences", he had no reason to love the Catholic Church's authoritarian stance on the subject.

The Execution of Giordano Bruno, 17 February 1600
IV.31

> La Lune au plain de nuict sur le haut mont,
> Le nonveau sophe d'un seul cerveau l'a veu:
> Par ses disciples estre immortel semond,
> Yeux au midi, en seins mains, corps au feu.

Translation:

> The Moon at full by night upon the high mount,
> The new sage alone with his brain has seen it:
> Invited by his disciples to become immortal,
> His eyes to the south, his hands on his chest, body in the fire.

Arthur Prieditus, in his book *The Fate of Nations*, suggests that this obscurely occult quatrain refers to the death of the brilliant Italian philosopher, Giordano Bruno.

Bruno was a young Dominican monk who independently, through his own astrological observations, came to the same conclusion as Nicholas Copernicus and Tycho Brahe – that Earth revolved around the Sun and not, as the Church insisted, *vice versa*. However, being more of a poet than a scientist, Bruno used his discovery as a basis of a new pantheistic philosophy. He identified the order in the universe as the "world soul" or God. All material things, he said, were manifestations of the world soul.

Naturally enough, he felt his new, "heretical" beliefs invalidated his vows as a monk and fled the Inquisition to the Protestant countries of northern Europe. After many years travelling and discussing his ideas (with John Dee, among others), he was invited to return south to Italy, under the patronage of a Venetian nobleman called Giovanni Mocenigo. Bruno was at first reluctant to return to the heartland of the Inquisition, but eventually allowed the enthusiasm of his Italian disciples to persuade him.

On Bruno's arrival in 1592, Mocenigo treacherously denounced the philosopher to the Inquisition. The Church incarcerated Bruno for eight years, tore out his tongue and finally burned him at the stake. However, his Neoplatonic philosophy lived on and, through its influence on Baruch Spinoza, won Bruno acclaim as the father of modern philosophy.

The Assassination of Henri IV, 14 May 1610
III.11

> Les armes battre an ciel longue saison
> L'arbre au milieu de la cité tombé:
> Verbine, rongne, glaive en face, Tison
> Lors le monarque d'Hadrie succombé.

Translation:

> The weapons battle in the sky for a long season
> The tree fell in the midst of the city:
> The sacred branch is cut, the sword opposite Tison
> Then the monarch of *Hadrie* succumbs.

Henri IV of France (formerly Henri of Navarre) was preparing for a major war in the spring of 1610. A disagreement over the succession in the otherwise insignificant state of Julich-Cleves had set him at odds with the House of Hapsburg – the most powerful royal line in Europe, ruling both Spain and the Holy Roman Empire. Neutral observers feared the conflict would set the whole of Europe ablaze.

On 14 May, Henri was attacked and stabbed to death on the Rue Ferronnerie, in the centre of Paris. The murderer was a pro-Spanish Catholic called Francois Ravaillac. He was caught and tortured to death. Despite the likelihood that Ravaillac was put up to the assassination by the Hapsburgs, Henri's widowed queen immediately made peace with her husband's enemies, and thus ensured peace in Europe (at least for a few more years).

The first line of Nostradamus' quatrain suggests an air war to modern minds, and thus apparently places the prediction in the post-1900 era. However, the other three lines seem to be specifically about the death of Henri IV.

The "tree" that fell in the "middle of the city" and the "sacred branch" are both poetic images of Henri – the last of the Valois family tree to rule France and, following his anointing and coronation, a sacred person. Ravaillac stabbed him on a street that adjoined Rue Tison, thus the "sword opposite Tison". Finally, the nickname "Hadrie" appears in several other Nostradamus quatrains – all apparently dealing with Henri of Navarre (later Henri IV).

In fact, records from the time of Henri's death actually mention sightings of a ghostly army in the sky over France (like those seen over English Civil War battlefields and over the Battle of Mons in World War I). Popularly considered a portent of the death of kings, this phenomenon may be what Nostradamus was referring to in the mysterious first line of the quatrain.

The Thirty Years' War, 1618–48
V.13

> *Par grand fureur le Roi Romain Belgique*
> *Vexer vouldra par phalange barbare:*
> *Fureur grinsseant chassera gent Libyque*
> *Despuis Pannons jusques Hercules la hare.*

Translation:

> In a great rage the king of Roman Belgium
> Vexed with barbarian warriors:
> Gnashing fury will chase the Libyan people,
> From Hungary as far as the Straits of Gibraltar.

Erica Cheetham argues that this quatrain describes the broad outline of the Thirty Years' War.

By 1618, the smouldering hatred kindled between the Catholic and Protestant nations of Europe exploded into war. On the Catholic side were Spain and France, loosely allied with Ferdinand II, the Holy Roman Emperor. On the Protestant side were Germany, Holland, Denmark, Norway and Sweden. Cheetham suggests that Belgium is mentioned in the quatrain because it was the geographical centre-ground between these factions. She adds that the terms "barbarian" and "Libyans" in the quatrain both describe the Protestant forces – all outlanders and heretics, in the eyes of the Catholic Church.

For over thirty years, up to the 1648 Peace of Westphalia, the war ravaged central Europe, killing and displacing thousands of people from eastern Hungary to western Spain.

The Last Days of Cardinal Richelieu, 1642
VIII.68

> Vieux Cardinal par le jeune deceu,
> Hors de sa change se verra desarmé,
> Arles ne monstres double soit aperceu,
> Et Liqueduct et le Prince embausmé.

Translation:

> Old Cardinal by the young one deceived,
> Shall find himself disarmed,
> Arles does not show the double is perceived,
> And Liquiduct and the Prince embalmed.

The most famous European Cardinal since the time of Nostradamus was Richelieu of France.[1] Erica Cheetham suggests that this quatrain accurately describes his final days.

In 1642, the 57-year-old Cardinal Richelieu – who had effectively run French national policy for over a decade – suddenly found himself supplanted in King Louis XIII's favour by the 22-year-old nobleman, Henri de Cinq Mars. Richelieu was quickly forced into retirement (politically "disarmed").

However, while he was staying in the town of Arles, the Cardinal's spies provided him with a copy of a treaty that had been treacherously made between Cinq Mars and the King of Spain. Although very sick, Richelieu travelled to Paris by barge to denounce his enemy ("Liquiduct", from line four, literally means "led by water"). Cinq Mars was beheaded, but both Richelieu and Louis XIII also died within the year. Both were embalmed.

---

1 The villain in Alexander Dumas' *Three Musketeers*, but also the man whose various political intrigues ultimately cemented over a hundred years of power and prosperity for his country.

The Age of the Sun King, 1643 to 1715
X.89

> *De brique en marbre seront les murs reduits*
> *Sept et cinquante années pacifiques,*
> *Joie aux humains renoué L'aqueduict,*
> *Santé, grandz fruict joye et temps melifque.*

Translation:

> The walls shall be turned from brick to marble,
> Seventy-five years' peace,
> Joy to humanity renewed the aqueduct,
> Health, abundant fruit, joys and mellifluous times.

This glowing picture of three-quarters of a century of happiness and plenty certainly fits the reign of Louis XIV – the "Sun King" of seventeenth-century France. De Fontbrune points to the beautiful Palace of Versailles, as the explanation of the first line. Built by Louis between 1661 and 1701, much of it faced with marble, it was the wonder of its day. Louis XIV's reign, from 1643 to 1715, was the longest in European history, just three years short of Nostradamus' "seventy-five years".

On the other hand, the reign of Louis XIV – although generally prosperous – was far from peaceful. Mainly for his own glorification, the king involved France in a series of foreign wars throughout the course of his life. In this light, it might be more optimistic to place this prediction among those yet to be fulfilled.

The Fall of Charles I of England and the Rise of Oliver
Cromwell
III.80 & III.81

> *Du regne Anglois l'indigne dechassé,*
> *Le conseiller par ire mis à feu:*
> *Ses adhera iront si bas tracer,*
> *Que le batard sera demi receux.*

Translation:

> From the English kingdom the unworthy one is
>   driven away,
> The counsellor through anger will be burnt:
> His followers will stoop to such depths,
> That the bastard will be half received.

Judging from the *Centuries*, some scholars believe that Nostradamus was rather emotionally involved in his visions of the English Civil War. His apparent descriptions of Oliver Cromwell drip with loathing and hatred – much as one might expect from an ardent royalist contemplating a regicide. Nevertheless, if we accept Erica Cheetham's reading of the above quatrain, Nostradamus fully understood that King Charles' downfall was mostly his own doing.

Charles showed himself "unworthy" of remaining king through his obsessive and irrational belief in his "divine right" to rule, and his refusal to recognize Parliament as a force that needed diplomatic handling.[2]

Two of Charles' councillors were executed for treachery – Lord Stafford was beheaded and Archbishop Laud was burned at the stake (as line two seems to predict). The followers who stooped "to such depths" in the third line might have been the Scots – to whom Charles surrendered himself in the hopes that they might join him, but who instead handed the king over to the Parliamentary forces. Finally, the "bastard" of the final line was probably Cromwell. Following the arrest and execution of King Charles, Cromwell had himself made Lord Protector – a king in all but name. However, he was never fully accepted by the people and, following his death, the British monarchy was restored.

> *Le grand crier sans honte audacieux,*
> *Sera eseu gouverneur de l'armée:*
> *La hardiesse de son contentieux,*
> *Le pont rompu cité de peur pasmée.*

---

2 An attitude that was to also doom Tsar Nicholas of Russia, 250 years later.

Translation:

> The great shouter shameless and proud,
> Shall be elected governor of the army:
> The audacity of his contention,
> The broken bridge, the city faint from fear.

This quatrain is the subject of some debate among writers on Nostradamus, but most believe it to refer to the rise to power of Oliver Cromwell. The prediction that the demagogue described in the first line will be "elected" to leadership of the army is important to this argument. Few military commanders since the days of ancient Rome have been elected rather than appointed to the position, but the radical Roundhead Parliament insisted on voting on every major decision.

Cromwell was certainly an audacious commander and the frightened city of the broken bridge, mentioned in the last line, could be Pontefract – a Royalist stronghold that suffered two grim sieges during the war. The Latin for bridge is *"pons"*, and *"fractus"* means broken: thus Pontefract equals "bridge broken" – a typical Nostradamus wordplay.

The Execution of Charles I, 30 January 1649
IX.49

> Gand et Bruceles marcheront contre Envers
> Senat du Londres mettront à mort leur Roi
> Le sel et vin lui seront à l'envers,
> Pour eux avoir le regne en dessarroi.

Translation:

> Ghent and Brussels march against Antwerp,
> The Senate of London shall put their King to death
> Salt and wine oppose him,
> That they may have the kingdom into ruin.

In 1648, Parliament brought Charles I to trial and found him guilty of wantonly shedding his people's blood. On 30 January, the following year, he was publicly beheaded in front of Whitehall.

During this time, Philip IV of Spain made great efforts to maintain the Spanish hold on Holland. Several attacks were made on rebellious Antwerp (as mentioned in line one), but the effort would ultimately prove fruitless. The "salt and wine" and the national "ruin" mentioned in the last two lines are explained by de Fontbrune as a warning of the economic difficulties England would suffer following the Civil War – during which both luxuries and basic necessities were scarce.

This is one of the most striking and oft-quoted quatrains of Nostradamus, as not only does it predict that an English Parliament would commit regicide – an unthinkable event in Nostradamus' day – but its numbering is also signifcant. Quatrain 49 seems to be a hint to the year (1649) in which the execution was to take place.

The Protectorate of Cromwell, 1653–58
VIII.76

> Plus Marcelin que roi en Angleterre
> Lieu obscure nay par force aura l'empire:
> Lasche, sans foi, sans loi saignera terre,
> Son temps approche si presque je soupire.

Translation:

> More Butcher than king in England,
> Born in obscure place by force shall rule the empire:
> Coward, without faith, without law the land bleeds,
> His time approaches so close that I sigh.

If we assume that Nostradamus considered "close" to be within a hundred years of his own death, the only candidate for this gloomy prediction is Oliver Cromwell.

Although a good strategist, Cromwell was also ruthless in battle and may therefore be described as a "butcher" (the Irish certainly thought so). However, to call Cromwell a "coward without faith" seems very unfair.

On 16 December 1653, Cromwell was elected Lord Protector of the Commonwealth for life – a role that gave him almost sovereign powers. Born a gentleman (but of a relatively poor family), Cromwell was popular with the people, but his political power always rested on his control (*"force"*) of the army.

Following Cromwell's death, in 1658, his son Richard took over as Lord Protector. He was not up to filling his father's boots, however, so Richard Cromwell resigned in 1659 and Charles I's son was invited to return and renew the monarchy. Charles II ruled from 1660 to 1685.

The Wreck of the French Fleet, 1655
III.87

> *Classe Gauloise n'approches de Corsegne,*
> *Moins de Sardaigne tu t'en repentiras:*
> *Trestout mourrez frustrez de l'aide grogne,*
> *Sang nagera, captif ne me croiras.*

Translation:

> French fleet, do not come near to Corsica,
> Much less Sardinia or you will regret it:
> You will all die frustrated help from the pig's snout,
> Swimming in blood, captive you will not believe me.

In 1655, much of the French fleet was wrecked in the Gulf of Lyons while sailing past the islands of Corsica and Sardinia. Erica Cheetham notes that the odd-sounding end of the third line contains a typical Nostradamus double meaning. *"Grogne"* could mean both "pig-snout" and "cape" in sixteenth-century French and, in fact, many sailors from the fleet drowned trying to swim to the Cap de Porceau (Cape of the Pig). The "captive" in the last line may have been the fleet's pilot, Jean de Rian, who had, earlier in his career, been enslaved by Algerian pirates.

This quatrain, like many others in the *Centuries*, reads like a dire warning. Yet here, Nostradamus used the same riddling style, devoid of specific details, as elsewhere. Even if Jean de Rian had read the quatrain and believed its warning, he would have had no information with which to save the fleet.

The Great Plague of London, 1665
II.53

> *La grande peste de cité maritime,*
> *Ne cessera mort ne soit vengée*
> *Du juste sang par pris damné sans crime,*
> *De la grand dame par feincte n'outragée.*

Translation:

> The great plague of the maritime city,
> Shall not cease until the death be revenged
> Of the just blood by price condemned without crime,
> Of the great dame not feigned outrage.

Most commentators believe this quatrain refers to the great plague outbreak in London in 1665. Although de Fontbrune suggests it might have, in fact, been a prediction of the 1720 plague outbreak in Marseilles, the former interpretation seems more likely because the third line echoes Nostradamus' indignation concerning the execution of King Charles. The disease arrived on trading vessels and killed thousands before it died out. All those that could walk or ride left London, and to survivors it must have seemed that the wrath of God had struck the city. The outrage of the "great dame" could be a reference to the old St Paul's Cathedral, to which some "unclean" plague victims fled for succour.

The Great Fire of London, 1666
II.51

> *Le sang juste à Londres fera faulte,*
> *Bruslés par fouldres de vingt trois les six:*
> *La dame antique cherra de place haute,*
> *Des mesme secte plusieure seront occis.*

Translation:

> The blood of the just will be required of London,
> Burnt by fire in three times twenty and six:

> The ancient dame shall fall from her high place,
> Of the same sect many shall be killed.

As the reader may have noticed, many of Nostradamus' quatrains are vague to the point of total obscurity. No amount of historical knowledge can help a researcher when the references given by the seer are both nebulous and highly poetic. Therefore, the above quatrain, with its clearly-stated date (66), stands out in the *Centuries* as plainly as a light in the fog. It is often quoted as one of the most convincing pieces of evidence for precognition.

As with *Century II*, quatrain 53 (see above), divine vengeance for the execution of Charles I seems to be regarded by the seer as the cause of a catastrophe befalling London: in this case the Great Fire of 1666.

This blaze, started by accident in a bakery on Pudding Lane, went on unabated for four days and destroyed 13,200 homes. Although amazingly few people were killed, this was due in part to the fact that so many had already died in the previous year's plague outbreak.

The figure given in the second line ($3 \times 20 + 6$) is remarkably accurate, and it should be noted that no other great fire has raged in London during the sixty-sixth year of any century since the time of Nostradamus.

Most commentators agree that the "ancient dame", mentioned in the third line, is the old St Paul's Cathedral – burned during the fire, along with eighty-seven other London churches (perhaps these being those "of the same sect" Nostradamus notes in the last line). Ovason points out that the Bank of England (the "Old Lady of Threadneedle Street") was also burned. Ovason also suggests that the blood of the just was not that of King Charles, but of the Protestant martyrs burnt by Bloody Mary in 1555 and 1556, during the seer's own lifetime.

The Rise of the British Sea Empire: the Mid-seventeenth Century to the Mid-twentieth Century
X.100

> Le grand empire sera par Angleterre,
> Le pempotam des ans plus de trois cens:

> *Grandes copies passer par mer et terre,*
> *Les Lusitainns n'en seront pas contens.*

Translation:

> The great empire will be in England,
> The all-powerful for three hundred years:
> Great armies will travel by land and sea,
> The Portuguese will not be content.

Another remarkable and (this time) quite unambiguous prediction by the seer. England was a third-rate power in Nostradamus' day. In both military and economic strength, the country lagged behind France and Portugal and was even further behind Spain and the Holy Roman Empire. Indeed, Nostradamus' readers in the sixteenth century might well have laughed at this quatrain, much as a Victorian European would have laughed at the idea of Japan becoming a world power.

Many historians date the rise of the British Empire from the reign of Queen Elizabeth I. On the other hand it is arguable that the foundations of the empire were not properly laid until after the English Civil War. If we use this more conservative dating, Nostradamus' three hundred years would take us to the late 1940s and the end of the British Raj in India – the date most historians would give as the end of Britain as a first-rank world power.

The final line of the quatrain may seem odd today, but this is only because Portugal has been so eclipsed by other nations in the last four hundred years. In Nostradamus' day, Portugal was a powerful trading state and had been awarded religious sovereignty over half the world by the Catholic Church. It might have been more accurate for the seer to predict that Spain would be discomforted by the rise of the British Empire but, all things considered, naming Portugal was not too inaccurate.

James II, William of Orange and the "Glorious Revolution",
1688–9
IV.89

> *Trente de Londres secret conjureront,*
> *Contre leur Roi sur le pont entreprinse,*

> *Lui, satalites la mort degousteront.*
> *Un Roi esleu blonde, natif de Frize.*

Translation:

> Thirty Londoners will secretly conspire,
> Against the King on a bridge the plot is made,
> He and his courtiers will not choose death.
> A blond King elected, native of Holland.

Although some students of Nostradamus believe this quatrain predicts the Guy Fawkes gunpowder plot, the last line seems to link it more firmly with the "Glorious Revolution" of 1688-9.

Following the death of King Charles II in 1685, his brother ascended the throne as James II. However, the new king was unpopular with his largely Protestant subjects from the start, because he was a Roman Catholic convert. His haughty and occasionally ruthless behaviour only served to make matters worse.

In 1688, a group of lords secretly asked James' Protestant sister Mary and her husband, William of Orange, to take the throne. William sailed with his Dutch army in November and, on landing and marching to London, found the city open and welcoming. James' troops had, it turned out, deserted him and the king and his close courtiers had fled to France rather than face imprisonment or death. Following a vote in Parliament, William of Orange was crowned William III of Great Britain – the only king in European history to have been elected (*"esleu"*).

Erica Cheetham offers an ingenious explanation of the odd-sounding second line. She suggests that the word "pont" might also indicate a sea crossing – she points out that William of Orange insisted on the English rebel lords secretly crossing to Holland, to sign a document of support, before he would undertake the usurpation of James' throne.

The word "blond" in the last line has proved confusing for many scholars, because William had brown hair. However, David Ovason points out that the word "blond" derives from the old Germanic word for "yellow" – so Nostradamus could have been deviously indicating William's title: "Orange".

11 The Brahan Seer

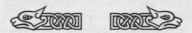

Kenneth Mackenzie, the Brahan seer, whose Gaelic name was Coinneach Odhar, is the most famous of the Scottish soothsayers. In a nation with a traditional place by the fire for the village prophet – whether a minister from the kirk or a descendant of Macbeth's demonic hags – Coinneach Odhar's accuracy of prediction won him a reputation to rival that of Nostradamus in France.

The Brahan seer became known to folklorists fairly late; stories about him were collected in the nineteenth century by writers like Andrew Lang and Hugh Miller, more than two centuries after his death around 1662 (although some had been chronicled by Alexander Cameron of Lochmaddy soon after that date). So, as we might expect, they lack the authenticity of records by actual contemporaries. Nevertheless, the consensus appears to be that he was born of a peasant family in the parish of Uig, on the Isle of Lewis, some time in the early seventeenth century (some say as early as 1600). When he later became a bondsman of the Clan Mackenzie, he moved to their estate at Castle Brahan, near Dingwall, on the coast of the Cromerty Firth.

The Brahan seer's first prediction is said to have saved his own life.

Mackenzie's father was a peasant farmhand, whose status was little better than that of a medieval serf. Even his surname, Odhar, simply meant "mud-coloured". However, his son was not content with a life of virtual slavery, and could be sharp-tongued about the failings of his betters. The story goes that, when he was bonded to a local farmer, he so infuriated the farmer's wife that she decided to murder him.

She waited until her husband sent Odhar off on his own to cut peat in a distant part of the farm. Since it was too far away for him to return for his midday meal, she knew that he would have to go without. So she prepared a bowl of milk and oats (and a noxious herb that would kill him before he could reach help) and took it to him by her own hand.

She found Odhar lying fast asleep on a low hill, known in local folklore as a fairy mound. Rather than wake him, and be invited to share the poisoned meal, the woman laid the bowl beside his shoulder and hurried away. Coinneach awoke, found the food and was about to wolf it down when he felt a cold pressure against his heart. Reaching into his shirt, he found a small, pearly white stone with a natural hole through the middle. (In Celtic mythology, "water-bored" stones were considered particularly lucky.) Holding the stone, Coinneach turned again to the bowl and suddenly knew that the food was poisoned. Lifting the stone to his eye, he even saw the farmer's wife preparing the dose. He tested his suspicion by offering the food to his dog, which ate ravenously and promptly died.

The legend does not say what revenge, if any, Odhar managed to exact, but the power of his first vision is said to have robbed him of sight in one eye.

It is said that Odhar could, if he wished, summon the power of second sight by peering through the hole in the stone, but that most of his prophecies came to him unbidden. This places him firmly within the Celtic tradition of the *taibhsear*: one who sees visions.

In Gaelic Scotland, the *taibhsear* was seen as a creature to pity as much as to respect or fear. His – or her – visions might descend at any moment and were often horrific. Far from cultivating second sight (or "the sight", as it is simply known), many *taibhsears* lived in hermit-like isolation, afraid that company or travel might spark ghastly revelations.

The visions themselves were said to slip into the seer's awareness as smoothly as an optical illusion. One Scottish author, a Dr Beattie, has speculated that the sight of the play of sun or moonlight over the broad landscapes of the Highlands might trigger psychic ability much as flashing lights can cause epileptic fits. Traditionally, the *taibhsear* would close his eyes and bend double if he came upon something that he suspected might be present only to his inner eye. If the vision was still there when he straightened up, then he knew it was real.

Second sight was generally hereditary, but might also be a gift from God, the Devil or some other supernatural agency. It is interesting to note that Coinneach Odhar is said to have had his first vision after sleeping on a "fairy mound". Such protuberances in the landscape are found across the Celtic and Scandinavian countries and usually consist of a prominent hump or an oddly shaped hill. The fairies said to live within were not the charming and childish "little folk" that Victorian authors claimed "lived at the bottom of the garden", but were powerful and dangerous magical beings. Their widely feared resentment led their human neighbours to refer to them as the "Good Folk" or "the Gentry", since even a slightly derogatory remark might lead to anything from a minor accident to violent death. Even today, some farmers refuse to plough over fairy mounds because they believe it will bring bad luck.

Historian Elizabeth Sutherland has suggested that the belief in fairy mounds might date back to the pre-Druidic ancestor worship of the Celts. These people buried their dead in man-made hillocks called barrows, where they would also offer sacrifices, both out of fear of the spirits and hope of their favour. Moreover, many beliefs involving spirit or ancestor worship – such as Japanese Shinto, Cuban Santeria and the Spiritism of Brazil – accept that the dead are able to induce visions of the future. These are not necessarily momentous – in fact, they may be amusingly trivial. On 12 April 1923, at a seance in London, the young medium Stella Cranshaw (better known as Stella C) described the front page of the *Daily Mail* dated 19 May – five weeks hence. She said that she glimpsed the words "Andrew Salt", with a picture of a small boy, and a white powder being poured from a bottle or tin. On that date, half the front page of the *Daily Mail* was taken up with an advertisement for Andrews Liver Salts, showing a small boy pouring the white powder from a tray – an advertisement that, as the makers confirmed, was prepared after the date of the seance.

However, where Kenneth Mackenzie was concerned, common sense suggests that his gifts came neither from the dead nor from the fairies, but that he was born with them. The story of the fairy mound is almost certainly a later accretion, as is another tale to the effect that Odhar's pregnant mother happened to be passing a cemetery when she saw all the dead leaving their graves. She placed her stick over the grave of the last to return to bar access. The latecomer proved to be a beautiful girl who identified herself as the King of Norway's daughter, and who presented the seer's mother with the pierced stone in exchange for allowing her back into her grave. This story has since proved to be an Icelandic legend that had been recruited for service in Odhar's biography.

So we are probably safe to assume that, like so many of his countrymen, the Brahan seer possessed second sight, which he probably inherited, and that tales of murderous farmer's wives and Norwegian princesses are irrelevant.

In due course, Odhar reputation as a prophet came to the attention of the lord of the clan Mackenzie, Kenneth Cabarfeidh (meaning "Staghead") Mackenzie, first Lord of Kintail, who lived in Brahan Castle on the mainland, north-west of Inverness. He summoned Mackenzie around 1622, but died shortly thereafter, and was succeeded by his son, who became the first Earl of Seaforth in 1623. The seer was then living in a farm cottage and working as a labourer, and this hard existence continued throughout the lifetime of both the first and the second earl. So Mackenzie slaved throughout two generations, until the third Earl of Seaforth, whose name was also Kenneth Mackenzie, succeeded to the title. He was roughly the same age as the seer, and seems to have liked him – enough, in fact, to allow him to retire.

The new life plainly agreed with Odhar and, as his fame spread across Scotland, he was invited to visit the homes of other clan leaders. From then onward, the seer is said to have spent much of his life wandering across the Highlands from one castle to another.

There were apparently those who felt that the gloom that characterized Odhar's predictions sprang out of his own rather dour temperament: but historical retrospect suggests that it was due rather to the fact that the centuries following his death were among the grimmest in Scotland's history.

Clan power enjoyed a brief renaissance during the rebellion under Bonny Prince Charlie in 1745, when the Highland clans rose against the English in an attempt to restore the Jacobite crown. They initially enjoyed considerable success, winning several battles with the terrifying Highland charge – a rush of berserk men armed with round shields, axes and claymores. Then at Culloden Moor, near Drummossie, in 1746, the English employed a newly invented weapon: the bayonet.

Owing to the time it took to reload their weapons, Redcoat musketeers were virtually defenceless once they had fired their first shot. At Culloden, however, with a fixed blade on the end of the musket, the English soldiers were, in effect, armed with a heavy spear as well as a rifle. The Highlanders were slaughtered in huge numbers.

At some point, the Earl of Seaforth "lent" Odhar to a gentleman of Inverness, who recorded many of his predictions. Crossing the moor of Culloden, the seer cried out: "Oh, Drummossie! Thy bleak moor shall, before many generations have passed away, be stained with the best blood in the Highlands. Glad I am that I will not see that day, for it will be a fearful time. Heads will be lopped off by the score and no mercy shall be shown or quarter given by either side."

This was duly recorded by the gentleman of Inverness.

After the defeat of Bonnie Prince Charlie, the English repression was long and harsh, culminating in the wholesale "clearances" in the nineteenth century, when thousands of Highland crofters were driven from their farms to allow aristocratic landowners to farm sheep or raise deer for hunting. If this was the future glimpsed by the Brahan seer, his gloomy disposition is understandable.

Coinneach Odhar has never developed an international reputation like that of Nostradamus, but this is not because he was any less accurate in his predictions – if anything, the *taibhsear's* plainness of language makes confirmation of his prophecies easier than for the enigmatic Frenchman. Yet, where Nostradamus described occurrences outside the borders of his own country, Odhar stuck only to events within Scotland and, usually, to whatever area he happened to be viewing at the time. This made his predictions both personal and poignant to his listeners, but less interesting to non-Scots.

The Rev. John Macrae of Dingwall recorded the following story of the Brahan seer. Asked by Macrae's kinsman, the elderly Duncan Macrae of Glenshiel, "by what means he would end his days", Odhar replied that he would die by the sword. That seemed unlikely, since the clan wars – in which Macrae had fought bravely – were over. But in 1654, during the English Civil

War, General Monk led a troop of Parliamentary soldiers to Kintail, and Macrae encountered a company of them in the hills behind his house. Addressed in English, which he did not understand, Macrae put his hand to the hilt of his sword, and was cut down – the only casualty of Monck's expedition.

On another occasion, Odhar announced that "a Lochalsh woman shall weep over the grave of a Frenchman in the burying place of Lochalsh." Again, it seemed unlikely, since there were no Frenchman that far north. Then the third Earl learned that a Lochalsh woman had, in fact, married a French footman, who had died young, and that since then she had been inconsolable, weeping by his grave in Lochalsh.

The seer also made long-term predictions, stating that in the village of Baile Mhuilinn, in west Sutherland, a woman named Annabella Mackenzie (*Baraball n'ic Coinnich*) would die of measles. Two centuries later, in 1860, a woman of that name lived in the village but, since she was ninety-five, seemed more likely to die of old age than disease. However, Odhar proved to be correct, and she died of measles.

Another startling prediction concerned an eight-ton stone that marked the boundary of the estate of Culloden and Moray. The seer spoke of the day when the "Stone of Petty" would be moved from dry land to the sea in Petty Bay. In a great storm on the night of 20 February 1799, the stone was uprooted and was swept 250 yards out to sea.

One prediction seemed so absurd, it led a local who had been writing down the seer's utterances to burn his notes. Standing in Inverness, Odhar gazed up at the neighbouring hill of Tomahurich and said (in his native Gaelic, the only language he spoke): "Strange as it may seem to you this day, time will come, and it is not far off, when full-rigged ships will be seen sailing east and west by the back of yonder hill."

One hundred and fifty years later, the Royal Navy constructed the Great Caledonian Canal, running from the North Sea diagonally south-west to a spot near Glasgow on the opposite coast. The link from the Moray Firth to the head of Loch Ness passed behind Tomahurich Hill.

Another geographical prediction began: "The day will come [his favourite preamble] when the hills of Ross-shire will be strewed with ribbons, and a bridge on every stream."

The seer was plainly talking about roads. In his day, and for some time after, the only Highland roads were rough cattle tracks. Anybody who has read Robert Louis Stevenson's *Kidnapped* will recall that the heroes spend most of their time wading knee-deep in trackless heather. It was not until the late eighteenth century that roads and bridges began to appear in the Highlands.

Odhar is also quoted as saying that there would be "a mill on every stream and a white house on every hillock." The "mill on every stream" sounds like a prediction of the Industrial Revolution. The mention of white houses must have struck his contemporaries as odd, since Gael houses in Odhar's day were invariably black – being roofed with turf and sooted with peat smoke inside and out. However, with the later influx of Lowlanders and English settlers, the whitewashed cottage has become the typical Highland home.

While Odhar's view of Scotland's future gave grounds for optimism, his predictions concerning his countrymen were less so: "The people will degenerate as their country improves and the clans will become so effeminate as to flee from their native country before an army of sheep."

This was hardly tactful. The Highland clans of the time were both powerful and proud; for Odhar to describe their descendants as effeminate might have been regarded as biting the hand that fed him. In Scottish histories dating from the early to mid-nineteenth century, the prediction is listed as "unfulfilled", but from the late nineteenth century the "Highland clearances", the eviction of crofters to make way for sheep farms owned by absentee landlords, suddenly revealed its accuracy. Thousands of legally unrepresented people faced either starvation or emigration. What was left of clan power, following the 1745 rebellion, now vanished forever. With the clearances came a steady drop in Scotland's population that has only showed signs of reversal in the second half of the twentieth century.

Odhar also predicted that: "The ancient proprietors of the soil shall give place to strange merchant proprietors, and the whole of the Highlands will become one huge deer forest; the whole country will become so desolated and depopulated that the crow of a cock shall not be heard north of Druim-Uachdair . . ."

This again sounds like a reference to the clearances.

"The people will emigrate to islands as yet undiscovered or unexplored, but which shall yet be discovered in the boundless

oceans. Afterwards the deer and other wild animals in the huge
wilderness shall be darkened and exterminated by horrid black
rains. The people will then return and take undisputed possession of the lands of their ancestors."

This "black rain", it has been suggested, was the industrial
soot of the nineteenth century – although it could also refer to the
nuclear fallout from the Chernobyl meltdown or the environmental and economic changes brought about by the exploitation
of North Sea oil. Many Scots emigrated to Australia or New
Zealand, "undiscovered" at the time of Odhar's prediction. After
North Sea oil, many Australians, New Zealanders, Texans and
Canadians of Highland descent returned to work on the oil-rigs.

Among his contemporaries, Odhar's reputation was based on
minute but accurate details he scattered through his prophecies.
For example, the Laird of Raasay, of the MacGille-challum
holdings on the Isle of Skye, once asked Odhar about the future
of his clan. The seer's answer was depressing: "When we shall
have a fair-haired Lochiel, a red-headed Lovat, a squint-eyed,
fair-haired Chisholm, a big, deaf Mackenzie and a bow-crook-
legged MacGille-challum, who shall be the great-grandson of
John Beg of Ruiga: he shall be the worst MacGille-challum that
ever came or ever will come. I shall not be in existence in his day
and I have no desire that I should."

The other families named were the owners of lands around the
Macgille-challum clan's own. At the later birth of a clan heir –
who also happened to be a grandson of a John Beg of Ruiga –
delight was mixed was a certain amount of misgiving. The
physical description of the neighbouring lairds given by Odhar,
and the bow-legs of the young MacGille-challum, were accurate.
This last Laird of Raasay was a wild spendthrift and bankrupted
the clan.

As we have seen, many of Odhar's predictions seemed improbable to the point of absurdity. One concerned the village of
Strathpeffer, which stands in a valley a few miles from the western
end of the Cromarty Firth (a long, narrow inlet of the North Sea).
To a visitor standing on the hills above the village, the valley
bottom appears to be below sea level: only a hilly ridge at its
seaward end seems to protect it from flooding. Visiting the valley,
Odhar prophesized: "When five spires rise above Strathpeffer,
ships will sail over the village and hitch cables to their tips."

So seriously did locals take this prediction that, in the early years of the twentieth century, when an Episcopal rector proposed building a church, a petition was raised to beg him not to include a spire on the building. The spire, of course, would bring the number of such edifices to Odhar's fateful five. The rector, knowing that the valley bottom was actually at least three or four feet above sea level, ignored the petition and added a spire to his church. Shortly before the First World War, a small blimp airship was hired to make an appearance at the Strathpeffer Games. By accident, the ship's grapnel line became entangled with the spire of one of the five churches. This seems to have fulfilled the prophesy in an unexpectedly unproblematic way but, with the threat of global warming and of rising sea levels, a threat still hangs over Strathpeffer.

Odhar had another prophecy concerning Strathpeffer: it concerned its sulphurous waters, which the locals shunned as poisonous: "Uninviting and disagreeable as it now is, with its thick crusted surface and unpleasant smell, the day will come when it shall be under lock and key, and crowds of pleasure and health seekers shall be thronging its portals in their eagerness to get a draught of its waters."

In 1818 Strathpeffer became a fashionable spa, and the pump room of its sulphur spring was kept locked.

An equally unlikely prediction was of a disastrous flood from a loch "above Beauly", a small town at the head of the Beauly Firth – there was no loch anywhere near. But in the twentieth century, a dam was built across the river Conon at Torrachilty, a few miles from Beauly, and in 1966 it overflowed and destroyed farm buildings and hundreds of sheep and cows in the village of Conon Bridge, "above Beauly".

Odhar also seems to have predicted the coming of the steam train to the Highlands:

"When there shall be two churches in Ferrintosh, a hand with two thumbs in I-Staina, two bridges in Conon and a man with two navels at Dunean: a black bridleless horse will bring soldiers through the Muir of Ord. I should not like to be alive then."

Local tradition affirms that all these conditions had been met when the railway was laid through the Muir of Ord in the nineteenth century. Whether it has ever carried soldiers is not recorded.

With such a naturally dismal and depressing prophet, it is not surprising that certain of his recorded predictions strike some modern readers as warnings of environmental disaster: "A dun hornless cow will appear in the Minch [an area of sea off Carr Point, near Gairloch] and make a bellow which will knock six chimneys off Gairloch House."

Gairloch House was a fortified structure in Odhar's day; its other name, *Tigh Dige*, meant "house of the ditch" and came from the defensive ditch that ran around it. This prediction caused confusion for some generations, since the house had no chimneys. Its subsequent replacement with a manor house (with the same name) has caused some disquiet, because the new building has six chimneys.

As to the "dun hornless cow", environmentalists have suggested that it might be a nuclear submarine, and that the "bellow" powerful enough to wreck six stone chimneys could be a nuclear explosion.

Eventually, the seer's second sight would lead to his own downfall. The instrument of that downfall was Isabella Mackenzie, third Countess of Seaforth.

Shortly after the Restoration of King Charles II in 1660, Kenneth the Earl of McKenzie-Seaforth was sent by the king on a mission to Paris, leaving his wife Isabella to mind the clan and property. As time went by and neither the Earl, nor any word of him, returned to Brahan, the countess grew increasingly worried. Eventually she sent for Coinneach Odhar and asked him to scry out the truth. The *taibhsear* replied that he was only occasionally able to force the sight to come, but when he gazed through the hole in his seeing-stone, he broke into one of his rare smiles.

"Madam," he is said to have announced, "there is no need to worry concerning your husband's welfare. He is well and merry."

When she pressed him further, the seer replied that the Earl was staying in a luxurious house with fine company in a foreign place he could only assume was Paris. As she asked for further details, any man of common sense would have claimed he could see nothing more, or at least asked to speak to the countess alone – for this encounter took place among a large gathering of family and principal retainers. Instead he seems to have allowed himself to succumb to his customary testiness, and told the countess that her husband was "on his knees before a fair lady".

She was naturally furious. Tradition has it that she was an unpopular mistress, and also that she was herself "wanton". If

Odhar's "sight" could reveal her husband's infidelity, it might come to rest on her own. Whatever the reason, she used her power as her husband's authorized representative to condemn him to death as a witch, for which the punishment was to be burned alive in a barrel of tar. Her decision had to be ratified by the elders of the Kirk, but they knew better than to cross the countess – or perhaps they genuinely felt that Odhar's powers came from the Devil. (Although the accession of Charles II brought a reduction of witch trials in England, in Scotland they reached a high point.) So they upheld the death sentence, and the seer was taken to the Presbytery at Chanonry Point, on the Moray Firth, for execution.

Awaiting death, the seer made the following prophecy:

> "I look into the future and I see the doom of the race of my oppressor. The long-descended line of Seaforth will, ere many generations have passed, end in extinction and sorrow. I see a chief, the last of his house, both deaf and dumb. His four sons will go to the tomb before him, one dying on the water, and he shall die in misery, knowing that his line is extinguished. No more Mackenzie men will rule over Brahan and Kintail.
>
> "His possessions will be handed to a white-hooded lass from the east, and she will kill her own sister.
>
> "It shall be known that these things are coming to pass by the existence of four great lairds – Gairloch, Chisholm, Grant and Ramsey – of whom one will be buck-toothed, another hare-lipped, another half-witted and the fourth a stammerer.

There would also, he said, be a "stag-like" Laird of Tulloch, who would kill four of his wives, although a fifth would survive him.

> "When the last Laird of Seaforth looks around him and sees his neighbours are these men, he will know his sons are doomed and his line ended."

It is said that he then hurled the "seeing stone" into Loch Ussie.

When the Countess told him that he would never go to heaven, Odhar replied: "I think I shall, but you will not. After my death, a raven and a dove shall meet above my ashes. If the raven lands first, you are right. If the dove, my word is truth."

When the barrel of tar – and the seer – had been reduced to ashes and cooled down, a dove and a raven were seen hovering over the remains; the dove, according to witnesses, landed first.

The seer was executed – probably in 1662 – near the modern Chanonry Point lighthouse, by the road from Fortrose to Fort George ferry, and the place is marked with a stone slab. What happened to the countess and her errant husband is, unfortunately, not recorded.

The history of the next century and a half bore out the seer's prophecies. In 1715 the Seaforths took part in the Jacobite risings against George I, and lost their titles, but these were restored in 1726. The Seaforths became staunch Hanoverians and prospered during the following decades. Although the title ceased to exist in 1781, when its holder died without an heir, the position of head of the Clan Mackenzie passed to a second cousin, Francis Humberstone Mackenzie. It was he who gave his name to the Seaforth Highlanders regiment, which he raised to fight in the revolutionary wars with France which began in 1793. In 1797 he was created Baron Seaforth of Kintail, became Governor of Barbados, and was a patron of Sir Humphrey Davey and the painter Sir Thomas Lawrence.

Yet this favourite of fortune was deaf, as a result of an outbreak of scarlet fever in his boarding school when he was twelve; later in life, his speech became affected and he would only communicate by writing notes. As the seer predicted, he was deaf and dumb.

His four sons died: the first, William, as a baby, the second, George, at the age of six, the third, Francis – a midshipman in the Royal Navy – in a skirmish at sea ("dying on the water"), the last, William Frederick – an MP for Ross – in 1814, of a particularly lingering and painful disease. At one point, when it seemed that William Frederick might pull through, an old family retainer was heard to comment: "Na, na, he'll nay recover. It's decreed that Seaforth must outlive his four sons." The grief-stricken Baron Seaforth would, in fact, die in the following year, 1815.

As the Edinburgh *Daily Review* pointed out in its obituary, Seaforth's neighbours were the buck-toothed Sir Hector Mackenzie of Gairloch, the hare-lipped Chisholm of Chisholm, the retarded Laird Grant, and the stammering MacLeod of Ramsay.

As Odhar foretold, Mackenzie's eldest daughter, Mary, who had married Admiral Sir Samuel Hood, returned from the East Indian station, where her husband had just died, to take over her father's estate, and her formal mourning dress included a white hood. One day, she was driving her younger sister, the Hon. Caroline Mackenzie, through the woods when the ponies bolted and the trap overturned; she was only injured but her sister died.

The Laird of Tulloch mentioned by the seer was a well-known ladies' man, and he might be said to have killed four of his wives in that they died in childbirth, presenting him, between them, with eighteen children. Because he was known as also having fathered thirty illegitimate offspring, he was known as "the stag". (Odhar called him "staglike".)

The widow Hood eventually married a man called Stewart and, over the decades, the Seaforth lands were gradually sold off by the Stewart-Mackenzies. In 1921, it seemed that Odhar's prophecy of the end of the Seaforth line might be inaccurate, when James Mackenzie-Stewart was created Baron of Seaforth and Brahan, but sadly he died without issue two years later and the title became extinct once again.

In 1877, the respected historian Alexander Mackenzie published *The Prophecies of the Brahan Seer*, which quickly became a bestseller in Scotland. In this book he freely admitted that almost all of his source material came from oral traditions, but added that since most Highland history has been passed down this way, he felt justified in its serious presentation.

In her conclusion to the 1977 edition of Mackenzie's *Brahan Seer*, the historian Elizabeth Sutherland hypothesizes that Coinneach Odhar might never have existed as an actual individual. Instead, she suggests, he might be a conglomeration of hundreds of years of *taibhsear* folklore – much as some historians believe the myth of King Arthur might be based on the exploits of several real warlords of post-Roman, Dark Age Britain. Understandably, most Scots reject the idea with contempt, just as most Englishmen reject the notion that King Arthur never existed.

But Elizabeth Sutherland mentions one intriguing piece of evidence for her thesis. After pointing out that there is no record that the Countess Isabella ever had a man burned to death, she suggests that the story may spring from a confusion with the case of Lady Catherine Munro of Foulis, seventy years earlier.

Lady Catherine was publicly tried for murder, attempted

murder and witchcraft in 1590. The Crown's accusation was that, thirteen years earlier, Catherine had tried to murder her stepson and her sister-in-law, first through the spells of several local witches, then by poisoning. In the course of testing the dosage of ratsbane to be used on her relatives, she was also said to have killed two servants. An Edinburgh jury packed with her relatives acquitted her, but the confessions of her magic-dabbling co-conspirators tainted her reputation for life.

We might feel justified in dismissing this identification of Countess Isabella with Lady Catherine Munro as far-fetched, but Elizabeth Sutherland supports it by pointing out that one of the male witches said to have aided Lady Munro, and later executed for dealing with the Devil, was named Coinneach Odhar.

Against this "collective" hypothesis, we can set the fact that so many of the predictions of the Brahan seer are highly specific and concern contemporaries connected with his part of the Highlands – and, of course, that so many of them later came true. With such a legacy, the Brahan seer's place in the history of prophecy is assured.

12 Nostradamus and the Eighteenth Century

For all his confusing obscurity, Nostradamus offers at least some notion of the time frame he has in mind – that is, how far into the future his prophecies stretched. *Century I*, quatrain 48 reads:

> *Vingt ans du regne de la lune passez,*
> *Sept mil ans autr tiendra sa monarchie:*
> *Quand le soleil prendra ses jours lassez,*
> *Lors accomplit et mine ma prophetie.*

Translation:

> Twenty years or the reign of the moon having passed,
> Seven thousand years another will hold its monarchy:
> When the sun ends his tired days,
> Then fulfilled and ends my prophecy.

The astrological "great lunar year" is equivalent to 320 solar years. Erica Cheetham points out that the great lunar cycle during which Nostradamus wrote the *Centuries* began in 1535. Thus 1535, plus twenty years (as mentioned in the first line) gives the year 1555 – the date the first book of *Centuries* was published. The second line, adding seven thousand years, therefore gives us the date 8555 AD.

On the other hand, *The Prophecies and Enigmas of Nostradamus* (editor Liberte E. LaVert) suggests the reader should multiply the twenty by the 320 years of the great lunar year. The result is 6,400. If we add 555 (1555, minus the thousand which Nostradamus himself would often leave out in the quatrains) we get 6,955 . . . just 45 years short of 7000 AD.

Of course, neither of these arguments can claim to be conclusive, but unless readers expect to live another five or six thousand years, the debate is rather academic. The one certainty about the above quatrain is that Nostradamus claims his prophecies stretch many millennia into the future.

If one expected the quatrains to be evenly spread over a 7000-year period, one could expect an average of thirteen or fourteen predictions to correspond to each hundred years. However, as the reader will doubtless have already realized, Nostradamus had his own ideas about distribution, and did not adhere to such a simple set of rules.

Nostradamus scholars claim to recognize "clusters" of predictions, concentrating on periods of history involving the seer's main obsessions – chiefly France, regicide and the fate of the Christian church. So it is hardly surprising that a disproportionate number of quatrains have been assumed to be about the last twelve years of the eighteenth century: the period of the French Revolution, the execution of Louis XVI, the suppression of the Catholic church in France and the rise of Napoleon. Of 952 quatrains, at least sixty are thought to cover the period between 1789 to 1800.

Nostradamus introduced the first edition of *Century VII* with an open letter to Henri II (the king whose death he had unobtrusively predicted in *Century I*, quatrain 35). Couched in the sycophantic tones that were expected of a writer addressing his royal patron,[1] and full of unusually obscure predictions – even for Nostradamus – the letter contains a sentence that leaves the reader feeling slightly stunned:

"Then the beginning of that year shall see a greater persecution against the Christian church than ever was in

1 "I have been ever since perpetually dazzled, continually honouring and worshipping that day, in which I presented myself before [Henri's 'immeasurable Majesty']." Introduction, *Century VII*.

Africa,[2] and it shall be in the year 1792, at which time everyone will think it a renovation of the age."

1792 was, of course, the turning point of the French Revolution. It was the year that saw the unsuccessful attempt to change France from a monarchical dictatorship to a democracy headed by a constitutional monarch – an attempt that soon collapsed into republican revolution. In the resultant bloodshed the king was guillotined and the Catholic church was persecuted. Tens of thousands of people were executed for "crimes against the people" – the first but certainly not the last time in European history that this charge would be used. Yet out of that brutal chaos there emerged a new liberal philosophy that would change politics forever. Just as Nostradamus predicted, it was "a renovation of the age".'

The Wars of 1700 (or 2025)
I.49

> Beaucoup, beaucoup avant telles menées,
> Ceux d'orient pat la vertu lunaire:
> L'an mil sept cens feront grands emmenées,
> Subjugant presque le coing Aquilonaire.

Translation:

> Long, long before these happenings,
> The people of the Orient influenced by the moon:
> In the year 1700 shall carry away great multitudes,
> Subjugating most of the Northern region.

This is one of the more confusing of the quatrains. Although one of the few to give a specific date, it is baffling in that the year 1700 hardly seems a turning point in history. If the figure is actually a Nostradamus riddle, it has yet to be solved.

The second line may refer to the Turks, whose banner was the crescent moon. The third and fourth lines describe this nation "influenced by the moon" sweeping away "multitudes" in 1700

2 Probably a reference to the Vandal persecution of Orthodox Christians in North Africa during the fourth and fifth centuries AD.

and conquering most of "Aquilonaire" (from the Latin *aquilonaris*, meaning "northern").

In 1700 AD, the Russians under Peter the Great defeated the Turks and took the towns of Azov and Kouban. At the same time, Charles XII of Sweden took Iceland and Peter the Great, as a result, declared war on him (this later became known as "the Great Northern War"). Although these were momentous actions in themselves, they do not seem to match the "subjugation" described by the quatrain, nor were the "people of the Orient" the winners. Even the seer's admirers concede that this prediction seems to be a "miss".

However, in *The Complete Prophecies of Nostradamus*, Henry C. Roberts suggests that Nostradamus started his dating not from 1 AD, but from the First Council of Nicaea[3] in 325 AD. Thus, if 325 is added to 1700, the result is 2025 AD. Roberts goes on to suggest that the quatrain predicts the invasion of Russia by China in the twenty-first century.

A Century of Turmoil, 1702–1802
I.51

> *Chef d'Aries, Jupiter et Saturne,*
> *Dieu eternel quelles mutations!*
> *Puis par long siecle son maling temps retourne*
> *Gaule, et Italie quelles emotions!*

Translation:

> Heads of Aries, Jupiter and Saturn,
> Oh eternal God what changes!
> After a long century evil times return
> France and Italy, what turmoil!

3 This was the fundamental debate over the future direction of Christianity. Father Arius of Alexandria insisted that Jesus was merely a human being and was therefore only a prophet, like Moses or Abraham. Athanasius (later Saint Athanasius) countered that Jesus was of the same substance as God and therefore was God himself. Athanasius won the argument and denounced Arius as a heretic.

Nostradamus, the grandson of a Jewish convert, may have considered this debate all important because it was there that Christianity finally divorced itself from its Jewish roots.

As we saw in the chapter on Nostradamus and astrology, his use of astrological imagery in the *Centuries* is apparently aimed at giving a rough dating system.

The first line mentions the planets Jupiter and Saturn and the sign of Aries. Since Jupiter and Saturn are both slow-orbiting planets, they align very rarely. The first alignment of Jupiter and Saturn in the House of Aries following the publication of the *Centuries* took place on 13 December 1702. The quatrain clearly predicts a turbulent century following this date and, indeed, the eighteenth century was an age of new invention, educated enlightenment and bloody revolution.

This interpretation is strengthened by the prediction in the third and fourth lines: that "evil times" will return after a "long century", shaking France and Italy. By 1802, Napoleon Bonaparte had consolidated his dictatorship of France and had conquered Northern Italy. Although this was a victory for the French Republic, the other major European powers became alarmed by Napoleon's expansionist policy and dedicated themselves to his destruction. The next thirteen years[4] were among the bloodiest in Europe's history – arguably an "evil time", even when compared to the upheavals of the previous century.

It should be noted in passing that the next conjunction of Jupiter and Saturn in Aries after 1702 was 2 September 1995. If the above interpretation of *Century I*, quatrain 51 is incorrect, then we ourselves may be facing a changeable century ahead.

French Wars in 1580 and 1703
VI.2

> *En l'an cinq cens octante plus et moins,*
> *On attendra le siecle bien estrange:*
> *En l'an sept cens, et trois (cieux en tesmoings)*
> *Que plusieurs regnesun à cinq feront change.*

Translation:

> In the year five hundred eighty more or less,
> There shall be a strange age:

4 Culminating with Napoleon's defeat at Waterloo.

In the year seven hundred and three (witness heaven)
Many kingdoms one to five shall be changed.

Erica Cheetham suggests that this quatrain predicts two periods of war in France. In 1580 (Nostradamus probably left out the thousands on the dates, for the sake of scansion) France was in the midst of the so-called "Seventh War": a religious civil war fuelled by the St Bartholomew's Day Massacre of Parisian Protestants in 1572. In 1703, Louis XIV was obstinately involving France in the Spanish War of Succession (see IV.2 and IV.5, later in this chapter). Cheetham suggests that the phrase "kingdoms one to five" in the last line refers to the lands that the war won for Philip V, Louis' grandson. On his accession to the Spanish throne Philip was, on paper at least, the ruler of Spain, Sicily, Milan, the Netherlands and America.

Henry Roberts, using his own eccentric dating system based on the Council of Nicaea (see I.49 above), adds 325 years to the above years and suggests 1914 (he assumes "580 more or less" equates to 1589) and 2028 AD. The first date, the beginning of World War I, was indeed a "strange age". From the second date, Roberts predicts there will be a "complete change in the line-up of nations".

The Spanish War of Succession, 1701–13
IV.2 & IV.5.

> *Par mort France prendra voyage à faire,*
> *Classe par mer, marcher monts Pyrenées,*
> *Espaigne en trouble, marcher gent militaire:*
> *Des plus grand Dames en France emmenées.*

Translation:

> By reason of a death France shall undertake a journey,
> Fleet at sea, marching troops over the Pyrenean mountains.
> Spain shall be in trouble, an army marches:
> Some great ladies carried away to France.

A French military intervention into Spain is clearly described here. Most Nostradamus scholars believe the quatrain to be a prediction of the Spanish War of Succession, which took place between 1701 and 1713.

In 1700, Charles II of Spain died, bequeathing his kingdom to Philip, Duke of Anjou. Although Philip was only related to the Spanish royal family through marriage, the issue would probably have passed without controversy had the new Spanish king not also been the grandson of Louis XIV of France. The joining of the two thrones under the ambitious Bourbon family was more than the other powers of Europe could tolerate. In 1701, England, Austria, the Netherlands, Denmark and, later, Portugal formed a coalition to remove Philip V from the Spanish throne. France and Spain naturally opposed them and war was declared.

The death mentioned in line one of the quatrain would thus be that of Charles II, and the "journey" could be that of Philip from Anjou (in France) to be crowned in Madrid. The second and third lines seem self-explanatory: France sends fleets and armies to aid Spain, the latter crossing the Pyrenees Mountains, which form a natural border between the two countries.

Erica Cheetham suggests that line four is a reference to the beginning of the whole affair. Some years before, two Spanish princesses were married into the French branch of the House of Bourbon, guaranteeing trouble if Charles II died without a male heir – as indeed he did.

> *Coix paix, soubz un accompli divin verbe,*
> *L'Espaigne et Gaul seront unis ensemble:*
> *Grand clade proche, et combat tresacerbe,*
> *Coeur si hardi ne sera qui ne tremble.*

Translation:

> Cross peace, under an accomplished divine word,
> Spain and France shall be united:
> A great disaster, and savage fighting,
> No heart so brave that will not tremble.

The peace "under an accomplished divine word", mentioned in the first line, might be Clement XI's papal bull of 1713. Although this bull had nothing to do with the Spanish War of Succession, Clement was an active peace-broker during the conflict and published his *Vineam Unigenitus* in the year that an armistice was finally achieved. The remaining three lines accurately describe the cause of the war (the political joining of the French and Spanish thrones) and the savagery of the fighting.

In 1711, after ten years of war across Europe, France and Spain were close to defeat on all fronts. However, Britain then decided that total victory might make the Austrian Empire too powerful, so the British government unilaterally offered peace to the Bourbon faction. Having lost such an important member, the "Grand Alliance" promptly collapsed. Individual peace treaties were signed by the separate nations over the next two years and, ironically, Philip V was allowed to keep the Spanish throne.

The Reign of Louis XV of France, 1715–74
III.15 & III.14

> Coeur, rigeur, gloire le regne changera,
> De tous points contre ayant son adversaire,
> Lors France enfance par mort subjuguera,
> Un grand regent sera lors plus contraire.

Translation:

> Heart, vigour, glory shall change in the kingdom,
> In all points having an adversary opposing,
> Then France will be ruled by a child through a death,
> The great regent will be very contrary.

Louis XIV of France died in 1715 – seventy-seven years old and exhausted from his efforts to win the Spanish War of Succession. His son was immediately crowned Louis XV. However, as Louis was only five at the time, Philippe Duc d'Orleans was made Regent. He was to rule France until 1723, when the king reached the minimum legal age of majority.[5]

Unfortunately France, which only a few decades before had been one of the strongest powers in Europe, was physically and

---

5 This was the first time a regent had ruled France since the publication of the *Centuries*.

financially exhausted, thanks to Louis XIV's foreign wars. Thus the Duc d'Orleans did indeed find the regency a "contrary" task, as noted in the last line of the quatrain. On the over-optimistic advice of a Scottish financier called John Law, Philippe printed vast sums of paper money (then a new invention) which caused inflation to go through the roof and, in 1721, bankrupted the whole nation.

> *Par le rameau du vaillant personnage,*
> *De France infime, par le pere infelice:*
> *Honneurs, richesses, travail en son vieil age*
> *Pour avoir creu le conseil d'homme nice.*

Translation:

> By the branch of the valiant person,
> Of weak France, through the unhappy father:
> Honours, riches, labour in his old age,
> For having believed the council of a nice man.

Louis XV, the son (and branch) of the valiant Louis XIV, was only thirteen when he took control of the now benighted nation. The reference to "the unhappy father" in line two might be a comment on the parental failing of Louis XIV: by fighting pointless wars and not producing a son earlier in his life, the old king left his very young heir with a huge task of reconstruction.

On the other hand, the word "father" may be another Nostradamus pun. In 1726, Louis XV appointed his old priest and tutor as Prime Minister. Father Fleury did his best over the next seventeen years and succeeded in partially stabilizing the economy. Unfortunately, in doing so, he imposed draconian taxes on the peasantry and effectively sowed the seeds of later revolution.

Louis XV was a lazy monarch and, for most of his 59-year reign, left the task of running France to his ministers. The result was gross corruption and mismanagement. Over a few decades, the British annexed most of France's overseas holdings, thanks to France's feeble generals. The "bourgeoisie" – the merchant class that had done very well in Louis XIV's prosperous reign – were taxed unmercifully and the French peasants were treated little better than serfs. At the same time, the clergy and nobility were exempted from all state tariffs. By the 1770s, the national situation was one of stagnation, decadence and growing social unrest.

Belatedly, in the last four years of his life, Louis XV realized that reform was urgently needed and took steps to balance matters. He restricted the rights of the nobility – who generally felt themselves to be above the law when dealing with "inferiors" – and imposed taxes on the church and the gentry. Unfortunately, his self-serving court officials blocked him at every possible juncture and the tremendous effort drove him to an early grave. This might be what Nostradamus was referring to in the last two lines of the quatrain. Louis lived a life of honour and riches, then spent his last years labouring to redress the work of Father Fleury (a "nice" but politically short-sighted man – *nice*, oddly enough, is an old French word.)

The King's efforts were all wasted. Louis' grandson, crowned Louis XVI, was as lazy and weak-willed as Louis XV had been as a young man. Within only a few years, the bureaucracy and nobility had reversed all Louis XV's reforms and France was on course for bloody revolution.

The Turkish/Persian Armistice, October 1727
III.77

> Le tiers sous Aries comprins,
> L'an mil sept cens vingt et sept en Octobre:
> Le Roy de Perse par ceux d'Egypte prins:
> Conflit, mort, perte: à la croix grand approbre.

Translation:

> The third climate comprised under Aries,
> In the year one thousand seven hundred twenty seven
>   in October:
> The King of Persia shall be taken by those of Egypt:
>   Conflict, death, loss, to the cross great shame.

This is another of the rare quatrains that contains an apparently precise date. While Henry C. Roberts translates the second line to read, "In the year 2025, the 27th of October",[6] other

6 He does this by adding 325 (see I. 49 above) to 1700 and adding a useful – if not wholly justified – comma to get the date, 27th October.

scholars – like Erica Cheetham and David Ovason – have little doubt that this is an accurate description of Middle-Eastern events in October 1727.

In that month, Shah Ashraf signed a peace treaty with the Ottoman Empire, ceding most of western Persia to them. (The word "Egypt" in the quatrain might signify the Turks, as it was then the most significant asset of their empire.) The Ottoman Turks, in return, ceased their invasion plans and formally recognized the validity of Ashraf's dynasty. Although the third line may seem to flatly contradict this interpretation – describing as it does the "taking" of the King of Persia – David Ovason believes that Nostradamus was indirectly describing the ignominious loss of half the Shah's kingdom. Ironically, Shah Ashraf did not live long to enjoy the peace for which he had paid such a tremendous price. He died the following year, in 1728.

The first line of the quatrain may seem rather obscure, but David Ovason points out that it is, in fact, a remarkably precise description of the land areas involved in the peace treaty of 1727. The term "third climate" comes from the work of the Arabic astrologer, Alfraganus. He divided the globe into seven *climata*, or "climates", creating a working, if rather arbitrary, system of latitudes. The "third climate" stretched, approximately, between twenty-eight and thirty-four degrees north, and included most of Persia, Afghanistan, Iraq and Arabia.

The second part of the line adds "under Aries", and Ovason points out that this is a reference to Ptolemaic astrology. Ptolemy invented a system called *"chorography"*, under which each country and land area was assigned to a particular zodiac sign. Persia, in this system, falls under Taurus, but Aries controls Syria, Palestine, Edom and Judaea – in fact, the precise area that Shah Ashraf ceded to the Turks. Thus, "the third climate comprised under Aries" may translate as "the Persian Empire, specifically the western provinces".

Despite this remarkable accuracy, the last line describing "conflict, death, loss, to the cross great shame" seems to have nothing to do with the rest of the prophecy. War was avoided and the Christians – who Nostradamus often signified with *la croix* – had nothing to do with the matter. Ovason again offers an explanation: he points out that the modern solidification of Islamic power dates from the treaty of 1727. As we have already seen, Nostradamus seems to have shared his contemporaries' horror of the Ottoman expansion and of Islam in general. Perhaps, says Ovason, the seer was summing-up, in eight words, the entire history of mistrust and outright bloodshed between Christians and Moslems since 1727.

Catherine the Great of Russia, 1729–96
VIII.15

> *Vers Aquilon grans efforts par hommasse*
> *Presque l'Europe et l'univers vexer,*
> *Les deux eclipse mettra en tel chasse,*
> *Et aux Pannons vie et mort renforcer.*

Translation:

> Towards the North great efforts by the masculine woman
> To vex Europe and the universe,
> The two eclipses will be put to flight,
> And will enforce the life and death of the Poles.

Several commentators take this quatrain to be a prediction of the rule of Russia's Catherine II.

Catherine was the wife of Grand Duke Peter of Holstein, the heir to the Russian throne (although he was actually a German). The Grand Duke was crowned Tsar Peter III in 1762, but was so dismissive of his new subjects that he was dethroned by the Imperial Guard within six months. Catherine, on the other hand, had gone out of her way to woo the Russian nobility, so now found herself crowned as ruling Empress. Peter was murdered a few days after he agreed to abdicate.

Catherine was an intelligent, strong-willed woman. A capable Commander-in-Chief, during her 34-year rule she won several wars, expanded Russia's borders and put down a major Cossack uprising. She was, at the same time, well versed in the liberal attitudes of the Enlightenment, but towards the latter part of her rule became increasingly oppressive and reactionary.

Her love affairs were legendary in her own lifetime; she had numerous lovers – ten of whom she made virtual consorts – and, when she died at the age of sixty-seven, the rumour went about that she had been crushed to death while copulating with a stallion.

Although this last scandal was a malicious falsehood,[7] it does give an indication of how much she impressed and worried her contemporaries. In an age when most women were still little better than chattels, Catherine earned her title, "the Great", and frightened Europe in much the same way that Napoleon would a few decades later.

The first line of the quatrain mentions "the North"[8] with a capital letter, as if it were a separate country or place. David Ovason also notes that, in Latin, *aquila* means "eagle". He suggests that Nostradamus was employing a double meaning: i.e. a northern country connected with an eagle. Imperial Russia's symbol was the double-headed eagle. Since the time of Nostradamus, Catherine II has been the only female ruler of Russia, and she was certainly a "masculine woman" in her style of leadership, all as described in the quatrain.

The second line describes the vexatious effect of the *"hom-masse"* on Europe and, rather improbably, "the universe". The first certainly fits Catherine, and Ovason offers a rather ingenious explanation of the second. The term *"l'univers"* may also be rearranged as *luni vers*: Latin for "towards the moon". This may give us the key to line three, which describes two eclipses being put to flight. If, says Ovason, we consider these eclipses to be Earth's shadow on the moon, we may see a poetic description of Catherine's two successful wars on the Ottoman Empire (whose symbol was the sickle moon).

It is the last line that leads most commentators to agree that Catherine is the subject of the quatrain. Throughout the late eighteenth century, Russia, Prussia (now Germany) and the Austrian Empire teetered on the brink of war. The main bone of contention was the buffer-area between them: Poland. In 1772 and 1793, these three super-states sliced off huge sections of Polish territory to be divided amongst themselves: the so-called "Partitions". Finally, in 1795, following a failed attempt at revolt in what was left of Poland, Catherine presided over the total division of Polish lands, removing the hapless nation from the map for 125 years. The Poles became serfs to the greater Russian

7 Catherine died of a stroke. Her lover, at the time, was a perfectly normal young man, forty years her junior.
8 *"Aquilon"*, derived from the Latin *aquilonius*, meaning "northern".

nation and, in the last year of her life, Catherine was the final arbiter of life and death over most of the Polish people.

The First Balloon and the Imprisoned Pope, 1783 & 1797
V.57

> Istra du Mont Gaulfier et Aventin,
> Qui par trou avertira l'armeé :
> Entre deux rocs sera prins le butin,
> De SEXT. mansol faillir le renommée.

Translation:

> One shall go out from Mount Gaulfier and Aventine,
> Who through a hole shall give notice to the army:
> Between two rocks the prize will be taken,
> Of SEXT. the Sun shall fail in renown.

This is one of Nostradamus' truly stunning predictions.

The Montgolfier brothers invented and launched the first hot air balloon in France, in 1783. Nostradamus' apparent pun on their name is too precise to be easily dismissed. Even the inventors' nationality is apparently hinted at by the seer: "Gaul" was the Latin name for France.

The balloon was utilized as a scouting device by French generals, aiding the Republican army's victory at the Battle of Flaurus in Belgium eleven years later. This battle consolidated French military power. This, in turn, allowed them to sack Rome in 1797. One of the Seven Hills of Rome is the "Aventine", the last word of line one.

Erica Cheetham suggests that the word "SEXT" in the last line is a shortening of "Sextus", and that "mansol" is derived from manens solus – "he who is solitary" – a reference, she says, to pontifical chastity. She believes that prediction in this line indicates Pope Pius VI – one of only two Popes since Nostradamus' day to be designated "Sextus".

Pope Pius VI was strongly opposed to the French Revolution, but was captured when Napoleon took Rome in 1797. The pontiff was forced to cede large areas of church land to the French – the "rocks", according to Cheetham, upon which the pope's temporal power was based. Pius VI died in captivity in 1799 (see below).

The Beginning of the French Revolution, 1789–92
VI.23, I.53 & V.5

> D'esprit de regne munismes descriées,
> Et soront peuples esmuez contre leur Roi:
> Paix, faict nouveau, sainctes loix empirées,
> Rapis oncfut en si tres dur arroi.

Translation:

> Defences undermined by the spirit of the kingdom,
> The people will be stirred up against their King:
> Peace, new made, sacred laws degenerate,
> Rapis never was in such great trouble.

By the late 1780s, France was on the edge of social and economic collapse. The lower orders were taxed to the hilt while the tax-exempted nobility wasted money like fools. King Louis XVI was aware of the problem and, over the previous decade, had assigned several reforming ministers to the problem. However, as he invariably failed to support them when they faced the vested interest groups at court and in the church, these men always failed.

In 1788, Louis was forced to call elections to the Estates-General: a parliament equally composed of nobility, clergy and commoners. (National democracy had been unknown in France since 1614.) The King hoped that a legislative body with lesser powers to his own might win peace with his critics, but the nobility and clergy tried to gang together to suppress the commoners and created even greater tensions. Thus the third line of the above quatrain might be describing this "new made" "peace," undermined by the "sacred laws" and entrenched attitudes of the right-wing factions.

"*Rapis*", mentioned in the last line, is almost certainly an anagram of "Paris" – the seer uses the word in several other quatrains in which he seems to have the French capital in mind. As the tensions within the Estates-General increased, the starving population of Paris became the centre of the growing insurrection and anti-monarchist movements.

> *Las qu'on verra grand peuple tourmenté,*
> *Et la loi saincte en totale ruine:*
> *Par autres loix toute la Christienté,*
> *Quant d'or d'argent trouve nouvelle mine.*

Translation:

> Alas how the great people will be tormented,
> And the holy laws in total ruin:
> By other laws Christianity is troubled,
> When new mines of gold and silver are found.

Matters were going rapidly downhill. In June 1789, the commons section of the Estates-General formed their own legislative body – the National Assembly – and voted themselves sole tax-gathering powers. When Louis ineffectually tried to suppress them, they retaliated by vowing to draft a constitution for France (thus threatening Louis with either a constitutional, legally restricted monarchy or an outright republic). In the face of growing insurrection, Louis capitulated and recognized the National Assembly as the new legislative body.

A few days later, on 14 July, the Parisian mob stormed, captured and demolished the hated Bastille prison on the bank of the Seine. Fearing further escalation of violence, the National Assembly quickly drafted the new constitution and issued 400 million *assignats* – paper money secured on the value of confiscated church and Crown lands. This helped to stabilize the economy for a short time, but inevitably sent inflation rocketing.

This issue of paper bills – as opposed to the more usual gold and silver coinage – may be what Nostradamus is referring to in the last line of the quatrain. The other three lines seem to concern the Assembly's disestablishment of the French Catholic church in 1790. Under the new constitution, priests and bishops were to be created only by the election of the populace, monastic orders were disbanded, church lands seized and all clergy had to swear allegiance to the state. Nostradamus would have been shocked by this humiliation of the church, and some scholars hear an echo of his prophetic anger in the above quatrain.

Souz ombre faincte d'oster de servitude,
Peuple et cité l'usurpera lui mesmes:
Pire fera par fraux de jeune pute,
Livré au champ lisant le faux proesme.

Translation:

Under the feigned pretext of removing servitude,
People and city usurp power:
He will do worse because of the trickery of a young whore,
Betrayed in the field delivering a false promise.

Following the storming of the Bastille, the people of Paris exercised great power of fear over the National Assembly, and the more radical and republican leaders used the threat of the mob to win themselves greater political leverage. This may be what Nostradamus is referring to in the first two lines above.

Louis XVI ruefully accepted his new role as a constitutional monarch, but soon found himself under house arrest in the Palais des Tuileries. Unfortunately, although the king retained the loyalty of many sections of French society, his popularity was undermined by the actions of his wife, the Queen consort, Marie Antoinette.

Popular history has recorded Marie Antoinette as a rather dim-witted[9] and out-of-touch woman. In fact, she actively connived with the reactionary elements of the National Assembly and openly corresponded with her brother, Emperor Leopold II. This last may seem natural enough, but the Holy Roman Emperor was violently opposed to state reform and was threatening war to topple the French constitutionists. An unpopular foreign national to begin with, Marie Antoinette's virtual acts of treason against France did much to get herself and her husband condemned. Nostradamus, if line three is indeed about the queen, clearly disliked her as much as her republican enemies.

The last line of the quatrain may refer to the false promise

9 Famously, when told that the poor were rioting because they had no bread, she remarked: "Let them eat cake . . ."

Louis gave to his captors, when he said he would not try to escape
– he and his family were originally held captive to protect them
from the mob. However, in 1791, the family tried to escape to
Austria, but were captured while still in the French countryside,
or "in the field".

Milk and Honey, Blood and Quicklime, 1792 & 1793
IX.20, IV.85, VI.92, I.57 & IX.77

> De nuict viendra par la forest de Reines,
> Deux pars vaultort Herne la pierre blanche,
> La maine noir en gris dedans Varennes
> Esleu cap. cause tempeste feu sang tranche.

Translation:

> By night will come through the forest of Reines,
> Two partners by a roundabout way *Herne* the white stone,
> The black monk in grey at Varennes,
> The elected cap. causes tempest fire blood slice.

This is perhaps the most hair-raisingly precise quatrain in the
whole of Nostradamus' *Centuries*. If a modern forger decided to
fake a prediction after the fact – with the help of a pile of history
books – he could hardly give a more accurately detailed version of
these events. Yet we know for a fact that Nostradamus published
this prophecy over two hundred and thirty years before the
episode took place.

In 1792, tiring of incarceration in the Palais des Tuileries and
fearing for the future, Louis XVI and the royal family escaped
through a secret door in the queen's apartments, boarded a waiting
coach and made towards the eastern border and the Austrian
Empire. They were initially heading for the small town of Varennes, but became lost in the dark and went a roundabout route
along the road to Reines (although one edition of the *Centuries*
prints "forest of Reines" – which does not exist – as "*fores de
Reine*" – the "queens' door", through which they escaped from the
palace). It was at this point that they were recaptured.

Before his attempted escape, Louis had some hope of survival.
Afterwards, he had next to none. Most of his subjects felt that a

king who tried to desert his country in time of trouble was no better than a captain who abandons his ship in a storm. Likewise, Nostradamus seems to blame Louis for the "tempest" of fire and blood that followed his execution, but this is unfair. Most historians now agree that Louis XVI was simply an inept ruler, not a tyrant; the mismanagement of his two royal predecessors had all but guaranteed a revolution before he was even born.

The word "*Herne*" in the second line is probably an anagram of "Rehne": a medieval spelling of "Reine" ("Queen"). The "white stone" also mentioned is rather obscure but, as the next line accurately describes the shade of the King's clothes when captured – "grey" – this might be a reference to Marie Antoinette's habit of wearing all-white outfits. Louis XVI was of a monkish temperament (this may also be a comment on his occasional celibacy, the result of bouts of stress-related impotence) although precisely why he should be described as a "black monk" is hard to guess.

The "elected cap." described as causing so much destruction in the last line of the quatrain is probably Louis himself; "cap." could be a shortening of *Capet* – an archaic French word for "King". Louis was the first constitutional (thus "elected") king of France.

The last word of the quatrain is "*tranche*": the French word for "slice". A chilling reminder of the sound of a guillotine – the recently invented execution machine (to whose design the king himself contributed a suggestion)[10] used to behead "enemies of the Republic".

> *Le charbon blanc du noir sera chassé,*
> *Prisonnier faicte men au tombereau:*
> *More Chameau sus piedz entrelassez,*
> *Lors le puisné sillera l'aubereau.*

10 This was one of the greatest moments of black irony in French history. In 1789, a Dr Guillotin was commissioned by Louis XVI to design a humane method of beheading criminals. The weighted, curved blade looked fine on paper but usually failed to sever fully the heads of the test animals. In the Tuilleries, Louis XVI happened to be passing one day and, on hearing Dr Guillotin's problem, suggested the use of a straight but angled blade. The suggestion worked perfectly – on the King's own neck as well as on tens of thousands of others.

Translation:

> The white coal chased out by the black,
> A prisoner carried in a tumbril:
> Like a camel his feet are tied,
> Then the last born will free the falcon.

In September 1792, the National Convention – the constitutionally reformed National Assembly – declared France a republic. Immediately afterwards the ex-king was tried as a traitor and condemned to death. On 21 January 1793, he was taken in a tumbril (a two-wheeled cart used to transport condemned prisoners) to the Place de la Revolution (now Place de la Concorde). There, bound hand and foot, he was beheaded by the guillotine.

Apart from the key word "tombereau" ("tumbril"), this quatrain is, on the surface, one of the most allegorically obscure of all Nostradamus' predictions.

The word "*Charbon*" (or "coal") in the first line may be a rhyme on "Bourbon" – Louis XVI's family name. White was the shade of the Bourbon standard and, as Erica Cheetham points out, Nostradamus often used *noir* as a partial anagram of *rein*, or "king". Although this gives a nonsensical reading to the whole line (i.e. "The white Bourbon flag will be chased out by the king") it does seem to hint to the identity of the prisoner in the second and third lines.

The word "*chameau*" ("camel") in the third line sounds ridiculous, not least because Louis was not hobbled like a riding beast, but was tightly bound hand and foot. However, in *The Prophecies and Enigmas of Nostradamus*, edited by Liberté E. Lavert (1979), it is suggested that the word *chameau* is actually a misprint of *chamois* – the little French deer that hunters bind tightly around the hooves to allow them to carry them home.

The last line may be a reference to the *Dauphin* – the heir to the French throne. Louis XVI's eight-year-old son – also called Louis – was held in the "protective custody" of the Republican government following his parents' execution. Unfortunately, this did not stop escaped French Royalists declaring him Louis XVII. This made him a threat to the Republic, so few people were surprised when he was reported "dead of tuberculosis" in June 1795. Nevertheless, rumours continued to circulate that he was actually alive. Indeed, over the next few decades, no less than thirty men came forward claiming to be the lost Dauphin (and the rightful King of France).

Young Louis was indeed the "last born" child of Louis XVI and Marie Antoinette, but we can only speculate on whether the term "free the falcon" refers to his survival.

> Prince de beauté tant venuste,
> Au chef menée, le second faict trahi :
> La cité au glaive de poudre face aduste,
> Par le trop grand meutre le chef du Roi hai.

Translation:

> The Prince of such handsome beauty,
> Intrigues against him, the second rank betrayed:
> The city of the sword consumed by the powder that burns,
> By too great a murder the head of the king hated.

Louis XVI was said to have been strikingly handsome as a young prince. Erica Cheetham suggests that the "intrigues" of the second line were the constitutional deliberations that lowered Louis to the "second rank" of constitutional monarch. The "city of the sword" certainly sounds like a description of Paris at this period, and the "powder that burns" might be a reference to quicklime – the caustic substance used to hasten the decomposition of the many executed bodies thrown into mass graves.

As with the death of Charles I in England, the monarchist in Nostradamus seems to consider Louis' regicide "too great a murder". Also, like Charles I, Louis XVI's freshly severed head was held up for a mob of former subjects to "hate" and ridicule.

> Par grand discord la trombe tremblera
> Accord rompu dressant la teste au ciel :
> Bouche sanglante dans le sang nagera,
> Au sol la face ointe de laict et miel.

Translation:

> By great discord the trumpet trembles
> Agreement broken lifting the head to heaven:
> A bloody mouth swims with blood
> The face turned to the sun anointed with milk and honey.

In fact, the death of Louis only brought about a greater level of social unrest in France. Lacking a king to blame for ongoing problems, the parties in the National Convention turned on each other. The ballot to execute Louis had scraped through on only 387 votes to 334, and much bad blood had been caused by the near-deadlock. Many agreements were broken, as mentioned in the second line, and it was certainly a time of "great discord", as it says in the first.

As noted above, Louis' severed head was held up to the crowd at his execution and, as gruesomely described in the third line, the mouth was wet with blood "vomited" as the blade cut his throat.

Nevertheless, the last line is the reason why many Nostradamus scholars confidently connect this quatrain to the death of Louis XVI: the French coronation ceremony involved the anointing the new king's head with "milk and honey".

> *Le regne prins le Roi conviera,*
> *La dame prinse à mort jurez à sort,*
> *La vie á Roine fils on desniera,*
> *Et la pellix au sort de la consort.*

Translation:

> The government takes the invited King,
> The captive queen condemned to death by a lottery,
> Life will be denied the Queen's son,
> And the concubine to the strength of a consort.

David Ovason argues that the four lines of this quatrain each predict the death of one of four of the central characters of the French Court.

Louis was "invited" to be a constitutional monarch by the government only a few months before he was "taken" and executed on 21 January 1793.

Queen Marie Antoinette was tried by a jury from all classes of people, chosen by lot. She went to the guillotine on 16 October 1793.

Louis XVII, "the Queen's son", was reported to have died in captivity on 8 June 1795. If he either died of neglect, or was murdered on the orders of the French government, it would still be accurate to say that his "life [was] denied".

The "concubine" in the last line might be Madame Du Barry: an ex-courtesan and the influential mistress of the late Louis XV. She was executed on 7 December 1793.

Ovason adds that each of the above deaths are presented in chronological order in the quatrain – except for the death of the Dauphin. He suggests that Nostradamus might have been offering us a clue that the boy actually died between October and December 1793, but that the matter was covered up for a year and a half. However, Ovason himself admits that there is no historical evidence to back this theory.

The Reign of Terror and the Cult of Reason, July 1793 to July 1794
    IV.11, VI.57, I.44 & VIII.98

> Celui qu'aura gouvert de la grand cappe,
> Sera induict à quelques cas patrer
> Les douze rouges viendront fouiller la nappe.
> Soubz meutre, meutre se viendra perpetrer.

Translation:

> He that will have covering of the great cloak,
> Shall be led to execute some cases,
> The twelve red ones will come to soil the cloth,
> Under murder, murder will be committed.

Several Nostradamus scholars believe that this quatrain is some unspecified or as yet unfulfilled prophecy concerning the papacy – the term "twelve red ones" being reminiscent of the Cardinal Bishops in the Vatican College of Cardinals. However, Jean-Charles de Fontbrune suggests that the seer was actually referring to the French Revolutionary Committee of Public

Safety – the twelve-man body that ruled over tens of thousands executions in the infamous "Reign of Terror".

Although the word "*cappe*" at the end of the first line of the quatrain literally translates as "cloak", de Fontbrune suggests that it is really a deliberate misspelling of "*capet*" ("king"), allowing a rhyme with "*nappe*" ("cloth") at the end of the third line. Thus the first line might be read: "He that enshrouds the great king." This is a direct description, de Fontbrune thinks, of Maximilien Robespierre: a leader of the radical Jacobin Party and the man who virtually forced the execution of Louis XVI on the divided National Convention.

On 13 July 1793, Charlotte Corday – a follower of the comparatively moderate Girondist Party – assassinated a leading Jacobin, Jean Paul Marat, in his bath. The resultant public anger allowed the Jacobins to seize control of the powerful Committee of Public Safety, and Robespierre had himself made chairman. Under the cover of "national security", the twelve-man committee set about persecuting their former opponents ("soiling the cloth" of liberty with their brutal corruption). Although some of the show-trials and automatic executions that followed were of actual rebels against the new Republic, many more were personal murders covered by a show of judicial nicety: "under murder, murder will be committed".

It is a popular misconception that a majority of the victims of the Terror were members of the French aristocracy. In fact, only eight per cent of the forty thousand people executed between July 1793 and July 1794 were aristocrats. A further fourteen per cent were bourgeoisie, and six per cent were members of the clergy. The remaining seventy-two per cent were commoners accused of minor or imaginary crimes. The new regime was already collapsing into paranoia and blood mania.

In some of the quatrains believed to predict the French Revolution, Nostradamus refers to the radical Republicans as "reds" – and this was indeed the colour of their banner. Nevertheless, from the repugnance the seer clearly felt for "les rouges", he might also have been thinking of the sea of blood for which they were responsible.

Celui qu'estoit bien avant dans le regne,
Ayant chef rouge proche á la hierarchie:
Aspre et cruel, et se fera tant craindre,
Succedera á sacré monarchie.

Translation:

He who was a good way to the front of the kingdom,
Having a red head near the hierarchy:
Harsh and cruel, and will make himself so feared,
He succeeds to the sacred Monarchy.

By the time Louis XVI came to trial, Robespierre and the Jacobin Party were already the main power within the National Convention. The ferocious Parisian mob gave strong backing to these radical "reds" while, at the same time, the Jacobins' moderate opposition was split into factions and lost popular support. The murder of Marat took place at just the right time to give Robespierre and his cronies the leverage to seize absolute power.

Although still nominally under the direction of the democratic senate, Robespierre and the Committee of Public Safety showed themselves so ruthless and arbitrary that no one dared oppose them. Thus Robespierre "succeeded the sacred monarchy" as a dictator in all but name.

En bref seront de retour sacrifices,
Contrevenans seront mis á martyre:
Plus ne seront moines, abbez, ne novices,
Le miel sera beaucoup plus cher que cire.

Translation:

In a short time the return of sacrifices,
Opposition shall be put to martyrdom,
There will no longer be monks, abbots, nor novices,
Honey will be more expensive than wax.

Even before the death of Marat and the rise of the Jacobins, the French Catholic church was under political siege – church property was confiscated and the monasteries abolished. On

23 November 1793, the Commune of Paris ordered all churches closed and denounced the local clergy as enemies of France. These measures quickly spread across the nation, and many churchmen ("monks, abbots [and] novices") were arrested and guillotined.

To replace Christianity, the Republicans instituted the "Cult of Reason": a semi-philosophical, humanist religion, based on the liberal ideas of the Enlightenment. Line one of the above quatrain is argued by Nostradamus scholars to predict the coming of the Cult of Reason as a new form of paganism. "Sacrifices" were not a part of the cult, but Nostradamus may well have seen the executed clergy as sacrifices to a pagan faith.

Before the revolution, the wax from beehives was more valuable than the honey because it was needed in great quantities to make votive candles for churches. Thus, as the last line of the quatrain suggests, honey became more expensive than wax when the Church was abolished and the demand for candles was greatly reduced.

> Des gens d'eglise sang fera espandu,
> Comme de l'eau eu si grand abondance;
> Et d'un long temps ne sera restranche
> Ve, ve au cleric ruine et doleance.

Translation:

> Of the churchmen blood will be spilt,
> As water in such great abundance;
> And for a long time it shall not be restrained,
> Woe, woe for the clergy ruin and grief.

Although there is nothing specific to link this quatrain to the persecution of the Catholic clergy under the Terror, it is an accurate description of their suffering. Since Nostradamus' day, the Catholic churchmen have only once undergone a similar period of state persecution – in Germany under the Nazis. Let us hope that the above quatrain refers to one of these two periods, and not to some future event.

Thermidor, July 1794
II.42

> *Coq, chiens et chats de sang seront repeus*
> *Et de la playe du tyran trouvé mort.*
> *Au lict d'unautrejambles et bras rompus,*
> *Qui n'avait peur de mourir de cruelle mort.*

Translation:

> Cock, dogs and cats will be replete with blood
> And of the wound the tyrant found dead,
> In the bed of another with arms and legs broken,
> Who was not afraid dies a cruel death.

By spring 1794, the ruling Jacobin party was beginning to experience major rifts. Robespierre and his followers insisted that the bloody slaughter of "enemies of the Republic" must go on, but many previously fervent Republicans had become sickened by the endless executions.

At the end of March, Robespierre acted characteristically to silence his critics: he arrested and guillotined them. However, the zealous ex-lawyer had gone too far this time. His inner core of supporters now saw that any of them might be next, and even the bloodthirsty citizens of Paris were growing tired of the daily butchery.

By June, the Republic's very successes were working against its leaders. The Terror had originally been justified by the danger of invasion by foreign nations, but major victories by the French army in Belgium had all but ended this threat. Robespierre continued to make radical speeches, calling for greater vigilance and more executions, but he was now swimming against the tide of public opinion.

On 26 July (8 Thermidor, under the newly instituted Republican calendar) Robespierre gave his last speech to the National Convention. He warned that many executions were still necessary, but this time failed to mention any names; the natural result was that everyone in the Convention felt under threat. The next day he was shouted down as he tried to speak, then he and his followers were arrested as they tried to leave. That night Robespierre was rescued by soldiers of the Paris Commune, who took him to the Hotel de Ville, but Convention troops quickly recaptured him. Robespierre was shot in the jaw during the second arrest, and spent his last night in agony. The next day he and a hundred of his closest followers were guillotined, without even the mock trial they had given so many others. It was 27 July – or the Ninth of Thermidor.

The first line of the quatrain is most reminiscent of the Reign of Terror. The Cockerel is the emblem of France and the Parisian mob was certainly animalistic in its thirst for blood[11]. By the beginning of Thermidor, however, even the Commune de Paris was satiated; in the previous month alone, the Committee of Public Safety had executed 1,500 people.

The second line is reminiscent of the assassination of Jean-Paul Marat – found stabbed to death in his bath. Why Nostradamus should hark back to this event, when apparently predicting the fall of Robespierre, is harder to explain.

The third line sounds plain wrong. Although we know that Robespierre was tied to a bed during the agonized writhings of his last night, his legs and arms were not broken. Yet, finally, paranoid monster that he certainly was, Robespierre showed bravery in the face of his own execution, echoing the last line of the quatrain.

The Death of Pope Pius VI, 29 August 1799
II.97.

> *Romain Pontife garde de t'approcher,*
> *De la cité que deux fleuves arrouse,*
> *Ton sang viendras aupres de là cracher,*
> *Toi et les tiens quand fleurira la rose.*

11 Indeed, during the Enlightenment, Parisian crowds would sometimes entertain themselves with cats and dogs – throwing them out of high windows and laughing uproariously when the unfortunate animals burst on the cobblestones below.

Translation:

> Roman Pontiff beware the approach,
> Of the city watered by two rivers,
> You will spit your blood there,
> You and yours when the roses bloom.

When the French Republican army under Napoleon took Rome in 1798, they also captured Pope Pius VI – an ardent enemy of the new republic. He was subsequently held prisoner at Valence, a city near the joining of the Rhone and Saone rivers at Lyon.

Still under arrest in the summer of 1799, Pope Pius suffered a severe bout of vomiting. This was so violent that it resulted in internal bleeding and caused him to spit blood. Thirty priests were also incarcerated with him, and some may have caught the same malady – thus the use of the phrase "you and yours" in the last line. The pope died on 29 August 1799, as the late roses were coming into bloom.

13 Scrambled Time

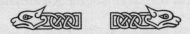

In his *Guide to Modern Thought*, C. E. M. Joad uses the phrase "the undoubted queerness of time". He is referring to one of the most famous of all cases of "retrocognition" – or, in everyday language, a time-slip.

The case to which Joad refers began on 10 August 1901, and concerned two English ladies, Miss Annie Moberly and her companion, Miss Eleanor Jourdain. Miss Moberly, aged fifty-five, was the daughter of a Bishop of Salisbury and was also the principal of St Hugh's College, Oxford, while Miss Jourdain, who was thirty-eight, was the first of ten children of the Rev. Francis Jourdain, Vicar of Ashbourne, Derbyshire, and she was the headmistress and part-owner of a private school for girls in Watford. She would later succeed Miss Moberly at St Hugh's in 1915.

Miss Jourdain had taken a flat in Paris, and furnished it in order that her schoolgirls should be able to go to Paris and learn French with a French mistress. In August 1901, the ladies decided to experience Paris for themselves. After several days of wandering around looking at historic sites, they decided to take the train to Versailles – although both of them suspected that they might find it boring.

After a long journey by bus and tram, they wandered around the Palace of Versailles, then sat down to rest by some open windows overlooking the gardens. They decided that there was still time to visit the two smaller palaces called the Trianons: the Grand Trianon, built by Louis XIV, and the Petit Trianon built by Louis XV, and given by his son Louis XVI to Queen Marie Antoinette.

The two ladies walked past the Grand Trianon, intending to go to the Petit Trianon. However, they managed to walk across the drive that led to the Petit Trianon, and instead went up a lane straight ahead. They saw a woman shaking a white cloth out of the window of a building at the corner of the lane, but did not ask her the way. Further up the lane, they saw some buildings, and saw through an open doorway the bottom of a carved staircase. Soon after that, they saw two men who looked as if they were wearing fancy dress – long, greyish-green coats and small three-cornered hats. They asked the way, and were told to go straight on.

At this point, to their right, they saw a cottage with stone steps, and a woman and a girl in the doorway – both wore white kerchiefs tucked into the bodice, and the girl's dress was down to her ankles, although she only looked about fourteen.

At this point, both the women experienced a curious feeling. Miss Moberly described it as "an extraordinary depression . . . which, in spite of every effort, steadily deepened". The trees struck her as flat and lifeless, as if, she said, they had been worked in tapestry. Miss Jourdain said: "There was a feeling of depression and loneliness about the place. I began to feel as if I were walking in my sleep; the heavy dreariness was oppressive."

Soon they came to the end of the path, and saw in front of them a wood. Overshadowed by trees was a light garden kiosk, circular, and like a small bandstand, in front of which a man was sitting. Miss Moberly comments: "Everything suddenly looked unnatural, therefore unpleasant."

The man, who was wearing a cloak and a large shady hat, looked at them, and proved to have a repulsive face, "its expression odious". They heard the sound of someone running towards them but, when they turned round, there appeared to be no one there. Then, they received a sudden shock when a man appeared ahead of them – in front of the large rock at the end of the path, and shouted at them in French that they were not allowed to go that way. This man was "distinctly a gentleman", tall, with large dark eyes and crisp curling black hair under a wide-brimmed hat. Miss Moberly said he looked like an old picture, and his face was glowing red. He then waved his arm and told them to go "this way . . . look for the house".

The two went towards a little bridge to their right and, turning their head to thank the man, found that he was no longer there. Yet, again, they heard the sound of running feet.

The bridge crossed over a tiny ravine, with a stream descending from above. They followed a narrow path under trees, skirted a narrow meadow of long grass, and came to the Petit Trianon. They were in the English garden, behind the house, and on the rough grass a lady was seated, holding a paper out at arm's length. They assumed that she was sketching. As they passed her, she noticed them, and they saw that she was rather pretty, although no longer young. "She had on a shady white hat, perched on a good deal of fair hair that fluffed round her forehead. Her light summer dress was arranged on her shoulders, in handkerchief fashion, and there was a little line of either green or gold near the edge of the handkerchief, which showed me that it was *over*, not tucked into, her bodice, which was cut low. Her dress was long-waisted, with a good deal of fullness in the skirt, which seemed to be short. I thought she was a tourist, but that her dress was old-fashioned and rather unusual."

They went up the steps to the terrace, and crossed to a paved walled courtyard, but then turned back. Facing them was a second house, and a young man stepped out of a door onto the terrace, banging it behind him. He had the jaunty manner of a footman, and called to the two women, saying that the way into the house was by the courtyard. He led them around through the French garden, parts of which were walled in by trees, and Miss Jourdain noticed that the feeling of depression was particularly strong there. Then they came to a broad way out into the avenue and, when they reached the front entrance, they felt themselves back in the ordinary world. A French wedding party arrived, and the two women followed the party round the house. Then they drove back to their hotel, and, oddly enough, did not even mention that afternoon's experience to one another. It was only a week later that one of them asked: "Do you think the Petit Trianon is haunted?" And the other said she agreed it was.

During the Christmas holiday, Miss Jourdain paid another visit to Paris, and decided to go and take another look at Versailles.

At first, everything seemed perfectly normal. She went back to the Petit Trianon, then walked along the little group of cottages in the grounds known as the Hamlet (*Hameau*). Yet when she crossed the bridge to go to the Hamlet, the feeling of unreality suddenly came back. She said it was "as if I had crossed the line and was suddenly in a circle of influence".

She saw a cart being filled with sticks by two labourers who wore tunics and capes with pointed hoods, one hood being red and the other blue. She turned to glance at the Hamlet and, when she looked back again, the men and the cart had vanished. This struck her as odd, since she could see for a long way in every direction.

On her way back from the Hamlet she passed a building which she saw from her map to be the smaller Orangerie; then she took the wrong turn and found herself in a wood so thick that she was unable to see anything through the trees, but she heard a kind of rustling around her which she compared to silk dresses of people out on a wet day. Yet there was no one visible. She felt as if she was surrounded by invisible people. She could even hear their voices talking in French. Then, as if they had gone past, she heard faint music like a band playing.

Whenever she decided to take any particular path, she experienced an odd compulsion to go down another. Finally, at the Orangerie, she was overtaken by a gardener and enquired how to find the Queen's Grotto, and was told to follow the path she was on.

Back in Paris, she made enquiries about which band had been playing there, but was told that, though it was the usual day of the week for the band, it hadn't played there because it had played the day before, on New Year's Day. Miss Jourdain went back to the Petit Trianon nearly seven years later, in September 1908. Here, once again, she felt that something strange had happened. After taking a number of photographs, she went back towards the old gateway and passed the old building of the Corps of Guards. There she saw two women sitting in the shade and disputing in loud voices. She also felt once again that there was something rather strange as she passed the guards' quarters.

"I felt as though I were being taken up into another condition of things quite as real as the former. The women's voices, though their quarrel was just as shrill and eager as before, seemed to be fading so quickly that the dispute would soon be altogether gone; from their tones the dispute was clearly still going on, but seemed to have less and less power to reach me

"I turned at once to look back and saw the gates near which they were sitting melting away, and the background of trees again become invisible through them, as on our original visit, but I noticed that the side pillars were standing steady. The whole scene – sky, trees and buildings – gave a little shiver, like the movement of a curtain or of scenery as at a theatre. At the same time the old difficulty of walking on and making any way reproduced itself, together with the feeling of depression described in 1901 and 1902. But I instantly decided to keep to my plans of going straight out by the lane, and, once outside the lane, things became natural again. But the sudden startling sense of insecurity left a deep impression, so little did I expect any repetition of the phenomena after the innumerable uneventful visits I had paid to the Trianon since the winter of 1902."

In fact, Miss Moberly and Miss Jourdain had paid another visit to Versailles in July 1904, together with a French woman. They retraced the route of their first visit up the lane and turned to the right on reaching the quarters of the Corp of Guards. Then everything was changed. The gardener's house was quite different from the cottage described by Miss Jourdain in 1901, and there was no trace of the old paths. Everything seemed to be on a smaller scale than they remembered. The kiosk was gone; so was the ravine and the little bridge, together with a cascade that had fallen from the rocks above their heads. Many of the trees seemed to have been cleared away.

The English garden was also not shaded by many trees and they could see the house and the Hamlet. Yet, instead of the tree-shaded rough meadow continuing to the wall of the terrace, there was now a broad gravelled space beneath it, and there was no longer either trees or grass. There was a large spreading bush on the spot where they had seen the lady sketching, and it seemed that it had been there a long time. They did not recognize the present staircase up to the terrace, nor the wall which they now had to go round to reach the staircase. The exit from the French garden was not so near the house as they had expected, or as broad as they recalled. They could certainly not find the thick wood in which Miss Jourdain had lost her way on the visit to the

Hamlet. Miss Moberly was depressed by the changes that had taken place since she last saw it in 1901.

They went again in 1905, and tried to find the building out of which the "footman" had come to direct them to the front of the house, and they concluded that it was the chapel – which was, however, in a ruined condition.

A year later, Miss Jourdain managed to get into the chapel but had to go in from the avenue, because there was now no entrance from the garden. Inside, she was able to see the door out of which the man had come, and saw that it was one that led to the Royal Gallery, but that the staircase to this gallery was completely broken down, so there was no way of getting up to it – or, obviously, of going out of the door onto the terrace. Both doors were bolted, barred, and covered with cobwebs. The guide told her the doors had not been opened during the lifetime of any man there. Not surprisingly, the two English women came to the conclusion that what they had seen was the Trianon as it had been in the past – they guessed that it was in the year 1789, when the royal family had been compelled to escape from the mob.

An Adventure, describing their experience, was published in 1911, and attracted very wide attention – it quickly went through three editions. It was not until another edition was issued in 1931 that the real names of the authors were revealed – in the 1911 edition, they called themselves Miss Morison and Miss Lamont.

This edition also contained an interesting appendix which seemed to make it clear that they were not the only persons to have experienced a "time-slip" at Versailles. In May 1914, they met Mr and Mrs John Crooke, and their son Stephen. The Crookes lived in a flat in rue Maurepas at Versailles between 1907 and 1909. The odd thing was that, although they saw busloads of tourists arrive at Versailles, they never saw anyone in the gardens – they were always empty and deserted. The only occasional exceptions were on days that they assumed must be some kind of holiday. Moreover, no wind ever appeared to blow inside the park. It all seemed so still and airless that they used to take their walks along the Marly Road to breathe some fresh air. As soon as they went inside the grounds the light in the trees and walks seemed so still and quiet that it got on their nerves, and they quickly went away.

As soon as *An Adventure* came out in 1911, they recalled seeing the sketching lady at the Grand Trianon. The first time she was in the garden and the second below the balustrade. Both times, she was dressed in a light cream-coloured skirt, white fichu, and white untrimmed flapping hat. The skirt was full and much gathered, and the lady spread it out around her. She appeared to be sketching, occasionally holding out her paper away from her, as if to judge it at a distance.

The Crookes said that the lady seemed "to grow out of the scenery with a little quiver of adjustment". They felt she was aware of their presence and, when Mr Crooke senior once tried to look over her shoulder at what she was drawing, she quickly moved the paper away.

Another woman, Mrs Kate Crooke, had seen a man in eighteenth-century costume, wearing a three-cornered hat, and Mr and Mrs Crooke had seen a woman in old-fashioned dress – they had also noticed the flattened appearance of the trees, and the large forest trees between them.

Mr Crooke had also heard music coming over the water when none was going on, and said that it was a stringed band playing "old music", which he enjoyed listening to.

The Crooke family mentioned "a curious hissing sound that sometimes came when things were about to appear, possibly suggesting some electrical vibration", and they said there was a vibration in the air when they "saw things".

The Crooke family had also seen grass growing right up to the terrace, where there was now simply a wide gravelled space, and the large bush on the spot where the two English women had once seen the lady sketching. Mr Crooke had seen a cottage near the Hamlet, and seen people in old-fashioned clothes looking out of the windows; he was not always able to see it – it appeared and disappeared in a most extraordinary way. Miss Moberly had also seen this cottage – but she saw it without a roof, and with three bare walls.

In 1938, a man called J. R. Sturge-Whiting, who was interested in psychical research, published a book called *The Mystery of Versailles – A Complete Solution*. Sturge-Whiting came to the conclusion that the two English ladies were simply deceiving themselves, and that they had simply got lost and taken the wrong route (which is admittedly easy to do at Versailles). Yet although Sturge-Whiting manages to sound convincing about a great many of the paths taken by the English ladies, he simply fails to take into account half the experience of the two ladies. If, as Miss Moberly says about her 1904 visit, "From this point everything was changed . . . we came directly to the gardener's house, which was quite different in appearance from the cottage described by Miss Jourdain in 1901."

In 1965, the French author Philippe Jullian published a biography of the French dandy Count Robert de Montesquiou (on whom Proust based Baron de Charlus), and also concluded that he had found a simple explanation for the "adventure" of the two ladies. He discovered that Montesquiou had taken a house near Versailles in the early 1890s, and often spent whole days in the park. His friend Mme de Greffulhe organized a fancy-dress party at the Dairy, and Jullian remarks that perhaps "the 'ghosts' . . . were, quite simply, Mme Greffulhe, dressed as a shepherdess, rehearsing an entertainment with some friends." But he was unaware that the Versailles "adventure" was in 1901, and that, by 1894, Montesquiou had already moved away to Neuilly – so the amateur dramatics took place seven years too early for Miss Moberly and Miss Jourdain. Nevertheless, Dame Joan Evans, the literary executor of the two ladies, was so convinced by these efforts at debunking that she decided to allow *An Adventure* to go out of print.

Besides, all these efforts to "explain away" what the lady saw fail to consider that Miss Jourdain became thoroughly familiar with Versailles in the years following 1902, and is quite certain that what she had seen in 1901 and 1902 was the "old Versailles", quite unlike the new Versailles with which she became familiar.

The two English ladies and the Crooke family were not the only ones who saw strange things at Versailles. In October 1928, Miss Claire M. Burrow, a mistress in a girls' school at Haslemere, Surrey, and her ex-pupil, Ann Lambert, went to the Grand Trianon with a party of visitors, but then went off on their own to the Petit Trianon. They also saw a deserted building with nettles round it, just about where the two English ladies had earlier seen the farm building, and they experienced the same feeling of depression. A woman looked down on them from the window of a farmhouse near the lake, and they noticed that she was wearing a kind of muslin mobcap. They turned and saw an old man who was dressed in a green and silver uniform approaching down an avenue. Yet when they called to asked him the way, he shouted sentence after sentence in a "hoarse and unintelligible

French, as if in great haste". Something sinister about his face caused the two women to hurry on, but when they looked back, he had vanished. It was not until the two women returned to England and told about their experience that someone showed them *An Adventure*. However, it was almost twenty years later when a French member of the Society for Psychical Research got in touch with the elder of the two women, who was able to recall the events in detail and to make a sketch of the man in livery they had seen. Miss Burrow told him that this man was wearing a long green skirted coat, with multiple collars edged with silver braid, large cuffs, stockings which she thought were white, buckled shoes and a stick with a knob and a tassel. He was wearing a three-cornered hat with a rather high turned-up brim, also braided.

By the sketch made by Miss Burrow, the French researcher was able to say that the man was wearing a "Roquelaure", a kind of overcoat with multiple collars which was worn between 1715 and 1773.

People continued to have curious experiences at Versailles. On 21 May 1955, a London solicitor and his wife were walking in the grounds towards the Hamlet and noticed on their left a wall with gaps in it and a deep muddy ditch on the other side. On their right there was open parkland dotted with trees. The weather was close and oppressive – just as when the English women were there. The solicitor's wife noticed an extraordinary feeling of tension in the air and felt unaccountably depressed. Then she saw three people coming towards her, a woman and two men, and the woman's dress was of a striking yellow, and fluffed out at the waist. Then men on either side of her were dressed in black. They were wearing black breeches, black stockings and black shoes with silver buckles.

And then, quite suddenly, the three simply vanished. Oddly enough, the woman had experienced a sense "as though a curtain were drawn across my mind, obliterating the vision" until her husband spoke.

It was the first time her husband had seen a ghost, although the woman had seen one several times before her marriage. They wrote down their account of what they had seen in 1957, when a journalist asked for accounts of the supernatural. They were questioned by someone at the Society for Psychical Research, who wrote down the details.

A man called Jack Wilkinson, a poultry farmer of Leven, near Kendal, together with his wife Clara and their four-year-old son, was also approaching the Grand Trianon from the nursery gardens on 10 October 1949, when they saw a woman standing on the top of the steps. She was wearing a light gold-coloured crinoline dress reaching down to the ground and a large picture hat and was carrying a stick or parasol. She had dark ringlets to her shoulders and looked as if she was in her late twenties. She seemed to be quite normal and solid and, as they moved towards her, she went to the other side of the balustrade. They looked away for a few minutes and, when they looked again, she had vanished. They went up on the terrace, but she was not there. Asked whether he felt any sense of depression, Mr Wilkinson said no, but that he noticed there was a certain quiet and stillness about the place.

Andrew MacKenzie, one of the most conscientious and reliable writers on the paranormal, mentions in his book *Adventures in Time* that he interviewed a certain Mrs Elizabeth Hatton who, in September 1938, was walking down the avenue in the park of the Petit Trianon, towards the Hamlet, when she saw two men dressed as peasants drawing along a little wooden trundle cart with logs of wood on it. They went close by without saying anything. Mrs Hatton turned to watch where they were going, and as she watched they seemed gradually to disappear.

It is MacKenzie, in his early book *The Unexplained* (1966), who makes the most thorough attempt to understand the Versailles incident, at least as far as the dating is concerned. He relies upon the work of A. O. Gibbons and his wife Ena, in their book *The Trianon Adventure* (1958) and G. W. Lambert, of the Society for Psychical Research, who published some of his own researches in the SPR journal for June 1962. They started from the assumption that Miss Moberly and Miss Jourdain made, that they had seen the Petit Trianon in 1789, shortly before Louis XVI and Marie Antoinette were arrested. Yet the researches of Mr and Mrs Gibbons revealed that this could not be so.

In fact, the gardens in 1789 and in 1901 were not so very different. This was a fact often raised by critics of *An Adventure*. In fact, as already mentioned, the Petit Trianon was built by Louis XV for his mistress, Mme de Pompadour. When she died, Mme Dubarry occupied the king's bed and moved into the Petit Trianon. This was on 9 September 1770.

Work on the house was still not finished – the kitchen block had not then been completed. The king also had a small menagerie and a farm in the grounds, and an early plan shows a broad carriageway leading to the avenue of the menagerie. The width between the gateposts was about sixteen feet.

At that point, the king decided they needed a chapel, and this was finished in the following year, 1773. Yet this also meant getting rid of most of the kitchen and providing space elsewhere – with the consequence that the avenue of the menagerie was closed around 1771. MacKenzie is convinced that the two English ladies saw the old kitchen block before it was changed into a chapel. Miss Moberly said:

> "The terrace was prolonged at right-angles in front of what seemed to be a second house. The door of it suddenly opened, and a young man stepped out onto the terrace, banging the door behind him. He had the jaunty manner of a footman, but no livery, and called to us, saying that the way into the house was by way of the *cour d'honneur*, and offered to show us the way round."

MacKenzie points out that a person dressed like this would hardly be in the chapel, unless he happened to be sweeping the floor. In fact, he was dressed for work in the kitchen, which is why he was not wearing livery, and the door from which he stepped *was* a kitchen door in 1771.

But Miss Moberly and Miss Jourdain mentioned that the house was shuttered – although, when the young man had led them around to the front, they were able to follow a wedding party inside, and the shutters had obviously been taken away. It is unlikely that anyone closed all the shutters in the house in a few minutes. What happened, MacKenzie thinks, was that the house seen by the two women was in fact the house as it was before the king and his mistress moved there in September 1770. The ladies also say that "the road from the garden to the avenue (through which the man ushered us) was not far from the chapel, and was broad enough to admit a coach. The present one is narrower and further to the west." This would be perfectly correct if the road they saw was the original avenue, and not the later one.

As MacKenzie points out, the odd thing is that the women

could not have got around to the front of the house by that way in 1901, because it would have meant walking through several solid walls. He speculates that they came out of their time-slip (or trance) when they arrived at the front of the house.

MacKenzie goes on to point out that there were two royal gardeners in those early days: Claud Richard, and his son Antoine. (It is stated in *An Adventure* that one man was older than the other and that they were dressed in "long greyish-green coats with small three-cornered hats".) The Gibbons' research shows that the two gardeners were dressed in green during the lifetime of Louis XV, who died in 1774, and that after that date, Marie Antoinette ordered that they should be dressed in red livery with blue velvet facings. So again, it sounds as if the two women saw the Richards in the time of Louis XV.

While the women were talking to the two men in green, Miss Jourdain saw a woman and a girl standing in front of a nearby cottage – a cottage that no longer exists. Mr Gibbons found an old map that seemed to show a cottage on this site, and he was later able to trace its foundations by probing in the ground with a poker. The "Kiosk" seen by the women has been dismissed as the Belvedere, or possibly the Temple of Love, but in fact, documents of the 1770s refer to a "circular pavilion".

Again, the tall rock at the end of the path actually existed in 1774. It disappeared when Marie Antoinette took over the Petit Trianon.

Another criticism that has often been directed against the two English ladies is why they did not see the merry-go-round built for Marie Antoinette. In fact, this merry-go-round had not been built in the time of Louis XV.

MacKenzie goes on to comment that he cannot really understand what there was about the site in the early 1770s – almost twenty years before the French Revolution – to create this peculiar atmosphere that led to "time-slips".

"What I cannot explain is why these hallucinatory experiences seem to apply to one particular period and not a dramatic one at that. The shadow of the Revolution had not yet fallen across France. There is a theory in psychical research that cases of telepathy, clairvoyance, or the appearance of apparitions involve an agent and a percipient or an agent-percipient. If this is so, who was the long-dead agent who presumably left some influence on the Trianons which could, in certain atmospheric conditions, 'trigger off' the hallucinatory experiences of certain visitors to the gardens in modern time?"

He then quotes the writer Jean Overton Fuller as providing a possible solution:

"My mother was a person with very strong reactions to places. Some she would not go near. Usually, retrospective research into the background of a place where she had been paralysed by terror afforded some reason to imagine it might have anciently been a site of Druidic human sacrifice. That did not explain her dislike and fear of Versailles. Her father had, since his second marriage, gone to live in it. I cannot deny that she may already have read *An Adventure*, but the impression created by its authors was not sinister, and I have heard her refer to the book with pleasant interest. Her dread was of the place itself. In 1928, when I was thirteen, we were invited. I knew Mother did not want to go, only she could think of no reason to refuse, as we were passing through Paris.

"After lunch, inevitably we were taken to the Chateau and its gardens. My grandfather, Col. Frederik Smith RAMC, loved it. In 1914, he had commandeered the Hotel Trianon as the No. 4LA General Hospital in France, and he walked down the Grand Avenue as if he belonged there, stopping to suggest to a gardener the treatment for an ailing bush. Mother managed to put on a smiling face until we reached the Petit Trianon. They wanted to take us in, and here she stuck her feet in as though resisting being pulled, and refused absolutely to go in or a step further towards it. Her revulsion and fear were most evident, and we had to come away.

"In the station, after we had settled into our carriage, there was still a delay of a few minutes before the train pulled out. I looked at Mother. She appeared still to be suffering from the ill effects of the place. Guessing at the way in which her thoughts were running, I said: 'They weren't executed here.'

"She flashed back at me, 'It was here their melancholy

thoughts returned while they were waiting to be executed.'''

This is an interesting theory, and it is worth considering. One thing is perfectly obvious: that Jean Overton Fuller's mother was "psychic" – that is to say, a medium. Andrew MacKenzie feels fairly certain that the same applies to Miss Moberly and Miss Jourdain. MacKenzie calls his original chapter on Versailles (in *The Unexplained*) "The Haunting at Versailles". The reaction of the average reader is to say: what does he mean, haunting? The people looked perfectly solid and normal. What is more – and this is perhaps the most baffling part of it – the two English women were able to speak to them. So how could it be a haunting?

The first answer is that most "ghosts" look perfectly solid and normal. People who have seen them do not know that they have seen a ghost. It is only in ghost stories – and films – that ghosts appear to be semi-transparent.

The Cambridge archaeologist T. C. Lethbridge wrote many books on his own experiences of the paranormal, and was completely convinced that ghosts are nothing more than "tape recordings", somehow impressed on their surroundings, so that sensitive people can somehow see them when they venture into these surroundings. Around the turn of the century, Sir Oliver Lodge suggested a similar theory about ghosts, which he called the "psychometric theory". "Psychometry" is the ability that certain people possess to hold an object in their hands, and to suddenly know all about its history. It is too well documented to be dismissed as imagination. A good psychometrist can hold, let us say, an umbrella, and not only describe what its owner looked like, but what happened to him and how he died. In the mid-nineteenth century, an American medical man called Joseph Rodes Buchanan conducted long and painstaking research into this ability, and finally coined the word "psychometry". He tested his "sensitives" with such things as sealed letters, and the sensitive was able to give an accurate description of the person who had written the letter.

Buchanan's friend William Denton, a professor of geology, tried the experiment of wrapping geological specimens up in thick brown paper, and allowing his "sensitives" to handle them. Again, they showed amazing accuracy. A fragment of lava from a Hawaiian island gave the psychometrist a picture of an ocean of fire pouring over a precipice; a pebble of glacial limestone produced a picture of being deep under the sea and frozen into ice. A fragment of bone from a piece of limestone caused the psychometrist (Denton's wife Elizabeth) to see a prehistoric beach with plesiosaurs lying on it. When he tried it a second time, some months later, she saw a picture of bird-like creatures with membranous wings, which sound like pterodactyls. A fragment of the horn of a chamois produced a fine description of the Alps. A fossil from Cuba brought a description of a tropical island. A fragment of mosaic brought back from Italy produced an accurate account of a Roman villa, and, moreover, of the dictator Sulla who had lived there. This was a particularly convincing case because, as far as Denton knew, the villa had belonged to the Roman orator Cicero, who was tall and thin, whereas the person Mrs Denton saw was "a fleshy man with broad face and blue eyes". This was altogether more like Sulla – as was her comment, when she saw lines of helmeted soldiers, that the man had something to do with them.

So it could be argued that what the two ladies saw at Versailles was not real and solid, but some kind of "psychometric impression" which came from their surroundings. As they were close friends, both of them felt and saw the same thing.

Yet this explanation is not altogether satisfactory. Seeing Versailles as it was in 1770 is not at all the same thing as having a kind of inner impression of the dictator Sulla from holding a piece of Roman tile. Yet at least it makes one thing clear: that human beings have some odd psychic faculty which can enable them to see the past.

Another more recent case offers another interesting clue. In 1977, Mrs Jane O'Neill, of Cambridge, wrote the following letter to my father, Colin Wilson:

"In October 1973 I was the first person to arrive at a serious accident; a car had driven head-on into a coach behind which I was travelling. I pulled the passengers from the wreck, waiting with them till the ambulance arrived. Afterwards, with my hands covered with blood, I drove to London airport to pick up a friend. Driving home, later that night, I began to 'see' all over again the dreadful injuries of the passengers. They continued for days; I am usually a very sound sleeper, but I now found that I could not sleep at all. The doctor said I was suffering from shock, and I was away from school for five weeks. [Mrs O'Neill is a schoolteacher.] A fellow teacher [Shirley] invited me for the half-term holiday to her cottage in Norfolk, where several inexplicable things happened. I would be sitting in her sitting room and would quite suddenly see very clearly before me a vivid picture. It would last a couple of seconds, during which my riveted attention was apparently obvious [and] Shirley would ask me what the matter was. I don't remember the sequence of these sights, but I remember them very clearly. After one, I told Shirley: 'I have just seen you in the galleys.' As I hardly knew her, I was astonished when she replied: 'That's not surprising. My ancestors were Huguenots and were punished by being sent to the galleys.' While wide awake, I also 'saw' two figures walking by trees beside a lake, and I knew, though I don't know why, that one of them was Margaret Roper [daughter of Sir Thomas More]. (My maiden name was Moore and I have wondered whether there is any connection with Thomas More.) I also 'saw' two strange animals facing each other, one a horse, the other resembling an armadillo, but tied in what looked like a string . . . after each of these I felt quite exhausted."

The scenes that came into her mind are known as "eidetic visions". Some people have such remarkable power of visualization that they can actually conjure up a picture of something that looks as solid as the real object. Jane O'Neill's shock obviously produced a similar feeling.

Two months later, Jane O'Neill visited the church at Fotheringhay with a friend, and spent some time in front of a picture of the crucifixion behind the altar. "It had an arched top and within the arch was a dove, its wings following the curve of the arch." Back in their hotel room, Shirley read aloud from an essay by Charles Williams that infinity was sometimes symbolized by a straight line meeting an arc. Mrs O'Neill commented that this was what she had seen in the picture in the church, "The upright of the cross meeting the curve of the arch with the dove."

"What picture?" asked Shirley and, when she was told, replied that *she* hadn't noticed it.

"She is very observant – much more than I am – so I was bothered by her remark. Two days later, I decided to phone the vicar and ask him about the picture. I got through to the post office and asked for his number, to be told they hadn't had a vicar for three years. I apologized and asked the postmistress if she knew the church. She said she knew it well because she arranged the flowers there every Sunday. I asked her if she could tell me about the pictures. She said there weren't any."

Two days later, the postmistress confirmed this in a letter – there was no painting.

A year later, the two women revisited the church. "While the outside of the building was exactly as I remembered it, I had no recollection at all of having been inside that church. It was much smaller than the one I had been in and there was no crucifixion. The dove – to my amazement – was not the one I had seen; this one is in a cloud and its wings are outstretched and not curved."

Colin Wilson's account (in *Mysteries*, 1978) goes on:

"In Joan Forman's book *Haunted East Anglia*, Mrs O'Neill discovered that people had reported hearing Plantaganet music issuing from Fotheringhay church. She wrote to Joan Forman, who put her in touch with Tom Litchfield, a Northamptonshire historian who had studied the history of the church. On December 13, 1974, Litchfield wrote her a long letter explaining that the present church was the surviving remnant of a former Collegiate church. The adjacent college and the cloisters and chancel had been pulled down in 1553 by Dudley, Duke of Northumberland, leaving only the nave which became the present church. A print of 1821 shows 'arched' panels on the east wall, behind the altar; 'the two central ones have a larger arch to embrace both, in the spandrel of which is the painting of a dove with outspread wings . . .

"Mrs O'Neill was inclined to believe that she had known Fotheringhay church in a previous existence and her experience was some kind of 'far memory'. Then one night as she lay awake in hospital (where she was being treated for asthma): 'I suddenly became aware that Nana (a nurse we had as children, who died of leukaemia twenty years ago) was there. I couldn't see her, but I knew she was there. And I found myself saying to her (not aloud): "You are outside time. Tell me about Fotheringhay." And she replied that the picture I saw was one of a pair; the other also had an arched top and was of a bright blue sky with gold stars and angels. Higher up on the wall in a niche, she said, was a statue of the Blessed Virgin (I can see it: very clearly) and on the corner of the wall, jutting out, a statue of the archangel Michael with a sword. I asked her when this was, and she replied: "1570". I asked her, "Was I there?" But she replied, "No".

"In 1976, Mrs O'Neill had been in Salle church, in Norfolk, when she heard the tramp of feet over her head. She knew no one was there and wondered if it could have some connection with the Civil War, when the church had been despoiled. After asking about the Fotheringhay experience as she lay in hospital, Mrs O'Neill also asked about the sound of feet at Salle church, and was told that what she had heard had taken place in 1680, and had been made by men storing grain."

The one thing that seems clear from the Jane O'Neill case is that the whole experience was triggered by her shock at the bus accident. It looks as if this made her far more "receptive" to a wider range of mental experience. In *The Doors of Perception*, Aldous Huxley mentions the theory put forward by the "time" philosopher, Henri Bergson, to the effect that our senses are not so much intended to let things in as to keep them out. He thinks that they may be filters whose purpose is to stop us from being overwhelmed by our experience.

In a book called *The User Illusion*, science writer Tor Norretranders reports that, during any given second, our senses pass on about eleven million bits of information to our brains. Of this eleven million, we consciously process only sixteen bits of information; we ignore the other 10,999,984 bits.

A shock like the one Jane O'Neill experienced makes our filter-system far less efficient. Fatigue does the same thing. Anyone who has driven a long distance can remember that sensation of closing the eyes, and seeing the road still going past. So it may well be that "psychics" are simply people whose filter systems are far less efficient than those of the rest of us.

The philosopher Kant actually argued that man *creates* space and time, in order to make his experience easier to handle. If this is true, then our impression that time is like a street down which we can only travel one way is an illusion.

Moreover, if it is possible for a psychometrist to hold an object in his hands, and somehow "know" about its past, then the past must still be there, somehow contained in the object, like a tape recording. Some people seem to have the power to replay this tape recording.

And sometimes, the recording replays itself, whether the person in question is willing or not. This happens particularly when we have been reduced to exhaustion by some kind of strain or tension.

An interesting instance occurred on a summer day in 1954 when a publisher and his wife decided to take a day off in the country. Their small publishing business had taken up an enormous amount of energy, and left them both exhausted. Early one Sunday morning, they set out from their Battersea home and took a bus that went towards Guildford, in Surrey.

The couple – who, in the account they provided for the Society for Psychical Research, preferred to be known as Mr and Mrs Allan – both woke up feeling intensely depressed. Neither of them mentioned this to the other because they did not want to spoil the day.

They had intended to get off the bus at a place called The Rookery, but they somehow managed to miss the stop and got off at the next stop, at a place called Wotton Hatch. Wotton had been the home of the diarist John Evelyn, and so they decided to go into the Evelyn family church, which lies at the end of a minor road. They came out of the churchyard, having spent rather more time there than they intended, and found themselves looking uphill at an overgrown path. They climbed up this for some time until they came to a wide clearing with a bench, on which they sat. To the left they could see a stretch of grass and then woodland, while on the right there was a steep drop downhill. Down in the valley, Mrs Allan was able to hear the sound of someone chopping wood and a dog barking.

When Mr Allan looked at his watch, he discovered that it was midday, and they decided to eat their sandwiches. Mr Allan was too depressed to feel hungry, and started crumbling his sandwiches for the birds.

Suddenly, the birdsong stopped, and there was a silence. Mrs Allan felt herself go cold with a sense of foreboding and fear. Then, without turning round, she felt she could see three figures standing in the clearing behind them. They seemed to be dressed in black clerical garb, and she was certain that they belonged to some time in the past. The central one had a round, friendly face, but the other two seemed to radiate hatred and hostility. What frightened Mrs Allan was her feeling that she had been able to see them without turning her head. When she tried to turn round, she felt paralysed.

She asked her husband if he thought everything had gone cold, and he touched her arm and said she felt like a corpse. Mrs Allan then said: "We must get out of here." And the two hastily descended. They found themselves on a path that crossed the railway line, went to the other side, and then lay down on the grass and fell asleep. Then they lost all recollection of what happened until, some time later, they took the train from Dorking.

The event preyed on Mrs Allan's mind, and she felt that she had to face up to it. So, almost two years later, she set out, alone, for Wotton.

At the churchyard, she felt that things seemed oddly different. She went inside, looked at the tombstones, then went to the churchyard gate, which should have led to the path at the bottom of the hill. Yet there was no path, and no hill. She could see woods half a mile to the west, but the fields around her were flat. Someone came past, and she enquired about the hill and the seat on which she had sat. The person she questioned was a local resident, yet had no idea of any place that resembled the one she was talking about.

When she returned home and told her husband what had happened, he told her that she must be making some kind of mistake. The following Sunday, he also went down to Wotton, and began by asking a local woodsman if he knew the place where they had sat on the wooden bench. The man said that, as far as he knew, there was no such place in this area.

Soon after this, Mr and Mrs Allan went along to the Society for Psychical Research and told their story to Sir George Joy, Honorary Secretary, and also G. W. Lambet, a member of the council. Unfortunately, the Society was in process of changing its headquarters, with the consequence that their account was somehow lost. However in July 1973, Mrs Allan told the story to Mary Rose Barrington, another member of the Society for Psychical Research. Mr Allan also added his own details.

Miss Barrington and another council member, John Stiles, went down to the Wotton area to investigate for themselves. They were able to verify that the land around the church was certainly flat.

Miss Barrington delivered a paper about the incident to the Society for Psychical Research in 1984. By that time, she and Mr Stiles had made two more visits to the area, and decided that there seemed to be no obvious normal explanation for what had happened – for example, that the Allans had simply lost their way.

Miss Barrington became convinced that she had at least found a clue to what had happened that day. It was in the diary of John Evelyn, who was a contemporary of Samuel Pepys. His entry for 15 March 1696 starts by talking about the sermon he had heard that day in Wotton church, and then mentions the execution of "three of the unhappy wretches (whereof one a priest)" who were part of a Catholic plot to assassinate William of Orange. Miss Barrington commented: "I cannot help associating Evelyn's three unhappy wretches, one a priest, with the three men in clerical types of garment, who sent such a cold shiver down the back of Mrs Allan. The thought of them may also have sent a shiver down Evelyn's back as he walked out of the church on that day and remembered the three executed assassins."

This, on the whole, seems a rather far-fetched explanation – that it was simply Evelyn's thoughts that had somehow been "recorded" and caused the Allans to pick them up two and a half centuries later.

But, in some ways, this case is even more puzzling than the case of Versailles. Hills do not simply disappear – not without modern earth-moving equipment – so it is difficult to know exactly what happened to the Allans when they came out of the churchyard and began to climb a hill.

Andrew MacKenzie, who tells the story of the Allans in his book *The Seen and the Unseen* (1987), returned to this subject of time-slips in a book called *Adventures in Time: Encounters with the Past* (1997). This, as he says in his introduction, is the first complete book to be devoted to time-slips – or what the Society for Psychical Research prefers to call "retrocognition".

His first case concerns three youths from the Royal Navy shore training establishment HMS *Ganges* near Shotley, in Suffolk, who went out on a training exercise on a bright Sunday morning in October 1957. Guided by bells, they approached a little village called Kersey.

They entered a lane leading to the Saxon church which they had seen through the trees and, as they came nearer, the bells quite suddenly stopped. As they turned a corner, they saw a dirt track on the right-hand side, with no houses, and on the left-hand side only two or three houses. The track ran down to a stream and rose to the northern end of the village, where there were more houses that were small, old and dirty. The three young men noticed that the village seemed to be completely empty. The only sign of life was a number of ducks who were waddling around the stream that ran through the middle of the village. They could see no cars, telephone wires, TV or radio aerials or anything else suggesting modern life.

They began to feel an odd sense of depression in the total silence. They knelt by a stream and drank from it, then jumped across it and peered into the window of a butcher's shop, in which they could see skinned carcasses of oxen, but they looked as if they had been there for a very long time, covered in green mould. This shop was also filthy and full of cobwebs. The youths, who were fifteen, peered through other windows in the house, but all they could see were empty rooms without furniture.

As they walked along, they began to feel that they were being watched. As they went up the silent village street, they broke into a run, and then paused at the top of the hill to look back. Suddenly, they could hear church bells, smoke hung in the air, and they could see the church behind the trees at the other end of the village. It was as if they had suddenly stepped back into the modern world. Thirty-one years later, this remarkable story was told in a letter by one of the three youths, now a middle-aged man, William Lang, who was a retired Navy wireless operator. He had emigrated to Australia in 1968 and, reading a book called *Hauntings and Apparitions* (1982) by Andrew MacKenzie, decided to write him an account of the experience. He also happened to know that another one of the three youths, Michael Crowley, was also in Australia, in Adelaide, South Australia, while William Lang was living in Leuras, New South Wales.

With considerable difficulty, Andrew MacKenzie succeeded
in tracing the third of the youths, Ray Baker, who responded to
an appeal in the *Navy News*. Unfortunately, he seemed to
remember very little.

In September 1990, William Lang and Andrew MacKenzie
visited the village of Kersey together and walked through it with
Hugh Pincott, of the Society for Psychical Research, and the
local historian Leslie Cockayne.

All the three youths clearly remembered seeing the butcher's
shop and the moulding carcasses hanging up. They recollected a
green painted door and windows with smallish glass panes. In
writing about it later, William Lang also recollected how the
colour of the vegetation suddenly changed as they approached
the village – it was October, and the vegetation was autumnal,
and then, quite suddenly, it became bright green, as if they had
walked from autumn into spring.

Michael Crowley was able to verify parts of the account – the
butcher's shop, the general air of desolation in the village, the fact
that there were no people, and no church or pub. The reason that
he had never taken any particular interest in the experience was
that, being a practical sort of person, he had simply not seen the
experience as in any way abnormal.

The third person, Ray Baker, said simply: "I did not notice
anything."

So what had happened? When MacKenzie visited the village, it
was certainly not a "grubby little place". Lang had described a
kind of footbridge made of a plank going across the stream,
although he had preferred to jump over it. Now, there is an
attractive footbridge. There are radio aerials and phone wires
everywhere. Nevertheless, as MacKenzie comments, it certainly
deserves the description of Sir Nikolaus Pevsner in his *The
Buildings of England* as "the most picturesque village in south
Suffolk". So it would seem that the Kersey seen by the three
youths was definitely not modern-day Kersey.

The village is first mentioned in an Anglo-Saxon will of about
990 AD. When William the Conqueror came, it was a thriving
community.

But in 1349, the growth of the village was suddenly checked by
the Black Death and a large proportion of the population died.
Then the village gradually revived and, by the end of the
fifteenth century, cloth-making had made it very prosperous.

When the woollen trade moved to Yorkshire, in the seventeenth century, Kersey once again became a farming village. In the mid-nineteenth century, there was a population of 800, but later on this dropped to its present level of about 350.

MacKenzie's own view is that the three youths entered the "circle of influence" as they climbed over the fence before entering the village, when the bells cut out, and they remained in a state of hallucination until they left at the northern end about half an hour later. "During this period of hallucination, the scenery of the present day was obliterated and that of an earlier period substituted for it. The people of the present day were also obliterated with the scenery, and we have the strange situation in which the village people who were around, as they must have been on that autumn day in 1957, were able to see the little group from HMS *Ganges* as they passed through the village, all squatted by the stream, but were themselves unobserved." MacKenzie wonders if this perhaps explains Miss Jourdain's feeling at Versailles when she could feel people around her, hear their voices, and actually feel clothes brushing past her, yet was unable to see anybody. Were these invisible people visitors from her own time, who were in the Versailles of 1902?

MacKenzie's own theory is that the village into which the two youths wandered in 1957 was, in fact, the village as it had been in 1349, during the Black Death. MacKenzie says:

"Mr Lang is not alone in finding the village a depressing place. On my first visit to Bridge House, from which the butchery business was once conducted, Mrs Finch and Miss Gladys King said there was a deeply unhappy feeling in the village marked by the fact that there had been fourteen suicides there in the last sixty years – a large number in such a small place. Both took seriously the suggestion that the village might be haunted. At the Bell Inn the landlady, Mrs Lynne Coote, a Yorkshirewoman, declared that the inn was haunted. I found it rather difficult to ascertain what form the haunting took but apparently she saw what she described as 'skeleton faces'. A former landlord had hanged himself there. Members of the staff of the inn agreed that the village was a sad place."

As we have seen, the retired Cambridge don, T. C. Leth-bridge, was convinced that ghosts are very often a kind of tape recording.

He and his wife Mina had moved from Cambridge after his retirement, to Hole House in Devon. On 22 February 1959, he was sitting on the hillside above the mill that was occupied by their neighbour. He saw her in the yard, and they waved to one another. Then, another woman appeared in the yard behind the neighbour. She looked in her late sixties, her face was rather dark, and she had a pointed chin. She was dressed in a dark tweed coat and skirt, and wore a long skirt and a broad-brimmed hat. Lethbridge assumed she was a guest staying at the mill.

Ten minutes later, Lethbridge and his wife saw the neighbour walking alone, and asked her about her guest. "So you are seeing my ghosts now, are you?" said the neighbour. It seemed that there was no one staying with her at the mill, and she had noticed no one with her in the yard ten minutes earlier.

The following year, Lethbridge and his wife decided to see whether there was anything in the story that ghosts appear on anniversaries, and went to the same spot on the hillside. Down below, they could see their neighbour working in her garden. Yet the "ghost" did not appear. What Lethbridge *did* notice was a kind of electrical tingling in the atmosphere. He was a good dowser, and he also noticed that the electrical tingling seemed strongest over a drain. As they walked at the side of a rivulet that ran from the drain, they both noticed the electrical tingling all the way along the running water. (Most dowsers say that water has to be running before they can detect it – the rod will not respond to still water.) At the same time, their neighbour, in her garden, heard a voice say distinctly "good morning", and one of her dogs came rushing up, barking, to see who it was. There was no one there.

Lethbridge came to the conclusion that the "ghost" had some-thing to do with the rivulet, which ran very close to their neighbour's garden. However, he had no idea what this observa-tion might mean.

In 1961, he stumbled on an interesting clue. On a grey, damp afternoon in January, he and Mina drove down to Ladram Bay to collect seaweed for the garden. Lethbridge noted that, as he stepped on to the beach, he passed into a kind of blanket, or fog, of depression – and, he added, fear. Mina went off looking for seaweed at the other end of the beach, then came hurrying back, saying: "I can't stand this place any longer."

That evening, when Mina spoke to her mother on the phone about what had happened, her mother commented that she had experienced the same depression on the same beach on Christmas Day, five years earlier. When Mina mentioned it to her brother, he remarked that he and his wife had had a similar feeling of horror and depression in a field near Avebury. Lethbridge asked: "What kind of weather was it?", and his brother-in-law replied: "Very warm and muggy."

Now Lethbridge recalled how he and his mother had been on a walk through the Great Wood near Wokingham when they had both experienced a sudden feeling of intense depression. A few days later, they heard that the body of a suicide had been found close to the spot where they had felt the atmosphere of gloom. Could it, Lethbridge now wondered, be something to do with the feelings that the man had somehow "imprinted" on the atmosphere before he killed himself?

In a spirit of experiment, he and Mina went back to the beach again the following Saturday. It was again a warm, drizzly day. They experienced the same "bank of depression" as they stepped on to the beach, and he noticed that it was near a place where a tiny stream ran down on to the beach. The depression, he now noticed, occurred around this stream, like a bad smell. Mina then pointed out the place where she had felt depressed the previous week, and they both noticed that the feeling was so powerful that it made them feel almost dizzy. It felt, he said, as if he had a high temperature and was full of drugs.

They went up to the cliff top, and Lethbridge began to make a sketch. Mina, meanwhile, wandered off and stood at the cliff top. When she came back, she told Lethbridge that she had experienced an unpleasant sensation as if someone was urging her to jump.

Back at home, Lethbridge thought this over. Their neighbour had died, after a quarrel with a farmer who lived on the other side of the mill, and she had told the Lethbridges that she intended to put a spell on his cattle. Lethbridge warned her against it, on the grounds that black magic often rebounds on the person who tries it. Their neighbour had died quite suddenly. Lethbridge noticed that after her death, there was an unpleasant feeling that hung around her house. He also noticed something else – that it had a quite definite limit – it was possible to step into it, and then step out of it again, as if it was a kind of invisible wall.

Now he remembered the tingling sensation alongside the rivulet when he had been waiting for the "ghost" to appear in the neighbour's yard. Could it be that such phenomena were something to do with water – or with the electrical field that surrounds running water? They had felt it on Ladron Beach – again close to running water.

He took his divining rod, and went to the spot from which he had seen the woman in the wide hat; then he noticed the stream that ran nearby, and that disappeared underground. He traced it with his dowsing rod, and discovered that it passed directly below the spot where he had seen the woman in the wide hat.

Could that, he wondered, be the answer? Was it possible that the electrical field of water could somehow record the emotions of human beings – and even their appearance? Could the electrical field of water be the "tape" that recorded ghosts?

Now most people involved in psychical research would agree that this is an over-simplification. There is some extremely strong evidence that ghosts are very often what tradition has always declared them to be – spirits. Yet Lethbridge was not particularly interested in spiritualism or life after death. His "tape recording" theory most certainly does apply to certain places that have an unpleasant "atmosphere".

It is clear that MacKenzie is suggesting something like the tape-recording theory to explain the "ghosts" of Versailles and the experience of the three young seamen at Kersey.

In the nineteenth century, such a theory would have seemed absurd. It seemed obvious that there is a fundamental difference between the world of "reality" around us and the world of illusion that a person in a fever might experience. All this changed with the discovery that the world is actually made up of atoms, which in turn consist mostly of empty space, like our solar system. In this space there are entities called electrons, which are negatively charged particles, and which are counter-balanced by positively charged particles, called protons. In the same way, when our eyes register an object, they are actually registering a stream of photons bouncing off the retina.

So the idea that the three young sailors might have walked into a "tape recording" of Kersey in the days of the Black Death, which seemed to them perfectly real and solid, is not as far-fetched as it sounds.

In a book called *The Mask of Time* (1978) Joan Forman quotes many cases of "time-slips". She mentions the experience of a friend, Mrs Anne Williams of Formby, Lancashire, who, on a summer afternoon, had been shopping with her brother in Southport, in Lancashire, and decided to have a cup of tea in the Kardomah teashop.

Just as Anne Williams had started to drink her tea, she noticed a change in the teashop:

"I noticed that all the angles of the room were out of order. The dado (i.e. frieze), the angle of the walls and ceiling, the whole perspective was wrong somehow. The very floor, as it ran into the distance, seemed crooked and out of true."

She tried closing her eyes, altering her position, yet the room remained as twisted as before. Even the people in the room seemed out of perspective. Then, after ten or fifteen minutes, the room returned to normal.

It sounds as if something she had eaten was not agreeing with her. Yet this seems to be contradicted by the fact that, when she went outside and mentioned to her brother that her eyes had seen the room distorted, he replied: "Good heavens, so did I. It gradually started when those two people [sitting opposite] lapsed into silence after talking to us." The experience had started for them at exactly the same time and ended at the same time.

Mr P. J. Chase told Joan Forman of his own similar experience. It was in 1968 and he was waiting for a bus near his place of work. Since he expected a long wait, he decided to walk along the road, to exercise his legs. After a short walk, he came to two cottages, which were thatched with straw and looked old. The gardens were particularly attractive – he noticed the variety of flowers and the presence of hollyhocks. One of the cottages had a date on the wall – 1837.

The next day, Mr Chase mentioned the cottages to a friend at work, and the man said that, as far as he knew, there were no cottages at that place.

The following evening, Mr Chase returned to the same spot, and discovered that the cottages were no longer there. In that position were two brick houses. Yet when Mr Chase enquired in the area from somebody who had lived there a long time, he learned that there *had* been two thatched cottages, which had been demolished many years before.

Presumably, this was not a case of some tragedy imprinting itself on the "atmosphere" of this spot. It sounds, rather, as if the cottages had simply left behind a kind of "tape recording" and Mr Chase, because he was in a thoroughly relaxed mood, somehow picked up this tape recording.

What would have happened if Mr Chase had knocked on the door of one of the cottages? Would it have been opened by a ghost from the past? Or would he have found that he was knocking on the door of one of the two brick houses?

Another letter, from Mrs Louisa W. Hand, quoted by Joan Forman, seems to suggest that she might indeed have seen past tenants. Mrs Hand described how, when she was eight or nine, in about 1920, she had lived in a small village called Cockey Moore, near Bury in Lancashire.

She was playing in the front garden of her grandmother's cottage, and then went back in, running through the open front door. Here, to her bafflement, the furniture was different, and the doorway to the kitchen and the opposite wall had vanished. Mrs Hand found it all very quiet, and everything seemed darker.

Thinking she had somehow run into the wrong cottage, she went out again. This time she made sure she went in by the right door. Still the surroundings were quite different. She went out into the garden and waited there a few minutes, then went back in – and found herself back in her grandmother's usual cottage. Joan Forman is certain that she walked back into the cottage's past.

But, of course, her grandmother's cottage had the same front door as the cottage in the past. Yet what would have happened if Mrs Hand had tried to sit down on the sofa? Would she have gone through it and landed on the floor? In *Adventures in Time*, Andrew MacKenzie recounts an experience that sounds like that of Mr Chase. John Watson, an engineer of Nottingham, wrote in a letter:

"In the summer of 1961, I had just finished my 'O' Level examinations and had a lot of time on my hands. One sunny afternoon, I was strolling aimlessly round Nottingham, a city I knew extremely well, having lived there all my life. I was somewhere near the castle, but was not sure exactly where, when I turned a corner and was suddenly struck by a feeling of having stepped into the past. I was looking into a narrow cobbled street, on one side of which was a row of half-timbered cottages with shutters alongside the windows and window boxes full of brightly coloured flowers – I seemed to think they were mostly geraniums. There was no one in sight and the street was surprisingly quiet for somewhere near a city centre. It was obviously a cul-de-sac so I did not enter the street but turned round and carried on towards the castle, being surprised to find such a picturesque spot which I did not know. I later described it to my mother and other relatives, all of whom had lived in Nottingham all their lives, but none of them recognized the street from my description. Since then I have often looked for the street but without success and I decided the street no longer existed.

"The sequel to this is that the Nottingham *Evening Post* ran a series of photographs of old Nottingham scenes, and I was interested to see, last year, a photo of the very street I had seen. The caption stated it to be Jessamine Cottages, but I had a strange feeling when I read the street had been demolished in the mid-1950s. My mother spoke to Dr Dick Iliffe of the Nottingham Historical Film Unit (to whom the film belonged) a few days later and he confirmed the date of the demolition. I suppose it is possible I had seen the street as a child, but I do not consciously remember doing so and in any case I am sure of the year in which I saw it, because of having just taken my exams."

Andrew MacKenzie checked with John Watson's mother, who confirmed that he had told her about the experience at the time, "and when a picture of this very place appeared in the *Evening Post*, he recognized it at once, only to read that the property was demolished quite a time before John had seen it."

Another similar story was passed on to MacKenzie by Mrs Gladys McAvoy, of Inverness. She describes how, in August 1966, she was in the village of Altandhu in Wester Ross, in the Scottish highlands. She and her family were staying at a holiday house that had been built for them. On 5 August Mrs McAvoy's husband took the children swimming, and Mrs McAvoy decided to walk to the other end of the village to see a crofter friend. She remarks that she was feeling "vague" and decided that it was the result of fatigue after a long drive the previous day. She was noticing the houses as she passed them, and found one particularly attractive.

"Because it lay at an angle to the road I could see down into the 'garden' – just a grassy (or cobbled?) square, as far as I remember. The house was of grey stone with the gable end nearest to the road, and what struck me as of more interest than anything else was the fact that it had a chimney at both ends (as is usual in croft houses) and that *both* were smoking. I felt sure that it was a very busy house, though no one was about."

Later that morning, her husband called to take her home from the friend's house, and she mentioned the house she had seen and asked if he knew who lived there. They stopped at the place from which she had seen the house – and from which her own house had been visible – but there was nothing there, not even a heap of stones.

About two weeks later, while visiting neighbours, she described her experience and asked them whether there had been a house there. Their curious reply was that "it will just mean that someone is thinking of building there". But finally they agreed that there had been such a house exactly where she saw it. It had indeed been a busy house with a large family. A daughter of the family, now ninety years of age, still lived in a nearby village.

In fact, the local postman built a house on the site of the house that she had seen.

Again, MacKenzie went to considerable trouble to verify the story, talking to Mrs McAvoy's husband and to the various friends concerned – all were able to verify it.

An equally puzzling case is that of a couple named Pye, who had gone to Falmouth, in Cornwall, for a holiday in June 1933. After ten days, they decided to spend the rest of their holiday on the North Cornish Coast, and decided to go to Boscastle. On 17 June 1933, they went to Wadebridge by train, and took a bus for Boscastle, passing Tintagel and Trevalga. They were on the lookout for some guest house or hotel where they could stay.

Close to Boscastle, not far between the top of the steep hair-pin bend that descends into the town, the bus stopped to let off a passenger, and the Pyes noticed that they were at the gate of a house on the left-hand side of the road. It stood back from the road and the garden was screened from the road by a hedge, over which the Pyes could see from the bus. The house was double-fronted and of a style of architecture that Mr Pye judged to date from the late 1860s. It had a fresh, trim appearance and seemed to have been recently painted. Its most striking feature were several large garden umbrellas of black and orange which shaded wicker chairs among beds of scarlet geraniums.

It certainly looked like a guest house, and they decided that it was just the kind of place they would like to stay. So when the bus halted in Boscastle, and they found the smell of seaweed disagreeable, Mrs Pye decided to walk back up the hill while her husband sat and rested.

When Mrs Pye had not returned, half an hour later, Clifford Pye became anxious. Finally, about an hour and a half later, she came back to explain that she had been unable to find the house. She had walked all the way to Trevalga, and found a boarding house there.

The Pyes agreed that it should have been impossible to overlook the house because of the bright umbrellas in the garden, and so, on the bus going back, they took great care to look out of the window. There was certainly no house where they had seen it – just empty fields. Later, during their stay at Trevalga, they made another search, but again failed to find the house.

But in this case, the mystery was solved, and proved to have nothing supernatural about it. Almost thirty years later, in 1962, Miss M. Scott-Eliott, a member of the Society for Psychical Research, set out to look for the house seen by the Pyes. On the outskirts of Boscastle, halfway down the steep hill, she found a house that looked similar to the one described by the Pyes. It was named Melbourne House, and a twelve foot wall and hedge hid the garden.

The late owner's nephew was able to tell her that the house had been painted brown – exactly as the Pyes had seen it – in 1932, that it had a centre flowerbed filled with scarlet geraniums, and that there had been wicker chairs on the lawn. Yet there never had been any umbrellas. These, in fact, were in the café at the bottom of the hill. They had black and orange stripes, just like those remembered by the Pyes. The solution to the mystery seemed to be that the Pyes had not realized that the house was not at the top of the hill, but halfway down it, and that they had somehow associated the umbrellas in the café with the garden of the house. The Pyes had made this mistake because it was nine more years before they wrote the account that appeared in *The Journal of the Society for Psychical Research*.

But this explanation certainly does not apply to one of the most interesting cases discussed by MacKenzie in *Adventures in Time*, even though it was also reported in *The Journal of the Society for Psychical Research* nine years after it had happened. Nevertheless, it was written down within two years of taking place.

In March 1938, a Mr J. S. Spence was taking a holiday on the Devonshire coast. He had walked along a beach exploring rocks and pools, towards a headland on the far side. He noted – as in so many of these cases – "As I went the atmosphere, which at first so much appealed, grew heavy and depressing.

"Eventually, in a little inlet in the headland, I came upon a cave which seemed large enough to enter on hands and knees. I felt very much afraid but curiosity drove me into it. A few yards down the tunnel, I noticed daylight ahead and after a further two or three yards I found myself in a vast cave which apparently extended to the further side of the headland as I was only in semi-darkness.

"Although there was clearly no one in the cave, I had an unpleasant feeling of being watched and scrambled back to the cove through the little tunnel as quickly as was consistent with self-respect. I now saw and found a little path by which I could clamber up the cliff and, once on top, I set out to climb to the summit of the ridge, less than a quarter of a mile away. I now felt even more depressed and lonely than before and had the impression that something was straining on a leash, so that one could almost hear the noise that something made, trying to break the bonds. However, I went on slowly, though waist-deep in bracken and bramble. After ten minutes or so I came upon a long old-fashioned type of wall made of slabs and stone and earth – no mortar. The stone looked very fresh and there were no creepers on it. As I passed through a gap, left as if for a gate, I noticed that the wall stretched about eighty yards or so over the grass, bramble and bracken to the edge of the cliff, which was there very high. Almost at right angles to it another wall sloped steeply down the hill and disappeared among the scrub and bracken on the headland.

"I was puzzled why the walls should be there but decided that if I were not to be late for lunch I must hurry on to my objective, a point where, according to a large-scale Ordnance map, I would find a solitary tree beside an old gate. On looking ahead I saw neither the tree nor the gate, but a mass of stunted trees, bent by the prevailing wind. The heat was terrific and the stillness awful, so I hurried on to get into the shade. As I went forward, the atmosphere became less charged and less tense and, for the first time since I had entered the cove about half an hour earlier, I heard a definitely real sound: a seagull flew over my head, screaming. Then, to my surprise, I saw ahead the lone tree and gate and I was also surprised to find on looking back that the grass seemed greener and fresher and the bracken less than when I had passed through it. The wall was apparently hidden behind the brow of the hill. My head was aching less and I could breathe more easily. When I got home I felt astonishingly weary and my good appetite had quite disappeared.

"The next day, I decided to set forth on the same walk about the same time. The sun was even warmer than the day before but the odd depressing feeling and the strange stillness had gone. On reaching the cove, I was surprised to find the tide right up, for the day before it must have been low to enable me to cross the beach to the cave in the headland. Surely, I thought, the tide cannot alter more than an hour a day? I turned back and climbed the hill behind towards the summit of the ridge and the wall. On reaching the top, I was amazed to find myself near the edge of a cliff and with no sign of a long new wall, and I thought I must have gone wrong. There was certainly a very old scrap of wall covered in ivy, with another portion leaving it at right-angles, but within a few feet it broke off at the end of a cliff. My eye then followed the branch wall, expecting to see it disappear in scrub, but it, too, stopped abruptly, very dilapidated, at the edge of the cliff.

"For a while, this puzzled me; then I gave it up and walked on. Almost at once, I was startled to see the lone tree and the gate. I was certain I had been in the same spot the day before and had seen only a mass of bent and stunted trees and I knew I had seen a long new wall. I came to the conclusion that I must have taken the wrong path and I decided to return the next day with a torch and a camera and explore the cave and find the wall. How I had come to miss my way in such a small area was beyond me.

"I reached the cove next morning to find the tide fairly full and I could not get across to the cave for a couple of hours. I distinctly remembered the little inlet in the headland where I had entered the cave at sea level but, on reaching it, there was no cave. I at last found, a few feet up in a pile of shale and hidden by a large boulder, an entrance to what was obviously a cave, but far smaller than it had been two days before. As a large pile of shale showed signs of collapse and there was hardly room to wriggle in, I decided not to risk it and walked back to find the path by which I had climbed the cliff. This was not to be seen, but further along I found another which led up to the headland.

"Here, to satisfy myself as to my whereabouts, I made my way through some bracken and over a stile to the end of the headland and then returned to where I expected to find the top of the path by which I had climbed the first day. The place, however, looked impossible to get down and I wondered how I had ever got up, so I decided to go along the cliff towards Dartmouth. As I reached the top of the cliff path the atmosphere seemed charged and unfriendly again. I had the same tight feeling across my forehead and felt the same sweat breaking out.

"There came that peculiar sensation of something straining at its leash. There was no particular sound to this effect, to which I could have stopped and listened, and possibly logically explained, but I received the impression, on a much larger scale, as it were, of a cart-horse straining at a wagonload of bricks which it could not possibly drag.

"I moved on mechanically through the ferns, which suddenly seemed to have become waist-deep again, and it was with considerable difficulty that I made any progress.

"I had forgotten about the wall until I came to it, in front of me with its new-looking slabs of stone, neatly placed into and against each other. Down to the left it stretched for some way, over grass and brambles and bracken to the edge of the cliff. Furthermore, another wall jutted away from it almost at right angles, and sloped sharply down the hill, nearly in the direction in which I had come, and disappeared amongst scrubs and undergrowth somewhere on the headland.

"I went up close to the wall and walked a few paces forward. I felt giddy, as if looking from a great height, but in front of me, without any doubts stretched the wall. On an impulse, I pulled out my camera, and attempted to find an object in the viewfinder, but my giddiness increased and I clicked the shutter with very little care. I put my camera away in my pocket and prepared to move forward.

"I had gone only one short pace, when I felt my left foot slip and go down as if into a rabbit hole. The shock threw me off my balance, and my left foot twisted so that I felt my body collapse. As I fell, my hand grasped wildly and came into contact with tufts of thick coarse grass, and I held on tight. My body came to rest on my twisted left foot, while my right foot shot into space. For a few moments, everything went black.

"When I opened my eyes, I immediately became aware of two things: the shrieking of the seagulls, and the very dangerous position in which I was. Two small sturdy tufts of grass, and a ledge a few inches wide, on which my left foot lay, had saved me from the rocks below. Almost immediately above my head was the broken fragment of an old ivy-covered wall.

"For some minutes, I clung to the grass and dared not move. When some composure returned, I realized the seriousness of the position. With great care, I gradually wormed my way to a cautious standing position, though the whole of my weight, until I could bring my right foot on to the ledge, had to be thrown on to the damaged left. Then I caught hold of a large tuft of grass further away from the edge of the cliff, tested it, and pulled my right leg up and on to the top of the cliff. The left leg followed slowly. I dared not look back, but carefully I manoeuvred my way on my stomach to a safe position some yards from the top of the cliff.

"After a few minutes, my mind cleared a little. The atmosphere had returned to normal, and the tremendous pressure that I had felt had gone. I looked to the right. The lone tree and gate were in their proper positions. Out in front, where the wall had stretched, was nothing but space, but some distance out at sea there was a group of rocks.

"Then, as if suddenly aware of my recent escape, I got up and as quickly as possible set off home. Down the slope towards the cove, I suddenly remembered the portion of the wall that had jutted out at right angles, which had appeared to

stretch to the headland, to be lost in brambles. So I went out
to the headland and, after a long search, found not far from
the edge of the cliff and directly in line with the tumbledown
bit, which could be seen on top of the ridge, a fragment of wall
buried in the bramble."

MacKenzie adds that a photograph of this section of wall taken
after the experience and one taken by Mr Spence just before he
nearly walked off the cliff edge accompanied his article in the
Journal.

MacKenzie then goes on to a lengthy criticism of Spence's
experience, which was published in the *Journal* in December
1947. Its author, J. T. Evans, identifies the area of cliff as Crab
Rock Point at Man Sands, near Brixham. The point of Evans'
criticism is that he believes that Spence simply took the wrong
path, and that his whole experience can be explained very simply
as a simple mistake. The editor of the *Journal* agreed with Evans
and commented: "the case is not evidential".

On the other hand, MacKenzie points out that Spence's
experience when he almost fell over the cliff can hardly be
explained as a sense of misdirection. He also points out that
Spence had the typical sensation of depression and unreality, and
the sensation of being watched. There was also the cessation of
bird calls and an unnatural silence. MacKenzie says: "In his
hallucinatory experience he 'saw' fields and wall which had once
existed but which had disappeared during cliff falls."

MacKenzie cites another case in which there can be very little
doubt that the experience cannot be explained away as some kind
of mental confusion.

On 2 January 1952 Miss E. F. Smith, of Letham, Angus, a
woman in her late fifties, attended a cocktail party at a friend's
house at Brechin, ten miles to the north of Letham, and stayed for
dinner. A fall of snow had been followed by rain so that, on the
way home, her car skidded into a ditch. Uninjured, Miss Smith
decided that her only course was to walk home, about eight miles.
So, with her little dog on her shoulder, she set out to walk
through deserted countryside with a few scattered farms.

Seven and a half miles further on, about half a mile from the
first houses of Letham, she saw what seemed to be moving
torches. She went on to turn left towards Letham at a T-junction,
so the lights were now on her right. As she walked on down the

winding road, she saw, in the middle distance, more figures carrying torches. Finally, these figures were only about fifty yards away, in the direction of some farm buildings.

The dog began to growl, and Miss Smith hurried on until she left the figures and torches behind her as she entered the village. Arriving home some time after two a.m., she went straight to bed. It was only on awakening the next morning that she realized what a strange experience she had had.

Twenty years later, Dr James McHarg, a member of the Society for Psychical Research, heard of her experience, and went to interview her. By then, she was in her seventies.

Based on the tape recordings he made that day, McHarg went on to research the area around Letham, and came to the conclusion that what Miss Smith had seen was "a vision of the aftermath of the battle of Nechtanesmere", which took place in 685 AD.

In this battle, which happened on 20 May 685 AD, the Northumbrians under their king Ecgfrith were beaten by the Picts, under their king Brude mac Beli. Ecgfrith had mounted an expedition, against the advice of St Cuthbert and other Northumbrians. Ecgfrith is believed to have been diverted from his route by a feigned Pictish retreat through a cleft in Dunnichen Hill, and they followed them. Then they realized that the Pict fortress was only a few hundred yards away. The Picts, with reinforcements, pursued the fleeing Northumbrians towards the mere at the bottom. Ecgfrith, his royal bodyguard and most of his army were killed. The exact site of the battle has not been determined, but Dr McHarg is convinced that it was in the area of Letham.

Miss Smith saw some of the figures carrying torches walking around the edge of a mere. She said of the figures who came closest to her: "They were obviously looking for their own dead . . . the one I was watching, the one nearest the roadside, would bend down and turn a body over and, if he didn't like the look of it, he just turned it back on its face and went over to the next one . . . there were several of them . . . I *supposed* they were going to bury them."

Asked about how they were dressed, she said: "They looked as if they were in – well, I would have said brown, but that was merely the light – anyway, dark tights, the whole way up . . . a sort of overall, with a rolled collar, and at the end of their tunics there was a larger roll round them too. And it simply went on looking like tights until it reached their feet. I did not see what was on their feet. But there weren't long boots." MacKenzie points out that a tracing from a photograph of an incised figure of a Pict warrior on a stone at Golspie shows a bootless figure, and gives the impression of tights, and also of a roll-necked tunic with what could be a "roll" at the bottom of it.

Asked about the torches, she commented that they were very long, and very red. Research about torches in Scotland revealed that they used to be made from the resinous roots of the Scots fir, which have a distinctive red colour. Dunnichen Hill was crowned with Scots firs.

MacHarg pointed out to Miss Smith that Dr F. T. Wainwright, head of the Department of History at Queens College, Dundee, had attempted to create a map with a vanished loch. Miss Smith had had the feeling that some of the figures with torches were trying to skirt the mere – or loch. MacHarg wondered whether Miss Smith might have seen the map, but she explained that, although she had met Dr Wainwright, she had not seen the map before her experience. In any case, MacKenzie suggests that it is unlikely that anyone but an experienced map-reader would have been able to work out exactly where the loch was supposed to be.

In view of Miss Smith's clear sight of the figures, of the torches they were carrying, there seems to be little doubt that she experienced some kind of time-slip – and the most likely explanation is that the battle of Nechtanesmere took place in that area.

Joan Forman has a similar story about a couple called White, who lived on the Isle of Wight, and who had a strange experience on the night of 4 January 1969.

They were on their way to dine with friends, and drove across the Downs. It was a dark night with towering masses of cloud, but there was a brilliant full moon. They began to climb the first hill approaching the Downs, with chalky pits to the left and fields to the right. It is a lonely area, and they were surprised to find that the fields appeared to be covered with bobbing lights, as though crowds of people were moving about. The Whites assumed that probably shepherds were working at night on their lambing.

At the top of the hill, they noticed that all the fields on their right were also ablaze with lights – "like a great city".

They halted the car, wondering what was happening, but certain that it was something quite normal, perhaps an agricultural exhibition. What puzzled them was that in the distance, what they thought was a simple cart track seemed to be a well-lit city street with buildings on either side. The lights were green, red and orange. Yet when they arrived at the farm track, it was the same as usual, dark and deserted.

Now feeling rather nervous, they looked forward to reaching an inn called The Hare and Hounds, at the crossroads to Newport and Merstone. When they turned the corner and saw the inn, they found that it was also bathed in light and surrounded by what appeared to be figures carrying torches. They were running backwards and forwards across the road. The fields on either side also seemed to be brightly lit. They noticed an exceptionally tall man with clean-cut features who ran directly in front of the car, and they were able to see that he was wearing a leather jerkin with a broad belt.

Dr White decided that it was time to stop and ask what was going on. Yet, when the car was close to the Hare and Hounds, everything suddenly became dark, "as if a switch had been thrown". The pub was in darkness, and all the people seemed to have disappeared from the road and the surrounding fields.

When they came back the same way, in the early hours of the morning, everything was back to normal.

The Whites made the observation that we have come to expect – that, during the whole experience, there was a feeling of oppressiveness and a sense of unreality.

The Whites now began to investigate, wondering if they had seen some kind of reflection from Portsmouth, across the Solent. Yet, of course, this would certainly not have explained the figures who were running around.

Sheila White, later a widow, suggested that the experience might have been either of the past or future. Roman legions had once camped and marched in that area, then known as Vectis. Roman camps were built with at least two streets intersecting at right angles. Around a permanent fort, they were built on a grid system. Torches were used for illumination.

But Vectis was also occupied by invading Vikings, who set up winter camps there in the late tenth century, and used the island as a base from which to attack the mainland. The dress worn by the tall man sounds more like Viking than Roman costume.

What would have happened if Dr White had stopped the car and asked the figure what was going on? Would it have answered him, like the figures seen at Versailles? Or would it have simply vanished into thin air?

At the end of *Adventures in Time*, Andrew MacKenzie has an interesting chapter called "Seeking an Answer". He begins by pointing out that time, as described in modern physics, does not "flow". Instead, we have an entity called space-time, which could be regarded as more or less permanent.

He goes on to quote Professor H. H. Price, who was the President of the Society for Psychical Research.

His presidential address was called " '*Haunting*' ' and the ' "*psychic ether*" ' hypothesis". "Images", according to Professor Price, are "dynamic rather than static".

This theory is close to what Madame Blavatsky calls "the akasic records", records that are supposed to exist of everything that has ever happened. According to this theory, everything that happens imprints itself upon a kind of "psychic ether" and the recording then remains, so to speak, in the archives, until somebody happens to take it out and activate it.

This is clearly not all that dissimilar to the theory of psychometry put forward by Joseph Rodes Buchanan in the mid-nineteenth century – everything that has happened somehow imprints itself upon some recording medium, particularly the walls of houses, and can later be "recovered".

At first, this idea seems completely mad. Yet then, the idea of radio would have struck scientists in the nineteenth century as equally mad. The same would have been true of (now old-fashioned) gramophone records, which can actually capture the sound of a complete orchestra in one single wavy line imprinted in wax. Yet we now know that this is not science fiction but fact. We might imagine that this "imprinting" process could only take place where human beings – or at least living creatures – are present. It is not too difficult to believe that the walls of a haunted room have somehow absorbed an impression of powerful and tragic emotions that took place in this room. Yet how can we explain William Denton's observation that a piece of volcanic lava from Hawaii gave the psychometrist a clear view of an exploding volcano, and lava pouring into the sea? Yet there are so many similar stories recorded by both Denton and Buchanan – as well as later investigators like Dr Gustave Pagenstecher – that there is certainly very strong evidence for the "akasic records" theory.

Consider this curious case cited by Andrew MacKenzie. In 1860, a Mr. Robert Palfrey was putting the finishing touches to a haystack he was thatching in Kingshall Street in Bradfield St George, a village near Bury St Edmunds. Looking across the narrow lane, he was startled to see a house and garden with roses and flowerbeds in full bloom. The house had solid red bricks and the flowerbeds were edged with the same red bricks planted slantwise and half-buried. There were two entrances with ornamental iron gates, which were closed. Mr Palfrey noticed that the air had suddenly turned distinctly chilly, although it was a warm June evening, and that he had the feeling that it was something unreal.

He told the story when he got back home, and his relatives went back to the spot – only to find that the house was certainly not there.

About half a century later, Robert Palfrey's great-grandson (who, in his account, prefers to use the pseudonym John Cobbold) apparently saw the same house. He tells how when he was twelve he used to go out with a butcher, Mr George Waylett, on his Saturday deliveries, and how they had just left one of the houses in Kingshall Street when there was a loud swishing "whoosh", as of air being displaced, and the air suddenly became very cold; the pony reared and bolted, and Mr Waylett was thrown from the cart. The boy then glimpsed a double-fronted red brick house roofed with pantiles, with three storeys and a distinctly Georgian appearance. There were flowerbeds in full bloom in front of it. Mr Cobbold managed to turn the pony and said that, as he did so, "a kind of mist seemed to envelop the house, which I could still see, and the whole thing simply disappeared; it just went".

"John Cobbold" published the article in an issue of *Amateur Gardening* on 20 December 1975 and, after it had appeared, a young man from the village told him that his father had seen the same house at least twice during the past ten years.

A story like this – particularly from a source like *Amateur Gardening* – sounds unreliable, for even if we can accept that John Cobbold has not made it up, there is still the chance that all kinds of mistakes and exaggerations have crept into it. In fact, Andrew MacKenzie arranged for Mr Cobbold to be interviewed by a Mr and Mrs Aves and a Captain D. Armstrong RN of Rougham, and John Cobbold actually came all the way from Cambridgeshire especially for the interview. He took the three witnesses straight along Kingshall Street, to a spot opposite a lane called Gypsy Lane, opposite which there was a gap in the hedgerow with an entrance to a field of winter wheat. Mr Cobbold indicated a point in the field and said that it was in this place where both he and his great-grandfather had seen the house.

Oddly enough, this is not the only phantom house seen in the area of Bradfield St George. Another account was sent to Sir Ernest Bennett, and printed in his book *Apparitions and Haunted Houses* (1939). He had made a broadcast five years earlier, and the account was sent to him as a consequence. It came from Miss Ruth Wynne, who ran a small private school in Rougham, at the Rectory.

Miss Wynne tells how she came to live in Rougham in 1926, and how on a dull, damp afternoon in October, they walked off through the fields to look at the church in Bradfield St George. They had to pass through a farmyard, and came out on a road. Opposite, they saw a high wall of greenish-yellow bricks. They followed this wall round the bend, and found tall wrought-iron gates. Behind the wall was a cluster of tall trees, and from the gates, a drive led away among these trees to what was evidently a large house. They could see a corner of the roof above a stucco front, in which there were some windows of Georgian design. They then went on and walked to the church, and then across the fields and home.

They discussed the big house with her parents, but thought no more about it.

The following spring, the two once again took the following walk, on what was once again a dull afternoon. Having walked across the farmyard, both stopped and gasped: "Where's the wall?" There was nothing alongside the road but a ditch, and beyond that a wilderness of tumbled earth and weeds. Only the trees were still there. Round the bend, there was no gate, no drive, no house.

Their first speculation was that the house had been pulled down since they last saw it, until they noticed a duck pond and other small pools among the mounds, covered with weeds, and it was obvious that they had been there for a very long time.

The two women told Miss Wynne's parents, who simply thought that they must have been mistaken.

The pupil who had been with Miss Wynne was called Miss Allington, and she replied to Sir Ernest Bennett's letter, verifying everything that Miss Wynne had said.

Andrew MacKenzie went to the trouble of calling at the Suffolk record office to check whether there had been a house on that site many years earlier – perhaps in the eighteenth century. He learned that no such house had ever existed.

Now, if we are convinced by these stories, and do not dismiss them as some kind of fantasy or mis-identification, then we find ourselves once again reflecting upon Dr Joad's remark about the undoubted queerness of time.

The truth is that there is a sense in which time does not really exist. If we imagine an infinity of empty space, it is obvious that nothing can take place in it – until some object intrudes into it. Time is something which is associated with objects.

Moreover, we all know that time can move at different speeds. For a child who is late for school, time seems very compressed. On the other hand, for a tree growing in the spring, time is obviously far more leisurely.

In fact, time is *process*.

We normally use clocks to measure time, but this is only a convention. It is just as easy to imagine, for example, dropping an effervescent tablet into a glass of water, and watching it fizz away until it dissolves. Time could just as easily be measured by this method. If we think of time as something happening, in this way, then we can suddenly see that it might easily leave some mark of its progress on its surroundings – for example, little bubbles that have floated out of the glass and made a thin spray of mist on the table around it. If we now think of a house in the same spot for several centuries, and many families growing up in it, we can also see that it could easily leave some kind of trace behind, some kind of mark. If the glass was removed, a person who possessed the same powers of reasoning as Sherlock Holmes could probably look at the table top, and deduce that a glass had been there some time before.

But perhaps a "sensitive" person – a so-called "psychic" – might have such *unconscious* powers of observation that he or she might actually see a house in the place where it had once been, as Mrs McAvoy saw the house with two chimneys in Altandhu.

It is also possible that there are certain times or conditions when some past event comes particularly close to the surface of the present, in the way that an old bloodstain might appear on a piece of oak floorboard. The time may well have been right for these conditions when Miss Smith seemed to see long-dead Picts turning over their fallen comrades with the aid of torches.

Another interesting clue seems to be afforded by the case of Anne Williams, already quoted, who went into the Kardomah tea-shop in Southport, and suddenly noticed the change in the room: "I noticed that all the angles of the room were out of order . . . the whole perspective was wrong somehow. The very floor, as it ran into the distance, seemed crooked and out of true."

We have already looked at the theory of Immanuel Kant that our senses are far more active than we think – that they actually impose a certain order on the things around us. Any scientist would tell you that colour in itself does not exist. When you look at a rainbow, you are not really seeing red, orange, yellow, blue, indigo and violet. You are seeing a number of different wavelengths, which your eye interprets as these colours – in other words, it simplifies its interpretation by turning the wavelengths into colours. The whole process has become unconscious – in the same way that we can read a sentence, and simply take in its meaning, without spelling out individual words and syllables.

So it is quite easy to imagine that, if the world that we appear to "see" is actually *interpreted* by our senses, then some slight change in our senses might make the whole world look quite different.

But perhaps the oddest thing of all, if we can believe these accounts of retrocognition, is that there seems to be some sense in which the past continues to exist. The wall seen at the top of the cliff near Brixham by Mr Spence was at the same time a newly built wall and an old wall that was falling to pieces. If Mr Spence was merely suffering from some kind of delusion when he saw the past wall instead of the present one, then we also have to suppose that the furze and bracken and trees were also the past version of furze and bracken and trees, and were merely some kind of appearance. In that case, why was Mr Spence not continually tripping over clumps of furze which existed in 1932 but not at the date – presumably in the past century – when the wall was first built? Why were the two English ladies at Versailles able to walk around to the front of the house, following the footman, when two walls had been built since then? The world in which they found themselves was obviously something slightly more than a mere appearance.

What is the explanation of this feeling of feverishness and unreality that seems to be experienced by just about everybody who has described a time-slip? Why do ordinary sounds seem to fade away?

If I try to play back an old video tape, perhaps made years before, on a recently purchased video recorder, I may get very poor results – the sound may seem distorted, the picture may jump up and down, and I become suddenly aware that the quality of a recording depends completely upon the machine it is played on. Yet, when I am looking at a picture on the television, I find it hard to imagine it flickering up and down, or looking less real. It seems so ordinary and "normal" that it is hard to think of it in terms of some kind of mechanical transmission which can run into problems.

We have the same feeling about the world that surrounds us. It looks so completely solid that we take its reality for granted. Yet if we happen to be feeling feverish, and we take a lot of medication, this normal and solid world suddenly becomes to seem slightly unreal. T. C. Lethbridge, we recall, described exactly this "feverish" feeling when he was walking on the beach at Ladram and experiencing an unpleasant feeling which seemed to emanate from the small stream that ran down onto the beach.

What was happening? Was he really sensing some past time? Was the "tape recorder" of his senses trying to play some unfamiliar tape recorded on another machine?

The one thing that emerges from all these speculations is that it is a mistake to regard this world around us as solid and real. Our senses could be regarded as tape recorders that play back the impressions that fall on them from the outside world. What we are watching is, in fact, a tape recording, not the "real world".

T. C. Lethbridge was convinced that our physical reality is only one of several worlds, which exist parallel to one another. He came to this interesting conclusion through dowsing with the use of a pendulum. Many dowsers prefer a pendulum to a divining rod, on the grounds that it is more sensitive and accurate. They most frequently use a small bob, usually a wooden bead on the end of a string about six inches long. This, they insist, can not only detect water and other underground substances, but can also answer "yes or no".

When Lethbridge moved into Hole House, he decided to try a much longer pendulum, and was startled to find that, according to its length, it responded with great accuracy to various substances, such as silver, lead, copper, iron, and even to objects like truffles, tomatoes and potatoes. If Lethbridge held the pendulum above a little heap of sulphur, and slowly lengthened it to seven inches (from a small ball of string that he held in his hand), the pendulum went into a circular swing over the sulphur. If he held it over an ivy leaf, it went into a circular swing at ten and a half inches. Carbon responded at twelve inches, mercury at twelve and a half, sand at fourteen, and so on, right down to forty. Lethbridge tried lengthening the pendulum beyond forty, and was surprised when it once again began to respond to the various substances at the usual length, plus forty – sulphur at forty-seven, mercury at fifty-two and a half, and so on.

Beyond eighty, it began to do the same thing all over again. Lethbridge was unable to continue his experiments beyond one hundred and twenty, because the pendulum was now becoming much too long and he had to stand on a balcony to use it.

Lethbridge made another curious discovery – that the pendulum not only responded to substances, but also to ideas and feelings. For example, he found that when he and Mina threw stones, the pendulum afterwards showed distinctly which of them had thrown the stones by responding at the appropriate rates for male and female – respectively twenty-four inches and twenty-nine inches. The pendulum also responded to such ideas as anger, sex, evolution and death. Death, significantly, was at forty inches. This led Lethbridge to the interesting supposition that what lies beyond forty inches is somehow in the "next world", beyond death.

Lethbridge tried making the pendulum respond to the idea of time, but it refused to do so at any rate below forty. However, at sixty – forty plus twenty – it responded to time.

Lethbridge concluded that the pendulum *ought*, in theory, to respond at a rate of twenty inches, but that it does not do so because we are *in* time, like someone being carried along the river in a boat, for whom the stream has no speed. In the "next" world, beyond forty inches, the pendulum responded to time – but, as far as Lethbridge could work out from his experiments, "time" in the next world is static. He admits that he does not understand what this means. He thought that objects might exist in this next world as if they were in glass cases in a museum – permanently still and unmoving. In the next world still, beyond eighty inches, the pendulum reacts normally for time, as if this world also has a flowing time, like our own, but at one hundred and twenty inches, there is once again no time.

Lethbridge concluded that different worlds, or "dimensions", somehow exist parallel to this one, but on a different vibrational rate, exactly like different radio stations – which do not interfere with one another because they are on different wavelengths.

Lethbridge's observations obviously provide us with a kind of theory to explain why time can behave so oddly – and why people can experience "time-slips". It will be remembered that Mr Cobbold experienced a kind of "whoosh" when the phantom house suddenly appeared. Perhaps what had happened was simply that two vibrational rates had somehow intermingled, in the same way that two radio stations can interfere with one another if their wavelengths are too close.

All this raises another strange speculation. If Lethbridge was correct in believing that forty inches is the rate for death, and that anything beyond that is in the "next world", then it would follow that the dead exist in a kind of timeless realm. This might explain the observation made in the chapter on the *Titanic* about the deceased Harry Kaulback, who was able to tell his wife – who was still in the world of the living – that their son Bill would be given command of a battalion. According to Kaulback, this would happen on 4 November 1942. In fact, it happened a month later.

Alan Vaughan explains, in *Patterns of Prophecy*: "This type of temporal confusion happens so often that Mrs Kaulback asked one of her communicators . . . for an explanation. He replied through her hand that . . . 'at times, the pictures are perchance taken from the mind of the boy and shown to you. And it must therefore be that we strive yet more earnestly that we see but actual deeds, for thoughts are not what we endeavour to collect. Sometimes, too, the visions slip from firm grasp, and we see what is about to be done perhaps at some future date. It is not easy grasping time between two planes; and in addition do we try to grip the different times upon your earth, therefore on occasion do we sadly err'."

In other words, the dead can foresee the future, but can easily get the timing wrong.

The UFO investigator John Keel is convinced that he has had

experiences of various strange entities who also belong to another dimension or vibratory level. In 1966, Keel went to West Virginia, where there had been a series of sightings of a huge winged figure, which was able to keep up with fast cars without even flapping its wings.

When Keel became deeply involved in these investigations, he suddenly became the subject of persecution of some curious entities. He tells stories of mysterious phone calls, people impersonating him or claiming to be his secretary, strange warning messages, and even arriving at a motel that he had decided upon on the spur of the moment, and finding a sheaf of messages waiting for him behind the desk.

In 1967, a hypnotized contactee began to "channel" a "spaceman" named Apol, who made exact predictions about a number of plane crashes. These plane crashes, says Keel, occurred exactly as predicted. Apol said that the Pope would be stabbed to death in the Middle East, and that this would be preceded by a great earthquake. There was, in fact, an earthquake in Turkey when the Pope was there on a visit, but it was not until three years later that a man tried to kill the Pope with a knife at Manila airport (halfway across the planet from Turkey, in the Philippines) – fortunately, without success. Keel was also told that Senator Robert Kennedy was in great danger, and that Martin Luther King would be shot in the throat while standing on his balcony in Memphis.

The date for the King assassination was given as 4 February 1968, but in fact took place two months later.

Apol warned him that there would be a major disaster on the Ohio River and, in due course, a bridge that Keel crossed frequently collapsed into the river during the rush hour traffic, killing hundreds.

Keel remarks about Apol:

> ". . . I felt sorry for him. It became apparent that he did not really know who or what he was. He was a prisoner of our time frame. *He often confused the past with the future* [my italics]. I gathered that he and all his fellow entities found themselves transported backward and forward in time involuntarily, playing out their little games because they were programmed to do so, living – or existing – only as long as they could feed off the energy and minds of mediums or contactees."

In fact, Mr Apol sounds more like a typical poltergeist than a "UFO entity".

If Lethbridge is correct, and the "next world" is static and timeless, it becomes understandable why some of its inhabitants should want to return to the realm of time that they knew in their lifetimes. Meanwhile, they would rather make contact with *any* human entity than remain stuck outside time.

The paranormal investigator Joe Fisher calls these entities "hungry ghosts", in a book of that title. He tells how, through a Toronto medium, he was contacted by a number of "discarnate entities" who told him highly convincing stories of their life on earth. A spirit with a Yorkshire accent described in detail the farm where it lived in the nineteenth century, while another "spirit" called Ernest Scott gave details of his wartime experiences in a bomber squadron in the RAF. Finally, a female entity called Filipa told him that she was a teenage Greek girl who had been his lover in a previous existence, three centuries earlier, in a village called Theros, on the Greek-Turkish border. Soon he was convinced that he was in actual physical contact with Filipa, whom he found to be extremely sensual.

On a trip back to England, he decided to verify this story of Ernest Scott, having no doubt whatever that it would prove genuine.

In fact, although the airfield existed, and so did the squadron with which Scott claimed to have flown, Ernest Scott himself was simply not in the squadron's records.

Fisher tried to track down the farm of the Yorkshireman, and again found that the geography was extremely accurate, together with many other details. Yet it was clear that the man himself had never existed.

The same thing applied to a man who claimed to be a World War I veteran named Harry Maddox. His stories of the war proved to be accurate enough, but he himself was simply not in the records.

In spite of all this, Fisher had no doubt whatever that Filipa really existed, and that he and she had been lovers in a previous existence. On a holiday in Greece, he tried to locate the village of Theros, where he and Filipa had been lovers three centuries earlier. There was no such village. Also, the town of Alexandropouli, which Filipa had mentioned as being the nearest large town, proved to be only *two* centuries old.

Like John Keel, Joe Fisher concluded that these spirits are caught in a kind of limbo, not sure of who they are or where they belong, and that their aim is to feed off the energy and minds of people living on earth.

Does all this explain the mystery of time-slips? Probably not – but at least it seems to provide us with some kind of framework for an explanation, perhaps to be filled in as we learn a little more about the nature of space/time.

14 Nostradamus and Napoleon

As we have already noted, the *Centuries* are Francocentric; large proportions of the predictions appear to be partially, or exclusively, about the fate of France. The seer dedicated whole series of quatrains to predicting what appear to be fairly insignificant events in French history, but totally failed to mention – for example – the American Revolution. Nostradamus devoted more of his quatrains to the French Revolution than to any other period of history, then dedicated even more to a figure who sounds very like Napoleon Bonaparte.

The quatrains that seem to be about Napoleon's career suggest that the prophet felt rather ambivalent about him. There seems to be evidence of distinct national pride when Nostradamus predicts a great French empire, yet Napoleon himself is described as destroyer, a butcher and a "fearful thunderbolt". There are several possible reasons for this mixed attitude. To begin with, Napoleon was no friend to religion, and Nostradamus seems usually to have put his Christian faith before his nationalism. Second, Nostradamus had a genuine horror of bloodshed – perhaps natural in a medical man – and Napoleon caused some of the bloodiest conflicts in European history. Finally, the seer's predictions suggest a clear knowledge of how short France's "age of empire" would be (he even gives the correct period of "fourteen years" in *Century VII*, quatrain 13).

In the end, perhaps the main difference between Nostradamus

and Napoleon was simply that it was one of the Emperor's policies never to calculate the human cost of his victories, while the seer knew that all victories are transient, and saw that individual suffering is all that really matters.

The Coming of Napoleon I
I.60 & VIII.1

> Un Empereur naistra pres d'Italie
> Qui a l'Empire sera vendu bien cher:
> Diront avec quels gens il se ralie,
> Qu'on trouvera moins prince que boucher.

Translation:

> An Emperor will be born near Italy,
> Who will cost the Empire dear,
> They will say when they see his associates,
> That he is less a prince than a butcher.

The future Emperor Napoleon was born in Ajaccio on the island of Corsica in 1769. The above quatrain describes an Emperor "born near Italy", and this was both physically and chronologically true of Napoleon; Corsica is equidistant between France and northern Italy and, only a year before Napoleon's birth, the Italian city of Genoa ceded the island to France. (Who knows how history would have differed if Napoleon had been brought up a citizen of Italy rather than of France?)

Line two of the quatrain is equally true of Napoleon, but it is also ironic in that that the French would not have had an empire without Napoleon.

The Emperor's associates certainly caused gossip, as lines three and four hint. Josephine – his first wife – was a Creole from Martinique in the Caribbean, and was virtually a second-class citizen in the eyes of "home-grown" Frenchmen. Furthermore, Napoleon appointed his brothers rulers of Spain, Naples, Holland and Westphalia, despite their total lack of training as governors. Aristocratic society across Europe was scandalized that such a low-born family could rise so high. The phrase "less a prince than a butcher" echoes this snobbish indignation, but it might also be a hint to the bloodshed caused by Napoleon's expansionist wars.

Napoleon's Father, Carlo Buonaparte, was a successful lawyer and became "Count Carlo" when France took over Corsica in 1768. Although the Buonapartes had never been a military family, Carlo pulled strings to have his second son, Napoleon, sent to the Brienne Military School in Paris. Ironically, it was Louis XVI who paid for the boy's scholarship. Napoleon graduated to a second lieutenancy in the artillery at the age of sixteen. When the revolution broke out, Napoleon joined the Republican side and was made a captain. He won national acclaim in 1793 at the siege of the anti-revolutionary port of Toulon: after his commanding general was wounded Napoleon's brilliant use of the artillery won the battle. He was promoted to brigadier general at the age of twenty-four.

The butcheries of Robespierre's Reign of Terror left the French army largely unaffected. The Committee of Public Safety avoided accusing military men of treason, just as a woodcutter does not saw at the branch he is sitting on. Thus Napoleon advanced his career and public standing in comparative safety.

In 1795, bread riots broke out in Paris. Following the fall of Robespierre and the Jacobins, the revolutionary government had undergone a political about-turn and was now right wing and reactionary rather than left wing and radical. Their efforts to stabilize the economy hurt the poor so severely that the army was needed to quell the riots. General Napoleon saw to it that the rioters were not only put down, but that he won credit as the "Saviour of the Republic".

> *PAU, NAY, LORON plus feu qu'á sang sera.*
> *Laude nager, fuir grand au surrez.*
> *Les agassas entree refusera.*
> *Pampon Durance les tiendra enferrez.*

Translation:

> Pau, Nay Loron will be more fire than blood.
> Swimming in praise, the great one will flee to the confluence.
> The magpies are refused entrance.
> Great Bridge Durance will keep them confined.

Pau, Nay and Loron are all small and historically insignificant towns in western France. However, Nostradamus gives the names in capitals – usually a sign that he wants us to find a hidden message. Sure enough, if read as an anagram, the message NAPAULON ROY (Napaulon King) can be constructed from the three words. Even in his own lifetime, Napoleon's name was occasionally written "Napaulon". Alternatively, the misspelling might be a subtle joke; early in his career, Napoleon simplified the spelling of his Corsican surname from "Buonaparte" to the French version "Bonaparte".

Although denigrated by his enemies as the "Monster of Europe", Napoleon was a tyrant only by the most liberal standards. Indeed, he invariably gave the nations he conquered better legal and social systems than they had ever previously enjoyed. On the other hand, his wars spread fire and ruin across the continent. So a retranslation of the first line could read: "Napoleon the King, a rule of military fire, but not of tyrannical bloodthirstiness."

The phrase "more fire than blood" might also be a comment on Napoleon's endless zeal. Like Alexander the Great and Julius Caesar, Napoleon seems to have lived for the glory of his military conquests and the acquisition of power. He is quoted as once saying: "Power is my mistress."

Erica Cheetham suggests the remainder of the quatrain concerns Napoleon's imprisonment of Popes Pius VI and VII. She derives this idea from the rather convoluted connections of the word "*agassas*" at the beginning of the third line. *Agassa* is the Provencal[1] name for a magpie. In regular French, the word for magpie is *pie*, which is also the French spelling of the pontifical name "Pius".

In *Nostradamus on Napoleon* (1961), Stewart Robb points out that the Durance River (mentioned in the last line) flows through the south-east section of France. It was here, in Valence and Grenoble, respectively, that Pius VI and Pius VII were imprisoned by Napoleon.

---

1 Nostradamus' native province.

Napoleon's Italian Campaign, 1795–98
I.93, III.37 & V.99

> *Terre Italique pres des monts tremblera,*
> *Lyon et coq non trop confederez:*
> *En lieu de peur l'un l'autre s'aidera.*
> *Seul Catulon et Celtes moderez.*

Translation:

> Italian lands near the mountains will tremble.
> Lyon and cockerel will not be in agreement:
> In a place of fear they will help one another,
> Only *Catulon* and Celts moderated.

By 1795, the French Republican army was powerful enough to move from defending their own borders to attacking their enemies. In that year, General Bonaparte led his troops across the Alps into northern Italy (then a possession of the Austrian Empire). His campaign was brilliantly successful and, by 1797, the entire peninsula as far as Rome was in French hands.

The second line of the quatrain mentions tension between "*Lyon et coq*". The city of Lyon sounds as if it is the subject, but Nostradamus used the spelling *lyon* for "lion" in other quatrains. Since the cockerel is the traditional emblem of France and the lion of Britain, is possible that this is a prediction of the growing enmity between these two nations in the 1790s. Before Napoleon's Italian campaign, Britain saw the new French Republic as detestable, but not as any great threat. However, as Napoleon's "Grand Army" grew in power, the British became increasingly worried about France. War was inevitable.

Later, when Napoleon was forced to abdicate in 1814, Britain became an ally of the reinstated French monarchy. This was partially through a mutual fear of the re-emergence of the French Republicans – as line three seems to hint.

Line four is difficult to fathom. The word "*Catulon*" sounds like Catalonia – a province of Spain – but Erica Cheetham translates it as "freedom", although she gives no explanation why. The word "*Celtes*" is usually translated to indicate the French – a Celtic race in the days of the Roman Empire.

Avant l'assult l'oraison prononcée,
Milan prins d'aigle par embushes decevez:
Muraille antique par canons enfoncée,
Par feu et sang à mercy peu receus.

Translation:

Before the assault the speech is pronounced,
Milan taken by the eagle deceived by ambush:
The ancient walls shattered by cannons,
In fire and blood few receive mercy.

The northern Italian city of Milan fell on 15 May, 1796. Before their assault on the Austrian garrison, Napoleon made a speech to his troops that later became famous across Europe:

"Soldiers, you are starving and half-naked. Our government owes you much but can do nothing for you . . . I will lead you into the most fertile plains in the world . . . There you will find honour, glory and riches . . . Are you wanting in courage?"

They were not. In fact, the French prepared to attack so threateningly that the Austrian garrison fled without firing a shot. Although this was not a victory "by ambush", as line two predicts, the emblem of the French Republican army was indeed an eagle.

The third and fourth lines of the quatrain could not be about the first capture of Milan – the town fell without bloodshed – but may refer to an event later that year. The citizens of the nearby town of Pavia revolted against the French occupying troops and were joined by the citizens of Milan. The rebellion was suppressed with great brutality.

Milan, Ferrare, Turin et Aquillaye,
Capne Brundis vexés par gent Celtique:
Par le Lion et phalange aquilee
Quant Rome aura le chef vieux Britannique.

Translation:

> Milan, Ferrare, Turin and Aquileia,
> Capua and Brindisi vexed by the Celtic nation:
> By the Lion and eagle phalanx,
> When Rome will have the old British chief.

By 1798, Napoleon's army (the "eagle phalanx") had captured all the territories mentioned in the above quatrain, including Rome.

The last line could be a reference to the Cardinal of York – the last direct descendant of the British royal line of Stuart – who died in French-occupied Rome in 1807.

The Egyptian Campaign, 1798–99
II.86

> *Naufrage á classe pres d'onde Hadriatique,*
> *La terre tremble esmeüe sus l'air en terre mis:*
> *Egypte tremble augment Mahometique.*
> *L'Heralt soi rendre à crier est commis.*

Translation:

> A fleet will be wrecked near the Adriatic,
> The earth trembles pushed into the air and falls to earth:
> Egypt trembles Mohammedan increase.
> The Herald is commanded to cry surrender.

Following his victories in Italy, Napoleon led an expedition against Turkish-held Egypt – through which he hoped to strike at the British in India. Although the French force defeated a much larger army of Mameluke mercenaries at the Battle of the Pyramids, their fleet was destroyed by the British (under Admiral Nelson) at the Battle of Nile. Without naval support, the expedition eventually had to be abandoned.

Whether the Nile can be considered "near the Adriatic", as it states in line one, is a moot point. Erica Cheetham suggests that the second line of the quatrain refers to the explosion of the French flagship during the battle, pieces of which rained down on the nearby shore.

Following this defeat, Napoleon besieged the Turkish-held city of Acre (in present-day Israel). When plague broke out among his troops, Napoleon attempted to use trickery to win the city: he sent a herald who demanded Acre's immediate surrender, hoping that the Turkish leaders would lose their nerve. Unfortunately, the Turks knew of the sickness decimating their enemy and refused the demand. The French were forced to withdraw and General Bonaparte returned to France.

Napoleon the Emperor, 1799–1804
VII.13, VIII.57, IV.54 & VIII.53

> De la cité marine et tributaire,
> La teste raze prendra la satrapie:
> Chasser sordide qui puis sera contraire
> Par quartorze ans tiendra la tyrannie.

Translation:

> Of the city marine and tributary,
> The shaved-head shall take the satrapy:
> Chasing off the sordid who oppose him
> For fourteen years he will hold the tyranny.

Napoleon won national fame for his defeat of the port of Toulon in 1793. Toulon is a "marine" city and its rebels were supported and "tributary" – as far as promises were concerned – to Britain. The term "satrapy", used at the end of the second line, is a Persian word for a governor/kingship, and may refer to Napoleon's promotion to brigadier general. However, the phrase that allows many writers confidently to attribute this prediction to Napoleon is "teste rase" or "shaven-head". His own soldiers nicknamed Napoleon "le petit tondu" – "the little crop-head".

The "sordid" opposition expelled in line three might be the defeated British support fleet at Toulon or, considering Nostradamus' ardent monarchism, it could describe the French Republican government that Napoleon overthrew in 1799.

From 18 Brumaire (9 November) 1799, Napoleon ruled as First Consul then, in 1804, as Emperor. His authoritarian, though not necessarily tyrannical,[2] rule lasted until April 1814 – just over fourteen years, as line four of the quatrain states.

> De soldat simple parviendra en empire,
> De robe courte parviendra à la longue
> Valliant aux armes en aglise on plus pire
> Vexer les prestres comme l'eau fait l'esponge.

Translation:

> From a simple soldier he will attain an empire,
> From a short robe he will attain one that is long
> Valiant in arms much worse towards the church
> He vexes the priests as water soaks a sponge.

The meaning of the first line of the quatrain, although self-evident, might just as easily refer to Adolf Hitler as Napoleon. The second line, on the other hand, neatly describes Napoleon's change from the short ceremonial robe of a First Consul to the flowing coronation robe of the Emperor of France.

Napoleon ended the persecution of the Catholic Church in France by guaranteeing freedom of religion in his new legal code. Unfortunately, Pope Pius VI had died in French captivity two months before the coup d'état that raised Napoleon to First Consul. The new incumbent – although naming himself Pius VII in remembrance of his martyred forebear – was reconciled enough to Napoleon personally to crown him Emperor in 1804. However, they fell out shortly thereafter and, in 1809, Napoleon annexed the Papal Estates and imprisoned Pius VII at Grenoble.

The friction between Napoleon's reformist/authoritarian regime and the conservative Church went on throughout his reign – a steady flow of insults and irritations like "water soaking a sponge".

> Du nom qui onques ne fur au Roy Gaulois,
> Jamais ne fut un fouldre si craintif:

2 Nostradamus may have been using the word "tyranny" in its original Greek meaning. "Tyrant" was first used to describe a usurper rather than a despot, and this is certainly a better description of Napoleon, who came to power through a coup d'état, but ruled fairly.

Tremblant l'Italie, l'Espaine et les Anglois,
De femme estangiers grandement attentif.

Translation:

> Of name never held by a French King,
> Never was there such a fearful thunderbolt:
> Tremble Italians, Spanish and English,
> Of female strangers he will be most attentive.

Although an emperor rather than a king, Napoleon was certainly the first French monarch of that name.

The description "thunderbolt" in line two also fits Napoleon. His speed of command caused the Duke of Wellington to comment that Bonaparte could handle batteries of cannon as swiftly as another man could handle pistols. Also, Napoleon's Imperial seal had at its centre an eagle gripping crossed thunderbolts. Lord Byron once wrote a poem about the French emperor that contained the line "Never yet was heard such thunder!" – a strikingly close match to the second line of the above quatrain.

Line three contains a distinct hint of national pride, but also states the truth: Italy, Spain and England were all invaded or threatened with invasion by Napoleon's armies.

Like many absolute leaders, Napoleon indulged his sexual passions with many women – French and foreign – yet he never allowed his amours to interfere with his work. In fact, quite the opposite is the truth.

In 1809, Napoleon divorced the Empress Josephine on the grounds that she had borne him no heir, and married Princess Marie-Louise of Austria. The match was primarily to link Napoleon's new dynasty with the ancient ruling house of Habsburg, but the forty-year-old emperor wooed the nineteen-year-old princess with touching and genuine romanticism.

The Failure at the Channel, 1804
VIII.53

Dedans Bolongne vouldra laver ses fautes,
Il ne pourra au temple du soleil,

Il volera faisant choses si haultes
En hierarchie n'en fut oncq un pareil.

Translation:

Within Boulogne he will want to wash himself of his faults,
He cannot at the temple of the sun,
He shall fly doing things too great
In the hierarchy he never had an equal.

Napoleon was famously dismissive of the British, calling them a "nation of shopkeepers". For a while, he considered invading the islands, and even started preparations at the Channel ports (such as Boulogne). However, in 1804 he abandoned the project in favour of attacking Austria. If he had invaded Britain, even with only partial success, it is arguable that his defeat at Waterloo would never have happened. So the "faults" mentioned in line one might be Napoleon's basic misjudgement of the danger that Britain posed to France.

The "temple of the sun", mentioned in line two, sounds like a typical Nostradamus classical allusion. In pre-Roman times, Britain had two famous shrines dedicated to the sun. The first was Stonehenge, and the second was a temple on the north bank of the Thames – over the ruins of which, Westminster Abbey was later built. Failing to invade Britain, Napoleon saw neither of these in his lifetime.

The last two lines are unspecific, but certainly fit Napoleon. In choosing to invade Austria, then Russia, Napoleon could be described as flying to "things too great". As to being his without equal in the "hierarchy", as line four describes, many military historians rank Napoleon as the most gifted soldier of the last two centuries.

The Battle of Trafalgar, 21 October 1805
I.77

Entre deux mers dressera promontaire,
Que plus mourra par le mords du cheval:
Le sein Neptune pliera voille noire,
Par Calpre et classe aupres de Rocheval.

Translation:

> Between two seas stands a promontory,
> Who will then die by the bite of a horse:
> The proud Neptune folds black sails,
> Through Calpre the fleet nears Rocheval.

In October 1805, a French fleet under Admiral Villeneuve was ordered to ship an army from Cadiz in Spain to southern Italy. The thirty-three ships were attacked by twenty-seven ships of the British blockading force at Trafalgar – a point midway between Cape Roche ("*Rocheval*") and the Rock of Gibraltar (a "promontory" between the "two seas" of the Atlantic and the Mediterranean). The word "*Calpre*" in the last line also sounds very like "*Calpe*" – an old name for Gibraltar.

The British fleet, under Admiral Nelson, split into two halves and attacked the French line of ships from two directions, out-flanking and decimating them. Twenty French ships were sunk or taken, and 14,000 Frenchmen were killed or captured. The British lost no ships and only 1,500 men. Among the British dead was Lord Nelson himself. As a sign of mourning, his flagship *Victory* raised black sails as it returned to port – an event apparently predicted in line three. David Ovason further adds that the first three words of the line – "*Le sein Neptune*" – contain a partial anagram of the name "Nelson"(i.e. – *Le SiEN NEptune* = NE L S EN).

Pierre Charles de Villeneuve, the French Commanding Admiral, was taken prisoner at Trafalgar. He was allowed to return to France in 1806, but on the way home committed suicide by pushing a long pin into his heart. David Ovason points out that line two may predict this if the word "*cheval*" ("horse") is read as a deliberate misspelling of "*cheville*" ("pin"). He further adds that, in Nostradamus' day, the term *cheval* also meant a wooden table across which condemned soldiers were tortured. Villeneuve killed himself from tortured guilt over Trafalgar.

The Spanish Peninsula War, 1808–14
IV.70

> Bien contigue des grans monts Pyrenées,
> Un contr l'aigle grand copie addresser:
> Ouvertes veines, forces exterminées,
> Comme jusque à Pau le chef viendra chasser.

Translation:

> Very near the great Pyrenees mountains,
> One will raise a great army against the eagle:
> Opened veins, forces exterminated,
> As far as Pau, the chief will chase them.

In 1808, Spain asked for French help in a war with Portugal. Napoleon complied and his generals soon conquered the small state. However, the Spanish were disturbed to note that strong French garrisons were being stationed in Spanish as well as Portuguese strongpoints across the Iberian peninsular. That same year, a palace revolution unseated Charles IV and installed a new Spanish monarch: Ferdinand VII. Napoleon forced Ferdinand to abdicate and crowned Joseph Bonaparte, his own brother, Joseph I of Spain.

The Spanish people rose in revolt against the French occupation force and were joined by their former enemy, Portugal. The British formed an alliance with the rebels and sent an army under Arthur Wellesley (later the Duke of Wellington) to Portugal. This might be what is meant by line two: the "eagle" being the banner of the French army and of Napoleon himself. Wellesley defeated the French in battle after battle, forcing them back towards, and eventually over, the Pyrenees. Napoleon did what he could from a distance, but was too busy with conquests in the east to take the field against Wellesley himself. The city of Pau – mentioned in line four – is in south-west France on the eastern slopes of the Pyrenees. It was one of the towns to which the French retreated following their total ejection from the Spanish peninsula in 1814.

Line three is grimly poetic, but is also accurate. The loss of 300,000 fighting men in the six-year Spanish conflict drained France of strength like a cut vein. Military historians believe that Napoleon's eventual defeat was as much a result of the Iberian war as it was of the retreat from Moscow and the Battle of Waterloo.

The Russian Disaster, 1812–13
IV.82, II.91 & II.99

> *Amas s'approche vendant d'Esclavonie,*
> *L'Olestant vieux cité ruinera,*

Fort desolee verra sa Romanie.
Puis la grand flamme estaindre ne saura.

Translation:

A mass of men approaches from the land of the Slavs,
The Destroyer will ruin the city:
He will see his Romanie quite desolated.
He will not know how to extinguish the great flame.

Napoleon's rule was aggressively expansionist. He not only saw himself as the founder of a new royal dynasty, but also as the man who would win France an empire to surpass that of Ancient Rome. War with his neighbours was inevitable.

In 1803, Britain declared war on France. Two years later, Russia and Austria joined Britain to form an anti-French coalition. Napoleon reacted with characteristic decisiveness, dropping plans to invade Britain and striking east into the Austrian Empire. He smashed the Austro-Russian forces at the Battle of Austerlitz on 2 December 1805. Then, in 1806, he annexed the Kingdom of Naples and the Republic of Holland, crowning his brothers Joseph and Louis as their new kings. In the same year Prussia joined the anti-French coalition, but Napoleon destroyed the Prussian armies at the battles of Jena and Auerstadt. The Russian army was also decisively defeated at the Battle of Freidland and, in 1807, Tsar Alexander I signed a peace treaty with the French. In 1809 Napoleon destroyed what remained of Austria's fighting strength at the Battle of Wagram.

By 1810, the Napoleonic Empire stretched from the Spanish peninsula to the borders of Russia – France was the major superpower of Europe. Indeed, due to Napoleon's socially reforming rule of the states he had conquered (not to mention the efficiency and size of the French Army), there seemed little reason for France not to maintain this powerful position. Then, in 1812, Napoleon's alliance with Tsar Alexander fell apart and the Emperor invaded Russia. Napoleon defeated the Tsar's army at the Battle of Borodino on 26 August and, by 14 September, had taken Moscow. It was at this point, when Napoleon was at the height of his military glory, that the Russian generals hit on the one strategy that could beat such a brilliant tactician – they chose not to fight him. With the Russian winter fast coming on, Napoleon needed to crush the remainder of the Russian army in one last battle, but the Tsar's troops refused to be baited. Moscow had been evacuated, stripped of provisions, then set on fire, so Napoleon's troops now had to raid the countryside to find provisions. Army discipline was already eroded when the first snows began to fall in October and, reluctantly, the Emperor ordered a retreat.

Line one of the above quatrain describes a mass of men approaching from "*d'Esclavonie*": "the land of the Slavs". This might describe Napoleon's invasion from the Slavic lands east of Germany, but the term "mass" seems to reflect better the chaotic return journey from Moscow. Staggering through snowdrifts, the troop's discipline soon collapsed and the French army became a straggling disorganised mob.

The city ruined by the "Destroyer" in line two sounds like Moscow – although it was Russian patriots who torched the city, not Napoleon. In fact, he was desperate to extinguish the fires, but could not, as line four seems to suggest.

If the word "*Romanie*" in line three refers to Romania being desolated, it was a stunning piece of precognition by Nostradamus: Romania did not exist before 1861. Although Napoleon's army did retreat just north of what is now Romania – and found it horribly desolate – most Nostradamus scholars think the line is a prediction that the retreat from Russia would eventually cost Napoleon his lands in the Romagna region of northern Italy (along with all his other conquests).

> *Soleil levant un grand feu on verra,*
> *Bruit et clarté vers Aquilon tendants:*
> *Dedans le rond mort et cris l'on orra,*
> *Par glaive, feu, faim, mort las attendants.*

Translation:

> At sunrise a great fire will be seen,
> A noise and brightness in the direction of *Aquilon*:
> Inside the round death and cries will be heard,
> From sword, fire, famine, death to those who waited.

Radical Russian nationalists set Moscow alight on the night of 16 September 1812. The occupying French did not fully realise

what had happened until dawn next day, by which time the blaze
was out of control. Line two contains the word "*Aquilon*" (Latin
for "northern"), which Nostradamus often seems to have used to
indicate Russia. Line three describes death and screams from
"the round". This fits the burning of Moscow – a roughly
circular city – as 15,000 wounded Russian soldiers were burned
to death in the inferno. The last line may also be a reference to the
suffering of these men, but sounds more a description of the
agonies of the retreating French army. All the way back to
French-held territory, the Russian army attacked the enemy
using hit-and-run tactics. French soldiers who managed to
escape the Russian harassment often met a grimmer end in
the cold.[3]

> *Terroir Romain qu'interpretoit augure,*
> *Par gent Gauloise par trop sera vexée:*
> *Mais nation Celtique craindra l'heure,*
> *Boreas, classe trop loing l'avoir poussée.*

Translation:

> The Roman land that the auger interprets,
> Will be greatly vexed by the French:
> But the Celtic nation will fear the hour,
> North wind, fleet driven too far.

As we have seen, Napoleon annexed the Papal Estates in 1809,
and lines one and two seem to predict this event (Nostradamus
often uses the word "auger" to indicate a pope). Lines three and
four, in turn, predict a fearful time for France, however, the
actual warning is infuriatingly vague. Erica Cheetham argues
that the disaster of the Russian campaign is described, because
the word "*Boreas*" is Latin for "north wind".

Stewart Robb, in *Nostradamus and Napoleon*, supports
Cheetham's interpretation by pointing out that the word

---

3 In *War and Peace*, Tolstoy used real accounts of the Russian campaign as
a basis for the experiences of his fictional characters. He describes the
Russians finding a group of French soldiers sitting round the embers of a
huge bonfire. The men had been scorched on their hands and faces from
sitting so near the flames, but all were dead – their backs frozen solid.

"*classe*", in the last line, had a meaning other than "fleet" in the early nineteenth century: the term was also used to describe Napoleon's conscripted troops. Since this piece of French slang was, naturally, not current in Nostradamus' time, readers must decide for themselves whether it is either a coincidence or an astoundingly precise prediction. Robb also suggests that Nostradamus was drawing a direct causal link between the theft of the papal lands and the later disastrous retreat from Russia.

Of the 600,000 men of the Grand Army that marched into Russia, only 30,000 returned alive. Any possibility of France holding on to her European empire disappeared.

The Escape from Elba, 26 February 1815
II.66

> *Par grans dangeriers le captif eschapé,*
> *Peu de temps grand a fortune changeé:*
> *Dans le palais le peuple est attrapé,*
> *Par bon augure la cité assiegée.*

Translation:

> Through great dangers the captive escapes,
> In a short time his fortune will change:
> In the palace the people are trapped,
> By good omen the city besieged.

Napoleon had stripped his empire of troops for the Russian expedition and now most of them were dead. Through 1813, he marshalled what forces he had left, but all of Europe was now allied against him and he could do nothing but retreat to Paris with the enemy hard on his heels. In April 1814, as Cossack troops were watering their horses in the Seine, Napoleon's generals forced him to abdicate.

The Allies agreed to peace with France provided Louis XVIII – Louis XVI's brother – was placed on the throne and Napoleon was condemned to lifelong exile. Bonaparte was sent to the small Mediterranean island of Elba, with a ceremonial guard of just under a thousand men. As a final veiled insult, the Allies allowed

Napoleon to keep the title of Emperor, but reduced his empire to Elba alone.

On 26 February 1815, Napoleon and his bodyguard escaped Elba and returned to mainland France. Louis XVIII sent a large army to crush Napoleon's thousand men but, when the forces met, the King's troops immediately joined Napoleon and followed him back to Paris. He was made Emperor of France once more on 20 March.

Although non-specific in detail, line one could describe Napoleon's escape – one of the most important in European history. Line two may be read in one of two ways: that the luck of the *"captif"* will dramatically change for the good or ill. Both were true of Napoleon. He went from exile to reinstated Emperor of France in a matter of weeks. However, although he sued the Allies for peace and even offered to abdicate in favour of his baby son, they pronounced him an "enemy of humanity" and declared war. By the end of June, he was a captive in exile once again.

Line three of the quatrain sounds odd but, as is often the case with Nostradamus, proves accurate when closely examined. Napoleon arrived in Paris on 20 March, and made his way to the palace followed by an ecstatic crowd. As Bonaparte alighted from his coach, the mob lifted him on their shoulders and carried him to the (hurriedly vacated) King's apartments. It was reported that this happy crowd so packed the palace corridors that nobody could get in or out for some hours – greatly impeding urgent state business.

The last line is vague. Paris had already been besieged by the Allies, and was besieged again following Waterloo. What "good omen" may have been connected with these events is unclear.

Waterloo, 18 June 1815
I.23 & IV.75

> *Au mois troisiesme se levant le soleil*
> *Sanglier, Liepard au champ Mars pour comattre:*
> *Liepard laissé, au ciel extend son oeil,*
> *Un aigle autour du Soleil voit s'esbattre.*

Translation:

In the third month at sunrise,
Wild Boar, Leopard towards the field of Mars to combat:
The Leopard wearies, lifts his eyes to the sky,
An eagle playing about the Sun.

When the former anti-Napoleon allies heard that he had returned to Paris, they immediately set about preparing a combined army to crush him once and for all. Napoleon, with characteristic swiftness, gathered his own troops and struck at his enemies before they could marshal their forces.

On 15 June 1815, the French army of 123,000 men crossed the Belgian frontier. Facing them were two military forces: an army of 116,000 Prussians and another of 93,000 British troops. These latter were commanded by Napoleon's old nemesis from the Peninsula War – Arthur Wellesley, now the Duke of Wellington. Had the Allied armies stayed together, it is doubtful that even Napoleon would have dared such odds, but the Prussians and British had foolishly separated.

On 16 June, the Prussians, under Field Marshall Blücher, were defeated and forced to retreat. Napoleon sent a third of his force, under General Grouchy, to chase the surviving 70,000 Prussians – hoping to destroy them or, at the very least, stop them reinforcing Wellington.

On the morning of 18 June, Napoleon attacked Wellington's force on a strip of farmland called Waterloo. The British (reinforced by a contingent of Dutch troops, but depleted by earlier fighting) numbered 67,000. The French had 74,000 soldiers and almost double the number of the enemy's cannons. Napoleon had never yet lost a battle with the odds so in his favour.

If the above quatrain is a prediction of Waterloo, it is one of the most strikingly accurate and poetic of all those in the *Centuries*.

As stated in the first line, the battle took place exactly three months after Napoleon's return to the French throne. It is also worth noting that the Emperor had regained power in March (the "third month") on the day before the vernal equinox – a date that would have been important to the astrologer in Nostradamus. This may explain the reference to "sunrise" at the end of the line.

The outcome of the Battle of Waterloo hung on whether

Blücher's Prussians could evade General Grouchy and reinforce Wellington. Line two seems to hint at this because the emblem of the Prussian army was a wild boar and the British lion might have been rendered as a leopard – Napoleon himself used to describe the heraldic British lion dismissively as "the Leopard of England".

The battle began at eleven thirty in the morning. By mid-afternoon, the British forces were sagging. The French attacks were being held, but it seemed only a matter of time before the British lines broke. Looking southward across the battle Wellington would have seen the French Imperial eagle standards "playing about the [sinking] sun", just as lines three and four seem to describe.

> *Prest á combatre fera defection.*
> *Chef adversaire obtiendra la victoire.*
> *L'arriere garde fera defension,*
> *Les deffaillans mort au blanc territoire.*

Translation:

> One ready to fight will desert.
> Chief adversary obtains the victory.
> The rear guard makes the defence,
> Those that fall away die in a white country.

At four in the afternoon, the army of 70,000 Prussians attacked the French right wing. Since the battle began, Napoleon had sent several messages to General Grouchy – who was still in pursuit of the rear of the Prussian army – ordering him either to engage the Prussian forces or stop following them and rejoin the main army. Grouchy did neither. Although his troops were "ready to fight", as line one states, Grouchy simply pursued Blücher, not even attempting to cut off his march towards Waterloo and Wellington. Although not really a desertion, Grouchy's failure to follow orders lost Napoleon the battle.

Wellington had long been Napoleon's "chief adversary", as line two describes. He had consistently beaten French armies in Spain and Napoleon's generals were afraid of him. Although Waterloo was the first battle in which Wellington and Napoleon had actually fought against each other, their personal enmity for one another was long-standing. The return of Blücher's Prussians to the conflict dashed any hope that the French might win the day so, as line two states, Wellington "obtained the victory".

The Allies lost 22,000 men in the battle, while the French lost 40,000. Certainly more Frenchmen would have died in the rout that followed the battle if the Old Guard (a regiment of fiercely loyal veterans) had not fought a valiant rearguard action – eventually being killed to the last man – an event apparently described by line three.

The meaning of line four is uncertain. It might be an out-of-place reference to the retreat from Moscow: men dying in a country white with snow. On the other hand, it could be a prediction of the return of Louis XVIII to the French throne. Louis' flag was Bourbon white. It was reported that the people of Paris were so anxious to curry favour with the new regime that, on Napoleon's second arrest, the city looked as if it was carpeted in snow because of the numerous white banners and cockades.

St Helena, 1815–21
I.32

> Le grand empire sera tost translaté,
> En lieu petit, qui bien tost viendra croistre:
> Lieu bien infime d'exigue comté,
> Ou au milieu viendra poser son sceptre.

Translation:

> The great empire will soon be translated,
> To a small place, which soon will begin to grow:
> A miserable place of small area,
> In the middle of which he will lay down his sceptre.

Following Waterloo, Napoleon returned to Paris. Although the Parisian populace begged him to fight on, the generals and politicians abandoned his cause. He fled to the port of Rochefort, but there surrendered to the British warship *Bellerophon*. His second and final exile was to the small Atlantic island of St Helena.

Nostradamus uses the word "empire" in the first line of the quatrain, as opposed to "kingdom" or "nation". Napoleon is one of the few leaders, since Nostradamus' day, to have "translated" a great empire for a "small place".

The end of line two may be a reference to Napoleon's hundred-day return to power after escaping Elba, but the rest of the quatrain sounds like a grim description of Napoleon's final site of imprisonment.

Napoleon died of stomach cancer on St Helena, on 5 May 1821 (although there is much evidence that he was poisoned). He was fifty-two years old.

15 The Tarot

Readers of the chapter on the *I Ching* will recognize that Jung's line of argument about synchronicity applies to any kind of fortune-telling, including foretelling the future with playing cards, dice, or any other operation that depends upon chance. This argument rests on an observation everybody has made – that some people seem lucky and others unlucky. There are some people who are always finding money in the street, and some people on whom tiles are always falling from roofs. Of course, the same person may be lucky or unlucky at different times; most of us have also noticed how, when we feel relaxed and happy, everything seems to "go right"; while, when we feel tense or gloomy, things go wrong.

Sceptics would argue that when we are tired and depressed, we make mistakes that cause problems, while when we are happy and wide-awake we avoid them. But if we reject this explanation, as many (including myself) do, then we are left with the interesting notion that a kind of "fate" clings around us and, to some extent, governs what happens to us.

An Australian mystic, Barbara Tucker (wife of the painter Albert Tucker), described an interesting experience when she was sitting in a room full of friends:

"All the people round me were laughing and doing the things people do at parties – and then . . . I suddenly saw all the connections between these people – how they all inter-connected – how all this show that was going on was not, in

fact, idle chatter. It was all interconnecting into their
relationships with one another in the most extraordinary
way."

An American writer and publisher, Frank DeMarco, speaks in
his autobiography of the effect of taking mescalin as a young man
and, after describing the way that it enhanced "the reality of the
world", goes on to speak of an experience that sounds very
similar to the one above.

"Mescalin had many effects on me – one was to shatter my
belief in coincidence. Several times in the course of that
long Saturday afternoon, I watched the interaction of five
people come to perfectly orchestrated peaks and lulls. I
refer not to anything externally dramatic, but to the temporary clarity of vision that showed me (beyond later
doubting) that more went on between individuals than their
ordinary consciousness realized. Thinking about the or-
chestration I saw then, I for a while referred to God the
Great Playwright. I didn't anymore know if I believed in
God or not, but it was suddenly very clear that something
was ordering the patterns I saw around me."

In both cases, there was a sudden powerful feeling that things
do not occur by "chance" – that there is an underlying pattern of
which our conscious minds are unaware. This pattern is, of
course, what the ancient Greeks referred to as "fate".
    In which case, it is perfectly conceivable that this fate can be
read in the lines of our hands, or in the *yin* or *yang* obtained by
throwing three coins, or in the pattern of tea-leaves left behind
when we have drained a cup of tea, just as our genetic code can be
read in a fragment of skin or hair.
    The origin of cartomancy (telling the future with cards) is
unknown, but it seems certain that the ordinary pack of fifty-
two playing cards came *after* the Tarot pack, and developed
from it. The Tarot contains four suits of cards numbered from
one to ten, and called swords, cups, coins and staves (or wands)
which became spades, hearts, diamonds and clubs. Besides
these, the Tarot also contains four cards to each suit labelled
King, Queen, Knight and Page, and called (for obvious reasons)
court cards. In addition, it has twenty-two "picture cards",

known as the Major Arcana (the others are called the Minor Arcana), with symbols such as the Magician, the Pope, the Sun, the Moon, the Devil, the World, and so on, making up seventy-eight cards altogether.

Their origin is something of a mystery. They are believed to have appeared in Europe in the time of the poet Dante (who was born in 1265 and died in 1321). The earliest-known surviving cards date from 1392, from a pack made for the mad King Charles VI of France by the painter Jacquemin Gringonneur: now there are only seventeen of them in the Bibliothèque Nationale in Paris. (More recently, their date has been questioned, and it has been suggested that they were made in Italy about 1470.)

So where did they come from, and why were they made? Romantic writers like to call the cards "the Tarot of the Egyptians", and to claim that they were originally known as the Book of Thoth. But although Jessie L. Weston claims that "parallel designs" are found on the ceiling of the temple of Rameses III at Karnak, and that this particular hall has twenty-two columns (like the twenty-two cards of the Major Arcana), there is no evidence whatever of playing cards in ancient Egypt. It is believed that the Persians had a pack of "picture" cards called *atouts*, which is why the Tarot trumps are still sometimes referred to as *touts*.

A far more likely suggestion is that the twenty-two cards of the Major Arcana are related to the twenty-two "paths" of the *Kabbala*, the Jewish mystical system in which ten circles – the highest of which represents God, the lowest the Earth – are joined by twenty-two lines. The *Zohar*, the second book of the *Kabbala*, was first written down in Spain in 1275 by the scholar Moses de Leon, and this sounds like the right date for the subsequent appearance of the Tarot pack.

The cards are not referred to by any of the medieval writers, or by Chaucer or Boccaccio, both writers who might have been expected to mention them if they had known about them. A French decree against gambling in 1369 does not mention cards but, by 1423, St Bernardino of Sienna was denouncing them as a creation of the Devil, and since then Tarot cards have often been referred to as the *Devil's Pack*.

Brother John, a monk of Brefeld in Switzerland, wrote of "a certain game called the game of cards", which had "come to us in this year of Our Lord 1377, in which game the state of the world as it is now is most excellently described and figured".

And so, to allow ourselves a little free speculation, we can imagine some Hebrew mystic, at the beginning of the thirteenth century, studying the paths of the *Kabbala* – one corresponding to the sun, one to the moon, one for the earth, and so on – and considering their significance for the kabbalist. Then, using the twenty-two letters of the Hebrew alphabet, he sets out to devise twenty-two cards based on these paths, which will symbolize every human situation. Perhaps, as with the *I Ching*, the original method of divination was extremely simple, like shuffling the pack and then taking out one card at random, which was an omen of a situation that the questioner wished to know about.

Naturally, he will need a Wheel of Fortune, for that idea is fundamental to the very idea of divination. This was an idea that played an important part in the Middle Ages – a fickle goddess turning a wheel to which all men are fastened, their fortunes rising and falling almost at random.

Then he will need such basic medieval concepts as Death, the Devil, Justice, Temperance, Ruin (depicted by a tower being struck by lightning), the Last Judgement, the Hermit, the Fool, the World, and so on. A man hanging upside-down from a kind of gallows – one of the most puzzling cards in the Tarot – may well have started out by symbolizing disgrace, but later became associated with hesitation, someone whose judgement hangs in the balance.

Now anyone who had created these basic twenty-two cards must have felt that this was too simple, and felt a desire to go on. The Tree of Life has four worlds or realms: Atziluth, Briah, Yetziah and Assiah, corresponding to the Divine, the world of Creation, the world of Angels, and the world of Matter. That may have suggested four suits, each of ten basic cards. And it would have been natural for these to represent the four major social classes of the Middle Ages: swords for the nobility, cups for the priesthood (like the chalice of the Catholic mass), coins for the merchant class, and clubs or staffs (most people do not understand the word "staves", and so we may as well modernize it) for the peasantry, the "churls". Then each suit will need a king, queen, knight and page. (The knight was dropped when the Tarot became ordinary playing cards, and the page became the "knave".)

Now it would hardly be an exaggeration to say that the invention of the cards had as much impact on the thirteenth century as the invention of the novel on the eighteenth, or of radio and television on the twentieth. One of the main everyday problems of that time was simply how people with leisure could keep themselves entertained. The nobles could go hunting in the summer, or play outdoor games like bowls, or practise archery; but in the winter there was nothing much to do between sunrise and darkness. There were dice, of course, but one easily grows tired of their limitations. So this fascinating pack of cards must have been a godsend. The simplest game would be to shuffle the cards, place them face downwards, then let each of the players take one in turn. The cards would have different values, and the winner would be the one who had the highest total.

In a fairly short time, many players dropped the Major Arcana from their packs, and played with the basic fifty-six cards of the Minor Arcana, then also dropped the Knight, reducing the pack to fifty-two. All the "mystical" significance disappeared; this was simply a game for whiling away the winter afternoons.

Not long after the time Tarot appeared in Europe (perhaps in Italy, where it is believed it is named after the River Taro), there also appeared the first gypsies – in the Balkans and Greece in the mid-fourteenth century, and in Europe in the first quarter of the fifteenth century. Their language suggests that they originated in northern India. Gypsy women had a strong tradition of fortune-telling. The Tarot being ideal for this purpose, it soon became as popular as palmistry, crystal balls or staring into a flame. (The Tarot cards were in Europe before the gypsies, so the belief that they brought them is inaccurate.)

Now, oddly enough, no one paid much attention to the Tarot until shortly before the French Revolution. Then a Protestant clergyman called Court de Gebelin, author of a massive work on the ancient world, saw some friends playing with a Tarot pack and, after studying the cards, announced that they were of ancient Egyptian origin – dating back to about 2000 BC – and had been created by the priesthood to encapsulate their secrets. A Parisian fortune-teller named Alliette went on to declare that the legendary founder of magic, Hermes Trismegistus, had been the first to conceive the idea. Under the name Etteilla (his own named reversed), Alliette produced his own Tarot pack.

In 1856, a book called *Dogma and Ritual of High Magic*

launched the "magical revival" of the late nineteenth century. It was by a Frenchman named Alphonse Louis Constant who wrote under the name Eliphaz Levi, and is a highly romanticized account of magic. The book – which has been popular ever since – consisted of two parts, each of twenty-two chapters, supposedly based on the Major Arcana of the Tarot, which he claims originated in the *Kabbala*. His pupil Jean Baptist Pitois, who wrote under the name Paul Christian, found a passage in the fourth-century neoplatonist Iamblichus, describing how initiates into the mysteries of Osiris were led through a passage with twenty-two pictures on the walls, eleven on either side, and became convinced that these pictures were the twenty-two trumps of the Tarot.

In 1889, a Tarot pack was designed by a Theosophist named Oswald Wirth, and was printed in a book called *The Tarot of the Bohemians* by "Papus", whose real name was Gerard Encausse, also the author of a book on the *Kabbala*. His book on the Tarot was translated into English in 1892.

The "occult" movement had spread to England through the novelist Bulwer Lytton, who popularized it in works like *A Strange Story*, and Lytton in turn was largely responsible for the British "magical revival" that included Macgregor Mathers, W. B. Yeats, Florence Farr, Aleister Crowley, and Dion Fortune. Mathers was largely responsible for the founding of the Order of the Golden Dawn, and one of its other members, Arthur Edward Waite, was responsible for designing what has now become the best-known Tarot pack, painted by Pamela Colman Smith. The problem with this Tarot is that it is heavily influenced by the pre-Raphaelites, and is romantic and sentimental. One has only to compare his design for the Fool with earlier designs (of which there are several in Richard Cavendish's excellent 1975 book *The Tarot*) to see how sugary it is; Waite's Fool looks like Prince Charming out of a pantomime.

Aleister Crowley also designed a Tarot pack, painted by Frieda Harris, altogether more "modern"-looking, in which some of the metallic surfaces seem inspired by Wyndham Lewis. In execution it is certainly superior to the Waite pack, yet seems full of that desire to impress with a suggestion of the wicked and the sinister which is so typical of Crowley. Crowley also wrote a guide to the Tarot called *The Book of Thoth*, which also insists on the deck's Kabbalistic connections.

Waite's book reproduces his own Tarot pack, and has a commentary on each card. He also outlines several methods of consulting it, one of which he claims to be "ancient Celtic".

The Celtic method, according to Waite, is to select a card that represents the questioner himself (or herself). This is called the Significator. Court cards (kings, queens, knights and pages) seem preferable. Or a card may be chosen which represents the question itself. So presumably a question about one's love life would be represented by the Lovers, about gambling by the Wheel of Fortune, about a law case by Justice.

The pack is then shuffled and cut three times. After that, the top card is taken and placed across the Significator. This will represent the main influence on the enquiry. Those who draw some card of ill omen, like Death, the Devil or the Tower struck by lightning need not be too concerned: Waite usually explained that the cards should be interpreted mystically, so Death may mean a rebirth of consciousness, the Devil the occult arts, while the Tower is a warning against falsehood.

The second card is laid across the first and shows the obstacles that might arise.

The third card, placed above the Significator, is the questioner's aim or ideal, or, alternatively, the best that can be achieved under the circumstances.

The fourth card, placed below, shows what has already happened.

The fifth card is placed behind the direction in which the Significator is looking, and represents what has just happened or is now happening.

The sixth card, placed in front of the Significator, shows what will be happening soon.

The first six cards will now be arranged in the form of a cross. The seventh, eighth, ninth and tenth cards are placed one above the other in a line on the right side of the cross.

Seven signifies the questioner himself (or the question.)

Eight signifies influences – his position in life, his friends, etc.

Nine signifies his hopes or fears, and ten signifies the final result.

Anyone who wishes to become an expert in Tarot reading should consult at least three standard books, the best probably being Papus' *Tarot of the Bohemians*, Waite's *Pictorial Key to the Tarot* and

Crowley's *Book of Thoth*. A good modern handbook is *Tarot and You* by Richard Roberts, which details a number of individual readings with the author's friends, and provides an excellent insight for beginners into how such readings are carried out. For those who are prepared for serious and relentless study, Mouni Sadhu's *The Tarot* is not simply an in-depth examination of the Tarot cards, but of astrology, the Kabbala, and "occultism" in general.

Divining with cards is far more often carried out with an ordinary pack of playing cards. Here, as with the Tarot, the first thing that is necessary is to memorize the meaning of the individual cards. We can say that, in general, hearts are connected to home and domestic happiness, clubs to friendship and influence, diamonds to work and money – the practical side of life – and spades to misfortune. (The ace of spades is regarded as a card of ill omen, while the nine of spades is virtually disaster.)

The table below is taken from Basil Ivan Rakoczi's article on cartomancy in *Man, Myth and Magic*.

The two simplest layouts are known as the "seven triplets", and the "lucky thirteen".

In the "seven triplets", the pack is shuffled and cut into three heaps. (This latter should be done with the left hand.)

Then from the top of each heap, a card is taken and laid nearby face-up. Then a second and third card is placed on top in the same way, forming three heaps of three. Four more heaps of three are dealt in the same way, making seven heaps. Then each of the seven heaps is spread, so the cards can be seen, and the interpretation commences.

Each group of three is considered as a separate situation.

For example, a seven of hearts would suggest good fortune, an ace of diamonds that this will involve marriage while a queen of spades might suggest that a false friend may act, or try to act, as the serpent in this Eden.

The remaining six groups of three are interpreted in the same way. What emerges is basically a complete character reading, with indications for the future.

The "lucky thirteen" method is closer to the "Celtic" method of the Tarot. The joker (a leftover from the Fool of the Tarot) is placed face upwards at the centre. Then, from a well-shuffled pack, form a cross by placing one card above and one below, then one at either side – all face down. Then place another four cards – face down – beyond each of these, lengthening the arms of the

cross. Finally, another four cards are placed in the spaces between the arms of the cross.

The four cards immediately next to the joker are turned up
first; these represent the influences in the present.

Next, the four outermost cards of the cross are turned up; these
represent the future. Finally, the four diagonal cards are turned
up; these represent minor or secondary influences.

The Fortune-telling Values of Standard Playing Cards

	Hearts	Diamonds	Clubs	Spades
1	Love; Marriage	An engagement	Conquest	A death
2	Friendship	Trouble	Enterprise	Treachery
3	Pleasure	Social activities	A kind gesture	Separation
4	Change	A legacy	Gaiety	Peace
5	An inheritance	A rendezvous	A lawsuit	A funeral
6	Originality	Forgiveness	Good news	A stroke of luck
7	Good fortune	Money	Success	Prudence
8	Company	Prosperity	Deception	Quarrels
9	A wish	A loss	Anticipation	Suffering
10	Home	Financial gain	Travel	Deprivation

The Jack of Hearts = A charming but faithless young man/woman who
may bring news.
The Queen of Hearts = A kind woman of noble demeanour.
The King of Hearts = A mature, generous man of good position: a
patriarch.

The Jack of Diamonds = A gifted, lucky young man/woman.
The Queen of Diamonds = A rich and glamorous woman.
The King of Diamonds = A rich man of the world: a tycoon.

The Jack of Clubs = An adventurous young man/woman who is given to
extravagance.
The Queen of Clubs = A practical woman of strong character.
The King of Clubs = A distinguished and powerful man: a diplomat.

The Jack of Spades = A serious-minded young man/woman who may be
an enemy.
The Queen of Spades = A seductive and treacherous woman.
The King of Spades = A forceful, possibly dangerous man: a soldier.

16 Nostradamus and the Nineteenth Century

It must be admitted that, when we come to the nineteenth century, the prophet's obsession with his own country begins to look like parochialism. He fails to foresee Dalton's atomic theory, Darwin's theory of Evolution, the discovery of steam power, the Industrial Revolution, the South-Sea Bubble or the American Civil War. Yet there are prophecies that appear to be detailed accounts of French political life over the same period.

The relative significance (or insignificance) of the events does not seem to have been the deciding factor. Nostradamus was apparently quite aware that France would become a secondary world power after the defeat of Napoleon Bonaparte, but he is always, at heart, a Frenchman. Before we condemn him as small-minded, we should perhaps ask if we ourselves – placed in a position of foreseeing the future – would not take more interest in our own culture than those of other countries.

The Fall of Sultan Selim III, 1807
I.52

> *Les deux malins de Scorpion conjoinct,*
> *Le grand seigneur meutri dedans sa salle:*
> *Peste à l'Eglise le nouveau roy joinct*
> *L'Europe basse et Septentrionale.*

Translation:

> The two evils of Scorpio conjunct,
> The great lord murdered in his hall:
> Plague to the Church by the new king,
> Lower Europe and the North.

The first line of this quatrain seems to be another of Nostradamus' astrological dates. The two planets of evil portent are usually accepted to be Mars (war) and Saturn (old age and decay). These conjoin in the sign of Scorpio around three times every hundred years, giving us fourteen such dates since 1555.

One such conjunction took place in 1807: the year that Sultan Selim III of the Ottoman Empire was deposed. (He was, in fact, murdered in the following year.) Erica Cheetham points out that one of Selim's titles was "*Seignoir*": just as the quatrain says.

The second two lines seem to link the quatrain to events around 1807. By that time the Catholic Church was in direct conflict with Napoleon, although the Pope himself had crowned him emperor ("new king") only three years earlier. Bonaparte had also "plagued" "lower" and "Northern" Europe by that time, defeating the Austrians, Prussians and the Russians in major battles.

The End of Napoleon's Luck, 1809–15
II.44 & I.88

> *L'aigle pousée entour de pavillions,*
> *Par autres oiseax d'entour sera chassée:*
> *Quand bruit des cymbees, tubes et sonaillons,*
> *Rendront le sens de la dame insensée.*

Translation:

> The eagle flying among the pavilions,
> By other birds shall be driven away.
> When the sound of cymbals, trumpets and bells,
> Restores sense to the lady insane.

Nostradamus scholars generally agree that when the seer mentions an "eagle", he is often referring to the badge of Napoleon Bonaparte. Following the Emperor's disastrous retreat from Moscow in 1812–13, his previously cautious European enemies found the courage to attack him. The image of a flock of lesser birds harrying an eagle over military pavilions is poetically reminiscent of these events.

The third and fourth lines depict music returning a lady to her senses. Such a vague outline is, needless to say, difficult to pin down to an actual event. Some Nostradamus scholars believe that the "*dame*" is France, returned to Bourbon rule under Louis XVIII with military pomp and music. Others suggest the lines may concern the mad jealousy of the Empress Josephine, divorced by Napoleon in 1809.

There is little in the quatrain to back the second interpretation, apart from the link with Napoleon's defeat in the first two lines; it is a traditional French belief that the Emperor's luck abandoned him when he abandoned Josephine.

> Le divin mal surprendra le grand prince,
> Un peu devant aura femme espousse.
> Son appuy et credit à un coup viendra mince,
> Conseil mourra pour la teste rasée.

Translation:

> The divine malady overtakes the great prince,
> A little while after he marries a woman.
> His support and credit become slender,
> Counsel will die away for the shaven head.

This quatrain also seems to predict the fall from luck of a "great prince". The "divine malady" mentioned in the first line sounds like another of Nostradamus' classical allusions. In ancient Greece, the human weakness that was supposed to provoke divine vengeance was *hubris* (conceit and overweening ambition) – a failing to which Napoleon was rather prone.

The second line connects this fall from grace with an ill-starred marriage. Again, this sounds like Napoleon's change of fortune after divorcing Josephine and marrying into the royal line of Habsburg.

The third line is only accurate of Napoleon after his retreat from Moscow in 1812. Even then, the Emperor's "support and credit" only ran short with his own politicians and generals – the French public was still enamoured of the emperor, even after Waterloo.

The last line is generally true of Napoleon's last years in power. A combination of absolute power, middle age, a crushing workload and chronic stomach ulcers made him less prone to listen to counsel that he did not agree with. The result was that sycophants surrounded him and his good counsellors faded into the background.

The last two words of the quatrain echo quatrain 131 of *Century VII*: "*teste raze*", or "shaven-head". Napoleon's troopers nicknamed him "*le petit tondu*", or "the little crop-head".

The Fall of Paris, 3 July 1815
IX.86

> *Du bourg Lareyne ne paviendront droit à Chartres*
> *Et feront pres du pont Anthoni pause,*
> *Sept pour la paix cantelleux comme martres.*
> *Feront entrée d'armee á Paris clause.*

Translation:

From Bourge-la-Reine they will not come straight to Chartres
And near the Pont d'Anthony they will pause,
Seven for peace crafty as martens.
Armies enter a closed Paris.

Following the French defeat at Waterloo, the allied elements of seven nations' armies entered Paris on 3 July 1815: Britain, Russia, Austria, Prussia, Sweden, Spain and Portugal. The seer is perhaps being insulting when he calls them as "crafty as martens",[1] but he also seems to admit that their mission was not one of conquest, but to bring peace (albeit on their own terms).

1 Small, wily carnivores – closely akin to weasels – native to northern Europe.

There was no battle for the French capital and the Allies easily occupied and "closed" Paris because the shattered French army had already left the city. Just as lines one and two describe, the remnant of Napoleon's Grand Army made its way to the Loire town of Chartres via Bourge-la-Reine, and even bivouacked a night under the Pont d'Anthony.

The 1815 Occupation of France
I.20

> Tours, Orleans, Blois, Angiers, Reims, et Nantes,
> Cités vexées par subit changement:
> Par langues estranges seront tenues tentes,
> Fleuves, dards Rones, terre et mer tremblement.

Translation:

> Tours, Orleans, Blois, Angers, Reims, and Nantes,
> Cities vexed by sudden change,
> By strange languages tents shall be pitched,
> Rivers, darts at Rennes, land and sea tremble.

The first three lines of the above quatrain seem to predict a foreign invasion of northern France, where all the cities listed in the first line are situated. Such an event has taken place several times in the last two centuries, but not between 1815 and Nostradamus' day.

The 1815 invasion is the most likely candidate for this prediction (to date) because the anti-Napoleonic Allies were a more mixed group of nationalities ("*langues estranges*") than in any subsequent invasion. The cities mentioned were also "vexed by sudden change" in this period: Napoleon fell in 1814, returned in 1815 to dethrone Louis XVIII, was dethroned himself and exiled a hundred days later, and Louis again became king.

The last line is less easy to fathom. Rennes is another northern French town that was briefly occupied in 1815, but no record of an earthquake or similar event is known from this time.

The Assassination of the Duc de Berry, 13 February 1820
III.96 & I.84

> Chef de Fossan aura gorge coupee,
> Par le ducteur du limier et laurier,
> La faict patre par de mont Tarpee,
> Saturne en Leo treziesme de Fevrier.

Translation:

> The Chief of the Fossan has his throat cut,
> By the keeper of hunters and greyhounds:
> The act committed by those of the Tarpian Rock,
> Saturn in Leo thirteenth of February.

Louis XVIII lived for nine years after the exile of Napoleon to St Helena. Although he initially persecuted the remaining French Bonapartists and Republicans, Louis was also increasingly attracted to the new liberal doctrines of state and kingship. However, this liberality ceased following the murder of his son and heir, the Duc de Berry, in 1820.

The Duc was stabbed to death while attending the opera on 13 February – the date given in line four of the above quatrain. The term "Saturn in Leo" is astrological: the sign of Aquarius rules Saturn, so when that planet is in the opposing house of Leo, it is said to be in a "malevolent" position.

The murderer was a Republican called Louvel. In the days of the Roman Republic, traitors were executed by being thrown off the Tarpean Rock; thus line three seems to hint at Louvel's political motivations. Line two could also be true of Louvel, who worked in the royal stables and might well have been in charge of hunting horses and greyhounds. Unfortunately, line one throws doubt on this interpretation, because the Duc de Berry did not have his throat cut. On the other hand, Erica Cheetham offers a link (if somewhat tenuous) between de Berry and the phrase "Chief of Fossan": de Berry's maternal grandfather was King of Fossano in Sardinia.

> Lune obscurcie aux profondes tenebres,
> Son frere passe de couleur ferrugine:
> La grand caché long temps soubs les tenebres,
> Tiedera fer dans la plaie sanguine.

Translation:

> The moon will be obscured by profound darkness,
> Her brother passes the rusty colour:
> The great one hidden a long time in shadow,
> Cools the blade in the bloody wound.

Erica Cheetham also connects this quatrain with the assassination of the Duc de Berry, but has to use some rather circuitous arguments to justify her translation.

She suggests that the first three lines poetically describe the Comte d'Artois – younger brother of Louis XVI and Louis XVIII. D'Artois escaped into exile during the revolution and remained there, "obscured by profound darkness", for over two decades. Cheetham translates the second line to read: "His brother becomes bright red in colour": taking this to be a reference to the execution of Louis XVI. The third line, she says, is a further comment on d'Artois' long period in the political wilderness. Even following the restoration of the Bourbon monarchy, d'Artois found that his reactionary, ultra-royalist views were out of step with the liberal trends at court.

Whether or not one finds the above argument overstretched, line four does sound a grimly accurate description of de Berry's assassination. As de Berry lay stabbed – the blade of the murder weapon literally cooling in his dying flesh – he is said to have moaned: "I am murdered. I am holding the hilt of the dagger."

Despite the accusatory sound of the last two lines of the quatrain, it is highly unlikely that the Comte d'Artois had anything to do with his nephew's murder. Nevertheless, he did gain by it. First, his elder brother Louis XVIII swung to ultra-royalist party and ended his liberal reforms. Second, d'Artois became the heir apparent following the murder; on Louis's death in 1824, he was crowned Charles X of France.

Pax Britannica
X.42

> *Le regne humain d'Anglique geniture,*
> *Fera son regne paix union tenir,*

Captive guerre demi de sa closture,
Long Temps la paix leur fera maintenir.

Translation:

The humane reign of English offspring
Shall cause the reign of peace and union,
Captive war half enclosed,
A long time the peace maintained by them.

This quatrain delighted British Nostradamus scholars in the nineteenth and early twentieth century, as it all but proclaims "Rule Britannia!"

As we have already seen (in the chapter on Nostradamus' predictions for the seventeenth century) the seer was apparently quite aware that the English would achieve an ocean-spanning "great empire"[2] – although England was only a second-rate power in Nostradamus' day. This quatrain goes even further by predicting that England would reign in "peace and union". Taking the two quatrains together, Victorians saw a virtual endorsement of the British Empire.

Whether British Imperialists were correct to claim their empire was so "humane" is matter for debate – but, ignoring this aspect, the quatrain does contain another striking prediction. In both the famous "British Empire" quatrains, Nostradamus refers to "England" and the "English" ("*Angleterre*" and "*Anglique*") – not to "Great Britain" or the "British". This is hardly surprising; England and Wales were only joined in the seer's own lifetime (in 1543); Scotland remained separate until 1707, and Ireland was treated as little more than a protectorate up to the 1920s. The idea of the "British Nation" was not widespread in the sixteenth century, nor was the possibility of the islands becoming a "United Kingdom". Nevertheless, line two of the quatrain predicts the "English offspring" (perhaps meaning the descendants of the English of the seer's own day) would rule a "union".

2 *Century X*, quatrain 100.

The Abandoned Heir, 1820
V.39

> *Du vrai rameau de fleur de lys issue*
> *Mis et logé heretier de Hetrurie:*
> *Son sang antique de long main tissu*
> *Fera Florence florir en l'armoirie.*

Translation:

> Out of the branch of the *fleur de lys* issue
> Placed and lodged as heir to Etruria,
> His ancient blood a long woven tissue
> Will make the coat of arms of Florence flourish.

Although the Comte d'Artois was named the heir to Louis XVIII following the murder of the Duc de Berry, there was another claimant to the throne of France. The Duchess de Berry was two months pregnant when her husband was killed. The resulting son was named the Comte de Chambord and, when d'Artois became Charles X, was declared the *heir apparent*.

However, the child's late birth was the cause of a national controversy. The Duc d'Orleans – himself in line to the throne, although not of pure Bourbon blood – accused the Duchess of trying to foist a bastard on the royal family. In 1830, following the July Revolution, the boy and his mother went into self-imposed exile in Venice. Northern Italy was also the home of the ancient people called Etruscans, their country being called Etruria (see line two above).

The Comte de Chambord was the last of the true French Bourbon line, but never attained his birthright. The Duc d'Orleans took the throne after the abdication of Charles X (as we will see below). Nevertheless, the Comte de Chambord lived a happy and productive life. In 1846 he married the daughter of the Duke of Florence. Both families – who shared the *fleur de lys* on their coats of arms – flourished through the union, just as the quatrain seems to predict.

The Murder of Louis Bourbon Condé, 1830.
I.39

> De nuict dans lict le suspresme estrangle,
> Par trop avoir sejourné, blond esleu:
> Par trois l'empire subrogé exanche,
> A mort mettra carte, et pacuet ne leu.

Translation:

> At night in bed the final one is strangled,
> For much bribery, blond elect:
> By three substitutes the empire enslaved,
> He is put to death document, and packet unread.

Erica Cheetham thinks this quatrain predicts the death of Louis Bourbon Condé. The last of the Condé line ("the final one"), Louis was found hanged in his bedroom in 1830. Although accepted as suicide, the rumour went about that he had actually been throttled in bed, then hanged from a rafter to disguise the strangulation marks. The public blamed Louis Phillipe, Duc d'Orleans.

If Condé was murdered, it was probably for the support ("bribery") he gave to the cause of the Comte De Chambord – son of the Duc de Berry and heir elect ("*esleu*") to Charles X. The "three substitutes", seen enslaving the "empire" in line three, could therefore be the three regimes that usurped the throne from Bourbons: Louis Phillipe, the Second Republic then Napoleon III.

Condé is believed to have left a will favouring the young Comte de Chambord, but this was apparently substituted for an earlier testament, favouring the son of Louis Phillipe, Duc d'Orleans. This may explain the meaning of the last line of the quatrain.

Citizen King, 1830
V.69

> Plus ne sera le grand en faux sommeil,
> L'inquietude viendra prendre repoz:

> *Dresser phalange d'or, azur, et vermeil,*
> *Subjuger Affrique la ronger jusques oz.*

Translation:

> No more will the great one be in a false sleep,
> Unease takes the place of repose:
> He shall raise the phalanx of gold, azure, and vermilion,
> Subjugating Africa and gnawing it down to the bone.

By 1830, the reactionary, 73-year-old Charles X had pushed France to the edge of another revolution. His overriding of the democratic Chamber of Deputies, his attempts to restrict the voting franchise and his draconian curbs on the free press roused the people of Paris to open rebellion. On 26 July they stormed and took the *Hôtel de Ville* – the centre of government. After three days' fighting, Charles saw that his troops could not regain control of the streets, so he capitulated to the rebels' demands and was forced to abdicate.

The leaders of the July Revolution called for a return to the Republic, but the liberal bourgeoisie managed to have Louis Phillipe, Duc d'Orleans, crowned as a constitutional and legally restricted monarch. As such, he was nicknamed "Citizen King".

This Louis Phillipe was the same Duc d'Orleans who had questioned the legitimacy of the Bourbon heir, the Comte de Chambord. He was also one of the men implicated in the death of Louis Bourbon Condé, not least because the dead man's estates were handed over to d'Orleans' son. He was clearly something of a political schemer, unwilling to risk an open attempt on the throne, but always plotting to that end. The first line of the quatrain, depicting a "great one" ending his pretence of sleep, poetically describes Louis Phillipe's election to the throne after a decade of plotting.

The second line also fits Louis Phillipe. Having achieved his end, he found kingship a mixed blessing. Over the next eighteen years, he must often have thought ironically of the comparative repose of his days as a schemer compared to the uneasy task of actually ruling a volatile and quickly changing France.

The third line mentions a "phalanx of gold, azure and vermilion". Louis Phillipe was the first king of France to adopt the revolutionary tricolour flag: three bars ("phalanx") of red ("ver-milion") white ("gold") and blue ("azure").

1830 was also the year that the French army captured Algiers. Over the next two decades, the French annexed and colonized all of Algeria. In French eyes, they were civilizing and bringing modern amenities to the Algerians. To the Arabs, however, the French were arrogant imperialists who treated them as third-class citizens. Troubles continued for the next century, culmi-nating in the 1954 War of Algerian Independence. This bitter conflict continued until the French were forced to give the colony independence in 1962.

Since that time, Algeria has had continuous misfortune. When the general election of 1992 was on the point of being won by the Islamic fundamentalist party, the military cancelled the ballot, seized power and declared a state of emergency. The resulting conflict between the military government and Islamic terror groups has been one of the most savage of the decade – both sides apparently targeting women and children in wholesale slaughters. French influence, backing the military regime, has been widely rumoured. If so, France can still be accused of "gnawing [Algeria] down to the bone", as Nostradamus seems to in the last line of the quatrain.

Napoleon's Bones, 1840
V.7

> *Du Triumvir seront trouvé les os,*
> *Cherchant profond thresor aenigmatique,*
> *Ceux d'alentour ne seront en repos.*
> *Ce concaver marbre et plomb metallique.*

Translation:

> The bones of the Triumvir will be found,
> When they search for a deep and enigmatic treasure:
> Those around will not be restful.
> This concavity of marble and metallic lead.

When Napoleon died in 1821, he was buried on his island of exile, St Helena. Louis XVIII or Charles X would have no more wanted the remains of the former emperor brought home than they would have considered building a marble tomb for the regicidal Robespierre. King Louis Phillipe, on the other hand, saw Napoleon's bones as a way to make peace with the still active Bonapartist faction and boost his own flagging popularity. In 1840, he ordered Napoleon's body disinterred and brought back to Paris.

The first line of the above quatrain describes the finding of the bones of the "Triumvir".[3] The First Republic – which Napoleon took over in the Brumaire coup – was run by a "Directory" of five men. One of Napoleon's first acts on taking power was to reduce this number to three – with himself as ruling First Consul. Thus he could certainly be called a "Triumvir".

The "deep and enigmatic treasure" mentioned in line two could be the secret of Napoleon I's seemingly boundless popularity with the French people – an approval that King Louis Phillipe hoped to find, through association with the dead emperor. It is some indication of the king's desperation that he attempted to make friends with the Bonapartists – a group dedicated to putting Napoleon's nephew, Louis Napoleon Bonaparte, on Louis Phillipe's throne.

Despite Louis Phillipe's efforts, the Bonapartists were certainly "not restful", as line three predicts. They had led two revolts against Citizen King in 1836 and 1840, and were only slightly mollified by the return of "their Emperor" to Paris.

The bones of Napoleon Bonaparte were reinterred with great pomp at *Les Invalides*, on the left bank of the Seine. As line four of the quatrain predicts, the body was placed in á lead coffin in a marble tomb.

The Reign and Fall of Citizen King, 1830–48
IX.89

> *Sept ans Philip fortune prospere,*
> *Rabaissera des Arabes l'effaict,*
> *Puis son midi perplex rebours affaire*
> *Jeune ognion abismera son fort.*

3 A Latin term for one of three joint rulers of a state.

Translation:

> Seven years Philip's fortune will prosper,
> Cutting down the Arab exertions,
> Then in the middle of a perplexing and contrary affair,
> Young *ognion* shall put down his strength.

The first seven years of Louis Phillipe's reign were troubled but fundamentally successful. Although disappointed Republicans and the starving poor often rioted, the Bourgeois Chamber of Deputies provided solid support for their "Citizen King". Arab attempts to block French colonization of Algeria were easily frustrated by Louis Philippe's troops (just as line two predicts) and France began to win back her prestige in foreign affairs.

Louis Phillipe was unhappy with his limited position during this period, but saw that he would go the way of Charles X if he attempted to increase the political power of the monarchy. This did not stop him establishing his Bourbon-Orleans family as the new French royal dynasty and dispensing honours and government posts to his personal cronies. The result was that, by the mid-point of his eighteen-year reign, corruption was rife in the Palace.

The "perplexing and contrary affair", mentioned in line three, could be the so-called "Eastern Question", concerning the decrepitude of the once-feared Ottoman Empire. As the Turks continued to lose their grip on Greece and the Balkans, it was becoming increasingly clear that Russia was growing stronger. Britain and France saw Russian expansion as a threat to the balance of power in Europe and tried various diplomatic measures to curb the Tsar's power. The Eastern Question was still unresolved when Louis Phillipe was toppled from his throne.

By the late 1840s, Louis Phillipe's corrupt regime had forced many of his former backers in the Chamber of Deputies to seriously consider the creation of a new republic. Although not attempting to rule as an absolute monarch, the king used his veto to block the social reforms that France desperately needed to modernize herself. Many therefore saw the monarchy itself as an obstacle to progress.

The end came in September 1848, the year of European revolutions, when the king sent troops to crush a Republican demonstration in central Paris. The resulting riot turned into a full-scale revolution and Louis Phillipe, like Charles X before him, was forced to abdicate and flee into exile. A group of Republican leaders formed the new government and declared the birth of the Second Republic.

Erica Cheetham connects this event with the word *"ognion"* in line four. She suggests that this word should actually read *"Ogmios"* – the Celtic Hercules – and can be seen as an image of resurgent French Republicanism.

The End of the Second Republic and the Birth of the Second French Empire, 1848–52
VIII.42

> Esleu sera Renad ne sonnant mot,
> Faisant le faint public vivant pain d'orge,
> Tyranniser apres tant à un coup,
> Mettant pied des plus grands sur la gorge.

Translation:

> The Fox is elected without saying a word,
> Playing the saint in public while eating barley bread,
> A tyrant after such a coup,
> Putting his feet on the necks of the greatest ones.

The constitution of the new French Republic created the post of President, to act in concert with the elected senate. One of the candidates for the first presidential election in 1859 was Louis Napoleon Bonaparte, the nephew of the Emperor Napoleon. Despite support for him from the Bonapartists, the political pundits ignored Louis Napoleon as a rank outsider; thus his landslide victory came as something of a shock to the French political establishment.

Louis Napoleon rode to power on a groundswell of popular support created by his uncle's undying popularity and his own daring escape from imprisonment by King Louis Phillipe in 1856. Nostradamus' description, in line one, of a foxy politician being elected without having to utter a word on his policies is therefore true of President Bonaparte.

Unfortunately for Louis Bonaparte, the presidency only ran

for four years, and the constitution banned further election of the same person. So, for two years, he pretended to be an ardent Republican while secretly plotting to overthrow the state. This situation fits the prediction in line two – a "saint in public" "eating barley bread" (a French equivalent of the British phrase, "feathering one's own nest").

On 2 December, 1851, the president of France staged a *coup d'état*. He declared the Second Republic dead and initiated the "Second Empire". He also claimed right to be called "the Emperor Napoleon" but, because the first Napoleon's son had been declared Napoleon II in 1815, Louis Bonaparte had to settle for the title "Napoleon III".

Nostradamus' term *"Tyranniser"*, at the beginning of line three, is a quite accurate description of the early part of Napoleon III's reign. He forcefully repressed political opposition, exiled his enemies, and his secret police – the *ratapolis* – were simply club-wielding thugs. So Napoleon III certainly put his "feet on the necks" of the "greatest ones" of the banned Republican movement, as line four describes.

The Attempted Assassination of Napoleon III, 14 January 1858
V.9 & V.10

> *Jusques au fonds la grand arq demolue,*
> *Par chef captif, l'ami anticipé:*
> *Naistra de dame front face chevelue,*
> *Lor par astuce Duc à mort attrapé.*

Translation:

> Below the great fallen arch,
> By the chief captive, the friend anticipated:
> Son born of a woman hairy forehead and faced,
> Then through cunning the Duke escapes death.

The first decade of Napoleon III's rule was dictatorial and repressive. Many Frenchmen must have anticipated or hoped for an attempt on the Emperor's life but, when this eventually happened in 1858, its source proved surprising.

In his younger days, Louis Bonaparte had been something of a political radical and had fervently supported the cause of Italian nationalism. Now, as Napoleon III, he was in a prime position to help his former friends, but (apparently) did nothing. A small group of Italian revolutionaries, led by Count Felice Orsini, decided to make him pay for this betrayal.

The conspirators tried to blow the emperor to pieces with a bomb as he left the Paris Opera on 14 January 1858. The explosion damaged the building ("the great fallen arch" mentioned in line one of the quatrain) and killed a number of innocent bystanders, but Napoleon III escaped with only minor wounds.

Line two may be a prediction of the arrest of Pieri – one of the three co-conspirators with Orsini – the night before the assassination attempt. This interpretation, coupled with the use of the word "cunning" in line four, allows Erica Cheetham to argue that Napoleon III escaped death through foreknowledge of the plot, although the history books offer no supporting evidence for this theory.

Line three has no obvious explanation in the context of the assassination attempt. Nostradamus throws in descriptions of strange births throughout the *Centuries*, possibly because he, like most of his contemporaries, believed such "monsters" were portents from God. Some Nostradamus scholars suggest he used these descriptions to make allegorical points to illuminate his message. Others believe he mentions them as concurrent events to provide a further method of dating his predictions. If the latter is true, the idea failed: accounts of freak births rarely find their way into the history books.

> *Un chef Celtique dans le conflict blessé,*
> *Aupres de cave voyant siens mort abbatre:*
> *De sang et plaies et d'ennemis pressé,*
> *Et secourus par incognus de quatre.*

Translation:

> A French chief wounded in the conflict,
> Near the cellar he sees his people struck dead:
> By blood and wounds and enemies pressed,
> And saved from four unknown people.

If, as Nostradamus himself claimed, his quatrains were deliberately mixed up to disguise their chronological order and relation to each other, V.9 and V.10 may have escaped his attention. Both have been argued to predict the assassination attempt on Napoleon III.

As noted above, the emperor was only slightly wounded in the bombing. His survival was due to the crowd of people between himself and the explosion, so – as line two states – he must have seen a lot of dead citizens as he was led away. The word *"cave"* in this line should be translated as "theatre", according to Erica Cheetham: *cavea* being a Latin name for a theatre.

The "four unknown people", mentioned in line four, could therefore be Count Orsini and his three co-conspirators.

With most tyrants in history, an assassination attempt tends to drive them towards ever more draconian policies. Fortunately, Napoleon III was an exception. By 1860, two years after the attempt, he had begun a series of liberal reforms that were to transform France from an absolute monarchy to a modern democracy.

It should be added that the vengeful Orsini was ignorant of the French Emperor's secret dealings with Italian revolutionary groups. The year following the bombing – undeterred by the bloody misunderstanding – Napoleon III launched a war to free Italy from the Austrian Empire.

Napoleon III and the War to Free Italy, 1859
V.20 & X.64

> *Dela les Alpes grand armée passera,*
> *Un peu devant naistre monstre vapin:*
> *Prodigieux et subit tournera,*
> *Le grand Tosquan á son lieu plus propin.*

Translation:

> Beyond the Alps a great army passes,
> A short while before a wretched monster will be born,
> Strange and suddenly,
> The grand Tuscan will return to his native land.

French troops crossed the Alps into Italy in early 1859 and, together with Italian revolutionaries and the Sardinian army, attacked the occupying Austrians. As a commander-in-chief, Napoleon III proved to have an excellent grip of modern warfare. A technically minded general, he used his new, long-range artillery and scouting balloons to great effect – decisively winning the battles of Magenta and Solferino by the middle of the summer.

The first line of the quatrain describes a "great army" crossing the Alps, but this could equally be about Napoleon I's invasion of northern Italy in 1795. However, lines three and four seem to link the quatrain with Napoleon III's war in Italy.

Early in the campaign, Leopold II, Grand Duke of Tuscany, was driven out of Florence by the pro-independence allies. He returned in disgrace to his native Austria, fulfilling the prediction that the "grand Tuscan will return to his native land".

The second line may be another of Nostradamus' "freak-birth" inclusions (see above). But Erica Cheetham suggests it might be a prediction of the birth, in 1807, of Giuseppe Garibaldi: the great Italian revolutionary.

Garibaldi was born poor ("wretched") but why Nostradamus should describe him as a "monster" is harder to say. Garibaldi's forces assaulted French troops holding the Italian Papal States in 1866, but the seer was usually above such national partisanship and, besides, Garibaldi fought for France in the Franco-Prussian War, four years later.

Of course, it is possible that Nostradamus was using the term "monster" in its ancient meaning: the word derives from the Latin verb *monere*, meaning "to warn". Even in Nostradamus' day, a "monster" was seen as more than just a freak of nature; such births were also seen as portents. Garibaldi – the forerunner of all twentieth-century, anti-imperialist revolutionaries – could certainly be seen as a portent of future things. However, one must then accept that Nostradamus meant "a short while" (in line two) to mean around fifty years.

> *Pleure Milan, pleure Luques, Florance,*
> *Que ton grand Duc sur le charmontera,*
> *Changer le seige pres de Venise s'advance,*
> *Lors que Colonne Rome changera.*

Translation:

> Weep Milan, weep Lucca, Florence,
> When the grand Duke mounts the chariot,
> Changing the siege of Venice advances,
> When *Colonne* changes at Rome.

Milan, Lucca, Florence and Venice are all cities in northern and central Italy – the region of the 1859 war – large areas of which were abandoned by the Austrians, following the precipitate withdrawal of the Grand Duke of Tuscany. The towns mentioned were delighted to be free of the yoke of the Austrian Empire, so perhaps the weeping mentioned in line one of the quatrain signifies tears of joy.

Venice was not freed until the near-collapse of the Austrian Empire, which followed the latter's war with Prussia in 1866. Whether this long-term Austrian occupation counts as a "siege", as line three states, is a matter of individual interpretation.

Rome herself did not join the unified Italy until 1870. Both Erica Cheetham and David Ovason suggest that the word "*Colonne*" in the last line may refer to the Colonnas – a great Roman family – but neither can offer an explanation as to what the line is actually meant to predict.

The Return of Savoy to France, 22 March 1860
V.42

> *Mars esleue en son haut befroi,*
> *Fera retaire les Allobrox de France:*
> *La gent Lombarde fera si grand effroi,*
> *A ceux de l'aigle comprins souz la Balance.*

Translation:

> Mars raised to the belfry,
> Will cause *Allobrox* to retire to France:
> The people of Lombardy shall be in such great fear,
> Of those of the eagle included in the Balance.

In late 1859, despite his successes in the war to free Italy, Napoleon III began to worry about his military situation. Austria was loosely allied with Prussia and the southern German states. If these latter decided to take the field on Austria's behalf, France would be in serious trouble. He therefore signed a peace treaty with Austria, leaving his former allies to fend for themselves. The Sardinians and Italians doubtless felt betrayed, but eventually managed to win independence without further French help.

France, nevertheless, demanded a reward for her efforts. On 22 March 1860, the new Italian king, Victor Emmanuel II, ceded the duchy of Savoy to French ownership as a reward.

The rather odd-sounding first line of the above quatrain is probably too literal a translation. Perhaps "a warrior [Napoleon III?] achieving the height of success" might be a better paraphrase.

The word "*Allobrox*" in the second line sounds very like the name *Allobroge*: a tribe that once dominated the Savoy region. This interpretation seems to be further confirmed by the mention of Lombardy in the third line (Lombardy is a region of northern Italy; Savoy is sandwiched between Lombardy and France).

The last two lines apparently describe the northern Italians ("Lombardy") throwing out the Austrians (the sign of imperial Austria was an eagle). Erica Cheetham translated "la Balance" as Libra, the scales, and equates this with Italy, presumably because Italy was "liberated".

The Franco-Prussian War, July 1870 to February 1871
I.92, VIII.43, IV.100 & X.51

> *Sous un la paix par tout sera clamee,*
> *Mais non long temps pillé et rebellion:*
> *Par refus ville, terre, et mer entamee,*
> *Mors et captifs let tiers d'un million.*

Translation:

> Under one the peace will be proclaimed everywhere,
> But not long after will plundering and rebellion:
> Because of a refusal town, land, and sea will be assaulted,
> Dead and captured a third of a million.

The expanding power in late nineteenth-century Europe was Prussia.[4] The brilliant but ruthless Prussian chancellor, Otto von Bismarck, dreamed of unifying all the Germanic states and saw war as the quickest method of achieving this. He started with a diplomatic campaign to annoy Austria – fully aware of how decadent and brittle the Holy Roman Empire had become. The resulting conflict, in 1866, became known as the Seven Weeks' War, which resulted in the swift victory of the Prussian army.

By 1870, Bismarck was ready to humiliate France as he had Austria. If he could make the French start a conflict, he felt sure he could use the situation to unify the disparate German states under one flag. To his delight, Napoleon III played straight into his hands. The Prussians had tried to place a member of their own dynasty, the Hohenzollerns, on the recently vacated throne of Spain. France, seeing that this might leave them with hostile forces on both east and western frontiers, demanded the candidate's withdrawal. Bismarck refused and Napoleon III declared war on 19 July 1870.

The French Emperor had set in motion important political reforms since 1860, transforming the nation from a totalitarian state to a free democracy headed by a constitutionally bound monarch. Unfortunately, Napoleon III's zeal for internal reform was not matched by his diplomatic skills in judging foreign situations. The French were quite unprepared for the war. They could only marshal 200,000 men, while the Prussians and their south German allies had 400,000. Only Napoleon III's personal conviction that he was a military genius can explain the appalling folly that led him to declare war against such odds.

The first line of the above quatrain echoes Napoleon III's complacent announcement in the late 1860s: *"L'Empire, c'est la paix"* ("The Empire is at peace"). Chancellor Bismarck had no intention of letting this situation continue.

Line two mentions "looting and rebellion"; the first is certainly true of the Prussian invasion force. The second came true when Paris rebelled on hearing the news of the dismal performance of Napoleon III at the Battle of Sedan. Although the Paris Commune continued to fight the Prussians, they now did it in the name of the "New Republic", not the Emperor.

4 A state situated across what is now northern Germany and Poland.

Line three describes the ruin of "town, land and sea", because of a "refusal". This might be the flat refusal of Bismarck to withdraw his Hohenzollern candidate's claim to the Spanish throne, thus causing the war.

The last line describes a third of a million "dead and captured". It is estimated that 299,000 were killed or wounded in the Franco-Prussian war – a figure relatively close to the seer's prediction.

> *Par le decide de deux choses bastars,*
> *Neveu du sang occupera le regne,*
> *Dedans lectoyre seront les coups de dars,*
> *Neveu par peur plaire l'enseigne.*

Translation:

> Through the decision of two bastards,
> Nephew of the blood will occupy the throne,
> Within *lectoyre* there will be blows of lances,
> Nephew through fear will fold up his standard.

The Battle of Sedan was the deciding moment of the Franco-Prussian War. The French had already lost four major battles, and had allowed the Prussians to split their forces down the middle. On the morning of 1 September 1870, over half the French army (120,000 men) found itself sandwiched between the Belgian border and a force of 200,000 Prussians. The French fell back on the town of Sedan, where they were surrounded and mercilessly bombarded. The French commander, MacMahon, was badly wounded early in the battle. When, in the late afternoon, Napoleon III himself arrived to take command, he immediately saw that surrender was the only possible course of action.

Seventeen thousand French soldiers were killed in the fighting; 83,000 were taken prisoner, along with Napoleon III himself.

Erica Cheetham suggests that the phrase "*le decide*", in the first line of the quatrain, should be translated not as "the decision" but as "the fall" – from the Latin *decidere*: to fall. Thus, the seer may have been referring to "the fall" of the "Citizen King", Louis Philippe, and the subsequent Second

Republic. Both might have been seen as "bastards" in the eyes of Nostradamus, an absolute-monarchist.

Napoleon III took the French throne, as described in line two, by right of being the nephew of Napoleon I. He was the only nephew of a monarch to attain the crown between Nostradamus' day and the end of the French monarchy.

The word "*lectoyre*", in line three, Erica Cheetham argues, is an anagram of *Le Torcey*. This suburb of Sedan was the scene of some of the bloodiest fighting in the battle.

Line four describes the "nephew" folding his standard through fear: a blunt, but essentially accurate description of Napoleon III's humiliating surrender.

> *De feu celeste au Royal edifice,*
> *Quant la lumiere de Mars defaillira:*
> *Sept mois grand guerre, mort gent de malefice,*
> *Rouen, Eureux au Roi ne faillira.*

Translation:

> Fire falls from the sky on to the Royal edifice,
> When the light of Mars fails:
> Seven months' great war, people dead by evil,
> Rouen and Evreux will not fail the King.

The first line of the above quatrain sounds like the Prussian artillery. Even with odds of two to one against, the French commanders initially believed that they could beat the enemy. From the very beginning, the war was fought on French territory, giving the French Army the advantage of fighting from their fortifications. However, this advantage was soon checkmated by the superiority of the Prussian artillery. As reports came in of French garrisons being blown to pieces in their forts, the captured Napoleon III may have bitterly remembered the words of his uncle and namesake: "The army that stays within its fortifications is already beaten."

The "Royal edifice" receiving "fire from the sky" could be the Tuileries Palace, destroyed by Prussian shells during the siege of Paris. The French capital was bombarded from late September 1870 to 19 January 1871. The Parisians fought heroically with crude, home-made weapons but, with the

French army destroyed, they had no hope, and surrender was inevitable.

Line two describes "the light of Mars fail[ing]". As we saw in the quatrain on the French annexation of Savoy (V.42 above), Nostradamus may have used the nickname "Mars" for Napoleon III (inappropriate as it may seem, in hindsight). The Bonaparte dynasty was emasculated by the Franco-Prussian War and, with their fall, the throne of France vanished – a stunning *Götterdammerung* for a monarchist like Nostradamus.

Line three describes "people dead by evil". This could also be a prediction of the siege of Paris, by the end of which the Parisians were reduced to eating dogs, cats and rats. Thousands died of starvation. As to the war lasting "seven months", the Franco-Prussian war continued from July 1870 to February 1871 – precisely seven months.

Rouen and Evreux, mentioned in line four, are both towns in Normandy. This area remained loyal to Napoleon III, even after he was captured by Bismarck. The rest of the France had declared itself a republic, in pure disgust.

> *Des lieux plus bas du pays de Lorraine,*
> *Seront des basses Allemaignes unis,*
> *Par ceux du siege Picards, Normons, du Maisne,*
> *Et aux cantons ce seront reunis.*

Translation:

> The lowest places in the county of Lorraine,
> Will be united with lower Germanies,
> By reason of the siege of Picardy, Normandy, and Maisne,
> And in cantons they will be reunited.

Following the surrender of Paris, the Prussian army occupied the whole of France ("Picardy, Normandy and Maisne"). Bismarck demanded territorial rights to a large part of Lorraine and, further south ("*plus bas*"), the region of Alsace. He also demanded five billion gold francs in war reparations. The French had no choice but to agree.

The debt was not paid off until September 1873, and only then did all the German troops leave French territory. France was reunited as a free country, as line four suggests, but why

Nostradamus uses the word "*cantons*" (a Swiss term for a county) is hard to fathom. Lorraine remained lost to France until 1919.

Bismarck got the German unity he had gambled for. King William I of Prussia was crowned Emperor (*Kaiser*) of Greater Germany in Versailles in 1871. France has remained a republic since the defeat and, considering modern political trends, is highly unlikely to ever be ruled by a monarch again. Napoleon III lived the rest of his life as an exile in Britain, dying during a routine medical operation in January 1873.

Louis Pasteur, 1822 to 1895
I.25

> *Perdu trouvé, caché de si long siecle,*
> *Sera Pasteur demi Dieu honoré:*
> *Ains que la lune acheve son grand siecle,*
> *Par autres vents sera deshonoré.*

Translation:

> Lost, found again, hidden for a long cycle,
> Pasteur as a demi-God is honoured:
> But before the moon ends her great cycle,
> By ancient ones shall be dishonoured.

This is another of Nostradamus' stunningly accurate predictions – even giving the name of one of the greatest French scientists of the nineteenth century: Louis Pasteur.

Throughout history, doctors had been unable to discover the fundamental cause of disease. In Nostradamus' day, for example, it was universally believed that "ill humours in the air", such as marsh gas, caused sickness. It was not until Pasteur, through his work on fermentation in wine and milk, hit on the concept of "microbiology" that the modern renaissance in medicine began.

Pasteur argued that microscopic objects called *bacteria* – discovered the previous century – caused the spoiling of liquids like milk. These tiny pieces of matter were alive, he insisted, and their life cycle produced acids as a by-product, making the milk sour.

If the milk were heated then sealed in an antiseptic bottle, it would be less prone to spoil – thus *pasteurisation* was invented.

He went on to argue that many diseases were the result of attacks on the human organism by "germs" – his name for dangerous bacteria. Although he was roundly attacked by traditionalist doctors – who refused to believe that something so tiny could harm much larger creatures, such as human beings – eventually his theory was proved correct. Quite apart from his discovery that anthrax, rabies and other illnesses could be prevented by vaccination, it is arguable that Pasteur's simple idea – that bacilli were a danger that must be tightly controlled – has saved most of us from premature deaths.

As we saw in the chapter on Nostradamus' life, it has been argued that his success against plagues might have been due to precognition of future medical practice, with its emphasis upon cleanliness. This would certainly explain why he singled out Pasteur as one of the most significant figures in history.

Line two describes "Pasteur" being honoured like a "demi-God". This is truer today than it was in Pasteur's own lifetime. As line four seems to hint, senior medical men ridiculed the theory of microbes for a long time; many died refusing to accept any of the growing evidence for Pasteur's "germs".

The Pasteur Institute was founded in 1889. This, Erica Cheetham points-out, was at the end of a 320-year lunar cycle. The most bitter criticism of Pasteur took place before this date, and therefore "before the moon end[ed] her great cycle", as it says in line three.

The first line of this quatrain is one of the most extraordinary in all the *Centuries*, because it seems to mean that the existence of microbes was known a long time before Pasteur's discoveries, but somehow became "hidden". In 1990, Robert Schoch, a geologist from Boston University, confirmed the assertion of the Egyptologist John Anthony West that the Great Sphinx of Giza was eroded by rain, not wind-blown sand. Schoch's own estimate of its age was around 7000 BC – older than any *known* civilization.

Is it possible that a forgotten civilization (which West calls "Atlantis" – admitting that this is merely a convenient label) built the Sphinx? West also believes that the remarkable sophistication of medicine in ancient Egypt was a legacy of this former civilization, which was destroyed (as Plato described in the

Timaeus) in a great cataclysm. Is it conceivable that this is what Nostradamus meant when he said that Pasteur rediscovered knowledge that had been "hidden for a long cycle"?

As to the last line about being dishonoured by "other winds" (*autres vents*, often translated as "old ones", or "*vieux*"), it might refer to Pasteur's dissenting colleagues, or might suggest a more disturbing possibility. Bearing in mind that, in Nostradamus' day, it was believed that diseases are caused by bad odours on the wind (which is why the wealthy carried handkerchiefs soaked in scent), it sounds as if Nostradamus is saying that Pasteur's discovery will be rendered useless by germs that are not so easily destroyed.

It is only towards the last part of the twentieth century that this possibility has presented itself. That is to say, Pasteur's discoveries can offer little to help us in the face of the more deadly viruses. These microscopic killers are simply DNA strands surrounded by inanimate protective casings. Unlike bacteria, they are not living organisms, and therefore cannot be killed by antibiotics. On the other hand they are not wholly inanimate, as they can reproduce – often with fatal repercussions for their host organism.

Viruses are the oldest creatures on the planet ("old ones") and can "hibernate" for millions of years.[5] A lone batch of a virus might literally hide under a rock for millennia, but can come to "life" the moment a suitable host uncovers it. Thanks to modern jet travel, this infection could spread across the world in forty-eight hours, just as new types of influenza (another occasionally fatal virus) do on a virtually yearly basis.

Both HIV and Ebola – viruses that kill ninety-nine to a hundred per cent of infected sufferers – may have originated in the jungles of Africa. They had probably been "hidden" there since before the birth of mankind, and only our modern incursions into the once untouched forests released them. Horrible as both these diseases are, they are relatively difficult to catch; the next virus to be "released" may be as lethal as AIDS and as easily caught as the flu . . .

5 The phrase of the visionary horror writer, H. P. Lovecraft, comes to mind: "That is not dead that can eternal lie . . ." Lovecraft called his hidden monsters – poised to destroy mankind – "the Old Ones": a close echo of Nostradamus' phrase.

The Dreyfus Affair, 1893–1906
I.7

> Tard arrivé l'execution faicte,
> Le vent contraire lettres aux chemin prinses:
> Les conjurez quatorze d'une secte,
> Par le Rousseau semz les enterprinses.

Translation:

> Arriving too late, the execution is done,
> The wind is contrary, letters intercepted on the way:
> The conspirators fourteen of a sect,
> By the Rousseau the enterprise is undertaken.

The Dreyfus scandal shook the turn-of-the-century French establishment. Alfred Dreyfus was an artillery captain assigned to the general staff in Paris when he was accused, in late 1893, of selling military secrets to the Germans. An anonymous letter to the German Embassy had been intercepted, containing a list of top secret documents. Someone thought the handwriting resembled that of Captain Dreyfus, who, because he was a Jew, was not popular with his superiors. Despite the doubtful supporting evidence, he was convicted and sentenced to life imprisonment in the prison colony called l'Île du Diable (Devil's Island).

Two years later, in 1896, Lieutenant Colonel George Picquart, head of the French intelligence service, found evidence that a Major Esterhazy was actually responsible for the "bordereau" (or list – as the document became known). However, when he presented this evidence to his superiors, he was ordered to remain silent and dismissed from his post. Whether through Picquart, or from their own investigations, Dreyfus' family discovered the same evidence against Esterhazy and published it. In 1898, the embarrassed military authorities were forced to send Esterhazy to trial, but they saw to it he was acquitted, despite the weight of the evidence.

Shortly after Esterhazy's trial, Picquart's successor, Lieutenant Colonel Hubert Henry, publicly confessed that he had discovered that the evidence used against Dreyfus had been forged. He was immediately arrested and killed himself in his cell.

In 1899, Dreyfus was brought back from prison to appeal his case. To the rage of the public, his guilty sentence was upheld, although his prison term was reduced to ten years. Ten days later, the new Prime Minister of France, Pierre Waldeck-Rousseau, ordered Dreyfus pardoned. He was reinstated in the army as a major and, rather ironically, awarded the Legion of Honour. He later fought with distinction in the Great War.

Esterhazy fled to England and later confessed to being the author of the *bordereau*.

Line one of the quatrain may predict the "execution" of Dreyfus' sentence, despite his known innocence by his judges; French justice "arriving too late" to save him from five undeserved years on Devil's Island.

The phrase "*le vent contraire*", at the beginning of line two, is the French equivalent of the English phrase: "the tide is against you". This may reflect the public indignation and anti-Semitic bigotry at the time of Dreyfus' first trial, or it might be a warning to the anti-Dreyfus conspirators that the truth would eventually be revealed. The "letters intercepted" in the second part of the line could be the forged documents that convicted Dreyfus, or the true evidence that Esterhazy was the guilty man.

Whether there were fourteen people, as described in line three, involved in the conspiracy to convict Dreyfus cannot now be verified. The mention of "Rousseau" in the last line may, in fact, be a hint that the Prime Minister who eventually pardoned Dreyfus was actually one of the conspirators. It is known that Rousseau was violently anti-Dreyfus, and it was almost certainly Rousseau who was behind the reconviction at retrial in 1899. He only pardoned Dreyfus when he saw popular indignation might cost him his own job.

The Dreyfus case had implications far beyond the embarrassment of the French government. The image of the military Establishment conniving to allow racism to triumph over justice caused a scandal that echoed round the world. The Dreyfus case was a watershed, the first of a series of scandals in which the establishment has been shaken by popular indignation or (worse still) derision.

17 Prophecy in the Twentieth Century

Edgar Cayce

Edgar Cayce (pronounced "Casey") was born on a farm in Christian County, Kentucky, on 18 March 1877. His father, Leslie Cayce, was also a Justice of the Peace, and was addressed as "Squire". He was not a particularly affectionate father, and Edgar had a difficult upbringing because he was so inclined to get into trouble – as one biographer (Joseph Millard) puts it: "It seemed to his distracted parents that every time they took their eyes off him, there would be a crash and a yell to signify another disaster." The father even hired an eleven-year-old boy to keep him out of trouble.

His maternal grandfather was an excellent dowser, and was always being asked by neighbours where they should sink wells. Cayce probably derived most of his psychic powers from this side of the family. Unfortunately, his grandfather was killed in an accident when Edgar was only four – his horse suddenly panicked when he rode it into a pond to drink, and he was thrown over its head into the water, then struck on the head by the horse's flying hooves.

Cayce was a dreamer at school, who never seemed to be able to remember anything. His teacher had to rap him on the knuckles again and again for not paying attention.

After his grandfather's death, Edgar saw the old man in a

tobacco barn, and his grandfather talked to him at length. Edgar told his mother and grandmother about the visit, but never mentioned it to his father.

Some time in his early years, Edgar conceived an enthusiasm for the Bible, and read it from beginning to end. He decided he wanted to be a minister, and to travel all over the world, saving heathens. He also prayed for the power to heal the sick. He later told how, at the age of ten, he woke up one night and saw a woman standing at the foot of the bed and creating a strange light that filled the room. He ran off to tell his mother about it, and she soothed him and told him to go back to bed. Once again, he saw the woman, who told him: "Your prayers are answered; you will have the power to heal the sick." Unfortunately, he was still so bad at his school lessons that his father forced him to stay awake one night, threatening that he would beat him until he learned them. Cayce claims that a voice told him that if he went to sleep, he would learn more than by staying awake. When his father came and awakened him, he knew his lessons. His father thought it was some kind of joke – that his son had been pretending to be stupid to stay at school as long as possible, so that he wouldn't have to start work. Edgar received another beating.

From then on, he claimed, he was able to go to sleep with a book under his pillow, and wake up knowing its contents.

It was soon after this that he revealed his ability to prescribe medicine. A baseball had struck him on the spine, and he suddenly became noisy and uncontrollable. Finally, forced into bed by his father, he seemed to fall asleep. Then his voice began to speak, explaining that he had had a shock from the baseball and that his mother should make a poultice from certain local herbs that were to be mixed with chopped onions. This was done and, the next morning, he was normal again.

In spite of his new scholastic abilities, he left school at the age of fifteen.

He was in his early twenties when the family moved to nearby Hopkinsville, and he began to work in a bookstore. At this point, he fell in love with a girl named Gertrude Evans, the daughter of a prominent architect, and the realization that it would take him several years of study to become a minister before he could marry her made him decide to abandon his dreams of the church. He took a job in a shoe store. Then, realizing that this was still not going to support a wife, he became for a time a salesman for a stationery firm, then an insurance salesman.

In the New Year of 1900, he suddenly lost his voice. Three months later, he could barely whisper. Cayce himself realized later that his illness was purely psychosomatic – a salesman cannot sell without a voice, and his unconscious mind was telling him that he had better things to do than becoming a salesman.

When a hypnotist named Hart came to the local theatre – stage hypnotists had been popular for the previous twenty years – he heard about Cayce's strange illness, and offered to restore his voice for two hundred dollars. Hart was known as the Laugh King and his act consisted of placing people under hypnosis on stage, and then making them do absurd things – just like modern stage hypnotists, who make people imitate Elvis Presley or climb imaginary ladders. Cayce's friends offered to finance the cure. Under hypnosis, his voice came back but, as soon as the hypnotist awakened him again, his voice vanished again.

Another hypnotist called Doctor Quackenboss tried to cure him, but only succeeded in putting him to sleep for more than twenty-four hours.

Finally, he met a man called Al Layne, whose wife ran a millinery shop while her husband studied hypnotism.

On 31 March 1901, Layne put Cayce into a state of deep hypnosis, and then told him that his unconscious mind could cure his problem. Cayce immediately replied: "The trouble is partial paralysis of the vocal chords, due to nerve strain. To remove the condition, it is necessary only to suggest that the body increase the circulation to the affected area."

Layne leaned over him and told him to increase the circulation to the affected area. Cayce's throat immediately turned a deep red colour. Then suddenly, Cayce said: "The condition is cured. Suggest the circulation returns to normal, then wake me up."

A few moments later, Cayce was shouting triumphantly: "I can talk! I can talk!"

When Cayce's explosions of sheer joy had subsided, Layne remarked: "You know, you sounded just like a doctor when you were in your trance. If you could look inside closed books when you fall asleep, maybe you could do the same thing with some-body who's sick." Cayce thought about this. "OK, I'll try," he said finally.

The next day, Layne placed Cayce in a trance, then said: "I

want you to check over my body and find out what's wrong with me."

"Yes, I can see your body clearly." And then Cayce began to talk as if he had had a lifetime of medical training. Layne was amazed. He had written down what Cayce said, including parts of the body, prescriptions and all kinds of instructions. When Cayce looked at Layne's notes, he shook his head in bafflement. "I've never heard of most of these things."

Nevertheless, Layne followed the instructions precisely. In no time at all, his health improved.

"But how do I do it?" asked Cayce.

"It's called clairvoyance."

"What's that?" Cayce asked, and Layne had to explain that clairvoyance meant the curious ability possessed by some people to know things that they simply should not know – for example, what is happening in other places, or what somebody they have never met looks like. The mind, Layne said, obviously has all kinds of powers that we do not even begin to understand. The fashionable psychotherapist Sigmund Freud would have said that it was the unconscious mind. Whatever it was, it was some kind of direct knowledge.

Layne was so delighted that he decided to set up his own office above his wife's millinery shop, and began to treat people by suggestion. He asked Cayce if he would be willing to be placed in a trance, and asked about the ailments of someone he had never met. Cayce agreed, on condition that he was not told the identity of the other person.

When he woke up, Layne told him that his diagnosis agreed exactly with what a doctor had told the patient – but the doctor had been unable to prescribe a remedy. Cayce had just prescribed one.

Cayce began to help Layne regularly – always refusing to take money. All Cayce needed to know was exactly where the patient was at the moment. They might even be sitting in Layne's outer office. Yet, when Cayce returned from his trance, he could always describe the ailment and prescribe for it.

On one occasion, a mother came to see him, frantic with worry – her child was choking, but an X-ray at the hospital had shown nothing wrong. Cayce was hastily put into a trance by Layne, and said that the problem was a celluloid shirt button that the child had swallowed – that was why it didn't show up on the X-ray.

The child was rushed back to hospital, and the shirt button found exactly where Cayce said it would be.

Cayce soon became so good at it that he could put himself into a trance, and treat the sick without even coming into contact with them. The only thing that reconciled him to this strange ability – which made him nervous – was that he felt he was doing God's work, which had been his ambition ever since he was a child.

Cayce never took money for his cures. He had discovered that he was a good photographer, and this made enough to keep Gertrude and his family.

When his son was eight, he lit some of the magnesium used for flashlight photographs, and lost the sight in one eye. An oculist recommended an operation, but Cayce went into a trance, and ordered that a bandage soaked in tannic acid should be placed over the eye. The boy's sight came back within two weeks.

On one occasion, a Kentucky businessman he was talking to over the telephone admitted his scepticism; Cayce promptly described him precisely, then told him the route he had taken from his home to the office that morning. The man was convinced.

One day, in his trance, he recommended a drug called Codiron, and gave the address of the supplier in Chicago. Over the telephone, the drug manufacturer admitted to being baffled – Codiron was a new product, and they had only decided on its name two hours before.

In 1906, Cayce even solved a murder in Canada. A woman had been found shot. Cayce stated that she had been shot by her sister because both were in love with the same man. He said that the woman had pushed the weapon down a drain, and gave its serial number. When the police recovered it, the sister admitted her guilt.

He even gave one of his clients a stock-market forecast which helped him to make a vast sum of money – but Cayce found that he had such a bad headache when he woke up that from then on he declined to try it again.

Cayce also had his failures. When Charles Lindbergh, the baby of the famous aviator, was kidnapped in 1932, Cayce was totally unable to suggest the identity of the kidnapper.

But on another occasion, consulted about a railway accident, Cayce declared that the blame should be placed on a trusted employee, and said that there would be another fatal accident unless he was dismissed. The vice-president of the company refused to dismiss him; he himself was killed in the fatal accident that Cayce prophesied.

This example shows clearly that Cayce was able to foresee the future.

In 1910, Cayce finally began charging a small fee for his help. This was because Dr Wesley Ketchum, a homeopath who practised in Hopkinsville, wrote an enthusiastic article about his successes, and sent it to the American Society of Clinical Research in Boston. When an article in the *New York Times* was published, Cayce found himself famous overnight. Suddenly, he was overwhelmed with requests for help. Even so, the fees he accepted merely paid for his time, and he remained basically a poor man.

In the 1920s, Cayce began to develop a new speciality: what he called "life readings". In one of his trances, he had said that he could see himself in a previous life on a raft on the Ohio River, fleeing from marauding Indians, who finally killed everyone in the party. In 1923, a Dayton printer named Arthur Lammers asked Cayce about past lives. Cayce said that he didn't believe in past lives, because the Bible said nothing about them.

Lammers replied that in the New Testament, the Jews who did not believe in Jesus asked whether he was Elias, which seemed to indicate that they believed in reincarnation.

Soon, under hypnosis, he was telling his subjects about their past lives – sometimes in India, China, Persia and Egypt. According to his biographer, Jess Stearn (in *The Sleeping Prophet*): "Cayce outlined how past life experience had influenced the present, and what the individual must overcome to fulfil this life."

Stearn goes on to add: "As he got deeper into life readings, he frequently spoke alien languages in trance, chiefly the familiar Romance tongues. Yet, once asked to speak Greek, by a Greek scholar, he broke into Homeric Greek, as though living in that period."

We have seen that Cayce was able to prophesy that a fatal railway accident would occur unless an inefficient employee was replaced, and how he was able to advise a businessman – who questioned him while he was in trance – about the stock market. In March 1929, Cayce warned a man not to invest in stocks and shares. When, that afternoon, a stockbroker described a dream that had worried him, Cayce said that it meant there would be a downward movement of long duration in the market, and advised him to sell his entire portfolio. On 6 April 1929, Cayce told another financier: "There must surely come a break when there will be a panic in the money centres not only on Wall Street, but a closing of the banks in many centres." So, by that time, Cayce had already started to talk about the future.

At the same time, it must be admitted that many of his prophecies do not seem to be accurate. This is the case with many psychics. Their prophecies come from the unconscious mind, and can be influenced by other minds. It would be a mistake to assume that, because he was such a brilliant healer, he was an infallible prophet. We have seen in the case of the Lindbergh kidnapping that Cayce was unable to offer any help.

All the same, his successes are remarkable. Before America became involved in the First World War, one of his readings stated that the war would spread across the world and involve America. Twice during the First World War, Cayce was summoned to Washington – exactly what happened is still unknown. In another reading, he predicted the breaking up of the Western Front in Europe, the end of the war, and the Russian Revolution of 1917. Yet during this same reading, Cayce stated: "On the religious development of Russia will depend the hope of the world." By 1998 – the time of this writing – it still seems as meaningless as it did at the time.

In December 1918, a new influence entered Cayce's life. The editor of a newspaper in Cleburne, Texas, wrote to ask his advice on business matters, and Cayce wrote back saying that he did not use his powers for financial gain – either his own or other people's. They began to correspond, and the editor told him that he believed in astrology. He asked Cayce's exact date and time of birth and, although Cayce thought that astrology was nonsense, he sent them. When the horoscope of Cayce came back, he was staggered at its accuracy. Moreover, horoscopes continued to come in from all over the world – at the request of the Texan editor – and what impressed Cayce was that they agreed so closely.

These horoscopes told Cayce, without exception, that a conjunction of planets on 19 March 1919, between 8.30 and 11 p.m., would be a good time for Cayce to ask important questions. Accordingly, Cayce went into a trance at that time, and his wife

Gertrude asked the questions. When she asked, "Do the planets have anything to do with the destiny of man?", the reply was: "They do". He went on to say: "The inclination of man is ruled by the planets under which he is born. In this way, the destiny of man lies within the sphere of the scope of the planets. With the given position of the solar system at the time of the birth of the individual, it can be worked out – that is the inclinations and actions, without the willpower taken into consideration."

"It" went on to tell him that he should live by the sea and should always have done so.

Later, following a suggestion made when he was in trance, Cayce moved to Virginia Beach, a small seaside village in Virginia.

Cayce's successes were remarkable. He prophesied the defeat of Hitler and India's independence. He stated that two American presidents would die in office, as Roosevelt and Kennedy did. But, asked in 1938 if there would be a war that would involve the United States between 1942 and 1944, he missed a golden opportunity by answering that this depended on whether there was a desire for peace. Asked what would cause such a war he replied: "Selfishness" – which is undoubtedly a simplification of Hitler's reasons for going to war.

In 1934, he declared that there would be born in America, in 1936, a baby named John Penniel, "who would be beloved of all men in all places when the universality of God in the earth has been proclaimed." Penniel would "come as a messenger not a forerunner", and bring to the earth "a new order of things". When this was about to happen, "the sun will be darkened and the earth shall be broken in several places" By 1998, by which time Penniel would be sixty-two, there has still been no sign of this world saviour.

This same reading made some very ominous predictions. "The greater portion of Japan must go into the sea. The upper portion of Europe will be changed as in the twinkling of an eye. Land will appear off the east coast of America. There will be upheaval in the Arctic and in the Antarctic that will make for the eruptions of volcanoes in the torrid areas, and there will be the shifting then of the poles." When that happens, he said, "frigid or sub-tropical" climates will become tropical. All this would occur before 1998. Obviously, another miss.

In 1941, a businessman was asking Cayce whether it would be

a good idea to move out of New York, in case it was finally bombed by Hitler or the Japanese. After advising the man to move out of New York, Cayce added that "Los Angeles, San Francisco, almost all of these will be among those that will be destroyed, before New York, even." Cayce said that this was all a part of great upheavals that would begin in 1958, and extend to the end of the century, when the new millennium would bring a new era.

But, at the same time that he was giving "life readings" that involved many ancient civilizations, Cayce also began to talk about Atlantis.

There are literally hundreds of references to Atlantis in Cayce's work, and many of these are contradictory. For example, one account declares that Atlantis was destroyed in 10,700 BC, while another claims that this was only the beginning of the end, and that Atlantis disappeared in 9,700 BC. In another reading, he declares that hordes of Atlantean refugees flooded into Egypt in 10,500 BC.

In another reading, he declared that the Nile had once flowed west, which has since been proved – it once flowed into Lake Chad, halfway between the present Nile and the Atlantic Ocean.

He also declared that a group of Essenes had lived near the Dead Sea, which was verified by the discovery of the Dead Sea Scrolls, two years after his death. Elsewhere, Cayce stated that the civilization of Atlantis had dated back to 200,000 BC, and that the Atlanteans had possessed some kind of "crystal stone" for trapping the rays of the sun; they also possessed steam power, gas and electricity. He also stated that, by the time of the final catastrophe, around 10,000 BC, the Atlanteans had mostly dispersed to Egypt and South America – statements that made sense to the Egyptologist John Anthony West, whose own studies convinced him that the Sphinx had been built by Atlanteans in 10,500 BC, and not in 2,500, as is generally supposed.

Cayce also forecast that Atlantis would begin to rise again in the area of Bimini in 1968 and 1969. In fact, underwater ruins that appeared to be the remains of ancient roads were found in Bimini at this time, but many archaeologists have disputed that they are ancient ruins, and, in any case, there has so far been no further sign of "Atlantis rising".

Cayce also declared that the Great Pyramid was begun in 10,490 BC and took a hundred years to build. The actual records of Atlantis and Ancient Egypt were placed in a Hall of Records, which is somewhere in the area of the Great Pyramid. (In another reading, Cayce declares that the Hall of Records lies between the right paw of the Sphinx and Nile river.)

Cayce declared "the pyramid was . . . built by Levitation, abetted by song and chanting, much in the same manner in which the Druids of England set up their huge stones at a later period."

According to Cayce, the Hall of Records will be rediscovered towards the end of the twentieth century.

It is difficult to summarize Cayce's life, as a psychic and a prophet. His accuracy is at times incredible, but it is unfortunately untrue, as Jess Stearn has stated, that "his batting average on predictions was incredibly high, close to one hundred per cent". However, his prophecies about the end of the millennium are by no means as grim as those of Nostradamus appeared to be. Foretelling in 1937 a planetary situation in which Neptune and Uranus would be in Sagittarius and Jupiter in Scorpio, where it would be joined by Mars in September, and Saturn in Libra, Cayce writes: "As I see it, the planetary forces will be manifested through the last four signs of the Zodiac only, which is bound to accentuate certain tracts both in nature and in people which will make for imbalances, for we are all part of the cosmic whole.

"I will plump for increased instability, social upheavals, a few earthquakes, and the discarding of outworn ideas upon society generally."

A situation not unlike that which Cayce describes occurred near the beginning of 1982, when all the planets in the solar system were in the same segment of sky for a time, a situation that occurs only once every 179 years. Great earthquakes were expected, and possibly a movement in the San Andreas fault which might well bring about the destruction of the West Coast of America. Fortunately, there was no catastrophe.

During the Second World War, Cayce's health began to fail. Floods of requests kept him busy, and he occasionally spent several hours of the day in a trance, giving readings. In autumn 1944, he had a complete breakdown. In a reading, he was advised to go to a nursing home near Roanoke, and asked: "How long should I stay?" The answer came back: "Until you are well, or dead."

Cayce went into the nursing home, but disliked the inactivity, and worried all the time about the people he could be helping.

Eventually he had a stroke that left one side of his body paralysed. He was only sixty-seven years old.

Shortly after Thanksgiving 1944, he came home to Virginia Beach; on New Year's Day 1945, he told a visitor: "I am to be healed on Friday, the fifth of January."

On the evening of 3 January Cayce died. Three months later, on Easter Sunday, his wife Gertrude also died. His sons, Hugh, Lynn and Edgar, continued the Edgar Cayce Foundation, as well as the Association For Research and Enlightenment, and the Edgar Cayce Publishing Company. The interest in his life and work has continued unabated – dozens of books about him have appeared since his death.

Wolf Messing

Although far less well known than Edgar Cayce, Wolf Messing, who worked mainly behind the Iron Curtain, has every right to be regarded as one of the greatest psychics and seers of the twentieth century. When Hitler made a pact with Stalin, Messing – who was Stalin's favourite psychic – nevertheless reported: "Soviet tanks will within a few years enter Berlin." The Germans heard about this and made official protests to the Kremlin.

Addressing an audience in the Opera House in Novosibirsk, in Siberia, Messing declared: "The war will end victoriously for Russia in May 1945, and most likely in its first week." He was out only by two days.

The West first learned about Messing in 1970, in a remarkable book called *PSI: Psychic Discoveries Behind the Iron Curtain*, by Sheila Ostrander and Lynn Schroeder, which startled everyone who was interested in parapsychology. Most people had assumed that the Soviet Union was rigidly materialistic in its outlook, and that it would not tolerate anything that looked like occultism or mysticism. Yet this was to overlook the natural mysticism of the Russian temperament, embodied in writers like Dostoevsky, Solovyev, and even Tolstoy.

The account of Messing's life had been published in the Soviet Union in 1965. His autobiography *About Myself* began serialization in *Science and Religion, nos 7 and 8*, although, as far as is known, it has not been published in full.

"I was born on 10 September 1899, in Russia, to be precise, on the territory of the Russian Empire, in the tiny town of Gora Kalwaria, near Warsaw."

Messing was a Polish Jew, born in a small Jewish village. As a child, he was presented to the famous Jewish writer Sholom Aleichem, and Aleichem said: "You will have a shining future!" Messing admits wryly that Aleichem said that to every other little boy.

Messing's family was intensely religious, and by the age of six, Wolf knew the Talmud virtually by heart. The rabbi decided that he should be sent to a religious school to be educated for the priesthood. However, the child flatly refused to go.

According to Messing, he then saw a strange figure clad in a white garment on the steps of the porch leading up to their house, which said to him: "Go to school! Your prayers will please heaven!" Then the figure vanished. Messing fell to the ground and lost consciousness. When he recovered, his father and mother were reciting prayers over him but, when he told them what had happened, they were delighted. Accordingly, Messing went to a religious school in another village.

But he was right about not enjoying religious studies. He bore them for five years, then decided to run away.

He crawled on board a train, and hid under a seat. He wakened from sleep to find the conductor peering at him and holding out his hand for his ticket. According to Messing, it was then that he first discovered his remarkable powers of mental suggestion. He held out a piece of paper torn from a newspaper, and willed the conductor to think that it was a ticket. The conductor took it in an uncertain manner, turned it over in his hands, and then punched it in his ticket punch. He asked: "Since you have a ticket, why are you hiding under the seat? Get up! In two hours we'll be in Berlin."

In Berlin, Messing got a job as the messenger in the Jewish quarter. One day, taking a parcel to a Berlin suburb, he collapsed and became unconscious. When he was found – half frozen – his pulse was undetectable, and he was taken to the morgue.

Fortunately, a medical student who took his pulse noticed a faint heartbeat, and Messing was moved into a ward. He was unconscious for three days. He was fortunate that the doctor who tended him, a man named Abel, was interested in telepathy and other psychic faculties. Abel explained to him that Messing had somehow induced in himself a state of catalepsy – a kind of

suspended animation. Soon, Abel and another psychiatric colleague named Schmidt, together with Schmidt's wife, began
training Messing in telepathy.

It might seem that the ability to induce catalepsy is hardly a
way of making a living. In fact, he was given a job in a waxworks
called the Berlin Panopticon, where Messing, who was billed as
"the wonder-boy", climbed into a transparent coffin, went into a
state of catalepsy, and stayed there like a corpse from Friday until
Sunday evening. For this, he was paid five marks a day.

He began training his psychic abilities by walking in the
market place and trying to "hear" the thoughts of people around
him – which were usually about their homes, and other such
practical matters. Sometimes, when the people had problems, he
would hear a voice telling him the answer to their problems, and
would accost them and tell them what he had heard. Often, when
he saw them again, they told him that he had been perfectly
correct.

When he was still in his early teens, he appeared at the Berlin
Winter Garten, playing a fakir, and allowing needles to be driven
through his flesh. He was also able to locate jewellery and other
valuables which members of the audience had concealed.

In 1915, he went to Vienna, where his success was remarkable.

It was there that he was invited to the home of Albert Einstein,
and was introduced to Sigmund Freud.

To test Messing's powers of telepathy, Freud gave him a
mental command: "Go to the bathroom cupboard, get some
tweezers, and pull out three hairs from Doctor Einstein's moustache." Messing did what Freud had ordered him to do.

After that, he toured the world, as far as Japan, India, South
America and Australia. He performed in every major capital from
Buenos Aires to Melbourne.

In 1927, Messing met Gandhi in India, and Gandhi tested
Messing by giving him the psychic order: "Take a flute from the
table and give it to one of the people in the room." When Messing
did so, the man began to play, and the snake emerged from a
basket and swayed to the rhythm of the flute.

Messing was deeply impressed by the Indian yogis, because
they could stay in a state of catalepsy for weeks, whereas Messing's abilities only allowed him to stay unconscious for three
days.

For ten years, Messing worked in Poland, and became famous

as a psychic. One day, he was summoned by Count Czartoryski, who offered him a large reward if he could locate some missing family jewels. Messing was flown to the Count's castle in his private plane, and there he began to suspect a small boy, the son of one of the servants. Messing asked the Count to have a large stuffed teddy-bear opened. The jewels were found inside it – the boy had taken them, like a jackdaw, together with other shining objects, and pushed them inside his teddy bear.

The result of this was that the Count used his influence with the Polish parliament to have certain anti-Jewish laws rescinded.

Messing also spent some time investigating spiritualism but, in the Russian journal, claims that he believes Engels, who said that spiritualism is merely a superstition.

But then, if Messing had taken any other point of view, his autobiography could certainly not have been published in the Soviet Union.

In 1937, Messing appeared in a theatre in Warsaw, and was asked by a member of the audience about Hitler's future. Messing replied immediately: "Hitler will die if he turns to the East."

Hitler had an intense dislike of anyone who made prophecies about his future. According to Messing, he placed a price of 200,000 marks on his head. So when the Nazis invaded Poland on 1 September 1939, Messing knew it was time to leave. For a few weeks, he had been in hiding in a Warsaw meat locker, but one night, when he went into the street, a Nazi officer asked to see his papers, then shouted: "You're Wolf Messing! You predicted the death of our Führer!" And then, still holding Messing's hair, he hit him with all his force in the jaw. Messing collapsed, with six teeth broken.

According to Messing, when taken to a police station, he realized that his life was hanging by a thread. Using all his powers of suggestion, he made the police assemble in one room, while he lay motionless, as if dead. When everybody was in the same room, Messing leapt to his feet and ran out, closing the door behind him and sliding the bolt.

That night, Messing succeeded in crossing the Polish border into Russia hidden in a wagonload of hay. His family later died in the Warsaw Ghetto uprising.

Messing was lucky; he fell on his feet. On first applying to the Ministry of Culture, he was disappointed to be told: "We do not need fortune-tellers in Russia." But some kind of demonstration

– presumably of telepathy – soon convinced them, and, very soon, Messing became one of the most popular stage entertainers in Russia.

In the following year, in 1940, he was about to begin a performance in the Byelorussian City of Gomel when he was interrupted by two green-uniformed Soviet police, who ordered him to come and get into a car. According to Messing's own account, he was already starting his performance on stage when the police walked in and told the audience: "The performance is over."

As the car drove away, Messing asked about his hotel bill and his luggage. The police told him that all this had been taken care of.

Finally, he was led into a building, which he thought was a hotel. Then a man with a heavy moustache walked into the room, and Messing was stunned to recognize Stalin.

Stalin began by asking him questions about some of his Polish friends, perhaps Count Czartoryski. No doubt the fact that Hitler had offered a 200,000-mark reward for Messing interested the Soviet tyrant.

He was soon convinced of Messing's genuineness, and asked him to demonstrate. Messing's task was to go into the Moscow Gosbank and use his powers to get the cashier to give him a large sum of money.

Messing used the same trick that he had used on the train guard on his way to Berlin. He walked up to the cashier and handed him a piece of blank paper. He then willed the cashier to hand over the money. The cashier glanced at the paper, then opened the safe and took out 100,000 roubles. Messing put them into his briefcase and went outside to join the two men waiting for him in the car. When they had verified that he had succeeded in his task, he went back into the bank, handed the bank notes back to the cashier, and also the piece of blank notepaper. The cashier was so stunned that he collapsed with a heart attack – fortunately not fatal.

Messing was then given an even more difficult task. He was taken into a major government office, and the door closed. Three sets of guards were ordered not to let Messing escape. Yet once again, Messing strolled out of the building without an exit pass. In the street, he turned and waved at the government official who was watching from the top floor of the building.

A few days later, Messing went to Kuntsevo, where Stalin's *Dacha* was situated, and strolled in, as if he belonged there. The guards stood back respectfully to let him pass. He walked down a hallway, then stopped at the doorway over the room where Stalin sat working on a pile of documents and papers, and walked in. Stalin looked up in amazement.

When asked how he had achieved this, Messing explained that he had simply willed everyone who saw him to believe that he was Lavrenti Beria, the head of Stalin's secret police. Yet Messing did not bear the slightest resemblance to Beria, who was bald-headed and wore pince-nez glasses – Messing had curly hair and wore no glasses.

As a result of these triumphs, Messing won Stalin's trust, and was allowed to tour throughout the Soviet Union.

According to Ostrander and Schroeder, Messing was allowed to describe himself openly as a psychic, when professors who were studying telepathy had to do so secretly.

Challenged to explain how a "psychic" could read people's minds – which, according to Marxian philosophy, ought to be impossible – the Soviet Academy of Sciences explained that Messing was apparently able to do so by observing almost imperceptible muscle movements and facial expressions.

Messing himself pointed out that this failed to explain why he was even better at telepathy when he was blindfolded.

A reporter who came to interview Messing described how, after Messing had tied on a tight blindfold, he then obeyed the reporter's mental suggestion to locate a copy of a magazine, find in it a portrait of Lenin, and decide whether it was a painting or a photograph of an actor playing Lenin. Messing did all this in silence until he announced, "It's an original portrait."

Messing's own comments on what he did were that, in addition to the scientific method of gaining knowledge, there is also *direct knowledge*. "Only our indistinct ideas about the meaning of time and its relation to space, and the past, present, and the future, make it inexplicable at present."

On the subject of free will, he added: "Of course there's free will. Yet there are patterns. The future is shaped from the past and the present. There are regular patterns of connections between them. The 'mechanism' of these connections is far from being known by most people, but I clearly know myself that it exists."

His method, he said, is to make an effort of will, which enables him to "suddenly see the final result of some event flash before me. The mechanism of 'direct knowledge' bypasses the logical cause and effect chain and reveals to the psychic only the final, concluding link of the chain." And he predicted: "The time is coming when man will understand all these phenomena."

Messing died, not long after Ostrander and Schroeder had met him, in 1972.

Gerard Croiset

The Dutchman Gerard Croiset was not primarily a prophet of the future, and he is best remembered for the many times he helped the police solve murder cases or cases involving missing persons. What is so extraordinary is that he was often able to state precisely when a missing person would turn up.

On 16 October 1959, an eighteen-year-old boy named Jan Steffen disappeared from his home in Antwerp. A Belgian newspaper reporter spoke to Croiset over the telephone, and was asked whether the missing boy was sixteen or seventeen years old.

"No, he is eighteen."

"Tell his father not to worry. I see the boy travelling farther away from Paris. Within three days, his father will hear some definite news."

The following afternoon, the father received a telephone call from Lyon, south of Paris, saying that his son was there, and wanted to come back home.

On 18 December 1958, an eighteen-year-old girl named van der Meiden left her home in the Hague. The father rang Croiset.

"Don't worry," Croiset said. "I see your daughter hitch-hiking on the way to the winter sports in Austria. I see her in the company of a girl friend about the same age . . . in three days, you will hear from her." Three days later, the girl was found, just as Croiset had predicted, in Austria.

Croiset was born in March 1909, the son of an actress and wardrobe mistress who never married. His father frequently left his mother to go away with other women. At the age of eight, he was placed in a foster home where he was unhappy. (Many psychics have had this unhappy childhood – it seems to nurture psychic sensibility.) When he was eleven, his father finally deserted his mother for good, and she married another man. Croiset lived with them, but he was still unhappy, intensely disliking his stepfather, and running away from home frequently. At thirteen, he became a farmhand, then a junior clerk in the office of a harbour master. He became a shop assistant, then a sales representative for a tea company, and finally an assistant in a grocery chain, a job he managed to hold for several years. He married the daughter of a carpenter when he was twenty-five, and his in-laws found the money for him to open a grocery store. Unfortunately, he was a poor businessman and, a year later, the business collapsed.

In 1935, visiting a watchmaker, Croiset picked up a stick lying on a table, and immediately saw images of the watchmaker's youth. He told the man that he could see an automobile accident, and a body lying on a grassy road. The watchmaker admitted that it was all accurate, and ended by saying: "You are a clairvoyant."

Croiset also possessed the ability to suddenly foresee the future. One Dutch friend who met him in 1933 became a member of a pro-Nazi group, and during the war wore a black Nazi uniform. As early as 1939, Croiset had warned him that he would wear a black uniform, and that he would spend several years in prison. At the end of the war, the man was arrested, and spent the next three years in prison.

Another of Croiset's friends was told: "In the future, you will make a long journey to a country where there are temples and pagodas. The people there are dark and wear big hats and large, coloured cloths around their waist. You will have a very difficult time. I see two bleeding wounds in your back. They are not fatal. Good times will begin for you afterwards."

In 1948, the man went to Indonesia, and visited many old temples and pagodas in Bangkok. He was shot in the back by a bandit, just as Croiset had foretold, and dismissed from his job. He started a law suit and won it, and suddenly his life became far more smooth – just as Croiset had told him.

Both these cases – like so many others – were recorded by Professor Willem Tenhaeff, the director of the Parapsychology Institute at the University of Utrecht, who was approached by Gerard Croiset after a lecture in December 1945. Croiset claimed that he had paranormal powers and offered to be tested. Tenhaeff agreed, with some misgivings. Croiset seemed to be rather a show-off, and was inclined to be boastful. He was also virtually illiterate. Yet the laboratory experiments soon proved that he possessed an extremely high level of psychic ability. Croiset explained: "When a warning feeling disturbs me, I get a vibration which is like a full-up feeling, and I expand like a balloon. I grow attentive. The paragnost [clairvoyant] in me is now at work . . . when somebody with a real problem comes to me, I see a lot of colours. These colours spin around in me very fast until they form a picture. These pictures shoot out as if they were flashing forward, like a three-dimensional film."

The book about him, called *Croiset the Clairvoyant*, by Jack Harrison Pollack (1964), is among the most reliable books of its kind. Chapter and verse is given for every case that it cites.

Tenhaeff records how a woman who lived in Entschede asked him in 1938 whether she should go to the Dutch Indies. Croiset told her that if she stayed in Holland, she would be involved in the war. It would therefore be best for her to go to the Dutch East Indies. There would be a war there, he said, but it would not last as long as the European war. He told her: "As a matter of fact, we shall lose the Dutch Indies. But then you will be back in the Netherlands, so you won't have to go through that transition period."

So Croiset not only foresaw the Second World War, but accurately foresaw what would happen to Holland during the war.

An army acquaintance named van de Berg asked Croiset in 1936 when he would leave his post in Tilburg. Croiset replied that he would go to Utrecht.

"Impossible – war would have to break out!"

"Then there will be war within four years," replied Croiset. In 1940, as he had foretold, van de Berg was transferred to Utrecht.

During the war, he was arrested as a Jew and spent some time in a German concentration camp. He somehow succeeded in returning to Entschede. There, he was able to help the Dutch Resistance. Passing by a house, he suddenly knew there were Jews hidden there, and that they were in danger. He warned: "The Germans will soon raid this house." The Jews were moved and when the Nazis raided the house, they were already elsewhere.

Asked "What has been your biggest disappointment in life?", Croiset told Pollack: "That human beings could be such beasts during the war."

In October 1959, an American girl named Carol, the daughter of a Kansas professor, was in hospital being treated for a nervous breakdown, and one day she walked out. Six weeks later, her father rang Tenhaeff in Utrecht, and made an appointment with Croiset over the telephone. As soon as they began to talk, Croiset began to receive images: Carol had walked out of the hospital and hitched a lift in a lorry, then in a large red car. Her father would hear news of her after six days. When the girl came home six days later, she verified that she had been given a lift in a lorry then in a red car.

In February 1961, Croiset was consulted by the New York police about the disappearance of a four-year-old girl named Edith Kiecorius, who had last been seen playing on the street. Witnesses had seen her with a woman, and the police believed that she may have been taken to Chicago. An airline offered to fly Croiset to New York, but he declined, saying that it would only confuse him. Holding a photograph of the girl, and a map of New York, he was able to state over the telephone that the girl was already dead, and to describe the area in which she was last seen alive. He also described the killer – a small, sharp-faced man of about fifty-five.

The police switched their investigation from Chicago, and began to search again in the neighbourhood where the child had vanished. In a nearby rooming-house, they found a locked metal door which they forced open. They found the child's naked body on the bed – she had been raped and beaten to death by a degenerate named Fred Thompson, who corresponded exactly to Croiset's description.

In February 1967, a girl named Pat McAdam had spent the night in Glasgow with a girlfriend, and was hitchhiking back to her home in Dumfries, when they accepted a lift from a lorry driver. The girlfriend was dropped off near her home, and Pat drove on in the lorry. She then vanished. The driver of the lorry, a man named Thomas Young, insisted that he had simply dropped the girl near her home.

A Scottish newspaper reporter went to see Croiset, who asked him to bring along some item belonging to her. He took her Bible with him. After holding it in his hand for a moment Croiset said: "The girl is dead." He went on to say that she had been killed close to a bridge, and her body thrown into the river. Near the bridge, he said, was a house with an advertisement sign on it, and in the garden they would find a car with no wheels, with a wheelbarrow propped against it.

Young's lorry had been seen parked close to a bridge on the River Annan, and Young had even admitted that he and Pat McAdam had made love there before he took her home. Near the bridge, the police located a house with an advertisement sign, as well as a car without wheels with a wheelbarrow propped against it.

Ten years later, the lorry driver was arrested for kidnapping and raping a sixteen-year-old girl, and in his home were found pieces of evidence that connected him to the sex murder of a woman called Frances Barker in 1977. Young was sentenced to life imprisonment, and boasted of having had sex with more than a hundred women in the cab of his lorry. Sadly, Pat McAdam's body was never found and the case remains officially unsolved.

One of Croiset's most remarkable achievements was his success in the so-called "chair test", first devised by Eugene Osty, a quarter of a century earlier. (Pollack states, mistakenly, that Tenhaeff was the first person to devise this test, especially for Croiset, but in fact, Osty devised it in 1925; in more recent years, the psychic Robert Cracknell has performed it with equal success.)

In this test, the psychic is taken into a room where some kind of meeting will occur later in the day – or perhaps several days ahead – and in which people are allowed to sit wherever they please. The psychic is then asked to describe the people who will sit in various chairs.

In October 1953, Croiset told Tenhaeff: "The person who will sit in that chair was away for a few weeks in another country. I see him walking in a large city. His shoe laces are loose. He leans forward to tie them. As he does so, I see a gentleman walking behind him who bumps into him."

The man who sat in the chair admitted that the incident had occurred in London.

In March 1950, a Dutch journalist who rang Croiset asking for proofs of his powers was told that the chair test would take place in a few days' time, and asked to pick a chair at random. The journalist suggested row seven, third chair from the right. Croiset said that his impression was that a slim lady with grey hair would occupy this chair and that she was involved in Christian social work. When the test took place, the chair proved to be occupied by a Protestant Sister of Mercy who did Christian social work and who was slim and grey-haired. She said that she had come to the meeting on impulse, and chosen the chair at random.

Tenhaeff carried out dozens of these chair tests, and described them in his book *Precognition*.

Croiset died in 1980, and his son continued to run the healing clinic that was one of Croiset's main preoccupations.

Peter Hurkos

Peter Hurkos, born two years after Croiset in 1911, was also a highly successful "psychic detective", often helping the police. Unfortunately, the chief book about him, *Psychic*, is by Hurkos himself, and so readers may feel that it does not have quite the same authenticity as Tenhaeff's book on Croiset. Yet this would not be entirely correct. Hurkos was extensively tested by the paranormal investigator Andrija Puharich, whose records reveal his amazing accuracy.

Peter Hurkos's real name was Pieter van de Hurk, and he was born in Dordrecht, near The Hague. His father was a house painter, and Peter joined him at the work when he was fifteen. In the winters, when there was no work outdoors, he shipped out as a sailor. He went on to become a stoker and chief engineer. In May 1940, the Germans invaded Holland and, after a short time, Peter went underground, and changed his name to Hurkos. He did a little spying for the Resistance, while continuing to work as a painter. He was working for the Germans, camouflaging their aeroplane hangers.

One day, in June 1941, he was painting an army barracks, leaning sideways on the ladder, when he lost his balance and plunged thirty feet to the ground. He says that his life passed completely before his eyes before he hit the ground, a few seconds later.

He woke up in hospital, with a broken shoulder and brain concussion. He was also blind.

When his wife came to see him, he asked after his son Benny. His wife said she'd left him with a neighbour, and suddenly Hurkos shouted: "Quick, go and get Benny! The room is burning!" But Benny proved to be perfectly safe. Five days later the house caught fire and firemen broke down the door in time to rescue the child.

One day, when Hurkos was nearly better, a new nurse came, and he told her: "Be careful or you will lose your valise." The nurse said: "How did you know?" She had already lost it on the train on the way to the hospital.

He turned to the patient in the next bed and said: "Your father died recently and left you a gold watch, but you have already sold it." The patient admitted this was true.

A few days later, a patient who was about to leave his hospital stopped by his bed, and as they shook hands, Hurkos suddenly knew with certainty that the man was a British agent, and that he would be killed shortly – he even knew the name of the street, Kalver Street. He told the nurse: "He is a British agent and he is going to be killed."

The man *was* murdered two days later, and his death almost cost Hurkos his life. A doctor and nurse came into his hospital room, with a man in a leather jacket. They asked Hurkos how he knew the man was going to be killed – they were certain he was a German agent. One of them held his arms while the leather-jacketed man pressed a pillow over his face. As he struggled for life, Hurkos gasped: "*Come aborrezo dar la muerte.*" He had spoken aloud the thought in the man's mind – How I hate killing – and the man let him go in astonishment, suddenly convinced, as Hurkos said, that he was a genuine psychic.

When he came out of hospital, four weeks later, Hurkos was still unwell. He could hear noises in his head and was unable to concentrate. He was unable to earn a living, and his inability to concentrate made it impossible to return to house-painting.

Then, one day, he was taken to a public performance given by a well-known psychic. Members of the audience wrote messages, which were folded and taken to the stage by the psychic's wife. The psychic would then burn the paper in a brazier, and repeat the message aloud. Hurkos's friend sent up a message. After the psychic had burned it he turned to the audience and said: "The message is from Peter Hurkos, and he says that he is a far better psychic than I am." He asked Hurkos to stand up and invited him onto the stage. The audience tittered with amusement. Asked about his method, Hurkos replied: "I touch things." The psychic handed him his watch. Hurkos held it for a moment, then said: "This watch contains a lock of blonde hair from a woman who is not your wife." The psychic's amused expression vanished. "Her name is Greta, and you take her from town to town with you. She is in the audience now." At this point the psychic interrupted hastily to ask him to return to his seat. As he walked back through the audience, Hurkos stopped by a young blonde girl, placed his hand on her shoulder and said: "This is Greta." He had sensed that her "vibrations" were the same as those of the lock of hair.

Hurkos was offered an engagement in a theatre, and was an immediate success. Soon after that, he became involved with his first criminal case. The Limburg police were trying to solve the mystery of a fatal shooting; the victim was a young coal-miner named van Tossing. Hurkos touched a coat belonging to him and told the police that van Tossing had been murdered by his stepfather because the stepfather was in love with the murdered man's wife. The gun, said Hurkos, was on the roof of the dead man's house.

The police found the pistol in the gutter of the roof, and fingerprints on it led to the conviction of the stepfather, Bernard van Tossing.

In another case, Hurkos demonstrated Osty's argument that once a link has been established between the psychometrist and the person he is concerned with, no further contact with the article is necessary. When a Captain Folken came to ask about his son, who had fallen overboard from a ship in the harbour, Hurkos touched some of the dead man's clothing and confirmed that he was drowned. The next day, Hurkos went to Rotterdam harbour and, as he approached the ship from which the man had fallen, suddenly had a flash of intuition. He was able to point to a certain spot and told the father that his son lay there, under forty feet of water, caught in some refuse. The police sent down a skin diver and recovered the body where Hurkos said it would be.

In the years immediately after the war, Hurkos performed in Belgium, Paris and Madrid – he impressed General Franco by his knowledge of certain obscure events in his past. He also helped the police in a number of criminal cases which he detailed in his autobiography *Psychic*. In 1948, he was invited to America by Andrija Puharich, who was testing telepathy. In his book *Beyond Telepathy*, Puharich tells a typical story about Hurkos. As they were watching the sunset, Hurkos suddenly burst out excitedly: "I see it . . . I see a hand. The wrist is cut and blood is coming from it." Puharich asked him if he knew what it referred to: after some thought, Hurkos said he thought it was something to do with an acquaintance named Jim Middleton, and his brother, Art. Puharich rang Middleton and warned him that his brother might attempt suicide. Middleton was amazed – he had just received a telephone call from his brother's psychiatrist warning him of the same thing. The brother was hospitalized. Later, he succeeded in slashing his wrists by using a pair of broken glasses – but a nearby attendant saved his life.

One of the strangest stories told by Puharich – off the record – was how he and Hurkos had been staying in a hotel in Mexico overnight and, since Hurkos loved to go off with prostitutes, Puharich had locked him in his room.

The next time Puharich went to the same hotel, the manager told him indignantly that Hurkos had managed to escape from the room after Puharich had gone to sleep, and had gone downstairs, and taken the manager's son – who was working as a telephonist – to a brothel. They had both made love to the same woman and, as a result, the boy now had syphilis.

Puharich confronted Hurkos with this, and pointed out to him that he probably had syphilis, too. Hurkos shook his head. "Ever since I became a psychic, I have been immune from syphilis." And apparently this was true.

Is it conceivable that psychic powers have the effect of making their possessor immune from transmitted sexual diseases? As far as I know, no physician has ever tested the hypothesis.

Like Croiset, Hurkos was prone to a certain innocent immodesty, which created a certain hostility amongst journalists. So when he failed, they were apt to publicize it.

The man who financed Puharich's research was a wealthy businessman, Harry Belk. Belk and Hurkos were close friends until, in June 1957, Belk's ten-year-old daughter vanished in the woods of North Carolina while playing. Belk rang Hurkos, who was unable to "see" anything. Yet, soon after hanging up, Hurkos saw a clear picture of the child lying drowned in six feet of water, near a boathouse. The girl's body was found precisely where Hurkos had said it would be, but Belk was bitter: "If he can see the future, why didn't he warn me?"

One of Hurkos's undoubted successes was a murder that took place in Miami, where Hurkos was living in 1958. A naval commander was shot in his apartment. A cab driver was shot to death a few hours later but, at first, the police did not connect the two murders. The Miami police approached Hurkos, who asked for a photograph of the cab driver, and asked to sit in the man's taxi. He immediately received an impression of a tall, skinny man with a tattoo on his right arm, and a slow ambling gait "like a sailor". He was even able to tell them that the man was from Detroit, and that his nickname was Smitty. He added that he had been responsible for another murder in Key West, in the course of burglary. The police checked and discovered that the naval commander and the cab driver had been killed with the same .22 pistol.

A check with the Detroit police revealed that Smitty was the nickname of Charles Smith who had been a member of a Detroit gang, but had been charged, among other things, with attempted murder. A waitress identified Smitty's photograph as that of a man she had heard boasting that he had committed two murders. Smith was arrested a month later, after a robbery in New Orleans, and was found guilty of both murders.

Less successful, from the criminological point of view, was Hurkos's involvement in one of the most horrifying murder cases of the late 1950s. On 11 January 1959, Carrol and Mildred Jackson were out driving with their two children in eastern Virginia, when they vanished. Another couple stated that they had been forced off the road that Sunday afternoon by a man in an old blue Chevrolet and, as the driver had walked back towards their car, they had reversed and driven away.

Two months later, two men found the body of Carrol Jackson in a ditch; his hands were tied and he'd been shot in the skull; underneath him was the body of his eighteen-month-old daughter, Janet, who had suffocated underneath him.

Later that month, boys playing in the woods came upon the bodies of Mildred Jackson and her five-year-old daughter, Susan; both had been subjected to sexual attack before being killed.

The police investigation seemed to have come to a dead end. A Washington psychiatrist asked Hurkos to see if he could help. In Falls Church, Virginia, Hurkos handled some of the belongings of the Jackson family, and described a house where, he said, the murderer had lived. It was a broken-down place on the edge of the woods, and the police were interested because one of their chief suspects – a trash collector – lived there. Hurkos went on to describe two men: one was the trash collector, and the other a tall left-handed man with a tattoo on his arm and a walk like a duck.

Hurkos led the police further into the woods, to a cinder-block shack – it was within a few hundred yards of the place where Mildred Jackson's body had been found. Hurkos told them that the killer had been there. A search of the area revealed an identity bracelet belonging to the trash man. The police had no further doubts. They arrested the trash man, who soon confessed to the murders. The newspapers ran such headlines as "psychic solves murder". But Hurkos had not solved the murder.

Soon afterwards, the police received a tip from a salesman named Glenn Moser, who told them that he was the author of an anonymous letter they had received several months previously, stating that the writer believed the killer was a jazz musician named Melvin Rees; Rees had once stated that he did not consider murder to be a crime and, on another occasion, when Moser asked him point blank if he had killed the Jacksons, had merely evaded the question. Now, said Moser, he had received a letter from Rees, who had become a piano salesman in a music store in West Memphis.

In the home of Rees's parents, police found diaries in which he described the murders and subsequent sexual violations. Rees was arrested in the music shop. He proved to be over six feet tall, with ape-like arms and a walk like a duck. Moreover, he had lived in the same house as the trash collector before the latter became a tenant. Rees was believed to have committed another sex murder in the area – a nurse called Margaret Harold – and to be responsible for four other sex killings in Maryland. He was found guilty of the murders of the Jacksons and executed in 1961.

Hurkos declared that his mistake had been due to unconsciously reading the minds of the police, who had already suspected the trash collector; but psychometry had enabled him to identify the real murderer. In fact, Rees *had* been living in the cinder-block hut in the woods at the time of the murder of Margaret Harold.

Nevertheless, the same newspapers that had proclaimed that Hurkos had solved the murder now denounced Hurkos and the whole notion of "psychic detection".

Hurkos belongs in this chapter because, like Croiset, he had an odd ability to foresee the future. When he demonstrated his powers in Paris in his early days, he was so successful that the police asked him if he would be willing to submit to a test. This took place in the court-room of the Palais de Justice in front of judges and policemen. On a table, there was a comb, a pair of scissors, a watch, a cigarette lighter, and a wallet. Not all these, apparently, were connected with the case.

Hurkos held each object in turn, then said that he could see a bald man in a white coat, probably a doctor, a railway, and a hill. He could see a small house with a barn, and a body lying between the barn and the house. There was someone or something named Nicole, and a bottle of milk was involved. The body, he said, was that of a woman, and the bald-headed man had murdered her. He saw him dead in his cell.

Everyone congratulated Hurkos. The bald-headed man was a doctor who had killed his wife with poison in a bottle of milk. The woman's body *had* been found between the house and the barn, and her pet poodle was called Nicole. Yet the doctor was still alive, and awaiting trial.

However, it was Hurkos who had the last word. Five days later, the doctor hanged himself in his cell.

In 1952, Hurkos had dreamed of disastrous flooding and, soon after that, Holland experienced its worst floods in years.

He also made the extraordinary statement that Hitler was still alive in Madrid; he said he was overcome with a feeling that Hitler had been through the city after escaping from the Berlin bunker. The following day, Hurkos was visited by two ex-Nazis and told that, if he wanted to stay alive, he should not go on making statements like that. In his autobiography, *Psychic*, he wrote: "I do not know whether Hitler is alive today, but I know he was living at that time."

Yet on the whole, all the evidence suggests that this was another one of Hurkos's "misses".

Hurkos died in 1988. His rather flamboyant lifestyle, and his love of publicity – and of money – led to a great deal of criticism – for example, from the magician James Randi, whose account of Hurkos in *The Supernatural A-Z* is entirely negative. Yet the accounts contained in Andrija Puharich's *Beyond Telepathy* and in Norma Lee Browning's *The Psychic World of Peter Hurkos* make it clear that, even though he disliked being subjected to scientific tests, Hurkos was one of the most remarkable psychics of the twentieth century.

Jeane Dixon

Randi was equally scathing about Jeane Dixon, the Washington prophetess who made her living in the Real Estate business. She is famous for her prediction of the assassination of President John F. Kennedy, which appeared in *Parade* on 13 May 1956, in the following words: "As for the 1960 election, Mrs Dixon thinks it will be dominated by Labour and won by a Democrat. He will be assassinated or die in office, though not necessarily in his first term."

In October 1963, she told Ruth Montgomery, a Washington journalist, of a vision in which the plaque labelled "Vice President" was removed from Lyndon Johnson's door, and that the man responsible had a two-syllabled name with five or six letters – she added: "the second letter was definitely an s and the first looked like an o". As a glimpse of the name of the assassin – Lee Harvey Oswald – this can hardly be faulted.

Again, on 1 November 1963, having lunch with a Washington society woman, Mrs Harley Cope, Jeane Dixon exclaimed: "He's going to be shot!"

Mrs Cope asked: "Who?"

"The President, of course!"

In an article called: "Premonitions of Kennedy's Death" in *Fate* magazine, John C. Ross reports:

> "John Gold, Washington correspondent for the *London Evening News*, wrote that he had talked with a dozen reputable men and women who reported that, in the two or three weeks before the assassination, Mrs Dixon had repeatedly referred to an impending tragedy in the White House.
>
> "One was Charles Benter, a former U. S. Naval officer and retired White House bandmaster. Benter told Gold that, on the Tuesday before the assassination, Mrs Dixon suddenly startled friends with whom she was dining by saying, 'The President is going to be shot'. The two women lunching with Benter and Mrs Dixon verified the statement.
>
> "Mrs Dixon said she had seen 'a dark cloud' hanging over the White House and was heard to say on one occasion that "the veil is drawing nearer".

"The witnesses who reported Mrs Dixon's predictions usually stated that they did not believe in psychic phenomena. One of them is John Teeter, executive director of the Damon Runyon Cancer Fund. He stated: 'All we can do is say exactly what occurred.'

"Mrs Dixon was so sure the President would be shot that she contacted a personal friend close to the family and asked her to warn him.

"She told the *London Evening News's* correspondent, Gold: "It was during the final days that I got most worried about Kennedy. Over the weekend, I drove past the White House and I had a vision of the building draped all in black. It got worse over the next few days. On Tuesday, while having dinner, I saw the President shot before my eyes. He was struck in the head. That was when I called out, 'The President has been shot'.

"On the day of his death, I was having breakfast with an old friend and by that time the White House was completely veiled in black.

"I said, 'Charles, this is the day – this is the day it has to happen.'

"Mrs Dixon is not a professional fortune-teller. On the contrary, she is a well-to-do businesswoman who, with her husband James, runs a Real Estate firm specializing in expensive Georgetown property. She believes that her talent is a gift and must not be commercialized upon."

As everyone knows, President Kennedy was assassinated in Dallas on 22 November 1963.

In an article called "A Gift of Prophecy", Norman Winski explains:

"At the age of eight, little Jeane's mother took her to a gypsy for a palm reading. Noticing the unusually strong markings of the psychic in Jeane's left hand – the Star of David with a double heart line leading from it, and another star on the mount of Jupiter – the gypsy proclaimed in awe and wonder that Jeane's prophetic ability would be acknowledged far and wide. Years later, a Hindu mystic was to tell Jeane that the markings on her hands occurred perhaps once in a thousand years.

"The following predictions by Mrs Dixon are a mere handful of the ones that history has seen come to pass:

"She predicted that China would go Red when such a possibility in no way seemed tenable to our government.

"During the Second World War, Franklin Delano Roosevelt summoned Mrs Dixon for unofficial consultations on the world situation. On one of their meetings, haggard and burdened with crushing responsibilities, the great President asked her if she could give him some idea of how long he had to live. She asked him if she could touch his fingers. As she picked up his vibrations she tried desperately to change the conversation, but Roosevelt kept bringing it back to the time he had left to live. Reluctantly, she told him: 'Six months or less'. He died in less than six months from the time of their first meeting.

"In 1952, she predicted serious race rioting would bloody our streets in '63 and '64.

"She warned cinema star Carol Lombard to avoid flying for a time. A short period later, the beautiful actress died in a plane crash.

"Mrs Dixon predicted Gandhi's assassination; the Marilyn Monroe and Dag Hammaskjold tragedies; the merger of the AFL and CIO [the two major American industrial Unions] when the possibilities seemed ridiculous; the Sputnik and the rise of Malenkov and Kruschev, only to be laughed at by Soviet expert Elmer Davies."

On the other hand, James Randi points out that Jeane Dixon has been wrong many times: "In 11 March 1956 issue, *Parade* magazine reported that Jeane said, concerning the 1960 Presidential election:

"Mrs Dixon thinks it will be dominated by Labor and won by a Democrat. He will be assassinated or die in office 'though not necessarily in his first term'.

"The election was not 'dominated by Labor'. She was correct on the winner's party, and the death prediction was in line with the Presidential Curse [which states that, beginning in 1840 with William Henry Harrison, and at twenty year intervals up to 1960, each President elected or re-elected in those years died in Office], since Kennedy fell into that pattern. Yet when 1960 arrived and the election was closer, Mrs Dixon declared that Richard Nixon would win the Presidency.

"The endless chain of Dixon's major failed predictions (Tom Dewey as 'assistant president', the fall of India's Nehru that never happened, Richard Nixon's return to Office, germ warfare in 1958 with China, a monster comet striking the Earth and the election of a female US President – the last two to have taken place in the 1980s – and the dissolution of the Roman Catholic Church before 1990) established that her actual written record is hardly impressive.

Charles Neilson Gattey has a chapter in his *Prophecy and Prediction in the Twentieth Century*, "A Chapter for Cynics", in which he points out some of the prophet's failures. For example, although seventeen major earthquakes took place between January and August 1970, the forecasters in the *American Astrology Magazine* missed every one. "Of the sixteen earthquakes predicted by them, they were right for only three minor upsets and failed to give any advanced warning of the worst disasters of the century to strike Peru on 21 May, when some 30,000 people perished."

In 1971, many psychics predicted that California would be destroyed by an earthquake and tidal waves in April.

"Members of spiritualist churches in Los Angeles and elsewhere were urged by their ministers to take refuge in the hills of Georgia and Tennessee, and many obeyed. Andrew Widrovsky of Santa Barbara described to reporters his awesome prevision of 'two titanic earth convulsions, followed by five tidal waves and a deluge of radioactive ash that will cover the entire south western part of the state', and announced that he had invented an 'anti-radiation belt' which, if worn, would save people's lives. These could be purchased direct from him.

"There was some confusion as to the date of the expected disaster. When the news broke that California's then Governor, Ronald Reagan, would be going away to Arizona on 4 April, the rumours spread that he had received a confidential warning from a friendly top psychic. Yet nothing untoward occurred that day, and the favourite date then became 18 April – the date of the terrible earthquake of 1906 that had destroyed San Francisco. Enterprising shop-keepers urged customers to buy protective helmets and fireproof clothing, while one store put on a 'How to be Best Dressed for the Earthquake' fashion show.

"The event was expected by most astrologers to begin at 3.15 p.m., and at 5 a.m. Joseph Alioto, San Francisco's mayor, gave a great Earthquake Party in its Civic Centre Plaza. Undeterred by having to rise so early, over 7,000 gathered to await the predicted havoc with song, dance and drink, and were entertained with earthquake scenes shown on a giant screen from the MGM movie *San Francisco*. Yet the elements did not rage that afternoon, neither did they the next day at 8.19 a.m., the time chosen by a group of mystics supported by the hippies of Haight-Ashbury."

Gattey adds:

"Not all scientists have derided the claims of astrologers. In 1959, Doctor Rudolf Tomascher, president of the International Geophysical Union, startled more orthodox colleagues by claiming that planetary positions did appear to be linked to earthquake incidence. His claim, based on a study of 134 earthquakes, was published in the scientific journal *Nature*. Tomascher selected Uranus as the planet to keep under close observation. Its position in relation to earthquake epicentres was the same far more frequently than it should have been by chance, the odds being 10,000–1.

"Within a short while, following the publication of Doctor Tomascher's paper, an earthquake destroyed Agadir in Morocco. He then commented that if its population had read *Nature*, they would have taken the necessary precautions while Uranus neared Meridian after the minor precursor shocks. Thus they might have saved their lives when the main quake occurred at 11 p.m., leading to over 20,000 deaths.

"Doctor Tomascher stressed that there was something unique about Uranus. 'It is the only planet the direction of whose axis coincides with the plane of its orbital revolution, so that any magnetic field issuing from it must have an influence quite unlike that of any other planet.'"

Jeane Dixon declared:

"Towards the middle of the 1980s, the earth will be struck by a comet. Earthquakes and tidal waves will be the result of this tremendous collision which will take place in one of the great oceans. It will be one of the worst disasters of the twentieth century. Although the approximate point of impact has already been revealed to me, I believe that I should not reveal it yet, but at a future date I will give more detailed information."

Gattey adds: "Mrs Dixon wisely did not do this, and was later hard put to find excuses for the catastrophe's non-occurrence." Gattey concludes with a quotation:

"The *Daily Telegraph*'s 'Peterborough' on 24 January 1987 quoted this extract from the *Bournemouth Evening Echo*: 'A blaze ripped through a Bournemouth store early today causing damage estimated at £10,000. The cause of the fire at Harper's is still being investigated. A clairvoyant at the store, George Lewis, said he did not predict the blaze because 'Sundays are my days off'."

18 Nostradamus and the Twentieth Century

As has already been noted in previous chapters, Nostradamus quatrains tend to be interpreted by different scholars to reflect their own personal interests. This is equally true of periods of history. Seventeenth, eighteenth and nineteenth-century studies of the *Centuries* tend to find interpretations that match their own historical background, only to be reinterpreted in the light of new events that seem to fit the predictions better.

Turning now to the events of the twentieth century, I am quite aware that I too might suffer from such a partisan outlook. Nevertheless, some of the "matches" of twentieth-century events and the seer's riddling quatrains are quite remarkable . . .

I'm afraid it is a fact that the only truly unbiased Nostradamus scholar would be one that shared the seer's gift for precognition.

Rasputin and the Empress Alexandra, 1905–16
VI.72

> *Par fureur faincte d'esmotion divine,*
> *Sera la femme du grand fort violée:*
> *Judges voulans damner telle doctrine,*
> *Victime au peuple ignorant imolée.*

Translation:

> By a feigned fury of divine emotion,
> The wife of the great one will be violated:
> Judges willing to condemn such a doctrine,
> The victim sacrificed to the ignorant people.

Grigory Yefimovich Rasputin was a holy man (*starets*) from the depths of Siberia. Born the son of a peasant in 1869, he spent his first thirty years working the land as an uneducated serf. He abandoned his family and his life as a farm labourer in 1901, taking to the road as a wandering preacher and faith healer. By 1905 he had made something of a name for himself and travelled to St Petersburg (the then Russian Imperial capital). It soon became a fashion among the aristocracy to visit the wild-looking, heavily bearded holy man – especially among the ladies, who found his powerful personality attractive, and vied for his favours.

The heir to the Russian throne, Crown Prince Alexei, was a haemophiliac – that is, his blood would not clot, so that cuts, or even bruises, could be fatal. One day in 1907 (when the child was three), a fall resulted in high fever. Rasputin (who had already met the royal family) was hastily summoned and, after he prayed for half an hour, the boy's temperature became normal. From then on, Rasputin was constantly in attendance at the palace, and the Tsarina's chief spiritual adviser. It is fairly certain (notwithstanding Nostradamus' suggestion of "violation") that he was never the Tsarina's lover.

Tsar Nicholas II was a kindly but vacillating character, who would have been much happier in private life. He and the Tsarina adored one another and lived in a private cocoon, which (since Russia was seething with revolutionary ferment) was disastrous both for them and the country. By the time World War I broke out, Rasputin, through the Tsarina, was a major power in the palace, and became the Tsar's adviser on political appointments – adding to Russia's chaos.

Not surprisingly, in class-obsessed Imperial Russia, many aristocrats hated the former serf (not least because he had many aristocratic mistresses). On the night of 29/30 December 1916, a group of Rasputin's enemies, led by the spoilt homosexual

Prince Felix Yusupov, invited the holy man to a party, where they laced his sweet wine with enough cyanide to kill an elephant.

Rasputin did not appear to notice. Yusupov shot him in the back, and he collapsed, apparently dead – only to stand up and attack Yusupov, ten minutes after being pronounced dead. More shots and blows from a steel bar subdued him, and he was finally dropped into the frozen River Neva through a hole in the ice. Medical examination later revealed that he had managed to untie one of his hands before he drowned.

If the above quatrain is indeed about Rasputin, it is clear that Nostradamus disliked him – the prediction reads like a scandal-sheet composed by one of the assassins. Yet there are undoubted similarities between the two men. Both were religious, both apparently had "second sight" and – not least – both were court favourites of powerful queens.

The first two lines describe "feigned" religious passion causing the wife of "the great one" to be "violated". This may be an echo of rumours in St Petersburg that the Tsarina was having an affair with Rasputin – which, as already noted, was probably untrue. Alexandra was too devoutly religious and adored her husband and family too much to have behaved in such a way.

The fact that Nostradamus used the word "violée" – a term more indicative of rape than adultery – may suggest that he is condemning Rasputin's violation of the Tsarina's trust (and undoubtedly his lecherous and drunken behaviour would have shocked her deeply).

The last two lines may predict two circumstances in this context; and, knowing Nostradamus' love of riddles, he could have intended both meanings. Influential people ("judges") in Russian society certainly condemned Rasputin's "doctrine" – it was generally supposed that he was a member of a sect called the Khlysty, whose religious ceremonies were believed to end in orgies. Or could the line suggest that it was the Russian people who passed judgement on their self-indulgent aristocracy? Line four – a "victim sacrificed to the ignorant" – may refer to Rasputin, but seems more likely to refer to the Tsar and his family, who were murdered in 1917 by Bolsheviks in Ekaterinburg.

Rasputin told the Tsar that, as the absolute ruler, he must act like a Tsar, not like a half-hearted democrat (a piece of advice that

Joseph Stalin seemed later to have taken to heart). If Nicholas had taken this advice, it might have saved Russia from revolution.

There seems little doubt that Rasputin had genuine supernatural gifts. Even his enemies had to admit he could heal apparently terminal cases by the touch of his hands and that his presence, even when drunk, was magnetic. However, what is less well-attested is his prophetic power.

In 1916 Rasputin wrote a strange document headed "The Spirit of Grigory Rasputin-Novyhk of the village of Pokrovskoe", which was found among his papers after his murder. It begins by stating that he had foreseen that he would not live beyond 1 January and that he had a message for the Tsar and the "Russian Mother" (the Tsarina). If "common assassins" killed him, especially peasants, the Tsar had nothing to fear and Russia would remain a monarchy for centuries to come. If on the other hand, he was murdered by nobles, the Tsar and his immediate family would all die within two years, and all Russian aristocrats would have died or been driven out of the country within twenty-five (by 1942).

By 1942, Russia was firmly in the tyrannical grip of the paranoid Joseph Stalin. Any surviving aristocrat in the USSR would have been living in anonymous poverty with his fellow Soviet citizens.

The Great War, 1914–18
III.18, II.1 & IV.12

> *En Luques sant et laict viendra plouvoir,*
> *En plusieurs lieux de Reims le ciel touché:*
> *O quel conflict de sang pres d'eux s'appreste,*
> *Peres et fils Rois n'oseront approcher.*

Translation:

> After a long rain of milk,
> Several places in Rheims struck from the sky:
> Oh what bloody battle prepared,
> Fathers and sons' Kings dare not approach.

Nostradamus seems peculiarly reticent on the subject of World War I. While he apparently dedicated many quatrains to conflicts such as the Napoleonic wars and the Franco-Prussian War, only a few seem to be specifically linked to the "war to end war" (to use H. G. Wells' phrase).

This may, of course, be our failure to understand certain quatrains, or it could be that Nostradamus was so preoccupied with minutiae that he failed to recognise a conflict on such a massive scale.

Line one mentions a "long rain of milk". Jean-Charles de Fontbrune and Henry C. Roberts feel that this is a poetic description of France's *"belle Epoque"*: a period of peace and plenty around the turn of the century.

On 28 July 1914, the Austro-Hungarian Empire declared war on the little nation of Serbia, after the Serbian nationalist Gavrilio Princip shot and killed the Austrian heir to the throne, Archduke Ferdinand, in Sarajevo. On August 1, Austria's ally Germany declared war on Russia, turning a local war into a European conflict. By August 4, Britain and France had entered the war on the side of Serbia and Russia. Eventually, thirty-two nations were drawn into the conflict, creating the planet's first "world war". Over twenty million people were to die, an unprecedented horror perhaps reflected in lines three and four of the quatrain.

Line two describes something falling from the sky on Rheims. This town in north-eastern France was close to several major battles in World War I. By the 1918 Armistice, the Germans had shelled and bombed Rheims to little more than rubble.

> *Vers Aquitaine par insuls Britanniques,*
> *De pars eux mesmes grands incursions,*
> *Pluies gelées feront terroirs uniques,*
> *Port Selin fortes fera invasions.*

Translation:

> Towards Aquitaine by British assaults,
> By them shall be great incursions:
> Rains and frosts make the terrain unsafe,
> Port Selin makes strong invasions.

The first line of the quatrain contains the word "Britanniques" – interesting, since Britain as a nation did not exist in the time of Nostradamus. However, as we saw in the chapter on Nostradamus and the Nineteenth Century, *Century X*, quatrain 42 seems to show that Nostradamus was aware that the British Isles would one day be unified as a single nation. Here he describes "British" assaults towards Aquitaine (a region of south-west France) and, in the second line, making "great incursions".

Much of the fighting in France took place in the north-east of the country, in and around Belgium on the so-called Western Front. This was a long way from the "Aquitaine", but the appalling weather, described in line three, is reminiscent of the conditions that made the trench warfare so grim.

Of course, the latter part of World War II also saw large British (liberating) "incursions" through south-western France, but line four of the quatrain seems to rule out this interpretation.

Francis X. King points out that "Port Selin" means "Port of the Crescent [moon]". This is one of the old names for Istanbul, the Turkish capital. Turkey was neutral throughout the Second World War, but fought on the German side in World War I.

The 1915 major Allied offensive ("strong invasions") in the Dardanelles (in north-west Turkey) was an unmitigated failure. Over half of the 489,000 British, French, Australian and New Zealand troops sent on the invasion were killed, captured or badly wounded.

> *Le camp plus grand de route mis en fuite,*
> *Gauires plus outre ne sera pourchassé:*
> *Ost recampé, et legion reduicte,*
> *Puis hors ses Gaules du tout sera chassé.*

Translation:

> The greatest army is routed and put to flight,
> But shall not be pursued further:
> They re-encamp, and the legion is reduced,
> They will be driven out of France.

The Germans mobilised almost 14 million men throughout the period of the war. Britain, by contrast, fielded only 8.9 million, France 8.4 million and the USA 4.3 million; only Russia came close to Germany's sheer numbers with 12 million troops. So the Germans could accurately be called "the [single] greatest army", as it says in line one. However, by the beginning of November 1918, this huge army was defeated and was in full retreat from the western front.

The end of World War I was not as complete a defeat for the Germans as the end of World War II would be. On 11 November an armistice was signed. Hostilities ceased immediately and the retreating German army was "not . . . pursued further", as line two says. However, they were completely "driven out of France", as it predicts in line four.

Line three describes "the greatest army" reforming after the rout, but then being reduced. Following the German surrender, the victorious Allies forced them to demobilize their army. The humiliating Treaty of Versailles allowed Germany a standing army of only 100,000 men, demanded enormous war reparations and annexed much of their most valuable industrial territory (making repayment of the reparations nearly impossible). It has been reasonably argued that these acts of vindictive revenge by the Allies all but guaranteed another major war with Germany.

The Russian Revolution and the Murder of the Royal Family, 1917–18
VIII.80

> Des innocens le sang de vefue et vierge.
> Tant de maulx faitz par moyen se grand Roge
> Saintz simulacres tremper en ardent cierge
> De frayeur crainte verra nul que boge.

Translation:

> The blood of innocents the widow and the virgin.
> Many evils committed by the great Red,
> Saints' icons soaked in burning candles,
> Of fear none will be seen to move.

Trying to determine which of Nostradamus' predictions refer to the Russian Revolution is complicated by its similarities to the earlier French Revolution. Both rebel factions were called

"Reds", both were republican and executed aristocrats, both were hostile to the church and committed regicide. Considering the seer's obvious predilection for French history, it is not surprising that many commentators prefer the French interpretation for quatrains that might refer to either. However, the reference to *"simulacres"* (*icons* – paintings of saints) suggests that it is Russia that Nostradamus has in mind here. (The French for statue is *statue*).

Following a popular uprising in March 1917, Tsar Nicholas II was forced to abdicate. A democratic provisional government was set-up, but in October the Bolsheviks (Reds) seized power. Nicholas and his family were held prisoner by the "Red[s]", who seemed to be at a loss as what to do with them. They were initially held at Tobolsk in Siberia, but in the spring of 1918 they were moved to Ekaterinburg. By July it seemed plain that "White Russian", counter-revolutionary forces were going to take the town, so the decision was taken to kill the royal family.

On the night of 16/17 July, the Tsar and Tsarina, their five children, their doctor and three servants were led down into the cellar of the house in which they had been held. The Tsar was given a chair to sit on and their gaoler, Yurovsky, announced: "Nicholas Alexandrovich, your followers have tried to set you free. They failed. Now you are to be shot."

"What?" Nicholas demanded.

"This . . ." said Yurovsky, and shot him in the chest with a revolver. The others fell to their knees and were shot by the rest of Yurovsky's firing squad. The Tsar's doctor, Botkin, the three servants and even the Tsarina's pet spaniel were killed as well. A week later, the Whites took Ekaterinburg, but the bodies had already been partly burned and buried in the forest.

The "great Red", mentioned in line two, is presumably Lenin. Nostradamus seems to have disliked the Bolsheviks as much as he did the French Jacobins, speaking of the "evils" committed by them.

Line three seems to be a prediction of the Communist persecution of the church, with overturned candles soaking the icons with wax; the Bolshevik government went on to abolish the Russian Orthodox Church, along with all other religions. The first and last lines may refer to the deaths of the Russian royal family, although the Tsarina was a "widow" for only the few seconds between her husband's death and her own murder. The children – a son and four daughters – were all "virgin[s]" when they were killed, and the monarchist seer seems to regard the shedding of "the blood of innocents" with indignation.

For many years after the executions, there was a persistent rumour that not all the members of the royal family had been shot. In 1922 a young woman in a German mental hospital told her psychiatrist that she was really the Grand Duchess Anastasia – the youngest of the Tsar's four daughters. She was about the right age and looked very like the Grand Duchess. Indeed, many of Anastasia's relatives were convinced that she was genuine. Now, however, we know that they were wrong. The bones of the Russian royal family were found buried in the Siberian forest in 1991; Anastasia's remains were identified by a DNA test.

Perhaps line four of Nostradamus' quatrain predicts the deaths of all the Tsar's family when it says, "none will be seen to move". Or perhaps he refers to the Stalinist terror that followed, when so many Russians were forced to watch their relatives being sentenced to execution or forced labour, but dared show no sign of dissent

The 1918 Influenza Pandemic
IX.55

> L'horrible guerre qu'en l'occident s'apreste,
> L'an ensuivant la pestilence,
> Si fort horribles que jeune vieux, ne beste,
> Sang, feu, Mercure, Mars, Jupiter en France.

Translation:

> The horrible war is prepared in the west,
> The following year will come the plague,
> So powerfully horrible that young, old, nor beast,
> Blood, fire, Mercury, Mars, Jupiter in France.

The First World War ended on 11 November 1918, having killed over 20 million soldiers and civilians in a four-year period. The great 1918 influenza pandemic (a worldwide epidemic) killed at least that many people again in a single year.

The First World War was certainly "prepared" many years

in advance, as line one states. From the end of the Franco-
Prussian war, in 1871, two military power blocks had been
developing in Europe. On one side were the Germans, the
Turkish Ottomans, the Austro-Hungarian Empire and Bulgar-
ia: the so-called Central Powers. On the other was France,
Britain, Russia and a number of smaller European states: the
Allies. Some statesmen felt that the tremendous military forces
built up by both groups would be a natural deterrent to war –
the prospect being too catastrophic for anybody to contemplate. In fact, the military jingoism that went hand in hand
with the keeping of such large standing armies ultimately made
war virtually inevitable.

The year following the Armistice of 1918 saw one of the worst
pestilences in modern history: the great flu epidemic.

The virus had, in fact, killed large numbers in America in the
months before the end of the war, but the greatest number of
deaths occurred later – one reason being the demobilization of
millions of troops. Crowded troopships and trains might have
been designed to incubate the disease, and thousands arrived
home, only to infect their families and then to die.

The final line of the quatrain – about "blood, fire, Mercury,
Mars, Jupiter in France" seems at first baffling – influenza is not
associated with blood or fire. But war is. The solution is obviously that the second line of the quatrain – about the plague –
should actually be the last. Then we have:

The horrible war is prepared in the west,
Blood, fire, Mercury, Mars, Jupiter in France
So powerfully horrible that (neither) young, old nor beast
    (shall be spared)
The following year will come the plague.

This becomes obvious when we reflect that the *"fort horrible"* of
line three obviously refers to the horrible war of line one, and that
this war took place mainly in France – which does not apply to
the flu epidemic. The references to beasts makes the same point:
although there is a type of flu virus (Influenza A) that can affect
birds, pigs and horses, the great flu epidemic was not notable for
animal deaths.

The League of Nations, 1919–47
I.47

> *Du lac Leman les sermons faschermont,*
> *Les jours seront reduicts par les sepmaines:*
> *Puis mois, puis an, puis tous deffailliront,*
> *Les magistrats damneront leurs loix vaines.*

Translation:

> Of lake Leman the sermons become troublesome,
> The days are dragged out into weeks:
> Then months, then years, then all will fail,
> The magistrates will condemn their own inept laws.

The 1918 Treaty of Versailles was a great disappointment to American President Woodrow Wilson. A liberal and a genuine idealist, he had all but begged his principal allies – France and Britain – not to impose humiliating reparation demands on the defeated Germany. His arguments were ignored but, to placate him, his fellow Allies agreed to the setting-up of a "League of Nations": an international debating chamber, whose main aim was the preservation of world peace.[1]

It was a laudable idea, but was ultimately doomed to failure by the imposition of war reparations aimed at bankrupting Germany. With hindsight, the greedy and vindictive demands made by Britain and France guaranteed another European war, so that the period 1918 to 1939 (between the Great War and World War II) might be seen as an interlude of peace in a single, major conflict.

The first line mentions a lake called "Leman". This was an old (but still widely used) name for Lake Geneva in Switzerland, a traditionally neutral nation and site of the League of Nations' conferences.

Lines one to three describe "sermons" stretching out for weeks, months and years, but ultimately failing. This is exactly

1 Ironically, America refused to join, much to the sorrow of President Wilson. The US remained outside the League for the whole of its existence, greatly reducing its political, financial and military potency.

what happened – endless sermonizing speeches (about the short-comings of other nations) and petty, self-serving arguments occupied most of the League's time, but the delegates ultimately failed in their main purpose: the prevention of another world war.

The last line describes "magistrates" condemning their own inept law-giving. Following World War II, the League admitted its failure, blaming bureaucracy and lack of legal "teeth".

Sixty-three countries belonged to the League at one time or another, and it scored certain successes in limiting international prostitution, drug-trading and illegal immigration. Unfortunately, it failed utterly in its major task as peacekeeper. The Nazis withdrew Germany from the League in 1933, when they began the process of re-arming in violation of the Treaty of Versailles. Japan also withdrew that year, when other League members criticized their savage invasion of China. When the League condemned the Italian invasion of Ethiopia in 1935, Mussolini simply ignored them. Finally, the League was powerless to stop the onset of World War II. When world peace was again restored in 1945, the League of Nations voted for its own dissolution, to be replaced by a stronger (US and Soviet backed) United Nations organization.

The Abdication of Edward VIII, 11 December 1936
X.22

> *Pour ne vouloir consentir à divorce,*
> *Qui puis apres sera cogneu indigne,*
> *Le Roi des Ilse sera chassé par force*
> *Mis à son lieu que de roi n'aura signe.*

Translation:

> For not consenting to a divorce,
> Which afterwards will be recognised as unworthy,
> The King of the Isles shall be chased by force
> Another substituted who had no sign of kingship.

Edward – known to his family as David – was the oldest son of George V of Great Britain, and succeeded his father in the first month of 1936, at the age of forty-one. A liberal with inclinations towards socialism (and an admiration for Hitler), Edward VIII was naturally at odds with his Conservative Prime Minister, Stanley Baldwin. This political difference would certainly have been glossed over, had the king not also been an incorrigible playboy, who enjoyed seducing other men's wives, and who, as monarch, believed that a king ought to rule, rather than be a rubber-stamp for Parliament.

He was naturally casual and careless – for example, he tended to leave top-secret documents lying around the Buckingham Palace for the servants to pick up (and read, if they happened to have friends in the German or Russian espionage services). It was indicative of Edward's work and lifestyle that he often gave such documents back to Baldwin half-read and covered with wine stains and cigar ash.

Finally, Baldwin started to withhold the more secret documents from Edward, as a matter of national security. However, the king's sex-life was a matter he could not deal with so easily. Edward had been having an affair with a respectable (but middle-class) English widow for some years. This, in itself, was hardly likely to cause raised eyebrows, particularly since he had no intention of marrying the lady.

The political problems arose when he threw over this mistress for a married American woman called Wallis Warfield Simpson. Even this might have been controllable, since the British press had no intention of exposing the affair; then Edward told Baldwin that Mrs Simpson had obtained a divorce, and that he intended to marry her as soon as possible.

Baldwin replied that, as official head of the Church of England, the king could not marry a divorcee. Unfortunately, Edward was so accustomed to getting his own way that this made no impression. The American press soon broke the story, and the more discreet British press – this was 1936 – had no alternative than to follow suite.

The general public was scandalized, particularly since Mrs Simpson was an American, and the idea of an American queen seemed as unthinkable as having W. C. Fields as king. Yet Edward would not be swayed. Finally, under considerable pressure, he announced his abdication. It was 11 December 1936. His younger brother was crowned George VI.

Line four describes a successor to the throne who lacks the "sign of kingship". This description certainly fits George VI, who was shy and had a bad stammer – although historians now classify him as one of the most successful monarchs in modern British history. In due course he was a major factor in boosting British morale during the Second World War.

General Franco and the Spanish Civil War, 1936–39
III.54 & IX.16

> *L'un des plus grands fuira aux Espaignes,*
> *Qu'en longue playe apres viendra saigner:*
> *Passant copies par les hautes montaignes,*
> *Devastant tout et puis en paix regner.*

Translation:

> One of the great men will fly to Spain,
> That will cause a wound that will bleed for a long time:
> Leading troops over high mountains,
> Devastating all and afterwards reigns in peace.

Spain was falling apart politically in the early 1930s. The worldwide economic depression had the effect of deepening the hatred between the left and right-wing factions, and partisan terror gangs stalked the streets at night.

On 18 July 1936, a fascist military *coup d'état* attempted to overthrow the government of the Second Republic. Much of the population in the countryside (which always tends to be conservative) backed the coup, but it failed in most of the major cities. Thus the two factions split the nation: the besieged, leftist government – the Loyalists – and the right-wing rebels – the Nationalists. A bloody civil war began.

One of the chief ("great") men of the Nationalist side was Major General Francisco Franco. A career military man, his attitudes had been brutalized in Spain's grim war to crush Moroccan independence in the 1920s. When the coup took place, Franco was commanding the colonial army in Morocco. Since the pro-Loyalist Spanish navy held the Straits of Gibraltar, Franco made a deal with the German Nazi government to lend his troops transport aeroplanes. Thus, as it says in line one, he literally "flew" back to Spain.

On his arrival, Franco swiftly deployed his troops and marched on Loyalist-held Madrid. The calculated brutality of his troops cowed the Loyalist enemy and impressed the Nationalists. Madrid eventually fell and Franco was made head of the Nationalist faction.

General Franco fought an all-out war – using ruthlessness and cruelty as strategic weapons. This made him a very effective commander, but meant that the Spanish Civil War was a "wound" in the nation's psyche that would "bleed" for generations – just as line two describes.

Troops certainly "passed over high mountains" (the Pyrenees) to aid both sides in the Civil War, as line three describes. Military aid was sent from fascist Italy and Germany to the Nationalists, and similar aid came from the USSR for the Loyalists – as well as thousands of young political activists from all over Europe, who hurried to fight in what they considered a war of ideology.

Franco, despite or perhaps because of his brutal methods, won the war – as line four seems to predict. He then kept his exhausted country out of the Second World War, and ruled "in peace" until his death, at the age of eighty-three, in 1975.

> De castel Franco sortira l'assemblee,
> L'ambassadeur non plaisant fera scisme:
> Ceux de Ribiere seront en la meslee,
> Et au grand goulphre desnier ont l'entrée.

Translation:

> From *castel* Franco comes the assembly,
> The ambassadors not pleased create a schism:
> Those of *Ribiere* will be in the mêlée,
> And the entry is denied to the great gulf.

This is a remarkable quatrain, since it names Franco and connects his name with Spain (the word "castel" is usually translated by Nostradamus scholars as "Castille": a town in Spain).

Francis X. King, in *Nostradamus* (1995), suggests that the "assembly", mentioned in the first line, and the contention of "ambassadors", mentioned in the second, are both predictions of the disagreement between Spain and Germany in 1940. As we have already noted, General Franco kept Spain neutral in the Second World War, but was willing to support his fellow fascists unobtrusively. Hitler asked Franco to help him take Gibraltar from the British, thus breaking their stranglehold on entry into the Mediterranean "gulf". Franco saw that this would violate his neutrality and flatly refused.

At the time, it was a political gamble to annoy a powerful neighbour like Hitler but, in maintaining his neutrality, Franco guaranteed his political survival when the Allies won the war.

The word *"Ribiere"* in line three is generally assumed to be a misspelling of "Rivera". General Miguel Primo de Rivera ruled a military dictatorship in Spain from 1923 to 1930. He went into exile when his government fell. His son José entered politics to clear his father's name and founded the Spanish fascist party, Falange, in 1933. As such, any "mêlée" involving Franco's fascists might have been said to contain "those of Rivera".

José Rivera may have either supported Franco's push for power or fought to head the Nationalist side himself, but we will never know because the Loyalists shot him in 1936.

Adolf Hitler, 1889–1945
II.24, III.35, IX.90 & III.58

> *Bestes farouhes de faim fleuves tranner,*
> *Plus part du champ encontre Hister sera,*
> *En caige de fer le grand fera treisner,*
> *Quand Rin enfant de Germain observa.*

Translation:

> Beasts wild with hunger swim rivers,
> The greater part of the field will be against Hister,
> In a cage of iron the great one is drawn,
> When the child of Germany sees the Rhine.

We know that Hitler himself read this quatrain as a prediction of his own future. Nazi propaganda made much of Nostradamus, claiming that the *Centuries* clearly predicted that Germany would conquer Europe and rule a thousand-year empire. It would, no doubt, have gratified Nostradamus, who delighted in ambiguities and ironies, that the Allies also used his work for propaganda purposes, as proof of their own inevitable victory. By now, the reader will have seen how easy it is to read varied and often contradictory meanings into the same quatrain.

The word *"Hister"* in line two is plainly a name, because Nostradamus gives it a capital letter. However, the River Danube used to be called the *"Ister"* by the Romans and, as we have seen several times already, the prophet was quite capable of referring to a place by its Ancient Roman name. Hitler almost certainly knew this fact, but it would not have dampened his enthusiasm, because the Austrian town of Braunau am Inn, where he was born, was on the River Danube. To Hitler, it would have seemed a clever play on words and an actual reconfirmation that it was he who was intended in the prediction.

The first line mentions ravening "beasts" crossing rivers. Hitler saw this as a prediction that his own troops (the Nazis liked to be described as blond beasts) would conquer to gain the *lebensraum* ("living-space") that his people needed. (With the benefit of hindsight, we could also interpret it as ferocious drive of the Allies, hungry for revenge against the Nazis.)

Line two can be read as predicting that most of Europe would eventually be "against" Hitler and Nazi Germany.

Likewise, the "iron cage" of line three could be a description of the steel-and-concrete bunker in which Hitler confined himself during his last days, and in which he took his own life. As a matter of passing interest, almost the exact phrase was used of an earlier dictator; in 1815, Marshal Ney was sent with a large French army to capture Napoleon (who had just escaped from Elba). Ney told Louis XVIII that he would "drag [Napoleon] back to Paris in an iron cage". In fact, as we saw in an earlier chapter, the whole army deserted to join Napoleon . . . including Marshal Ney.

The last line seems baffling, until we recall the transposed lines of the quatrain about the flu epidemic of 1919. If we transpose lines three and four, then the quatrain states that the rest of Europe will be against Hitler when he crosses the Rhine and attacks France.

> *Du plus profond de l'Occident d'Europe,*
> *De pauvres gens un jeune enfant naistra:*
> *Qui par sa langue seduira grande troupe,*
> *Son bruit au regne d'Orient plus croistra.*

Translation:

> In the deepest part of Western Europe,
> Of poor people a young infant will be born:
> Who with his tongue will seduce many people,
> His reputation will increase in the eastern kingdom.

The above quatrain matches the lives of both Hitler and Napoleon, but the reference to western Europe tends to favour Hitler – Napoleon was born in Corsica.

Hitler's father, Alois Hitler, was a badly paid border official. Napoleon's father was a lawyer and a count, but could not afford to send his son to military school and had to petition a scholarship from Louis XVI. Line three describes this "infant" seducing many people with his tongue. Hitler made his political career as an orator; we now tend to think of him as a ranting demagogue, but contemporaries like Albert Speer noted that Hitler could "seduce" just about any audience by matching his tone to their sensibilities. Napoleon, of course, was primarily a general, but even he had a famous ability to inspire his troops with his speeches before battles . . .

Finally, line four describes the leader in question increasing his reputation in the "eastern kingdom" (presumably meaning Eastern Europe). We can only assume that Nostradamus was being ironic here. Both Hitler and Napoleon dreamed of crowning their military achievements by conquering Russia, and both lost their reputations for infallibility in their Russian campaigns.

> *Un capitaine de la grand Germanie,*
> *Se viendra rendre par simulé secours,*
> *Un roi des rois aide de Pannonie,*
> *Que sa revolte fera de sang grand cours.*

Translation:

> A captain of greater Germany,
> Will come to deliver simulated help,
> A king of kings to support *Pannonie*,
> Whose revolt will cause great bloodshed.

In Nostradamus' day, "Germany" consisted of a number of independent principalities. Yet the term "captain of greater Germany" suggests that the seer knew that the country would one day come under the domination of a single ruler. This would have then been considered as unlikely as England forming a union with Wales, Scotland and Ireland – which, however, Nostradamus also foresaw.

There is a single, complex meaning contained in these four lines, not two, three or four sub-predictions as the quatrains usually contain. The seer predicts that the "captain of greater Germany" will offer "simulated help" to "*Pannonie*" ("*Panonia*" was the classical name for Hungary). This will make him a "king of kings", but the resultant bloodshed will be very great.

The quatrain fits Hitler perfectly. He was indeed the sole *Führer* ("leader") of "greater Germany"; in fact, the Third Reich was often referred to by the Nazis as *Grossendeutschland* ("greater Germany"). The Hungarians sided with the Germans in World War II but, following terrible losses on the Russian front, they secretly sued to the Allies for peace. Hitler invaded his wavering ally and set up a puppet government. He described this invasion as "help" for the people of Hungary, but his troops then arrested and murdered hundreds of thousands of Hungarians.

Hitler's invasions certainly made him a "king of kings", but the war he started shed the lifeblood of an estimated 80 million people, 55 million of whom were civilians.

> *Aupres du Rhin des Montaignes Norique,*
> *Naistra un grand de gens trop tard venu.*
> *Qui defendra Saurome et Pannoniques,*
> *Quon ne sçaura qu'il sera devenu.*

Translation:

Near the Rhine from the mountains of *Noricum*,
Will be born a great man of the people but he comes too late.
Who will defend Poland and Hungary,
It will not be known what became of him.

The word "*Norique*" in the first line sounds like "*Noricum*", the ancient name for Austria. Hitler was an Austrian who led the Germans – a people whose national river is the Rhine. He was "too late" because land war to build an empire had become, by 1939, a thing of the past. Hitler and his slavery-based Third Reich were a throwback to a more savage, bygone age.

Line three might be read as a question: "Who will defend Poland and Hungary?" On the other hand, German troops certainly did defend these countries, not least from the Poles and the Hungarians. Again we may catch a whiff of prophetic irony from the seer.

The last line states that it would not be known what happened to this "great man of the people". This is also true of Hitler. Although official sources accepted that he killed himself in the Berlin bunker, the fact that his body was never recovered fed rumours that he had survived and was living secretly in South America. Given the lack of evidence, it is possible that this belief may never be disproved.

The Nazi Swastika
VI.49

> *De la partie de Mammer grand Pontife,*
> *Subjugera les confins du Danube:*
> *Chasser les croix par fer raffe ne riffe,*
> *Captifz, or, bagues plus de cent mille rubes.*

Translation:

> The Pontiff of the party of *Mammer*,
> Subjugating the borders of the Danube:
> Chasing the iron cross by hook or by crook,
> Captives, gold, jewels more than a hundred thousand rubies.

The first line of the quatrain describes the "Pontiff of the party of *Mammer*". This could be a neat description of Hitler with the added twist of a typical Nostradamus double meaning . . .

"*Mamers*" was the Sabine name for the god Mars but, by adding another "m", the seer gives a second indication: that of "*Mammon*", the demon of money and greed. The Nazis certainly had a near-religious respect for war and militarism, and coupled this with an undisguised love of wealth. In fact, a third meaning may also be extracted from this single word, provided the reader is willing to extrapolate on an extrapolation . . . The Sabines were a tribe in central Italy – the same country to form the first "fascist" party, which the Germans copied and called the National Socialist (or Nazi) Party.

The Nazis certainly subjugated the "borders of the Danube", as line two predicts, and their bravest soldiers "chased" hopes of winning the Iron Cross ("*croix par fer*") as it says in line three. Many Nostradamus translators have also read a prediction of the Nazi Swastika in this line. "*Raffe ne riffe*" is a French version of "by hook or by crook". Some scholars simply translate the line: "chasing the crooked iron cross."

We may take line four, with its gold, jewels and rubies, as Nostradamus' shorthand for the vast amount of wealth the Nazis' plundered from banks, museums and chateaux in the territories they overran, although "rubies" could also be a poetic image of all the blood shed during the war.

World War II, 1939–45
II.38, II.39 & II.40

> *Des condamnez sera fait un grand nombre,*
> *Quant les monarques seront conciliez:*
> *Mais l'un deux viendra si malencombre,*
> *Que guere ensemble ne seront reliez.*

Translation:

> There shall be a great number condemned,
> When the monarchs shall be reconciled:
> One will come to such a bad encumbrance,
> That their reconciliation will not last long.

These next three quatrains are commonly thought to describe the run-up and early part of the Second World War.

The first sets the tone for all three in its first line, describing "great numbers condemned". With over eighty million dead and millions more maimed and dispossessed, this description certainly fits World War II. One could also accept Erica Cheetham's interpretation that it is a prophecy about the Nuremburg War Crime Trials that followed the downfall of the Nazis. Over one hundred and twenty Nazi war criminals were eventually "condemned" to death.

The quatrain's link to the Second World War is seen in the remaining three lines, which echo the events of the Hitler–Stalin Pact. In August 1939, Joseph Stalin and Adolf Hitler shocked the world (and their own nations of Russia and Germany) by announcing a non-aggression treaty ("the monarchs shall be reconciled"). These previously mortal enemies even cemented their friendship by jointly invading and partitioning Poland the following month.

Informed and understandably cynical political commentators saw, however, that the alliance was simply a ruse by both parties. Hitler's army was still too small to defeat the massive Soviet armed forces. Stalin, on the other hand, could not launch an attack on Germany because he had – unfortunately – shot almost his entire officer corps in the previous decade of purges.

Until these weaknesses could be repaired, both leaders had good reason to delay their otherwise inevitable conflict. Line three goes on to predict that one of these "monarchs" would meet a "bad encumbrance" that would lead to a crumbling of their reconciliation (in line four). Hitler successfully invaded France in spring 1940, but found his attack on Britain barred by the English Channel and the Royal Air Force. Thus "encumbered", he decided simply to contain the British, and turned his attention and resources to preparing to stab his Soviet "ally" in the back. He beat Stalin in the treachery stakes – invading the USSR in May 1941.

Other commentators have speculated that the alliance between Hitler and Mussolini might be meant – certainly, Mussolini had become an "encumbrance" long before the end of the war.

> *Un an devant le conflict Italique,*
> *Germaines, Gaulois, Hespaignols pour le fort:*
> *Cherra l'escolle maison de republique,*
> *Ou, hors mis peu, seront suffoque mors.*

Translation:

> A year before the Italian conflict,
> Germans, French, Spanish for the strong:
> The school house of the Republic will fall,
> Where, except for a few, they suffocate to death.

In 1939, the Italian dictator, Benito Mussolini, told Hitler that Italy would not be ready to support the Germans in the war until 1942 at the earliest – the Italian army was simply too small and badly trained.

However, in 1940, Mussolini was overcome by his own greed. He saw how easily France had fallen and calculated that Britain and Russia might also fall before 1942. This would obviously leave little of value for him to conquer for his own empire. So Italy entered the war with an undertrained army which, as a result, lost virtually every battle it fought.

If we take this quatrain to be a prediction of the Second World War, then "a year before the Italian [entry into the] conflict," would be 1939. The second line of the quatrain supports this interpretation, because it matches the political affiliations of western Europe in that year. Fascist Spain was friendly towards Nazi Germany – as were a significant section of France's ("*Gaulois*") right-wing politicians – those that formed the heart of the quisling Vichy Government after the German invasion.

Hitler's *blitzkrieg* invasion took France by surprise in the spring of 1940, and seems to be predicted in line three. France was the first modern European republic and, as we saw in previous chapters, disseminated her political philosophy both by argument and force. To call France the "school house" of modern republicanism would be far from inaccurate. Certainly, the Nazi invasion caused the "fall" and flight of the French Republican Government.

France, although unable to field troops for most of the war, lost an estimated 675,000 of her citizens – many of whom might be said to have "suffocate[d]" under the crushing Nazi rule.

> *Un pres apres non point longue intervalle,*
> *Par mer et terre sera faict grand tumulte:*
> *Beaucoup plus grande sera pugne navalle,*
> *Feux, animaux, qui feront plus d'insulte.*

Translation:

> Shortly afterwards not a long interval,
> By sea and land there is made a great tumult:
> Greater than ever will be naval battles,
> Fires, animals, which will make great affront.

This quatrain is clearly supposed to be a continuation of the previous prediction (or predictions) as line one refers back to it.

The European war did not become a "world war" until Japan entered on the Axis side in December 1941. This was after the fall of France and the collapse of the Nazi-Soviet pact (apparently predicted in the previous two quatrains); a year and a half later came the Japanese attack on Pearl Harbor. The major land and sea battles of the war ("great tumult[s]") did not occur until after this event, just as line two seems to predict.

The major sea battles in the Atlantic – predicted by British and German military planners at the start of the war – never took place. Apart from the hunting and destruction of the German pocket battleships, the main battle in this area was a cat-and-mouse conflict to crush the U-boat menace (see below). However, the American–Japanese war in the Pacific turned on several major sea battles (Coral Sea, Midway, Leyte Gulf and the Marianas "Turkey Shoot"[2]). These "naval battles" were certainly "greater than ever" (i.e. than those that went before them) because of the new giant aircraft carriers deployed by both sides.

Line four is puzzling, with its fire and animals. Erica Cheetham suggests that it is a comment on "animals" who can "fire", describing riflemen, or perhaps tanks and submarines.

However, the word *"insulte"* ("insult" or "affront") at the end of the line may suggest another meaning. The Nazis slaughtered millions like "animals" in concentration camps, "fire[ing]" the bodies in huge incinerators. This, it is now universally agreed, was an "affront" to humanity.

The Battle of the Atlantic and the Holocaust
IV.15 & III.71

> *D'où pensera faire venir famine,*
> *De là viendra le rassasiement:*
> *L'oeil de la mer par avare canine,*
> *Pour de l'un l'autre dorna huile, froment.*

2 So-called because the once fearsome Japanese "Zero" fighters were so heavily out-gunned by the new American planes.

Translation:

> From the place famine will be thought to come,
> From there will come plenitude:
> The eye of the sea like a covetous dog,
> One gives oil and wheat to the other.

Hitler relied on his U-boats (submarines) to reduce Britain to starvation. He knew that the UK had too high a population-to-land ratio to be self-sufficient in food, so cutting the supply route from America, across the North Atlantic, would eventually starve the besieged nation into surrender.

So the U-boat "wolfpacks" ceaselessly hunted cargo ships making their way to and from America. Hundreds of vessels were torpedoed and one out of four Allied merchant seamen did not live to see 1945.

Fortunately, the U-boat fleet was always kept under strength for the task allotted them because Hitler ordered his limited number of armament factories to build tanks rather than submarines. As a result, Allied technology had enough time to counter the U-boat threat, and the new sonar and radar equipment had turned the Battle of the Atlantic against the Germans by the mid-point of the war. Nine out of ten U-boat crewmen were killed as their "iron coffins"[3] were depth-charged or rammed by destroyers. This was the worst casualty rate of any service on either side of the conflict.

The first two lines of the quatrain seem to suggest an overall historical view of the Battle of the Atlantic. Hitler and Churchill both knew that the Atlantic seaways were the key to winning the war in Europe. If America could be physically barred from intervening, Russia would stand alone, except for a starving, weaponless Britain.

Nevertheless, thanks to the bravery of the British, American and Canadian merchant fleets, vital supplies and, later, troops made it across the Atlantic in a continuous stream throughout the war.

The third line is one of Nostradamus' most poetically striking. Up to the end of the nineteenth century, this description ("the eye of the sea like a covetous dog") was simply a puzzle. Yet the invention of the "submersible torpedo boat" in 1906 could have

3 The bitter nickname U-boatmen gave to their submarines.

provided a clue to any contemporary Nostradamus scholar with an interest in military inventions. The new German *U-boot* could fire a torpedo while under water by aiming with a telescopic periscope: "the eye of the sea [hunting] like a covetous dog".

The fourth line is connected with the second – an apparent prediction that the U-boats would fail to inflict starvation on Britain. However, the inclusion of the word *"huile"* (oil) is striking. Crude oil was as vital as food to Britain during the war because it was made into petrol.

> *Ceux dans les isles de longtemps assiegez,*
> *Prendront vigeur force contre ennemis:*
> *Ceux par dehors mors de faim profligez,*
> *En plus grand faim que jamais seront mis.*

Translation:

> Those of the islands that have long been besieged,
> Shall use vigorous force against their enemies:
> Those overcome outside will die of hunger,
> As great a famine as has ever been known before.

The first two lines seem to echo the prediction given above: Britain besieged, but fighting back and ultimately winning against Hitler.

The second two lines seem to predict something much darker. There was, in fact, great starvation in German-occupied countries ("those overcome") during the war, but this was not a historically unprecedented famine, as line four seems to predict. On the other hand, if we take the line to mean a *man-made* famine, we might see a prediction of the deliberate starvation of millions in Nazi concentration camps: the first time in history that so many people were murdered in this cruel way.

Pearl Harbor, 7 December 1941
IX.100

> *Navalle pugne nuit sera superee,*
> *Le feu naves l'Occident ruine:*

> *Rubriche neufue la grand nef coloeree,*
> *Ire à vaincu, et victoire en bruine.*

Translation:

> Naval battle night is overcome,
> The fire in the ruined ships of the West:
> A new coding the great coloured ship,
> Anger to the vanquished, victory in a fog.

Just after dawn ("night is overcome") on 7 December 1941, the Japanese navy launched a massive air attack from its carrier ships, secretly anchored off the Hawaiian coast. The target was the US Pacific Fleet docked in Pearl Harbor. (The war vessels were painted camouflage-style – and this might be what Nostradamus means by "great coloured ship[s]" in line three.) Japanese bombers and fighters sank eighteen ships, including eight battleships, destroyed almost 200 aircraft (most of which did not have time to get off the ground) and killed nearly 3,000 people.

The Japanese government had actually issued a declaration of war a few hours before the attack but, because of American bureaucratic bungling, the fleet at Pearl Harbor had not been informed that they were at war and so were taken by complete surprise.

In fact, it is rumoured that the Americans had intercepted and translated the Japanese coded orders to attack Pearl Harbor some days before. However, US President Franklin D. Roosevelt ordered the information to be suppressed, so America could enter the war as an ally of Britain: an attack by Germany's Japanese ally would have given him the necessary leverage to budge his solidly anti-war Congress.

Whether that is true is still a matter of some debate. However, line three, with its mention of a "new coding", might suggest the interception of the Japanese signal.

The last line speaks of "anger to the vanquished". This might be a reference to the rage of the American people over the Japanese "sneak-attack". Overnight, the country went from being largely pacifist to being fervently militaristic.

The words "victory in a fog" are harder to understand in this context, but they may refer to the fact that the Japanese attack failed to sink the US carrier ships which were out on exercises at the time. Missing these ships "in the fog of battle" was a major disappointment to the Japanese. Their survival gave the Americans just enough foothold in the Pacific to launch a counter-offensive. Arguably, these American carriers were the main reason Japan lost control of the sea and, ultimately, the war.

The Bomb, 8a.m., 6 August 1945
II.6

> *Aupres des portes et dedans deux cités,*
> *Seront deux fléaux et oncques n'apperceu un tel:*
> *Faim, dedans peste, de fer hors gens boutés,*
> *Crier secours au grand Dieu immortel.*

Translation:

> Near the gates and within two cities,
> There will be two scourges the like of which have never
>   been seen before:
> Famine within plague, people thrust out by the sword,
> Crying for succour to the grand God immortal.

The Allies' atomic fission bomb project was originally aimed at destroying Berlin, but Germany collapsed before the weapon could be made ready. However, mainland Japan was still holding out, and American military planners were certain that tens of thousands of US servicemen would die in the planned invasion. Therefore Harry Truman – the new American president, now Roosevelt had worked himself to death – gave orders to drop single atom bombs on the coastal ports of Hiroshima and Nagasaki, in the hope of shocking the Japanese into surrender.

The first bomb exploded over Hiroshima at just after 8a.m., on 6 August 1945: 129,558 people were killed. The second bomb was dropped on Nagasaki three days later: 66,000 people were reported killed or severely injured. By Second World War standards, these casualty figures were comparatively light. For example, six months previously, 135,000 people had been killed in one night in the German town of Dresden by a "conventional" air raid. Nevertheless, Japan surrendered.

Erica Cheetham translates the word *"portes"* in the first line as "harbours" rather than "gates". Given Nostradamus' penchant for deliberate, riddling misspellings, it is not unreasonable to suspect that he added an "e" to the French word "*port*" ("harbour") to make "*porte*" ("gate"). Both Hiroshima and Nagasaki are harbour towns.

The second line speaks for itself. The atom bombs were unquestionably "scourges". And certainly, such weapons had "never [been] seen before", in the history of warfare.

Line three sounds like a description of acute radiation sickness. Victims first suffer total loss of appetite or extreme nausea. Deterioration of the body's cell structure follows, appearing as "radiation burns" on the skin. In such extreme cases, death is usually inevitable. Nostradamus – a veteran of numerous plague outbreaks in his own time – may well have described these symptoms as "famine within a plague".

The last line may be a prediction of the despairing prayers of the bomb victims, but it also seems to carry an undertone of the prophet's own horror.

The Founding of Israel, 1947
III.97

> *Nouvelle loi terre neufve occuper,*
> *Vers la Syrie, Judee et Palestine:*
> *Le grand empire barbare corruer,*
> *Avant que Phoebus son siecle determine.*

Translation:

> A new law will occupy a new country,
> Towards Syria, Judea and Palestine:
> The great barbarian empire crumbles,
> Before the cycle of the Sun is determined.

The British army captured Palestine – the former Jewish homeland – from the Turks in the First World War. They promised the Palestinian Arabs independence in exchange for their support, but they had also promised the Jews (whose help they also needed) a homeland in Palestine. After the war, the British continued to occupy Palestine, and delayed when asked to fulfil their (mutually exclusive) promises. Thirty years of revolt and terrorism followed.

After the Second World War, exhausted and sick to death of the "Palestine Problem", the British announced (in 1947) that they would pull out by mid-1948. The newly formed United Nations was left to sort out the mess and they, partly out of guilt about the Holocaust, supported the Jewish demands: over fifty per cent of Palestine was to be given over to Jewish rule. The Palestinians were naturally outraged, and the neighbouring Arab states of Syria, Egypt, Lebanon, Jordan and Iraq supported them.

After a year of war, the Jews – or, rather, the Israelis – had beaten off their attackers and subdued their own Arab population. Israel was back on the map for the first time in almost two thousand years.

Being of Jewish stock himself, one might guess that Nostradamus would have had a special interest in the rebuilding of the State of Israel.

Although the above quatrain gives no indication who would rule this "new land", the position the seer gives in line two is exactly correct. The third and fourth lines describe the crumbling of a "great barbarian empire . . . before the cycle of the Sun is determined." From a late twentieth-century perspective, it is hard not to see this as an accurate prediction that Soviet rule in Russia would collapse before the end of the second millennium (2000AD).

The Crushing of the Hungarian Revolution, 1956
II.90

> *Par vie et mort changé regne d'Ongrie,*
> *La loi sera plus aspre que service:*
> *Leur grand cité d'hulements plaincts et crie,*
> *Castor et Pollux ennemis dans la lice.*

Translation:

By life and death the kingdom of Hungary will be changed,
The law will become more bitter than service:
Their great city will howl lament and cry,
Castor and Pollux are enemies in the field.

As noted above, Hungary fought on the German side during the first half of the Second World War, but was treacherously invaded and brutally occupied by their former ally. The Soviet Army was therefore welcomed as a liberating force by most Hungarians. Sadly, by the mid-1950s, the rejoicing was over. Stalin's rule was little better than the Nazi occupation, and many Hungarians dreamed of a return to democracy. In 1956, student demonstrations in Budapest – calling for an end to compulsory Russian language courses – quickly spread the unrest to the whole country. The communist puppet regime was ousted and multi-party democracy was reinstated. The new Hungarian leaders – egged on by promises of aid and military assistance from the West – declared Hungary a "neutral nation". Stalin sent in the tanks.

Desperate pleas for help were sent out from the last free radio station in Budapest ("[the] great city will howl lament and cry") but the western governments ignored them, for fear of starting another war. The free Hungarians fought back with the few weapons they had, but had no chance against the massive Soviet invasion force.

The last line of the quatrain describes "Castor and Pollux" as "enemies in the field". Castor and Pollux were Greek (and Roman) twin heroes. In 1956, communist Hungarians joined the advancing Russians and fought to suppress their fellow Hungarians.

The Soviets shot hundreds of "counter-revolutionaries" and imprisoned thousands more. The Communist regime was reinstated as an absolute state, where even whispered dissent could lead to the death sentence; so the "law [became] more bitter than service" – or perhaps we might translate the word "service" as "slavery".

Fidel Castro in the USA, 1959
VIII.74

> *En terre neufue bien avant Roi entré,*
> *Pendant subges lui viendront faire acueil,*
> *Sa perfidie aura tel recontré*
> *Qu'aux citadind lieu de feste et receuil.*

Translation:

> Into the new land the King advances far,
> While the subjects come to bid him welcome,
> His perfidious action shall have the result,
> That to the citizens it is a reception rather than a feast.

As the English called America "the New World", the French of Nostradamus' day called the newly discovered continent "*le Terre Neuve*". It is hard to believe that Nostradamus could have used this phrase, in line one of the above quatrain, without realizing that it would make his readers think of the Americas.

Although the rest of the quatrain is too vague to offer an obvious historical incident, it does seem to echo Fidel Castro's ill-fated diplomatic trip to the USA in spring 1959.

Cuba had been a thoroughly corrupt dictatorship, but in 1956 the young political exile Fidel Castro and his brother Raoul sailed back to the country with eighty fellow revolutionaries. Seventy were killed on the beach by a government ambush, but the Castros escaped. They launched a popular revolution and, by December 1958, had taken Havana and driven out the former dictator, Fulgencio Batista, into exile.

The USA viewed the Cuban revolution without enthusiasm. The American government had backed the corrupt Batista regime, and now Castro started to talk of "land reform" and nationalisation of the (largely American-owned) oil and sugar industries: a socialist plan, bordering on communism.

In the spring of 1959, Castro flew to Washington to try to win American support. He was rudely denied a meeting with President Eisenhower, and instead met with Vice-President Richard Nixon. According to Castro's version of events, Nixon was cold towards him. The Cuban revolutionary explained that he was not a communist, but merely wanted to help his country's transition into the twentieth century. He added that he could not do this without the help of one or other of the two rival superpowers – the USA or the USSR. Nixon reported to Eisenhower that Castro was a communist and should not be helped in any way. So Cuba sided with the Soviet bloc.

The language of the last three lines of the quatrain is subtle, but Castro *was* seen as "perfidious" in the rather paranoid eyes of post-MacCarthy America, so his welcome was chilly: a forced "reception rather than a [joyous] feast".

It is interesting to wonder how the world would look today if Nixon had been diplomatic and friendly to Castro; it is possible that Cuba might have joined the western powers and, at the very least, the world might have been saved the emotional trauma of the Cuban missile crisis.

The Kennedy Assassinations, 22 November 1963 and 5 June 1968
IX.36

> *Un grand Roi prins entre les mains d'un Joine,*
> *Non loing de Pasque confusion coup coultre:*
> *Perpet. Captifs temps que fouldre en la husne,*
> *Lorsque trois freres se blesseront et meutre.*

Translation:

> A great King taken into the hands of the Young,
> Not far from Easter confusion knife state:
> Permanent captives times when lightning is above,
> When three brothers are wounded and murdered.

President John F. Kennedy was killed (almost certainly by multiple snipers) as his motorcade passed through downtown Dallas on 22 November 1963. His younger brother, Senator Bobby Kennedy, was shot dead when walking through the kitchen of the Ambassador Hotel, moments after winning the Californian nomination for the Democratic leadership on 5 June 1968.

Both assassinations caused widespread shock, so it is not surprising that subsequent Nostradamus scholars should have searched the quatrains for predictions of these murders. Of course, bearing in mind that Nostradamus' interests never strayed too far from France and Europe, it is perhaps not surprising that there seem to be few "hits". It is true that about half a dozen quatrains have been linked to the Kennedy assassinations, but all rely on rather remote connections – so that, for example, any mention of "brothers" and death in the same quatrain has been seized upon.

Another example, *Century II*, quatrain 57, describes the "fall" of "the great one to death, death too sudden and bewailed". True, the snipers' bullets that killed Jack Kennedy struck "too sudden", and his loss was certainly "bewailed", but the link is hardly convincing.

The above is one of the most-quoted "Kennedy quatrains". I offer it here in order to allow the reader to judge the material for themselves. Also, if it is about the Kennedys, it seems to predict that Senator Edward Kennedy will follow his two older brothers in being murdered.

Line one may be a description of John F. Kennedy winning the presidency (the youngest man ever to do so) after the retirement of President Eisenhower.

Line three describes "lightning from above", and this has been linked to the overhead sniper shot that burst Kennedy's skull.

Line four describes "three brothers wounded and murdered". Whether the remaining Kennedy brother of that ill-fated generation, Edward, needs to be cautious of knives around Easter, as it suggests in line two, is a matter for conjecture.

Space Exploration, 4 October 1957 to the present day
IX.65

> *Dedans le coing de luna viendra rendre,*
> *Ou sera prins et mis en terre estrange,*
> *Les fruitz immeurs seront à la grand esclandre,*
> *Grand vitupere à l'un grande loiange.*

Translation:

> He will be taken to the corner of the moon,
> Where he will be placed in a strange land,
> The unripe fruit will cause a great scandal,
> Great shame, to the other great praise.

The Space Age began on 4 October 1957, when the Soviets launched the world's first orbital satellite: *Sputnik 1*. The USA, caught napping, hurried to catch up in what became known as the "Space Race". However, the Russians beat them again, sending up the first manned rocket into orbit on 12 April 1961. In 1969 the Americans at last won the initiative when, on July 20, they were the first nation to put a man on the moon.

The first line sounds odd – but close examination shows that it is an accurate description of the Apollo 11 "Moonshot". The astronauts did not, strictly speaking, "fly" to the moon. Their rocket was fired on a predetermined trajectory in much the same way that one of those circus performers known as a "human cannonball" is shot into a distant net. Since they had minimal control over the spaceflight, it would therefore be accurate to say that the astronauts were "taken" to the moon.

It certainly sounds paradoxical to speak of a "corner" of a spherical object – until we remember that, to Nostradamus' contemporaries, the moon was a flat plate. We now know that although it is a ball that revolves round the Earth, the Moon does not rotate on its own axis, so it always presents the observer with the same "face". The Sea of Tranquillity, where Apollo 11 landed, is in the upper left-hand corner of that face.

The "strange land" of line two is certainly an apt description of the barren lunar surface on which the astronauts touched down (or in Nostradamus' words, were "placed").

Various writers have connected lines three and four with the Challenger shuttle disaster. On 28 January 1986, seventy-three seconds after take-off, this space shuttle exploded, killing the six NASA crewmen and a young teacher called Christa McAuliffe – the first civilian to be invited on a NASA space mission. Francis X. King suggests that the "unripe fruit" mentioned in the third line is a reference to the faulty shuttle design that led to the disaster. He also concludes that the "great shame", mentioned in line four, was the public anger (and a cut in funding to NASA) over the incident – the "great praise", he suggests, was the public enthusiasm for Neil Armstrong and his fellow moon-walkers.

Conspiracy theorists have added another interpretation to the words about "great shame" – in fact, two. The first is the suggestion that the moon missions never actually took place. Discovering that the mission was not technically possible with their underdeveloped ("unripe") technology, NASA, they claim, faked the landing at a secret movie set in the Nevada desert.

The other theory involves the so-called "Face on Mars". In 1976, NASA scientists studying the Viking Mars-Orbiter photographs found what they thought looked like a mile-long construction on Martian surface. This object appeared to be a giant sculpture of a human face looking directly upwards. Ever since then, the "Faceists" (as they call themselves) have argued that there is a cover-up of evidence of alien artefacts found by NASA and the Soviet Space Agency. They suggest that the governments involved do not believe that the mass of the human race is psychologically mature enough to face the vast implications of the finding of the remains of extraterrestrial civilisations – one might say that they think we are the "unripe fruit" Nostradamus speaks of.

If either of these theories were true, it would certainly involve "great shame" for the governments involved. In which case, presumably the conspiracy theorists who revealed the hoax would reap the "great praise".

The Iran-Iraq War, 1980 to 1988
V.25

> Le prince Arabe Mars, Sol Venus, Lyon,
> Regne d'Eglise par mer succombera:
> Devers la Perse bien pres d'un million,
> Bisance, Eygpte, ver. serp. invadera.

Translation:

> The Arab prince Mars, Sun, Venus, Leo,
> The Kingdoms of the Church overcome from the sea,
> Towards Persia very near a million,
> Turkey, Egypt ver. serp. invades.

This quatrain seems to be one of the most chillingly accurate in the *Centuries*.

In September 1980, Iraq invaded its giant neighbour Iran. Iraqi President Saddam Hussein ("the Arab prince") was prompted by greed for land, by the belief that Iran (having just suffered bloody Islamic revolution) would be militarily weak, and by a fear that their Islamic fundamentalism would be exported to his own repressed population.

Initially Iraq – a nation between landlocked Iran and the seas of the Mediterranean and the Persian Gulf – did well. As it says in line two, "the Kingdoms of the Church" (Islamic, priest-led

Iran) were "overcome from [the direction of] the sea". However, the Iranians rallied their nation and, by 1982, had driven the Iraqi troops out of Iran.

The war continued because Iran wanted to punish Iraq. This led to more than five years of brutal fighting, much of it from World War One-style trenches, with both sides employing poison gas.

The directions Nostradamus gives are quite correct in the context of this conflict. The Iraqis attacked towards "Persia", the old name for Iran, beyond which (to the north-north-west) lay "Turkey". The Iranians, on the other hand, directed their attacks towards Baghdad – beyond which (to the south-west) lay "Egypt". Although both Turkey and Egypt were not directly involved in the Iran-Iraq War, it is possible that the seer is indicating the sweeping directions of attack. (It should also be noted that neither Iran nor Iraq existed in Nostradamus' day, so he would presumably have been vague about their precise boundaries.)

The first line gives one of Nostradamus' astrological combinations, which David Ovason suggests are a complex method of dating the predictions. This conjunction of Mars, the Sun and Venus in the House of Leo is rare. The last such event was on 20 August 1987.

The Iran-Iraq War actually lasted into 1988, but United Nations peace resolution 598 – whose acceptance by Iran signalled the end of the conflict – was passed on 20 July 1987.

Erica Cheetham suggests that "ver. serp." may be short for "vera serpens" (Latin for "true serpent"), perhaps an unflattering description of Saddam Hussein.

Exact casualty figures in the eight-year conflict could not be ascertained by either side; Nostradamus' figure, "near a million", is as close as the Iranians and Iraqi can come themselves.

The Fall of Soviet Communism, 1989
V.81, IV.32 & II. 89

> *L'oiseau royal sur la cité solaire,*
> *Sept mois devant fera nocturne augure:*
> *Mur d'Orient cherra tonnerre esclaire,*
> *Sept jours aux portes les ennemis à l'heure.*

Translation:

> The royal bird over the city of the sun,
> Seven months together gives nightly warnings:
> The Eastern wall will fall and lightning shines,
> Seven days the enemies shall be at the gate.

Growing unrest in the Soviet Bloc countries in the 1980s led Russian president Mikhail Gorbachev to introduce sweeping political and economic reforms. One by one the former Soviet client states followed suit. Revivified opposition parties then swiftly – and usually bloodlessly – toppled one absolute communist government after another.

The Berlin Wall had been a symbol of repression and anti-western paranoia since it was erected in a single night on 13 August 1961. Berlin, although deep within communist Eastern Germany, had been split down the middle in the post-war agreement between Stalin, Churchill and Truman. The prosperous, capitalist, western-ruled half of the city was a permanent temptation to East Berliners. The Wall, with its watch towers and machine-gun nests, was erected down the thirty-mile, east-west city boundary by the East German government to prevent East Berlin from becoming totally deserted. Between 1961 and 1989, at least seventy people were killed trying to cross the wall.

In 1989, Hungary suspended its border agreement with East Germany, and allowed thousands of East German citizens to cross into Austria and thence West Germany. This exodus drastically undermined the authority of the East German government, and they were finally forced into holding free elections which, of course, they lost. The Berlin Wall was immediately torn down by joyous Berliners – often aided by the former border guards.

The first line could be a description of the Brandenburg Gate, a triumphal arch in the middle of Berlin, closed by the building of the Wall in 1961, and the "royal bird" the statue of a winged Angel of Victory that stands on top of the Gate. For Nostradamus, "the city of the sun" would be an accurate description of Berlin, the capital of north Germany, whose astrological ruler is Leo – the principal sun-sign.

Seven months "of warnings" is also a fairly accurate estimate of the period of demonstrations and minor riots, on both sides of the Berlin Wall, before the Wall came down.

> *Es lieux et temps chair un poisson donra lieu,*
> *La loi commune sera faicte au contraire:*
> *Vieux tiendra fort plus osté du millieu,*
> *Le Pánta chiona philòn mis fort arriere.*

Translation:

> In places and times when meat is replaced by fish,
> The common law will be against it:
> The old stands fast then is removed,
> The Things held in common among friends is set aside.

Soviet communism fell because its internal infrastructure was corrupt and rotten. As stated in line one, the Soviet population often had to eat fish because the state shops could not provide meat.

The "common law" of line two sounds like Nostradamus' way of speaking of common public opinion. As line three states, the old order stood fast until it was removed.[4] "*Panta, choina philon*" in line four is a Greek phrase that literally translates as "things shared in common among friends", an apt characterisation of the ideal of communism.

> *Un jour seront demis les deux grands maistres,*
> *Leur grand pouvoir se verra augmenté:*
> *La terre neufue sera en ses hauts estres,*
> *Au sanguinaire le nombre racompté.*

Translation:

> One day the two great masters will be friends,
> Their great powers will be increased:
> The new land shall be at the height of its power,
> To the man of blood the number is reported.

4 For three days in August 1991, the world looked on gloomily as Soviet military hard-liners attempted a *coup d'état* to return Russia to absolute communist rule. Fortunately, political reformers, led by future Russian president Boris Yeltsin, with the aid of the citizens of Moscow, peacefully disarmed the generals and went on with the dismantling of the communist, one-party government.

American president Ronald Reagan naturally welcomed the liberalization of Russia – a country he had described, only a few years earlier, as "the Evil Empire." There was a warm friendship between Reagan and Mikhail Gorbachev ("the two great masters will be friends").

Economically speaking, both the west and the east gained by the cessation of the cold war – military budgets were cut, allowing urgently needed funds to be siphoned elsewhere.

We have already encountered the term "new land" in Nostradamus (see *Century VIII*.74 above). Here, in line three, it also seems to indicate the United States, which became the world's most powerful country after the downfall of Soviet communism.

The "man of blood" of line four sounds like Mikhail Gorbachev, who had a large "port-wine" birthmark on his forehead. When Russia and America agreed to nuclear disarmament, observation teams from both sides checked that the missiles were genuinely destroyed, then reported the figures to their respective leaders.

1990s Political Environmentalism
III.76

> *En Germanie naistront diverses sectes,*
> *S'approcant fort de l'heureux paganisme,*
> *Le coeur captif et petites receptes,*
> *Feront retour à payer le vrai disme.*

Translation:

> In Germany diverse sects are born,
> Approaching very near to happy paganism,
> The heart captive and small receivings,
> They will return to pay the true tithe.

Although this quatrain has been linked to the creation of Protestant sects in the sixteenth century (Cheetham) and the rise of German fascism in the 1930s (de Fontbrune), I am personally inclined to see it as a reference to growth of political environmentalism in the last two decades of this century.

Most of Europe and America's political parties have embraced certain environmental policies, although they are often aimed simply at netting the "hippy" vote.

The first green-specific politician to win office in a national parliament was the Swiss, Daniel Brelaz, in 1979. In 1981, four "greens" were elected to the Belgian parliament. However, it was not until 1983, when Petra Kelly and twenty-seven other environmentalists were elected to the German Bundestag, that politicians realized to what extent environmentalism could be a vote winner. (This seems to be indicated by the reference to Germany in line one.) Since then, the environment has figured as widely in political debate as unemployment or defence spending.

As to "happy paganism", in line two, environmentalism has often been associated with nature worship, paganism, and even Wicca (white witchcraft).

Lines Three and four seem to suggest the gradual disillusionment experienced by greens faced with "small receivings" from uninterested or cynical governments. The result described in the last line – "they will return to pay the true tithe" – sounds like a reference to the immense cost of repairing the natural environment if the warning is unheeded.

Doomsday, July 1999
X.72

> L'an mil neuf cens nonante neuf sept mois,
> Du ciel viendra un grand Roi deffraieur.
> Resusciter le grand Roi d'Angolmois.
> Avant que Mars regner par bonheur.

Translation:

> In the year 1999 and seven months,
> From the sky will come the great King of terror.
> Resurrecting the great King of *Angolmois*.
> Before and after Mars will reign happily.

This has been one of the most quoted of the quatrains, and has (understandably) caused most apprehension. Writing, as I am, in the autumn of 1998, I must confess to considerable curiosity as to what the world will look like after July/August 1999 – while recognizing that I am writing for a reader who knows the out-come (or lack of it).

The first line is certainly unambiguous, and is one of the few times the prophet gives a specific date.

Line two is obviously the crucial one – who precisely is the great "King of terror", and why does he come from the sky? In the nineteenth century, the Second Coming or the advent of the Antichrist was feared. Following the publication of H. G. Wells' *War of the Worlds* in 1898, an attack by Martians became a popular alternative. The Cold War raised the spectre of a pre-emptive nuclear strike but, when this ended, this was replaced by fears of terrorist germ-warfare, meteorite strikes and, in an echo of the turn of the century, extra-terrestrial invasion.

The word *"Angolmois"* could be a reference to Angoumois, a province in south-western France, but since this area has never had a "King" of any note, the accepted view is that the word as an anagram of the French word *Mongolois*: "Mongols".

The only "King of the Mongols" Nostradamus would have been likely to have heard about was Genghis Khan. This thir-teenth-century warlord, with his wild horsemen from the steppes, conquered China, then turned his attention westward, marching across Persia and Turkey, and on into Europe as far as Germany. Even in Nostradamus's time, three Centuries later, the memory of Genghis Khan still made Europe shudder. Specifi-cally, Genghis Khan was probably the only person that Nos-tradamus could have known to be responsible for the slaughter of hundreds of thousands, perhaps millions of people.

Line four will come as no surprise to any student of modern history. "Mars", the god of war, has certainly had a "happy" reign in the late twentieth century. Yet, Nostradamus says this bloody rule will continue after 1999 – therefore we are not speaking of the end of the world . . .

19 The Future in Your Grasp?

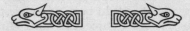

Chiromancy – foretelling the future by studying the hand – sounds, at first, even more absurd than astrology or divination by playing cards. Yet anyone who has had any experience of it knows that, for some reason, it actually seems to work.

I was present – although very young – when a palmist at the Blackpool fairground looked at my father's hand, and told him, among other things, that he should beware of an accident during the next week or so. She added that it would not be life-threatening, but that it could be dangerous. For the rest of that holiday, my father drove with unusual care.

About a week after we returned, we went out in the boat when the sea was choppy. Further out, it was rougher than it looked, and my father decided to go back home. My mother asked him to drop the rest of us off at a nearby beach, about 200 yards away. Long before we reached the shore, it became obvious that the sea was too rough to beach the boat. At that moment, the engine cut out, and a large wave picked us up and dumped the boat down on the rocks, which came straight through the bottom. No one was hurt – we were merely soaked and a little shaken. It was not until it was all over that we remembered the palmist's prediction.

But why should the lines on my palm predict the future any more than the scratches that form over the years on the face of my watch?

French palmists of the nineteenth century held the view that everyone is subconsciously aware of what the future holds for them, and the lines that form on the palm as the body matures reflect that future.

We will see in the last chapter that the Huna of Hawaii hold a similar belief. They believe that the "high self" (or superconscious mind) knows our future because it actually constructs it. In that case, there seems to be no good reason why this future should not be indicated on the palms of the hands (in fact, only the right hand is supposed to tell the future – the left is the character, what we are born with).

One of the best modern books on palmistry is *The Palmist's Companion: A History and Bibliography of Palmistry* by Andrew Fitzherbert (Scarecrow Press, Metuchen, New Jersey, 1992). The following account is indebted to Fitzherbert's introductory pages.

We have seen that, in the nineteenth century, the astrological revival was due to a French artillery officer named Paul Choisnard. The modern palmistry revival was also due to a French military man – a captain named Casimir D'Arpentigny who, in 1843, wrote a book called *La Chirognomie* (which means "knowledge of the hands"). Not long after that came *Les Mystères de la Main*, by Adrien Desbarrolles.

Palmistry, of course, did not begin with them. In a chapter called: "Where Did Palmistry Come From?", Fitzherbert offers short histories of ancient Chinese palmistry, as well as Arabic, Indian and European palmistry. He notes that European palmistry began during the late twelfth century, and that there are a dozen or so works in Latin. By 1600, palmistry was extremely popular yet, by 1700, it had almost vanished. The reason, presumably, is that the century of Newton and Leibniz came to regard it as so much nonsensical superstition.

After D'Arbentigny and Desbarrolles, palmistry suddenly achieved a new popularity during the great "magical revival" in the second half of the nineteenth century, when it was associated with such names as Eliphaz Levi, Rosa Baughan, Edward Heron-Allen, and, above all, the flamboyant Irishman who called himself Cheiro, and who claimed that his real name was Count Louis Hamon.

Cheiro may certainly have been highly inventive where his own biography was concerned, but he was undoubtedly one of the great palmists of all time. His work *You and Your Hand*

(1932) remains one of the best books on palmistry ever written.

Even Cheiro's real name is not certain, although it may well have been Louis Warner, the name under which he worked as a stage hand in a theatre when he first came to England. He was born in Ireland in 1866, went to England as a young man, and finally became a palmist in London at the age of twenty, setting himself up in Bond Street. He spread stories claiming that he had studied palmistry in India for two years, worked as an archaeologist in Egypt, and had toured Europe as a child. During this time, he claimed that he had been kidnapped by gypsies, because they saw at a glance that he was clairvoyant. All this is apparently untrue.

Soon he was claiming to be the Count Leigh de Hamong, but changed this to Louis Hamon before the First World War, because he felt that his original *nom de guerre* sounded German.

In 1900 he went to Paris, and read hands at the Paris Exhibition. Then he inherited a French vineyard and a champagne business and bought two Paris newspapers. One of these collapsed immediately, while the second, the *Anglo-American Register*, aimed at Americans living in Paris, kept going until shortly before the First World War.

He became deeply interested in spiritualism and mediumship, and recorded many of his own experiences in *True Ghost Stories*. During this time, he also became interested in astrology, and was mainly interested in the sun signs.

According to Fitzherbert, Cheiro became a secret agent for the British Government and was in Russia before the Revolution of 1917, using his work as an occultist as his cover. This was the period when Rasputin and various other "mystics" were immensely popular in Moscow and St Petersberg, and Cheiro must have found it easy to make an impression. Fitzherbert states that he was "active in Russian politics prior to the overthrow of the Czar". He apparently ran the Russian postal service for a time and, after the war, began to travel in Asia and South America. It was during his travels that he met a widow named Mena Harris, and married her when he was almost fifty. They lived in Ireland, where Cheiro ran a chemical factory, which was burned down during the "troubles".

In the mid-twenties, Cheiro and his wife moved to Hollywood, where he had a contract to write silent film scripts – which unfortunately fell through with the arrival of talkies. He then turned once more to palmistry, and became the favourite palmist of many film stars. He died at his home in 1936, at the age of seventy, probably of lung cancer – he was a heavy smoker. Fitzherbert notes that a story told by Frank Edwards, in one of his "stranger than fiction" books, to the effect that Cheiro had been imprisoned for fraud and was found lying in the gutter one day, and died on his way to hospital, is apparently completely untrue.

One of the best modern astrologers, R. K. Naylor, wrote of him: "He would often tell the most amazing stories which would afterwards turn out to be true. Yet later he would casually mention some simple, quite believable thing which would turn out to be – well, poetic imagination!" Yet in spite of his Celtic imagination, Cheiro remains one of the greatest "occultists" of the late nineteenth and early twentieth century.

Adrien Fitzherbert, an Australian, describes how his own introduction to palmistry came at the age of fourteen, when he came across *The Complete Guide to Palmistry* by someone who called himself Psychos. Having studied this for a while, he began reading the hands of his school-friends, family and teachers, and was amazed how often he was right.

Certainly, palmists would claim that what they are doing is basically scientific, and could be picked up by anyone. Yet most good palmists will also agree that very often they simply "know" all kinds of things about someone's hand as soon as they take it in their own and stare at it. Sometimes, this works best the very first time, and tends to become diluted later.

If you look at either of your hands, but preferably at the left, you will notice that there are three major lines. One of these runs across the top of the hand parallel with the base of the fingers. This is the "heart line". Slightly further down, again running across the palm, is the "head line". Finally, running in a wide curve around the base of the thumb is the "life line".

The heart line, as the name suggests, is concerned with the affections. The head line is concerned with the mind and intellect. According to Cheiro, it can show in advance such things as brain deterioration. The Line of Life, according to Cheiro, "is that line traced what is called the ball of the thumb. By its position, depth, freedom from breaks, islands, length etc., may be judged the general health, constitution, and duration of life that may be expected."

Many people have a line that runs down from the second finger to the centre of the wrist – this is the Line of Fate. Cheiro says that it should be understood as the line of individuality or personality, and that it shows the character of the individual.

Parallel to this, running from the third finger downwards, there is the "Sun Line", which Cheiro also describes as the line of success. He remarks that a successful preacher may have this line, or a successful criminal.

The shape of the hand is regarded as just as important as the lines. Fitzherbert gives a good example of the way this operates. Describing a young man of twenty-two, he says:

"He races round on a motorcycle and has a casual job in an electronics shop. In his spare time, he is a research officer with the UFO Society, and gives absorbing lectures on the topic. He is friendly and popular and likes to chase women. All of this can be clearly perceived in his hands.

"The shape of the hand, with its almost square palm and long fingers, indicates a communicator. Lecturing and writing are common activities with hands of this type; known as the 'Air Hand', this type often features Loop fingerprints with a few long thin lines.

"There are gaps between his fingers, big spaces. This shows an independent, non-conformist approach. No wonder he goes in for motorbikes and flying saucers. His Loop fingerprints make him good-natured. The way he spreads his fingers out shows extroversion. This combination will make him reach out to people and run around a lot.

"What about the casual job? Well, his Fate Line is pretty weak, and keep in mind those gaps between the fingers. This man will not want to be tied down to much. Yet the print has a Loop of Seriousness, so he's not really a light-hearted guy, for all his unconventional ways. The unpaid job as research officer suits him nicely.

"Chasing women is not uncommon with young males. But check the strong Heart Line with the Girdle of Venus about it. Sex and love and romance are certainly heavy on his mind. The hand is broad across the base, which shows a love of physical pleasures as well as a strong libido."

Here we can see just how much a skilled palmist can see in the lines of a hand and in its shape.

Another example Fitzherbert gives is – as he says – a "complete eccentric". The hand is far less regular than that of the young motorcyclist, and Fitzherbert comments: "Even the most amateur Palmist could see that there is something wrong with this hand. The lines are all disturbed." He adds: "The whole hand is long and thin. This is a sensitive, highly strung formation. The hand is covered with lines showing a lot of restless nervousness. The little finger is very long, typical of a great talker. There are gaps between the fingers, as in the previous case, to show independence. The little finger is especially wide, revealing the trouble he has with his love-life."

By now, many readers will be feeling inclined to dismiss palmistry as pure delusion. But, like astrology, it has been subjected to scientific examination, and Fitzherbert devotes a whole chapter to it.

He speaks of "the first major statistical investigation of Palmistry", which was made by Elizabeth Wilson for her M. A. thesis at Columbia University, New York, in 1924. She took handprints from psychological college graduates, a number of institutionalized schizophrenics, and a number of grossly subnormal people, kept in an institution because of a low IQ. The first thing that she noticed was that the hands of the abnormal people had shorter lines than the hands of the normal people, and that the abnormal hands tended to contain far more breaks in the lines. She also discovered a study of schizophrenic hands that noted differences in hand shapes between sufferers from manic depression and those with schizophrenia.

Next came the Polish psychologist, Dr Charlotte Wolff, whose early studies concerned youths from a home for delinquent boys. Using careful statistical methods, she demonstrated the preponderance of defective features in their hands, especially structural defects in the little finger and abnormalities in the Fate Line (including the complete absence of this line). She made similar studies with schizophrenics and separate studies of catatonic schizophrenics. All these produced positive results, and she confirmed Wilson's findings as to the special prominence of Head Line abnormalities in mentally disturbed people.

Fitzherbert also speaks of the Israeli psychotherapist Ms Yael Haft-Pomrock who, since the 1980s, has submitted many papers on palmistry to psychological journals. In 1982, in collaboration with Doctor Yagal Ginath of Ben Gurion University, she made a study of the hands of hospitalized schizophrenics, comparing them with a control group of normal people, and found distinct differences. One of her students, Shoshand Ayzen, studied three groups of children, one normal, one suffering from mild learning disabilities, and one with acute learning problems, and showed that they could be clearly distinguished by their hand features.

So, like astrology, palmistry has been subjected to scientific analysis, and found to be basically sound.

Now in fact Cheiro had also been concerned with the implications of palmistry for abnormal psychology. In *You and Your Hand*, he has a section entitled "The Murderer's Mark", which begins by emphasizing that no line can be taken on its own – they need to be taken in association with other lines.

He is speaking about the way that the Head Line and the Heart Line can actually cross one another in the so called "murderer's mark".

"In the case under examination, these propensities became abnormal, the affectionate and natural desires became subjugated or completely annihilated, the result being an absolute disregard for other human beings. The subject on whose hands this mark appears becomes obsessed with the idea of obtaining money at any cost, and will stick at nothing to gratify this desire.

"In such an example, murder for gain becomes a methodical study rather than the simple act of killing in a sudden outburst of passion or rage. This mark is more often found on the hands of those who use poison, or some other secret means of getting rid of their victims."

Cheiro goes on to say: "During my professional career, I came across several examples of the 'Murderer's Mark'. One instance was that of Doctor Meyer, who became known as 'the Chicago Poisoner'. Impressions on paper were brought to me on the occasion of my first visit to the United States by the reporters of the *New York World*, who wanted to test my powers."

Dr Henry Meyer, sentenced to life imprisonment in 1893, was involved in extremely complicated schemes to defraud the insurance companies by murdering people he had insured for large sums of money – including his wife's maid. His complex schemes involved persuading various associates to assume false names. His total number of victims – including criminal associates – seems to have amounted to about half a dozen.

"[The reporters] submitted about a dozen impressions of hands without giving the slightest clue as to whom the hands belonged. (In all these tests, I was successful in accurately describing the character and class of life each person lived.)

"When I came to the impressions of Meyer's hands, I was struck by the fact that the lines on his left were normal in every way, while on the right the Head Line had risen out of its place and cut into the Line of Heart . . . I summed up the impressions before me by stating 'The owner of these hands undoubtedly commenced his career in a normal way. He was even likely to have been a religious man in his early years.' I even ventured the idea that he might have commenced life as a Sunday School teacher. Later, the desire for wealth came into his brain, as distinctly shown by the upward trend of the Line of Head in the right hand. I went on to describe how his entire nature had changed under the continual urge to acquire riches at any cost until, finally, murder for money became as nothing in his eyes.

"My remarks noted down by the reporters were as follows: 'Whether this man has committed one crime or twenty is not the question. As he enters his forty-fourth year, he will be tried for murder and condemned to death. It will then be found that for years he has used his intelligence and whatever profession he has followed to obtain money by crime, and has stopped at nothing to achieve his ends. He will be sentenced to death, yet his hands show that his life will not end in this manner. He will live for years – but in prison.'

"When the interview appeared in the *New York World* it was disclosed that these hands I had read were those of Dr Meyer. He had just been arrested in his forty-fourth year, and a few weeks later was convicted of having used his profession as a doctor to poison wealthy patients whom he had insured for considerable amounts of money.

"He was sentenced to die by the electric chair. The sentence was appealed against. Three trials took place.

At the third, he was again condemned to death. A week before his execution, he requested that I would come and see him. I was taken to his cell in Sing-Sing, New York. As long as I live I shall never forget such an interview.

"'Cheiro,' gasped the now completely broken man, 'at that interview you gave the reporters, what you said about my early life was true. But you also said that although I would be sentenced to death my life would not end in that manner – that I would live for some years – but in prison. I have lost my third and last appeal – in a few days I am to be executed. For God's sake tell me if you stand by your words that I shall escape "the chair".'

"Even if I had not seen his Line of Life going on clear and distinct, well past his forty-fourth year, I believe I would have tried to give him some hope. Even though I could hardly believe what I saw, I pointed out that his Line of Life showed no sign of any break – so I left him, giving the hope that some miracle could still happen that would save him from the dreaded 'chair'.

"Day after day went past with no news to relieve the tension. The evening papers full of details for the preparations for the execution fixed for the next morning were eagerly bought up. I bought one and read every line.

"Midnight came. Suddenly boys rushed through the streets, screaming, 'Special edition'. I read across the front page, 'Meyer escapes the chair. Supreme Court finds flaw in indictment.' The miracle had happened – the sentence was altered to imprisonment for life. Meyer lived on for fifteen years. When the end did come, he died peacefully in the prison hospital."

Cheiro goes on to say: "Murder as the outcome of a sudden fit of passion may be foreseen by the summing up of various flaws of temperament whose cumulative effect will produce the ungovernable impulse to murder.

"One of these indications is what is known as the 'clubbed thumb', otherwise called the 'murderer's thumb'. The 'clubbed thumb' is so designated from the fact that it has every appearance of being a 'club', and the curious thing about it is that those who possess it generally kill their victim by employing a club or some heavy article to strike the fatal blow.

"The 'clubbed thumb' is in itself the signification of an animal nature. It indicates that people possessing such a formation have little or no control over themselves in a moment of rage or passion. They simply strike their enemy down when they 'see red' but, once the paroxysm is over, they frequently quickly regret their impetuous action."

One of the interesting things about this account is Cheiro's remark that Meyer's left hand showed no sign of this 'murderer's mark'. So obviously what is being suggested is that Meyer actually *developed* this mark as a result of focusing his attention on making money by crime.

All this is verified by a Canadian palmist called Gale Small-wood-Jones. In an essay called "Anatomy of a Serial Killer"[1], she describes how, in 1982, she was in a post office in Buffalo, New York, when she saw some posters of America's most wanted criminals.

She had been studying palmistry for over five years, and was therefore familiar with fingerprints. Her description of the fingerprints of criminals was "squirrilly" – which she defined as "sort of crooked and strange".

"For the next twelve months, I tried to get hold of more FBI posters. To no avail. I did not know anyone on the 'inside', and was told that the FBI did not release their information to Joe Q. Public."

Fifteen years later, her ex-husband – who happened to be Adrien Fitzherbert – sent her a copy of a book called *Crime and Mental Disease in the Hands*, by Paul Gabriel Tesla.

"I opened it up and found seventy-four of the most amazing hand-prints I had ever clapped eyes on. I think I gasped . . . I felt overwhelmed.

"Paul Tesla, working with the Bartow, Florida, Police Department, was able to obtain the hand-prints of some of the worst serial murderers and rapists in the American prison system. These include the prints of Ted Bundy, Charles Manson, Gary Heidnik and Wayne Williams. I took up his book again this year, during a winter storm

1 A copy of which she sent to my father, Colin Wilson, for reasons that will become obvious in its text.

which had me housebound. I carefully read the text which Mr Tesla had written about the killers' hands. He seemed to focus on the minutiae of skin ridge patterns. I saw something else.

"My first clue was in the opening pages of hand-prints. At first glance, I thought they were a left hand and right hand of the same person. Then I realized they were both right hands. Reading the text, I found that the two prints belonged to two different killers. Yet they could have been brothers, so identical were they. At the same time, I had never seen a hand-print like them. I took a deep breath and turned the pages.

"I am not a psychologist. In fact, I dropped out of High School and do not hold any degree in higher learning. But I knew I was looking at something important when, after twenty years of studying the human hand, I was given a sheaf of prints unlike any I have ever laid eyes on. I decided to go through a small number of hand-prints of killers, say thirty, and make notes on them. Looking at the unusual features, it was obvious that many of the hands shared the same traits. I made a list of what I consider to be the ten most outstanding features in the hands of these killers.

"Then I got a good night's sleep. The following day, I picked thirty random hand-prints of men whom I have printed over the years. (It was Cheiro who invented the method of taking palm prints in black ink.) These guys cover every socio-economic background, age and profession. I then went through each print to score my pals against the ten features found in killers' hands. The results were startlingly low. (Whew!) . . . I sent a letter to the FBI's Serial Killers Unit in Quantico, Virginia, but they did not answer. Who else would care?

"Not long after, my daughter asked me to look in on her cats. She is a bookworm, like every member of my family. On a shelf in her flat I saw the words, *Written in Blood*, and recognized one of my favourite authors, Colin Wilson. I opened the book at random as I poured from the box of Purina. The cats crunched as I read, '. . . The serial killer is a recognizable type; in case after case, the same patterns repeat themselves with almost monotonous regularity: deprivation of affection in childhood, sadism towards animals, fear and distrust of women, alcohol and drug abuse, resentment against society, high dominance, and the tendency to escape into a world of fantasy.'

"Jeez, that was pretty well the psychological profile I had found in their hand-prints. Then Mr Wilson quotes American psychologist Joel Norris, who has studied serial killers: '. . . The majority of serial killers are physically and psychologically damaged people . . . almost all of them have scars on their bodies, missing fingers, evidence of previous contusions and multiple abrasions on and around the head and neck area. Perversely, he is wishing for death . . . for he is suffering from a disease that is terminal, not only for his numerous victims but also for himself . . . the serial killer can no more stop killing than a heroin addict can kick the habit.'

"Colin Wilson commented: 'All this would seem to suggest that the problem of serial killers is virtually insoluble – at least until some great social transformation has created a society in which there are no alcoholic parents or abused children.' Yes! But certainly not every abused child turns into a serial killer.

"And Norris again: '. . . As our understanding of the serial killer syndrome developed, we realized that these profiles could lead to the development of a diagnostic or prediction instrument that would identify individuals who might be at risk . . .' By now I was nearly shaking. Everything I was reading about convicted killers had been evident in the killers' hand-prints I'd found in Paul Tesla's book.

"I decided to write to Colin Wilson and tell him what I had told the FBI about the hand-prints of the killers. He replied immediately and asked me to put it all in writing. Since it will take a book to present this information properly, I will give the briefest outline of what I found in the hands of the killers.

THE RECIPE FOR A SERIAL KILLER
(A psychological profile taken from the hand-prints of thirty killers)

"*Take one unwanted child.* Give him parents who have no inclination to love or nurture. Make the parents so wrapped up in their own neuroses and/or addictions that they only notice the boy when he needs to be punished. Make that punishment brutal. Add sexual abuse at an early stage so that the child has no possibility of knowing what 'normal love' may be. Mix well in an atmosphere of poverty, emotional deprivation and constant betrayal. Give the child physical handicaps, a gimpy leg, bug eyes or a stutter. As he grows into a man, bless him with a powerful natural energy and strength that finds no healthy outlet. Throw in a strong inclination to indulge the baser instincts – sex, drugs and thrill-seeking – and make him, like an eternal child, want them *now*. Toss in a natural proclivity to throw caution to the winds along with the feeling that he is 'a boat without an anchor'. Make this guy a Doer; *he has energy to burn*, and anger like you wouldn't believe. Although he suffers from an inferiority complex, his 'dominant' nature puts a chip on his shoulder and makes him feel aggressive inside. Give this man a short fuse. What you have is a time bomb waiting to go off.

"But there is more to complete the picture. The above RECIPE is what *shaped* these men, basically environmental causes. There are three additional clues from my list of ten most common features which may have a genetic or medical base. Since I am not a scientist or a doctor, I do not know for sure. These clues are found in the dermatoglyphic patterns of the fingerprints and in the swelling found in both the fingers and the thumbs of the killers.

"In 1892, the world-famous palmist, Cheiro, published a book in which he described 'the Murderer's Thumb'. Then, in 1901, W. G. Benham produced an impressive study of thumbs in which he corroborated Cheiro's theory about 'the Clubbed or Murder's Thumb'. Both men were careful to stipulate that this condition is only dangerous when found on 'a poor hand'. When it is found on an otherwise healthy, well-balanced individual, there is no fear of having found a killer. But the owner will certainly be known for his or her temperamental outbursts. The great English stage designer, Gordon Craig, had a superb pair of Clubbed Thumbs. He was a powerful and gifted man, tall and handsome, but he burned many personal bridges when he went into uncontrollable rages.

'Of my thirty hand-prints of killers, eighty-seven per cent of them have a variation of the Swollen or Clubbed Thumb. Of my thirty male friends, there is *not one* with this distinctive characteristic. This thumb pattern is thought to occur in about one in every hundred persons.

"Unusual fingerprint patterns were found in ninety per cent of the killers' hands, but in only seventeen per cent of the control group of male hands. And the Swollen Fingertips (said to indicate excess energy and possibly an enlarged heart – a condition similar to Reynaud's Disease) were found on fifty-five per cent of the killers, as opposed to only three per cent of my men friends.

"I quote from Erin Pizzey's book *Prone to Violence*, (Hamlyn Paperbacks, 1982), written after she had worked with battered families for ten years. 'It is not the physical attacks that do the worst of the damage; it is the slow destruction of a human soul in the hands of people already suffering from their own violent natures . . . In bringing up children, you may slowly decimate any sense of self they have, so that their inner world is destroyed. And then you commit the equivalent of soul murder, and the resulting adults will be the walking dead.' And in another paragraph, she describes the psychological results of a violent childhood. 'What they need is for society to understand that the chaos, anarchy and drama of the violent relationships which they have lived through has created with them a *special urge* (my italics) to continually relive the excitement of what they have left behind.'

"So what does all this mean? It would appear to indicate that a serial killer is both born and made. All of them fall within a socio-economic category which ensures they will receive minimum aid or attention. More important, if the patterns which are most significant, the ones which occur so seldom in ordinary men but so commonly among the killers, can be studied by the scientific and medical communities, there is a strong possibility that these men can be helped."

Undoubtedly, what Gale Jones has discovered is staggering. At the same time, it is so amazing that the average person is bound to dismiss it as some kind of delusion.

What she is saying takes us to the heart of one of the main

topics of this book – how far human beings are shaped by their environments, and how far they can actually shape themselves. When we have discussed synchronicity, we have pointed out that it looks as if the unconscious mind is somehow able to shape events – either that, or there is some little spirit dancing around us and shaping them for us.

Again, the whole subject of "psychometry" – the way that events are somehow able to imprint themselves on things connected with them, so that a good psychometrist can "read" them when he holds an object in his hand – seems to suggest that matter can actually be moulded by our mental states.

Now, we have the science of palmistry widely regarded as a superstition or a confidence trick, apparently telling us that our minds, and the events of our life, can somehow shape the palm of the hand.

This obviously raises many questions. We presume that people who have clubbed thumbs are born with them. So, in this case, it seems obvious that what we might call the "hand evidence" precedes the events that seem to be related to it. On the other hand, Cheiro is saying that the right hand of the poisoner Meyer has somehow changed as he becomes increasingly obsessed with the idea of obtaining wealth by crime.

And what about the fingerprints that Gale Jones saw in the Buffalo Post Office? Fingerprints form fairly early in life, and remain the same for the rest of our lives. So presumably the fingerprints of serial killers like Ted Bundy, Charles Manson and Gary Heidnik (who imprisoned and murdered a number of women in Philadelphia in the 1970s) showed signs of violence from birth.

If, in fact, Gale Jones's conclusions were accepted by the FBI and other police forces, we might well find serial killers arguing that they're not guilty because they were not born with the "murderer's mark" on their hands.

Presumably the solution here is similar to the one we have already considered in the chapter on astrology. Most astrologers would assert that our horoscopes only determine what *kind* of a person we are. Yet every baby who is born at the same moment does not live the same lives as all the others. There are obviously many other factors that determine who we are and what we do.

If Gale Jones is correct about the importance of fingerprints and palm prints and the shape of the hand, then it would seem that fate – or some other force – has imprinted our destiny on us in precisely the same way as the positions of the planets at the moment of birth. It seems to be an example of what Hermes Trismegistos meant by: "As above, so below."

Only one thing seems unarguable: that the criminal is a person with a fairly low level of self-control, and therefore with a limited capacity for freedom. Perhaps this is the answer to the various paradoxes that arise when we discuss astrology, palmistry, and the mystery of time. We can only understand them when we recognize that the answers do not lie in the purely physical realm, like the answers to problems in physics or chemistry. The answers lie in the human capacity for freedom, and in the individual's determination to exercise it.

Cheiro himself obviously recognizes these two factors: the element in individual destiny defined by character, and the element defined by choice. His advice to those who intend to study palmistry is as follows: "To be able to read character alone is helpful to all, but to be able to look far into the future and aid others by counsel and advice is something so nearly divine that the recompense this study gives is beyond all price."

20 Nostradamus and the Future

There is an important question we have yet to address: does Nostradamus offer us any clues to *how* he actually foresaw the future?

In *Nostradamus: Prophecies for Present Times?* (1985), David Pitt Francis offers one of the most systematic analyses of the *Centuries* so far. He splits the predictions into two sets – long-term and short-term – and examines them, virtually word by word, with a statistical approach. For example, he assembles the magical and astrological references, and shows that – contrary to popular belief – the predictions contain a comparatively small proportion of such mystical material.

He also argues that many of the quatrains containing political, geographic and ecclesiastical information can be interpreted as short-term predictions concerning Nostradamus's own period, not sweeping predictions of far distant future events.

Francis then sets out to show that Nostradamus was a penetrating and well-informed commentator on contemporary history who, out of caution, disguised his political, social and religious opinions as opaque predictions of future events. The result was the Rorschach ink-blot effect we discussed earlier: how every commentator has managed to read his own period of history (and his personal views) into the quatrains. Francis goes on to argue that leaders like Napoleon and Hitler deliberately set out to try to fulfil their personal interpretations of

Nostradamus's predictions – leading, they hoped, to their personal glorification.

Nostradamus: Prophecies for Present Times? sounds like the rationalist's answer to the Nostradamus enigma – except that Francis feels obliged to admit that some of the quatrains actually foretell specific future events. He seeks to explain this by suggesting that Nostradamus copied them from Biblical predictions – which, oddly enough, he believes to be genuinely precognitive. This view may well be correct, but it is hardly logical to try to demonstrate one unproven assertion by depending on another.

So, regretfully, we have to acknowledge that Francis is doing what every other writer on Nostradamus has done – finding evidence for what he can personally accept in the *Centuries*. Apart from leaving no doubt that Nostradamus was a highly intelligent man with a wide knowledge of politics – which was already self-evident – Francis has shed little light on just how the Seer of Salon accurately foretold the future.

The obvious place to seek further enlightenment is Nostradamus's own writings. The very first two quatrains of the first book of the *Centuries* seem to be a guide to how he saw into the future. *Century I*, quatrain 1 reads:

> Estant assis de nuict secret estude,
> Seul reposé sur la selle d'aerain:
> Flambe exiguë sortant de solitude,
> Fait prosper qui n'est à croire vain.

Translation:

> Sitting at night in secret study,
> Alone reposing over the brass tripod:
> A slender flame emerges from the solitude,
> Making prosper that which is not in vain.

The meaning of the first line seems self-evident, and we know from other sources that Nostradamus always conducted his studies at night. Line two may remind readers of the Delphic oracle. The pythia, we recall, sat on a bronze tripod above the sacred fissure in the ground, from which emerged mystical vapours. Any classically educated contemporary of Nostradamus would have recognized the mention of a brass tripod.

The last two lines are harder to interpret. Line 3 might suggest the arrival of a precognitive vision in the gloom or, more mundanely, that the seer is lighting a brazier – perhaps, it has even been suggested, containing hallucinogenic herbs. The last line is usually taken to mean that Nostradamus knew that the *Centuries* would "prosper" and that his prediction would not, ultimately be "in vain".

Century I, quatrain 2:

> *La verge en main mise au milieu des BRANCHES,*
> *De l'onde il moulle et le limbe et le pied:*
> *Un peur et voix fremissant par les manches:*
> *Splendeur divine. Le divin pres s'assied.*

Translation:

> The wand in hand is placed in the middle of the
>   BRANCHES,
> He moistens with water his foot and garment hem:
> A fear and voice makes him tremble in his sleeves,
> Splendour divine. The divine sits near.

The last two lines are probably poetic descriptions of the terrifying, but euphoric effect of Nostradamus's predictive practices on his senses, while the religious aspect of the last line is unmistakable.

The last word of the first line seems to be another of the seer's historical allusions – "BRANCHES" in capitals underlining the hint. Branchus was a demi-god in Ancient Greek mythology. He possessed the gift of prophecy and could bestow it upon his followers. The fourth-century chronicler Iamblichus of Chalcis gives the following description of the prophetic rite of the Branchus worshippers:

> "The prophetess of Branchus either sits upon a pillar, or holds in her hand a rod bestowed by some deity, or moistens her feet or hem of her garment with water . . . by these means . . . she prophesies. By those practices she adapts herself to the god, whom she receives from without."

The similarity to lines one and two of the above quatrain is so obvious that one can only assume that Nostradamus had read Iamblichus. Whether he is actually suggesting that he received inspiration from Branchus is an open question, which in turn leads us to the subject of Nostradamus's religious beliefs.

Nowhere in his work can we confidently infer his personal convictions. Various commentators have seen in Nostradamus's writings evidence of faiths as diverse as Catholicism, Protestantism, Judaism, and Paganism – some have even hinted at intercourse with powers of darkness.

This latter theory points to *Century I*, quatrain 42 as evidence:

> *Le dix Kalende d'Avril de faict Gothique,*
> *Resuscité encor par gens malins:*
> *Le feu estainct assemblé diabolique,*
> *Cherchant les os du d'Amant et Pselin.*

Translation:

> The tenth of the Calends of April calculated Gothic,
> Resuscitated by the wicked people:
> The fire put out, a diabolical assembly,
> Seek for bones of the demon of *Pselin*.

We have already considered the meaning of the first line in Chapter 9 (Nostradamus seemed to have foreseen Pope Gregory XIII's calendar change that was implemented decades after the seer's death). This quatrain also seems to offer another hint as to Nostradamus's predictive methods. The last line almost certainly refers to the Byzantine philosopher Michael Psellus, who wrote *De Demonibus*. In spite of its lurid title, this tome was in fact a treatise on the history of magic. The passage Nostradamus had in mind could be the following, from Psellus's section on the history of prophecy:

> "There is a type of predictive power in the use of the basin, known and practised by the Assyrians . . . Those about to prophesy take a basin of water, which attracts the spirits of the depths. The basin then seems to breathe as with sound . . . Now, this water [in] the basin . . . excels a power

imparted to it by the charms which have rendered it capable of being imbued with the energies of the spirits of prophecy . . . a thin voice begins to utter predictions. A spirit of this sort journeys where it wills, and always speaks in a low voice."

From other hints the seer dropped, it seems likely that he used a bowl of water much as a fortune-teller might use a crystal ball (see the discussion on "scrying" in Chapter 7).

The mention of Psellus's church-forbidden treatise on magic could have led Nostradamus to a charge of heresy. So it is possible that the "wicked people" referred to are those from whom he had to disguise the reference. Which in turn might mean that the Catholic church was the "diabolical assembly" who sought to extinguish the "fire" of knowledge. Again, we are reduced to guessing, probably just as Nostradamus meant us to be.

Yet there is one quatrain – *Century II*, quatrain 13 – that seems to be a direct (if still obscure) statement of Nostradamus's religious beliefs:

> *Le corps sans ame plus n'estre en sacrifice.*
> *Jour de la mort mis en nativité:*
> *L'esprit divin fera l'ame felice,*
> *Voyant le verbe en son eternité.*

Translation:

> The corpse without soul no longer at the sacrifice.
> At the day of death it is brought to birth:
> The spirit divine makes the soul rejoice,
> Seeing in the word eternity.

The first line may be seen as a direct rejection of Catholic belief. On the Day of Judgement, the souls and bodies of the dead will, according to the *Book of Revelations*, rise from the grave. So for Nostradamus to speak of a corpse without an attached soul might have been regarded as heresy if it had been stated in a more direct fashion.

Line two has been seen as a statement of Nostradamus's faith: reincarnationism. Specifically, he seems to say that the soul of a dead person is "brought to [re]birth" on the day of his death.

If this is so, then line three can be interpreted as an echo of the Buddhist belief in the "Great Soul": that universal entity with which all lesser souls struggle to blend through gradual purification over numerous lives. So the last line sounds like a depiction of the Nirvanic state – in which the universe and eternity can be viewed as one by the purified soul.

On the other hand, a Catholic could choose the opposite interpretation. The first line means that the dead can no longer attend Mass ("the sacrifice"). Lines two and three offer hope, showing the departed soul "rejoice[ing]" through "[re]birth" to the "spirit divine." Line four is an echo of the first words of the Bible: "In the beginning was the word . . ." Thus Nostradamus may be saying that the soul attains "eternity" through the word of God.

Typically, Nostradamus manages to create fertile ground for argument, but does not leave enough clues to allow anyone to reach definite conclusions.

The magic practices Nostradamus describes are straight out of antiquity, but leave us none the wiser about how precognition might be attained. Perhaps, where Nostradamus was concerned, it was not "attained", but came naturally – in fact, in his Epistle to Henri II, he says: "I will confess, Sire, that I believe myself capable of presage [precognition] from the natural instincts of my ancestors . . ."

Perhaps, like Mother Shipton, Kenneth Mackenzie and Edward Kelly, Nostradamus was a "natural seer". Any ceremonies he conducted simply helped to focus his inborn talents. This would suggest that genuine prophets are not made, but can only be born.

The Millennium Bug, Midnight 31 December 1999
I.22

> *Ce que vivra et n'ayant ancien sens,*
> *Viendra leser à mort son artifice:*
> *Austun, Chalan, Langres et les deux Sens,*
> *La gresle et glace fera grand malefice.*

Translation:

> That which lives but has no senses,
> Will cause its own death through artifice:
> Autun, Chalan, Langres and the two Sens,
> Hail and ice cause great damage.

Francis X. King makes the thoroughly up-to-date suggestion that this description of something that lives without senses could be Nostradamus's attempt to describe a computer. He further suggests that the "death through artifice" in the second line could be reference to computer viruses – the "artifice" being the efforts of hackers to vandalize the information stored in other people's systems.

However, the wintry conditions mentioned in line four and the implication of "death" rather than just inconvenience (most viruses are simply irritating, not catastrophic) sound to me like a prediction of the "Millennium Bug".

For a long time, computer hardware designers failed to realize that, since their programs could not recognize the turn of the century, the internal clocks in their silicon chips would go haywire during the first second of the new millennium. Literally uncounted numbers of silicon chips across the globe could fail at this moment – nobody, at the time I am writing in 1998, has any idea what the result will be.

Over the last twenty years, "millennium bugged" chips were wired into almost every vital system on the planet, but nobody thought it necessary to note where many of these theoretically everlasting chips were. The simple problem of detection and replacement of all these chips will be a tremendous task in itself, especially after 1 January 2000.

The least consequence we can expect – in our computer-dependent society – will be systems like traffic lights and our household appliances failing *en masse*. The worst is the Armageddon scenario of the world stock market collapsing, most power stations and water pumping stations failing, a famine created by lack of refrigeration, hospitals plunged into inactivity and a worldwide collapse of social and organizational systems – all this beginning, literally, in the blink of an eye.

An article in the American magazine *Wired* (August 1998)

reports that many of the computer specialists hired to deal with the "bug" have given up the project and are purchasing remote farm shacks, personal electricity generators, large quantities of tinned food and shotguns . . .

Natural Disasters

The following are some of the many Nostradamus predictions that seem to deal with natural – or possibly man-made – disasters. As with the other quatrains examined in this chapter, none have a specific date or historical detail to tie them to a past event, so I am listing them as "yet to come to pass".

Floods and Droughts
I.17, III.12, IV.67 & IX.31

Global warming – which, as at the time of writing, has yet to be conclusively proved – might reduce some areas of the globe to deserts while, at the same time, melting the polar icecaps and flooding lowland areas.

> Par quarante ans l'Iris n'apparoistra,
> Par quarante ans tous les jours sera veu:
> La terre aride en siccité croistra,
> Et grans deluges quand sera aperceu.

Translation:

> For forty years the rainbow will not appear,
> For forty years it will appear every day:
> The dry earth will grow more parched,
> And there will be great floods when it is seen.

The biblical reference to God's rainbow, which signalled the end of the Great Flood, is plain. Whether the seer was also using the figure "forty years" as a poetic echo of the Bible's "forty days and forty nights", or is literally predicting four decades of flooding and drought, is a matter of opinion.

Par la tumeur de Heb, Po, Tag, Timbre et Rosne,
Et par l'estang Leman et Arentin,
Les deux grands chefs et citez de Garonne,
Prins mors noyez. Partir humain butin.

Translation:

By the swelling of the Ebro, Po, Tagus, Tiber and Rhone,
And the lakes of Geneva and Arezzo,
The two chief cities of the Garonne,
Taken, dead, drowned. Human booty divided.

The Ebro and Tagus rivers are in Portugal, the Po and Tiber in Italy and the Rhone in France. Geneva is in Switzerland and Arezzo in central Italy. The two chief towns of the Garonne region (with such grim futures) are Bordeaux and Toulouse.

L'an que Saturne et Mars esaux combuste,
L'air fort seiché longue trajection:
Par feux secrets, d'ardeur grand lieu adust,
Peu pluie, vent chault, guerres, incursions.

Translation:

In the year that Saturn and Mars are equally fiery,
The air is very dry long meteor:
From hidden fires a great place burns with heat,
Little rain, hot winds, wars, invasions.

The astrological configuration in the first line is a relatively common one, so specific dating of the prediction is not possible. Drought and wars at the time of a meteor or comet are foretold.

Les tremblement de terre á Montara,
Cassich saint George à demi perfondrez,
Par assoupie, la guerre esveillera,
Dans temple á Pasques abismes enfondrez.

Translation:

> The trembling of the earth at *Montara*,
> *Cassich* saint George shall be half sunk,
> Drowsy with peace, war arises,
> At Easter abysses open in the temple.

"*Cassich*" in line two could be a reference to the ancient Greek *Cassiterides*, or "Isles of Tin": their name for the county of Cornwall in Britain (the island of "saint George"). "*Montara*", where the earthquake originates that will leave the English southwest "half sunk", is hard to place. There is nowhere in Cornwall with this name, but it is worth noting that there is an inactive earth fault line that runs along the south Cornish coast. Local legend holds that, as recently as the tenth century AD, a major earthquake drowned a whole region of South Cornwall, called Lyonesse, beneath the Atlantic.

Famine
I.67 & III.42

> *La grand famine que je sens approcher,*
> *Souvent tourner, puis estre universelle :*
> *Si grand et long qu'un viendra arracher,*
> *Du bois racine et l'enfant de mamelle.*

Translation:

> The great famine I see drawing near,
> Turns one way then another, then becomes universal:
> So great and long that they pluck,
> The root from the tree and the child from the breast.

Unlike many of his often egotistical profession, Nostradamus was a seer who rarely used the personal pronoun. His use of it in this quatrain seems to make it all the more chilling.

> *L'enfant naistra à deux dents en la gorge,*
> *Pierres en Tuscie par pluie tomberont :*
> *Peu d'ans apres ne sera bled ni orge,*
> *Pour saouler ceux qui de faim failliront.*

Translation:

A child will be born with two teeth in his mouth,
It will rain stones in Tuscany:
A few years after there will be neither wheat nor barley,
To feed those that are weak with hunger.

Once again, Nostradamus seems to be dating this prediction by
a freak birth. It is not unknown for children to be born with a few
teeth – Louis XIV was, for example. Of course, the word "gorge"
can be translated as "throat" as well as "mouth" – this would
suggest an altogether more unpleasant birth abnormality, reminiscent of radiation or chemically induced mutation.

A Nuclear Meltdown in the Mediterranean?
II.3 & II.4

Pour la chaleur solaire sus la mer,
De Negrepont les poissons demi cuits:
Les habitans les viendront entamer,
Quand Rhod, et Gannes leur faudra le biscuit.

Translation:

By heat like the sun upon the sea,
Around Negrepont the fish are half broiled:
The inhabitants will cut them up,
When Rhodes, and Genoa are in want of biscuits.

According to Erica Cheetham, "Negrepont" is the Italian name
for the island of Ruboea. What form of "heat like the sun" is
involved is not clear, but it would take a vast amount of energy to
half-cook fish in open water. The possibly of the meltdown and
explosion of a nuclear engine, like those that power nuclear
submarines, naturally leaps to mind. Alternatives – such as
meteor or comet impacts with the earth – are equally alarming.
The second two lines seem to hint at starvation caused by the
disaster. "Entamer" literally means "to cut up" – perhaps this is a
description of the animal autopsies that would be a part of the
clean-up operation.

> *Depuis Monarch jusque aupres de Sicile,*
> *Toute la plage demourra desolée:*
> *Il n'y aura fauxbourg, cité ne ville,*
> *Que par Barbares pillé soit et volée.*

Translation:

> From Monaco as far as Sicily,
> All the sea coast will be left desolate:
> There shall be no suburbs, cities nor towns,
> Which will not be pillaged and violated by Barbarians.

There is no specific reason to link this prediction with the disaster of the preceding quatrain, other than that it follows directly in *Century II* and deals with roughly the same area of the world. If the predictions are connected, the last line may undermine the "nuclear meltdown" theory – looters would hardly risk stealing from an area affected by radiation.

Economic Collapse
VIII.28, IV.50 & X.81

Several of the quatrains seem to point to major international economic problems. Whether they refer to several such periods in history, or to one major economic crisis, is unclear.

> *Les simulacres d'or et argent enflez,*
> *Qu'apres le rapt au lac furent gettez,*
> *Au desouvert estaincts tous et troublez.*
> *Au marbre script prescript intergetez.*

Translation:

> The copies of gold and silver inflated,
> Which after the theft are thrown in the lake,
> Being discovered that all is destroyed by debt,
> All bond and scrip will be cancelled.

Paper money – "copies of gold and silver" – was undreamed of in Nostradamus's day, as was inflation, yet the seer seems to have foreseen these economic commonplaces of the future.

This prediction may already have happened. Lines three and four are reminiscent of the Third World Debt Crisis of the late 1980s. Throughout the 1970s, the world banks lent vast amounts of money to impoverished nations, then increased the interest payments to an impossible extent. Finally, when Mexico threatened to default, it was realized that the whole world economy could collapse as a result. (The banks relied on the regularity of the debt payments to secure their own borrowings – if the Third World nations had refused to pay *en masse*, the banks would have collapsed, taking every currency in the world with them). Partial debt-cancellation was hurriedly organized with the aid of the major governments (and their taxpayers' money) and the disaster was narrowly averted.

> *Libra verra regner les Hesperies,*
> *De ciel et terre tenir la monarchie:*
> *D'Asie forces nul ne verra paries,*
> *Que sept ne tiennent par rang le hierarchie.*

Translation:

> Libra will be seen to reign over the West,
> Holding the rule over heaven and earth:
> No one will see the strength of Asia fail,
> Until seven have held the hierarchy.

Libra is an astrological sign of wealth and prosperity. "*Hesperies*" literally means "the West", but also seems to be one of Nostradamus's codenames for America.

This quatrain may describe the 1997–98 collapse of the Asian "Tiger" economies. For many years, the forum of the world's seven most industrialized capitalist nations (Canada, France, Germany, Great Britain, Italy, Japan and the USA) was called "G-7" (for "Group 7"). In 1997, Russia applied to join the group and the title was changed to "G-8". This may be the end of the "hierarchy" of seven, mentioned by Nostradamus in the last line. Shortly afterwards, the previously bullish Asian-Pacific economies unexpectedly collapsed through bad investment and massive state corruption.

Mis tresor temple citadins Hesperiques,
Dans icelui retiré en secret lieu,
Le temple ouvrir les liens famelimilieu,
Reprens ravis proie horrible au milieu.

Translation:

A treasure placed in a temple by Western citizens,
Withdrawn within to a secret hiding place,
The hungry serfs will throw the temple open,
Recaptured and ravished a horrible prey in the middle.

Some commentators have suggested that this quatrain predicts a major economic crisis, which will prompt impoverished Americans to raid the Federal Gold Reserve. Given that, in an economy that has totally collapsed, food would be more valuable than gold, I have my doubts about this interpretation.

Future War

As the reader will have noticed, most of Nostradamus's quatrains are given over to predicting conflicts of one sort or another. Many writers, since the Second World War, have found clues in the *Centuries* pointing to a catastrophic, possibly terminal third world war, some time in the near future.

I personally see no evidence to back this conclusion.

Certainly, Nostradamus often predicted horrendous battles and great loss of life, but he never suggested that these quatrains should be linked to form a picture of a single, humanity-destroying Armageddon. On the contrary, he seems to suggest mankind still has at least a few thousand years ahead of it.

I suggest that the *Centuries* suffer from the same problem as military history books: no matter how well-written, a history consisting solely of one war after another will give the reader the impression that mankind is constantly in a state of conflict. While it is true that there is usually a war going on somewhere on the globe at any one time, concentrating on this aspect of history misses the fact that most people down the ages have lived peaceful lives.

The following are some of the seer's many non-specific military and warlike predictions. I include them in this chapter because all seem to have some modern or futuristic aspect.

War Towards the End of a Century
I.16

> *Faulx à l'estang joint vers le Sagitaire,*
> *En son hault auge de l'exaltation,*
> *Peste, famine, mort de main militaire,*
> *La siecle approche de renouvation.*

Translation:

> A scythe joined with a pond in Sagittarius,
> At the high of its ascendancy,
> Plague, famine, death from military hands,
> The century approaches its renewal.

The "scythe" is the sign of Saturn, and the "pond" (or lake) may be Aquarius. The quatrain seems to say that when Saturn is in Aquarius with Sagittarius at the noon position towards the end of a century, a terrible war will take place. Unfortunately, this astrological event is too common to give us a specific date.

Missiles or Submarines?
I.29

> *Quand la poisson terrestre et aquatique,*
> *Par fort vague au gravier sera mis:*
> *Sa forme estrange sauve et horrifique,*
> *Par mer aux mure bien tost les ennemis.*

Translation:

> When a fish that is both terrestrial and aquatic,
> By a great wave is thrown upon the shore:
> With its strange, smooth and horrible shape,
> From the sea the enemies soon reach the walls.

This quatrain has reminded modern commentators of sea-launched, intercontinental ballistic missiles or cruise missiles ("fish" that can travel over water and land). The second line suggests, on the other hand, a beached submarine.

Less alarmingly, Henry Roberts suggests that this is a prediction of the landing craft hitting the beaches during the Normandy, D-Day landings in World War II.

Peace Followed by War

> Les fleurs passés diminue le monde,
> Long temps la paix terres inhabitées:
> Seur marchera par ciel, serre, mer et onde,
> Puis de Nouveau les guerres suscitées.

Translation:

The plagues pass away the world grows smaller,
For a long time the lands are inhabited peacefully,
All will travel safely through the sky, the land and the sea:
Then wars will begin again.

This is a remarkable quatrain as it matter-of-factly predicts the advent of air travel. Line one even seems to quote the modern cliché that, as travel methods become faster, the world seems to be getting smaller.

A long period of peace, when "plagues" are eradicated and all travel is safe, has yet to materialize. Unfortunately – as the seer predicts – when it does, it won't last.

Air War
I.64

> De nuict soleil penseront avoir veu,
> Quand le pourceu demi-homme on verra:
> Bruict, chant, bataille, au ciel battre aperceu:
> Et bestes brutes à parler lon orra.

Translation:

> At night they will think they have seen the sun,
> When the pig half man is seen:
> Noise, chants, battles seen fought in the sky:
> And brute beasts will be heard to speak.

This quatrain sounds positively like science-fiction. Seeing the "sun" at night suggests a giant, possibly nuclear explosion or fire. A pig-like half-man could be a colourful description of a man in breathing gear – perhaps a pilot in an oxygen mask or a soldier in a gas mask. The third line may be a prediction of air battles, or it could be a portent of visionary sky battles, like that reported over the First World War Battle of Mons. The last line is very odd, but it could be a prediction of military vehicles with computerized voices or even a description of genetically enhanced animals.

Destruction in New York
I.87

> Ennosigee feu du centre de terre,
> Fera trembler au tour de cité neufue:
> Deux grands rochiers long temps feront la guerre,
> Puis Arethuse rougira nouveau fleuve.

Translation:

> Ennosigee fire from the centre of the earth,
> Will cause the new city to tremble:
> Two great rocks will war on each other for a long time,
> Then Arethuse will redden a new river.

"Ennosigee" in the first line is probably a distortion of the Greek word ennosigaeus, meaning "earth-shaker". Modern commentators generally translate the Nostradamus phrase "cité neufue" as "New York", although, of course, any newly built city could be meant.

"Arethuse" sounds like Arethusa, the Greek nymph who was transformed into a stream. Erica Cheetham, on the other hand, suggests it might be a cross between the word "Aries" (the Greek god of war) and the letters "USA".

War in the West
I.91

> *Les dieux feront aux humains apparence,*
> *Ce qu'il seront auteurs de grand conflict:*
> *Avant ciel veu serin espee et lance,*
> *Que vers main gauche sera plus grand afflict.*

Translation:

> The gods will make it appear to mankind,
> That they are the authors of a great conflict:
> The once serene sky will show sword and lance,
> The left will be the most afflicted.

"Sword and lance" in the sky, in line three, sounds like an exchange of missiles and/or warplanes. The political concept of "left" and "right" was unknown in the Nostradamus's day, but on European-made maps, the "left" is the western hemisphere, so several Nostradamus scholars have linked this quatrain with a war that damages American soil.

A Slaughter of Fugitives
III.7

> *Les fugitifs, feu du ciel sus les piques.*
> *Conflict prochain des corbeaux s'esbatans,*
> *De terre on crie aide secours celiques,*
> *Quand pres des murs seront les combatants.*

Translation:

> The fugitives, fire from heaven on their pikes.
> The next conflict will be that of the crows,
> They cry from the earth for heavenly aid,
> The soldiers draw near the walls.

The first three lines seem to paint a grim picture of fugitive troops[1] being fired on from above, leaving only crows to fight over their dead bodies.

In early 1991, a coalition of allies led by the USA waged the Gulf War to eject Iraqi troops from the small Arab state of Kuwait. By late February, the Iraqi army was in full retreat down the Kuwait–Iraq highway. Despite the fact that many of these troops were unarmed and therefore, under the Geneva Convention, refugees, the Allies killed thousands with air-strikes.

Germ Warfare
III.75

> Pau, Verone, Vicence, Sarragousse,
> De glaives loings terroirs de sang humides.
> Peste si grance à la grand gousse,
> Proche secours, et bien loing les remedes.

Translation:

> Pau, Verona, Vicenza, Saragossa,
> Foreign swords wet the land with blood.
> Plague will come in a shell,
> Though relief is near, the remedy is still far off.

Three of the places mentioned in the first line are in Italy, a country with a history of foreign invasions and plague outbreaks. (The same applies to Spain, where Saragossa is located.) The disturbing aspect of this quatrain is the word "*gousse*" in line three. This translates as "husk" or "shell". The implication – that the "plague" will come from a sealed container (possibly an artillery shell or a missile) – causes germ warfare to spring to mind. The last line seem to predict that, although there will be medical facilities for the afflicted, an actual cure for the plague will take a long time to find.

---

1 "Pikes" might be translated as any long weapon, such as rifles.

A Brutal Air Invasion of France
III.82

> Friens, Antibor, villes autour de Nice,
> Seront vastees fort par mer et terre,
> Les saturelles terre et mer vent propice,
> Prins, morts, troussez, pillés, sans loi de guerre.

Translation:

> Frejus, Antibes, the towns around Nice,
> Will be greatly devastated from sea and land,
> Locusts with favourable wind by land and sea,
> Captured, dead, trussed-up, plundered, without law of war.

The towns in the first line are in the South of France. There has only been one invasion of France from this direction since Nostradamus's day: the Allies' second French front in 1944. Unlike the Normandy landings, this assault went largely unopposed by the retreating Germans (since the troops encountered so little resistance, they dubbed the front the "Champagne Campaign"). The savagery – described in lines two to four – seems to rule out this easy-going invasion, so we must assume that this quatrain refers to the future.

The word "locusts", in line three, may be a poetic description of a modern piece of technology; given the context, airborne troop-carriers seems a reasonable assumption. The ignored "loi de guerre" ("laws of war") may be the Geneva Convention – a dire prediction for France.

Holy War in the Skies
IV.43

> Seront ouis au ciel les armes battre:
> Celui an mesme les divins ennemis:
> Voudrant loix sainctes injustement debatre,
> Par foutre et guerre bien croyans à mort mis.

Translation:

> Weapons will be heard fighting in the sky,
> In the same year the divines will become enemies:
> They will unjustly debate the holy laws,
> Through thunder and war the true believers will die.

Here Nostradamus seems to predict the advent of aerial warfare, almost as a subtext to a quatrain about a religious conflict. As already noted, it is difficult to pinpoint the seer's exact religious leanings, but here he plainly foresees "true believers" being bested and slaughtered in a modern war.

American War?
IV.95

> *La regne à deux laissé peu tiendront,*
> *Trois ans sept mois passée feront la guerre.*
> *Les deux vestales contre eux rebelleront,*
> *Victor puis nay en Armorique terre.*

Translation:

> The reign left to two they shall not hold it long,
> Three years seven months pass and they go to war.
> The two vestals rebel against them,
> The victor will be born on *Armorique* soil.

This quatrain foretells a falling-out between two great powers. Given the context, it is reasonable to suspect the word "vestals" in line three is actually a corruption of the word "vassals", and refers to two rebelling vassal nations or peoples.

The key word in this quatrain is *"Armorique"* in line four. Armorica was the ancient Roman name for Brittany. Yet most modern interpreters translate *"Armorique"* as "American." If they are correct, it is certainly a striking fact. The word "America" was only coined by the mapmaker and bogus explorer Amerigo Vespucci around 1512 (we now know he barely set foot across the Atlantic). The name did not come into common usage until at least a hundred years later, so it would be remarkable if Nostradamus indeed mentioned it in this quatrain.[2]

Understanding of the quatrain will probably only be possible after the event – just as the seer meant it to be.

Rocket Attacks on the West?
IV.99

> *L'aisné vaillant de la fille du Roy,*
> *Repoussera si profond les Celtiques:*
> *Qu'il mettra foudres, combien en tel arroi,*
> *Peu et loing puis és Hesperiques.*

Translation:

> The valiant eldest son of the King's daughter,
> Will drive the Celts back very far:
> He will use thunderbolts, so many in such an array,
> Few and distant then deep into the West.

The grandson of a leader will press the "Celts" very far, according to the first two lines. "*Celtiques*" is apparently used elsewhere in the *Centuries* to indicate the French.

Line three describes this man using arrays of "thunderbolts"; since line four describes them reaching "deep into the West", Erica Cheetham believes that this is a description of strategic missiles or battlefield rockets. The word "*Hesperiques*" is given a capital letter, indicating that it is a specific place. Henry Roberts suggests it is Spain – the far west of Europe – but most other Nostradamus commentators translate the word to mean America.

Chemical War in Greece
V.90

> *Dans les Cyclades, en Corinthe et Larisse,*
> *Dedans Sparte tout le Pelloponnesse:*

2 In fact, he certainly seems to have done so in a later quatrain (see X.66 below).

Si grand famine, peste par faux connisse,
Neuf mois tiendra et tout le chevronesse.

Translation:

In the Cyclades, Corinth and Larissa,
In Sparta and all the Peloponnese:
Shall be great famine, plague through false *connisse*,
Nine months throughout the whole peninsula.

The places described in this quatrain are all in southern Greece. A catastrophe is plainly predicted, but its cause is harder to guess; the words "false *connisse*" are clearly the key to the mystery. "*Connisse*" could mean "exertion" (from the Latin *connissus*) or "dust" (from the Greek *konis*). Given the context, the latter seems more likely.

"False dust", Erica Cheetham suggests, might indicate a man-made plague and famine – i.e. chemical or biological warfare. However, it is worth noting that Nostradamus also uses the image of a plague combined with a famine in *Century II*, quatrain 6 (see the chapter on Nostradamus and the twentieth century). There, apparently predicting the atom-bomb destruction of Hiroshima and Nagasaki, he describes "famine within plague". If we are right to see this as a prediction of the effects of radiation poisoning, we might be justified in seeing "false dust" as nuclear fallout.

The ill-maintained, former Soviet nuclear power stations in the Balkans spring to mind . . .

Aerial Bombing
VI.34

Du feu volant la machination,
Viendra troubler au grand chef assiegez :
Dedans sera telle sedition,
Qu'en desespoir seront les profligez.

Translation:

The machine of flying fire,
Will trouble the besieged great chief:

> Within there will be so much sedition,
> That those abandoned will be in despair.

The "machine of flying fire" in line one is reminiscent of twentieth-century bomber aircraft. Unfortunately, there is no indication as to which conflict the quatrain might refer to. The London Blitz in World War Two is one possibility; thus making Prime Minister Winston Churchill the "besieged great chief", in line two. However, the Nazi attempts to break British morale by mass bombing raids failed – in contradiction to the prediction of lines three and four.

Another candidate for this quatrain is the mass bombing of Baghdad during the 1991 Gulf War (this time with President Saddam Hussein as the "great chief") but, again, the morale of the Iraqi civilians held, despite the devastation.

The Burning of New York
VI.97

> *Cinq et quarante degrés ciel bruslera,*
> *Feu approcher de la grand cité neufve,*
> *Instant grand flamme esparse sautera,*
> *Quant on voundra des Normains faire preuve.*

Translation:

> The sky will burn at forty-five degrees,
> Fire approaches the great new city,
> On the instant a great scattered flame leaps up,
> When they will want proof of the Normans.

There are several possible cities sited around the forty-fifth parallel, to which this prediction may point. For example, the description in line three of "scattered" fire is reminiscent of the Great Chicago Fire of 1871, when high winds spread flames faster than they could be put out and 17,500 houses were destroyed in a single night.

The description of an "instant . . . great . . . flame" has struck many modern commentators as a sixteenth-century description of an atomic explosion. This interpretation places the prediction squarely in the future, as Hiroshima and Nagasaki are nowhere near the forty-fifth parallel.

New York City (*"cité neufve"*) is between the fortieth and forty-fifth parallels.

The Poisoning of New York
X.49

> *Jardin du monde au pres du cité neufue,*
> *Dans le chemin des montaignes cavees,*
> *Sera saisi et plongé dan la Cuve,*
> *Beuvant par force eaux soulfre envenimees.*

Translation:

> Garden of the World near the new city,
> In the road of the hollow mountains,
> It will be seized and plunged into the Tank,
> Forced to drink water poisoned with sulphur.

The phrase "new city", in line one, has convinced many people that this quatrain describes the poisoning of New York (the phrase also occurs in I.87 and VI.97 above) but, of course, any newly built metropolis might be referred to.

Nevertheless, Francis King points out that New York's neighbour, New Jersey, has dubbed itself "the Garden State" in recent years ("Garden of the World near the new city"). Also, the phrase "road of the hollow mountains", in line two, certainly sounds like a description of New York's wide streets running beneath towering skyscrapers.

The last two lines seem to be a prediction that somebody will poison the city's water supply with "sulphur" (just as hippies threatened to pour a pint of LSD into Chicago's city reservoir in 1968).

Famine and Chaos from Space
VI.5

> *Si grand Famine par unde pestifere.*
> *Par pluie Longue le long du pole arctique,*

Samarobrin cent lieux de l'hemisphere,
Vivront sans loi exempt de pollitique.

Translation:

The great Famine by a pestilent wave.
Through Long rain will come the length of the arctic pole,
Samarobrin a hundred leagues from the hemisphere,
Living without laws exempt from politics.

We have seen the description of famine linked with pestilence twice before in the *Centuries*: both times sounding ominously like radiation sickness. The second line seems to describe the cause of the famine falling in a "long rain" over the Northern hemisphere.

The source of this pestilence is perhaps indicated in line three. "*Samarobrin*" (possibly another of Nostradamus's riddled or anagrammed names) is described as being "a hundred leagues from the hemisphere". Any object that high above the Earth would be in orbit; in other words, an orbital satellite or space station.

Another possibility is that Nostradamus is describing the detonation of a comet in Earth's upper atmosphere. The eminent astrophysicist Sir Fred Hoyle suggested in the 1970s that complex amino acids (a basic building-block of life) might exist in the interstellar clouds out in space; although controversial at the time, his theory has since been proved correct. Hoyle went on to suggest that apparently spontaneous outbreaks of plagues like the Black Death might be the result of comets (basically balls of frozen cosmic debris) plunging through our atmosphere and depositing new viruses on those below.

The last line seems to suggest social chaos following the disaster. It should be noted that in the sixteenth century, people living "exempt from politics" would not mean a utopian ideal, as some might see it today. "Politics" in Nostradamus's day simply meant "good sense".

The Shaking of the Vatican

The Irish Saint Malachy is said to have made a pilgrimage to Rome in 1139. On cresting the last hill and looking down on the Holy City, Malachy is said to have had a vision of the 111 popes from Celestine II (who reigned for less than a year in 1124) to the end of the papacy. His short, poetically descriptive Latin motto for each future pontiff was carefully noted and the document was given to the incumbent pope, Innocent II.

That, at least, is the legend attached to the "Malachy Prophecies". Many scholars now doubt that Saint Malachy was responsible for the predictions at all – a forgery around 1590 being generally suspected. Nevertheless, even if we accept this later date, the predictions have still proved disturbingly accurate.

For example, the papacy of Benedict XV (1914–22) was predicted with the epithet *"Religio Depopulata"* ("Religion Depopulated"). Benedict's reign covered the period of the Great War and the 1918 Influenza pandemic, during which millions of Catholics – as well as those of other religions – died.

John XXIII (1958–63) had been the Patriarch of the port city of Venice before his election. The motto given by Malachy was *"Pastor et Nauta"* ("Pastor and Sailor").

John Paul I (1978) was given the motto, *"De Medietate Lunae"* ("The Middle of the Moon"). John Paul I died less than a month after his election. The date was 28 September: exactly in the middle of the lunar cycle.

The present pope (as of this writing in autumn 1998) is John Paul II. His "Malachy" motto is *"De Labore Solis"* ("The Labour of the Sun"). John Paul II is, of course, Polish – the first pope from Eastern Europe which, from Rome, is the direction of the rising sun. Despite his age and failing health, he has insisted that he will not retire and will "die in harness" – "labour[ing]" for the church to his last breath. He was born on 18 May 1920: a date which was marked by a total eclipse of the sun in the northern hemisphere.

The "Malachy Prophecies" list only two more popes to come. After John Paul II will be *"Gloria Olivae"* ("Glory of the Olive"). John Hogue suggests, in *The Millennium Book of Prophecy* (1994) that this pope might broker reconciliation (the "olive-branch" of peace) between the Arabs and Israelis as a non-partisan third force.

The last pope of the prophecy is referred to in these lines:

'*During the last persecution of the Holy Roman Church, there shall sit* Petrus Romanus [*Peter of Rome*], *who will feed the sheep amid great tribulations, and when these have passed, the*

City of the Seven Hills [Rome] *shall be utterly destroyed, and the dreadful Judge will judge the people."*

The "dreadful Judge" is usually seen as the God of the Last Judgement, but the prophecy might also be a prediction of a more "mundane" disaster for the city of Rome, or might simply be a poetic description of the collapse of Roman Catholicism as an organized faith.

Nostradamus seems to have partially supported this latter possibility in the *Centuries*. Several of his quatrains hint at major disruptions at the Vatican and a fundamental reorganization of religious practice and belief in the future.

A Controversial Pope
III.65 & V.56

> *Quand le sepulcre du grand Romain trouvé,*
> *Le jour apres sera esleu Pontife:*
> *Du Senat gueres il ne sera prouvé,*
> *Empoisonné son sang au sacré scyphe.*

Translation:

> When the sepulchre of the great Roman is found,
> The next day a Pope is elected:
> The Senate will not approve of him,
> His poison blood in the sacred chalice.

The last two lines of the quatrain sound like a prediction of the death – suspected as murder – of Pope John Paul I in 1978. At this time, much of Italian public life was being manipulated by a secret Masonic group called the *P2*. Leading politicians, judges, military men and (so it is rumoured) Catholic cardinals were members of P2, forming a web of corruption that spread across the whole nation.

Pope John Paul I was certainly not one of these tainted men and, on his election in August 1978, announced that he would personally study the books of the Vatican Bank to weed out illegal transactions and punish those responsible. He was found dead in his bed a month later – only a few days before he was to announce his findings. The Vatican (which is literally a state unto itself) blocked moves to hold an autopsy. Subsequent rumours declared that John Paul was given poison in his bedside bottle of stomach medicine.

As the quatrain says, the "Senate" – or the corrupt powers ruling Italy – did not approve of a reformer being elected pope. The last line mentions poison.

On the other hand, the first two lines of the quatrain do not fit this interpretation; as far as I can ascertain, there was no archaeological discovery in Rome the day before the election of John Paul I. Therefore this quatrain could also be a prediction of a future, unpopular pontiff, whose "poison blood" would stain the "sacred chalice", although whether literally or metaphorically is impossible to judge.

> Par les trespas du tres vieillart pontif,
> Sera esleu Romain de bon aage:
> Qu'il sera dict que le seige debisse,
> Et long tiendra et de picquant ouvrage.

Translation:

> By the death of the very old pope,
> Shall be elected a Roman of good age:
> It will be said that he weakens the seat,
> And he shall live long through stinging labour.

There have certainly been many "very old" popes since Nostradamus's day, but few "of good [presumably 'young'] age". None of even relatively youthful age has, since the mid-sixteenth century, lived to reign a long time. It is therefore likely that this unpopular pontiff, who will "weaken the seat [of the Papacy]" has yet to be elected.

The Breaking of the Old Religion
I.15, I.96 & II.8

> Mars nous menace par la force bellique,
> Septante fois fera le sang espandre:
> Auge et ruine de l'Ecclesiastique,
> Et plus ceux qui d'eux rien voudront entendre.

Translation:

Mars threatens us with warlike force,
Seventy times this will cause the spilling of blood:
The clergy will be exalted and reviled,
And more from those who wish to learn nothing from them.

Mars was the Roman god of war, and is here predicted to cause seventy conflicts – when, how and of what scale is unclear. The first two lines are a typical Nostradamus warning: chilling, but too obscure to be precise. The only difference in this case is the use of the word "us" in line one – suggesting Nostradamus's personal interest in this quatrain.

As we have seen, Nostradamus was a devoutly religious man (even if we cannot guess his denomination). The second two lines of the quatrain may suggest that the cause of the seventy episodes of bloodshed will be religious or, alternatively, that after a long period of war, religion itself will be attacked.

The third line suggests a confused debate, with the clergy alternately "exalted and reviled". The last line may hint that the cause of the friction will not be religious differences, but pure lack of interest in the clergy's teachings "from those who wish to learn nothing from them."

The diminishing congregations in modern churches may be indicated.

> Celui qu'aura la change de destruire,
> Templus, et sects, changez par fantasie:
> Plus aux rochiers qu'aux vivans viendra nuire,
> Par langue ornee d'oreilles ressasie.

Translation:

He who is charged with destruction,
Temples, and sects, changed by fantasy:
He will harm the rocks more than the living,
By ornate language ears filled.

An influential religious reformer is "charged" (i.e. given the task) of destroying "temples, and sects, changed by fantasy". Perhaps this indicates an attack on "cults" or, alternatively, a move away from the religious traditionalism which many people now feel has undermined the "true" meaning of religion.

This predicted reformer humanely concentrates on changing the material of the faith, or faiths ("the rocks"), rather than persecute the believers ("the living"). Perhaps the last line indicates that he uses persuasion to defeat dogmatism: filling the ears of his audience with "ornate language".

> *Temples sacrez prime facon Romaine,*
> *Rejecteront les goffres fondements,*
> *Prenant leurs loix premieres et humaines,*
> *Chassant, non tout, des saincts les cultements*

Translation:

> Temples consecrated in the early Roman fashion,
> Rejecting the tottering foundations,
> Sticking to their first humane laws,
> Expelling, not all, the cults of the saints.

Unlike the two quatrains above, this prediction seems to solely concern the Christian church. A return to simple practices of the early church fathers and a following of more "humane" laws is indicated. The "tottering foundations" of the previous religious practices are rejected.

Erica Cheetham suggests that this might not have been a prediction, but an endorsement of Protestantism. Catholicism might be described as a "cult of the saints", and Protestantism rejects this (while still rejecting "not all" saints). We have earlier noted James Randi's assertion that Nostradamus was actually a secret Protestant.

Taken together, these three quatrains seem to point to a fundamental reform of Christianity. Considering that Nostradamus seems to claim that his predictions cover a period of several thousand years, such a notion is highly plausible.

We might, on the other hand, see these three predictions as quite separate and unconnected events.

The Antichrist

It is a popular misconception that one of the pivotal figures in the Bible is the Antichrist. In fact this person is only referred to briefly in the First and Second Epistles of St John, where he is simply the denier of Christ. The "Beast" in *Revelation xiii* is also assumed to be the Antichrist. He was expected by the early church to appear before the end of the world, and was much discussed in the Middle Ages, when theologians felt the need for a balancing "enemy" for Jesus.

Lucifer was elevated to the position of the Archfiend in much the same way. In fact, the Devil hardly appears in the Bible and, when he does, is more of a mischievous tempter rather than the "Great Adversary".[3]

In Nostradamus's day, the label "antichrist" was used for a wicked person as well as Christ's adversary – just as today one might call someone a "devil" without meaning they had horns and lived in Hell.

Nostradamus mentions no less than three "Antichrists" in the introductions to the *Centuries*. The first two have been linked by commentators to Napoleon and Hitler. The last, and most terrible, is thought to be yet to come.

In fact, the main body of the *Centuries* only contains two direct mentions of an "Antichrist": X.66 and VIII.77.

> *Le chef de Londres par regne l'Americh,*
> *L'isle de l'Escosse tempiera par gellee:*
> *Roi Reb auront un si faux antechrist,*
> *Que les mettra trestous dans la meslee.*

Translation:

> The chief of London by the rule of the Americas,
> The isle of Scotland suffers frost:
> King Reb will have a false antichrist,
> Who will bring them into discord.

3 Bernard Shaw suggested in *Man and Superman* that most modern Christians derive their knowledge of Satan and the afterlife more from Milton's *Paradise Lost* than the Bible.

We can almost certainly discount this quatrain in the present context, because Nostradamus himself admits that he is predicting a *"faux"* ("false") antichrist. In other words, a wicked man, but not the "true" Antichrist.

Nevertheless, this quatrain is still very interesting. It has a word at the end of line one that is almost certainly "America", a name that was barely in circulation in the mid-sixteenth century. Either Nostradamus obtained this name through precognition, or he had a surprisingly up-to-date knowledge of what was going on in the realm of global exploration.

The name *"Roi Reb"*, at the beginning of line three, could mean "King Reb", or it might be a prediction of the Highland bandit and rebel called Rob Roy. This was the nickname (meaning Robert the Red) of Robert MacGregor (1671–1734): a freebooter and brigand immortalized and romanticized by Sir Walter Scott in the novel *Rob Roy* in 1817. The link with Scotland in the second line may tend to support this interpretation. Also, during the period of Robert MacGregor's life, the British fought a series of wars with France over the ownership of the North American territories, beginning with the King William's War of 1689 to 1697. Twenty-nine years after MacGregor's death, in 1763, Britain won the French and Indian War, confirming London's "rule of the Americas".

> *L'Antechrist trois bien tost anniehielez,*
> *Vingt et sept ans sang durera sa guerre.*
> *Les heritiques mortz, captifs, exhilez.*
> *Sang corps humain eua rougi gresler terre.*

Translation:

> The Antichrist three very soon annihilates,
> Twenty-seven bloody years his war will last.
> The heretics dead, captive, exiled.
> Blood human corpses water red hail cover the earth.

The first line may predict that the "Antichrist" will annihilate three persons or groups of persons. Commentators have suggested that the three Cold War superpowers (Russia, America and China) might be indicated, or that three continents will be devastated by the war of line two. Alternatively, line one could mean that Nostradamus's "Third Antichrist" ("*Antechrist trois*") will simply be universally destructive.

The 27-year war predicted in line two rather undermines those interpreters that see this quatrain as a prediction of a total nuclear holocaust: even using only smaller "battlefield" nuclear weapons, such a war would be unsustainable for such a period. A 27-year "conventional" war (although quite possibly still using limited numbers of weapons of mass destruction) seems more likely, from the point of view of military logistics.

The religious aspect of the "Antichrist War" is reinforced by the description of the unpleasant fate of "heretics" in line three.

The grotesque description of the result of the war in line four is as lurid as any in the *Centuries*. Different writers on Nostradamus have seen in it evidence of nuclear fallout, chemical and biological weapons, genocide and the extinction of the human race. Yet all these interpretations are essentially the expressions of the fears of individual commentators; a non-presumptive reader could only say that a savage destruction of human life is predicted.

Nostradamus commentators have linked other quatrains to the "Third Antichrist". The following are some of the most often quoted of these predictions:

I.50

> De l'aquatique triplicité naistra.
> D'un qui fera le jeudi pour sa feste:
> Son bruit, loz, regne, sa puissance croistra,
> Par terre et mer aux Oriens tempeste.

Translation:

> Born from the three water signs,
> One who makes Thursday his holiday:
> His fame, praise, reign, and power will grow,
> By land and sea to the Oriental tempest.

The three water signs are Cancer, Scorpio and Pisces. Since an individual can have only one Sun sign (i.e. the sign he is born under), we must assume that Nostradamus means us to see that two of the signs are prominent elsewhere in the horoscope of the "one" predicted.

Thursday is not a weekly holiday in any major religion, but it may be worth noting that the American celebration of Thanksgiving always falls on this day.

II.29

> L'Oriental sortira de son siege,
> Passer les monts Apennins voir la Gaule:
> Transpercera le ciel les eaux et neige,
> Et un chacun frappera de sa gaule.

Translation:

> The Oriental will come out of his seat,
> Crossing the Apennine Mountains seeing France:
> Transported through the sky the waters and snows,
> And shall strike everyone with his rod.

The middle two lines strongly hint at aerial, perhaps even orbital travel. The "rod" of the last line may be a beam, such as a laser.

II.62

> Mabus puis tost, alors mourra viendra,
> De gens et bestes une horrible defaite:
> Puis tout à coup la vengence on verra,
> Cent, main, soif, faim, quand courra la comete.

Translation:

> Mabus will come, and soon after dies,
> Of people and beasts there will be horrible destruction:
> Then suddenly vengeance will be seen,
> One hundred, hand, thirst, famine, when the comet passes.

"Mabus" seems to be a name, perhaps of the Third Antichrist.

V.54

> *Du pont Euxine, et la grand Tartarie,*
> *Un roi sera qui viendra voir la Gaule,*
> *Transpercera Alane et l'Armenie,*
> *Et dans Bisance lairra sanglante gaule.*

Translation:

> From the Black Sea and Central Asia,
> A king will come to see France,
> He will pass through Alania and Albania,
> And in Istanbul will leave his bloody rod.

Tartary was the medieval name for what we now call Central Asia, but some Nostradamus translators prefer China (in Nostradamus's time, the word could mean either). Alania is a region of Southern Russia. The quatrain is so reminiscent of II.29 above, that one is tempted to believe they both predict the same event.

VI.33

> *Sa main derniere par Alus sanguine,*
> *Ne se pourra par la mer guarantir:*
> *Entre deux fleuves craindre main militaire,*
> *Le noir l'ireux le fera repentir.*

Translation:

> His hand finally through bloody *Alus*,
> He cannot guarantee his safety by sea:
> Between two rivers he will fear the military hand,
> The black angry one will make him repent it.

Erica Cheetham suggests that "*Alus*" could be the name (or an anagram of the name) of the Third Antichrist. Henry Roberts, on the other hand, suggests it is a partial anagram of the words "all US".

VI.80

> *De Fez le regne parviendra à ceux d'Europe,*
> *Feu leur cité, et lame trenchera:*
> *Le grand d'Asie terre et mer à grand troupe,*
> *Que bleux, pers, croix, à mort dechasssera.*

Translation:

> From Fez the kingdom stretches out across Europe,
> The city burns, and sword slices:
> The great one of Asia land and sea a great army,
> That blue, Persia, cross, driven to death.

Fez is a town in Morocco. As we have seen before, *"crois"* seems to be Nostradamus's shorthand for Christianity.

Food for Thought

The one question that each generation has asked since the publication of the *Centuries* has been: "What does Nostradamus predict for *my* time?" In the case of men like Louis Pasteur and Adolf Hitler, the answer was personal but, in general, Nostradamus foresees the fate of nations.

The following quatrains might predict pivotal changes for the present generation:

21 June 2002 AD
VI.24

> *Mars et le sceptre se trouvera conjoinct,*
> *Dessoubz Cancer calamiteuse guerre:*
> *Un peu apre sera nouveau Roi oingt,*
> *Qui par long temps pacifiera la terre.*

Translation:

Mars and the sceptre conjoin together,
Under Cancer a calamitous war:
A short while after a new king will be anointed,
Who for a long time will bring peace to the Earth.

Erica Cheetham suggests the "sceptre", in line one, is Jupiter (the "King of Planets"). A Mars-Jupiter-Cancer conjunction is very rare, the next being due on 21 June 2002.

2007–2008 AD
X.74

> *An revolu du grand nombre septiesme,*
> *Apparoistra au temps Jeux d'Hecatombe,*
> *Non esloigné milliesme,*
> *Que les entre sortiront de leur tombe.*

Translation:

The year of the revolution of the great seventh number,
It will appear at the Games of *Hecatombe*,
Not far from the great millennium,
When the dead will leave their graves.

The millennium mentioned in line three could, obviously, be the year 2000: the next millennium date following the publication of the *Centuries*. If this is so, then line one would seem to point to the "revolution" (or end) of the "seventh" year before or after the millennium. Since 1997 passed without fulfilling the predication, 2007 is the next in line.

"*Hecatomb*" is a Greek word for a sacrifice of a hundred sacred animals. Such massive sacrifices took place only at great public events – such as the Olympic Games ("Games of the Hecatomb"). The Christian Emperor Theodosius discontinued the ancient Olympics at the end of the fourth century AD, so they were only a distant memory in Nostradamus's day. However, in 1896, the Olympic Games were started again. 2008 – the year resulting from the "revolution" of 2007 – is an Olympic year.

The last line of the quatrain presumably refers to the Last Judgement, when the dead will rise from their graves. Indeed, if we add *Century X*, quatrain 72 (discussed at the end of the chapter on Nostradamus and the twentieth century) – with its description of a "King of terror" descending from the sky – we may note a close match with fundamentalist Christian beliefs. There the great "Antichrist War" is followed by the Second Coming of Jesus Christ, who rules the Earth in perfect peace for a time. Then comes the end of all material things, with the dead rising from the grave at the Last Trump.

The trouble with this interpretation is that Nostradamus clearly says elsewhere that his predictions for mankind run much further into the future. In his introductory letter to *Century I*, Nostradamus described the contents as "prophecies from today [1 March 1555] to the year 3797". Later, in *Century I*, quatrain 48, he seems to add to this figure by hinting at a predictive limit of seven thousand years (see Chapter 12). How can Nostradamus predict the events leading to the Last Judgement starting in 1999, if the human race has at least 1798 years of history to run?

David Ovason suggests that Nostradamus's "religious" quatrains were added to appease the ever-watchful church. The protection of Queen Catherine de Medici was enough to save Nostradamus from charges of witchcraft, but Catherine herself might have faced excommunication if she shielded a man who published heresies. In effect, Nostradamus may have had to include predictions that the world would end around the second millennium, because that is what the church insisted was going to happen. He may therefore have left uncommented the fact that he continued to predict for events after the "Apocalypse", as a contradiction that spoke for itself, but could not lead to heresy charges.

Nostradamus gives the reason for his deliberate obscurities in his *Preface to my Son*, in the first volume of the *Centuries*. He writes that he initially feared that if he "were to relate what will happen in the future, governors, secretaries, and ecclesiastics would find it so ill-accordant with their auricular fancy[4] that they would go near to condemn what future ages will know and perceive to be true.

4 The world as they hear and perceive it.

"This it is," he continues, "which has led me to withhold my tongue from the vulgar, and my pen from paper. But later on, I thought I would enlarge a little, and declare in dark abstruse sayings . . . the most urgent of future causes, as perceived by me, be the revolutionary changes what they may, so only not to scandalize the auricular frigidity of my hearers, and write all down under a cloudy figure . . ."

His use of the phrase "auricular frigidity" is cautiously diplomatic – he certainly means "dogmatic preconceptions".

This may explain why Nostradamus made his predictions so obscure, but why did he not make more practical use of his gift? The death of his patron, King Henri II, is a case in point. Nostradamus met the king years before the tournament that would end his life so painfully. Even allowing for the king's lack of interest in the *Centuries* (or, indeed, books in general), Nostradamus must have been able to find some way to impress upon him to avoid jousting on 10 July 1559.

Nostradamus's general statements about his gift of precognition offer a plain, but grim answer to the mystery. The seer believed that the future was immutable, that the events he foresaw were pre-ordained and could not be changed. It was not that Nostradamus chose not to save Henri, but that he knew the king was destined to die and nothing could change the fact.

So rather than an all-knowing magus, perhaps it would be nearer to the truth to see Nostradamus as an agonized but impotent observer – much like a war-correspondent who witnesses atrocities, and can only report them. The reader may remember the Scottish *taibhsears* discussed in Chapter 11, who preferred to be solitary hermits rather than meet people whose misfortunes they might suddenly foresee.

Yet is this all that prophecy can tell us – that our fate is immutable and cannot be changed?

Now, according to the Church, the future is preordained by God and is immutable. A strong influence on the doctrine of predestination was the work of the pagan philosopher Boethius (480–524AD). He argued that the whole history of the universe, from beginning to end, is already formed and that the gods are actually "outside" its process. So even if the gods are all-knowing, they are also be powerless to interfere.

A modern cosmologist might say that the whole universe is a kind of complex mathematical equation and, since there is no such thing as chance in mathematics, then our past, present and future were all pre-ordained from the moment of the Big Bang.

However, mathematics is not all we need to unravel the mysteries of space/time. In the quantum world inside the atom, the law of cause and effect does not operate as it does in our everyday world . . . Indeed, Hugh Everett Jnr's Parallel Universe theory suggests that a new universe is created every time our universe faces an alternative. Every time you flip a coin, according to Everett, three almost identical universes have just been created: one in which the coin landed heads-up, one in which the result was tails, and one in which the coin landed on its edge. "You" are in only one of those universes, but that does not mean that the other two "yous" in the other two universes are any less "real" or self-aware.

Quantum theory is beyond the scope of the present work,[5] but we can see that it suggests an alternative to Nostradamus's' deterministic view of the world. In the non-deterministic world of the quantum, consciousness travels through time down a road of near-infinitely branching possibilities. And it becomes conceivable that, through conscious decision, a person might navigate chosen paths rather than living mechanically.

In fact, we shall see in the last chapter that the paradoxical nature of time may allow both for a fixed and predictable fate and for a world in which free will can operate – a world where, as Buckminster Fuller once said, "I seem to be a verb".

5. I recommend to those looking for a simple approach to quantum physics, Fritjof Capra's *The Tao of Physics* and John Gribbin's *In Search of Schroedinger's Cat*.

21 The Mystery of Time

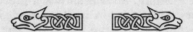

In his book on synchronicity – which we have already discussed in the chapter on the *I Ching* – Jung talks about foreknowledge of the future, and mentions the case of a friend:

> "I remember the story of a student friend whose father had promised him a trip to Spain if he passed his final examination satisfactorily. My friend thereupon dreamed that he was walking through a Spanish city. The street led to a square, where there was a Gothic cathedral. He then turned right, around a corner, into another street. There he was met by an elegant carriage drawn by two cream-coloured horses. Then he woke up. He told us about the dream as we were sitting round a table drinking beer. Shortly afterward, having successfully passed his examinations, he went to Spain, and there, in one of the streets, he recognized the city of his dream. He found the square and the cathedral, which exactly corresponded to the dream-image. He wanted to go straight to the cathedral, but he remembered that in the dream he had turned right, at the corner, into another street. He was curious to find out whether his dream would be corroborated further. Hardly had he turned the corner when he saw in reality the carriage with the two cream-coloured horses."

Now Jung feels that synchronicity – impossible coincidences – and precognition of the future are closely connected. He obviously feels that man's unconscious mind exists outside time, and that that is how people can have glimpses of the future in dreams. In synchronicities, it again looks as if the unconscious mind is playing tricks on our everyday self, which feels that it is trapped in time.

Jung notes an example from his own experience concerning fish. On 1 April 1949, he wrote about an inscription about a figure that was half man and half fish. There was fish for lunch that day. Since it was 1 April someone mentioned the custom of making an April fool of someone – but in German, they're called *April fish*. In the evening, he was shown a piece of embroidery with sea monsters and fishes in it. The next day, Jung saw a former patient for the first time in years, and she had dreamed of a large fish, the night before.

A few months later, he wrote about these coincidences in a book, and then walked to a spot by the lake, near a wall – he had already been there several times that day. This time there was a foot-long fish on the wall.

Most of us have had some similar experiences of minor coincidences in a row, one after the other. They do not surprise us. We can easily imagine that when Jung had fish for lunch, discussed April fish, saw the embroidery with fishes, and heard the patient's story of her dream of fish, he somehow felt that this kind of repetition was natural and normal. He probably did not even feel great surprise when, after writing down this sequence, he then found a fish on the sea wall. It is as if some unseen force was making us aware of its presence.

In this same book, Jung repeats the famous story about M. Fortgibu, from Camille Flammarion's book *The Unknown*. Here is Flammarion's own version of the story:

"Emile Deschamps, a distinguished poet, somewhat overlooked in these days, one of the authors of the libretto of Les *Huguenots*, tells of a curious series of fortuitous coincidences as follows:

"In his childhood, being at a boarding school in Orleans, he chanced to find himself on a certain day at table with a M. de Fortgibu, an *émigré* recently returned from England, who made him taste a plum-pudding, a dish almost unknown at that time in France.

"The remembrance of that feast had by degrees faded

from his memory, when, ten years later, passing by a restaurant on the boulevard Poissoniere, he perceived inside it a plum-pudding of most excellent appearance.

"He went in and asked for a slice of it, but was informed that the whole had been ordered by another customer. 'M. de Fortgibu,' cried the woman at the till, seeing that Deschamps looked disappointed, 'would you have the goodness to share your plum-pudding with this gentleman?'

"Deschamps had some difficulty in recognizing M. de Fortgibu, an elderly man, with powdered hair, dressed in a colonel's uniform, who was taking his dinner at one of the tables.

"The officer said it would give him pleasure to offer part of his pudding to the gentleman.

"Long years had passed since Deschamps had even thought of plum-pudding, or of M. de Fortgibu.

"One day, he was invited to dinner where there was to be a real English plum-pudding. He accepted the invitation but told the lady of the house as a joke, that he knew M. de Fortgibu would be of the party, and he caused much amusement by giving the reason.

"The day came, and he went to the house. Ten guests occupied the ten places at table, and the magnificent plum-pudding was served. They were beginning to laugh at Deschamps about his M. de Fortgibu, when the door opened and the servant announced: 'M. de Fortgibu.'

"An old man entered, walking feebly, with the help of a servant. He went slowly round the table, as if looking for somebody, and he seemed greatly disconcerted. Was it a vision, or was it a joke?

"It was the time of the Carnival, and Deschamps was sure it was a trick. As the old man approached him, he was forced to recognize M. de Fortgibu in person.

" 'My hair stood up on my head,' he said. 'Don Juan, in Mozart's opera, was not more terrified by his guest of stone.'

All was soon explained. M. de Fortgibu had been asked to dinner by a friend who lived in the same house, but had mistaken the number of his apartment."

There is really in this story a series of coincidences which confounds us, and we can understand the explanation of the author when the remembrance of a thing so extraordinary occurred to him: 'Three times in my life have I eaten plum-pudding, and three times have I seen M. de Fortgibu! A fourth time, I should feel capable of anything . . . or capable of nothing.'

Now here we can see why Jung feels that precognition and synchronicity are part of the same mystery. In both cases, we feel as if fate is talking to us. What it seems to be saying is: "You take it for granted that you are a slave of time, that you are born and have to die, and that you spend most of your life living by the clock, rushing to work, rushing to appointments, rushing to catch trains. You feel that you are simply a physical creature living in a physical universe. But I tell you that you are mistaken. You are like a prince who believes he is a frog . . ."

There is another point to make about Jung's story of the friend who visited Spain. It would strike us as altogether less extra-ordinary if Jung's friend had simply dreamed of the city, and its Gothic cathedral, before visiting it. After all, the city has existed for centuries, and millions of people have lived there. We might say that a great city exists in the "collective unconscious" of mankind. Seeing it in a dream would then belong to the class of events that Flammarion calls "distant sight in dreams", and to which he also devotes a chapter of *The Unknown*.

But as soon as we add the detail of the carriage and the two cream-coloured horses, this explanation loses all plausibility. The young man must have felt that he was taking the right-hand turn *of his own free will*. So to see the two cream-coloured horses is altogether more bizarre. It means that he foresaw some chance event – a local citizen deciding to take a drive, perhaps on the spur of the moment – months before it happened. Somehow, this stretches credulity far more than foreseeing some extra-ordinary event, like the sinking of the *Titanic* or an attempt on Hitler's life . . . As we have seen, no one can read the story of the *Titanic* without feeling it was somehow "predestined" And while we are still trying to absorb the amazing implications of Jung's story, the Fortgibu anecdote seems to reinforce them. To encounter M. Fortgibu three times, always in association with plum-pudding, seems to belong in the same category of un-believability as encountering two cream-coloured horses in a dream, and then in reality. We feel suddenly that we are dealing with a strange world that obeys different laws from the one we live in.

In fact, Flammarion has a whole chapter dealing with similar cases. His own mother told him frequently how, before she and her husband left a small country town to move to Paris, she dreamed of Paris several times, particularly a wide street that led to a canal, across which there was an elevated bridge. "Some little time after her arrival in Paris, she went to pay a visit to one of her relations who lived in the rue Fontaine-au-Roi in the Faubourg du Temple and, upon reaching the canal, she was very much surprised to recognize the bridge, the quay, the whole appearance of the neighbourhood, at which it was impossible that she could have had any knowledge, either by means of pictures or in any other way."

Flammarion goes on: "This dream is very difficult to explain. It would seem to prove that the mind is capable of seeing at a distance, and during the night, details which conform by day to the image remaining in the brain. This, however, is hard to believe. I should prefer to suppose that persons who had come from Paris had told my mother of the existence of this kind of bridge, and that she had forgotten their account which reappeared in the dream. But my mother affirms positively that no one ever spoke to her either of the Paris canal or the suspension bridge."

Flammarion also tells how his father had accompanied one of Flammarion's sisters, together with her husband and children, to live in the little town of Nogent. All the children were in good health. Yet Flammarion's mother dreamed that she received a letter from her husband in which she had read the sentence: "I am the bearer of a sad piece of news. Little Henri had just died in convulsions, with hardly any previous illness."

"My mother, on awakening, said to herself: 'It is nothing but a dream; it is all imagination and deception.' A week afterwards, a letter from my father contained precisely this very phrase. My poor sister had lost her youngest child in consequence of convulsions."

Occasionally, an anecdote of Flammarion's raises our doubts, because it sounds just a little too much of a good story.

"In a little town in the centre of France, La Charité-sur-Loire . . . there was a young girl of ravishing grace and beauty. She, like Raphael's Fornarina, was the daughter of a baker. Several suitors aspired to her hand, one of whom had a great fortune. The parents preferred this young man, but Madame Angela Robin did not like him, and refused him.

"One day, driven to extremity by the persistence of her family, she went to church and prayed to the Holy Virgin to come to her aid. The following night she saw, in a dream, a young man in the dress of a traveller, wearing a large straw hat and spectacles. On awakening, she declared to her parents that she absolutely refused her suitor, and that she should wait, which caused them a thousand conjectures.

"The following summer, the young Emile de la Bedolliere was induced by one of his friends, Eugene Lafaure, a law student, to make a journey into the interior of France. They stopped at La Charité, and went to a subscription ball. On their arrival, the young girl's heart beat tumultuously, her cheeks coloured a deep red; the young traveller observed her, admired her, loved her and, some months afterwards, they were married. It was the first time in his life that he had visited that village."

Now obviously, this story could be explained in perfectly rational terms. If she had dreamed of a young man with one blue eye and one brown eye, and a large wart on his nose, and her suitor had corresponded exactly to that description, we might agree that it sounds very much like dream-precognition. As it is, we must say that there is at least a fifty per cent chance that the young man in the straw hat and spectacles was not the person she actually married.

On the other hand, we must remember that Flammarion, as well as being an astronomer, was also one of France's foremost psychical researchers, and that he would be unlikely to cite stories which could be so easily explained away.

He tells a story repeated to him by a certain M. Goupil, a civil engineer of Cognac, who described how, at Tunis, in 1891, he was playing a game of billiards with a hairdresser who declined a second game of billiards on the grounds that he had to go home because he was expecting the doctor. He was concerned about his little nephew, who, on the previous day, had had a hallucination. He had suddenly cried out: "Here is a woman who wishes to take my little cousin away – I don't want her to be carried off." The hairdresser admitted that the boy had never before been subject to hallucinations, but said that he thought it might be some kind of fever.

For several days afterwards, M. Goupil asked the hairdresser after the health of his little girl – who was a few months old – and was always told that she was perfectly well. On the fourth day, the hairdresser told him: "We have lost my little girl – she was taken from us in a moment." (Goupil thought that it was croup.) And Goupil confessed that he had been expecting precisely this because of the nephew's vision of the woman.

Flammarion adds: "Can chance be called in here? No. There is something in all this which is unknown to us, but which is real."

However, it was Goupil's opinion that the figure of the woman was some kind of representation of death. Modern accounts of "death-bed visions", in which the dying see family members who have already died, makes it more likely that the woman was some family member. Yet the implication – as we have seen elsewhere – is that "spirits" appear to be able to foresee the future.

Another case cited by Flammarion has the odd pointlessness which seems typical of certain kinds of precognition. It was told to Flammarion by an "honourable ecclesiastic".

"I was at school in Miort. I was fifteen or sixteen years old. One night I had a singular dream. I fancied that I was at Saint Maixent (a town that I knew only by name) with my school-master. We were on a little square near a well, opposite to which was a drugs store, and we saw coming towards us a lady of that place whom I recognized, because I had once seen her at Miort, in a house where I was staying. This lady, when she accosted us, began to speak of such extraordinary things that in the morning I mentioned the matter to my school-master . . . he was very much astonished, and made me repeat the conversation. A few days after, having to go to Saint Maixent, he took me with him. Hardly had we arrived there before we found ourselves on the square that I had seen in my dream, and we saw the same lady coming towards us, who had with my master the same conversation, word for word, as in my dream." (This deposition is signed by Groussard, Curé of Saint Rade-gonde.)

This story could be paralleled with a story told by Charles Dickens, and quoted in the book *Noted Witnesses For Psychic Occurrences*, by Walter Franklin Prince.

In his diary on 30 May 1863, Dickens wrote:

"Here is a curious case at first-hand. On Thursday night in last week, being at my office here, I dreamed that I saw a lady in a red shawl with her back towards me (whom I suppose to be E). On her turning round I found that I didn't know her, and she said, 'I am Miss Napier.' At the time I was dressing next morning I thought: What a preposterous thing to have so very distinct a dream about nothing! and why Miss Napier? for I had never heard of any Miss Napier. That same Friday night, I read. After the reading, came into my retiring-room, Mary Boyle, and her brother, and the lady in the red shawl, whom they present as 'Miss Napier'. These are all the circumstances exactly told."

Flammarion himself mentions that he asked for accounts of "premonitory dreams", and received dozens of examples, which he goes on to quote for another forty pages, but there would be no point in mentioning more of them. All bear a fundamental similarity to the ones already quoted. Flammarion concludes: "The human being is endowed with faculties whose nature is still unknown to us, but which permit him to see from a distance into space and time. This is what we have wished to demonstrate by a mass of satisfactory evidence."

Flammarion became president of the Society for Psychical Research (UK) in 1923. In his presidential address, he concluded: "There are unknown faculties in man belonging to the spirit, there is such a thing as the double, thought can leave an image behind, psychical currents traverse the atmosphere, we live in the midst of an invisible world, the faculties of the souls survive the desegregation of the corporeal organism, there are haunted houses, exceptionally and rarely the dead do manifest, there can be no doubt that such manifestations occur, telepathy exists just as much between the dead and the living as between the living." He died in 1925, two years after this address.

What strikes us as so ironical when we read *The Unknown* (*L'Inconnu*), published in 1899, is that Flammarion's books on astronomy made him famous in Europe and America, and brought him many honours in France, while a book as obviously important as *The Unknown* simply failed to arouse widespread interest. As we read it, its conclusions seem so forceful and so undeniable that it is difficult to understand why the book did not cause the same revolution in understanding as his books on astronomy. We are forced to recognize that the kind of conclusions that Flammarion expressed during his presidential address failed to arouse widespread interest, simply because scientists can see no way of using them as the guidelines for some applied science. The result is that Flammarion is now remembered – at least in France – as a famous astronomer, while his books dealing with psychical research are virtually forgotten.

The problem, of course, is that the idea of being able to foresee the future seems to contradict our common experience. When, in addition to that, it seems to have no possible scientific explanation, we find it very hard to take seriously.

Let us see if we can make some sort of preliminary attempt at a scientific explanation of what is involved.

Jung has spoken of synchronicities so absurd that they appear to defy normal explanation. He mentions that Flammarion worked out that, in one case, the odds were more than eight hundred million to one against.

Jung then goes on:

"The writer Wilhelm von Scholz has collected a number of stories showing the strange ways in which lost or stolen objects come back to their owners. Among other things, he tells the story of a mother who took a photograph of her small son in the Black Forest. She left the film to be developed in Strasbourg. But, owing to the outbreak of war, she was unable to fetch it, and gave it up for lost. In 1916 she bought a film in Frankfurt in order to take a photograph of her daughter, who had been born in the meantime. When the film was developed, it was found to be doubly exposed: the picture underneath was the photograph she had taken of her son in 1914! The old film had not been developed and had somehow got into circulation again among the new films. The author comes to the understandable conclusion that everything points to the 'mutual attraction of related objects', or an 'elective affinity'. He suspects that these happenings are arranged as if they were the dreams of a 'greater and more comprehensive consciousness, which is unknowable'."

But then, as we have seen in the chapter on the *I Ching*, Jung's hypothesis of an "acausal connecting principle" is far from satisfactory. Somehow, Flammarion's view that we possess unknown powers has far more appeal. The truth is that all of us experience a certain sense of the unreality of time. Admittedly, it seems that we are trapped in time – particularly when we are tired. Yet as soon as we fall asleep, time disappears. Even when we are wide awake, we often have a feeling that we are the spectators of life as well as the actors in it. Most scientists would dismiss this as an illusion. Yet the fact remains that when we read stories like Dickens' description of seeing "Miss Napier" in a dream, we do not dismiss it with the comment "that is absurd – he must be lying". We are perfectly willing to accept that Dickens is telling the truth, and that therefore, our normal view of time is somehow mistaken.

The most famous of all twentieth-century time philosophers is John William Dunne, the son of General Sir John Hart Dunne, who was born in 1875, and achieved overnight fame for his book *An Experiment With Time* in 1927.

In that book, Dunne begins by relating an incident that occurred in 1899, when he was staying at a hotel in Sussex. Dunne dreamed that he was having an argument with a waiter about the correct time, and that he claimed that it was half past four in the afternoon, while the waiter maintained that it was half past four in the morning. In his dream, Dunne then took out his watch, which had stopped at half past four. A moment later, he awoke.

He struck a match to look at his watch, and found that he had left it lying on a chest of drawers. It had stopped – at exactly half past four.

Assuming that the watch must have stopped at half past four the previous afternoon, and he had merely forgotten about it, he rewound it, but left the hands exactly as they were because he was not sure of the real time.

On coming downstairs, the next morning he looked at the nearest clock, and found that his own watch was only two or three minutes slow – roughly the amount of time that had elapsed from waking up and finding the watch on the chest of drawers. So the watch must have stopped at the very moment he was dreaming that it had stopped.

Some time later, he was lying in bed in Sorrento, in Italy, wondering what time it was. His watch was out of sight, so he decided he would try and see the time "clairvoyantly". He closed his eyes, and fell into a semi-doze and, a moment later, found himself looking at the watch, which seemed to be encircled by white mist. It showed about two and a half minutes past eight. He sat up and reached for his watch on the bedside table. This also showed that it was two and a half minutes past eight.

Dunne concluded that he had some odd ability to see around corners. Then, in 1901, an incident changed his mind. He was at Alassio in Italy, having been invalided home from the Boer War, and dreamed one night that he was in a little village in Sudan, not far from Khartoum. Then he saw three men dressed in ragged Khaki uniforms, their faces dusty and sunburned. He asked what they were doing, and one replied: "We have come right through from the Cape", while another one added: "I've had an awful time. I nearly died of yellow fever."

The next morning at breakfast, he saw the headline in the newspaper: THE CAPE TO CAIRO – EXPEDITION AT KHARTOUM. The story also mentioned that of the three men in the party, one had died of enteric – not yellow fever.

Of course, the paper – the London *Daily Telegraph* – had taken some time to get from London to Italy, so all this had happened some weeks before. This was actually the first time that an expedition had travelled all the way from the Cape to Cairo.

In the following year, he was camping with his unit near the ruins of Lindley, in South Africa. He dreamed that he was standing on the upper slopes of some hill or mountain, and that jets of vapour were spouting out of little cracks in the ground. He dreamed that the place was an island of which he had dreamed before, and which was in danger from a volcano. He was able to recall the explosion of Krakatoa, when water got into the heart of the volcano and blew it apart. He felt a sudden urgent desire to warn the four thousand inhabitants – somehow he knew that there were four thousand. There followed a nightmare in which he was trying to persuade the authorities to evacuate the island with ships.

The next *Daily Telegraph* had a headline: VOLCANO DIS-

ASTER IN MARTINIQUE – PROBABLE LOSS OF OVER 40,000 LIVES.

Dunne was struck by another observation. There were actually forty thousand killed in the explosion, but the first time he read the newspaper headline, he read it as four thousand – and only realized the real figure later. So it struck him that possibly his dream was, in fact, a dream about *reading the newspaper* in the future – not actually about the Martinique disaster.

This was supported by the fact that, when the final figures came in, they were nothing like four thousand or forty thousand.

These "future dreams" occurred so often that he finally decided to perform an experiment.

What finally decided him was that, in 1917, when he was in hospital recovering from an operation, he read a paragraph about a combination lock, and then recalled that in fact he had dreamed about a combination lock the night before. When two other men in the hospital also described how they had had precognitive dreams, he began to wonder whether perhaps precognitive dreams were not abnormal but perfectly normal. Perhaps, he thought, everybody has them, but we simply forget them.

So he tried keeping a notebook and pencil at the side of his pillow and, as soon as he woke up from a dream, he would try to remember the details, and then write them down.

To begin with, his experiments did not seem particularly successful. Then one day, when he was out shooting, he lost his way and wandered on to land where he probably had no right to be. At that time, he heard two men shouting at him from different directions, and a dog barking, and made for the nearest gate. He managed to slip through it just a few moments before the men came into view. When he got back home, he looked at his "dream notebook" and found written in it for the previous night: "Hunted by two men and a dog".

What surprised him even more was that he had no memory whatsoever of any such dream. He could not even recall writing it down. Which is why he came to the conclusion that we could easily have many dreams of the future, and simply forget all about them.

A few days later, he read a novel in which someone hides in a large secret loft in the roof of an old house, and later in the story has to escape from the house by way of the chimney. He discovered that he had written down that he had dreamed of being in a secret loft in a house, and had to escape by way of a loft which led to the chimney.

He then began to try and persuade other people to experiment with their dreams. A young lady he calls Miss B. had dreamed she was walking up a path and found that it ended in a five-barred gate which should not have been there, after which a man and three brown cows passed on the other side of the gate. The next day, waiting at a station, she walked to the end of the platform and found a five-barred gate leading on to a road, and as she reached it, she saw the man driving three brown cows and holding the stick over his shoulder like a fishing rod, exactly as in the dream.

Dunne goes on to describe various other dreams by various people he persuaded to join the experiment, and they make it perfectly clear that they all had precognitive dreams – although, for the first few nights, they had no success whatever.

All this led Dunne to a theory which he called "Serial Time", by which he means that time actually consists of a whole series of "times". He argues that if you can feel that time is passing – either quickly or slowly – then you must have some standard by which you are measuring it. In other words, if you call the time which is passing in the present moment Time 1, then you must be measuring it against another kind of time called Time 2. But presumably this second kind of time can also go fast or slow, and so must be measured against another kind of time which you must call Time 3. And so on to infinity. Moreover, when you are simply observing the present time, you might say that "you" is a kind of observer, whom you could call Observer 1.

But as soon as you begin to think about time, and think, "Oh dear, it's passing very slowly," then you are standing back from Observer 1 – in other words, the second kind of time is observed by Observer 2. That suggests that there are also an infinite number of "yous".

The playwright J. B. Priestley became a close friend of Dunne's and went on to write a series of three "time plays' about these various paradoxes – which Dunne had gone on to write about in books with titles like *The Serial Universe* (1934), *The New Immortality* (1937) and *Nothing Dies* (1940).

In his own book *Man and Time* (1964), Priestley talks about Dunne's theories, and explains that he feels Dunne is making a mistake to have so many observers. Priestley writes:

"There is Self 1 which, because we are self-conscious, is always an object. There is Self 2, which may be a subject or an object. This self observes Self 1, but can be in its turn observed by Self 3. This last self is never an object; there is no other self to observe it; we can put Self 3 on paper, as I am doing now, but we are not in practice aware of our own Self 3; it is ultimate. Let us see how the three selves work.

"Self 1 says, 'I disagree with Dunne . . .' (It is saying this, so to speak, in the battle, in the welter of opinions, feelings and prejudices.) Self 2 says, 'I know that I disagree with Dunne . . .' (It says this out of the battle, and is ready to talk or write on the subject.) Self 3 would probably say nothing, not caring a rap about Dunne; but, if compelled to speak, it would probably say; 'I, Self 3, know that Self 2 knows that Self 1 disagrees with Dunne . . . and this is something I might possibly have to take into account.'

"In moments of great stress, Self 3 dominates the other two and takes over. Here is an actual instance that I remember. Self 1 heard terrible sounds in an aircraft, found himself hurled out of his seat and hit by a piece of luggage. Self 2 knew there was about to be a terrible accident. Self 3 said: 'Well, well, I shall know in a moment what it feels like to be fried alive.' Unlike the other two selves, Self 3 does not really care; it is as if it goes along with the other two just for the ride."

And so, according to Priestley, we do not have to assume that there are an infinite number of selves – just three. And that third self is the one of which we are all aware – that has an odd feeling that nothing out there is really genuinely real. Whenever something awful happens or seems about to happen, we feel that this is simply an illusion. If you heard the number of the winning National Lottery ticket announced and realized that you had bought it, you would feel tremendous excitement, and yet your "Observer 3" would be looking on with indifference. If, on searching your pocket, you realized you had lost it, you would feel that Observer 3 was simply a fool who had no idea of what to take seriously. In fact, you would feel rather as if he was a stupid child who fails to recognize the seriousness of events because he is too inexperienced. And yet this Self 3 continues to observe our lives and to assure us that, no matter how this may seem to Self 1, and even Self 2, it is not really all that important. Whether he knows that because he has some profound knowledge which is hidden from Selves 1 and 2, or simply because he lacks the seriousness, it seems impossible to say.

In his last book, *Intrusions?*, published after his death in 1949, Dunne makes an admission that will certainly confirm the scepticism of those who feel that the whole theory of Serial Time is nothing but self-deception. He admits that, ever since childhood, he had been possessed by a certainty that he would bring an important message to mankind. "Intrusions" were moments when some supernatural power intervened to remind him of his destiny. A medium in South Africa had told him at a seance that he was to become the greatest medium the world has ever known. So when Dunne began to have his curious experiences of "dreaming the future", he felt that he had finally embarked on his destiny.

On the other hand, if Flammarion is right, and we possess some kind of unknown power of which we seldom make use, then Dunne's belief in his "destiny" may simply explain why he put so much effort into trying to understand something that no one else had so far noticed. In other words, his belief in his own destiny simply *activated* the "unknown power" which remains dormant in most of us.

This notion of *activating* some unknown power may go a long way towards explaining the mystery of synchronicity.

Let me offer a personal illustration. Before I started this chapter, I went to the shelf that contained Jung's complete works, and looked in the General Index, to find what he had to say about precognition. It turned out to be under the heading "foreknowledge". There are not many entries – in fact, only references to four volumes. Volume Ten has two entries, the first being for paragraph 636. (For some reason, Jung prefers to refer to paragraphs rather than pages.) I looked at this, decided it contained nothing to my purpose, and looked at the second, which I read as paragraph 894. I turned over a whole block of pages casually, and found myself looking at paragraph 894. I was just congratulating myself on this piece of synchronicity when I realized that paragraph 894 also contained nothing of interest to me. I then looked again in the General Index and found that I had misread it, and in fact the entry was paragraph 849.

So I had misread it as 894, turned over a huge block of pages, and found myself looking at 894. Was this an example of some kind of "hidden power" inside me leading me to turn to the right page?

I find that I seem to have quite an ability to wake up at some exact time that I decide upon before I fall asleep. On one occasion, I had to catch an early train, and set the alarm on my watch for four fifty-five a.m. I woke up in the dark, and wondered what the time was. So I turned on the light and looked at my watch. It was, in fact, four fifty-six – somehow, the alarm had failed to work. Yet I had nevertheless awakened exactly on time.

So it is as least possible that I somehow unconsciously turned over exactly the right number of pages to take me to paragraph 894. If so, this would be an example of the "unknown power" that Flammarion talks about.

This, at all events, seems to support Flammarion's argument that we all possess some "unknown power", but that this is not activated unless we possess some sense of urgency like my need to get up to catch a train.

But what exactly are these "higher faculties", and how do they work? There is obviously no chance of explaining them in terms that would be acceptable to a materialist, because the materialist simplifies the whole question by arguing that such powers do not and cannot exist. And if we believe that that is untrue, then we have to begin by recognizing that any kind of answer is bound to go beyond the limits of science as we know it.

But that need not alarm us. Science depends upon logical categories, and logical categories are not necessarily complete. Our language, for example, is an attempt to fit our experience into logical categories – like the seven colours of the spectrum, or the sounds of the musical scale. Yet we all know that there are many colours and many sounds which do not fit the spectrum or the musical scale. There are probably two dozen shades of red, as well as the colour brown, which do not exist in the language spectrum. In other words, the problem with language is that it is too crude. How could I describe to someone the difference between the taste of two different types of tea? Or between a lemon and a lime? Or between a honeydew melon and a galia melon? It is easy enough once you have experienced the tastes, but we have no words to express them.

In 1936, a remarkable American writer called Max Freedom

Long wrote a book called *Recovering the Ancient Magic*, about the beliefs and the magic used by the priests of Hawaii, known as *Kahunas*. Although very few copies were sold, and the plates of the book were destroyed during the war in the bombing of London, Long received so many letters of appreciation about the book that he decided to enlarge it. It was republished in 1948 under the title *The Secret Science Behind Miracles*. Although this must be among the worst titles ever chosen, the book has nevertheless remained a classic.

Kahunas were the ancient priests of Hawaii, before Christianity came along and displaced them. Yet even after the religion was outlawed, it continued to be practised in remote parts of the Hawaiian islands.

Max Freedom Long, born in 1890, went to Hawaii in 1917, where he met a doctor named William Tufts Brigham, curator of the Bishop Museum in Honolulu. Brigham was perfectly aware that the Kahuna priests of Hawaii were capable of performing miracles. For example, they were actually able to cause death by something they call the "death prayer".

Long became a schoolteacher in a remote valley, and tried to find out all he could about Kahunas. It was difficult – the Hawaiian natives refused to speak about their ancient religion. But Long heard a story about a Christian minister who had challenged a Kahuna magician to a contest of prayers, and Long found the minister's diary, which described how member after members of his congregation died mysteriously. Finally, the minister persuaded someone to teach him the death prayer, and the Kahuna magician died within three days. Long also met a young a Hawaiian who had experienced the magic of the Kahunas. He had walked into a forbidden temple to demonstrate that he was not afraid, but his legs became useless and he had to be carried home. The local doctor could do nothing and he had to go to a Kahuna to be cured.

Brigham was able to tell Long all that he had learned about the Kahunas, but that was not very much. But when he was back in America, in 1935, Long suddenly had an inspiration. It struck him that the Hawaiians must have special words to describe their beliefs, and that these words must be in the dictionary. Since Hawaiian words are built up from shorter words, it ought to be possible to gather important clues from their sacred words. He looked up "spirit" and found there were two words: *Unihipili* and

Uhane. And he remembered that Christian missionaries declare that man has two souls.

Later, Long discovered that the Hunas (the Indians of Hawaii) believe that man has three souls – besides the *Unihipili* and *Uhane*, there is one called the *Aumakua*. He concluded that the *Unihipili* is what Freud called the unconscious – man's "lower self". The *Uhane* is the conscious everyday self – what might be called the "middle self". And the *Aumakua* is what might be called the "higher self", or the "super-conscious mind". The Hawaiians had apparently believed that, in addition to his unconscious mind, man has a super-conscious mind, which is as far above everyday consciousness as the unconscious is below it.

The eminent psychical researcher F. W. H. Myers had also suggested a similar theory in his classic work *Human Personality and its Survival of Bodily Death*. Myers called the "self" that is able to exercise unknown powers the "subliminal self". In his 1961 introduction to a reissue of Myers's book, Aldous Huxley suggested that it might be simpler to say that man has a Freudian unconscious – a kind of basement – a conscious ego, and a super-conscious mind, a kind of attic, of which we are all totally ignorant. These three "selves" seem to correspond to the three selves of the Hunas – which might be called the "low self" (unconscious), the "middle self" (conscious mind) and the "high self" (super-conscious mind.) The low self, say the Hunas, lives in the solar plexus, and its purpose is the manufacture of a vital force called *mana*. This is a life force that is created from food, and is used by the two higher selves, but stepped up in vibratory rate.

Although the low self is the servant of the middle self, it is often refractory and disobedient. It likes its own way. It is naturally violent and emotional like a spoilt child. The middle self, say the Hunas, should attempt to discipline the low self and raise it, rather than descend to its level. The human beings who give way to the tantrums of the lower self are going in the opposite direction to the true path of their evolution.

This can be seen in most criminals (particularly sex criminals).

According to the Hunas, the high self could be regarded as man's guardian angel, and *it knows the future and can control it*.

So it sounds as if the high self is the part of us which is in charge of synchronicity and such things as dream precognition.

The middle self – the "everyday you" – can, in fact, get in touch with the high self. But the problem is that it has to do so via the low self. It is as if the telephone line passes down through the low self before it goes up to the high self. And since the low self is usually in a state of negative emotion, the crackling on the line makes it impossible to communicate. It is only when the low self has achieved a state of calm, or has been disciplined to behave itself, that it is possible to get through to the high self, and to learn the future.

The death prayer, according to Long, depends upon "low selves" which have become detached, usually through death. These low selves are, for example, responsible for poltergeist disturbances. They are what are known as earthbound spirits, stupid but not particularly malevolent.

Middle selves that have become detached after death have no memory – since memory is a function of the low self. These are what are called ghosts, and they exist in a kind of permanent present, unable to escape it.

It would be a mistake to assume that the low self is simply a kind of juvenile delinquent. In fact, Long's group came to refer to the low self as "George", and pointed out that George can be extremely valuable. He has all the penetration of a child, so that if one asks George what he thinks of a certain person, he is likely to go straight to the point. The middle self may feel that a certain person is intelligent and convincing; George can see at a single glance that he is a crook.

According to Long, it is possible to get in touch with George and hold conversations with him. A person who has established this kind of close relation with "George" is in a far better position for establishing a fruitful relation with the high self.

The high self, as already stated, can foresee the future, and may well be the person who is responsible for those glimpses of the future that Dunne wrote about in *An Experiment With Time*.

According to Dr Brigham, the Kahunas can also look into the future and change it for their clients. But this is only possible if the client is not under the domination of the low self, because the low self tends to change its purposes and objectives from moment to moment. Long writes:

"Just how this mechanism works is uncertain, as it belongs to the next higher level of consciousness, but the Kahunas spoke of the forms as "seeds", which were taken by the *Aumakua* (high self) and made to grow into future events or conditions.

"The Kahunas considered it of great importance for the individual to take time out at frequent intervals to think about his life and decide in exact terms what he wished to do or wished to have happen. The average person is too much inclined to let the low self take the helm, which is dangerous because it lives under the domination of the animal world where things happen illogically and as if by accident. It is the business and duty of the middle self, as guide for the low self, to use its power of inductive reason and its will (to control the low self) in making plans for the task of living and seeing that proper efforts are made to work according to those plans."

Long adds: "A large part of the Kahunas' magical practice in days gone by was aimed at seeing what crystallized future lay ahead for the client, then procuring changes in that future to make it more desirable."

Long gives an example of how this can be done.

"In the year 1932, in Honolulu, I owned a camera shop which was hard-hit by the depression and the lack of tourist trade. Threatened with the loss of everything, I went to a Kahuna for help.

"The Kahuna was a Hawaiian woman of about fifty. I had known her for some time and, when I told her that I was in trouble, she set to work at once to see what could be done to right my affairs. We went into a small dining room, and sat down at the table. While she smoked and listened, I told of my difficulties.

"I was faced with the necessity of selling out my business, with the stock and fixtures, or facing bankruptcy. The only person in Honolulu who could buy my store to an advantage was my competitor. He owned a larger and older camera store.

"I had gone to him three times to try to get him to buy me out at a very low figure, but could not interest him. I had paid a real estate man a round sum to try and make the sale, and he had failed. It began to look as if I would have to lose everything. My lease had but a few weeks longer to run, and

to renew my lease for the five-year period at an advance in
rent was out of the question.

"When I had explained everything and had answered a
few questions, the healer asked me to think very hard for a
little while and then tell her exactly what I wanted to have to
come to pass. I thought it all over again, then said that I
wanted to sell my business and stock and fixtures to my
competitor for eight thousand dollars, which would be a
great bargain even in bad times. I wanted to help my
competitor amalgamate my business and his own, and after
that I wished to return to the Coast and to be able to do
some writing. I was quite definite.

"The healer asked more questions. She would say, 'And
if that happens that way, are you sure that it will not make a
difference in your plans?' She explained that I must overlook no possible contingency and must weigh each step and
consider its probable results. I had to consider all the small
details and imagine how each thing would work out and
react on some other part of the plan.

"The idea was to prepare to make the 'Prayer' to the high
self. The thought forms of the prayer had to be unmixed
with doubts and uncertainties. They had to stand out clear
and sharp and definite. Any overlooked angle of the affair
might bob up later to upset the working out of the plan.

"The healer told me that, in her experience, most people
sent to the high self a continuous jumble of conflicting
wishes, plans, fears and hope. Each day and hour they
changed their minds about what they wished to do or
become or have happen. As the high self makes for us
our futures from our averaged thoughts, which it contacts
usually during our sleep, our futures become a hit-and-miss
jumble of events and contrary events, of accidents of good
and bad luck. Only the person who decides what he wants
and holds to his decision doggedly, working always in that
direction, can present to the high self the proper thought
forms from which to build the future as desired and planned
and worked toward.

"After an hour of discussion, the healer was satisfied. She
announced that the next step was to contact the high self
and ask whether or not the plan was such that it could be
made to materialize.

"Instead of using the crystal-gazing arrangements of a black smooth stone swished with water in the bottom of a calabash bowl, she brought out a glass tumbler, filled it with water, grated half a teaspoonful of yellow ginger root into the water to cloud it and act as a physical stimulus to ward off spirit influences of the poltergeist type, should such be near. The grating was done with the thumbnail from a small piece of fresh ginger root out of the garden that afternoon. It was then evening.

"The healer then asked for a silver dollar as a preliminary part of her fee. This acted as a physical stimulus to her low self, as it represented a reward for work and service – thus appearing as a good thing to the low self. The dollar was placed under the tumbler. She then shaded her eyes from the overhead light and sat for a short time looking down at the surface of the clouded water.

"Soon she began to see images and get messages by some form of inner voice. She would remain in a trance-like state for a moment or two, rouse to speak to me and to tell me what she saw, or to ask a fresh question. This continued for perhaps seven or eight minutes.

"The visions in the crystal were all symbolic, and if the symbols were things she had learned by experience to know as good, she counted the answer favourable to my plans. She said she saw a door being opened, then, a little later, a sheaf of wheat. She asked what these things might mean to me or if I had been thinking about them – wishing to be sure that she was not seeing them in my mind instead of from the high self via the low self. When she was satisfied that the answer was favourable, she said, 'The god tells me that your prayer can be answered. The door is open. Your path is not badly blocked, even if the door was not open all the way. I will now ask what we must do for our part of the work.'

"Again she gazed into the water and entered the state in which she could see with psychic senses. She began to see my competitor, who was also a good friend of long standing. She described his appearance and checked with me as to whether she was seeing him accurately or not. She saw his office at the rear of his store and checked that with me. She also saw the man whom I had hired to sell my business and who had failed. When this psychic examination of the matter was finished it was growing late.

" 'Have you hurt anyone?' the healer asked. 'Why is the door not wide open and why is your path a little blocked?'

"I could think of no injury I had done anyone, and said so.

" 'Do you feel that you would cheat if you sold your store for eight thousand dollars?' was the next question.

"I assured her that I would consider the deal most fair.

" 'Then it is the little sin ideas which eat you inside because of your Sunday School or Church training,' she decided. 'Most of the good people, especially if they are good church people, have things like that. To get rid of the feeling of guilt and clear your path to the god, you must fast until one o'clock for three days and, while you fast, you must not smoke. After three days, give a gift to some person in need or to some charity. This gift must be large enough to hurt you a little – almost more than you can afford. This will make you feel deep inside you that you have done enough to balance all your little sins. After you have done these things, come to me again.'

"The healer was prescribing very excellent physical stimuli to impress the low self in me that it was making amends for such acts as it believed to be sins. I had no way of finding out what these small guilt complexes might be, but that made no difference.

"I carried out the orders during the next three days, finding them difficult enough to impress my low self not a little, as I had been blessed with a good appetite and at that time I loved to smoke. My gift was made to the Salvation Army, this being to my mind a good charity organization.

"Again arriving in the evening, I sat with the healer at the round table. She again made use of the tumbler mechanism in the same way, and after a few minutes saw the door again, this time wide open. Announcing that my path was now unblocked, she pushed the tumbler from her and reopened the question of my plans. Had I made any changes in my plans? Was I still sure I wanted everything to happen just as I had stated?

"When assured that my plans were clear and unchanged, she made ready to make the prayer for me to the high self.

"When a Kahuna prayed to his or her high self, asking aid for a client, the prayer automatically went to the high self of the client as well. This involves a belief that all high selves are linked together in some way we cannot understand and can hardly imagine. They are 'many in one' and 'one in many'. They are Unity in Separation. They have bonds closer than those of bees in a hive. They have learned to work as a unit, but each does individual works. We cannot grasp this, but, from the results obtained through contact with the high selves, this seems to be the nearest we can come to understanding the matter.

"To make the prayer, the healer rose and walked slowly back and forth, breathing heavily. After a few minutes, she paused beside the table, and said quietly that she would now make the prayer to the god for me, and then – looking as into a distance – began to speak in Hawaiian, slowly and with great force. She voiced the prayer once, then repeated it, then repeated it again.

"This thrice-spoken prayer was offered word for word and idea for idea as nearly as possible, the full force of the suggestive will being mustered to cause the low self to carry the high self the thought forms which were being made by the carefully and firmly repeated prayer.

"The high self was contacted by the low self after a direct command from the middle self of the healer, the tumbler not being used, as at this time no return answer was expected or requested. When the prayer has been thrice spoken, the healer resumed her chair and took a cigarette. She smoked and rested after her effort. She had accumulated extra vital force and had presented the prayer as a set of thought forms on a flow of vital force.

"Soon the tumbler was brought into action to see what message could be had from the high self, and what instruction might be given.

"In the water surface in the tumbler appeared (to her) a scene in which I did several things. It was an enactment of what the high self had caused my future to be. The old future was torn down and a new one had been instantly constructed for me.

"The old future had undoubtedly contained all the business failures which seemed inevitable to me and which I feared and so visualized as I worried. This probably would have been my future, if I had not the help of the high self in changing the bad to the desired good.

"We do not know the exact way in which the high self makes the future for the low and middle selves of which it stands as 'guardian, parental spirit'. We can only guess that the thought we make into thought forms are used in some way in shaping the future. At least, the thought forms tell the high self what we hope, fear, desire and plan. It seems that our futures are made from these thought forms with all care being taken not to intrude on our free will. We must be allowed to exert free will and, unless we ask for help, it must not be given, lest the free will be cancelled.

"We cannot say why, but we can understand that such condition of affairs can be.

"Because of our mental limitations, we cannot conceive of a future made of invisible material, but still containing all the events and conditions which will materialize from minute to minute and hour to hour and day to day, for as far ahead as the invisible outline of the future is 'crystallized'. Perhaps the future is made like the shadowy bodies of the low and middle selves, and as are the thought forms. Perhaps thought forms are made to grow into events. The Kahunas did not know. We cannot know. However, so long as we know that the future is made in some such way and that it can be seen ahead in so far as it has been made, and that IT CAN BE CHANGED, that is all we need to know.

"The healer saw the new future in her tumbler of water and described to me the things she saw that I must do, also telling me why. She seemed to get the idea of why things were done in some psychic way connected with the psychic vision. The usual method of the high self of giving symbols was not used here.

"'The god tells me,' she would say, or, 'The god shows me.'

"She saw me going to my competitor with a paper in my hand. She said that on the paper I had written out my proposition to sell, the price, and all details. She said that the god had told her that this man was the kind who would like to see everything written out on paper, otherwise he would say 'no' from force of habit.

" 'You write it all out,' she instructed. 'Then, next Tuesday, at a quarter after two, you are to go to see him. He will be in his office sitting at his desk and doing nothing. You put the paper on his desk and say, "Have a look at these figures, will you? I'll be back in about ten minutes." Then you go off and in ten minutes you come back. He will be finished reading your paper and will say to you that he will buy your business.'

"To me, this was unbelievably explicit and detailed. I asked how she knew, and she told me that she saw me doing it in my new future, and that the god made her understand why the proposition had to be written out.

"I marvelled at the instructions and promised to obey them to the letter.

"At a quarter after two on the following Tuesday, I went into my competitor's place of business with my proposal carefully typed out in full. I found him, as had been foreseen, idly sitting at his desk. I placed the paper before him and asked him to look it over, saying I would be back in ten minutes.

"In ten minutes I returned, and he was waiting for me. 'I'll take you up,' he said. 'I'll give you my check for a hundred dollars to bind the bargain and you can make out a bill of sale.'

"So, with the help of the healer and the high self, the deal was closed. The price stipulated in the prayer was paid me. I stayed on to help get my business amalgamated with that of my competitor.

"With the deal completed, I reported back to the Kahuna, paying her all she would allow, which was little enough, considering the great service she had rendered me.

"Some time later, when I was about to finish up my business affairs and leave for California, the healer ran a check on my future for me to see about the part of the plan I had made which included a desire to do some writing.

"She made a fresh prayer, asking that I be allowed to write, and then inspected the future with the aid of the high self via the low self, to see what instructions were given for me. As she had done in the case of the sale of business, she now did for the writing.

" 'You will write eight books,' she said, after a long look

into her improvised gazing crystal. 'That is as far ahead as the god shows me. Eight books.' She sighed. 'But you will have to be very patient. It will be a long time from the first book to the eighth. Many things will happen and it will not be easy, although the last four books will be easier than the first four and come faster.'

"That glimpse of the future which the healer got for me dates back to 1932. Now, in 1947, the first four books are water under the bridge."

In fact, as the Huna predicted, Long wrote eight books in all. After such an experience, Long was naturally anxious to establish where the Hunas came from originally, and whether their magical practices were known elsewhere. But that was made doubly difficult by the fear of the "death prayer". When people became the victims of the death prayer, they first lost the use of their feet, then of their legs, and then the paralysis gradually spread upwards until they died.

Dr Brigham told Long a story about a young Hawaiian boy who accompanied him on an expedition up Mount Mauna Lowa to collect plant specimens, and how, halfway up the mountain, the boy began to experience paralysis in his feet, then in his legs. Other Hawaiians who were in the party assured Brigham that the boy was the victim of the death prayer and, on questioning, the boy admitted that the old Kahuna in his village had warned everyone to have no dealings with the white people, on pain of death.

An old man among the Hawaiians begged Brigham – who was regarded as a magician in his own right – to counter the death prayer. Brigham, who was quite sure that he had no magical powers, finally had to agree. He knew that the agents who carried out the orders of the Kahuna were supposed to be spirits – "low selves" separated from the rest of the being by death. But these spirits are also highly suggestible. Brigham stood above the sick boy and began to argue with the spirits, telling them that he realized that they were fine and intelligent creatures, and that it was a great pity that they had been enslaved by the Kahuna. He told them that their real destiny was to go to heaven and that, in killing the boy, they were simply obeying the will of an evil man. Some of the listening Hawaiians actually began to cry, because they were so moved by Brigham's argument.

Finally, Brigham ordered the spirits to go back and attack the Kahuna. After a very long wait, Brigham felt a strange sensation as if all the tension had gone out of the air. At that moment, the boy discovered that he was able to move his legs. Not long after, Brigham went to the boy's village, and was told that the Kahuna was dead – it had happened on the night Brigham had wrestled with the spirits. The Kahuna had awakened with a scream and begun to fight off spirits, but because he had failed to put protection on himself, he was vulnerable, and died before morning.

It can be seen why Long had so much difficulty in learning anything about the religion of the Kahuna, and the death prayer.

But after the publication of his first book, *Recovering the Ancient Magic*, he received a letter from a retired English journalist called William Reginald Stewart, who was able to throw an extremely interesting light on the possible history of the Hunas.

Stewart had been in Africa, working as a correspondent for the *Christian Science Monitor*, when he heard about a woman who possessed magical powers, and who belonged to the Berber tribe, the aboriginal people of North Africa. Stewart was so interested in these stories that he hired guides and set out to find the tribe in the Atlas Mountains. There he discovered the female magician, who was known among her fellow Berbers as a *Quahuna* – obviously the same word. With a great deal of persuasion, he was adopted by the tribe, and also made the adopted son of the magician. Her name was Lucchi, and her seventeen-year-old daughter was also beginning to train as a *Quahuna*, so Stewart was allowed to become a second pupil.

According to Lucchi, there were originally twelve tribes of people who had magicians called *Quahunas*, and they once lived in the Sahara desert when it was green and fertile. (The Sahara *was* green and fertile once, but we have no means of discovering exactly when.) Then, said Lucchi, the rivers had dried up and the tribes had moved into the Nile valley. It was there that they used their magic to build the Great Pyramid. They became the rulers of Egypt and were highly regarded because of their magic.

Lucchi went on to tell how the prophetic powers of the *Quahunas* enabled them to see that a time of intellectual darkness was due to fall on the earth, and that the secret of their magic might be lost. So the twelve tribes began to hunt for isolated lands to which they might go to preserve their secret (for which the Hawaiian word is "Huna"). The world was explored – not physically, but by psychic means. (All ancient magicians and Shamans are traditionally believed to be able to leave their bodies.) Eventually, they discovered that the islands of the Pacific were empty, and made their way there via a canal to the Red Sea, then along the African coast and across India. But the twelfth tribe decided to stay in Africa, and moved to the Atlas mountains. There, they lived for centuries, preserving the secret and using its magic, until the only *Quahuna* left was Lucchi.

Much of what Stewart learned from Lucchi corresponded closely with what Long had said in his book. Stewart also described Lucchi's magical powers, how she was able to heal, control the weather (a traditional power of witches) and exercise her power over animals.

Then, Lucchi was suddenly killed. Two raiding parties began to shoot at one another, and a stray bullet killed the last of the *Quahunas*. This was before the First World War, and it was thirty years later that Stewart read Long's first book and contacted him.

It would seem possible, then, that Kahuna magic originated in Africa, before the building of the Great Pyramid, and that it had spread from there to the Pacific.

Long comments that Hawaiian legend states that the Hawaiians once lived in a homeland far away, and that they saw the land of Hawaii by "psychic sight". Their voyage began at the "Red Sea of Kane", and they then moved from land to land in large double canoes.

Long also adds that traces of Kahuna magic can be found in India.

Long's account of the Kahunas is obviously of great importance in this discussion of time. Mystics have always insisted that time is some kind of an illusion, and that man's essential spirit lives in a realm of timelessness. Here is an example taken from a book called *The Common Experience*, edited by J. Cohen and J-F. Phipps, which contains many accounts of religious experience selected from material collected by the Religious Experience Research Group at Manchester College, Oxford.

"I was in the garden, muddling about alone. A cuckoo flew over, calling. Suddenly, I experienced a sensation I can only describe as an effect that might follow the rotating of a kaleidoscope. It was a feeling of timelessness, not only that time stood still, that duration had ceased, but that I was myself outside time altogether. Somehow I knew that I was part of eternity. And there was also a feeling of space-lessness. I lost all awareness of my surroundings. With this detachment I felt the intensest joy I had ever known, and yet with so great a longing – for what I did not know – that it was scarcely distinguishable from suffering.

"How long I stood, or would have gone on standing, I do not know; the tea-bell rang, shattering the extra dimension into which I had seemed to be caught up. I returned to earth and went obediently in, speaking to no one of these things."

Dozens of similar passages could be quoted from *The Common Experience* and other similar books on mysticism.

If we take these seriously, then it would seem that there is a "timeless realm" which is available to human beings in certain moments of intensity.

In fact, all this makes sense, even in the light of our common experience. When we are bored and tired, time seems to drag. When we are happy and excited, it flies past. This is because you are exercising more free will. Your concentration brings a sense of freedom, and it is freedom which causes time to pass more quickly.

In other words, the less we exercise our sense of freedom, the more we feel bored and tired, the slower time becomes. The more we exercise our freedom, the more interested and excited we become, the faster time moves. So time is not something that simply rolls on whether we like it or not. The hymn that says "time like an ever rolling stream/bears all its sons away . . ." gives us a false impression. It makes us think of someone standing at the side of a river, watching it flow past. But time does not flow "past" us. We are in the middle of it, and the less we exercise freedom, the more we are subject to time. But the more we exercise freedom, the less we feel ourselves to be the slaves of time. What obviously happened to the man "muddling about" in his garden was that the sight of the cuckoo and its sound as it called, somehow triggered a sensation of happiness and freedom. This had the effect of hurling him into a sense of timelessness.

Time depends upon *us*, upon our power of focused attention. In a remarkable book called *On Time*, Michael Shallis quotes another passage about time "standing still".

"Now I Joseph was walking and I walked not. And I looked up to the air and saw the air in amazement. And I looked up unto the pole of the heaven and saw it standing still, and the fowls of the heaven without motion. And behold there were sheep being driven and they went not forward but stood still; and the shepherd lifted his hand to smite them with his staff and his hand remained up. And I looked upon the stream of the river and saw the mouths of the kids upon the water and they drank not. And all of a sudden all things moved onwards in their course."

This is from the Apocryphal Gospel of James.

In a book called *The Relevance of Bliss*, Nona Coxhead quotes an account of a man called Derek Gibson who was travelling to work by motor-cycle when he suddenly realised that the sound of his engine had faded away:

"Then everything suddenly changed. I could clearly see everything as before with form and substance, but instead of looking *at* it all I was looking *into* everything. I saw beneath the bark of the trees and *through* the underlying trunks. I was looking *into* the grass too and all was magnified beyond measure. To the extent that I could see moving microscopic organisms! Then, not only was I seeing all this, but I was literally *inside* it all. *At the same time* as I was looking into this mass of greenery, I was aware of every single blade of grass and fold of the trees as if each had been placed before me one at a time and entered into.

"My world became a fairyland of vivid greens and browns, colours not seen so much as felt. Instantly also my mind was not observing but was living what it was registering. 'I' did not exist. Power and knowledge surged through my mind. The words formed in me – I can remember clearly – 'now I know', 'there is *nothing* I could not answer. I am a part of all this.''

A writer called Warner Allen actually wrote a book called *The Timeless Moment*, after a similar experience:

> "It flashed up lightning-wise during a performance of Beethoven's Seventh Symphony at the Queen's Hall, in that triumphant fast movement when 'The morning stars sang together and all the sons of God shouted for joy'. The swiftly flowing continuity of the music was not interrupted, so that what Mr T. S. Eliot calls 'the intersection of the timeless moment' must have slipped into the interval between two demi-semi-quavers. When 'long after' I analysed the happening in the cold light of retrospect, it seemed to fall into three parts: first, the mysterious event itself which occurred in an infinitesimal fraction of a split second; this I learned afterwards from Santa Teresa to call the Union with God; the Illumination, a *wordless* stream of complex feelings, in which the experience of Union combined with the rhythmic emotion of the music like a sunbeam striking with iridescence the spray above a waterfall – a stream that was continually swollen by tributaries of associated Experience; lastly, Enlightenment, the recollection in tranquillity of the whole complex field of experience as it were embalmed in thought-forms and words."

Why do these "timeless moments" occur so infrequently?

The answer, obviously, is that our everyday consciousness is fairly mechanical. From the moment we get up in the morning, we are thinking of the practical things that we have to do, and of the practical measures we have to take to do things efficiently. This state is obviously a long way from the state we have described – of being "in control". Clearly, what happens in these mystical experiences is that, for some reason, we feel far more in control of ourselves than under normal circumstances. We notice that even when we are setting out on a bright spring morning and feeling curiously optimistic and relaxed. Somehow, energy seems to be bubbling up in us, and we no longer feel ourselves to be the slaves of time. When you are travelling to work on a bus, you see the passing scenery as something solid and inevitable, something that almost intimidates you with its permanence. But when you are setting out on holiday, the passing scenery seems to arouse a tremendous excitement in us, and it is this excitement that seems to give us power over it. As soon as we feel happy and excited, we have taken the first step towards "the timeless moment".

The medium Eileen Garrett writes:

"There are certain concentrations of consciousness in which awareness is withdrawn as far as possible from the impact of all sensory perceptions . . . Such withdrawals of consciousness from the outer world are common to all of us in some measure . . .

"What happens to us at these times is that, as we withdraw from the environing world, we relegate the activities of the five senses to the field of the subconscious, and seek to focus *awareness* (to the best of our ability) in the field of the superconscious – the timeless, spaceless field of the as-yet-unknown."

The mention of the "superconscious" immediately reminds us of the Kahunas and the "high self". And, as we have seen, the Kahunas are certain that the high self has the power to rise above time, to see the future. All of which means that the average human being is like a person who is struggling in a river and being swept along, while the super-conscious mind stands on the bank.

All this leads us to raise once again the question that has recurred throughout this book: if it is possible to foresee the future, then does that not mean that everything that happens is rigidly pre-destined, and that human beings have no free will at all?

Jung's story of the two cream-coloured horses makes it seem that the answer has to be yes. On the other hand, the views of another great teacher of the twentieth century, George Ivanovich Gurdjieff, suggests that this must be qualified. He was of the opinion that most human beings are little more than penny-in-the-slot machines, responding quite simply to stimuli from the outside world, and that therefore, they have little or no free will. On the other hand, anyone who becomes aware that his life is almost entirely mechanical has arrived at the point where he can begin to change this. It requires, according to Gurdjieff, a tremendous and continuous effort, but by making such an effort, human beings can begin to learn to become non-mechanical.

Gurdjieff's chief disciple, P. D. Ouspensky, tells an interesting story to illustrate the point. Gurdjieff made an important distinction between what he called "personality" and "essence". When a baby is born, says Gurdjieff, it only has "essence", its essential response to the world. At the age of six or seven, the child begins to develop "personality" – that is, to become aware of itself as a person among other people – *in response* to other people. When this happens, says Gurdjieff, "essence" often ceases to grow altogether, while "personality" takes over. Some people who appear to have a powerful and vital personality are totally empty inside; their lives are little more than a mechanical response to other people and their environment. Their essence ceased to develop as a child.

'In *In Search of the Miraculous*, Ouspensky describes an extraordinary experiment performed by Gurdjieff to show his pupils the difference between essence and personality. Two people had been chosen for the purpose of the experiment: one a prominent middle-aged man with an important position, the other a rather scatter-brained young man whose conversation tended to be wordy and confusing. In some way, either by hypnosis or a drug (Ouspensky declined to be specific), both were plunged into a semi-trance-like state in which "personality" vanished. (Kenneth Walker, another Gurdjieff follower, says that Ouspensky told him that Gurdjieff used a drug on this occasion.) The older man became completely passive. Asked about the war – about which he had been expressing the most heated opinions before – he said that it did not interest him. The young man, on the other hand, talked seriously and simply, making excellent sense. Gurdjieff explained that the young man had a reasonably developed "essence" which had become overlaid with awkwardness, a tendency to overreact to other people, so he appeared a nervous fool. The older man had little "essence" left; he had developed a bombastic and opinionated personality, but there was nothing underneath.'[1]

According to Gurdjieff, only people with "essence" have some possibility of exercising free will and changing their future. A man like the politician responds to each challenge entirely predictably and mechanically.

It was after he had met Gurdjieff in 1912 that Ouspensky

1 *Gurdjieff: The War Against Sleep* by Colin Wilson

began to write one of his most important books, *A New Model of the Universe*. In this book, there is a remarkable chapter called "Experimental Mysticism", in which the whole mystery of time is explored and expressed with unprecedented clarity.

Ouspensky describes how, even before meeting Gurdjieff, he had begun to experiment with some method – which he refuses to specify – for achieving heightened states of consciousness. It is virtually certain that what Ouspensky did was to sniff nitrous oxide – "laughing gas" – which has the effect of inducing euphoria and often "mystical" experiences.

Ouspensky explains that: "A change in the state of consciousness as a result of my experiments began to take place very soon, much more quickly and easily than I thought. But the chief difficulty was that the new state of consciousness which was obtained gave at once so much that was new and unexpected, and these new and unexpected experiences came upon me and flashed by so quickly, that I could not find words, could not find forms of speech, could not find concepts, which would enable me to remember what had occurred even for myself, still less to convey it to anybody else."

He goes on to explain that the first sensation he noted was a kind of *duality* in himself. It was as if he was suddenly watching himself from outside as well as having the experience induced by the gas. This change came, he says, about twenty minutes after the start of the experiment. "When this change came, I found myself in a world entirely new and entirely unknown to me, which had nothing in common with the world in which we live, still less with the world which we assume to be the continuation of our world in the direction of the unknown."

He goes on to say that the chief problem with explaining himself is that the whole experience was so strange and new that it was virtually impossible to find words for it.

Ouspensky went on to say: ". . . In this case, I saw from the very beginning that all that we half-consciously construct with regard to the unknown is completely and utterly wrong. The unknown is unlike anything we can suppose about it. The complete unexpectedness of everything that is met with in these experiences, from great to small, makes the description of them difficult."

Then he goes on to pinpoint one of the most important things about this experience:

"First of all, everything is unified, everything is linked together, everything is explained by something else and in its turn explains another thing. There is nothing separate, that is, nothing that can be named or described *separately*. In order to describe the first impressions, the first sensations, it is necessary to describe *all* at once. The new world with which one comes into contact has no sides, so that it is impossible to describe first one side and then the other. All of it is visible at once at every point; but how in fact to describe anything in these conditions – that question I could not answer.

"My personal impression was that, in the world with which I came into contact, there was nothing resembling any of the descriptions which I had read or heard of before.

"What I first noticed, simultaneously with the 'division of myself into two', was that the relation between the objective and the subjective was broken, entirely altered, and took certain forms incomprehensible to us. But 'objective' and 'subjective' are only words. I do not wish to hide behind these words, but I wish to describe as exactly as possible what I really felt. For this purpose I must explain what it is that I call 'objective' and 'subjective'. My hand, the pen with which I write, the table, these are objective phenomena. My thoughts, my mental images, the pictures of my imagination, these are subjective phenomena. The world is divided for us along these lines when we are in our ordinary state of consciousness, and all our ordinary orientation works along the lines of this division. In this new state all this was completely upset.

"First of all, we are accustomed to the constancy of the relation between the subjective and the objective – what is objective is always objective, what is subjective is always subjective. Here I saw that the objective and the subjective could change places. The one could become the other. It is very difficult to express this. The habitual mistrust of the subjective disappeared; every thought, every feeling, every image, was immediately objectified in real substantial forms which differed in no way from the forms of objective phenomena; and at the same time objective phenomena somehow disappeared, lost all reality, appeared entirely subjective, fictitious, invented, having no real existence.

"This was the first experience. Further, in trying to describe this strange world in which I saw myself, I must say that it resembled more than anything a world of *very complicated mathematical relations.*

". . . A world of mathematical relations – this means a world in which everything is connected, in which nothing exists separately, and in which at the same time the relations between things have a real existence apart from the things themselves; or possibly, 'things' do not even exist and only 'relations' exist."

Ouspensky goes on to say that he tried experiments under many conditions and in varied surroundings, and gradually became convinced that it was best to be alone.

"When I tried having someone near me during these experiments, I found that no kind of conversation could be carried on. I began to say something, but between the first and the second words of my sentence, such an enormous number of ideas occurred to me and passed before me, that the two words were so widely separated as to make it impossible to find any connection between them. And the third word I usually forgot before it was pronounced, and in trying to recall it I found a million new ideas, but completely forgot where I had begun. I remember for instance the beginning of a sentence: 'I said yesterday . . .'

"No sooner had I pronounced the word 'I' than a number of ideas began to turn in my head about the meaning of the word in a philosophical, in a psychological and in every other sense. This was all so important, so new and profound, that when I pronounced the word 'said', I could not understand in the least what I meant by it. Tearing myself away with difficulty from the first cycle of thoughts about 'I', I passed to the idea 'said', and immediately found in it an infinite content. The idea of speech, the possibility of expressing thoughts in words, the past tense of the verb, each of these ideas produced an explosion of thoughts, conjectures, comparisons and associations. Thus, when I pronounced the word 'yesterday', I was already quite unable to understand why I had said it. But it in its turn immediately dragged me into the depths of the problems of time, of past, present and future, and before me such possibilities of approach to these problems began to open up that my breath was taken away."

Ouspensky's sense of time was completely altered.

"It was precisely these attempts at conversation, made in these strange states of consciousness, which gave me the sensation of change in time which is described by almost everyone who has made experiments like mine. This is a feeling of the extraordinary lengthening of time, in which seconds seem to be years or decades.

"Nevertheless, the usual feeling of time did not disappear; only together with it or within it there appeared as it were another feeling of time, and two moments of ordinary time, like two words of my sentence, could be separated by long periods of another time.

"I remember how much I was struck by this sensation the first time I had it. My companion was saying something. Between each sound of his voice, between each movement of his lips, long periods of time passed. When he had finished a short sentence, the meaning of which did not reach me at all, I felt I had lived through so much during that time that we should never be able to understand one another again, that I had gone too far from him. It seemed to me that we were still able to speak and to a certain extent understand one another at the beginning of this sentence, but by the end it had become quite impossible, because there were no means of conveying to him all that I had lived through in between."

Ouspensky goes on to describe how, in these states, there was a curious connection between his breathing and the beating of his heart – when he breathed faster, his heart beat increased, and when he breathed slower his heart beat slowed down. After a while, he began to feel a kind of pulse spreading throughout his body, and "suddenly a shock was felt through the whole body, as though a spring clicked, and at the same instant something opened in me. Everything suddenly changed, there began something strange, new, entirely unlike anything that occurs in life. This I called the first threshold."

He goes on to say that, in many cases, he did not go further than this. But sometimes:

"It happened that this state deepened and widened as though I was gradually plunged in light. After that there came a moment of yet another transition, another kind of shock throughout the body. And only after this began the most interesting state which I attained in my experiments.

"The 'transitional state' contained almost all the elements of this state but at the same time it lacked something most important and essential. The 'transitional state' did not differ much in its essence from dreams, especially from dreams in the 'half-dream state', though it had its own very characteristic forms . . . In the 'transitional state', which as I learned very soon, was entirely subjective, I usually began almost at once to hear 'voices'. These 'voices' were a characteristic feature of the 'transitional state'.

"The voices spoke to me and often said very strange things which seemed to have a quality of a trick in them. Sometimes, in the first moments, I was excited by what I heard in this way, particularly as it answered certain vague and unformulated expectations that I had. Sometimes I heard music which evoked in me very varied and powerful emotions.

"But strangely enough, I felt from the first day a distrust of these states. They contained too many promises, too many things I wanted to have. The voices spoke about every possible kind of thing. They warned me. They proved and explained to me everything in the world, but somehow they did it too simply. I began to ask myself whether I might not myself have invented all that they said, whether it might not be my own imagination, that unconscious imagination which creates our dreams, in which we can see people, talk to them, hear their voices, receive advice from them, etc. After thinking in this way I had to say to myself that the voices told me nothing that I could not have thought myself.

". . . Once I asked a question referring to alchemy. I cannot now remember the exact question, but I think it was something either about the different denominations of the four elements: fire, water, earth and air; or about the relation of the four elements to one another. I put the question in connection with what I was reading at the time. In answer to this question a voice which called itself by a well-known name told me that the answer to my question would be found in a certain book. When I said that I had not got this book, the voice told me that I should find it in the Public Library (this happened in St Petersburg) and advised me to read the book carefully.

"I enquired at the public library, but the book (published in English) was not there. There was only a German translation of it in twenty parts, the first three being missing.

"But soon I obtained the book elsewhere in English and actually found there certain hints very closely connected with my question, though they did not give a complete answer to it."

Ouspensky concluded that in these 'transitional states', he went through the same experience as mediums and clairvoyants.

Ouspensky explains how he came to distrust these transitional states, and decided that he would only accept as real anything that he could not have imagined himself.

"I passed the second threshold, which I have already mentioned, beyond which *a new world* began. The 'voices' disappeared; in their place there sounded sometimes one voice, which could always be recognized, whatever forms it might take. At the same time this new state differed from the transitional state by its extraordinary lucidity of consciousness. I then found myself in the world of mathematical relations, in which there was nothing at all resembling what occurs in life.

"In this state also, after passing the second threshold and finding myself in the 'world of mathematical relations', I obtained answers to all my questions, but the answers often took a very strange form. In order to understand them, it must be realized that the world of mathematical relations in which I was did not remain immovable; this means – there was nothing in it that remained as it was the moment before. Everything moved, changed, was transformed and became something else. Sometimes I suddenly saw all mathematical relations disappear one after another into infinity. Infinity swallowed everything, filled everything; all distinctions were effaced. And I felt that, one moment more and I myself should disappear into infinity. I was overcome with terror at the imminence of this abyss. Sometimes this terror made me jump to my feet, move about, in order to drive away the nightmare which had seized me . . . Infinity attracted me and at the same time frightened me and repelled me. And I came to understand it quite differently. Infinity was not infinite continuation in one direction, but infinite variation at one point. I understood that the terror of infinity results from a wrong approach to it, from a wrong attitude to it. I understood that with the right approach to it, infinity is precisely what explains everything, and that nothing can be explained without it.

"At the same time, I felt that in infinity there was a real menace and a real danger."

Ouspensky explains that the most important thing about this experience was a state of intense emotion.

"This emotional state was perhaps the most vivid characteristic of the experience which I am describing. Without it there would have been nothing . . . I took in everything through feeling, and experienced emotions which never exist in life. The new knowledge that came to me came when I was in an exceedingly intense emotional state. My attitude towards this new knowledge was in no way indifferent; I either loved it or was horrified by it, strove towards it or was amazed by it; and it was these very emotions with a thousand others, which gave the possibility of understanding the nature of the new world that I came to know.

". . . further, in this world there was nothing dead, nothing inanimate, nothing that did not think, nothing that did not feel, nothing unconscious. Everything was living, everything was conscious of itself. Everything spoke to me and I could speak to everything. Particularly interesting were the houses and other buildings which I passed, especially the old houses. They were living beings, full of thoughts, feelings, moods and memories. The people who lived in them were their *thoughts, feelings, moods.* I mean that the people in relation to the 'houses' played approximately the same role which the different 'Is' of our personality play in relation to us. They come and go, sometimes live in us for a long time, sometimes only appear only for short moments.

"I remember once being struck by an ordinary cab-horse in the Nevsky, by its head, its face. It expressed the whole being of the horse. Looking at the horse's face, I understood all that could be understood about a horse. All the traits of horse-nature, all of which a horse is capable, all of which it is incapable, all that it can do, all that it cannot do; all this was expressed in the lines and features of the horse's face. A dog once gave me a similar sensation. At the same time the horse and the dog were not simply horse and dog; they were atoms, conscious, moving 'atoms' of great beings – 'the great horse' and 'the great dog'. I understood then that we are also atoms of a great being, 'the great man'. Each thing is an atom of a 'great thing'. A glass is an atom of a 'great glass'. A fork is an atom of a 'great fork'."

Understandably, Ouspensky felt a strong desire to try to pin down what he had seen in this state.

"Once, I remember, in a particularly vividly expressed new state . . . I decided to find some formula, some key, which I should be able, so to speak, to throw across to myself for the next day. I decided to sum up shortly all that I understood at that moment and write down, if possible, in one sentence what it was necessary to do in order to bring myself into the same state immediately, by one turn of thought, without any preliminary preparation, since this appeared possible to me all the time. I found this formula and wrote it down with a pencil on a piece of paper.

"On the following day, I read the sentence, 'Think in other categories.' These were the words, but what was their meaning? . . . I could not recollect it, could not reach it.

"I remember once sitting on a sofa smoking and looking at an ashtray. It was an ordinary copper ashtray. Suddenly I felt that I was beginning to understand what the ashtray was and, at the same time, with a certain wonder and almost with fear, I felt that I had never understood it

before and that we do not understand the simplest things
around us.

"The ashtray roused a whirlwind of thoughts and
images. It contained such an infinite number of facts, of
events; it was linked with such an immense number of
things. First of all, with everything connected with smoking and tobacco. This at once roused thousands of images,
pictures, memories. Then the ashtray itself. How had it
come into being? All the materials of which it could have
been made? Copper, in this case – what was copper? How
had people discovered it for the first time? How had they
learned to made use of it? How and where was the copper
obtained from which the ashtray was made? Through what
kind of treatment had it passed, or how had it been
transplanted from place to place, how many people had
worked on it or in connection with it? How had the copper
been transformed into an ashtray? These and other questions about the history of the ashtray up to the day when it
had appeared on my table.

"I remember writing a few words on a piece of paper in
order to retain something of these thoughts on the following
day. And the next day I read: '*A man can go mad from one
ashtray.*'"

Ouspensky explains that what he means is that in one ashtray it
was possible to know everything. By invisible threads, the
ashtray was connected with everything in the world, not only
with the present, but with all the past and all the future.

"My description does not in the least express the sensation
as it actually was, because the first and principal impression
was that the ashtray was alive, that it thought, understood
and told me all about itself. All I learned, I learned from the
ashtray itself. The second impression was the extraordinary
emotional character of all connected with what I had
learned from the ashtray.

" 'Everything is alive,' I said to myself in the midst of
these observations. 'There is nothing dead, it is only we
who are dead. If we become alive for a moment, we shall feel
that everything is alive, that all things live, think, feel and
can speak to us.'

"Once, when I was in the state into which my experiments brought me, I asked myself: "What is the world?'

"Immediately, I saw a semblance to some big flower, like a rose or a lotus, the petals of which were continually unfolding from the middle, growing, increasing in size, reaching the outside of the flower and then in some way again returning to the middle and starting again at the beginning. Words in no way express it. In this flower there was an incredible quantity of light, movement, colour, music, emotion, agitation, knowledge, intelligence, mathematics, and continuous unceasing growth. And while I was looking at this flower, *someone* seemed to explain to me that this was the 'World' or 'Brahma' in its clearest aspect and that the nearest possible approximation to what it is in reality – 'If the approximation were made still nearer it would be Brahma himself, as he is,' said the voice.

"These last words seemed to contain a kind of warning, as though Brahma in his real aspect was dangerous and could swallow up and annihilate me. This again was 'infinity'."

In this state, Ouspensky describes how once, in Moscow, he was for a few seconds able to see the faces of people at a great distance.

He tells another very interesting story about the ability to see into the future.

"Another instance occurred during the second winter of my experiments in St Petersburg. Circumstances were such that, the whole of that winter, I was unable to go to Moscow, although at that time I very much wanted to go there in connection with several different matters. Finally, I remembered that, about the middle of February, I definitely decided that I would go to Moscow for Easter. Soon after this, I again began my experiments. Once, quite accidentally, when I was in the state in which moving signs or hieroglyphs were beginning to appear, I had a thought about Moscow, or about someone whom I had to see there at Easter. Suddenly, without any warning I received a comment that I should not go to Moscow at Easter. Why? In answer to this I saw how, starting from the day of the experiment I have described, events began to develop in a definite order and sequence. Nothing new happened. But the causes, which I could see quite well and which were all there on the day of my experiment, were evolving, and having come to the results which unavoidably followed from them, there formed just before Easter a whole series of difficulties which in the end prevented me from going to Moscow. The fact in itself, as I looked at it, had a merely curious character, but the interesting side of it was that I saw what looked like a possibility of calculating the future – the whole future was contained in the present. I saw that all that had happened before Easter resulted directly from what had already existed two months earlier.

"Then in my experiment I probably passed on to other thoughts and on the following day I remembered only the bare result, that 'somebody' had told me I should not go to Moscow at Easter. This was ridiculous, because I saw nothing that could prevent it. Then I forgot all about my experiment. It came to my memory only a week before Easter, when suddenly a whole succession of small circumstances brought it about that I did not go to Moscow. The circumstances were precisely those which I had 'seen' during my experiment, and they quite definitely resulted from what had existed two months before that. Nothing new had happened.

"When everything fell out exactly as I had seen, or foreseen, in that strange state, I remembered my experiment, remembered all the details, remembered what I saw and knew then what had to happen.

"In this incident, I undoubtedly came into contact with the possibility of a different vision in the world of things and events. But, speaking generally, all the questions which I asked myself referring to real life or to concrete knowledge led to nothing."

All this becomes comprehensible in the light of what Max Freedom Long said about the high self. Ouspensky was able to see that a certain inevitable sequence of events would prevent him from going to Moscow – in other words, a completely mechanical sequence which he could foresee. And it happened exactly as he had foreseen – the mechanical sequence simply proceeded automatically, like a music box that has been wound up.

When Max Freedom Long asked the Kahuna woman to alter his future, she explained to him that he had to make a decision and then stick to it, without any possibility of changing his mind. It seems obvious that the 'high self' was able to precisely foresee a certain sequence of events, and also to see the small gap into which free will could be inserted, changing the direction of the events.

Ouspensky also has something extremely interesting to say about the subject of death.

"The experience was connected with the death of a certain person closely related to me. I was very young at the time and was very much depressed by his death. I could not think of anything else and was trying to understand, to solve the riddle of disappearance and of men's interconnection with one another. And suddenly within me there rose a wave of new thoughts and new sensations, leaving after it a feeling of astonishing calm. I saw for a moment why we cannot understand death, why death frightens us, why we cannot find answers to any questions which we put to ourselves in connection with the problem of death. This person who has died, and of whom I was thinking, could not have died because he had never existed. That was the solution. Ordinarily, I had seen not him himself, but something that was like his shadow. The shadow had disappeared. The man who had really existed could not have disappeared. He was bigger than I had seen him, 'longer', as I formulated it to myself, and in this 'length' of his there was contained, in a certain way, the answer to all the questions.

"This sudden and vivid current of thought disappeared as quickly as it had appeared. For a few seconds only, there remained of it something like a mental picture. I saw before me two figures. One, quite small, was like the vague silhouette of a man. This figure represented the man as I had known him. The other figure was like a road in the mountains which you see winding among the hills, crossing rivers and disappearing into the distance. This was what he had been in reality and this was what I could neither understand nor express. The memory of this experience gave me for a long time a feeling of calm and confidence.

Later, the ideas of higher dimensions gave me the possibility of finding a formulation for this strange 'dream in a waking state' as I called my experience."

It can be seen that here Ouspensky is coming very close to the idea of a 'world line', as expressed by the astronomer Percy Seymour, and mentioned in the chapter on astrology. A person, including his life and death, could be seen as a four-dimensional line.

Ouspensky also had an experience concerning his own father.

"I was thinking about another person also closely related to me who had died two years before. In the circumstances of this person's death, as also in the events of the last years of his life, there was much that was not clear to me, and there were things for which I might have blamed myself psychologically, chiefly for my having drifted away from him, not having been sufficiently near him when he might have needed me. There was much to be said against these thoughts, but I could not get rid of them entirely, and they again brought me to the problem of death and to the problem of the possibility of a life beyond the grave.

"I remember saying to myself once during the experiment that if I believed in 'spiritualistic' theories and in the possibility of communication with the dead, I should like to see this person and ask him one question, just one question.

"And suddenly, without any preparation, my wish was satisfied, and I *saw* him. It was not a visual sensation, and what I saw was not his external appearance, but *the whole of his life*, which flashed quickly before me. This life – this was he. The man whom I had known and who had died had never existed. That which existed was something quite different, because his life was not simply a series of events as we ordinarily picture the life of a man to ourselves, but a thinking and feeling *being* who did not change by the fact of his death. The man whom I had known was the *face*, as it were, of this being – the face which changed with the years, but behind which stood always the same unchanging reality. To express myself figuratively, I may say that I saw the man and spoke to him. In actual fact, there were no visual impressions which could be described, nor anything like ordinary conversation. Nevertheless, I knew that it was *he*, and that it was he who communicated to me much more about himself than I could have asked. I saw quite clearly that the events of the last years of his life were as inseparably linked with him as the features of his face which I had known during his life. These events of the last years were the features of the face of his life of the last years. Nobody could have changed anything in them, just as nobody could have changed the colour of his hair or eyes, or the shape of his nose; and just in the same way it could not have been anybody's fault that this man had these facial features and not others.

". . . at the same time, I understood that nobody could be responsible that he was as he was and not different. I realized that we depend upon one another much less than we think. We are no more responsible for the events in one another's lives than we are for the features of one another's faces. Each has his own face, with its own peculiar lines and features, and each has his own fate, in which another man may occupy a certain place but in which he can change nothing.

"But, having realized this, I saw also that we are far more closely bound to our past and to the people we come into contact with than we ordinarily think, and I understood quite clearly that death does not change anything in this. We remain bound with all with whom we have been bound. But for communication with them it is necessary to be in a special state.

"I could explain in the following way the ideas which I understood in this connection: if one takes the branch of a tree with the twigs, the cross-section of the branch will correspond to a man as we ordinarily see him; the branch itself will be the life of the man and the twig will be the lives of the people with whom he comes into contact."

Ouspensky ends by repeating an important comment:

"Nothing that I am writing, nothing that can be said about my experiences, will be comprehensible if the continuous emotional tone of these experiences is not taken into consideration. There were no calm, dispassionate, unexciting moments at all; everything was full of emotion, feeling, almost passion."

Ouspensky explains that "the strangest thing in all these experiences was the coming back, the return to the ordinary state, to the state which we call life. This was something very similar to dying or to what I thought dying must be.

"Usually this coming back occurred when I woke in the morning after an interesting experiment the night before. The experiments almost always ended in sleep. During this sleep, I evidently passed into the usual state and awoke in the ordinary world, in the world in which we awake every morning. But this world contained something extraordinarily oppressive, it was incredibly empty, colourless and lifeless. It was as though everything in it was wooden, as if it was an enormous wooden machine with creaking wooden wheels, wooden thoughts, wooden moods, wooden sensations; everything was terribly slow, scarcely moved, or moved with a melancholy wooden creaking. Everything was dead, soulless, feelingless.

"They were terrible, these moments of awakening in an unreal world after a real one, in a dead world after a living, in a limited world, cut into small pieces, after an infinite and entire world."

All of this makes us aware with great vividness that the real problem of human existence is the sheer dullness of our senses, and the plodding, moment-to-moment *ordinariness* of our thoughts. We are trapped in a world in which nothing seems to be happening. Everything seems to be moving in slow motion. As far as we can see, the purpose of this slow motion seems to be to give us a sense of security, a feeling that we can rely on life, and upon everything being the same when we wake up every morning.

But it could also be seen that the problem with this state of this "security" is that it traps us in a world that scarcely moves. Evolution in this world is extremely difficult, because everything moves so slowly.

This at least begins to allow us a glimpse of a possible answer to this question of time. This world in which we live is basically mechanical, so it *is* possible to foresee the future. Imagine that you are standing on a hilltop, looking into the distance at a train which is still several miles away. You can hear its whistle, and although it disappears around bends and behind trees, you are still fairly certain that, sooner or later, it will be passing below you. Of course, there is always a slim chance that this may not be so. Something may go wrong with the engine, and the driver may stop the train. Or perhaps the tracks are broken. But on the whole, this is not very likely. Sooner or later, the train will almost certainly pass you.

The same happens with our mechanical world. Events could, in theory, be seen well in advance, by somebody standing on a kind of hill.

According to the Hunas, the high self stands on such a hill, and can consequently foresee the future. It can also see that, if for some urgent reason you wish to change what is going to happen, some definite action has to be taken to stop or divert the train.

This obviously has a bearing on our everyday lives. If I am dominated by the low self, then I shall be inclined to vacillate and change my mind. This means that what has happened to me in the past will almost certainly continue to happen to me in the future. I remain trapped in a kind of feedback loop, an inevitable circle of events.

The high self may wish to improve my lot, but it can do nothing, because my tendency to vacillate will mean that it would be pointless for it to try to influence me.

If I wish my life to be lived on a more meaningful level, then the first thing I must do is to try to introduce some sense of determined purpose. If my future conduct remains reliable and foreseeable, then some kind of plans can be made for me. But unless I give my life this kind of direction and purpose, this is an impossibility.

It can be seen then that the question of time is by no means an abstract question. When we are prepared to follow it through, it points us towards some quite definite conclusions. Above all, it tells us how we should live if our lives are to be meaningful rather than meaningless.

Acknowledgments

I note the many expert sources I have relied upon in the compilation of this book in the body of the text, and can recommend all of them to the interested reader. There is rarely total agreement in such a nebulous field, but dogged research and profound inspiration seem to be commonplace.

I must especially thank Gale Smallwood-Jones for allowing me to reproduce a large section of her article on serial crime and palmistry: *Anatomy of a Serial Killer* (see Chapter 19).

Likewise, my deep thanks to Nicholas Campion of the British Astrological Association for allowing me to print a large section of a letter to my father concerning the astrological birth chart of James Maybrick (see Chapter 8). I would also like to thank Shirley Harrison who drew my attention to Nicholas Campion and the Maybrick material, which is due to be published in an updated edition of *The Diary of Jack the Ripper*, Blake Publishing.

As the reader will see, both these fascinating articles have proved central to my argument in these sections.

I offer profound and loving thanks to my father, Colin Wilson. Few would question his longstanding reputation and encyclopaedic knowledge in the field of parapsychological research. His help and advice in the preparation and completion of this book have been quite indispensable. I have been profoundly lucky in knowing him not only as a loving father and brilliant writer, but also as a kind and patient teacher of authorship.

Finally, I would like to thank my fiancée, Lucy, whose gentleness and love over the past year of monumental research has often been the only barrier between myself and stress-induced spontaneous human combustion.

Index